LOVE YOU DEAD

MAX HOUDEK

Copyright © 2016 Max Houdek
All rights reserved
First Edition

PAGE PUBLISHING, INC.
New York, NY

First originally published by Page Publishing, Inc. 2016

ISBN 978-1-68409-081-5 (Paperback)
ISBN 978-1-68409-082-2 (Digital)

Printed in the United States of America

Dedicated to my mother, who is as much a polar opposite of the mother depicted in this book as possible

My mother once told me that, "You can paint over a wall as many times as you like, but do it enough, and you'll start to paint it the same colors over and over again, just because you can't remember what color it was in the first place." Keep in mind, this is the same woman who often claimed that the world had gone to shit ever since we set the Blacks free and let the faggots start to marry, but I still found some wisdom in that.

I can't remember what colors the walls in our home were anymore. I can't remember if the kitchen drapes had ducks or tulips on them. I don't remember the way to the bathroom from my old room anymore, and for some sick reason, that worries me sometimes.

"Jesus will judge them all someday, just you wait and see. On That Day, that righteous day, the ground will open up, and while your aunt and I and all the other righteous, church-going peoples who follow the Lord's Holy Law ascend to the kingdoms of heaven with our Savior, Jesus Christ, while all the sinners and nonbelievers burn in the fires of Satan come again on this earth, where will you want to be on That Day, Gwen? Having the flesh torn from your bones with the sinners, or with your aunt and me in his kingdom of righteousness?"

I didn't have an answer then, I don't have one now.

The only thing difference between then and now is that now I know that when That Day finally did come, my mother did not ascend with some holy savior. Oh, no. In fact, it was only several hours before her own flesh was ripped from her bones and her skull was crushed in.

Ironic, isn't it?

He could see his breath tonight, even though it was only September—early September if his memory could be trusted. The wind still held a crispness that reminded Marshall Meers of leaves turned crimson and brittle and the famous pumpkin pie from Frank's Diner over by Logan's Point Theaters on Thirteenth and Elm. He zipped his jacket up a bit further, just below the neckline, and turned the heat up on the dashboard of his beat-up, old '83 Chevy Ridgeback. A small fog has settled in, covering most of the streets and giving the night an eerie feeling from the get-go. Marshall often felt fear in his line of work; he couldn't imagine many other gravediggers who didn't. Tonight was no different from many others, when all the conditions seemed right for a terror of horror-movie proportions to spring at him out from the darkness, which would wind up ending like all the others did—with him sitting at home, his feet up, and a bottle of Maker's held loosely between his trembling fingers.

After twelve years, he often thought about the first day he began working for Loganville Cemetery—a misguided twenty-something, fresh out of high school (he had been held back twice), who saw nothing in front of him but an early reservation there anyway. He had heard a lot of his friends complain about the miseries of life in a small town, but they never knew the true, utter bullshit of being a failure in a small town. From the day Marshall came out of his no-good mother, he was tainted—marked as a failure, born of his failure mother who would have spent his entire miserable existence within Loganville's twenty-mile limits. Everyone said, "Just accept what you got. You'll be happier if you appreciate what God's given you." At least that's what the good Father McMatherson said every Sunday, repeating some old prewritten speech about the key to living peacefully in God's "glory."

Marshall had accepted his lot in life, no doubt, but it brought him no happiness—just a couple addictions and an inferiority complex, which brought along the several failed marriages and an unhappy kid or two. Nothing a couple grams of OxyContin couldn't fix. He had tried to score some from Benny, whose cousin said he could grab some from his old, deaf grandmother, but he had bailed out on the last minute. Meers had to accept that the only friend he would have tonight would be his oldest: good old Al Cohol—God's medicine man.

The moon cracked through the layer of dark clouds and gave the road an entrancing glow as Marshall pulled up the gates of the cemetery, the closing lyrics of "Bohemian Rhapsody" echoing off the ancient stones. He often thought they might crumble from the stray sound wave of one of John deacon's destructive bass lines. Some of the structures here dated well back into the eighteenth century.

He killed the engine and hopped out of the behemoth of a truck. The familiar feeling of gooseflesh snuck up his arms as he started for the gate. He was so nervous he nearly dropped the keys as he was getting the heavy Henderson's padlock off. The fog made the air even chillier than it had been during the last few hours of twilight, and Marshall found he had to zip his jacket up the rest of the way just to stop the shivering. Or did that have nothing to do with the cold?

It was true that he had been frightened plenty of other nights in his years working at the cemetery, but he had refused to admit to himself the fact that there was something different about this night. The air was different; there was something about the chill that was just... colder. He couldn't place his fingers on the right word, but it hung in the back of his mind with some kind of certainty that he couldn't place. He had always considered himself a rational man—if not an entirely bright one. He had gotten into a couple of fights in his youth, mostly over his family name, but he always knew when to walk away; he always knew when to get out with what he had left.

And that feeling was deep within him now, gnawing at his legs, telling him to turn and run and never come back, that something was different—terribly, horribly different. But he knew better than to listen to the ravings of a frightened mind, especially one that was as rattled as his was. That's what the liquor was for—to calm him down, to steady him. That's how it worked if you told yourself enough. He wiped his lips after his gulp, drips of apple-brown whiskey falling on his pants.

He wiped them gingerly and reached into his pocket, slipping the list from his pocket. "So who's the lucky stiff today?" he joked aloud to himself on liquid confidence. He regretted it soon afterward.

When the veil of silence fell back over the cemetery, Marshall felt his flesh stiffen again. Another sip would fix that. He obliged his fancy and finally looked at the name. Sarah Marsden. No, wait, that couldn't be right. He had gone to school with Sarah Marsden. Hell, he had sixth-period English with her in the tenth grade, for Christ's sake.

But sure enough, there was here name, embellished into the paper with his boss's usual artistic scrawl. He often thought about complaining to his boss about this chicken scratch, along with a long list of other things; but he knew to hold his tongue, mostly since he knew the man only tolerated him because he was close friends with Marshall's aunt—plus, from all accounts, the man was batshit crazy.

It's not like the man was some kind of hermit that lived isolated deep in the middle of Makers Woods out by Route 64, but he did live out of town. A stupid thing to carry weight anywhere, but there were plenty of old traditions held onto in small towns, regardless of their stupidity. Plus there had been stories—not the usual stories that followed a mystery man with a lot of money (like scandalous, soap-opera style affairs or family embarrassments), but weird stories—ones about animals disappearing, the more exaggerated ones involving people, and the noises that came from the woods near his house. Well, they were the closest things you got to local legends out here, and Marshall was not one interested in snooping further into any of them.

He instead turned his attention to Sarah Marsden as he made his way toward the plots he had been digging yesterday in preparation for the usual "shipment" of bodies that came every weekend. Usually, he would dig them the night before, leave them open in the morning—marked off for safety purposes, of course—and find them filled with a fancy-polished wood coffin in the morning, waiting for him to fill them. He assumed this would be how he would find Sarah, and he was not disappointed. He looked down into the grave and saw the usual woodbox, albeit a fraction fancier than most he usually saw, with wood that seemed to glow in the misty light.

He had read her name that morning, when he first checked his list. He had forgotten by choice, he remembered—another gift from his good friend Al. He had been so distraught by that silly name he got so drunk that he almost slept straight through his shift into tomorrow. Some might consider that an overreaction; for a few annoying others, it might seem a cry for help. But based on the way memories of her were creeping into mind even now, he knew it had been necessary.

He took another sip from his flask before pocketing it again.

He remembered that she came from money. She would always show up to school wearing expensive new shoes straight from New York or Paris or other fancy places that Marshall had no place knowing about. One quarter, she had been seated in front of him, and she often wore tight, bright-colored pants that stuck tight to the shapes of her wide hips. Many days he would clearly make out the shape or even the top of her thong, as fancy as any other piece of clothing on her. He tried talking to her several times over the course of high school, fully expecting to be shot down, spat on, and kicked aside like the trash that he was; but she surprised him by treating him warmly, with respect even. At least that's how it seemed to the naive fool he was at the time. He even got the absolutely retarded idea in his head that she might've even taken a liking to him from the way she smiled and laughed whenever he made even the dumbest jokes. Once, he even swore he saw her catch him staring at her exposed undergarments and giving him a wink of approval. But he must've been imagining it. She showed her true colors soon enough.

The idealistic moron he was back then even decided to go and make a bigger fool of himself by asking her out, in front of all her rich, fancy, country club friends. They all laughed right away. Sarah sat thinking for several seconds, and he almost believed she was going to say yes, but she was only twisting the knife in deeper. She made a disgusted face and gave a hard, "No," then began laughing along with the rest of her jackals—so hard that she started crying.

He thought of her now, her beautiful face marked by decay and maggots that crawled through her pearl skin; and he thought of getting right in her once lovely, stunning, happy, hope-filled face and scream, "I don't care that you don't want to fuck me, you fake, cancerous human shit stain!" He wanted to laugh in that rotting face of hers.

The thought passed in an instant but left him just as disturbed as it would if it had been there his entire life. For some reason, it felt like it had. He dismissed it with another sip of his Maker's bottle—the thought of Makers Woods and its legends drifting through his mist-rattled mind—and started to pile dirt on top of Sarah Marsden.

The work was done sooner than Marshall thought it would be, and he finished flattening the mounds of dirt that separated him and Sarah Marsden by six beautiful feet. He worked on finishing the last few sips of his bottle in his own private celebration and stumbled drunkenly over to a random pile of graves, his old fears forgotten in an in instant of drunken adventurousness. He walked past several different graves he had seen before, remembering a few, mostly ones with humorous names like Henry Fuquitt and Norma Bottoms. His eyes moved in a bit of a dizzy frenzy and settled on one grave covered in scratches and moss, one that he was sure he recognized: Jonathon Longwarden, the Once and Future King of Loganville. Marshall did a drunken curtsy in front of the grave while chuckling to himself.

He heard the laugh echo. But after several seconds, he started to wonder if it really was an echo… or had it been someone else laughing? It had sounded unusual. The feeling of gooseflesh returned, and suddenly, Marshall Meers regretted the first time he ever put an alcohol bottle to his lips. It was a thought that gave him more fear than he had ever felt in his pitiful life, and he suddenly wanted nothing else than to get the hell out of this graveyard. But as he looked around, he realized that the mist had covered any sign of where he was.

There was the odd laugh again—not quite an echo, not quite a voice, something stuck horribly in between. He began to shiver again, the cold turning on him. He knew he had been to the Longwarden grave before, but for the life of him, he could not think how to get out of the graveyard. It was like a fog hung over his memory, one that surpassed any intoxication he had ever known, one that shook his very being.

He began to move very fast at that point, shuffling over weeds and lumps of dirt, and as he passed over each one, he saw their roots stretching down, deep down, into the bodies beneath him, draining them, feeding on them...

The laugh came again, and Marshall twisted his body wildly, afraid of every direction but deciding on one that seemed to hold a vague outline of familiarity. He jogged toward it now, his visions of bodies growing stronger with every passing moment, until it was all he was aware of and his movement through the rows and rows of dead became nothing more than something he paid mild attention to, like driving late at night when you're too tired to focus all your attention on a route you've gone down a million times before.

He wanted them to stop, and he wanted to shove a bottle of the strongest tequila he could find and probably finish the whole thing in one gulp, just to bring the darkness back when he closed his eyes, the peace to his mind. The laughter had turned into a steady buzz, a hum that settled like a smoke in his ears. He wanted it to stop. He wanted it all to stop. What was so fucking funny about all this? All this death? What was the fucking point?

His torso slammed heavily into the edge of a large stone tombstone, and Marshall fell heavily to the ground, retching as soon as his face rested on the icy dirt. The smell of vomit was burned into his nostrils as he lifted himself on top of the headstone in front of him. His strength was fading him, and all he could see was Sarah Marsden's decaying face laughing at him, cackling like a banshee. But he knew that was crazy because she was *fucking dead*. He struggled in place, trying his best to get to his feet, to get out of this terrible place—this evil fucking place. What's so funny, Sarah? What's the fucking joke?

A cold wrapped itself around his ankle, which felt like what he had always imagined freezing to death felt like: a numbness with a frightening warmth. It tightened around his bones, and he looked down to see a hand—a gray, withered hand reaching from the ground—its fingers, some missing joints, wrapped tightly around his foot. There was a sharp pull, and his foot disappeared over the edge of dirt that marked Marsden's grave; and the world disappeared to a blinding pain as he felt his bones mashed, snapped, chewed down to dust.

When he opened his eyes, he was instantly drawn to his attacker: a face he had been dreaming of almost every night of his lonely, pitiable life—the same face he had seen with worms crawling through her eyes, just like they were now—the face of Sarah Marsden.

He broke out into laughter, then terrifying, gleeful laughter, which mingled with the cool autumn breeze and became one with it and disappeared before anyone had time to realize it was there.

ACT I

A Musician, a Prophet, and an Iconoclast Walk into a Bar...

I prophesied just as I'd been commanded. As I prophesied, there was a sound and, oh, rustling! The bones moved and came together, bone to bone. I kept watching. Sinews formed, then muscles on the bones, then skin stretched over them. But they had no breath in them.
—Ezekiel 37:7

I should warn you princess—the first time tends to get a bit messy.
—Freddy Krueger, *Freddy Vs Jason*

You've got red on you.

—Various, *Shaun of the Dead*

I fucking hated that picture. That's the thing I remember the most about living there—that stupid picture of Jesus descending from heaven as the world burned around him, bathed in what my mother loved to refer to as "holy fire." When you look back on some of the shit that woman said over the years… I don't honestly know if I believe that she was crazy or just a truly, deeply hateful woman—one born with judgment in her bones. I almost feel sad for the bitch at this point in my life, especially looking back at how everything turned out.

People always ask me why—out of all the years of degradation and mental abuse—I resent a stupid goddamn picture (painted by a religious fundamentalist that was half crazy himself) the most. It was because that picture was what she fucking stood for, what she believed in and gave all her most secret, most evil, fucked-up desires to. Pardon my language.

If you knew the woman, you'd understand. Every other person from Loganville, the ones still alive—actually alive—will tell you the same damn thing. They'd agree. That woman talked about That Day more than anything I can remember. She believed in That Day coming and saving her from the world she resented so much. It was her golden fucking ticket.

She told me over and over about That Day and how "impending" it was—again, her words, not mine—whenever I was bad or acting out. She told every person she resented about it, and that was everyone she knew… except my aunt, of course—her mighty right hand, her Watson. They talked out at town meetings, shouted racist remarks at bingo nights, and ran church events into the ground with itinerary straight out of sinners in the hand of an angry God.

But none of it affected my mother. It didn't matter to her. She was on a mission more important than the whispers of small-town "heathens." She had spoken to the Lord himself. She was his holy vessel.

She was the fucking Prophet of Loganville. Again, pardon my language.

Mother did not want her to go to school that day.

There was a speech about safe sex at school today, and to hear of such sinful things would surely corrupt her soul. She was young and incorrigible—a weak, corruptible thing. She was a stupid teenage girl. How could anyone expect her to know anything? Of course, she must have fallen for all the traps that their generation had left for her and become a complete moron—a walking shell, only able to be filled by credit card purchases.

She'd heard it every day. Her mother made sure of that. Her mother managed to have the strictest views in a town with less than 1500 residents, something not easily accomplished. It took an expert in the arts of close-mindedness to accomplish that. Gwen did not often admit to herself that she hated her mother, but after seventeen years in close quarters, it had become really hard not to anymore. It was horribly depressing in a way.

She had come to the age where nostalgia became something sweet. Often, she found herself dreaming fondly of the time she was in grade school, a simple girl who actually enjoyed her friends and thought the world was a place worth exploring. The past had gained its first level of varnish, which gave it a glisten to make even the worst of heartbreaks something brighter. She remembered the stillness of the house in her youth when she was left alone to pray while her mother and aunt would go out to "fix the wrongs of the world," which would occupy most of the day—sometimes weeks at a time. She always had enough food, drink, and when she was really little, a babysitter; but she had usually been on her own. She had grown up on her own. It became what she was used to.

Maybe that was why she felt so disgusted when she saw all the other kids at her school bending ass over backward to try and fit into the outline of the person backed by the media that week. It seemed similar to dangling a carrot in front of a horse to get it to take you where you wanted. She knew that most of her rebellious attitude came from youth, yet that youthful part of her seemed to desperately want to fight back against some corporation, to stand for something, but even the media had turned that into another stereotype—meta on top of meta.

All she knew is that when she looked upon Claire Dunmark's pale face, heavily covered in the pastiest makeup imaginable, she could not think of anything but a walking doll—another bland product of the new world. She could no longer tell if all her spite came from her pride or her loneliness anymore. After a while, they all sort of blended into the same kind of tasteless emotional paste.

Stacey's heavy locker slam is what finally woke her from her mental drifting.

"Lost in your own hateful thoughts again, dearie?" she predicted through bright red lips that smacked against a piece of fruit-scented gum.

"You're getting creepy with your mind-reading."

"Eh. Some call it a gift, others a curse, but enough about my ass, we don't have all passing period to talk about it, unfortunately."

"That might be the saddest thing I've ever heard."

"It's truly a tragedy," Stacey laughed as they started walking down the hallway side by side, too close for Gwen's taste, although she'd never admit it.

She wasn't yet ready to admit to all her friends just how much she actually despised them. That would come in time… she hoped.

"So who were you mind-murdering this time? Sarah Glick? Stephen Barry? Oh, I know! It has to be perky Claire Dunmark over there, oblivious to her own pitiful existence, isn't it?"

When Gwen could not hide her smile in time, they both began to cackle almost evilly, delighted in their own shared sense of cattiness. Gwen did not usually like actively engaging in "the art of being bitch" as much as Stacey and her cohorts, but she did call out those that deserved it from time to time as well; and when the time came along, there was no one better to have on your side than Stacey Robinson.

Stacey was the Queen of the Bitch at Loganville West, competing solely with Veronica Métier, who some declared deserved to be both the King and the Queen. Stacey and Veronica had once been the best of friends until one of the many trivial love triangles of the Loganville school system set the two at odds. While Gwen really wasn't too fond of either of them, Stacey eventually had managed to win her over to her side after defending her against one of Veronica's attacks. Gwen tried to keep one rule to separate herself from all the bitter, angry people of the world: respect those who respect you.

Stacey had once sent a girl to a mental hospital for two and a half years because she had called her a "manatee spawn," worthy only of "porking old perverts by the docks." She had once ripped the hair out of a school counselor for telling her that she was out of line, but she had never once treated Gwen like she was anything less than human—which was something she could not say about Veronica Métier.

"Did you finish your paper for Fitzmartin? I tried to get a hold of Marcie's copy, but she told me to shove it. Can you believe that bitch? I swear to God, one of these days, that girl is going to come crawling to me for something, and she ain't gonna get shit from me. She gets high off that stupid shit, I swear, Little Ms. I'm-Better-Than-You-Because-I-Gave-a-Shit-About-a-School-Assignment, makes me wanna barf."

Stacey started to look at her nails, and Gwen felt a sudden urge to hit her, if she wasn't so right about the fact that Marcie Connell was Little Ms. I'm-Better-Than-You-Because-I-Gave-a-Shit-About-a-School-Assignment.

"You can have mine, although I don't really have a choice now. You may be able to get away being conniving with other stupider people, but I'll actually call you on it."

"And that's why I love ya, dearie. You're the only one in this school who can keep up with me."

"I'm sure you say that to everyone."

The bell rang and gave the statement a sudden silence that seemed to give a shadowy weight to their conversation. Gwen felt weird draped in that silence, colder than she had felt all day. Goose bumps started to creep up her flesh, starting from the bottom of her foot and spreading to the back of her neck. She got the horrid feeling that someone was watching her, and when she turned, she could have sworn that she had seen someone's head slip past her visibility—just for a moment, but a moment long enough to make her almost completely sure...

Stacey's laughter made her cringe, and when she began to eagerly shake her, the feeling to hit her suddenly rose up in her belly again.

"Worried that the teachers might find see us not in class? I'm so terrified."

She cackled again, and Gwen was instantly reminded of the green witches from cartoons and Halloween decorations.

"Let's just go. The sooner it starts, the sooner it's over, as I always say."

She didn't actually always say that, but it seemed right to say at the time.

Frank Rogers did not often have to deal with people, working as a janitor inside of city hall. Every now and then, people would ask him where Mr. So-and-So's office was, and he would gladly point them in a direction he was only half confident about, just so that they would leave him to his work in quiet, where he wasn't on the buzzer anymore. In school, when teachers had asked him questions, he would quickly spurt out the first answer that came to his mind, just to get the spotlight off him a little quicker—even if it might mean being wrong (as it often was) and enduring several moments of spite-filled laughter.

The only person he ever had to really talk to his whole life would be his momma—and Mr. Klunesberg, of course. His father had never paid him enough attention to have a conversation with him in the nine years that he was in Frank's life. Frank had never considered himself a people person, or a very outgoing one. There was a time in his more rebellious youth (inspired by the love), a good woman—the *only* woman—had made him daring enough to go against the law more often than he'd like to admit; but if there had ever been any lingering traces of that life left, Mr. Klunesberg had taken care of that with the same efficiency he brought to the rest of his life.

"Frog? Is that you?"

The voice echoed through the halls, bouncing off steel pipes long rusted and walls colder than bone. At first, Frank believed that the voice was only in his mind, and he began to welcome it with the embrace one would give a long-lost friend who decided to stop by for a catch-up and a cup of coffee. When the footsteps followed, the heaviness identifying their owner immediately, Frank soon wished that it had been voices in his head he was hearing instead of the creature that lay behind him.

"What brings you up here? You shouldn't be cleaning this wing of the building until everyone's gone home. I thought I made this perfectly clear the last time we talked about this."

Mr. Klunesberg's glasses shone bright against the backdrop of his face, making it seem darker than it really was, almost like a mask of shadows. His mustache had been recently trimmed as parts of his upper lip bore the familiar trace of red that Frank recognized on the days that he was just a little nastier than normal.

Reginald Gregory Klunesberg was not an especially rude man. He never berated his coworkers or spoke negatively of them—at least not to their faces—that Frank knew of. There was a subtlety to his nastiness that made it all the much worse. It wasn't the words that he would say to you that would take all the strength out of you; it was the way he said them—the bitterness that was drizzled over every polite criticism, the nasty undertone to each inquisition; the way that his eyes looked you over, inside, and out, with a contempt that regarded you as something lower than his shoe. That's what took all your self-confidence and made it his... ammunition.

"I know, sir, and I'm sorry, but there was a large group of people outside asking about some trouble over at Loganville Cemetery. Now, normally, I wouldn't pay any mind to people like this, especially when I'm in the middle of doing my lawn work. You know how Mabel gets if she sees that the flowers are off in front of her office. But they were talking about that missing gravedigger, Marshall Meers, and well, sir… well, I and Marshall used to be drinking buddies. We would get drunk down by Mickey's every night for up to, well… eight years, I'd say. The bar over on Thirtieth, you know, the place with the Christmas lights up all year round? Well, anyway, I'm rambling. I only talked to them because Marshall's disappearance it… well, really took me by surprise, sir.

"And well… I guess these people saw my interest and started talking to me and trying to get me to come up and get you, sir. I held out for a while. Told 'em how you didn't like to be bothered and all, 'specially when you're working, but they kept hollering about their daughter and calling Marshall a 'sicko' and 'pervert' or something."

"Their daughter?"

"That's right, sir. Sarah Marsden, the dead girl whose body went missing from the graveyard the same night Marshall… well, Mr. Meers, disappeared."

Klunesberg's eyes went glassy, and he no longer looked entirely like a man. His eyes seemed pale, and the rest of him looked like nothing more than a shade against the wall.

"I'm glad you brought this information to me, Frog."

The name.

Frank cringed as Klunesberg wrapped his wispy arms around his shoulder and started walking him down the expansive, old Gregorian architecture–inspired hallway. A painting of some saint that Frank didn't recognize caught his eye as he passed, and he took note of the look of horror on the man's face as the lion tore his spleen out, and he felt a twisted sense of envy.

"Can I be really frank with you, Mr. Klunesberg, sir?"

"Of course, Frog."

That fucking name. I hate that fucking name.

"Well, sir…" his eyes shot toward the floor, before warily backing up to meet those creamy white pools, "the weirdest thing about this whole thing is that Marshall Meers was talking about that girl the night he disappeared. He kept talking about poppin' a… well, becoming aroused by her in one of his classes."

"That only strengthens my worst suspicions, Frog."

Stop calling me that fucking name. Everyone calls me that now. It's all your fucking fault.

"Have you considered the fact that he was a madman, a deranged psychopath? Someone who secretly... got off on this sort of thing?"

"I talked to that man the night he died... sir," Frank tried to calm himself. He must not forget his place. "He talked no different than he did any other night I'd known him."

"They say it's always someone you'd never suspect," his eyes narrowed behind the gleaming lenses, "even someone like you, Frog."

You ruined my life.

Frank's eyes dropped to the floor, afraid to meet those inhuman ones anymore. "All I'm saying, sir, is that why would a man talk about a girl he hadn't seen or even mentioned in nineteen years, start bragging about her the night before he ran off with her body?"

"When else would they talk about it, except for the night before they plan to perpetrate the deed? Come on, Frog, I figured you more intelligent than that, at least."

"I guess you're right, but..."

The debonair smile that had once looked like something out of an old Fred Astaire movie disappeared within an instant, and only for an instant, but Frank's blood ran colder than ice water.

"Well, either way, my dear, dear Frog," he lifted his eyes over the ridges of his glasses and bored his vision into Frank's temple, "it's better not to draw attention to such a grisly subject, especially in the fall when election time is so near. It puts people in a bad mood, and I don't need people in a bad mood. The committee needs people happy and patriotic, and a necrophiliac gravedigger does not inspire that sort of feelings in people. So we should keep this event to ourselves as much as possible, all right?"

The stare hardened, and Frank swore his ears began to ring.

He managed a pained nod, and that smile twisted into something a demon would wear to church. "That's my Frog." He reached his hand out to straighten Frank's collar and did so flawlessly despite him twitching whenever his hand got too close. "Now, it's time for you to head back down to the basement. And remember what we talked about. You are to show yourself up here as little as possible, am I understood? That's a good, Frog. Start now, and get downstairs as soon as possible."

Frank tried to bring a smile to his face—something to cover the terror, the self-loathing. He pictured shoving a .34 in Klunesberg's mouth and blowing his brains all over his office's freshly painted walls. That did it.

"What do I tell the people outside? The girl's family?"

The smile disappeared, again only for an instant. "Tell them to go fuck themselves—politely, of course, not word for word like last time, thank you."

She noticed him right away but only pretended to notice after she had counted to a hundred in her head. She let her eyes wander over to his, a shade of blue so pure that she thought she had missed and stared straight into the sky. He grinned—a cocky grin, one that made the girl in her squeal. Her face somehow remained calm. His hair was blond... almost silver. In one motion, he pushed himself forward off the wall, and instead, he began sauntering toward her. Don't smile.

Stacey had already begun tapping her fingers gently against her arm, but she had trained herself to ignore her when needed at this point in her life. She felt his stare piercing right through her and felt her heart beat rapidly for the first time in a long time.

He turned with such suddenness that her breath almost exploded out of her. His smile turned into something sly, and he began to laugh as he disappeared among the trees that marked the edge of Makers Woods. A weird feeling washed over her then, one of true, bitter disappointment; and she relished it, so much that she almost laughed.

"Who the hell was that? Have you been a dirty whore behind my back, Gwennie?" Stacey's voice had a hint of jealousy in it. You could always tell when the word *whore* slipped out too. "I hope he's not one of those vampire faggots. Why can't anyone just be emo anymore like a normal person? So who is he, Gwen?"

"I have no idea. But I'm gonna find out."

LOVE YOU DEAD

I remember alabaster.

When I dream of my childhood, everything is covered in alabaster, coated in it. I wish I could point a finger at the thing that caused my alabaster walls to crumble and fall, to decay from within, to become something I hate to think about. I want the world to be alabaster, like it is when I was young, despite the fact I know it's just as sick and twisted as it looks when I think about it now. I know I can't make it better, and I can't go back and change anything. After many, many painful years, I've accepted that. Trust me. But I just wish I could believe they were these treasured moments again. I want the delusion back. Is that sick of me to think? To want that? Is that what I've become?

I'm filled with hatred for whatever it is that caused this whole… incident, as they like to insist we call it, and I want nothing more than to direct it at something, to point my finger at someone; but every time I try, it always seems to be pointing right back at me, especially after investigating just what the cause was.

That's what I remember most now.

And compared to that truth, alabaster seems almost like a blessing.

She heard her mother before she even got all the way up the stairs to her front door.

"His light, let us follow it to heaven. Let us bask in his embrace."

It sickened her that this had become her usual—that she walked up every day to a woman, half mad with religious fervor, two steps away from being Henrietta White's evil stepsister.

She walked in quickly, trying to skirt by unnoticed into the oasis of her bedroom, but her mother's eyes snapped open before she had taken her first step and were locked in a disappointed glare before she had taken her second.

"Ah, the sinner returns home. We were just praying for you."

Gwen scratched her ear. She did it whenever she needed to occupy her hand from flying across her mother's face.

"I must have done something to seriously threaten my immortal soul to require your holy intervention, Mother," she said stoically.

Her mother smiled, while her aunt tried her best to pick up the slack of her mother's fallen grimace and failed, as usual, coming across more as teacher's pet that an ardent follower.

"You were an hour late coming home today, dear daughter. You worried your aunt and I near to death."

"Your aunt and me."

"Watch your tongue, young lady," her aunt piqued in, doing her best impersonation of a parrot.

"Why, because I said something that was right? I know that's something that seems out of place in this house, but surely in this democratic country of ours…"

"Stop it, Gwen. You know exactly what your aunt means. You are being especially sinful today, trying to attack your aunt… and me… right before you have even come in and taken your jacket off." She turned to face Gwen's aunt. "You were right, Meredith. There was definitely a boy involved. Only that type of demon could rile her up so and turned her into the sinful… beast before you."

"I should probably retire to my room before the urges overcome me then," Gwen said through gritted teeth, her pride overpowering her usual levelheadedness in these situations.

"How dare you—"

"Meredith, it's all right. Her words are result of the evil inside of her, nothing more, nothing we are not used to handling from her." Her mother locked her misty, jade eyes on her. "Now, Gwen, you may go to your room, if that's what you really want. I could lock you in again, if that's what you really want. You could stay there until our Lord Jesus comes and the dead rise…" goose bumps spread up her spine faster than she ever thought possible, "if that's what you really want."

Gwen started to look away, but her mother was on her feet in moments and had wrapped her spiny fingers around the base of her chin and pulled her forward, boring her eyes into her very soul.

"I can see the sin in you. Stay here, Gwen. Stay and kneel before him, our Savior, and he will wash you clean, baby, my sweet darling child. He will set you free from the shackles of sin, and if you let him inside of you, your dirty, corrupted soul shall become one with his and be made clean in his image. You will be one with me, Gwen, and your aunt, and every other Christian soul on God's green gift. Don't you want that, sweetie? Don't you want to stop fighting it?"

Those swirls of mystic green light her mother called eyes seemed to hold her, give her a comfort that sickened her and wrapped her in grip of sad, undeniable childhood memories. She sucked in a heavy mouthful of air and wretched free, the gooseflesh feeling like a burning, itching rash.

"No! Get off of me!"

Her mother threw her to the ground, her head falling clumsily against the spotless carpet. She slammed her bony, vicelike grip around Gwen's skull, and began to shove it into the carpet, like she was trying to push her to hell itself.

"Repent for your sins, and be set free! You sinful spawn of my own sin-ridden loins, cast of your desires, and accept the savior Jesus Christ into your soul!"

"Get off! Get off! Get offffff!" Gwen swung at her mother to no avail, her arm flailing blindly at her mother's head.

"I cast you out, demon! You are no child of mine! Separate your parasitic self from this sweet child's soul—my child's soul—that the devil, in all his unholy cruelty, has deemed fit to take from me! Give me the holy child that I was so promised, I, your prophet, your Word, oh, Lord, your humble servant, who asks for so little in return other than your own divine retribution!"

A quick elbow to her mother's left breast, and she was free, slamming into the hallway as soon as she could move. She burst into her room, slammed the door behind her, and collapsed against it. There was no lock on her side. No safety. The one place any kid was given to call their own—and hers was a fucking jail cell for as long as she could remember. No place felt like a home; she almost envied orphans, as sick as it sounded.

The banging began a minute later, the horrible screaming serving as a harbinger of its arrival. She let the first few tears fall, counted to three, and sniffled the rest back. She would not be weak; she would not give her mother that easy victory.

She passed her hour against the door in silence, listening to her mother's psalm verses and religious chants through the pinewood. Every once in a while, she would throw in several derogatory terms, harsher than those she heard at school, when her religious piety failed her. Gwen remained relatively still throughout this, except for the times when she had to arch her back to shake the stiffness from her bones. The wood often felt cold against the ridge of her spine, making her shiver, or at least that's what she was telling herself.

She entertained herself with mundane activities, like counting the dust motes in the streaks of sunlight that spilled onto the center of her desk and the corner of her bed and trying to catch those that came close enough to her face. The bare white walls of her room seemed to cement her further into the ground every time, but she told herself she had plans to buy posters, if she could only get them past her mother's prying gaze. Coupled with screams and shaking door, it was like her mother was still there, slamming her face into the floor, trying to exorcise her like she was a demon—a sickening creature.

She fought back the tears with a quick breath.

The screaming stopped exactly an hour and seventeen minutes after it had started and was followed by the echoes of feet creaking on the floorboards down the hall… and then back, with a sharp click right above Gwen's head where the doorknob protruded like a rain cloud. The footsteps started again, and then silence sank into the room—sweet at first, then sticky and filled with a gnawing dread that nestled in the back of your mind like a tick.

Tensely, Gwen reached for the door handle, and when her gentle fingers found it, she wrapped them around it in a frantic flash and twisted it. It held firm. Her cell had become sealed—solitary confinement for the night.

Her gray sheets matched hideously with her bright-blue pillows, but she did not have any say in the matter. Her mother had only given her the privilege to choose what she wore, but only after she'd convinced her at age seven that the clothes were her own, not Momma's or God's. Her mother had forcefully agreed after a week of shameful silence but had removed everything from Gwen's room, claiming that everything in the house belonged to her and, "especially," she had added, God. So now, the walls were bare. The sheets were there out of their necessity, nothing more, and her desk contained nothing but pencils, notebooks that were often rifled through, and a Bible that reappeared every time it was disposed of. Her dresser was modest, with barely enough room for her small wardrobe of T-shirts, several blouses, a sundress or two, a couple pairs of jeans, shorts and skirts, and a four pairs of shoes crammed underneath the bottom. She had done her best with what she had been given. And even though she did often look down on the traditional "girly girl" image, she could not help but delight in clothes.

    She stretched as soon as she got up from the door, taking note of the slight indent that had begun to form there over the years—the bumps again. Gwen threw her backpack on the bed and soon followed after it, losing herself in the stiff comfort of the mattress. Her mind wandered, and soon, fifteen minutes had passed. The sun had begun to creep down to the tops of the McCrery and Hull houses across the street and had turned a sickened orange color that had moved to the floor in her room (white). She sat up lazily, slightly hunched over her stomach, and began to rub her eyes, as if it would get the sleep out of them. The next step she knew was to get to her feet; that would wake her up. She followed her own advice and hopped gently to her feet and started over to the window, hoping that a sunset might serve as a good replacement memory for this night. She would need something pretty beautiful to block this one out.

    She had never really believed that you could actually repress anything when she was little, but she learned quickly that with enough distractions, it was pretty simple—almost frighteningly simple. It made it hard, remembering who you were sometimes. She had learned that the hard way—on her own, like everything else. Her mother shunned any kind of free-thinking as the devil's work and believed that God would raise the child that she was too weak to raise herself. But as Jesus could probably attest while hanging from the cross he was "destined" for, God was a shitty father.

The sun warmed Gwen's cheek as she opened the window, close to immovable after years of being unopened and unused. Only recently had Gwen been able to figure out how to open it without her mother hearing: by twisting the squeaky lock just far enough to the left so that the window would slide up gently enough with only a squeak or two that would be written off by any pious, listening ears. Her mood brightened instantly in the waning grips of sunlight, and she was surprised to find a smile on her tear-streaked face.

She surveyed the neighborhood, shooting a glance at Mrs. McCrery sitting on her porch across the street, slowly rocking back and forth while attempting to read *To Kill a Mockingbird* for the umpteenth time before she would give up and switch back to Nora Roberts. Josh and Jacob Flitz were playing a game of tag that looked much more like tormenting young Susie Carter, who was lying in the dirt with a skinned knee after a particularly rough shove. The old couple that always waved when you greeted them but never introduced themselves were walking their Schnauzer down Apple Orchard Boulevard, the dog tugging at the leash as they passed every tree. As slow and pitifully boring Loganville was regularly, today it seemed even more corpse like than it had before.

Something caught her eye then. The boy she recognized from school was sitting down past Harold Street, near the O'Conners' backyard but in the Markers' yard behind them. They were famous for having the best playground in their backyard—with a full swing set that even someone as big as Hank Marker with his bulky, Homer Simpson frame could swing on—but even more famous for never being home to use it.

And there was that weird boy, swaying back and forth, just far enough to blur his features but just close enough to recognize him—or at least, she thought. He had what looked to be a guitar in his hand, and when she stuck her head a little further out the window pane and held her breath, she could hear the mournful melody drifting tandem with the breeze. It chilled her bones, and her skin began to crawl again, but her heart began to flutter. She was shocked by how much she liked it—how right it felt, how much it stirred her. A cold went up her back, and it felt like a gentle, probing, loving hand. She welcomed it and let it slip over her body like a long-lost lover. She had known so very few, even less, real lovers; but this one felt like one she had always known, always wanted.

This was beautiful enough. This memory would do.

Matt Métier awoke with the dreary realization that he had work in several minutes, and the hangover that greeted him was still a sweeter friend than the girl that lay next to him. This was yet another girl whose name he did not remember and was more than confident that after five minutes of talking to her, he would not want to know it. But the urge needed to be satisfied, and he had stopped giving a shit about who satisfied it a long time ago.

He coughed and felt his lungs shake and felt an ache spread through him that could only be blamed on the cheap whiskey from last night—or was it rum? He couldn't remember and was proud of it. He preferred his memories as blurs; things seemed a lot better when you couldn't make them out clearly. He stood, letting his nakedness bathe in the dipping sunlight, and coughed again. The girl stirred from her sleep and started to groan, but when he had turned to look at her, she had turned to her other side; and Matt started to realize why he had left with her. He smiled, amused by his own shallowness as nothing else but his supposed flaws seemed to provide him with any actual happiness anymore.

His flat was a single room, tucked cozily in the attic of a nice English couple who had grown tired of pretending to be shocked when they saw a new girl on their property every week. The rafters were made of wood from the old world—polished, varnished, and stained with a type of mastery that Matt was sure he hadn't put into anything in his entire life, let alone something as unimportant as a damned rafter. Still, he often looked up at those rafters; the ones he stared at late at night when the urge kept him awake were the pride of some man's life—a man from the early days of Loganville whose only lasting connection to this world were those stupid fucking rafters. And he didn't have anything nearly as nice as those.

He hadn't even started work yet, and he already wanted a drink.

He took a quick shower and was pleased to see the nameless girl had left by the time that he walked out, dripping water on the hardwood floorboards. The flat grew cold often at nights, and before he had crossed half of it, he was already shivering. He threw on clothes quickly before nearly stumbling down the stairs. After trying to forcefully shove his keys into the ignition more than once, he realized he was still running on fumes from the night before, much like his engine probably would be. Sure enough, the needle barely rose above the entire three-block drive to Terri's; but he ignored it, like usual, until the uninterrupted dinging finally made him pull into a station. For now, he pulled into the parking lot, not bothering to lock the old Honda, and walked into the bar with his usual disinterested gait.

Greg nodded to him as he passed, and Matt managed a quick wave while heading behind the bar. Grabbing his apron, he started to throw it on; while Rodrigo, ignorant to his very presence, continued serving drinks to several mothers from the edge of town who had been staring greedily at his crotch the entire time.

Matt's gaze drifted down to the obscene amount of cleavage produced by the little black leather dress of the middle-aged woman on the left, blue veins zigzagging down her breasts like a river map. He suddenly found himself rock hard down there, his eyes widening with the dreaded realization that the urge had set on him before the night had even begun.

Dead dogs with their entrails torn out; a baby with a crushed skull; a naked, defiled nun, tits saggin', blood soppin' from her legs.

Rodrigo had noticed him, gave him a nod, and exchanged the usual pleasantries before hanging his apron on the pegs besides the Bacardi and Tanqueray and heading back into the kitchen, lighting a Camel cigarette dangling from his lips as he went. Matt and Rodrigo had talked at work several times, but the one time Matt had actually hung out with him, the guy had invited him over to his coke-slinging cousin, Pedro, who kept waving his recently purchased .44 in people's faces. He hadn't responded to any of his invites since.

Now, it wasn't like he hadn't had a gun pointed at him before; it was the comments that annoyed him. They kept calling him the LA kid. He was starting to suspect that it wasn't a title of respect—more of a reminder that, as big as he talked, he had gone to Los Angeles and wound up back here, ass deep in debt without a cent to his name. The urge had gotten the better of him out there. He had gone to try and escape it—at least to try and hide it away from his family, especially Veronica. He was tired of his mother hearing the rumors of her son's weeknight expeditions to the club off of Route 17—the one where the girls took their clothes off, you know, all the way off and, if you tipped well enough, might give you something extra in the back room. He was tired of his dad's questions about the checking account, the nudey mags, the rubbers, every girl that he brought home, or the "weekly rotation," as his family liked to call it. He was tired of the way Veronica would look at him with that painful stare of hers, like a sick puppy dog.

Then the drugs had started. It's not that he was addicted to anything in particular; he just liked having something to get the images out of his mind, if even for a little while. The desire was always there, the nonstop stream of images—girls he wanted to fuck, girls he had already fucked, girls that he made up that he wanted to fuck. Every time he closed his eyes, they were there, and he wanted them; he needed them. He couldn't think of anything else, not unless he fried his brain beyond recognition. The thrill he got from sex, the rush of it, even just masturbating in the shower in the morning, the buildup to the final climax, that split second of pure, unbridled happiness that consumed your entire being, that one millisecond where *stress* was only a word in a dictionary, that one miniscule moment where life seems finally... worth it... and then it's gone. There's the release, beautiful and tranquil, where the mind empties. All the thoughts, those little troublemakers, go out the window. There's peace; the only thoughts are your own, your real thoughts, unaffected by the world that has otherwise consumed you.

He slammed down a shot of vodka.

Tits saggin', blood soppin' down her legs, bullet hole in the center of her head.

"Excuse me? How much will that be?"

The woman with the cleavage started to wave her hand parallel to his face. He noticed the hollow twinkle of the diamond ring on her finger and the way it coiled tightly like a metallic serpent around the knuckle, the poison in its fangs. He found himself aroused again.

You sicken me. "Sorry, ma'am, didn't catch the order. Say it again for me."

"Two banana daiquiris, if you know how to make 'em." She flashed a smile at him, her pearl teeth impossibly white and shining like a fluorescent, so bright that it gave off a buzz that rang painfully in your ear.

"They're not my specialty, but I can make those for ya. That'll be eighteen bucks, ma'am."

Her slim, swanlike hand dipped into the hemline of her shirt, and she slipped out a twenty and a ten and slid it across the bar, gently, like she was stroking the arm of a lover.

"Make 'em strong."

"Now that, ma'am, is my specialty."

Taking a piss, when you look down and see it's mostly blood. A mother holding her baby, stillborn, twisted, and deformed. You sicken me.

He took a shot of the Cuervo before pouring it into the blender, along with half a banana and the daiquiri mix. As he placed the lid on, he noticed Frank Rogers sit down on the far end of the bar near the door—a much-appreciated distraction. He finished the drinks quickly, taking note to do enough to earn his tip but paying no more mind to the women when he placed the drinks in front of them. They thanked him lustily, but his attention was already on Frank.

"Well, if it isn't ol' Mr. Rogers, come to visit me once again. How's the neighborhood?" Matt said gleefully as soon as he was near enough to be heard.

Frank looked up at him slowly, in a daze, as he often was—probably lost in thoughts about his boss as per usual. It was a well-known fact inside of Mickey's that Frank Rogers despised his boss, even more so than most people hated their bosses.

"Oh, hi there, Matt," he mumbled, his eyes making contact with Matt's sporadically and each time only for a few seconds. "How's business tonight?"

"Not sure, just started. Looks pretty slow, though. You're only my second customer, other than the fine ladies of Hover's Bay Trailer Park over there." *Tits saggin', blood soppin' down her legs, bashin' her brains from her head.* "How's Klunesberg today, Frog?"

Frank shot him a look—a scared, wild look—one Matt recognized as a mix of fear and distaste for his ill-assigned moniker.

"Nothing out of the ordinary."

"So still being a prick then?" Matt laughed, while Frank merely smiled.

An awkward silence fell on the conversation, while Frank stared off into his feet. Matt knew to wait until Frank was ready to say something. You couldn't rush him, but the thing Matt really liked about Frank was that the wait was usually worth it. They had once gone shot for shot 'til closing and ended up pissing on a frozen lake on the outskirts of Hodgekiss Highway, talking about the mysteries of life until 6:00 a.m., right before the sun came up and killed the buzz. You could always trust Frank to be interested in talking about the deeper things, and he would actually listen, not just wait for his chance to talk.

"He was talking about Marshall today. Klunesberg, I mean."

Matt's breath trickled down into this stomach and hung there like stomach flu. He wanted to throw up. "Did they find him? Is he... dead?"

"No, no, nothing like that. The girl who disappeared, the dead girl, you know, the one Marshall was talking about the night he... well... he disappeared. Her family was protesting outside of city hall, asking for answers about the body. Klunesberg was talking about how he was a psycho who ran off with the body over his shoulder and a hard-on in his pants."

"Oh, what a load of horseshit!" Matt screamed, unaware of his anger as he slammed his palm on the chilly wood of the bar; it felt like it was made of bone. "I mean, shit, I knew this Klunesberg guy was an asshole for the way he treated you, Rodge, but I wasn't aware he was this much of piece of shit. Where does he get off saying that kind of stuff about Marshall? He didn't know the guy, and if he did know him, he damn well wouldn't be blaming him in the first place. This town, I swear…" His voice trailed off, hand in hand with his thoughts. He felt his eyes pulling themselves to his right, to where they were sitting, waiting for him with their legs practically spread. It would be so easy… It would feel so good… to forget it all, to forget Marshall, Frank, Veronica…

"I tried telling him, Matt, I did. Matt? Matt?"

His eyes snapped back to Frank, whose eyes were finally locked on Matt's watery blues. The girls told him they liked the way you could see flecks of green at times, almost like his eyes were an actual ocean. Then he would slide his hand up into their shirt, beneath the stiff confines of the bra, fingers dancing around the outer grazes of their nipple.

Pus drippin' from the corner of your eye, old, wrinkled lips gummin' on your dick, you sick fuck. "Do you want a shot? On me?" Matt poured two shots without waiting for an answer and took them both himself before pouring another two and sliding one in Frank's direction.

"Jesus, Matt, how many is that already?"

"As much as I need to make it through the night. You now how rough this job can get, hearing everybody's shit every night." He brought a hand sloppily across the bottom of his chin, wiping up the residue. His breathing finally seemed to slow, and he swore he could hear a poison song playing somewhere, but he couldn't tell which direction. Frank looked at his shot like it was about to mug him but took it nonetheless, his face tightening afterward. Matt followed suit, the burn taking more of a toll than usual, and he soon tasted vomit at the back of his throat.

"I just don't get it. Why would he even talk about that girl if he was about to run off with her corpse that night? That just ain't Marshall. He wasn't bright, but he was sensible, for Christ's sake. And he definitely wasn't a necrophiliac, I can swear to that. I just want some answers, and there's none to be found. I feel like I'm losing my mind a little bit here, if it wasn't lost already."

"Cheers to that." Matt poured another two shots.

"Thanks, but I'm fine." Matt shrugged and took both of them again, grimacing heavily and giving a loud whoop followed by a sharp intake of air and a laugh that spoke of nothing but drunken merriment. Frank's eyes met his again, and that hint of fear was more present than it had ever been. "Can I ask you something, Matt? Something just between us and no one else and something that you will try to answer with complete and total honesty?"

"Of course." The look worsened, and Matt desperately wanted it go away.

"I went to the grave. Last night. After the cops had cleared out of course. The ground had been dug up in one solid hole, maybe only a couple feet wide, maybe five all around, and it went straight down to the coffin, which had been torn open. Now, I'm asking you, Matt, and again this is in complete confidence, but what person trying to dig up a body would dig a hole like that? Why would he go through all the work of digging the hole if he was just gonna take the body and split? Doing unnecessary work? Now that especially doesn't sound like Marshall.

"Now, I've been talking to this kid who's been snooping around city hall lately. Bright kid, real bright actually, a bit of an oddball, but his intentions are good. Says he's Marshall's cousin, although I never asked Marshall about it… Anyways, he's been talking to me about weird stuff happening at that graveyard and asking questions about. Says there's something wrong with the place. I can vouch for it. When I was there, I couldn't stop shivering, even with two jackets on. I'm getting worried, Matt. I'm worried that something bad is going to happen and that it's going to happen very, very soon."

There was another awkward silence that settled over the air around them, making it feel heavy and dry. Matt poured himself another shot, letting the joyful buzz of intoxication set in, before he broke the silence. "So what exactly are you asking me here, Matt? In complete confidence, of course?"

He poured another shot in Frank's glass, who eyed it before throwing it back like a high school student desperate to get drunk for the first time. "Do you think I'm losing my mind?"

Tits saggin', blood soppin' from her legs. "I think we're all losing our minds."

He filled the shot glasses again. The two lifted them high in the air, clinked the glasses lightly, their eyes meeting, exchanging a solemn look of morbid understanding, and threw the shots back. When the glasses came down, a dull echo rang out that stuck to the rafters like mildew for the rest of the night.

She had woken up several hours before dawn had peaked its nosy head over the horizon, bordered by the hills of the cemetery, which seemed to turn its radiance into something almost ironic and sickening. The autumn chill sat in the air like an old friend come to visit, like he did every year, something familiar with all the annoyances that came with anything you became used to.

Gwen's eyelids hung heavy with a weight that she was also familiar with, one she usually bore after a night of troubled sleeping. Sleep had come easy enough, but the dreams she had had... She could barely remember anything about them, like most dreams, but she remembered the feelings they left. She felt the weight on her chest, the tightness in her stomach, all the usual discomforts of terrible, unbelievable sadness. Gwen could remember following something, somebody—somebody she had trusted. They were important in some way, but still she could not remember even a distinction of their face. Her mother was present, like she often was in her dreams. Gwen had once heard that dreams were the minds way of working out the problems of the day in a subconscious form, and if that was true, her mother would be in her dreams every night for the rest of her life—a concept scarier than anything a nightmare could produce.

Shooting a quick glance over her shoulder, Gwen slipped her stiffening fingers into her backpack and found the pack of Camel Menthols at the bottom. She popped open the lid, slightly crushed from her algebra book, and pulled out a slightly flattened cigarette, taking note to not pick the lucky. The lighter was a bit harder to find, as she patted several pockets to no avail before finding tucked into the inside pocket of her gray cotton hoodie. The thing was still slick with morning dew acquired from its night spent in the bushes in the backyard, which were somehow immune to the prophet's all-seeing gaze.

She lit the cigarette as she walked and caught herself looking at the lighter, a silver Zippo with her uncle's initials penned into the bottom—the only thing she had gotten from her uncle after he passed away. The day her uncle died was the day her aunt had died as well, the aunt who had once given her a stuffed bear for her fourth birthday, the friend she had kept longer than any other. After Frank's death, Meredith had fallen into a depression so deep that Gwen's mother was sure that sin would have claimed her. Instead, her desperation had led her to her sister's doorstep.

She finished her cigarette and stomped it out before she made it halfway to school, so she decided to take the long way that went down Johnson, cutting out the traffic that clogged up on Mulberry. The town of Loganville was a lot smaller than most, especially those usually deemed suburbs, and a hell of a lot further from most civilization than the name implied. During the 'fifties and the economic boom, the town moved closer to Skowhagen, close enough to get the designation, one that sold houses with the promises of a quiet, trouble-free life. After the money dried up, and the witch hunt of McCarthyism had turned everyone cynical and frightened again, the town slunk back into the woods that birthed it—factories closing, farms becoming farms—and became desolate and overgrown. But it kept the name suburb and the sleepy dreariness that came with it, one composed of empty, deserted streets that made the town seem like one comprised entirely of spirits that moved things about when you weren't looking.

Her shortcut took her past the Church of Saint Francis, her mother's second home—which is probably why she knew it so well by now—and the east side of the city hall building that stood on Main, as well as the place where she had her first kiss with Bobby Loth in the seventh grade, if you were willing to go a bit out of the way down Denmark. She usually was, as she had fond memories of Bobby Loth (they called him Bobby Sloth). He had been a true gentleman, although all boys in grade school usually were; most of them were more afraid than the girls. Too bad he had moved to Columbus in eighth grade.

The smell of fall was in the air, a crispness that sparks memories of tart cakes and nights spent in hoodies, laughing with friends as you crunch through dead, cracked leaves. It always brought a casual grin to her face, especially when walking through the autumn chill. Walking seemed to calm her more than anything else; the stillness gave her time for her thoughts, the only things her mother couldn't control.

After the bench of Bobby Sloth, you came to the edge of the park that came to the edge of Loganville West's east parking lot, a gargantuan behemoth of concrete that clashed sharply with bright grass and ancient trees of the park like polar opposites crammed side by side by some kind of brutal magnetism. Even from across the park, Gwen could see very few cars in the lot, most in staff spaces, and she wasn't surprised. She usually arrived before anyone else. Her cheap brick of a phone, received only as a means of keeping tabs on her every movement, read 6:45 a.m.

Mornings at the house of the holy prophet consisted of a breakfast made up of oatmeal and an orange, confession of one's sins and prayer assignment, and more of the prophet's ravings about the destruction of morals by the homosexuals and the Blacks and the coming of Jesus to bring the holy, the clean (the white), up to heaven to be saved and given eternal life. Needless to say, after a decade or so, she had begun waking up early and getting to school before Sylvia and Meredith Sinais' eyes opened to behold yet another day without their Savior coming to rescue them.

As she passed through the rolling curves of the park, over the stiff wood chips and under the rusted steel monkey bars and yellow plastic slide covered in morning dew and something that smelled like Keystone Light—she swore she could hear that same melody from the night before, the one played by the boy who sat in the graveyard with his old, chipped guitar. It was silent again by the time she entered the parking lot, stumbling over the first parking block, like she did every morning, always noting to remember it the next day, only to forget in her insomnia-clouded trek. She got past Marcy Grunt's Honda when she saw Veronica, talking with Christine Johansen and Kim Hasing—one a cheerleader, the other a representative on the student council—neither a fan of a religious freak's daughter who frequented the library and talked about the conformity and complacency of modern society in regular conversation.

Gwen darted around the west side of the gymnasium, hoping to sneak in the side door before the Witches of Westwick decided to take notice of her, but they had spotted her long before she had them and made their move quickly to block her path.

"Good morning, Gwen. You're here early. I assume you came to use the shower since your house probably doesn't have one. Too sinful, I imagine," Veronica said with her brightest smile.

"Veronica, good to see you're still stuffing your bra. Christine. Kim."

Gwen started to move by, when Kim spoke up, "What's it like being the daughter of the craziest bitch in Loganville? Does it worry you that you're gonna inherit her title one day and all the pressure of living up to it?"

Her conscience, her better instincts, and her gut all told her to just keep walking, but still she whirled about, trying to keep her face as expressionless as possible.

"Well, if that's true, Kim, I guess I'd have to say I'd feel better than inheriting the title of biggest slut in town—although you won't have to worry about living up to anything, not with all the guys you've already blown before…"

The slap came quick and harsh across her face, over before she saw it coming, stinging more after the fact than when it had happened. Christine jumped forward and wrapped her fingers, tipped with bright pink nails that spelled out her name (and an additional heart), around Kim's arms and pulled her back. Kim eventually shook Christine off and started walking back toward the front doors, but not before casting one last spiteful glare into Gwen's soul. Christine looked back as well, with a look of odd glee and sympathy that made Gwen feel like there was some sick joke she was unaware of, but then again she often felt like that.

"Where do you get off?" Veronica was staring hard at her, her face filled with tight anger that added an unnatural age to it. She moved close enough so that her breath bounced wet and heavy across Gwen's cheeks. "You think you're so clever, that you're above all of us, despite the fact that your mother is a fucking psychopath and your father never gave enough of a shit about you to stick around. Somehow you've convinced yourself your quirks make you a smart, clever, Zooey Deschanel–type of girl with a heart as big as her eyes, but you're not, Gwen. You're just another crazy bitch like your mother."

She wanted to hit her then harder than she had hit anything in her life, but the utter originality of it after Kim's slap stopped her firmly in her tracks. Mr. Straus, standing just over by the gym doors, had begun to stare, so Gwen lowered her voice.

"And what makes you better, Veronica? You're father's money? Or his mistresses? Your mother's outfits? Or is it her drinking problem? Or is it because you think that just because you dress better than me, have a better phone than me, and have let more boys feel your tits than me, you have the right to be an obnoxious twat to me and everybody else in this school?"

Veronica's hazel-green eyes flickered for just a second, but they did not waver from Gwen's. Her cheek had begun to burn and had gone a shade of rose red.

"You're going to die alone, Gwen, with no one to remember you or care that you were here. No one will give a shit. If I saw you on the side of the road, your mouth dry and bloody, I would not give you water, and I think a lot of people at this school would feel the same. People at least like me. I have friends, people who care about me. You have nothing and no one. Even your crazy mother can't stand you. I know I'm better than you, Gwen. I know I'm better than most people. I've made myself better than them. Sure, I might've started with an advantage, but that doesn't mean that I'm still not better than all the freaks at this school, like you."

Gwen chuckled, turning Veronica's grin into a scowl. "I think, very soon, Veronica, you're going to see just how ordinary you really are."

Her mouth dropped open awkwardly, and a weird gasp of frustration came out, something Gwen had never seen Veronica do, in all the terrible years of knowing her. A wave of satisfaction swept her, and she followed it around the gym to the fields in the back—not looking back, thinking that made the moment that much better. She slipped behind the bleachers toward the school's south entrance, but as she did, she saw the same boy from the night before standing by the gate, guitar slung at his side like a third arm and a smile on his face, his aquamarine eyes locked on hers.

Both of her cheeks had gone scarlet as she scurried inside.

When I was six, I got lost in Makers Woods for seven hours.

I had been visiting a friend's house… Natalie Peterson, a member of my Sunday school, if I remember correctly, but who can be sure anymore? Anyways, I tried to cut through because I had stayed out a bit later than I was supposed to, and in those days, my mother still believed that pain was the best communicator of God's love, especially for his youngest and most foolish—the one most prone to sin, you see. My mother's methods varied over the years, like different chapters of the Bible. I always found it a little funny that they couldn't see how much like us God really was. He went from being trusting and naive, to vengeful and filled with spite for his own creations, until he finally wiped them all out. Then he got tired of destroying every person to ever have a dirty thought and decided to settle down and start a relationship with a group of people, fighting together through various setbacks, including the death of a child. That's just how I saw it, at least, and everyone always told me I was too smart for my own good.

But I'm rambling again. I always do when talking about the past, but who doesn't? Well, as I was saying, I ended up taking a wrong turn down a path I hadn't explored very much. I stayed relatively calm. I always thought of myself as a levelheaded child, but when the sun started to go down and the shadows started to cover everything, it was hard not to feel like I was in a horror movie. I began running all over, my head whirling about, just looking for something, anything I recognized, until I finally found the side of Ms. Mable's general store with the picture of the cow drinking the large jug of milk with sunglasses on it. I had never been happier to see that cow. I usually thought the thing was pretty weird, until that moment of existential relief.

I arrived home past ten o'clock, and my mother was waiting for me in the blue cotton armchair, her wooden switch clenched in her white knuckles. She hadn't even called the police. She told me that God had told her I would be back, and it would be her job to reprimand me for my sinful actions. I guess she thought that I had been out whoring around or doing drugs even though I wasn't old enough to actually know what any of those things were. After getting several welts, I ended up going to my room and crying my eyes out. They were red for days afterward.

Like most parts of my past, I pushed that night deep down where it'd stay hidden and turn nasty inside me. The only time I really ever talked about it before now was to my aunt several days after it happened back when she was still Meredith Reinhart. She laughed when I told her; it was the weirdest thing. She told me that the same thing happened to my mother when she was a little girl.

It seems her father, my grandfather, had staged a similar welcome for her. Turns out, on top of everything else my mother was, she wasn't very original either

The way the wind blew in from the window screen across the back of her neck caused the hairs back there to stand on end, sending electricity down her spine, like fingers caressing her neck, lulling her into a heightened sense of serenity. Sleep kept knocking on her door, her eyes dipping beneath her lids every few moments that Mr. Letcher's voice droned on about the ratifications of certain French amendments during the Revolution of 1795 and their effect on modern democracy. Gwen had lost interest after hearing about Marie Antoinette's beheading, something she had been eagerly waiting to hear about since she first heard about her ideas regarding the consumption of cake. Now, all she could think about was the graveyard that stood on the hill on the edge of town and how dreadful it looked from her window, so ominous, and even that was putting her to sleep.

The bell ring came sharp and quick, yet she stirred awake slowly, her eyes fluttering open as if in a struggle with an unseen force.

"Geez, you look dead."

Her eyes opened instantly, half expecting to see a flash of golden hair but was almost taken aback when the shaggy brown curls of Billy Raimi replaced them—a casual grin hung on his face, respectable and showing just enough teeth to be professional in any situation. Gwen could always tell when people practiced their smile in a mirror. Anyone could tell that Billy spent a lot of time in front of a mirror. He wasn't anything remarkable to look at, but his hair, messy as it was, would always be shiny from hair gel and posed into a nice symmetrical position, no doubt hoping that symmetry would make up for his large nose and eye that were too widely spaced.

"Yeah, and you look like a Jewish Chewbacca," Gwen said, drowsiness causing her words to blend together.

Billy laughed, though it was strained, his obvious insecurity about his gleaming Jewfro—as the kids colloquially called it—showing in his less-than-enthusiastic chuckles. He would never dare not laugh at one of Gwen's jokes, though. Gwen expected it every time now, so she had stopped trying to actually be funny around Billy and see what she could get away with by stringing silly words together.

"So do you plan to spend the rest of the day with Mr. Letcher or the night as well?"

The joke to cover it up came next, something casual about her promiscuity or her interest in someone else to make it seem like he was disinterested in her any sort of a sexual way, all the while trying to conceal the stiffer spot in his pants. Gwen knew the routine by now. Like any teenage girl, she wasn't exactly happy with how she looked, but she knew how some of the boys stared at her. Their eyes focused, dead-centered on her breasts or her ass, desperate to shove their dicks into something that would fit them. She understood the desires well enough, she supposed; she had them herself from time to time. Still, she didn't like at the way boys openly stared or the way they seemed to take a weird sort of pride from it. Too many of her generation took pride in the smallest of victories; too many tried to build themselves pedestals on empty beer bottles and falsified sexual accomplishments.

Then there were the kids like Billy, whose pride came from those who said it was okay to feel any. She didn't want to think of Billy as spineless, but it was the closest word that came to mind and still sounded close to polite. Billy was infatuated; in that, he liked the idea of something more than what that something actually was—for example, the people who still believed the church was the word and will of Jesus Christ even though it was more interested in gay bashing than feeding the homeless, or the people who believed that America was still focused on preserving freedom when it was more concerned with listening in on its own citizens' conversations.

Billy's problem was not that he saw his country or his church as something it wasn't, but he saw Gwen as his salvation—the perfect girl who would fix all the problems in his life just by letting him shove his lips uncomfortably against hers; the girl who would make him more noticed by his father just because she agreed to attend a feature film at the local theater with him on Friday and let him slide a hand up her shirt and fondle her tits on Saturday; the girl who would cause all his insecurities to disappear just because she would lay on her back for him.

Billy had told her all his problems on day 1, causing all of Gwen's interest to fade within seconds; but since Gwen, unlike most of the girls in school, continued to listen, Billy had marked her as "one of the good ones"—one of the girls who would save him. You could tell by the way he looked at her, the way his gaze hung an extra second longer than everyone else's and how his eyes always went to her when asked a question, as if he was noting whether she was listening or not. It was the same way he looked at Francine Kleenwich and Marcie Fowler. She couldn't really blame Billy or any of the other people she considered infatuated for feeling like that. When she had first met Bobby Loth, she had been the same way, before she grew out of it. Maybe that's why she hated it so much; it reminded her of her younger self.

"Well, you know how much I need the extra credit," she finally responded, giving her best sultry smile and flipping her hair back.

She managed to catch a quick look of Billy's reddened face, his eyes wide as a dog that had just been given his first bowl of water on a dry day. That look struck a painful chord deep in Gwen's stomach, like sour guilt bubbling over into her throat. She felt bad for Billy then and for not loving him as much as he wanted. She couldn't remember exactly when she had turned so cynical and narcissistic toward the world, when she could rant and bitch as naturally as she could breathe. Many considered the cynical to be twisted form of the bitter and lonely, and Gwen couldn't disagree with that. Loneliness had been something she carried with her for her whole life, like a backpack filled with rocks you couldn't take off and you became used to, so much so you forget it's there. And when you forgot something was there, it was a part of you, wasn't it?

"C'mon, I'll walk you to lunch."

"All right, let me grab my things," Gwen said, desperate for something to distract her from her thoughts that had turned against her quicker than usual this school day.

Grabbing the books hung on the thin steel shelf beneath her seat, she threw her things into her gray torn backpack with the word "bitch" written in large pink highlighter by Bobby in her freshman year. He had laughed his ass off at that, and Gwen had too—out loud, at least. Inside, she kept thinking about what her mother and everyone else would think. Even recalling that made her feel sick; she hoped the walking might settle her stomach.

The staunch yellow walls of Loganville West greeted her like a nostalgic trip to an old relative whose relation you couldn't remember, and she could smell the bitter rust of the puke, laurel green lockers before her fingers ever brushed against them. Every corner was marked by some past event—some comedies, mostly tragedies—that would play themselves out in her mind every time she walked through them.

"Ugh, I hate this school," she said, passing the hallway where Sarah Bennise had shoved her into a locker a year ago after Gwen had told her that it was stupid to be upset over a text message that her boyfriend had sent three nights ago, especially since he was probably having sex with half the school anyway—which he was.

"I know, right? I hate everything about this shitty place. Loganville West has gotta be the worst school within a fifty-mile radius."

"Do you ever wish you could change it all? That you could go back and make all those stupid mistakes right? Say all the things you thought of three hours afterward?"

They passed the lunchroom door where Jack McCrayer had asked her to the Homecoming Bash her freshman year. He would cheat on her three days afterward with Nicole Peters, sending her a breakup text message while his other hand was servicing Nicole "Lover Of" Peters through her unzipped Dungarees.

"Well, I don't know if I regret ever talking to the guy who broke my heart," he paused to laugh, making sure she understood he was completely, 100 percent straight. Good, predictable Billy. Next would be the red herring to hide his interest in her.

"But I mean, yeah, everybody wishes they could change things. I would love to go back and retake that test in economics from last week, and I would certainly love to have practiced asking out Claire before screwing it up as royally as I did." Bingo. "Why do you ask? Do you wish you could just go back and stop your younger self from ever coming to this terrible place?" He laughed again, somewhat shakily.

"I guess. Not like I really have a choice on that, unless I just go back and run away from all this. It's just that everywhere I look, I think about all these things I wanna change, about all these stupid, vain people talking about the latest reality show, or whatever, I don't know. Maybe I do just need to run away."

"Where would you go?"

"Someplace that has no people whatsoever."

And it was then, right after the words had left her distractingly chapped lips and right before she was to share more chide comments on the spring break choices of young women her age, she saw *him* again—because if there was a God, he was one sadistic, irony-loving bastard.

The boy with the soft green eyes and the golden blond hair, like crumbled-up maple leaves and honey. The same boy she saw last night, playing at the edge of the graveyard, and again this morning, watching her from the football field. He emerged from the crowd of bumbling, confused high school students—either talking or bumping into those that were talking—and almost became immersed in what seemed like an ethereal glow as the lights came down over him. He was all she could look at. For once, there was something that commanded all her attention, and it was a boy, of all things. Irony really was a bitch.

"Gwen? Gwen! You still with me?" *No.* "Or are you completely asleep now?"

Billy tried to laugh, but the way he shook the chuckles awkwardly from his throat, Gwen could tell he knew what she was looking at. A small smile selfishly slipped onto her face.

"Who is that?" she said in a half whisper.

Her eyes were trying to pull his toward her, but she knew as soon as his olive eyes migrated anyway in her direction, hers would probably bury themselves into the floor, like lovesick ostriches.

"Who?"

"The blond kid in the gray hoodie."

"With the ratty jeans?" He, of course, decided to highlight that feature.

"Yeah."

Her heartbeat slowed considerably as he walked past her and his eyes drifted ever so slightly to where she stood, feet planted, buried into the floor. Their eyes met for only a brief second, one that contained more meaning than any hour-long documentary she saw on the Discovery Channel ever could, and a smile flashed across his drawn lips.

"I think his name is Rag... Rahj... something weird like that. Oh, yeah, Range, that was it," muttered Billy, taking a while to say something he knew right away. "Range Barnfell, I think. He lives outside of town on a farm or something, I heard. A lot of people apparently see him wandering around at night, doing weird things, like playing guitar in people's yards or drawing weird pieces of graffiti on buildings around town, probably just some psycho country bumpkin."

Her eyes stayed on him until he slid through the half-cracked exit door of the school and watched as he closed it soundlessly shut behind him, alerting no teachers that his school day was ending at noon instead of three thirty today.

"I think he seems pretty cool," Gwen said and felt a strange warmth inside her, as it was the first thing she had said in a quite a long time that she was absolutely sure she meant.

The hollow buzz of the fluorescent lights was ever present inside Marty's Old-Fashioned Diner. It was a fact that Vel Veshkin knew all too well. It rattled around inside her head—day in, day out—for the past thirteen years, five months, twenty-three days. The days when she was hungover, the kind of hungover where even the mention of food made vomit jump to the back of her throat and any sound was accompanied by a dull yet piercing ache, were the worst.

Today was one of those days.

She scanned the restaurant once more from behind the counter, her eyes darting from white plate to white plate, from scuffed coffee mug to spotted glass. As soon as she saw that no one could possibly need anything, or at least was far enough away from her to not notice her slip away, she darted back to the kitchen and grabbed her coat from the hooks near the back door by the creaky, old ice machine that she was sure was bought from the old McDonald's that used to be down on Hickory—the one that got closed down after they had found the dull Hickam boy masturbating back in the freezer storage. She remembered the awkwardly dignified way Gloria Hickam tried to carry herself into church that week. Oh, to see the patron saint herself brought down to the level of the common folk... Vel had wanted to get a painting of that look on her face to hang above her bed at night.

Smiling, Vel made her way out into the back parking lot, stumbling over the crack outside the door frame like she always did, and pulled the pack of Newport 100s from the back compartment of her teal purse—or suitcase, as she liked to call it. Every time she went to buy another one, she swore she would get a smaller one and organize her shit, but she would always come back with one more expensive… and larger than the one she had before.

She lit the cigarette and let it dangle gently from her lips as she slid the black lighter back into her bag. The wind chill crept up on her slowly, settling into her bones like late fall rains into an old house's foundation. With it came the memories usually attached to the fall weather—old Halloweens spent running down the trick-or-treat paradise that was Denmark Avenue, football game in the bleachers eating terrible Loganville East popcorn, looking disdainfully as Gloria Hickam snickered to Bobby Ferrman about her. Vel tried to stop thinking about Gloria, but once she got going, one thing would remind her of another horrid thing the supposed saint had done to ensure Vel's life was as difficult and miserable as possible. The personal attacks like the name-calling and cellulite jokes behind her back stung well enough, but it was Gloria's complete likability with every other person that tore Vel to pieces. Every small success in Gloria's life stung like a venomous needle to Vel, slowly filling her with the painful acknowledgment that someone so despicable could get so far and be so well liked by people that wouldn't giving a passing notice to Vel.

After being diagnosed with depression, Vel left the state to spend time in a rehab clinic for a brief addiction to painkillers that had led to the… accident. Vel took a long drag as she heard the low rumble dance out from the trees around the edge of the road. It came in a low, primal pattern that caused tension to wriggle up her spine. The lustrous black Escalade came rounding around the turn of the Interstate, like a bat out of hell, its brights robbing Vel of her vision for a moment as it pulled up through the crackling gravel parking lot.

The car screeched up, turning at a rigid angle at the last second to avoid scraping up against a nearby Honda, and left the car placed defiantly across two spots. The front left tire was even jammed between the two cement markers near the curb. He hopped out of the front seat heavily, almost dramatically, fries falling of his mouth that was already involved in a very stressing conversation.

"And that's why I never fuck Latina chicks anymore. I was cleaning up for almost like three days afterward. I'm surprised you guys didn't even notice it back there. Fucking coochie juice errywhere, I swear."

"This is why I really didn't wanna hang out with you, Tyler. You coulda fucking told me that before I sat back there for a half hour."

"Not my fault my nigga Frog here called shotgun. You need to quit being such a busta, Matt. It's just a little coochie watah. Pussy sauce. Nattylube. Your bitch ass just needs to chill the fuck out and come have some pancakes with his homie."

Tyler walked up, his arm around the bald old janitor everybody called Frog. And Matt Métier, the handsome little bartender from Terri's down on Forty-Third—who resembled Chris Hemsworth with a dash of McDreamy and a reputation that matched, all of them sporting a bad case of the glossy eyes and dumbfounded gaze of the forlorn drunkard—came up behind him as Tyler looked her up and down as he often did. Tyler looked like a mix of Steve Buscemi and that skinny kid from *Hustle and Flow*—and maybe a pug.

"How's it goin' tonight, Tyler?"

"Who the hell is Tyler? Am I supposed to know this motherfucker? How many times I gotta tell you, ho, my name is Tranze. The Tyga Killer. T-Rock. T-Bones. Any of those will do, bae, but I don't know this Tyler fool you be talking about."

Vel tried not to chuckle as the flush came upon his pale cheeks.

"Ah, right, I forgot," Vel said with a sideways scoff and exhale. "What are you delightful young men up to tonight?"

"Oh, Velma, you always spoil an old guy like me," Frank said, his cheeks rising high in a grin that encompassed his whole face, it seemed.

"Had a bit of the good stuff tonight, have we, boys? Eh? What's the occasion?"

Matt stepped forward—or stumbled forward, rather.

"Drinking for our buddy Marshall, smoked a little bit for him too. By the way, mind if I grab one of those from you?"

"Sure thing."

She passed him a cigarette, making sure his finger slid all the length of hers as she handed it to him. He gave her an odd look before putting the cigarette in his mouth and pulling a Zepplin Zippo lighter from his pocket.

"The gravedigger? Didn't he disappear?" She always thought the guy reminded him a little bit of John Malkovich in the 'nineties when he still had hair.

"Yes, ma'am, nobody's seen any sign of the poor bastard."

"It's an awful shame. He was nice, always tipped well."

Frank's face turned back into the one of gloom that Vel usually saw when she saw him floating around town.

Tyler leaned in closer to her. "Shit's got my homies, Frog and Matty Ice, real depressed and all that, so I was bringing 'em out, showing 'em a good time, trying to get their minds off all that sad bullshit."

"Well, look at you, a regular humanitarian, like Brad Pitt."

"Yeah, 'cept I sure as hell wouldn't be adopting any Black children. I be getting enough the ol'-fashioned way as it is, you know what I'm saying?"

Vel gave him a discerning look then, the ones she would save for every douchebag that would hit on her on the late-night diner shifts especially during football season came round and the tourists from Mackinrow, fresh from leaving their wives for the first time all year, would sneak ass pinches under the table and leave disgusting drawings on the receipt stubs along with motel room numbers.

"Man, fuck this, I'm hungry. Let's bounce inside. C'mon, Frog!"

Frog nodded glumly before giving a warm smile to Vel and shuffling after his outrageous companion as they headed into the diner. Matt remained behind, inhaling past the halfway mark on his cigarette.

"Always the classy one, isn't he?" A warm smile had inched its way onto Matt Métier's face while she had been busy imparting Tyler with death stares.

She could definitely understand his reputation among the women of Loganville. That smile could melt through the iciest woman's heart; even if the last man she had been with had beaten her bloody, it'd be hard not to find comfort in this boy's dimples.

She had heard the stories about Matt as well—all the ones about his late-night activities, his *numerous* late-night activities all through Speckford County.

"He certainly tries really hard, doesn't he?" Vel affirmed, straightening the glasses on her nose and suddenly feeling self-conscious about them again for the first time in years. She almost swore she could hear Gloria's catty laugh rattling off the trees.

"So… how long have you been working here now, Vel? Ten years?"

His piercing green eyes hit her then, reminding her there was a little Channing Tatum to him as well, irises like seawater that seemed to wash over you. She could have sworn she felt the sting of salt in her nose.

"Thirteen years, five months, twenty-three days, sweetie."

She took a puff of her cigarette and stared at Matt, letting her lust dance across her lips as she inhaled slowly. Matt's grin only widened, and suddenly, a warmth stirred between her legs that she had not felt in years—not since Roy Hill from the lumberyard on Forty-Five had taken her to that restaurant, the Gilded Lily, the night he had proposed to her. He beat her senseless then and there after she had refused. She still got uncomfortable sitting in any restaurant that wasn't a diner or a cheap fast-food chain.

"Did you hear about the Kanye West and Kim Kardashian baby?" Vel said, leaning forward on her toes like she used to for the boys in high school—her classic "ready and willing" play whenever the boy was moving too slow for her rabid yet sensible taste. It hadn't worked very well back then, and she was mortified to be doing it now. But this young buck had her head swimming.

"I did not."

"They named her North West. Can you believe that? How crazy can some people be?"

"I guess I can." He shuffled closer then, tossing his cigarette butt to the ground, the flame spiraling like an out-of-control space shuttle tumbling from the heavens. "Why would you think I'd know anything about that?"

He got even closer so that his chest was right in front of her and seemed to keep the breaths from escaping her throat, which had seemed to have gone dry. She could feel a tingle shoot through her then, like a static spark that seemed to pull all the tension from her and replace it with urges she knew all too well.

"I just figured… you know… your sister might have been talking about it… or something. I don't really know what I'm saying."

Almost instantly, a tension rippled through his body, noticeably at first and then more reserved, as she knew he was trying to hide it. His gaze left her and went to the ground.

"Excuse me. I think Frog is looking for me to save him from our mutual friend."

He brushed past her then, not forcibly, but almost as if she wasn't even there, which somehow seemed to make it almost worse. She wanted to call him out for the jackass that he was right there, but her own shame held her back. How could she be stupid enough to think that a handsome young thing would have any interest in her, someone who had peaked before she had her first period? Gloria's laughing face hung in her mind, like a painting that had always been there until the curator decided it was time to pull it from the basement for display once again.

She let out a heavy sigh of air and looked up at the night sky, the stars looking like crystal tears, she thought, or some kind of beautiful garbage John Hughes would write about in this situation. Several streaks of light popped up like LEDs on a switchboard, and Vel found herself wishing that one of those stray chunks of space rock would come down and crush her into dirt to spare her the embarrassment of walking back inside.

"Did you hear? Some lady got hit by a meteor!"
"Bullshit!"
"No joke, man. I swear to God."
"Where the fuck did some chick got hit by a meteor? And why am I just learning about this now?"

"Don't you go on the Internet, dickhole?"

"I broke my last MacBook and have a goddamn Motorola Razer. Give me a fuckin' break."

"Your life sounds pretty gay, man."

"Fuck you, Derrick."

"Susie McAllister posted about it last night, said it happened a couple of blocks away from where she was."

"Here?"

"Not here, dumb shit. You probably would've *heard* it then."

"Suck a dick, Derrick!"

"Where was she?"

"Up in Fair Oaks. She was on the south side, and apparently, it landed up north near Castle Rock."

"By Marcus Field?"

"Yeah, couple blocks away from where Saturday practice was."

"Shiiiiiit."

"I know, right?"

"I heard it landed in Castle Rock but that it was near a church. A Baptist one. Mormon? One of the crazy ones."

"How do you know it hit a girl then, Zach?"

"That's what Susie said. I messaged her and got the whole story from her."

"What the hell was she doing over in Fair Oaks anyway?"

"She was with some dude from Penbrook."

"Penbrook? So what you're trying to say is that he's a douchebag?"

"What's she doing with some dude from Penbrook?"

"Yeah. Why isn't she at *my* house sucking *my* dick, like usual?"

"She met him at some party last Thursday, at Barry's place."

"North's catcher?"

"Yeah."

"Where was I?"

"You were drinking with us and Mary and Kelly down by my uncle's bar, remember? Jack went off with Kelly, and you took a piss on her clothes?"

"Fuck, yeah, I do, great night."

"Well, anyway, Susie just heard this super loud bang outside, like thunder if you were right next to it in the cloud. Her and this Penbrook guy go running out and see this huge fire burning a couple miles away, and they drive over, or at least as far as they could, 'cause there was traffic backed up there for blocks. They run over, and the police already got the area taped off and shit. The thing had rammed right into the side of a church and into the graveyard. I'm talking dead bodies thrown up everywhere, tossed all over the ground. She said she even saw a skull hanging from a tree branch."

"Whoa."

"Yeah, there was some girl they had off to the side and covered in a blanket, trying to calm her down. Apparently, her mother had been in the church, setting up for some kind of picnic for Thanksgiving the church was organizing. She said the girl's eyes were just… gone. Dead. Nothing there at all."

"Damn, I can't believe that happened like ten miles from here. I drove up there two days ago to buy weed."

"Speaking of driving for drugs, Greg, are you still giving me a ride over to your guy's place?"

"Yeah, to get some goodies?"

"Does he have that new stuff you were talking about?"

"Yeah, he should have a couple pills left at least. He had like crates full but was selling a lot. There was like a straight-up line last time I was there. Swear to God."

"Well, we gotta stop at a gas station so I can grab cash."

"You trying to come, Derrick?"

"Fuck Derrick, he can't come."

"Why can't I come?"

Like a cherubim descending from a lofty hall above, the morning bell rang and saved Gwen's conscious mind from any more of the drivel that had been shoved into by the open drainage pipes sitting several desks away from her. She lifted her head slowly from her arms, feeling her forehead stick uncomfortably to her forearm. The spot was red when she looked down at it and shaped like a skull… or at least it looked like one to her. I guess she could see why someone would call her a nut for saying it looked anything close to a skull. The left eye was smashed and half a forehead higher than the right, and the jaw had no visible bottom; but every inch of her swore that a tiny red skull was smiling back at her.

The heavy buzz of room 232's large fluorescent lights droned on to the tune of dozens of conversations, pouring from the mindless mouths of her classmates, talking about the sports game that ended just a second before the buzzer and how that made it better than the previous game that ended without anyone diving across the floor; about the party where Jeannie Sayers barfed all over Roy Lopez's dick; and about how last week's biology test was worse than most of the other ones before it because it covered things from before winter break—which was simply unthinkable and declared to be about as cool as "a flaming hot gerbil up your ass."

Homeroom was the tip of the iceberg that she called her school day. Every day seemed to pass slower than the one before, each grinding minute clicking past like a rusted gear in a clock that had no business running anymore.

"All right, everyone. Sit down and get out something to do. I don't care what it is, as long as it is school related and not on your cell phone, which may I remind you, Ms. Hawkins, are supposed to be in your locker. Why don't you run down there now for me? And try not to get—ahem—lost, Ms. Hawkins, because after ten minutes, I'll let Vice Principal Hemstry know you're on the loose, all right? Craig, I'm sure Ms. Bern can figure her bra out all on her own if you'd like to take your seat back on the other side of the room. And try not to flip me off on your way back this time… Well, at least you tried. Do you want the pink slip now, or when I see you at detention? All right, two slips in detention it is. Quiet down now, people. I guarantee Mr. Nelson is not nearly as interesting as he thinks he is."

Mr. Jonas did his best to settle the class down to the point where the only sound was the hum of the lights and the few occasional whispers from those past the first two rows of the classroom. Finally, when a dull sleepiness had overtaken all but the most boisterous and talkative (see, *insecure*) students, he took a seat behind his wooden desk covered in cracked splinters and dry-erase graffiti dicks and opened up his laptop and began to laboriously check his baseball fantasy league draft picks.

Gwen began to giggle, just thinking about the look of excitement on his face when he had told her after class about his upcoming season and how his wife had already changed the Wi-Fi password on him three times in an effort to keep his habit down. His small, beady eyes would bounce around behind his large frames glasses anytime he talked about it, like a dog that had just been flashed its favorite toy. This was often done when Gwen would stay after class to ask about some other faraway place that she fantasized about during homeroom that day.

Every time, Mr. Jonas would bring up a long list of beautiful-sounding churches from the Renaissance or talk about the new pieces that would be displayed at some of the museums there this time of year, along with a long list of hostels that he had stayed at when he had traveled abroad during his late twenties. He would smile at her, ask when she was planning on going to Europe, to which she would always reply, "Soon." While Gwen had never even been out of the state, let alone the country, to just hear of a place that wasn't... *this* one, just seemed to make everything a little less excruciating.

Today she was thinking of Athens, of the Parthenon stacked high on a crumbling peak against the Marengo sunset that gleamed against the pure marble bodies that stood pure, beautiful, and immovable. She sighed as she opened her eyes to the crisping yellow pages of her math book, an unfinished problem asking for the y to an x she didn't much care about.

A cold gust from the cracked window caressed the back of her neck and brought the familiar smell of green grass and rusting window screens. A tingle shot down her spine, and she started to drift into a place between sleep and the waking world. She struggled to keep her eyelids open, but the tingling wave had already began to seep through her.

In the darkness of her eyelids, she saw a slow glow start to rise, a heavy orange glow like the sunset in Athens, except with a deeper shade of red, like blood—a familiar sight, yet unsettling at the same time, like something seen in a nightmare not remembered. It seemed to start pulsing slowly, growing brighter and brighter as the whispers around homeroom slowly seemed to get louder and louder, crescendoing into a wild scream that seemed too guttural to be anything made by a human. A throbbing pain shot through her temple and caused her to sit up in her chair, shaking the drowsiness like a dog shakes water from its fur.

Blinking, she saw that she had drifted off to sleep for a grand total of three minutes and fifteen seconds, with nine minutes to go before they even passed the halfway mark. With boredom seeping in, she started to stare around the room and caught Jimmy Grefleski slamming his tongue through a finger-made vagina right in Susie Bern's direction. Marla Hawkins had returned from her locker while Gwen had been drifting off and was now furiously tapping away at her phone screen, buried in the crease of the junior-year biology textbook with a family of giraffes enjoying leaves far more than Gwen had ever enjoyed anything in her own life. She was almost jealous of a bunch of giraffes. She caught a quick glimpse of Craig in the back row flipping off a freshman girl she didn't recognize before he promptly redirected it at her.

With a grimace, she turned toward the window and looked out at the track field, dirty brown grass growing over the unused forest track near Makers Woods. She remembered running out there during her freshman year with the old girls' volleyball coach watching them all, who got fired after he allegedly was caught having sex with a member of his team, after providing her with the plenty of liquor and cocaine, of course, if the rumors were too believed—which in a town as small as Loganville, they always were. Gwen remembered the way he used to make Marcie Kennick and Zedoya Klunesberg run extra laps because they were "talking" even when the two weren't near each other all class. It definitely wasn't because the duo had the biggest tits in the freshman class. They had stopped using the old track after a new one was built around the football field, and while Gwen missed running near the tall oaks and expansive shrubs, she conversely supported the lumping of all the jocks into one large, easily avoidable spot.

And suddenly, she saw him sitting there, leaning back against the trunk of one of those decrepit old oaks, an old guitar on his lap, and she felt stupid for not seeing him earlier. His bright blond hair was buried beneath a plain white hoodie that hung loosely off of his shoulders, the sleeves pushed up all the way to the elbow. His eyes never made it up past the neck of his guitar, as if it was the only thing that existed.

Her stomach lurched as she stood up, as every instinct of her body told her to sit back down and keep staring at the math problem until an answer that seemed close enough to a real one came to her, yet she pushed on and walked straight toward Mr. Jonas desk. Gwen could feel the eyes on her when she stood up, but she ignored it as best she could.

"Uh, Mr. Jonas," she said, trying to keep her eyes away from the window, "can I use the washroom, please?"

"Well, this is normally the part where I, the well-spoken and incredibly handsome teacher, am supposed to ask, 'Well, I don't know, can you?' but for the sake of cheesiness everywhere, I'll just give you a hall pass instead," Mr. Jonas said, digging through one of his drawers overflowing with papers, many of them crude sketches, including a laminated copy of a doodle someone had made of Mr. Jonas "enjoying a healthy, wholesome meal of dicks" that he proudly showed to new students.

"Thanks, Mr. Jonas."

"Oh, you're most welcome. You know how much of a struggle it is to fill one of these bad boys, Gwen. Student name? Reason of departure? They act like I'm some kind of educated man here."

Mr. Jonas finished scribbling his quick cursive on the small yellow slip, the unusually large amount of hair on his knuckles brushing against his desk, and leaned in close to hand it to her.

"Now, don't tell your friend Ms. Hawkins this, but I left the time back blank. Just because I can trust you a little bit more than I can the rest of these ravenous dogs. But that's just between us."

Gwen couldn't help but chuckle as Mr. Jonas gave her a quick wink, leaning back in his chair with a satisfied grin on his face as he looked again at his laptop screen.

"You're the best, Mr. Jonas."

"I know. I know. If I had a nickel for every time someone told me that, I'd be able to buy that second Ferrari for my third summer home down in Barbados," he chuckled, his eyes still darting around his computer screen before turning back to Gwen with a look of genuine interest and concern that always took her by surprise, probably just because how little she had ever seen a look like that before. "That reminds me, Gwen. How's the vacation plans coming? The trip to Helsinki? When was that again?"

"Soon. There's still a couple things I need to get in order first, like lodging," *Mother*, "the airline," *Mother*, "schoolwork," *Mother*, "Money." *Mother. Mother. Mother.* "There's a lot more planning than I thought."

"Ah, Gwen! I took for you the rugged idealist, just picking up a bag and jumping on a plane, finding yourself someplace you've never been, marveling at how just like when you were young, the world is a stranger again. There are new things to see, to understand, to feel! Ah, and now I'm rambling again, Gwen, look what you've done, making me feel like one of those old-timers telling kids to get off my lawn and sitting on hemorrhoid pillows.

"But I understand, Gwen, I do. It's hard to do what you want at your age, especially coming from a household like yours." His face grew more haggard then, withdrawn almost, and his eyes drooped down to the glowing screen once more. "If you ever need any help, Gwen… with the trip I mean, or anything really, never hesitate to come and ask me for it, all right?"

A weight seemed to fall on her then and snuggled warmly inside her chest, like a cat forcing its way onto your lap. Guilt welled up inside her, urging her to tell this man, a man who seemed genuinely interested in her well-being and, by all reasons of common sense, she should tell everything that was wrong with her world—her mother's wild prophecies that kept Gwen locked in her room on Friday nights; the bruises from every "demon" that had been cast out of her; the cold basement floor against her skin; their eyes looking at her, dressed in white robes, chanting, looking down on her…

"Of course, Mr. Jonas, but I gotta…"

"Ah, yes, of course! Go! Go! I didn't mean to hold you up. And by the way, this next bit's just for the other kids. Take your time, all right?"

Gwen struggled to nod, to let the chance slide all the way through the cracks of her fingers. With a final wink, Mr. Jonas slinked back into his chair and slipped back on the role of homeroom monitor, distant and uncaring.

"And hurry back, young lady! I wanna see some actual homework done today! Fee fi fo fum and all that!"

With one back glance toward the window, she started out the door, managing to catch one last middle finger from Craig as she walked past the trash can that held the door to the hallway. As she turned down the adjacent hallway leading to the school's practice fields on the west side, she could hear Mr. Jonas having a shouting match with Craig and smiled.

Shoving past the light metal doors that led out to the gym, she cut a quick left over to the rusted fence when she started to hear a simple melody drifting over the permeated gusts of the fall breeze. She stopped for a moment to listen and realized that she had no idea what she was doing out here. She had no plan. She was just walking up to some random boy she had seen yesterday, and what was she gonna say? "Hey I just wanted to let you know that I saw you in the hall the other day and thought you were breathtakingly hot"? Right in viewable distance of her entire homeroom? Was she really going to look and act like a total slut just to speak to this random boy for a couple of minutes?

Gwen started toward the fence again, and as she came around the large corner of the gym, she saw him sitting there against the dead tree, the melody washing over her once again. Her doubts seemed to drain away with it as her breath caught in her throat; her head seemed lighter and her thoughts, distant and hard to grasp. A couple steps more and she could finally make his face out clearly, from the cracks of stubble on his pale cheeks and evergreen tint of his eyes. A couple of steps closer and she could finally make out the song as one she recognized—Bob Dylan's "The Times They Are A-Changin'." Her aunt had played it for her back when she was more than her mother's other half. She remembered the way her voice wavered when she sang it after her husband had passed, almost as if she was afraid of what the words meant.

Before she realized it, she was standing right in front of him, watching him as his fingers danced across the tight coil strings. His face never left the guitar and never once met her face or even seemed to acknowledge that she was there. At first, she wanted to run away, to apologize, to do anything to make this horribly awkward moment go away; but a grin came over his face, one that seemed to be for her and kept her feet firmly in place. He finally arrived at the final chorus, his fingers slowing and the tune dropping to just above a whisper. When he struck the final G chord, the note seemed to pulse through the air around her and brought goose bumps to her flesh.

Silence fell, no longer awkward, but almost important, as if words would have only made it worse. He lifted his head slowly, and their eyes met. The grin on his face became a toothy smile as he set his guitar down, the neck resting against his twisted steel seat.

"I wasn't really expecting an audience."

"Your song was very nice."

"Dylan fan?"

"Sorta. I've only heard a couple of his songs, but I really like 'Subterranean Homesick Blues,' and 'Blowin' in the Wind,' of course."

He chuckled and pushed himself up from the ground, his feet sliding off the slick grass.

"What? Surprised I know who Bob Dylan is?"

"Kinda. I mean, I'll admit I don't expect most kids our age to be self-admitted Dylan fans, but I think part of me knew you did."

"How do you mean?"

"Not entirely sure, just a feeling really. I kinda thought it the first time I saw you, actually, something about you that made me think we might have a bit in common."

A soaring sensation from under her breast filled her. "You've seen me before? Why didn't you come up and introduce yourself then?"

For some reason that Gwen couldn't quite understand, he laughed again, folding his arms over his chest. "I guess I prefer girls brave enough to come up to me first, ones not interested in the guy doing all the work for them."

"Does that mean you're not brave then? It seems a bit lazy on your part, really."

"I guess I can see your point there. Maybe I've been the scared one the whole time without even realizing it."

"It makes sense, I hate to break it to you. You could always do it now, I guess. Start a new leaf. Make today the first day of the rest of your life."

He smiled at her then, a genuine one, his eyes meeting hers again and really looking with an intensity she had never really seen before.

"The name's Range. Range Barnfell."

"That's a weird name."

"Well, this fresh-start thing's really going smoothly."

"I'm sorry. It just is."

"I bet your name is at least a thousand times weirder than mine."

"My name is Gwen."

"Wow, what a mouthful. That's definitely the weirdest name I've ever heard."

"I think it's weirder you think the name Gwen is weird, honestly."

"I'm sure your last name is plenty weird."

She almost told him then, before she stopped herself, the word catching in her throat like honey. The thought of her mother flashed through her mind, the local legend, the Monster of Loganville, and she, her daughter, in every right a freak, just like her mother. Her eyes darted to the ground, and she had already twisted her foot in the wet grass when he stuck his hand out in front of her.

"Good to meet you, Gwen Noname. That is a pretty weird one."

A smile snuck onto her face, and she placed her hand in his, feeling the roughness of it almost immediately. She reluctantly let go when he did, the silence blanketing them again.

"Why are you playing your guitar all the way out here? Shouldn't you be in class?"

"Shouldn't *you* be in class?"

"Good point. But why out here?"

"I like to go places that inspire me really. See, right here you can see deep out into Makers Woods, and there's this small break in the tree line and the light drips through like a prism. Helps me focus on something beautiful."

Gwen looked out at the woods and saw the sun, fighting to break through the heavy overgrow and casting rays of light, splintered to prisms of every color over the abandoned track. Muddy footprints filled with dirty rainwater seemed to shine like lagoons, and drops of water cascaded from the pine needles, filling the air with a deep earthy scent.

"There's something about places like this that fill me with peace—not just a calmness, but real, actual peace that loosens the muscles in your neck and replaces the weariness with satisfaction. If I could just capture that… that feeling… in a sound… that's what I sometimes think the meaning of my life is: to capture the perfect sound, the all-calming, all-pleasing chord that could give meaning just like those rays of light."

"I like that idea."

"Really? Most people say it's weird, too 'heavy' or 'deep' or something. Say I should focus on being a doctor or something, or just give up and apply to Starbucks."

"No, I think I understand what you're saying—the feeling when you see something really beautiful, like a mountain range or someone you don't like getting punched in the face, or… like a sunset in Athens, something that just makes sense in a world where a lot doesn't. I think it's a noble idea. Better than mine. To just run around the world, trying to find some view worth staring at for the rest of your life, even when you have no idea where to start looking."

"Seems pretty brave if you ask me."

Almost abruptly, she looked at him, saw the smile he carried on his face, and felt the spot where her heart was dropped away, never to be heard from. A desire stirred deep within her, one she had been trained to fear yet one she craved to give in to.

"Can you meet me somewhere tonight? If you're free?"

She struggled desperately not to choke on her own drool at this point. "I think I can. Where did you have in mind?"

His teeth flashed again as his smile grew wider, almost stretching across the entire lower half of his face, like the grin of a madman.

"The cemetery."

"Frog! Frog! Have you found that damn busted vent yet? I've been waiting up here talking to poor Ms. Hickam for almost a half hour now, and we both fear we are going to run out of things in this world to talk about before you ever finish. I swear to God above, I don't understand how it can be so hard for some people to understand instructions. I mean, you tell 'em the same thing over and over, and they still can't actually get through their thick skulls what you actually want done. The working-class in this country are so lazy compared to what China has. If I could only outsource a good janitor, you know what I mean?"

"Oh, Mr. Klunesberg, the things that come out of your mouth. A girl might think you were the devil himself with all that wit and charm."

The laugh boomed down the stairs, through the darkness of the basement that reeked of shit and mold, sending the hairs on the back of Frank's neck up on end.

"I assure you, Mrs. Hickam, that while I may appear devilish, this church is my sanctuary, just as much as it is yours."

"Call me Gloria, please, and again, Mr. Klunesberg, I can't thank you enough—"

"Harry."

"Excuse me?"

"Well, if you've given me the privilege to use your heavenly name, you should have full access to mine."

The sickening taste of yesterday's fajitas rose up Frank's throat.

"Oh, well, in that case... Harry, I can't thank you enough for sending your man—Frank, was it?—over to help us fix that antique heating system down there. It starts to become quite the bother in the cooler months. If our fund-raisers were a little more successful,

I think we'd finally be able to rip them out and put the new ones in, but you know how times are…"

Frank hesitated for a moment when he realized she used his real name; at least, he thought she did. Did he hear her right? Or was his wishful mind tricking him once again into thinking that there was some part of this town that wasn't breast-fed on Klunesberg's loquacious jabbering?

No… she actually called you by your name.

"Ever since that horrible incident with the Meers boy, the church has been pretty understaffed. Then I show up here this morning with a chill that would make an Alaskan shiver, I swear. I told Mr. Hickam and sent him down to the basement to work on the thing, but he comes back up more confused about the problem than when he left, wouldn't you know it? Then the poor thing had to go right to work, leaving me alone here with no idea how to fix this thing before the fund-raiser this weekend."

Frank stared down at the rusted riveted-steel coal furnace and couldn't help but scoff as he tightened the new, nonstripped screw into the grill frame, wrapping up his three and half minutes of actual work on the damn thing.

"Well, I am always happy to lend me and my team's service to everyone in this lovely town whenever possible. I try to think of myself in a somewhat humanitarian light, not exactly a Bill Gates if you will, but maybe more of a Steve Jobs. And Frog here is the really the best man for any job just because, well, honestly, he's got enough time on his hand to figure out whatever the problem is."

No.

The laughter from upstairs came again, lower and heavier, so heavy that Frank could feel it in his bones as his breaths started to come rapid-fire. His doctor had warned him about the effects of extreme stress on the body and had even tried prescribing him various pills (Zoloft, Ambien, etc.), but Frank had turned them down despite Dr. Yancy's insistence that his case was one of the most severe that he had seen, and he had studied at John Hopkins down in New York. Even so, the pills didn't seem to do much other than make him drowsy and the idea of taking more to the point of being so pilled out that you couldn't even recognize the signs of stress instead of actually dealing with them had not yet reached the point of being a seemingly better alternative to him yet.

"Frog?"

No, no, no, no, no.

"An affectionate little nickname I've given our good chum down there. It seems to have caught on very well among the community."

The quick, painful breaths soon turned into hyperventilation, and Frank found himself regretting not bringing his old inhaler, even though he hadn't used the thing since before the 9/11. Unfortunately, he had gone through his medication on his new one so fast the doctor couldn't prepare a refill fast enough, and Frank was stuck with this antique.

"That sounds like a sweet nickname. I wasn't aware you were so close with your workers, Mr. Klunes—ah, I mean, Harry."

"Ah, yes, I always try to think of my operation as something of a large family instead of just a workplace, makes worker morale a lot better and just provides a more zen-like place for me to go instead of thinking of it as a traditional job."

Don't listen to him… no, no.

"That sounds lovely."

"It is. Not only does it make my life a little easier, but what I really hope is that it makes it a little better for my workers. Like I said, I'm a humanitarian, or consider myself one, at least. I feel a little wrong for talking about it when the man's downstairs, working so hard—at least we can hope he is! But I think for Frog, that idea is especially important."

No, no, no… shut up… shut up now… no, no.

"Sometimes I feel like I'm the man's only friend—the scorpion to his Frog, if you will."

Don't call me that.

"Well, our Lord and Savior Jesus Christ can be his friend as well, as he has been to you and to me. Salvation is truly anyone's who is willing to accept him into their heart and mind and be as he commands them to be."

"A truly noble ideal to strive for, Gloria, and one that I hope poor Frog will one day realize so that he can join us up here in the light, instead of toiling away in the dark."

All of Frank's equilibrium seemed to fall away, snatched by some unseen, unknowable force that left him feeling withered and on the verge of some irrationality that seemed sweet and all-encompassing—a blinding white rage that seemed so much brighter than the darkness in front of him.

"You and those marvelous words of yours, Harry. I really think you'd appreciate the stained glass in the funeral parlor, if you've got the time, of course. There's a lovely design of the Holy City of Jerusalem with just a stunning recreation of the Dome on the Rock. It's truly marvelous—awe-inspiring, really. There's even a lovely series of verses from Matthew 27. Its beauty really must be seen to be believed."

"Ah, Matthew is one of my favorite books, Mrs. Hickam. It's like you know me already. Please lead the way."

The steps began, like chalk squeaks on chalkboard on a dry, early summer day, and Frank could picture the slight, awkward step Mr. Klunesberg would take, pausing just a second to let the shapely Mrs. Hickam pass in front of him, providing him with a better view. A rage, blinding white in its ferocity, trickled down the back of Frank's spine, wound his fists into tight balls, and ground his teeth together like he was trying to turn them to nubs. *I'm gonna find you while you sleep.* Rational thoughts seemed inaccessible, and all Frank wanted was to take everything thing that was this… fury… and bring it all down on his snarky—*Slit your throat… smear the blood over your sheets*—narcissistic little face. That smile he wore, that… perfectly placated look of inadequacy, of simply existing and believing that by that right alone, he was the most perfect being—*Blowtorch those glasses until they're part of your skin*—under God's green earth. This inescapable rage swept him forward, slamming his fist into the side of the cold steel, regretting so immediately after the surge of pain to his lower right knuckles.

That was when he heard the moan.

At first, he thought it was merely by-product of his display of aggression, but as the rattling stopped, the moaning continued—a slow, lurching sound of sorrow that echoed from behind the grill of the furnace, bouncing from one of the dozens of pipes that crisscrossed throughout the entire basement. His anger ebbed away unnoticed, forgotten almost immediately; and when the terrible sound came again, Frank began to shiver, even though he couldn't really figure out why. Opening the grill and placing his head inside with careful hesitation, he turned his ear toward the pipes and waited for the sound again. When it did finally come again, he realized that it seemed to be almost more muted now, even farther away than it had seemed seconds before. There was something else strange about it, but he couldn't quite pin the oddness of it on any one thing in particular.

Pulling back, he realized the sound was coming from down the hall behind him. He wheeled about quickly, expecting Klunesberg to be standing there, hatchet in hand, with a wild smile on face, ready to finish the job he had started decades ago. Instead, there was only darkness, and when Frank finally gathered enough courage to take a step out into the hall, he discovered that was all that was out there as well. A putrid smell, one that had hung in the air since he first stepped beneath the floorboards, seemed stronger, more stomach-churning than it had before—a smell that clung to your nostrils like it was right underneath them. Still, the moans and bitter, resolute sighs came with a steady rhythm, becoming almost stronger, more oppressive with each passing moment spent within the tight confines of the shadowy basement corridor.

A sickening pain overcame his stomach when he realized that the off-putting feeling, the shivers that were creeping up his forearms, was coming from the fact that even though he could hear each sigh and moan like they were right near him, there was not a single intake of breath, or any kind of breath, other than the mock exhalation draped in the mask of rueful agony.

Louder and louder they got, with a dull hum growing in the air and a scratch on the old mortar bricks steadily building. And for some reason, Frank found his legs moving him down the hall toward the sound that only brought dread to his ears. He found himself almost entranced, terrified by his own seemingly impending doom, but even more terrified by the glee he felt inside, thinking about it.

"Frog! Frog! Have you finished yet? What's taking so long? Need I remind you that you still have to attend to the mess hall back at city hall before the agricultural meeting at eight? Mrs. Hickam and I have finished our tour…" The two of them giggled at some intrinsic joke contained within his words that only they understood. "And it's really time we were to be leaving. Save whatever else is down there for tomorrow. We will be coming back then. Now, hurry up, Frog, and meet me at the truck."

Stopped dead in his tracks, Frog seemed to relish the idea of walking away into that dark hall and hoping for the end he felt for himself down there. It seemed so blissful in comparison. Peaceful.

And yet, the moaning had stopped, silence filling the corridor like cement. He turned back toward the splintered wooden stairs back up to the altar and began his ascent, wondering why the trip up, not down, seemed so much like one into hell.

When he reached the landing, he saw that the two snickering high-school-students-stuck-in-fifty-year-old-bodies had already departed for the parking lot, leaving him alone to shut the large oak doors of the cellar by himself. Frank shuffled over and grabbed the cold black steel handle. With a hefty grunt and all the energy he could muster, he pulled helplessly at the thing until a mix of exhaustion and shame allowed him to drop it back down the three inches he'd lifted it. Every part of his body still felt clenched, like all the stress had made his body forget how to actually release any sort of tension. The corners of his eyes began to tighten and itch, and Frank suddenly wanted a drink of bourbon more than he had ever wanted one in his life.

As if on cue, his bartender appeared before him, bursting through the door like a character in a bad sitcom.

"Frank? Frank? Oh, shit, there you are! Hurry up! We gotta go!" Matt exclaimed as he rushed over to his side and grabbed his arm, lifting him from his slumped position over the still-open cellar and dragging him toward the door.

"Matt? What in God's name are you doing here?"

A wicked smile broke across Matt's face—the kind of smile he got when he saw something, usually a woman, or wom*e*n—he wanted.

"Oh, I didn't come here for God. I came here for you, good buddy. We've been looking all over town for you until we finally heard from Ms. Cavendish over at city hall that you were over here doing God-knows-what for Klunesberg on your day off. How the hell did you let the scumbag fuck-talk you into this shit again, Frankie?"

A small pit formed in his chest, just like it did anytime someone asked why he let Klunesberg do what he did to him. He kept waiting for the answer to come himself, almost more than Matt was; but when none came, he simply let his eyes drop to the floor, eyeing a stain that seemed to be having a far better existence than he was.

"You gotta stand up for yourself, man. Just tell the guy to fuck off."

"You know I can't just do that."

Frank tried to keep the bitterness out of his voice, but it came anyway, a vehemence that seemed far too great to have any sort of control over. Matt seemed struck for a moment but quickly reeled back to his normal exuberant self, more focused on whatever desire had gotten into his crazy head than Frank's defensiveness.

"Well, it doesn't matter now anyways. And besides, there are better ways for somebody to get back at their boss than giving them a nice piece of 'go fuck yourself.'"

Before he realized it, they were standing outside of Tyler's oversized black Escalade, the door sliding open slowly by itself as Tyler bent over in the passenger seat. Matt shoved Frank in before he had a moment to protest and then quickly leaped in behind him. With a quick slam of the door, Tyler shot up and stared back at them with bloodshot and glossy eyes.

"What the fuck did I say about how to close my door, motherfucker? You think this is just some kind of no-consequence shit where you can just slam another nigga's shit, bust it up, and just act like that shit didn't even happen?"

"Your door's fucking fine, Tyler. Now can you just drive the damn car? We don't exactly have all the time in the world here. We are supposed to be on the Interstate ten minutes ago."

"Man, I am getting my shit in order, son. You may want to just run in there all carefree like a punk ass, inexperienced little bitch, but a true gangsta like me is about to be prepared for this shit." He rustled through the layers of garbage on the car floor, occasionally shaking ash and receipts from his hand. "And what the fuck did I say about calling me Tyler? It's fucking Tranze, bitch, Tyga, fucking anything else but that white-bread shit. I got a goddamn image to maintain here, 'ight?"

"Why are we supposed to be on the Interstate?"

"I'll explain on the way, Frank, I swear." With a quick turn, he was facing Tyler again. "What the fuck are you even looking for?"

"Never mind, ya bitch, I already found the damn thing."

Tyler's blond head popped back up for a second to be covered again by a brown film. Stretching the long brown fabric over his nose, Frank instantly recognized the panty hose and turned back to Matt, only to be greeted by a ski mask.

"Are those fucking panty hose?"

"Yeah, what the fuck else was I supposed to use?"

"I don't know, maybe a ski mask like every thief ever?"

"Man, bank robbers use fucking panty hose for this shit. Ain't you ever seen a movie?"

"I have. That's why I brought ski masks for me and Frank."

"And why the fuck didn't you bring one for me, motherfucker?"

"You said you had everything!"

"Yeah, I do! I have fucking panty hose!"

Frank grabbed Matt's shoulder so hard he hurt his own fingers covered in a thick wool coat and spun him back toward him.

"Why the hell do you have a ski mask for me?"

"Tyler, start driving. Frank, you're gonna have to trust me on this one, all right?"

The car lurched forward quickly, throwing Frank into the window. A cold, stinging pain went through his forehead as he looked back at Tyler, his hand wrapped around a Cobalt pistol inside his open glove box.

"What exactly am I supposed to trust you on here, Matt? What is this?"

Tyler looked back at Matt and gave him a wide grin, exposing the set of golden grills that Tyler sported over his plain white incisors; and Matt matched it, with eyes glinting like a wolf that was prepared to make a kill.

"Remember how I told you there were other ways to get back at your employer?"

"Yeah?"

"Well, this is one of 'em."

"How drunk are you right now?"

"Pretty damn drunk," Matt said with an excited whoop that was met with a long howl from Tyler, who lifted an almost-empty forty-ounce of Mickey's and tilted it back, keeping his hand with the pistol firmly on the wheel for all to see.

The little bit of gold left in the bottle disappeared into a foam that hung at the bottom of the glass when Tyler tossed it wantonly out the open window, cackling as it smashed against an old Chevy Camaro idling in front of the hospital emergency room drop-off.

"I got a tummy full of Henny, boy! And I'm lookin' to do some damage! Fuck, yeah! We're gonna show that motherfuckin' boss of yours what's up, Matty. Gonna run up in there, guns blazin' like we're Samuel Muthafuckin' Jackson, poppin' that cold steel right up in that old bastard's teeth. Let's see him garnish your fuckin' wages then, the old prick. I'm personally gonna give him the old 'slap across the face with my dick' move. Make 'em feel like the bitch that he is."

Frank exhaled slowly, trying to catch his breath when Matt forcibly pried open his fingers and shoved an old service revolver into his blistered palm. The wooden butt of the gun seemed to be the heaviest thing that he had ever held, even though he knew that couldn't be true. The thing was barely bigger than his palm, and Klunesberg would often joke at the size of them, saying that, "despite having perhaps the most feminine hands in maintenance, they did they best work."

"Just what exactly is going on here, Matt? You guys aren't planning on hurting anybody now, are ya?"

"Not if we can help it, Frank, I promise you that. *Tranze* here is just talking out his ass like he always is. You know I wouldn't involve you in anything you couldn't handle."

"And what exactly is that?"

"Just a little bit of armed robbery, maybe with a bit of destruction of property, if all goes as planned."

"I ate a shit ton of Taco Bell right before this, so I think we're all straight on that destruction of property, bitch. I'm gonna wreck that toilet, dawg. I feel that shit growling already."

"What the fuck, Matt? Armed robbery? You're gonna give me a heart attack!"

"Frank, relax. I shut the bar down an hour ago, even though nobody was even in the place. Put up a sign saying we were closed for maintenance and everything. It's deader than good ol' Sarah Marsden in there." Frank narrowed his gaze at that. "There'll be no one there except us, and the place has one camera in the back alley to stop bums from stealing the old liquor bottles. The only reason we brought guns is the off chance that some other robbers decided to show up and rob the crap shack because it's so fucking easy to right now."

"And if those motherfuckers do show up, the Tyga Killer and his boys, Matty Ice and Frog, will blow their asses all the way back between their momma's legs. I'm leaning. I got my nine. I just did five lines of the purest Columbian sugar you've ever seen, and I got no fucking problem shooting any motherfucker that gets in my way."

"But why, Matt? Why risk your job, you're home? Because you can't stay here after this. You know your boss is gonna be able to figure out it was you eventually. Is it really worth it? Just for a little bit more money? You already make off well enough from the bar every night."

Matt's face grew taunt, and in the gaps between the streetlights, when a swift shade of darkness fell over the car, his face seemed almost frightening in the intensity of his features.

"Trust me when I tell you, Frank, the asshole deserves it."

"Yeah, Frank, this piece of shit bitchass was fucking embellishing my boy Matty's paychecks every week, all because some bitch enjoyed getting Matty's dick rammed inside her instead of him," said Tyler, who turned back to look at Frank with his face away from the road long enough to send Frank's foot to the imaginary brake on the ground.

"Embezzling paychecks, moron, not embellishing."

"Is that true, Matt?"

His hardened eyes relaxed back to their usual carefree expression as he met Frank's stare. The road seemed nonexistent at the speed the car was going, giving Frank felt a sudden burst of adrenaline numb his arms and legs and filling him with visions of firing his gun right into Kluneberg's open, squirming mouth.

"It is. So is the thing about the bar being empty. Nobody will ever know we were in there until next Saturday when the money is counted for our monthly inventory. We'll already have gotten the money squared away in a separate account, and Mr. Stiffle won't be able to figure which of the employees he's been bending over a table all these years finally lubed up and fucked him back. And by that time, Tyler and I will already be out of the country, and they won't ever think mild-mannered Frank Rodgers assisted a robbery."

"Won't they suspect you when you don't show up to work tomorrow? This whole thing seems insane, Matt."

"I'm on vacation for the next week, friend. As far as they're concerned, they think I'm heading up to Canada for a trip to a brewing company. Not really a lie, I just left out the part about staying up there indefinitely with their money—which, like I said, they won't even know is missing until the inventory next Friday.

"Come on. Don't look at me like that. Don't act like you've never thought about taking revenge on a shitty boss, especially with the boss you've got. I've heard all the stories, Frank. You open up quite a bit after your tenth drink. You've shared quite a few stories about the 'glory days' over a shot of whiskey—which is why I'm asking for your help, Frank. We can't do it without you."

The image flashed again, the one with the gun in Kluneberg's mouth—*Don't fucking call me Frog, you low-life sorry excuse for a degenerate piece of human waste*—only this time, he let his finger melt over the trigger and squeezed, a flash of red decorating the silk curtains behind his sobbing, grimacing face as it fell limp and saggy.

"All right, this *one* time I'll help you. As long as you're 100 percent sure the cops won't show up tonight."

"Franky, my nigguh, I can guaran-fucking-tee there will be no fucking pigs anywhere near our dicks tonight, you feel me?"

The screech of the police radio was what shook Bruce Vencini from his restless sleep. The smell of fresh roasted coffee caused his nose to twitch, and at first, he thought he was going to sneeze, until he heard the voices trickling down the hall from the bull pen and kept himself silent.

"So the missus looks at me, her eyes wider than Stevenson's wife's ass, the dog still rolling around on the ground like a thing possessed, mind you, and goes, 'Well, John, are you happy with what you done? You've gone and scared the damn thing to death,' like the dog was about to curl up like a fucking roly poly right there and turn to dust, like a goddamn fart or something. I had to remind her that it was her fault for shouting in front of the kids about whatever nonsense she was going on about earlier—something about a church fund-raiser or whatnot, I wasn't listening.

"Anyways, I grab the dog by the collar and practically yank the li'l bitch's neck clean off the way she's struggling and writhing and such, like a 'spic after you give 'em a good bashing with the ol' night capper… What? Oh, would you calm your ass down. The closest thing we got to a 'spic around here is Bruce, and his lazy ass is passed out back in his cozy new office, fuckin' equal-opportunity bullshit, just like I was telling you the other day, George. Besides, even if the fool can hear us, I'm sure most of the niggers hate the 'spics more than we do."

The laugh that followed made Bruce uneasy, not because McCulley's words made him want to smash his face against the hard pinewood desk—quite the opposite, in fact. He worried because he didn't feel anything from them anymore. He supposed, that should be a good thing, that the words of dumb, ignorant racists were just that to him; but he could never shake the fact that something felt wrong about his placidity.

"So I finally get some water splashed on the mutt's face, and it goes off barkin' and yippin' at its own cheeks, like some kind of Rain Man, and I still have Sheila screaming directly into my guldarn ear. I swear I caught more spit in there than words. So I had to give her a bit of the ol' Christian affection, if you catch my drift. Then she starts hollering about how she's gonna call down here and demand they throw me behind bars. I had to crack her a few more times after that—and she finally picks up the phone, so I yank it free from her and said, 'Forget it, honey, I'm going down there later... Now, what was it you wanted me to tell the boys?'"

A chorus of hoots and hollers arose from the crowded station hall as all the listeners of John McCulley's lovely story of domestic abuse sat around their revered brother-in-arms, celebrating his job well done in keeping the status quo quite firmly established throughout Loganville. That seemed like every cop's job nowadays, at least according to all the news he watched during his lazy day's sitting in the station bull pen, waiting for someone to call complaining about annoying kids running around too close to their yards at night or to report strange sounds they heard coming from the woods, ignorant to the idea that animals might actually reside there. It seemed even worse than usual lately, especially now that half the force was two towns over in Castle Rock dealing with the forest fire that had started out by the Highway 83 junction. It had begun to spread out from the site of impact to Route 12 and Northern Pressway Pass by the Hardee's. Bruce found himself hunched over his desk, his cheeks numb and coated in a gloss of fresh saliva. The only calls that had come all night was from someone that was so drunk most of the call was barely intelligible, and the other was from a wild, religious zealot nutcase who claimed the apocalypse was starting tomorrow and that all the police should be ready to be mobilized at any moment against the rising armies of Satan—including the "Jew Scum," the "Babylonian whores," and the "hoodie niggers." When Bruce had informed the screeching shrew of a woman that he was himself one of those "hoodie niggers," there was an uneasy silence before a deafening dial tone that rattled his eardrums like he'd been standing right next to a speaker at a death metal concert.

"That's quite enough stories about the bruises on your sweet wife's face for one night there, John, which reminds me we should really have a chat about that in my office one of these nights."

The captain's voice was like an alarm clock that shook the last bit of sleep from Bruce's eyes, and his reproach of McCulley was like breakfast in bed. Despite being separated by a window with drawn shades, Bruce could see the exasperated guffaw on McCulley's face without even having to look at it.

"Luckily enough for you, we're too swamped with shit as it is to try and add one more turd to the bowl. Can I get someone down to Route 12 to investigate a broken-down Toyota '94 Seabreeze that's on the side of the road? I need at least three of you on this one, it could be a big one. We got reports of sightings of one Marshall Mears—that's right, Logan County's Most Wanted—coming down Twelve, and someone called in, saying they saw someone sitting in the Toyota with the lights on. So we got no other choice than to assume this is our boy, driven south by the forest fires from that grand old space rock that God himself sent down to smite that poor, confused sonuva bitch.

"Now, who's gonna step up and be the hero tonight?"

Bruce wanted to jump up from his chair but feared that everyone in the next room might hear. Instead, he let his feet gently push his chair out far enough to slide up and out to the hallway. Looking down the small, four-roomed corridor that led out back to the alley and contained the four offices—two administrative, two personal—Bruce felt a sudden sick feeling in his stomach, one that caused a general air of lightheadedness, of unwell, throughout his caffeine-riddled body as he thought of the words McCulley had managed to spit out in between his tales of wife beating wonder: that awful alliteration—affirmative action—that hung over his head and turned his blood to ice.

"All right, Henrickson, you owe me one after that Easter vacation robbery. Take Wenshaw with you in the Durango, and bring the .421 from the gun cab and place it under the truck flap along with some riot gear in case things get way worse than they should. I'm talking some helmets, a shield, and a couple stun grenades, all right? Leave the rocket launcher in your Yaris, got it? Remember, you wanna be a hero, not end up on the wrong side of the bench with the media calling you the next Zimmerman, all right?"

"How many secondaries are we talking here?"

"One on your thigh, Rambo, and that's it. Now, who's my third guy gonna be? Not much to choose from here, guys, so don't make me make it awkward here. I don't wanna have to force one of ya to go."

As soon as Bruce turned the slight corner, he caught sight of Sheriff Nottingull's gentle face, etched with wisdom lines that spoke more to his experience than they did his actual age. A young man trapped in a withered, ruined body—the thing you always noticed about the sheriff was his eyes, vibrant and hazel, like pine bark at the beginning of autumn that turned the forests into backdrops worthy of hymn and song (or, at the very least, a postcard), eyes that seemed to understand everything in front of them, a spark of genuine interest while most were simply glazed over or barely focused on anything.

"I can go if you need me to."

With a quick turn—but not quick enough to hide his age, like Bruce knew he tried to do on occasion—Nottingull's eyes fell on him, and a smile stretched the wisdom lines even deeper into his stoic features.

"Ah, Bruce, thank you for volunteering. Unfortunately, I had already planned to come and find you about something else I need taken care of," he said, turning back to face the half-dozen officers muddled around the coffee machine on Steinburg's desk in the middle of the bull pen. "McCulley, why don't you go? Save yourself from a talk with me and your wife? Can't pass up on that offer, I'm sure."

"You got it, Sheriff."

"Fan-fucking-tastic. I need you guys to have left fifteen minutes ago, so if I were you, I'd be hopping in the squad car by now. And that would be after I got done fucking your sexually unsatisfied wives and taking yours out to a nice dinner afterward, McCulley, so let's hustle. Pull the panties out of your assholes, and let's go! Let's go!"

With a slew of faked and overenthusiastic effort, the half-dozen cops turned into a quarter dozen; and the remaining quarter quickly removed themselves from the sheriff's wandering gaze that might catch the fact that they're coffee was a bit more Irish than it had any right being while they were on duty.

He tried to keep his face stern and statuesque, to betray no hint of the disquieting sickness that he felt bubbling in his stomach as he followed the sheriff to his office at the very back of the bull pen, the only office in the building not located in the back hallway. The door bore his name—*Hank Nottingull, Sheriff of Logan County*—in an offset Arial font that seemed both professional and hokey at the same time and stirred a chuckle from Bruce's chest every now and then when it caught his eye. It calmed him little now.

"I used to coach high school basketball up in Macinroe County, did I ever tell you that?" Hank said as they entered his office, shuffling over to his chair. "Same basic principles. Give 'em some inspiration and insults about their sexual inadequacy, and they jump up like you just told 'em they won the lottery. Works every time."

As he went to sit down, Bruce went to shut the door, like he usually did, but Hank shot out a quick wave of his hand to dismiss the idea.

"It's quite all right. There's no sensitive information for this case. Besides, all those boys out there don't want me to smell the Jim Bean on their breath, so I doubt any will ever be within earshot."

The shakiness in his voice betrayed the real reason about the growing suspicions of what was said behind closed doors. Sometimes he wondered if Hank honestly didn't think that Bruce noticed it, or if it was just one of many things that he liked keeping to himself; and if there was something Hank was keen on keeping to himself, you couldn't pry it out with a crowbar.

"You think they've been drinking, do ya?"

"Quit playin' around with me. Just 'cause I look like an old man doesn't mean I can't put my own pants on and remember what day it is. I know a man who's had a couple sips from the bottle when I see one. Now, whatever drugs these kids are doing nowadays, that's a whole other story. There was a bust down over in Grenville of some new drug going around. Some prescription, pharmaceutical garbage that a couple of repeat narcotics offenders got their hands on through some government testing and are now selling for the purpose of getting whacked out of your gourd so far you can't even stand up without swearing you were dying or dead."

"What new drug?"

"Cataboxil, I think, is the legal name, but narcs on the street have heard it been called Pussy, or more commonly, Frankenstein, due to the catatonic state that it's said to induce."

"Why pussy, though?"

"Well, if you want to be technical, it's a play on the cat part of Cataboxil, but the kids call it that because everybody wants it, real cute, huh?"

"Oh, yeah, clever," Bruce said, leaning uncomfortably in the cold wooden chair, the kind you would find inside vice principal's offices at a school—the type of chair you'd sit in when you knew you were about to get an earful of bad news. "So did you bring me in here to offer me drugs, sir, or was there something about a special case you had for me?"

Hank shot him a quick, dismissive look and scratched the back of his head, right beneath the bottom crop of his long but stringy auburn hair.

"It's more of a case that I don't want you to come on. You remember my brother-in-law? Greg? Greg Stiffle? Well, anyway, he asked for me to personally keep an extra eye of security on his place tonight as a favor in exchange for letting me and Helen borrow his camper last June for the trip up to Minnesota."

"When you went up by Big Stone over by Ortonville? You know, I got a cousin who lives up over in Itasca county by Dohasett. Great place right by a couple of lakes, used to go up there with my Auntie Jessica for a couple summers when—"

"Quit distracting me, boy, I did not come in here to chat. I came in here to ask you to watch the precinct while I head down there with MacEnroe and Asworth to guard the place from some supposed robbery my brother-in-law keeps nagging me about."

The words felt cold and indifferent, and a look in the sheriff's eye gave Bruce the impression that he was trying especially hard to make them seem that way. The unease in his stomach quickly turned to fire, and he found that he could almost taste the bitterness on his tongue.

"I'm sorry, Sheriff, but if I can speak freely, that is complete horseshit. Why in the hell would you step out of the station tonight to go sit and wait on some nonexistent robbery when you just sent out a squad to go and pick up the most wanted criminal for a hundred miles? All for some… hunch that your brother-in-law has about his precious fucking bar?"

The youthful glimmer in Hank's eyes faded, dulled down to a sickly grayness that made Bruce regret his words before he even finished speaking them.

"Watch your mouth. For your information, the lead I sent McCulley and his goons on came from old Ms. Havesh, and she calls in reporting demons in here backyard every week, so if Bobby Brown and the boys come back here with that psychopath, I'll eat my own hat. Now you listen good, Bruce, I understand you're eager to get out there and make a real name for yourself, to prove your worth as deputy. Trust me. I get it. I really do. But let me make this perfectly clear. You're treading a very dangerous line right now. I want you to know that before you speak again. My asking you this should be treated as a privilege, not like I'm asking you to pull shit out of the toilets with your bare fucking hands."

Bruce had a thousand of responses lined up at his mouth, ready to tear through him, but he held them back. He could feel the eyes behind him, watching like a cheetah watches its prey at the watering hole, waiting for its guard to drop even the slightest.

"Can I at least come and stake out this place with you? Since you're so hell-bent on spending your night twiddling your thumbs and humming 'Master of the House' to yourself."

The look in his eyes could've frozen a stove top, his pupils narrowing into tiny saucers that Bruce could feel probing his face, digging for something much deeper behind it.

"You and I both know that can't happen."

"Listen, if something does happen down there and isn't just you're paranoid brother-in-law talking about how some employees been running off with some staplers, you're gonna need me to—"

"You're staying here, and that's final, Deputy Vencini." His voice dropped to a whisper, and his fingers curled around the edges of the desk, his hands shaking. "People talk enough about your promotion as it is. The city council's been breathing down my neck about your lack of experience and your family's background. I stuck my neck out for you here. I put my family's well-being on the line with this one, so when I ask you to lie down in a pile of shit, the only thing I want to hear out of your mouth is, 'For how long?' Is that clear?"

Like usual, the sheriff's face was a mask that concealed everything. Any sign of weakness didn't get through, only a gaze that implied his mind was already set in its way and any word of disobedience would be met with a steely silence.

"Yes…"

"Yes, sir."

Bruce couldn't recognize the eyes that peered back at him anymore. These were a deep and dirty brown, like bourbon that had been spilled on a shag carpet. "If you don't mind me asking, *sir*… what reason does your brother-in-law have to believe that there's gonna be a robbery tonight?"

The sheriff stood quickly and pulled his gun belt with the silver .45 glinting in the low hum of the fluorescents and started back toward the bull pen without granting Bruce with so much as another wayward stare.

"Just a hunch he has about some of his employees. Apparently, one of them shut the place down early without consulting him, probably just some slacker trying to get the night off, but I'm going to look into it."

With that, Bruce was left alone and confused in the small, bright office that smelled of cleaner and cigarettes, even though one hadn't been lit in the building since the 'nineties. He found himself finding the urge to turn and yell back something clever, something witty, something to take the sting of failure from his chest, but his gaze never left the burgundy rug. Later, he would regret it, but then again, he seemed to regret everything—especially now.

"Asworth! Knope! Don't look so tired, boys, we've got a fun-filled night ahead of us of singing 'Kumbayah' and sending a couple of would-be robbers to meet their new cellmates. Open your fucking eyes, Asworth, and grab a couple of Mossberg's from the armory. I feel a shitstorm coming, fellas, and ask McArthur, he'll vouch for me. I'm never wrong. It may not show up 'til tomorrow, or the day after, but she's coming.

"Believe me, she's coming."

After telling the story for so many time over the years, the night doesn't feel real anymore. Sometimes when I wake up at night with it still fresh in my mind, I convince myself it was all just a cheesy young-adult novel I had read or a sappy movie I would sneak out to see on the weekends, laughing at every contrived word. Everything about it seems too perfect.

It sounds almost cliché to think something like that could be real. And I'm sure by many definitions, it wasn't. But I can still feel that moment when I look back at it. I still yearn for it, even now, after everything that happened. It could be nostalgia; it could be one of my many forms of PTSD, like my inability to go anywhere near a basement.

The thing about that night is I keep asking myself how things would be different if I hadn't gone; if I hadn't excused myself early from dinner to practice my prayers in my room before bed while my mother made her usual warning call to the authorities about the oncoming apocalypse she made every week; if I hadn't slipped through the upstairs window and scurried down the neighbor's tree; if I had just stayed in and fallen asleep that night instead of meeting Range at the graveyard, would... would people still be alive? Would I still be alive? Would...

Let me set the record straight for you now. I don't regret a goddamn thing that happened. I can't anymore. But I dream about things being different. Those are the dreams I like to have, the ones I wish had more often.

Usually, my dreams are filled with blood and screaming.

The wind bit deep, turning the cool autumn night into a chilly winter one. Gwen had worn an old gray sweatshirt with a faded *Tigers Softball* logo on it, even though she had never played for the Tigers but had attended one game with Bobby Sloth and left with one stuffed into the deep stretching compartments of her backpack that she usually reserved for hiding smokes from her mother.

The smell of burning leaves hung in the air, like an incense left burning too long, and Gwen quickened her pace in attempt to clear the scent from her nostrils. Yes, that was why she was rushing. It definitely wasn't excitement carrying her forward.

She slowed herself then, checking the time on her phone and realizing she still had three minutes until she was officially late—which she wanted to be. Her friend Stacy's sister had once told her in the first grade that whoever shows interest first will always be the one who has to try and keep the other one interested. They already know the other person will do anything, so what's to stop them from asking for it? When Gwen had asked how the boy would know she *was* interested if she never showed it, the question was quickly laughed off. She had never gotten to test it as she barely had to wait to talk to Bobby before he had professed his middle-school heart to her.

It wasn't the best advice she had ever gotten, but it's not like she had any "game" to speak of—if people even still said that. Besides, she didn't want to come across as some sappy, sucked-too-long-at-the-Nicholas-Sparks-teat teenage bimbo in the first place. She still slightly resented her own feelings about the matter, but she was finding it harder and harder to deny them. She was completely smitten with someone she had barely even spoken to—like someone who was completely, 120 percent, grade A insane.

By the time she reached the Deckard's farm, the worms in her gut started to twist at thoughts of the graveyard that lay just several blocks in front of her. The peak of the gate appeared as she crossed

Jacob Deckard's last roll of barbed wire, and the cold in the air seemed to grow heavier. It stuck to her spine like a thin veneer and brought goose bumps to her arms, even when she buried them against her chest. The ash trees that surrounded the Deckard's driveway burned amber in the twilight sun, canary leaves crunching beneath her feet like old candy wrappers.

    Gwen became aware of the hum of a chord, barely audible like a whisper on the wind yet sweet like something she knew by heart, even though she was certain she had never heard it before. The tone swelled inside her, stirring a warmth she almost had forgotten was there—one that reminded her of sparklers on balmy summer nights and catching june bugs with the neighbor girl whose name she never got to know before her parents fled in fear from the Prophet of Loganville's judgment. The sound grew louder and took shape into a melody that she did recognize, but only briefly, as the song she had heard earlier that day after she had agreed to his odd request, awkwardly walking back to her study hall while watching Range pluck away on the strings of guitar that seemed a couple of decades older than he was. Had he also played it the night before when he saw him by the graveyard?

    It seemed to sound brighter than it had then.

    She caught sight of him then at the basin of the hill leading down to the cemetery, perched on a section of fence that had been twisted and pulled out of shape into something like a hanging bench on a makeshift porch that had long become overgrown with dirty spinach-colored weeds. His head was dipped, lost in the workings of his fingertips, unaware of Gwen's slow approach down the embankment. Slowing and slipping behind an elm, she let herself gaze while she tried to regain what was left of her usual ironclad composure. When she caught herself admiring the way his hair seemed to match the color of the golden clouds closest to the edge of the sky, she snapped the hair tie around her wrist and yelped as it cracked across her skin, turning it slick and red. What was happening to her? All her pride stemmed from the idea that she would never lose control of herself to the whims and fancies of a passing lunk with pretty eyes and a broad chin; but when actually faced with them, it seemed like thinking wasn't even an option. It sickened her.

Collapsing into the base of the tree, Gwen let the grass slide between her fingers as she wondered how to proceed, slowly clunking the back of her head against the sharp bark, like some sort of penance her mother would assign for her sinful thinking. That thought actually made her gag.

The melody grow quicker and more frantic as the minutes passed, and Gwen's mind toyed with the idea of whether playing hard to get or the straightforward approach would allow her to keep some of her dignity; but both seemed to end with her utter admittance that her feelings seemed to no longer be her own. A chill rocked her body even though the breeze had died down and the night had become silent, like a play was starting soon and everyone had finally found their seats.

After a while, a shout snapped Gwen out of her mind and back into the prewinter night.

"So are you gonna stay behind that tree all night, or were you planning on saying hello at some point?"

Gwen felt a drop of sweat from beneath her arm slide down her bra and through her undershirt, and she found herself way too excited that she had put on deodorant that day. Swaying to her feet, she patted the dirt off the back of her jeans and down by the cuffs of her Converse before whirling around to face the serpent that awaited her at the base of the hill.

"If you saw me, why didn't you say hello to me first? I mean, you're the one who invited *me* here, I should point out."

His smile fit snuggly underneath the sharp edges of his cheekbones, the small bags above them giving his face a haunted look that reminded Gwen of pictures she had seen in a pamphlet about insomnia her friend Marcie had shown when her parents had put her on Xanax for the first time.

"I actually never saw you come down. I just noticed your leg sticking out from behind that root five minutes ago."

Gwen could feel her cheeks starting to burn, and she was sure that she must have started to look like a beet that had been cooked for several minutes too many.

"That still didn't stop you from saying something then, now, did it?"

"I guess you've got me there. You still haven't told me why you didn't say hello, though."

"To be honest, I was listening to the song, and I kinda started thinking about other things, I guess."

"Like what?"

"What do you mean?"

"Well, what did you think about? And I want specifics, nothing like 'you know, things,' or 'stuff,' or anything impersonal like that. What did you actually see when you closed your eyes? What did the song make you think of?"

"I don't know. Summer nights from when I was a kid, old friends that I haven't seen in I don't know how long. One girl in particular, her name was Maricola. Her family lived in one side of the house next to ours when the landlord was renting it out as a duplex. We used to play in each other's yards even though she didn't speak a single word of English—well, other than the ones she picked up from her father when he would drive her to school, so she'd run around when we were playing freeze tag, you know, running to try and get to home base on the elm tree, and she'd scream, 'Outtathaway, ashhole,' at the top of her lungs. Mom gave her parents quite the lecture after hearing that.

"Her parents bought her this type of slide that came with those colorful plastic ladders attached. For the first couple months, she would climb over to see me and bring me things from her *abuela*, mostly chocolate coins and tangerines. That was until Mom caught her again, decided to lecture her herself before bringing her back to her parents. Her family moved away a little bit after that.

"I don't think I've thought about that since it happened, and that was more than ten years ago, at least."

Gwen watched for any change in his face to indicate some easy confirmation of pure disgust, especially after she realized she almost mentioned the fact that her mother's sermon of the switch was why Maricola's family no longer occupied the house next-door to theirs. However, it didn't seem to faze him; his face remained intent, his interest leaking into pale blue eyes.

"Does that make you feel sad? Or just regretful?"

"I'm not entirely sure. Maybe both, they usually go hand in hand, don't they? Boy, you really know how to entertain a girl with witty conversation, don't ya?"

Gwen felt a pang of regret as he appeared wounded, only briefly. His eyes left hers and disappeared back into the stretch of graves behind him, and Gwen wasn't sure if she had noticed because she was still studying his face like a piece of classical Russian literature or because he simply had wanted her to see it.

"I'm not very good at conversation starters, I guess."

The smell of dirty charcoal hung in the air like a whiff of summer's bad breath. The boy named Range dropped his gaze back down to the neck of his guitar as his fingers slid across the silk and steel strings, seemingly screeching in protest as they dragged across the edge of each fret.

"It's kind of weird that they have the school so close to here," he added over his haunting concerto, almost like he was unaware his hands were doing anything at all beneath his shoulder blades.

"I can see what you mean."

"About the school?"

"No, about not being very good at starting conversations."

"Oh."

The silence stuck to the air like a thick caramel, weighing heavily on Gwen's chest. Her breath seemed to catch in her throat every time his eyes came near her, but they stayed focused on the task beneath him, occasionally looking down at the pale mocha building across the crumbling asphalt cracks of the highway. Gwen followed his gaze and reexamined the old elementary school that she had attended back when her hair had ponytails and the misguided aspiration of spreading the wonderful lessons her mother had prepared for her to the rest of the class. Fortunately, that endeavor had only lasted the first few days of Ms. Enfield's kindergarten glass, but the names stuck with her for the rest of the year. She couldn't recall much about her years walking the halls of Lincoln Elementary, but she remembered the names. They still swam in the blackness of her eyelids every night before sleep came for her—Bible Freak, Nun-in-Training, Gwen Craz-cee, one of the more creative ones, a riff on Spiderman's famous lover, Jesus's Girlfriend. When the *DaVinci Code* had become annoyingly popular, some of the few that actually had read it started using Mary Magdalene instead. As the years went on, the names became vulgar variations, spoken with an edge of bitterness even though the reason behind them was now as familiar to the kids as that day's analysis of Oliver Twist, or had become completely merged with the boogeyman that was her mother—the town's not-so-secret shame. The one that showed up to every town meeting and was answered with groans and the shuffling of chairs as people began to shift uncomfortably in their seats at the mere glimpse of the cut of her dress. The one that went to funerals for open members of the local LBGT community just to tell the parents that Satan was giving their baby what he had always really wanted down in hell. After her sister's funeral, Betty McArthur had thrown Gwen up against the lockers in gym and gotten a few good punches before Gwen had pinned her to the ground, feeling the thick blood from Betty's nose stick to her knuckles, the smell of rust swimming in her head. Despite her younger self's naive hopes of simply fading into obscurity and starting anew, the names only got worse, turning into whispers of "bitch" and "cunt" held under breaths as she walked by, the gazes behind them carrying the real weight. At least they were no longer related to her mother. She had made her own awful reputation. She could take some solace in that.

"What's so weird about the school being there? It used to be an old processing plant for a lumber yard before it was a school, and some kind of huge factory before that. That's why the gym roof looks more like an old assembly line than a place for kids to play kickball when it rains. I mean, I guess, looking back, it was kind of weird to look out the window and just see a field full of dead people across the road. You could always see it from Mr. Thompson's classroom. And the back wall of the computer lab faces out that way. Every now and then, you'd hear about a kid who went to bathroom and swore that he saw ol' Muddy Zelda standing there, her thumb raised like she was looking for her midnight ride.

"You remember that story? About the girl whose prom date stood her up, so she decided to walk out by the old graveyard, asking passing cars for a ride back home, but she was hit and killed, and now her vengeful spirit stalks the graves at night, covered in mud from the car that struck her and looking for men to give her a ride so she can cause their cars to crash into a tree or something like that. I mean, that was pretty creepy as a kid, especially when it got darker earlier during the last few days of winter and you had to walk the road home by yourself."

Although his eyes didn't move from the strings, a small smile had taken over Range's face, and Gwen become quite sure that her face must look like a ripe baby tomato.

"That's definitely a scary story. I don't know. I guess I just thought, putting the beginning and the end that close to each other just seems… wrong, doesn't it?"

He chuckled, and Gwen smiled despite herself, although she wasn't quite sure that he was laughing at the same joke she was. She suddenly felt on the outside, like this whole night had really been one long, drawn-out joke, and soon Veronica and her cronies would come skulking out of the bushes with a GoPro and wine coolers and a grin that ate shit for breakfast.

Despite knowing her anger was most likely misplaced, she walked around him to find his gaze and force it on herself, determined to not come out looking like a fool from this.

"So do you just carry that guitar everywhere you go?"

The devilish grin on his face stuck there as he finally looked up at her, his dark pupils awash in a sea of emerald that captured her there for longer than she wanted to admit to herself later. She had to remind herself to breathe after she started to feel the oxygen leaving her brain; she felt like she was drunk on the cheap wine stolen from the gas station where the attendant spent hours in the small washroom always marked with an "Out of Order" sign, oblivious to the kids always hanging right outside the sliding glass.

"There are times when I leave it at home, but for the most part, yes, I carry it with me most places I go."

"So that makes you one of those guys who always brings a guitar to the party to show everyone his awesome new cover of 'Wonderwall'?"

He laughed harder than she expected him to—more than she wanted him to, because it only seemed to make the vice on her chest tighten further.

"I guess, ashamedly, I am, although I try to never play 'Wonderwall' anywhere near any social gathering."

"But you can still play 'Wonderwall,' of course?"

"Like every other person who has picked up a guitar, yes, I can. I can play it for you now, if you really want, although I would have to judge you for it a little bit." His attention returned to his dancing fingers, his knuckles contorting into twisted forms, sharp, and curled around themselves like snakes.

"So why do you carry that guitar around everywhere you go then? Seems kind of like a pain in the ass," Gwen asked, regret tainting the words as soon as they fell out of her mouth.

The smile on his face seemed to change. Gwen wasn't entirely sure if it was just the way that the last few beams of sun leaking over the sea of elm trees that was turning his face into a very visage of some Norse god—illuminated in his wisdom and fierce passion that seemed to teethe beneath his crystalline eyes—or if it was just her imagination juxtaposing itself onto this crumbling reality. A warmth made itself known. Beneath the awkward silence and sweaty palms, there was something that made the discomfort... comfortable. Gwen felt like she wanted to be anywhere else in the world and yet nowhere else at the same time.

She was now entirely sure that she was completely and totally insane.

"It's a bit of an obsession, to be honest. I always find myself thinking about this song. Well, I don't know if *song* is exactly the right word for it. More of this... sound. It's something I've had in my head for as long as I can remember—before I could even talk, I think. My mother called it the family curse when I finally mentioned it to her. I didn't really understand what she meant at first, but then I remembered something, from the night my dad left."

"I'm sorry to hear that."

"Don't worry, I'm not. I don't think of him much, other than that night. Not because he left, it was before that, before he even had his bags packed. He was sitting in on the bed in my mother's room, perched right on the edge. I remember because she used to have these sheets with clouds covering them, like an entire horizon's worth of clouds on every square inch, and I'd always hang off the edge and pretend I was flying. When I walked in on my dad, though, I'm not sure why, but I thought he was falling.

"I was pretty young at the time. I couldn't have been more than a year old. My mom doesn't even think I actually remember it, but I do. I almost ran right across the room, ready to snatch him back, or catch him or something, but I stopped when I heard it. He was playing that song, the one I heard in my head before bed every night and heard every morning before I realize the darkness is no longer just the last lingers of a bad dream. It didn't last very long, it might have only been a few notes of it, really. But I knew that was it. He was trying to find the same song, the same sound as I was. I think, he was trying to get it out of his head. That maybe, if he was able to write it down, see it for what it was, just another collection of notes and times arrangements, it would stop. That if he was able to share this sound with someone else, anyone else, he could find something close to peace. I don't think he ever would have, not with my mom and me, at least."

A gust of wind interrupted him, throwing the edges of Gwen's gray hoodie into wild fits at her side. The hair in her eyes turned the world into a milky yellow haze, and when she was finally able to clear the very last struggling strand from her vision, the world seemed to be covered in purple blanket of twilight.

"Do you think maybe you just heard your dad playing that song when you were a baby and latched onto it when he left? Maybe you're just hearing that song over and over again because you want to see your dad again?"

"I can see my dad from here actually."

He turned around in his corrupted metal chair and pointed to a small patch of graves near a sycamore tree and a crypt adorned with blushing cherubs that would find themselves right at home in her mother's collection of paintings adorning the living room walls. Most of the plots were below ground and impossible to read, but his finger seemed to lead to a small group of three, one covered in an usually large amount of cracks. The grass on top of all of them was plagued with murders of dandelions, crabgrass, and plantains.

Gwen's eyes narrowed, and she shoved her hands deep into the pockets of her hoodie, the hairbands on her wrists pulling tight against the skin. She was sure there would be slick red skin there when she pulled them out.

"You know what I meant," she said.

He grinned again as he started to play, the sad melody starting with the same phrase as it had before, one that she heard repeated the most as the minutes, passing like seconds, went by.

"I used to think I was crazy, inherited some kind of folie à deux. I really did," he said, frown lines appearing at the sides of his smile, almost like he was forcing it there like a poster that keeps falling off from the wall. "I tried to convince myself that I had heard that song before, that somehow those notes weren't some random assortment that my grief-addled mind cobbled together. It made things easier for a while, to tell myself that I was the crazy one.

"But the song never went away, it's still there, like it always was. My father's lawyer brought us his effects after he passed, and I dug through every underground recording I could get my hands on. I asked my mother for anything she might have, any song he might have been working on writing, or a recording of a show he especially liked that they wouldn't have found buried in the couch folds with the other ones. I almost came up empty-handed until I decided to hum the song to her. The small phrase I had heard that day. It was only a couple bars, a few seconds maybe, but her eyes seemed to… dull, if that makes sense. All the life just left them. They looked like eyes you'd see staring back at you from a pale face of plastic in a dark room, the kind that make you double take to make sure you shouldn't expect cold hands around your threat if you look away.

Any color that her face might have had had left her, beads of sweat cutting through the stray splotches of powder, like rivers through an arctic forest.

"She told me she knew *that* song. She had heard that song every night of her life for years because my father hummed it in his sleep. When she had asked him about it, he had told her it was just something he had heard in his fast-paced job busting tables at Marinelo's. Belief was easy to feign for a while, even though the answer sat in her stomach like nest of cockroaches. When months passed with the humming continuing every night without fail, she pushed the issue again. He… well, let's just say she showed me the scar from when she tried to ask him more about it."

The wind grew louder, like a train that was approaching faster than you expected it to, drowning out the sounds of crunching leaves and shrill wails of strings and causing Range to snap out of the trance he seemed to talk himself into. His hand slipped weakly off the neck of the guitar, before he wrapped it back around like an eagle's talon gripping a branch for dear life.

"This song… this sound," Gwen said, suddenly aware that she was shouting to hear herself over the bursts of banshee wails, "what exactly does it *sound* like? Is it supposed to be that… sad?"

His eyes caught hers again, and when she was unable to keep them locked on his without her heart going out of control, she forced herself to look anyway—to lose herself in the body of water that was his gaze. Despite her fear, the only thing she found there was a comfort so foreign she wasn't sure if it could even be called a comfort, but the warmth betrayed its unfamiliarity.

"Yes. That's exactly what it is, I think, the exact sound of tragedy—a sound that perfectly encapsulates everything about sadness, the dark beauty that it holds, the dark demons that accompany it. That's the sound I'm looking for, a perfect sound—something that taps into that deepest and purest vein of human emotion, the ultimate connection between any two people, if only because it's universal that everyone has felt this type of honest disappointment with the world around them.

"My dad may not have gotten a lot right in his life, but I think he was right about this. Maybe if I can pick it apart, see it for exactly what it is, and understand it… if I could help other people understand it, share it with them… maybe it would stop. Maybe for once, I could shut off everything and actually hear the world moving around me instead of the same unchanging drone that turns all my thoughts against me.

"But like you said, maybe I'm just crazy and want my dead father to show me some overdue affection. Who knows?"

With that, he turned back to his guitar, retreated back into his shell of sound, the familiar refrain ringing off the cracked and crumbling walls of the sepulchers and mausoleums that spotted the kaleidoscopic horizon like an outbreak of acne before prom night. A chill came in with the breath of the wind, biting into the back of her neck and pulling the hairs there up with it. Gwen's hand wrapped tightly around her arm, hoping that her own support would be enough to allow her to speak the words she was dreading without collapsing underneath the cumbersome weight of her growing unease. She started to speak, but the words clogged her throat like water going down her windpipe. At first, she thought he hadn't noticed, and she had bought herself a reprieve, time to gather her thoughts and decide if the urge to divulge the horror show that was her family was a sign of unwavering trust or one of undiagnosed madness, a type made rare by its severity. But when the sound of ringing steel and vibrating acoustic hollows died down and she found her eyes locked with his once again, the words seemed to pour out of her without even a thought of protest.

"I know what you mean. My… my mother… I'm sure you've heard all the legends by now, the Great Prophet of Loganville and her dirty little shame. Well, I'm the dirty little shame."

She waited for the usual reaction—the slow spread of disgust across his thin mouth, twisting it to a sneer that mirrored every mother's when she heard just exactly whom her daughter was bringing over for dinner that day, the same broad eyes that the kids got when they hear from the whispers in their ear just who that quiet, blond girl skulking down the hallway is. She knew she had screwed up any chance for this night to end without some excruciating embarassment, and while she tried to tell herself this was a good thing, that she could retreat back to her state of proud isolation, it felt like a chink had been made in the armor she wore, one that exposed a weak spot she had spent years trying to convince herself wasn't there.

"I actually don't know anything about a prophet. Well, not from Loganville, at least. Why do they call her that? She preachy or something?"

At first, Gwen wasn't sure exactly what had happened. Moments earlier, she had convinced herself that the world was ending, but now that the moment had passed and she was still standing here, she found herself quite unprepared.

"I guess you could say that. You're messing with me, right? Or you're just trying to be nice? That's it, right? I don't know a single person in this town that hasn't heard of my mother."

"Well, that's awfully conceited of you to say."

"Not if you knew my mother."

"Well, I thought I made it pretty clear that I don't."

Gwen found herself at a loss of words again. She had never started a conversation with someone with a completely blank slate. Every encounter she could remember, she had to fight the judgments that came before she ever opened her mouth. She was always the underdog, fighting to give her words meaning in a world that had long ago decided that they were insignificant, all for something that had never been her choice. Now she was talking to someone that didn't think of her as an embodiment of her mother's words, but as Gwen. He only saw Gwen, the real Gwen… and she was absolutely terrified.

"She's the very definition of a zealot. She's convinced the world has become nothing but a den of sin, a place for the unconverted and the sinners to spite God's name and gift, and she's foretold its downfall probably a hundred times now. A couple of years ago, there was meeting at the community center over the participation of the citizens in an upcoming rally to support the growing AIDS epidemic in the more rural communities. And my mother strolled in, riding a horse so high no one could meet her gaze, and padlocked the doors shut before anyone knew what was happening, telling everyone there that the only solution was to wait for God to purge the homosexuals of their sin through fiery destruction and that we all should await the coming end-times together, praying for salvation and damning the worst amidst our ranks—which, in her own noxious view, was pretty much the entire town. She read off a list of the town's dirty laundry, right there in front of all of them, like Ms. Gugino's affair with the town's registered deacon or the fact that Maria Bennet's second child was actually conceived by her first daughter's kindergarten teacher. She exposed them all.

"But then she kept going, kept talking about these terrible, awful things, and nobody knew what she was going on about—about the earth trembling and splitting apart, swallowing everyone, about how poor Mrs. Gennaro would be struck down by God in an audacious display to highlight the tragedy of losing such a beautiful, God-fearing soul. This went on and on, with more and more outrageous claims, each one making the crowd more frightened, angry, and bitter.

"I was sitting in the corner for the whole thing. I don't remember how old I was, maybe six or seven—old enough to know where I was but not why I was there, at least at the time. After enough of the town's 'sins' had been aired and picked apart like buzzard feed, the crowd finally turned on her, tired of waiting to see which one of their secrets would be exposed next. The fire department had shown up around that same time and was working on breaking down the large steel doors, but my mother's padlock was twisted through one of the handles. They were left with cutting through the iron links, removing the hinges, or just knocking the damn things down. They went with the quickest and easiest option, and they started slamming this battering ram into the doors like you see SWAT teams do. Every time they hit the door, it sent this booming across the gymnasium, like a herald of trumpets getting louder and louder. People started to scream to be heard over it, and others started to scream to be heard over them, the booms of the battering ram stirring them up like dogs barking at a supersonic whistle.

"My mother took these as sign that God was finally answering her faith and started to speak from the Book of Revelations, the part about the seven trumpets sounding before the apocalypse. As she was howling her head off about a seven-headed dragon emerging from a sea and a mountain falling from the sky, people who had finally had enough, mostly men who had only come with the promise that this would buy them an hour of peace to watch the game later that night, started calling my mother a 'hippo-crate' and pointing to me—*at* me. I had covered my ears because the ram was getting so loud, so I don't remember anything that they were saying, but I remember their eyes. I'll always remember those.

"There wasn't an ounce of empathy in them. All of them were cold and bitter, piercing me yet going right through me. I couldn't tell the ones that were looking at me apart from the ones that were locked on my mother as she continued her exhortation, her eyes to the ceiling as if she was expecting it to be torn off at any moment and God's hand to pluck her from the linoleum floor like a gum wrapper.

"That's how people looked at me from then on. Some hid it behind listless, dead eyes that were careful to keep any affection hidden as well, and others wore it like a favorite suit, but they were always there, beneath smile and scowls alike.

"When the firemen finally got the doors down, my mother was on me in a second, pulling my arm off my head so hard that it almost popped out of its socket. The sheriff got to her before she could escape through the back door into the parking lot. Before I knew what was happening, I was sitting on an uncomfortable wooden bench beneath a police blotter while men walked by, afraid to speak to a six-year-old girl, their eyes betraying their real sentiments better than their procedural buzz words ever could. My mother kept her sermon up until they processed her and released her to my aunt on bail. Every time the door to the holding cells swung open, you could hear her voice reverberating through the whole building. I hate to admit it, but for a second, she really did sound like the voice of God.

"But it was worse than that. People talked about the event constantly. It might've faded into the backs of everyone's minds, a story to be brought up on drunken nights when traumatizing events suddenly become hilarious. But then what she said started coming true. There was an earthquake less than a week later, one so bad it ended up triggering a sinkhole on the Hanlon farm that pulled the entire farmhouse down, killing the family that lived there while they slept. This event alone caused enough nervous whispers. Only a few people remembered my mother's words at that point, and only the most paranoid—or enlightened, depending how you look at it—were able to put the two together. But then Mrs. Gennaro was struck by lightning in the church parking lot on her way to play organ for the local theater production of Oklahoma. Then the Saskans got a nasty divorce that resulted in Carrie Saskan's disfigurement and Lucian Saskan's suicide, and a fire closed down Main Street for several months, and people realized that everything correlated with what my mother said. They were finally as afraid of her as I was. They worried about what she might say next, what horrible future she might predict, what terrible thing she might *will to happen.* It gave her power, one inspired by fear, but power nonetheless. All it got me was spite, spite at being her daughter.

"I'm surprised you hadn't heard of *that*, at least. That's where she first got her nickname."

Range's face was serious, but his eyes were soft and perceptive. "I'd heard rumors, but I don't put much stock in those, like I do most things I haven't seen with my own eyes."

"When we got home, I tried asking my mom what had happened, why she had done what she did and why the townspeople seemed to hate her for it so much, why they hated *me* so much for it. But I was only met with a dark silence as she sat in her chair staring up at her painting of Jeremiah lamenting the destruction of Jerusalem while my aunt began to unpack in the other room. Finally, with all my confusion tasting like anger, I asked her why she lied—why she was *wrong*—about the world ending, and her eyes snapped to me so fast I wasn't sure she hadn't been looking at me the whole time. There was no love in her eyes when she looked at me anymore. If any part of her had ever seen me as her daughter before that, it died that day. Now, I was only her mistake, her ultimate sin before God, brought forth in human flesh. She locked me in my room for two weeks for that..."

His face didn't change while she spoke, and when she finished, his silence seemed to cling to Gwen's skin like a loose Band-Aid clinging to a spot of hairs that she wanted desperately to pull off. A bell tolled down the street, the large church tower conducting a symphony to send the sun off as it slipped into the abyss beneath the sky. Gwen thought of Apollo pulling his chariot back into pillared heights of Mount Olympus and wondered if he felt the same exhaustion with his day as the husband pulling into his remodeled garage, whose workdays have begun to blend into a blur of dotted lines and handling paychecks that gave the boss's brother-in-law more money than Apollo had seen in his life. Did Apollo get jealous of Zeus on his lofty throne as he resigned himself to another night on the couch, pretending to watch whatever was in front of him?

The stone gargoyles that dotted the bell tower like ticks on a beast shook with each thunderous crash of brass that turned the tower into a trumpet of the angels. For a moment, Range looked no different from the saints and martyrs that adorned the lower roofs and parapets. Looks of regret and agony etched into faces meant to inspire hope and compassion; they always frightened Gwen when her mother had dragged her to mass. They looked scarier in the dark morning before the sun showed up, which was when they usually did, so that the prophet could rest herself directly in front of the voice of God.

"I've never really told that story to anybody before. I guess I never really had to. I know it probably wasn't the most appropriate story for a first date, but I guess, I got a little... carried away by the memory, like I was watching an old movie, my own personal Zapruder film."

Several seconds passed before Gwen realized her mistake, but when it came upon her, it came like a tidal wave that swept through a factory that specialized in making the heaviest bricks in the northeastern United States. She saw the wolfish grin had returned to his slender face, and she could taste fresh bile in the back of her throat.

Certainly, throwing up would ruin this night just as perfectly has anything else Gwen was planning on saying instead.

"It was a little awkward of you, I have to admit," he replied, chuckling to himself and turning back to his guitar.

She swallowed the shame in her throat and felt as her chest began to tighten. Her thoughts irrationally turned to how much shampoo she had used in the shower before she left and whether or not she had remembered to actually use deodorant or if she had just convinced herself she had again, before she realized how much of an utter loon she sounded like.

"Excuse me? Did you just say that *I'm* the awkward one here? This coming from the guy whose bright idea of getting to know a girl is inviting her out to a graveyard in the middle of the night? You're lucky you're kinda cute, or else this would have seemed extremely creepy, you know that, right?"

It had been awhile since she had flirted with anyone, but she thought this was how you were supposed to do it. At this point in the night, she was having a hard time observing what she had to lose.

She caught his gaze again and drank in his smile, feeling the warmth hit her stomach like a shot of expensive bourbon. She started listing closer to him, making herself seem trepidatious, not too eager. That was how it was done. You had to play hard to get but not entirely out of reach, close enough to grab what you want for yourself if you have to.

"Well, it's good to know I'm cute, I guess," he said, setting the guitar to his side.

It sunk down into steel net that held it and its owner off the ground, and he motioned to her with his now-free hand as he stepped over the lame excuse for a fence and onto the darker, heavily trod grass of the cemetery. Tentatively, Gwen slipped her fingers through his and swung her leg over the makeshift seat, sliding down the links onto the other side.

"I'm not the best with this, even though I planned out exactly what I was gonna say in this situation probably a good hundred times before I saw you coming over the embankment. When I saw you, all the words kind of just… flew out of my head, like someone had kicked my chest in and taken every bit of me it could."

His eyes drifted back down to the grave in front of them, the name Maria Lemtrobe written in fine cursive that seemed to look more like an autograph than a eulogy. The date of death stood on April 6, 1965, more than enough time to turn the woman who might have been just as infatuated, just as naive as Gwen herself, into a collection of bones and strips of fraying skin. Scrunching up her face, she was able to put the horrific image out of her mind. A shovel was leaning against the tombstone next to hers, the grave beneath it made up of fresh dirt—a darker mix that stuck out from the old, crusted ground around it. The thought of a slightly *fresher* dead body did little to comfort her.

Suddenly sick of the dead, the living, and anything in between other than the pair of tender eyes and soft lips that stood before her, she found her face getting inexplicably closer to his as if on some kind of track that had been lain down years before. Tired of fighting what she knew to be real—terrifyingly, sickeningly real—she gave in to the gentle pull of his body.

When he turned back and noticed her, she saw an endearing flash of nervousness crack his cool exterior, and a lump in his throat dropped like something out of an old Saturday morning cartoon. His body seemed to be stuck in that same force, and as they neared each other, she could feel tingles already spreading through her body like ants burrowing beneath her skin.

A pained expression accompanied his face as he pulled back and placed his hand tight around her arm.

"Unfortunately, there's another reason I brought you out here tonight. I need to show you something."

Gwen's disappointment was palpable, but before she could voice her confusion, she realized that the tingles she had felt before were still there, and any comfort she might have mistaken them for earlier was now gone. All that was left was the feeling that they were being watched by someone.

Scanning the horizon like a mother looking for a lost child, Gwen was met by the same dark, abandoned streets that had greeted her when she had arrived an hour ago. There was no one around but them, the martyrs, and the gargoyles.

A scream unlike anything Gwen had heard drifted over the sky, a wail that seemed to be struggling to sound like something human. It often broke into frequencies that only the dogs several doors down could hear, their loud barking only adding to the screeching nighttime symphony. Gwen slammed her hands over her ears, the sweat sounding in her canal like a leaky faucet. After remembering everything about that day with her mother all those years ago, she suddenly felt like she was there again, a frightened six-year-old girl in the middle of a squirming, volatile crowd crying for blood and vengeance. The breath seemed to leave her lungs as if a vacuum had opened around her.

She looked up to see Range above her, screaming something she couldn't hear over the unearthly wailing. The scream turned into a low rumble, capturing his attention to the grave in front of him, the stone shaking and crumbling like finely driven snow. The left corner fell to the ground in pieces, soon followed by the entire right side, leaving only Maria's date of birth and part of her first name as the only evidence of her existence.

Without warning, just as it had come, the shrill scream ended; and Gwen found her composure returning to her slowly, as if all the blood was rushing back into her. She turned to Range, ready to ask for a damn good explanation as to what in God's name just happened; but before she could even stand, the dirt in front of her began to slide and part, like quicksand that you would see in the old movies.

Something rose up from the center: one digit twisted in the wrong direction—the joint, which no longer bore any skin other than a loose flap that looked like stained yellow parchment, pointed sickeningly upward like a man caught in prayer. Mounds of dirt fell from between its fingers as the bones, muscles long dissolved into the earth, clenched and tightened into a fist before they fell to the loose ground like an eagle's talon.

And slowly, the decaying hand began to try and pull itself up from the confines of its grave.

A Shitstorm

And the Lord will send a plague on all the nations that fought against Jerusalem; their flesh will rot while they stand on their feet, their eyes will rot in their sockets, and their tongues will rot in their mouths. Their people will become like walking corpses, their flesh rotting away.

—Zechariah 14:12

But sin never dies. Sin never dies. I should've given you to God when you were born, but I was weak and backsliding, and now the Devil has come home.

—Margaret White, *Carrie*

That's my mother you're pissing on!

—Lionel, *Dead Alive*

The smell of beer and piss radiated from the very floorboards of the bar, stamped in by thousands of disinterested feet gliding across the dimly lit establishment for their next quick fix, whether it came in a frosted glass or a tight dress. Matt equated the odor with his job now and all the stress that came with it, which only served to reinforce his resentment for the place. When he was young, that same smell brought dreams of red-faced nights spent amidst friends, many he believed to be permanent fixtures in his life. Now he wasn't sure if he could even remember all (or any) of their names and what state they had moved to or whom they had married. Whatever their excuses for leaving were, Matt never paid much attention to. As far as he was concerned, they were out of his life and there was no point wasting thoughts on them. All that mattered was what was in front of him: his town, his cock, and a drink.

It was weird to think that he would never wake up within its small borders again.

"How's it coming on the safe, Frankie?" He called into the next room, his impatience getting the better of his manners at this stage of the evening.

"I thought I told you to quit rushing me!"

"All I'm saying is, I didn't think it would take you this long, or else I would've just done the safe myself. I've practiced on the one at my place for months now."

"Then why in the hell did you ask me to help?"

"I honestly didn't expect you to come with us, Frank. And seeing as I learned most of the things I know about it from you, I figured, you know, you'd be a little bit quicker than I was."

"Well then, either put your lips to good use on me while I finish up here, or else shut them up because right now, your bitching's doing nothing for nobody. At least that way, I'd be able to get a good blowjob before I end up handing him out to neo-Nazi's in prison. I mean, did you bastards plan any of this out past 'get inside and take the money'? 'Cuz that really seems like all you guys got."

The shots had given Frank a sharp tongue and a penchant for vulgarity, like they often did, and while Matt didn't particularly enjoy being spoken back to, he had to admit this was the Frank he preferred.

"You forgot the part where we drive away, fam," T-Rock said from across the bar, his back pressed against the heavy wood doors, sliding the barrel of his Remington M887 through the gilded handle as a type of makeshift stand. A suppressor made out of duct tape and PVC pipe hung loosely from the end, shaking with each wobble of exhaustion from his arms.

"We were planning on getting in and out in fifteen minutes. We passed the twenty-minute mark awhile ago. The stopwatch on my phone doesn't go past that."

"Goddammit."

There was a loud bang as Frank took out his frustration on the safe; part of him prayed God would cut him some slack for all the years of abuse and just have the thing pop open like a broken piggy bank, cash spilling out onto the floor. Reaching into the bag at his feet, he pulled out a long bit drill and twisted the eight-inch head into place before turning his attention back to his steel mistress. Rubbing his fingers gently over the uneven paint of the Hamilton until he found the indentation, he pressed the drill head hard against it and turned it on, hoping that his speed wouldn't result in sloppiness.

His ears were met with a roar that squealed like pigs in a slaughterhouse. Sparks shot from between the collision of steel, and for a brief flash, they looked like fireworks permeated with shrapnel. Even though the thought didn't last longer than several breathless seconds, Frank knew that if he kept it up, things would get worse, and that would be of no benefit to everyone—not with the time already a hotter commodity than unclaimed oil fields. Frank's finger slipped from the grip of the drill, the head whirring to a stop and sending shavings across the green shag rug of the office, which Matt had often criticized as looking imported straight from 1973.

However, that same horrible screeching continued, even as Frank let the drill clatter onto the floor, its shrillness seemed to be growing with each second that passed, piercing Frank's eardrums like rusty spoon unflinchingly shoving its way through. His hands clawed their way up to his ears, where he cupped them hoping that a vacuum would provide some relief from that inhuman noise, but it came through just the same, impervious to the howling crescendo.

"What in the holy fuck was that?" came Tyler's muffled voice from the front of the bar, the low register still making it through his sweaty palms.

It took Frank's brain a second to put together the fact that since he could hear his voice so clearly, the noise must have abated, at least for the time being. Hopefully, the sparks would be kept to a minimum now that the head had already cut several centimeters above the lock.

"Frankie! Are you all right in there, buddy?"

"I'm fine!" Frank called back, wiping the sweat from his brow and looking back at the door to the office, the name Caplin emblazoned in dark, glue on letters across the frosted glass.

"What the hell was that noise? Did you hear that? Tyl—I mean, Tranze, you heard it, right?"

"You fucking serious? Of course, I heard that shit, 'cuz my ol' deaf grannie with her giant-ass hearing aids could'a heard that shit."

"Was it some type of alarm?"

"It was the drill! It was just the drill."

Frank wasn't sure if he was trying to convince himself of the fact or explain it to his friends, but it seemed to cover both fields pretty well. Tentatively, he picked the drill back up and returned to his work, letting his eyes drift around the room, whose time capsule–like qualities became more apparent the more time you spent in it—which was probably why Matt was familiar with it enough to joke about it. It was no secret that Matt often found himself berated in this very office and coming right back out to pour himself a drink and relate the story to Frank, Tyler, and the rest.

The desk looked like one the teachers in elementary schools used to have—thick oak with enough drawers to keep every confiscated yo-yo and drawing of the instructor performing various acts of sexual congress with dogs and cats. The lamp looked like it probably still ran on a Clapper. Frank was tempted to test his theory but didn't feel like dropping the drill and screwing up his line to the tumbler, which he was proud to note was looking smoother than any job he remembered himself doing before. Either his mind was slipping and all the better jobs had sunk into oblivion along with the rest of his happy memories, or his mind was slipping and he was an old codger thinking his shady work was some of his best. Either way, it was no time to let complacency screw him up now.

Back to the walls his gaze went, where there were many pictures of the man named Caplin, with his wiry frame and beady, little eyes hidden behind the large black frames, bearing more of a resemblance to species of weasels than a man, shaking hands with many of Loganville's many movers and shakers. There he was, standing with the mayor at fund-raising event that bore a banner for the year 1998. Alongside that one was a photo op with a man Frank recognized to be the governor, who resembled someone he couldn't put his finger on, along with a woman he could only assume to be his wife. Caplin was standing with his own wife then, a fine piece of woman with a modest bosom and lips that wouldn't look out of place on a magazine insert. There was even a picture of the two meeting with Tom Selleck, his trademark mustache catching Frank's eyes as he moved over the man's private museum to his own life.

He still remembered his nights watching *Magnum P.I.* over at Sarah's house, his hands wrapped tightly around her shoulders, fondling her breast as Magnum shoved some perp's head into the table. That night, she had told him she loved him as he entered her, used his name even—his *real* name—him loving the feeling of her hair as it fell across his arm. How wonderful it had been.

She also left during an episode, one where Magnum met with a duchess and ended up showing her his mustache for a closer inspection. She made sure to call him Frog several times then, sneering at him and telling him that being called Frog was the best compliment he could hope for, as at least, they had spines to call their own.

His attention came back as his eyes reached one of the last pictures on the wall. At first glance, there was nothing different about it from the many others—Caplin dressed in his Sunday best, his hand wrapped like a vice grip around his wife's shoulder—but the face on the end caused the drill to veer sharply into the side of the safe; and a sharp whine rang out, the force nearly snapping his arm in two before he was able to regain control.

However, the damage had already been done. He had seen Klunesberg's face, and his voice was already ringing around in Frog's head like a clinical migraine.

Don't fuck up now, Frog. Everybody here is counting on you. You wouldn't want everybody to see you as you really are, now, would you?

"Shut up. Shut up. Shut up," he whispered to himself as he repositioned the drill, forcing it past the side tunnel created when his hand had slipped and back into the groove.

"Would you get your fucking face out of your phone for five minutes? You do realize what the lookout is supposed to be doing, right? The concept isn't new to you, is it?"

Was that voice real or just in his head? The fact that he had to ask himself worried him more than either answer would.

"Of course, I know what a fucking lookout is, fam. You think I ain't ever hit a lick before? A nigga's just trying to put some pussy aside for after, you feel me? I know you of all people know what I'm talking about. They don't call you Matty Ice because you be lookin' like Vanilla's younger brother."

"Why don't you just sort that shit out later?"

"I can't control when the bitches be thirsty, Matty."

Frank's attention drifted back to the picture. He tried to stop himself, but it only delayed what he knew to be inevitable. He allowed a quick glance at the smudged black-and-white photo, a banner that read "New Year's Eve '06" across it hanging just behind the group of couples sitting around a well-fashioned table. He saw Caplin leaning over and speaking to another man, who bore a tired face with eyes that seemed to sparkle despite the fact. Something about him seemed horribly familiar and turned his stomach into a boiling, writhing mess.

"Why aren't you planning on getting outta dodge right after we get out of here anyway? They're gonna know that we knew each other from high school. Hell, they even arrested both of us at that pep rally party down by Cutter's ravine. You're pretty much asking to get yourself thrown in a police interrogation room. And when that happens, that becomes my problem."

"Man, calm down, Matty, I ain't about to be goin' and getting myself arrested for a piece of poon. I got this pussy on lock to leave with me. Told that bitch I loved her and shit, so all I's gots to do is swing by afterward, and then I got myself some road head for the drive. You criticize, nigga, but when you be looking down that long stretch Interstate to Canada, you're gonna be wishing you had a pair of wet lips around your dick. Besides, we both know a true gangsta would shoot his way out before any cops brought him into some jail cell."

"If I had wanted someone sucking my dick, I would've just gotten a ride with you. Who's this chick you got leaving with you anyway? Can we trust her to keep her mouth shut if you ends up getting fed up with your tiny cock?"

"She's cool. Like I said, I got this bitch on lock. You remember Irene Palmer? The girl with the big ol' tittays."

"Yeah, last I heard of her, she had a muffin top to match those tits, and chlamydia too."

Frank tried to place the man in the photo, with his sparkling eyes and bushy mustache that seemed more at home in a 'seventies porno film than on anybody from the twenty-first century. The sickness in his gut caused him to turn away, but the grinning face that appeared again only brought most of his lunch up into the back of his throat. The drill slipped again, scratching against the steel and twisting sharply out of his grip. After shutting his eyes tight and an unpleasant swallow, Klunesberg's face left his mind; but his voice remained, a scornful whisper in the back of his ears.

They're gonna be upset with you if you keep messing up, Frog. It's really only a matter of time before they turn on you like everyone else did. You should understand that by now.

Sweat falling from his brow clouded his vision. Dragging the back of his hand across his forehead seemed to only make him warmer and stir up his already-squirming stomach.

"Frank, is everything all right in there? Do you need me to come and finish it up?"

See? What did I tell you? They realized they don't need you. You're just an old man who never took the time to realize there wasn't any time left. A failure. A waste.

"I'm fine, Matt, I was breaking into safes tougher than this before you figured out what that small pink worm between your legs was for."

Footsteps echoed from down the hall, a shadow growing beneath the door like a weed. "Are you sure? I could just run in there and check the—"

"I said I got it, all right?"

Breathing heavy, Frank could hear Matt back away, his soft footsteps growing quieter and quieter until they disappeared completely. Regret came in the next few gulps of air, tasting worse than the vomit had moments before.

Useless and unpleasant. God, how they've put up with your incompetence so long is really astounding. I almost admire them for it. Why don't you just save everyone some time and put that drill through that thick skull of yours?

Placing the warm plastic grip back into his soaked palm, Frank muttered to himself, "Why don't you just shut your fucking mouth?"

Angrily, he shoved the drill back into the small groove and squashed the trigger. Almost immediately, the drill veered into one of the side pockets from his previous transgressions and spun out of his control and back onto the ground with a heavy clatter. Rage filling his body like a fever and turning his vision to a ruby haze, his fingers curled round the drill and threw it across the room, flying awkwardly on the battery heavy side into the desk and spilling its contents over the floor.

After, he was sitting in a shamed silence for a while, waiting to see if the voices would continue mocking him until he was well and truly gonzo and to temper his own anger, which was spiraling into dangerous extremes. His father had often beat him when he was young, for errors in his manners, bad grades on his report cards (when he bothered to check them), even for things that were well beyond his control, like when the bank refused to remortgage the house after his mother's passing. While Frank couldn't deny his unhealthy fear of Michael Klunesberg, he knew deep down that he was more frightened of becoming a puppet to his rage like his father was.

Shuffling over to the coffee-stained floor in front of the desk, Frank leaned down to grab the drill when another photo caught his eye. This one was fortunate to no longer have the sick visage of Frank Roger's malicious higher-up, but it did have the man with the shining eyes and bushy mustache. In this photo, he was standing next to the scrawny Caplin, his large arm wrapped tight around his wiry frame, the golden pointed star bright on the lapel of his shirt. Frank's trembling hand managed to raise it all the way to his face to make sure he wasn't seeing a smudge or evidence to his worsening sanity; but when he confirmed the badge was very much real and remembered that he had seen the sheriff in person many times passing through city hall, the photo clattered back to the ground and shattered, the glass pocketing the carpet like land mines.

"Matt, get your ass in here now!"

The booms of footfalls reverberated down the hallway again, a dark shadow materializing behind the frosted glass shortly after. As soon as Matt's figure passed through the doorframe, Frank's hands were around his collar, forcing him back against the wall of the office. The door slammed shut behind him with force of the impact, keeping a muffled shout from Tyler from being anything more than mush of plosives, which wasn't much different from what usually came out of the boy's mouth. Frank slammed his hand against Matt's chest, his eyes wide with confusion for a just a moment before his hand rushed up to pull Frank's off of him. Instead of the back of Frank's hand, his fingers found the crumbled piece of celluloid from Caplin's desk, and a shamed understanding spilled onto his features, his mouth tight and eyes thin.

"So you did know about this? How could you be so goddamn stupid, Matt? The sheriff's brother-in-law? That's who you wanna pull a fuckin' safe heist on? And you have the nerve to get me involved in all this stupid petty revenge shit?" Frank said, losing his grip and turning to face the back wall, the shelf of liquor, his only true friend, greeting him. "All because you're too much of hot shit to put up with the regular day-to-day bullshit of having a job that, God forbid, might not be the one you saw yourself in when you were still sucking on your mom's tits. No, the life of a small-town bartender isn't fast-paced enough for the California kid, is it? Not enough girls throwing their panties at your feet everywhere you go? Too many guys smaller than you treating you like the dirt off the heel of their boot so you gotta bring me down with you just so you can feel like you showed them? Fuck, Matt."

"Hey, don't get all pissed off at me just because I have the guts to stand up to my piece of shit boss and you can't even say your name without pissing yourself," Matt shouted, his eyes darting to the floor in shame as soon as he said it. A silence descended onto the dark office, twisting its decorations into demons that watched the scene with a gleeful delight.

See. They know you're mine. Everyone knows. Every person in this small piece of shit town knows you're nothing, no better than a leech, a sucker fish that feeds on the filth, the leavings of others for sustenance. The pieces of dead skin I leave on the bed sheets each morning carry more impact on this world than you do. Just admit it. Tell him he's right. Do it. Go on now, Frog. Do what I say.

Frank found himself face-to-face with his boss on the wall, the moving lips home to the horrible voice from his head. The small creature in the photo began to laugh, a deep and terrible thing, like something you would hear from a soldier still shell-shocked from having seen his best friend from back home blown to bits in front of him. The low guttural chuckle bellowed out through the room as the face twisted into one of his father, with his eyes nothing more than sickly pale orbs in his rotting skull.

"Listen, Frank, I'm sorry I said that. But what does it matter? So what if Caplin's the sheriff's brother-in-law? The guy probably thinks he's as big of a piece of shit as we do. I'll still be hundreds of miles away before I'm supposed to show up for my shift tomorrow night. It doesn't change anything."

Frank's eyes darted hastily to Matt to see that his face, although softer, was unchanged; and when he looked at the picture again, Kluneberg's grinning visage and silence was all that greeted him. Shaking his head, hoping that it was just exhaustion toying with him but finding himself less and less convinced, Frank turned back to Matt, his discomfort worn on his sleeves.

"The last thing you want is to rob someone who can call in favors from the law. This guy could get every border patrol office from here to Aroostook County, an eight-by-ten poster of your face within an hour. Hell, the guy might even know a couple mounties, for all we know."

Matt opened his mouth, but only a heated breath escaped, a very sudden and real apprehension growing on his features. There came more muffled shouting from the front, Tyler's voice growing louder and more frantic by the second. Frank gave a final hard look at Matt, watching as the slow realization of a terrible error spread across his face until it was no longer amusing. Reaching out to comfort him, Frank thought of Kluneberg's words in his head and opened the door and strode out into the hall instead.

"Would you fags quit bummin' each other or whatever the fuck ya'll niggas is doing back there and get up here now? We got popo out front!"

Frank cast one last bitter look at Matt before darting quickly through the door, glad that he had decided against taking the Berretta Tyler had offered him in the backseat of the van before they came in through the freezer entrance in the back alley. If he was going to go to jail, at least he wouldn't have added time for carrying a firearm. When he arrived at the front of the building, he stopped and stared for a while at the bar, thinking of the times spent there beneath a bottle of cheap whiskey, swapping horror stories from the job with the likes of Greg Finnster and Billy Riggs, even Matt joining in to bad-mouth Caplin when he could pull himself away from the customers and the fan club of girls that followed him around like he was

Elvis reincarnate. The only one of them that probably had any *actual* horror from their job was Marshall.

    Frank remembered a time when he had showed up one Thursday, soaking wet, down to the very bone, three hours past his usual calling time, grumpier than a skunk while the rest of the usual were well and truly smashed. When all the rambunctious ne'er-do-wells were finally at attention, he told them about the grave he was digging, a plot for some rich yuppie who died flipping over their snowmobile on vacation in Hafjell (on Klunesberg's recommendation, as Frank later learned from one of his many half-assed memorials that always seemed to start with a trite story tangibly related to the person before veering off onto boastful tangents). The family had their own burial plot near the center of the cemetery where a lot of the town's famous names were buried—Yawfellow, Longwarden, Farsnworth, and so forth. While he was squaring away the last clumps of soil from the pit and checking his measurements to assure that the hole was wide enough to accommodate the rather large, expensive coffin with fine golden bouquets of marigolds overlaid on the top, there came a horrible rumbling from the ground beneath the hill. He could feel the tremors shaking the soil loose beneath his feet. The side of the plot nearest the bluff started to collapse, a hole forming almost instantaneously with the release of a chunky, sickly green liquid that poured out from the growing chasm. The substance began to fill the bottom of the grave as Marshall tried to pull himself up from the muck; but his feet, slick with mysterious liquid, couldn't get a strong enough hold, and he fell backward into the slime. The side of the plot near the hill continued to erode away beneath the force of the sludge, the top soil falling into the abyss and pulling the shining white coffin into view as the ground under it started to fall away. Soon, its shadow covered Marshall completely, and when he was sure that he was about to be crushed in the slimy pit, an onlooker who was visiting his father's grave at the time dropped his hand down to Marshall and pulled him onto the grass, sliding on his belly, like a seal, as the heavy alabaster box tumbled down into the earthen pit.

    Marshall swore that the grass smelled fresher than any grass he had smelled before in his life, and he had worked as a landscaper for a couple years out of high school. After thanking the man for saving his life and before heading off to tell his boss about the accident, he looked down into the pit once more and saw the dirty green sludge swallow up the golden marigolds, large bubbles slowly rising to the surface. Firefighters figured an old, undiscovered sewage pipe that had been running through the hills when the factory was still operating must've finally burst; and since the sludge had stopped just over the top of the coffin, they weren't worried about excavating it any further, other than draining the plot the best they could.

Marshall had told that story to bright red faces and was greeted with slaps on the back of his damp overalls and bellows of hearty laughter, despite the awful smell he dragged in with him; but even to this day, Frank could remember the hesitation behind his grins, the dullness to his eyes as he spoke of it. He could remember the genuine fear that Marshall had from his brush with the reaper. And now he was gone.

Matt came striding quickly into the room, making his way behind the bar and to the collection of liquors that lined the spotty glass shelves behind it. Pulling the red pour top from a bottle of Jim Bean, he lifted the bottle to his lips and took a long swig, the kind usually reserved for impressing other collegiate minds at the local keggers he often spent most of his time at when he wasn't working the bar; but there was no one here worth impressing. Matt knew that there was only one way out of this situation, one that was undoubtedly of his own design, although it was hard not to find angry ideas regarding Tyler's incompetence or Frank's spinelessness.

"They pulled up just a minute ago. Two cruisers, one's got cherries spinning and is talking on the radio to the other piggies. Wait. Wait. Hol' up, looks like one of 'em is getting out of the car, some gray-haired cracker motherfucker."

"Does it look like he knows we're in here?"

Tyler pressed the shotgun against the steel door handle, giving himself a quick view of the parking lot. "Can't tell, but the fucker's coming this way with his piece raised," he said, before looking back at Matt, his face filled with an unusual calm that Frank wouldn't have believed the kid possessed unless he saw it as clearly as he did now.

"You want me to take care of him before he gets in here? This nigga always preferred his bacon smoked."

Pulling himself up from behind the booth in which he had tucked away, Frank looked out of one of the nearby windows and saw the sheriff moving from his cruiser and out to the center of the parking lot, talking into the small radio hanging from his shoulder while the standard issue Glock G41 stood level with his eyes, their bright aquamarine gleam visible even through the dirty pane of glass.

"Wait a minute. Somebody else is coming up to him. Some skinny motherfucker, looks like that ferret my niece Trisha used to have, pasty mo'fucka. Now he's coming up while the pig's hanging back. The other guy doesn't seem to be packin' anything."

Frank cast a quick, desperate look at Matt, but he never saw it. He was already back to the lone bottle of Jim Bean. Matt poured himself another shot of bourbon, downed it with a quick snap of his head, and poured himself another and took that one as well. When he felt the tension leave his muscles and the calm seep into his chest like mildew on the attic rafters, he turned back to the entrance, placing his palms flat against the organic sandalwood bar where they had rested so many times before, feeling unnaturally comfortable amidst the sticky stains of spilled liquor and human spit—almost like those very things were what lay beneath his skin. Breathing deep, he saw the nights spent here with Frank and the other working stiffs, drinks spilling over in their hands, doing lines of coke picked up from Sweet Mick in the alley with Tyler and his cronies, locking the doors early with several of the more… open-minded Saturday night patrons when the urge became too strong to spend the entire night staring at cleavages dangled in front of him like a carrot in front of a mule. He briefly considered one more shot of the good stuff, especially when he saw the dark, damp splotches left by his hands when he pulled them from the bar, but decided against it, as he knew the grip on his senses needed to be as tight as it could be. Slowly and with another deep, chest-filling breath, he pulled the Browning Hi Power from the holster tucked underneath the back of his cotton shirt.

"Oh, shit, that's the stiff, isn't it? I thought I recognized him. Well, shieeeeeeeeet. Looks like Matty Ice wants to handle this one himself. You know I ain't gonna deny my boy that."

The dumb grin he wore was no different than the ones he'd seen on Tyler's face many times before, even when passed out on the cold tiles of the bathroom floor after one too many RumChata's; but this was the first time the malice hidden behind it became sickeningly apparent. The many faces of celebrities from the movie stills pinned to the wall, like a sad attempt at a twisted backwoods Applebee's, seemed to be smiling wider as well—sharing a secret joke that Matt thought he must've known at some point but was lost to time, buried deep within him where the rest of the things that weren't wanted were stored. His therapist had advised him to build a sort of memory museum in his mind when he was younger and still naive enough to believe that someone else could understand what he was going through, like it was just another crossword puzzle placed in front of them with their morning coffee.

The man, with his dark, slicked-back hair in an off-kilter widow's peak and teeth small and distractingly white—which made a small, tittering sound as he sat listening, the tips clicking against each other and producing a note not unlike the cartoons where the small mouse is all too happy to play the cat's ribs like a xylophone. The man told him that the museum could be his own design, a personal Versailles if he wanted it to be, with twisting mazelike corridors that would keep anyone but him out and booby traps that would give Indiana Jones a run for his money.

Instead of taking the good doctor's advice, Matt had made something more akin to a basement, deep below his diaphragm in the small nook between his back and his hips. There was where he kept the worst offenders, where he kept the urge and all things brought forth from giving himself over to it. It would bang around down there, knock things off the shelves—which looked a lot more like ones you'd find behind a bar than in a stuffy, old museum—but it did its job. And other than the occasional ache, one that even the best chiropractor couldn't seem to unkink, it did its job of keeping the beast at bay. Matt thought of sharing his victory with the doctor, laughing about the intended museum when a simple dark cage would've been suitable, that all his years of training and expertise meant nothing when applied to a problem that wasn't some example in a rotting, overpriced textbook; but the good doctor disappeared from the country without a trace before he ever got the chance.

The room grew silent, like someone had drained the life from it. The dust motes that danced through the air, like indiscernible fairies caught in a spotlight, seemed brighter, sparks shooting from the air like fireworks. Tyler backed silently away from the door, his pasty frame dissolving into the shadows. The last bit of him that Matt could make out was the barrel of his shotgun raised point-blank at the entrance—a steel viper waiting for its prey.

Matt found himself back in the basement of his mind, clearing space on one of the decaying, shoddily constructed shelves by pushing aside the faces of girls whose names he couldn't remember, if he had ever known them in the first place. There were always plenty more where that came from. He often saw their faces rising out of the swampy blackness of his dreams, the colors drained from their faces and baring fangs that would emasculate the count himself. He often awoke with the bitter taste of copper in his mouth, as if he had been sucking on pennies and battery acid.

As he turned to leave this place of shadows and denied fantasies, he found himself in a hallway smelling of juniper blossoms and sweat. The arcadian stripes that lined the walls seemed to be blurring like flip-book pages being thumbed through, twisted shapes in the forms of horned creatures bending over each other in motions that were all too familiar. Thrusting, writhing forms dancing all around him like a tainted burlesque, he started down the hallway toward the lit door frame at the end. He had walked down this hall before, many times before, to many different outcomes at the end. Yet he knew what awaited him behind this one.

The picture frames mounted on the wall held faces with eyes burned out, dark gaps of white that seemed to hide more than any shadow could. The mouths were stretched and twisted into monstrous forms, like a snake that had unhinged its jaws right before swallowing whole the mouse that had dared wander too close to the abyss. Still, they watched him as he passed. The demons on the wall continued to fornicate to the horrific pounding of the drums, a beat that he had felt in the pit of his stomach at every interval of every day. It occupied his thoughts during the daylight hours. It kept him from the wisps of slumber at night. Louder and louder the hammering rhythm grew, an appetite for flesh behind it, that sweet release behind the horrible ache he felt behind every passing second.

The door stood before him, the cold brass handle emblazoned with a sunflower that had caused its owner to choose the room in the first place. When his fingers slowly coiled around it, he expected to feel a chill but was met with a horrible, searing pain that caused him to jerk backward violently. He heard the noises from within the door, like they were right next to his ear canal. With each whimper, the door seemed to tremble and shake. With each grunt, Matt's teeth clenched tighter, silently squealing, blurring with the building symphony of distress.

With a slow creak, like a rusty knife being sharpened, the door opened. Outside of the basement tucked away in his head, in the bar snuggled tightly behind the Walgreen's and Family Feed Store, coming from a parking lot smaller than some rich folk's driveways, Greg Caplin walked cautiously into the establishment that he paid for with insurance money from his previous failed business attempts—ignorant to the 16.8 mm slug poised to enter his brains and drag them kicking and screaming into the pallet wood wall on the other side of the room. Matt knew that the scene in front of him wasn't really there, but he couldn't stop it from playing, from bending reality into some obtuse obelisk near undecipherable.

"Hello? If anybody's in here, they better… Ah, I should've fucking known. Matt Métier's here to pick up a little bonus for all his hard work, is he? And he's got himself a gun too, how about that."

"That's not all he's got, fam," Tyler said, moving out of the darkness like a ninja that had left the dojo content after his first class. The end of the barrel met Caplin's greasy forehead, the mole on the right side of his brow fitting perfectly within it. "I'd pay the man a little bit more respect if I were you. Or else you're gonna end up trying to hold your guts in through yo' asshole."

Caplin turned, letting the steel scrape against his skin and leave his brow a bright slick red. "I see you've really brought the cream of the crop for this job, Matthew. Glad to see you take this one about as seriously as your other one."

Tyler quickly brought the butt of the gun across Caplin's thin nose, drawing blood that splattered like watercolor against the door. "I'd watch that mouth around me too, pole smoker. I'll let my boy Matty deal with his own business, but that ain't mean a nigguh's just gonna stand here jerkin' off while you're insultin' him."

Spitting the blood to the floor, Caplin began to laugh, softly at first but rising to a frantic cadence. "That piece of shit hasn't finished a single thing in his life. If you want to keep yourself from being some *actual* nigger's sex doll in the slammer, I'd suggest you finish me off yourself. There's no way this apathetic loser, who's more interested in chasing a bit of easy pussy than doing something with his life, is going to do anything to me."

A scream—a horrible, earth-shattering scream that sang of bruised knees and ice cream dreams, of innocence shattered on the floor like cheap china. The sound became one with the demons around him, the pounding of the drum turning into a numbing cacophony. The memory kept replaying itself in front of his eyes, the raw flesh, the stained sheets. He wanted desperately to make it go away; whatever was in front of him *needed* to go away, or he was sure the tattered remains of his conscious would be lost to the dark depths of the cellar.

"There. You see? He's not gonna do anything, what a surprise. Now, take me outside so I can—"

A boom, and then the ring of absolute silence. The Hi Power recoiled sharply in his hand, but the bullet had stayed directly on its course. The spot of blood behind Caplin had turned to a matte, a Rorschach test on the wall. Matt tried to find meaning in it but found nothing, only a fuzzy numbness, like anesthesia at the dentist's. Caplin's body, somehow limper and more serpentine than it was before, collapsed onto itself and down into a growing body of blood spreading across the floor, seeping between the floorboards and congealing with the spit and dried liquor; the floor was now lined with what appeared to be veins.

"Shots fired! I repeat, we got shots fired inside, looks like we have a man down, requesting ambulances and any responding officers to the scene. I repeat, we got a 314, robbery in progress, at 154 Jennings Boulevard, requesting ambulances and any responding officers. Suspects are armed and dangerous. There appear to be three of them, the first one is cooped up behind the entryway, and there seems to be another—"

"Shut the fuck up, pig!"

With a quick thrust of his boot, Tyler sent the heavy bar door flying outward and sent several round toward the sheriff perched behind the front of his cruiser, one of the two stray parking lot lights yards above his head and casting his shadow large across the uneven asphalt. The radio dropped from his hand as they went up to cover his head and pull himself down further into the cover. Bits of steel flew from the frame around him, bullet holes appearing in the hood like zits before a prom date.

"That's right, motherfuckers! Drizzy ain't got shit on me! That nigga was on Degrassi, getting his bitchass put in a wheelchair while I was out on the street killing po' like they're in season. Who wants some of the Tyga Killer? Huh? Anybody else want a bit of jizz from my cold steel dick here?" Tyler shouted gleefully, his voice shaking in fits as he strolled out into the lot, buried beneath shadows and the bandana he wore wrapped around the lower half of his face.

"Sir! Put the gun down. We will exercise lethal force if you keep making it necessary."

One of the officers ran around the side of the car, crouched low near the hood, shouting something at the sheriff that became gibberish as it echoed off the inside of the bar. The sheriff's head rose up from beneath his steel cover for just a second, but Tyler had already seen his opportunity, his eyes filled with stills from *Scarface* that had ran past his eyes more time than he would ever care to count. A quick pull of the trigger sent the slug shattering across the hood of the car, the lead balls ricocheting off and tearing off part of the sheriff's skull. His shadow twisted and shrunk down to a small shapeless form, mixing with the crimson stains that decorated the ground between bright yellow parking lines.

"Ohhhhhhhh, shit! I bagged me a piggie! Hell, yeah, fucking right! Ya'll faggots see that shit? That's whats coming for ya'll next if you don't back the fuck off. Or else, ya'll gonna have to say hello to—"

Shots rang out in the crisp night hair, fizzling like fire crackers with heavy booms that echoed deep into the night. Tyler dropped down quickly as the volley of gunfire bounced off the ground around him. He saw pebbles fly up off the ground in front of him, flying at him as if possessed. There was a burning sensation that begun to emanate from his shin, like someone had set fire to the muscle beneath his skin and the bones were trying desperately to break free as they roasted alive. Falling backward, a trail of blood fell upon the loose stones of the pathway as he witnessed the gaping wound in his leg for the first time. The fine blue stitchings of his Nike track pants were stained with a deep, wet crimson and a singed hole, draped in blackened fringe surrounding the mass of pulpy flesh that was his shin. A buckshot had torn off most of the flesh from the right side, and the rest had been tossed over itself like a carpet, barely covering the sight of bone.

Matt, firing the Browning at the back cruisers and sending them back behind their makeshift cover, pushed through the swinging doors, careful to keep his back leg propped against one so that it wouldn't shut behind him. Wrapping his hand tight in the folds of the huge cotton hoodie, he began to drag the screaming, hysterical mess that was once his friend back into bar, leaving a blood trail that Freddy Krueger would've admired. Once inside, Frog—who had thrown himself against the wall to the side of the heavy doors when Matt had leaped over the bar after Tyler—slammed a pool cue through the handles as soon as they crossed one another.

"Here! Help me tip this gaming machine over," Matt called frantically, letting Tyler fall limp to the floor while he moved over to the glowing beacon in the corner beside the door, lights flashing across pictures of black garbage bags bursting at the seams with money and blond, buxom women (who had passed through Matt's mind during many a trip to the men's room during his breaks on slow nights when he found the pickings too slim to satisfy the urge), with words "Filthy Rich" emblazoned across the top in glow bulb letters.

Throwing his weight behind it, the machine began to teeter; the thin steel legs dug deep into curved grooves on the floor left from years of slowly sinking into the dead wood. Frank quickly added his own back into it, and the machine gave a final groan before crashing down in front of the doors, barely missing Gregory Caplin's thin rat face. With one last hard boot, Matt turned back to the shaking white lump on the floor, the right leg of his track pants almost entirely red, giving him a motley look that made him chuckle despite the tension sticking to the air, while he began dragging him into the cold bathroom floor.

"Are you seriously laughing right now, you punk-ass motherfucker? What is so goddamn funny about this? Have you seen my leg? It looks like they tied a buzz saw to a dog's dick and let him go at me."

"It doesn't look that bad, you big pussy. After getting hit by a Mossberg while standing out in the open, you should be happy the thing's still attached by more than a thread of skin. Frank, check that back window up there and make sure it's open. There should be a latch at the bottom of the lower right pane. Do you see it? The small knob?"

"The damn thing's jammed!"

"Try the window behind the stall."

The sound of the heavy work boots beneath Frank's feet echoed off the slick tiles as he dashed into the stall, bursting through the sickly green-painted door and onto the rim of the toilet. The noise mixed with Tyler's incessant bleating kept Matt unsure as to whether this was all actually happening or if he had slipped back into his hallucinations.

"It's open! If the panel tilts back far enough, I think we can slip through."

"Where's the van parked?"

"In the forest preserve parking lot. You can get to it through the woods back here. If we sneak through here quiet enough, we might be able to make it to the tree line and to the car before they figure out where we've gone. That should buy us enough time to lose 'em before we start making for the border."

"Sounds like a plan. Now help me lift this dead weight up and through."

"Can you please not use the word *dead* around me, you insensitive dickcheese. I'm fucking bleeding out here, man. I don't wanna die, not before I can tell people I took one of those fuckers down with me. What's respect worth if you can't even see people giving it to you, you feel me?"

"Sure, I feel you, and quit your bitching. You're not gonna die. We both know you're a shit doctor. When you watch house, you think every patient's got chlamydia."

"One nigga totally had it once, you know that."

"Jesus Christ, can we just get the fuck out of here, or do you two want to make out a little more before we go to jail? Hurry, hurry!"

Hefting Tyler to his remaining foot and wrapping his damp arm around his shoulder, Matt walked over to the far stall. Catching his reflection in the large stretch mirror in front of the sinks one last time, he saw the horrific grin his face wore and flinched when he recognized it from the demons he saw dancing on the walls in the hallway buried deep within his own dark insides. Tyler stepped awkwardly on his mangled leg and let loose a howl of exasperated pain. The pounding on the front door outside the bathroom seemed to increase in its viciousness.

"Shh, we need to do this silently, or else we're fucked."

"You go through first, Frank. That way, I can pass him through to you and he doesn't fall on his leg and give us away to the cops."

"You mean the pigs."

"Shut up. And that way, if things go south, at least you can get to the van and get out of here safely. They haven't seen you yet, Frank, you can still go back to your life and act like none of this shit ever happened. I'm sorry about this, Frankie boy, I really am."

"What? Are you serious right now, Matty?"

"I appreciate the thought," Frank said, lifting his legs up to the small gap between the top pane and the turned-open bottom. He pulled himself through and tumbled onto the dirt and grass below. Standing quickly, before he had an opportunity to dissuade his insanity, he turned back to the window and held his hands up to help Tyler through. "But I ain't leaving you guys that easily. I've dealt with way worse-looking situations than this bit of spilled milk. At least, I finally have an excuse to quit my job."

"Thatta boy, now up *you* go. Make sure you breathe in and hold in all that fat of yours when you go through. When you get your leg up and through, you're probably gonna feel a lot of pain, but you've gotta keep that big mouth of yours shut for once. Do you think you can do that?"

"Fuck off, Tranze can handle a bit of pain."

"You can have my dick to suck on if you want, that should keep your mind off it."

"Ha-ha, remind me to laugh my fucking foot off, asshole." With that, Matt hoisted Tyler to the window with his good leg. He passed through seamlessly, like a dolphin trained to leap through hoops in between hours of captivity; but the pane shifted as he fell, catching on the bloody hole in his leg with a sick crack. Moving frantically, Frank clapped his hand down across Tyler's mouth and felt the wanton slobber as the horrible wail disappeared into his palm.

Matt yanked the glass back into position, causing Tyler and Frank to collapse into a pile on the earth below. There came a heavy thud as the gaming machine fell from its side onto its curved plastic back. Practically throwing himself through the small opening, the duo managed to clear the landing zone just as Matt descended on top of them.

Standing and patting his pants free of the dirt and mud, he took a quick, instinctual look around and saw that they were alone in the small enclosure behind the bar, tree branches providing a dark cave from the lights of the parking lot and police cruisers. They could hear sirens on the night wind and wasted no time carrying their injured companion and themselves into the dark woods, a trail of blood left in their wake.

Vel watched as the man laid the bouquet of roses down upon the sculpted Grecian pillar, the magenta pillow providing a beautiful contrast for their crimson petals. Freshly lit candles sent the aroma of lavender bath oils into the air and the music, something you would expect to hear in the lounge of an Italian dignitary or connoisseur of high culture, maybe Bach? Beethoven? One of the old guys that everybody seems to talk about when talking about "classical" music. Vel always considered Madonna to be more classic than of that stuffy old music, but her opinion never seemed to carry much weight outside of her own shrinking social circle. At this point, it was more of a social line.

"The roses have been laid out. Now we'll see whom our bachelor is going to be giving them to. Steve?"

That brief second of hesitation before he walked from behind the curtain had the breath stuck in her throat like a bad case of phlegm after a passing cold. Sarah's eyes grew wide when she saw him, like they always did. It was sort of her shtick, something that would keep the cameras focused on her. Molly would always bite her lip and lock a steely gaze on Steve as he entered. Maybe it was an attempt to appear cute and innocent or a way to remind him of the blowjob she had reportedly given him on their last big date. It was just conjecture, of course, but the church of TMZ was rarely wrong.

When the cameras finally made their way across the crowd of squirming women, they came into focus on a hallway of candles and long, oriental drapes that stood in contrast to the crumbling plaster of the Spanish villa, its walls marked with paintings of fields of poppies and large verdant sunflowers in Tuscany and busts of famous Grecian figures whose names she was sure she had learned from Bill and Ted back when she was still in high school. Vel hadn't retained too much of the more boring aspects of her education (matters of foreign diplomacy being one of the top offenders), but even she was slightly entranced by the hodgepodge of culture that was laid out before her eyes.

But all was quickly forgotten when Steve's shining visage, held in the light like some exhibit at a museum, appeared center frame. His jaw, wide and set, held a mouth that sent quivers throughout her body as she imagined it going places that would've made her blush back in high school. Luckily, she had grown up a lot since then, which was more than she could say about the rest of the girls she knew back then—with their whispers and sideway glances that seemed to be all-knowing in their smug superiority. Who were they to judge?

The pair of sparkling blues brought her back to the fuzzy screen above her, the ABC watermark spoiling the technicolor fantasy that she had passed the last few hours of her shift in. The smell of gristle sizzling on a cast-iron skillet that probably dated back to the Civil War and Boris's incessant shouting about a soccer—no, *football*—team from one of the Slavic countries had droned on like static in the background of her daydream. She only seemed to notice them when an advertisement of some starlet, like Emma Stone or Kirsten Dunst, talking about their supposed skin problems and the salvation they found in a new type of skin cream from Revlon that was guaranteed to revolutionize the way you washed your face. When looking in the mirror every morning and seeing the cruel mocking grins of blackheads staring back at her, usually on the tip and bridge of her nose, she was actually convinced a revolution might actually be in dire need.

The early-morning darkness was still draped over the outside world, the smell of wet dew and fog coupled with the aroma of dead leaves and thick petroleum from the BP across the street. The smells, the glowing green eye of the BP logo constantly watching her like a paranoid shift manager, and the fresh pot of Maxwell's house were the only thing that kept her from the wistful dreams that played out behind her eyelids—the same ones you could catch on channel 6 every night at seven.

This early, however, all that was on were reruns of the previous evening's developments. Vel had watched this particular episode, in which LaTrice, Sarah, and Hillary would be sent home with their hopes of marital bliss and, more importantly, future stardom shattered—unless they were asked back next season, of course. But that was only if you were memorable. Vel could hardly tell Hillary and Sarah apart with their platinum hair and dimples that seemed to have been put on by a Barbie factory employee. They even seemed to laugh the same. LaTrice, however, had started the season off by talking about how he she believed the poor to be leeching off the rich in the country, so there appeared to be a bright future in Hollywood ahead of her. Vel could feel the envy bubbling in the back of her throat.

 The second hands on the clock ticked drearily by, superimposing their will on the feeble lives passing in and out around them. Vel remembered from the cartoons she used to watch when she was little, Bart Simpson, or some other rebellious grade-school hero, would set the clock to meticulously tick away the seconds faster than usual and end the school day early or get themselves out to the recess yard that much quicker for hotly contested games of tetherball and kickball. Vel often fantasized of pulling the same trick and watching as the hours of her shift flew by, her boss none the wiser to the altered time stream, leaving her pockets just as full and her day twice as empty. The more time she could spend at home engrossed in the lives of those she'd come to care for, the better, in her opinion.

 There was the hope that sometime someone might come and whisk her away from the monotonous flow of the diner and show her just how the other half lives, the ones whose worries peaked at trying to figure out which of the many parties they were going to attend that night or which house to stay in during the upcoming winter. She knew there was the drama drummed up for the ratings each week, and Velma had to admit that she ate up every bout of bitter hair-pulling and extramarital dilemmas that they threw her way; but she also knew that most of it was there just as a way to give people like her something to relate to. They wanted the more naive to think that they were just like the rest of us, that their fame and success brought them no easy solutions to life's problem, but Vel was never convinced. She couldn't be. If there was ever a thought that the worries about the wrinkles seeping across her forehead, or the frets about the way her breasts had begun to sag down and out like someone was trying to tie them around her back, or the ideas that this week's meager tips would not be enough to cover the cable, the rent, *and* food, or the terror that she would still be alone as the months continued to blur into the wasteland of her thirties... She didn't know if she could go on without the hope that one day, she'd be able to breathe deep without feeling them heavy as stones at the bottom of her stomach.

"Are you deaf or just stupid? Yoohoo? Little Ms. Thing who served me this watery piss you call a coffee, I've asked for the check five times now, and all you've done is make goo-goo eyes at that tee-vee faggot's dimples. Now, can I get some goddamn service?"

Vel's lip stuck out in a deep pout, the taste of her cinnamon lip gloss fresh on her tongue. "I'm printing it now, mister. You've got to give it a minute."

"Woman, how many minutes do you need to print a piece of paper? You haven't touched that register since Kennedy was still in office, I swear to God. Just a write a blasted number on a napkin, and I'll pay ya that way. I got a round of golf tomorrow with the circuit judge, and I don't got time for some bimbo to be daydreaming about getting a good stuffing."

"Watch your mouth, sir."

"Get me a damn check, and I will."

The old codger's face was resolute in its stubbornness. If Vel was worried about her own wrinkle problem, this man must've gone Code Orange decades ago. Most of his skull was bald, with the few tufts of hair that remained tucked behind his ears, with some even hiding in his ear canal barely visible behind the drooping lobes. He looked like Clint Eastwood if the few remaining tones of muscle had turned to floppy flaps of skin.

"Fine."

Pulling a napkin from her apron and the silver pen that had been gifted to her for her fifth-year anniversary of working at Mickey's, she wrote the man's total down, making sure to include a healthy tip before scribbling a heavy underline and sliding it down the counter.

"There's your total for the grits and bacon. I gave you the coffee for free since it wasn't meeting of your high standards, sir." She actually hadn't.

Initially, he kept his face skeptical while he looked down at the numbers like they were some type of ancient hieroglyphics found on a tomb wall.

"Now, that's more like it," he said finally, reaching back into his trouser pockets and pulling out a three-fold wallet of old, dirty leather that caused Vel to wrinkle her nose even though she was far down the stretch of white counter. He pulled out several loose bills, crumpled and torn, one even marked with one of those bright red stamps that gave instructions on how to track where the bill had been online.

"You tell ol' Mick I'll be back next Weds after I get back from a trip down to Florida to visit my grandson for his graduation party. He just finished up his premed at Florida State, like his old man did, breaking my old Husky heart. And I expect less sass next time, you hear that? I'll let Mick know next time I see him about your curtness, missy. Wouldn't be the first time I've mentioned it to him."

Putting on his old, tattered hat that looked like something out of an old serial that a newsboy would wear while screaming about his "Extra scoop!" (a job now completely taken over by Maria Menounos and Mario Lopez and their green screen), he made for the revolving door. With a quick tip of his hat to Mr. Heron and his wife in the corner booth and one reluctant, purely out of an outdated sense of courtesy tip of the brim to Vel herself, he pressed and turned himself out of her life.

The tight vice of anxiety on the back of her skull seemed to loosen its grip, but only like a beast would, while readjusting its fangs for another, more powerful bite that would tear through the jiggling flesh of its prey. A quick spin of her head back to the comforting glow of the old Panamax suspended in the corner above the kitchen porthole, a steady steam rising like a smokestack from a church belfry and briefly obscuring the screen. Soon, she was met with solace of Steve's glinting smile, his dentist's teeth looking more like the teeth from the Grecian busts around him than any of the girls' he spoke to.

As Vel tuned back in, she saw that McKenzie was walking back with tears flooding the creases of a smile, a bright rose clutched in her gloved hand, looking like a still from *Beauty and the Beast*. There was that deep-seated spite within her that pointed out the crow's feet that also sat beneath her pale lilacs. There was a brief interlude where the announcer motioned and spoke to the obvious fact that only one lone rose sat on top of the satin pillow. After what seemed like an eternity of zoom-ins and pan-outs on that damned rose, making it look so tantalizing, she felt a desperate need to reach out and pluck it from the colored fuzz of the television pixels. The camera came back to Steve's smug grin, casually showing off his pearly white while his gaze drifted into the lens of the camera, breaking the ultimate rule of show business. Just as his thin lips spread and a thick wad of spittle flew across the screen, there was a bright cut to a yellow background, loud blaring trumpets heralding some sort of morbid messenger. A large 7 flew across the screen before coming to rest in a snug corner at the bottom, a banner following behind it like a line of ducklings behind its mother. Written in big, chalky letters across it were the words, "Robbery at Bar Downtown Leaves One Dead, Several Injured."

The matte soon disappeared in a sweep, replaced by a feed to an empty newsroom, the chairs behind the desk still turned out facing the back wall from the night before. The image seemed wrong to her, like a boat floating on its side or a room that had been turned over while you were out for just a brief stop at the local Osco Pharmacy. It was like an episode of *Keeping Up with the Kardashians* that focused solely on Chloe.

As quick as a flash, a woman dressed in a bright-red jacket and skirt combo with the white blouse underneath—some kind of Vutton number, only half tucked in—appeared in the first chair. The makeup on her face seemed hastily plastered on, the bags under her eyes looking like something out of an old Droopy Dog cartoon and the rouge covering her cheeks making her seem more at home on a street corner in the early hours than on television—well, at least not the type of television you could show at a diner.

"Good eve—good morning, from everybody here at channel 7 news, as we bring you this early-morning breaking news report. This is Lacey Chastain reporting. Residents of the Loganville area have been asked by authorities to remain in your homes and keep the doors and windows locked until further notice as there are suspects from a recent robbery gone bad still on the loose in and around Somerset and neighboring counties. We don't have many reports on the identities or descriptions of the perpetrators, but authorities have confirmed that the suspects are armed and dangerous and should *not* be approached if seen. Instead, authorities recommend calling 911 and hiding out in a room with few windows or entryways to keep yourself safe and out of harm's way.

"Now, as I stated earlier, we don't know much about the actual identities of the suspects, but we do know that the one casualty from the robbery gone wrong was one Gregory Caplin—local property magnate, humanitarian, and owner and operator of local bar Mickey's, at which the attempted robbery took place. Caplin, known around town for his lively appearances at many community-organized events and rallies for many different organizations, from PETA to the American Heart Association, had been recognized recently by the Loganville Academic Association for the renovation to several wings of the Bellacosté Library at a benefit gala just this past Tuesday. He leaves behind a wife and two daughters."

Pictures of Greg Caplin's face played across the screen like a school PowerPoint project—various faded pictures of him with tight striped bike shorts and the blond curls held up in a make-do Afro with spray so thick you could smell it through the polaroid and newer ones where his balding locks were folded tight over his head like cross-stitchings. Vel thought he looked like a weasel, a Steve Buschemi–type without the hard folds of his face that gave him an abstract attractiveness. The only thing Caplin's mug seemed to give her was an overwhelming desire to bury her knuckles in it.

"We do have reports that Loganville Sheriff Hank Nottingull was critically injured in the ensuing firefight with the suspects and was rushed down to Whitehall General around four seventeen this morning. The sheriff is said to be in critical condition, although there have been no further information since his admittance to the ICU."

There were several audible gasps from around the diner as an image of the old, gray-eared sheriff's smiling visage was superimposed on the screen. Old Ms. Jordan dropped the mug from her already-shaking fingers and gasped louder as it shattered across the linoleum tiles, sending chunks of white shrapnel everywhere and the thick black coffee between the cracks, like tar pits. Vel's own mental computer wasn't able to process the information for a moment, the shock still settling into the back of her mind, like someone trying to get comfortable on a hammock that was tightening around them like a net.

Gradually, life started to seep into the early-morning crypt that went by the name Blue Stone Café during its operating hours, although anyone who lived in town could tell you that their only coffee options were regular, decaf, or the very popular "go fuck yourself"—which was a hit with tourists, usually of the Starbucks variety. Vel always felt a small pang of sympathy for them. She believed that turning the Blue Stone into something more akin to a Starbucks or a Caribou or the one with the cup that smiled at you like it knew something about the coffee you did not, would bring a newer, fresher clientele into the place. Not only liven up business, but turn the place into a cultural hot spot of Northeastern Maine—the place kids came after their drama and athletic clubs let out, on their way out on their adventures for their night at houses abandoned by the parents to their ever-innocent child's trusting hands or to secluded campfires deep with Tuskegee Woods out by Bartlett.

Vel had even heard talk about a rave being thrown no more than a couple weeks ago in one of the old, abandoned factory buildings that had closed nearly a century ago, passing back and forth between owners whose eyes were always bigger than their stomachs, the cost of refurbishing and getting the building up to code more than their small-town business aspirations. The place had been condemned shortly after the fire that had claimed the lives of several of the workers back before regulations concerning proper safety during work hours were anything more than passing nag of a site manager's conscience. The charred wallpaper curling from the wall, like the fingers of a beast made of ash, and shadows and constant groaning under the slackened support beams gave it the cheerful nickname Ol' Beezel's Place—which Vel had to admit had always been slightly impressive in its academic inspiration, although she suspected the heavy "Dante's Inferno" curriculum that remained a staple of the Loganville education system might've had something to do with it.

Back in the 'eighties—right after Vel had graduated and started the first of her two years at the beauty college up by Seeboomook Lake—two young lovers had gone missing, and every report from people that had spoken to them that day confirmed that they had plans to visit Ol' Beezel's Place later that night after attending a late-summer graduation party for the girl's cousin. The name Sarah stuck out in her mind for some reason. No, that wasn't right. That was the name of the cousin throwing the party, not the dead girl. Her name was Susan something. Susan Merangue, if Vel's memory served—which, when it came to the names of people in her actual life, it often didn't. The way she looked at it, if your name was big enough to be on television every few days, it was probably worth remembering.

The police had searched throughout the property and the surrounding grounds, sorting through artifacts lost to time, but not gone long enough to swing back around to the side of value or cultural importance. When nothing turned up, the case was initially dismissed as nothing more than a couple of lovers getting too caught up in a moment and running off together to the wilds of Toronto to start a life together, and soon, probably while on the back of a speeding bus, realization about the reality of their situation would set in and bring them back to their parents' doorstep with unpaid bills in hand and bags of dirty laundry underarm. However, when reports came in about several prior cases of *domestic* (used loosely since the couple still lived with their respective folks) violence against the missing Susan, APBs started to flood the airwaves again.

Several weeks after the disappearance, a couple of young kids were out, playing a round of Buckaroo Banzai out in the woods. One boy, while pretending to blast lizard men in the face with his space blaster—which happened to look a lot like a stray tree branch—had tripped over what he originally thought to be an overgrown root buried in covering of dead leaves. There was a large oak nearby after all, its branches stretching high into the clouds and blocking out most of the sunlight that had managed to break through the cracks of precipitation. Upon closer inspection, he believed it to be an old couch discarded in haste instead of at a proper Goodwill or Rent-a-Center.

When finally he pushed aside the crinkling cover of wet leaves and bore witness to the clammy, pale skin clinging like wet putty to a stray femur bone, he reportedly screamed so loud that sheriffs two counties over had shown up at the scene without anybody telling them about it.

The bodies were discovered several miles south of Ol' Beezel's Place—the boy's body pressed up against the tree as if he had been crawling away from something, and the girl's, practically in his lap, slumped over like someone who had too many drinks and was looking for comfort in a familiar armpit. The boy (Vel thought his name was Mark, although she might've been confusing him with a doctor on *Grey's Anatomy*; he had one of *those* faces—innocent blue eyes, disarming smile, she remembered thinking when looking at his face in all the papers) had had his throat ripped out, the tattered remains of his Adam's apple hanging like a badly tied necktie into the nook of the girl's neck. There were other bite marks around the arms and legs. Susan's, in particular, had almost been entirely consumed by passing animals—coyotes, bears, and the like. The coroner originally chalked it up to an animal attack at first glance, until they noticed that the bite marks on the male's arms were of a different variety than those he sported on his neck. The marks on his neck, despite being weeks old, were still teeming with copious amounts of bacteria; and there were burns on his fingertips, some down to the bone.

But his body was not the one that had turned the case from an open-and-shut accident to one that sat cramped in a flimsy box on a shelf in a dark room, the deep crimson stain of "Unsolved" plastered on the front. It was poor, old, innocent Susan, her mouth filled with blood and bits of skin far more than you'd ever expect to find from any type of internal hemorrhaging. And there was the cause of death: her head had been blown open so wide that half of her brains were spilling out on top of the dead boy's groin. Not to mention the bullet holes…

"Vel! Vel Veshkin, can you believe it?"

The voice made the hair on the back of her neck stand at attention like their long-lost drill sergeant returning to town for a visit after the war's long end. They knew their place perfectly, almost like an instinct; and a cold dread stuck to her bones like mildew clinging to decaying rafters, weakening it little by little, the small groans and creaks being the only indication of their gradual failings. That voice was a spell that awoke monsters deep within her psyche—not the ones with sharp teeth and bloody claws, but the ones that whispered in the shadows, sheltered by the dark.

Dark voices filled with malice that pointed out the fact that her love handles were slowly growing more noticeable every week, even after starting to drink some of those Weight Watcher's shakes that somehow managed to taste just like a chalkier batch of Ovaltine but claimed to be the solution to all her flabby woes. The voices that pointed out the fact that her cell phone, despite being attached to her hand for most of her conscious hours (and some of the unconscious ones when she fell asleep with it crammed underneath her growing second chin), actually only received texts updating her about her data usage and letting her know that she lost yet another radio contest for Maroon 5 and Beyoncé tickets.

With these voices came the images—the nightmares that held her mind within their slimy fingers; their blur of colors and cacophony of sounds burned into the blackness of her eyelids like a film reel. The bitter laughing and horrible pointing, the names repeated over and over behind her back ("Veshkin the Mex-ee-can!" "The Neanderthal!" "Good Ol' Shitstain Veshkin!") the voice—*her* voice—inside Vel's own mind, repeated like a chant or a prayer—seemed to bounce across the room like a super ball and find her, even when she told herself she wasn't actually listening.

Slowly, the sick realization dawned on her that she would have to turn and face the owner of that voice and that she had already spent an awful long time with her pupils gazing listlessly into the black haze of the early-morning sky. As the wind threw leaves across the lot like a disgruntled garbageman, Vel turned with the breeze and met those icy blue crystals that were locked on her like she imagined a lioness examined her prey before tearing its throat out and chewing on the stringy bits that remained.

"Oh, my goodness! It really is you! I wasn't sure of it myself for a while there, so I kept my mouth shut, but as you walked by and I looked up at that awful bit of news on the television, and I saw those trademark purple frames you used to always wear, I was certain it was you. However are you doing, darling?"

There was a hint of New England in her voice now—not much, not enough to convince anyone that it was her natural cadence; but there was enough drawl on certain words and a slight twist of several vowels that gave the impression she wanted people to notice the upgraded status of her own diction.

"Oh, I'm doing just fine, although I'll be a lot better once my shift ends in a couple hours. How are you doing, Olivia? I thought I'd heard you'd moved down to New Hampshire after college."

Olivia's face was much unchanged from her high school days. Her lips were still full and pouty with enough lipstick that you could make out the heavy cracks on the surface, looking like a photo from the Mars Rover they showed in between updates on the Kardashian baby photos. The beauty mark on her cheek still sneered at her whenever it caught her attention, and the constant droop in her eyelids (rumors would have you believe from the large doses of Qualudes she had been taking in between homerooms) imbued her dry recounts of her own life with a hint of menace—a venom that began to itch just as it got beneath the surface.

The only way you'd really be able to tell the difference between the former prom committee and yearbook club official president and her adult socialite self, without getting close enough to examine the creases and wrinkles, was by the noticeable absence of the large wart that had sat firmly upon the crest of her brow like the topper of a Christmas tree. It was that beautiful face's Achilles's heel—the one thing that caused the boys to make names behind her back ("the Wicked Witch of Loganville West") and the source of insecurity that led her and her gaggle of prized hens against plain, boring Vel Veshkin, picking apart her many flaws and laying them before her was definitely an easy way to forget her own meager ones.

But now, that wart—that unsung hero that had often kept a bubbling prepubescent ego in check—had been replaced by nothing more than a small red dot, barely larger than a small blackhead, a grim tombstone for a fallen ally.

"You heard correct, actually. A small, little town called Claremont down in the southwest tip, a lovely little place. You absolutely have to visit there sometime. Don't get me wrong. Loganville always had its share of small-town charm, but Claremont is like something out of a fairy tale. There's this lovely park that used to be a horse farm—you can still see the large farmhouse at the top of the ridge and visit on the weekends. I was just telling Tom. Oh, that's my husband, by the way, you'll simply have to meet him. He's out in the Honda, trying to make a call to Triple A after he realized this dummy forgot to get another spare tire after the ski trip last fall. He's a truly wonderful man."

A smile slid across her face, those pouty lips turning up into a Cheshire grin. The cat had found the long, stringy, nerve-filled tendon on its prey that was about to make dinnertime into something far more playful.

"You might've heard of him, actually, Tommy Jarvis? His grandfather started one of the most successful manufacturing plants in Claremont back in the early nineteenth century." (Every word's a deeper twist of the knife.) "They just recently opened up another processing plant in northern Berlin. Oh, not the one in Germany, of course! If only my Thomas was *that* successful. Berlin, New Hampshire, I mean.

"Anyways, I was just telling Tom that Claremont seemed like something more akin to a European city than an American one. Don't you go thinking we're not proud army boosters over there or anything, but it's the atmosphere, you know? I joked to Tom that sometimes I think we should be the ones named Berlin! There's even a small castle by one of the old mills near Nottingham Spring. Tommy actually proposed to me there in one of the old trebuchets, looking down at the expanse of the hills with several hundred candles spread out like he was King Arthur and me, his Maid Marian."

"You mean, Guinevere?"

"Excuse me?"

Her mouth hung open, like someone had run the back of their hand across it, almost as if by instinct. In the bright, translucent glow of the phosphorescent lights overhead, the heavy application of dark eye shadow couldn't mask the darker shadow in her skin behind it.

"You said, 'Like King Arthur and Maid Marian,' but King Arthur was married to Guinevere. I know because Keira Knightley played her in a movie once, opposite Clive Owen. Maid Marian was in love with Robin Hood."

She had often dreamed of Clive Owen in the dead of the night when the sweat clung to her body like a lover's hands and the stray gusts of winds turned into his voice—a whisper in her ear, gently cooing—as her fingers slipped beneath the curled lace ribbon on the top of her underwear. If only she had looked like Keira Knightly, she could've pulled herself from the sludge of this town back before age had slowly thrown a fog over the clarity of her dreams.

"Oh, well, yes, I suppose that's what I meant then. Oh, how silly of me! Blabbering away about my life and not even having enough courtesy to stop and ask you about how you're doing."

You knew exactly what you were doing. You probably had that whole speech prepared years ago.

"So what's new with you, Velma? Is there some handsome beau in your life I need to meet before Tom and I leave?"

Olivia's eyes sharpened and found their way to the center of Vel's face. She could practically feel them boring their way through her skull, sensitive to any change—darting eye, held breath, or drop of sweat that would give away the steely facade Vel had managed to keep throughout the long-winded piece of rhetoric. The image of their faces, laughing at her, judging her unworthy, sprang back into her mind like a flashback in a comic book; and she could almost see the rest of them standing behind Olivia, mimicking the hidden sneer she wore behind the veneer of a concerned old friend. The hairs on her neck felt like stones, weighing her down.

Then, without warning, Matt's face was there before her, almost shining in a glow suited for a cherubim in an old fresco.

"There is, actually. Although I doubt you'll get to meet him as he's currently out of town on business."

As if she had needed another reason to be happy she had spoken to Matt the other day and learned his upcoming travel plans. He had hesitated when he told her, when he talked about visiting an old flame at her apartment in Quebec, his eyes uncharacteristically falling to the dirt and gravel beneath his feet. It was almost like he hadn't expected to be coming back, but Vel hadn't allowed herself to believe that. Only because she knew if she did, the last bit of her strength might fail her. Looking back at the television screen as more pictures of the sheriff became plastered across it, she was realizing, lie or not, it was a good thing he had left when he did.

"Well, that's a shame. I was really looking forward to meeting him. Are you and Mr...."

"Métier, Matt Métier. And no, we're not. We just moved in together a couple months ago." The words felt stiff and unnatural, like drywall in her mouth. Still, an uncomfortable lie was still easier than dealing with Olivia Jarvis's judgment.

"Ah, I see. Well, it's good to hear you're doing well. You know, when we pulled up to this place after the blowout, I thought about whether or not I'd see you in here. I remember ordering fries and chocolate shakes from you here on Friday nights while on dates with George Blum and company, always wearing those huge purple frames of yours. I think that's why I didn't recognize you at first. That, and I almost didn't expect you to still be working here. How long ago was that? College, was it?"

The grin returned in full force, draped in false sympathy.

"Have to pay the bills somehow. So, Olivia, what brings you back into town at such an early hour of the morning?"

She seemed to take the bait of the subject change with an air of confusion, followed by a cautious passivity. It seemed the idea of talking about herself contented her more than the nectar of humiliation gained from the tidbits of Vel's homebound existence.

"Tommy wanted to power-straight through Carroll County by night, a lot of open fields and nothingness. Better to see it at night when you at least got the stars to look at, he says. You know how men are. Once they're set in their ways, there's no stopping them."

Vel nodded in modest enthusiasm, praying for a customer to pull their eyes from the screen and rescue her with one of their usual inane orders.

"We were actually coming back into town to attend a social event hosted by Gloria Hickam. You remember Gloria, don't you?"

There it was. While never spoken, the name had hung over the conversation like a storm cloud, infusing every word with electricity. Vel tried to answer but found that her voice had left her, and while she wanted to be upset, she probably wouldn't have stuck around if she was in its position either.

From the curtains at the back of her mind, Gloria stepped back onto stage, pulling the cobwebs from her sequin dress and paying them as much attention as she would give a fly—or someone who came from a family whose net worth was less than six figures. The grin she wore was painted on, wide and open with her pearly whites bared for the world to see. Her skin was as pale as milk and seemed to gleam in the stage lights, like it was made of some type of greasy porcelain.

A living doll—one that fed on nightmares and insecurities and projected them back at whoever was nearest. Vel wasn't entirely sure if the Gloria that had taken residence in the gloomy pits of her mind was some monster, her deformities simple exaggerations, or just a carbon copy of the real thing.

"No," she managed to squeak out, Olivia's eyes licking up any taste of fear they could find. "I mean, yes, I do remember her. I just haven't seen her in a while, that's all. We don't really run in the same circles."

"Ah, I guess things really haven't changed. I was so looking forward to seeing you at the benefit, maybe even with the man you had managed to sink your claws into. I'll talk to Gloria about getting you an invitation. Do you think Matt would be able to make it? It's this Saturday at the local Presbyterian church over on Grove. Will he be back by then, or will his... business keep him out of town this weekend?"

Yes, Vel, will the lovely Matt be able to join us *this weekend? I mean, I might just let you attend my social event, just to see what dog shit looks like after fifteen years of decomposition.*

"I don't think he would be able to. He's trying to close a deal with some particularly stingy clients of his out in Sarasota."

"Well, the man at least seems driven. What is this business of his that he's pouring so much of himself into to spend time away from a catch as lovely as you?"

Even a garbageman would want to pick up a couple hours of overtime if they were coming home to Vel Veshkin.

Olivia smiled again, and Vel restrained her hands from finding new real estate around her thin gizzard of a neck.

"He's in the liquor business. He owns a couple of bars around town and is trying to secure a deal with a small brewery up there to get one of their famous pilsners on tap. They're notorious for signing contracts only after one or both of them are under the table, so Matt plans on staying the weekend."

"Oh, sounds like good people. What's the name of this brewery that he covets enough to travel all the way to the Great White North to get some for his bar? I'll have to order a case for the next time the book club gals meet over at the estate."

Her bony fingers, shielded by garish rings, tapped against the table in a slow, steady rhythm complemented by the gaudy bracelets that jingled with each spritely bounce of her wrist. Unflinchingly, her eyes surveyed Vel from head to toe. The widening grin that accompanied the gaze did nothing to comfort her mounting terror. Somewhere from the recesses, Gloria laughed—a nasally whine, unpleasant enough to make Fran Drescher cover her ears.

"Nosy Hen Lager."

Hmph. A bit "on the nose," wouldn't you say, Velma? Olivia wasn't winning all those pageants for her looks, but she's got enough brain cells firing to catch on to that one. But I think you knew that, didn't you? Don't tell me you finally grew a pair of balls to complement that mustache of yours?

At this point, a full frontal lobotomy seemed like a healthy alternative to the rest of this conversation.

"Well, I certainly hope it doesn't make poor Matthew's bar too popular, or else he may end up like our poor friend, Mr. Caplin. Such a shame. All the best ones seem to die so young, don't they? Gloria was just telling me about how nice a man he was and how he had helped with the arrangements for the benefit at the church. The man was very generous."

Vel was sure that Gloria had been very generous with Mr. Caplin as well. *Well, don't you just know me* so *well, Velma? You judge only because you cannot have, just like the rest of them. You condemn only what you desire most.* Looking back at the old, dirty antique with the pictures of Matt's boss and his brother-in-law plastered all over the screen, Vel wasn't sure if she should laugh or start to pull her hair out like Britney Spears had done when she couldn't take the outsiders looking in anymore. She supposed there was always time to do both.

The scene changed to an overhead shot of the bar and the parking lot, the shadow of the helicopter looming over the neon glow like a phantom. Beneath the heavy illumination of the searchlight beating down on the smoking asphalt, you could make out the large pool of congealing blood, like the stains from old meat in a disregarded freezer.

After a quick transition, the sleep-deprived anchor was back on the screen, a stack of papers strewn about in front of her. Gathering up several off the top, her hollowed eyes turned back to the camera with a smile that would've looked more at home in a Hammer production.

"We have no official statement on the identities of the subjects, although one of our sister stations is reporting that several squad cars are gathering near the entrance to Makers Woods on reports of figures stomping about the grounds. We have asked some of our senior correspondents to weigh in on the story and to give us a good idea of just what is happening. Joining us is our crime analyst, Jake Rodgers."

The camera cut to a man with slicked back hair and large black frames dressed in his Sunday best, a bright-red tie straining against the rest of his jet-black suit.

"It's good to be here, Lacey, despite the circumstances, of course. And while I would've preferred they never happened at all, I do wish they could've waited until the sun came up. Fortunately, I was already on my way to the station when I got the call."

"So, Jake, would you argue that there is a connection between this incident here in Loganville and the increase in crime that we've seen lately in the greater Somerset area?"

"It's a very interesting question, Lacey, and there's several things to keep in mind. Firstly, we do not have a lot of information, as of this minute, on the motivations of the suspects or even who they are, their background, or various other crucial pieces of information to build a strong enough case to argue that there is a relation, but I think it's fairly safe to say that there is, based simply on the patterns that we've seen over the past week in various parts of the state, not just Somerset. The key thread tying all these incidents together is the extreme brutality displayed by the individuals involved."

"Now, just to recap for our viewers that missed your piece yesterday on the increase in violent crime statistics by over 400 percent in the past week, could you give us some possible explanations behind such a dramatic increase? Is something like this common?"

"It is very common. Very common. You always have many different factors contributing to the crime rates in this country, and this spike really appears to be no different than many others we've seen over the years. With massive layoffs from several key factories, such as Haylon Nash and CloudCo, along with the recent closing of several large housing projects near Portland in the past few months, there's been a steady increase in vagrancy and petty crimes since April. Admittedly, it's peaked this week, but with the recent meteor strike not far from our own front doors that left many unfortunate citizens without them, it's easy to see that there's a lot of desperate, destitute people out prowling the streets right now."

The shine of the bright studio fluorescents reflected in the large glasses Jake Rodgers wore blocked out any view of his eyes, leaving only two blank slates of chalky white snow. Coupled with his monotone recitation of ruined lives and the early hours that Vel had always noticed seemed to give the world an extra little ethereal glow, the broadcast seemed like something from another planet—like a Discovery Channel documentary on mankind from an outsider's perspective. Vel wondered what alien life forms could learn from a *True Housewives of LA* marathon.

"Earlier, you said that recent cases have been marked by excessive brutality. Do you think you could comment a little more about that?"

"Yes, certainly. Well, once you examine the data and the circumstances involved of the crimes, it all stems from recent callbacks from a pharmaceutical company that have been making big headlines in the past few months. The company, Solmed International, recently released a new type of depression medication onto the market back in early January. Reports from June indicate that many patients prescribed the drug Cataboxil, nearly a quarter in fact, later committed suicide after taking the drug for several months. After an investigation by the FDA, it was found that the testing of Cataboxil had been rushed and pushed through by the company CEO, Marcus Philstrum, in hopes of cornering the market before the release of a competing antidepressant later in the year. What the official testing discovered was that in large doses, Cataboxil has a highly psychotropic effect similar to that of psilocybin mushrooms, or PCP, similar to that of certain designer drugs. This led to reclassification by the DEA to a schedule 1 narcotic and led to the immediate recall of all Cataboxil pills from the market.

"Unfortunately, a large drug trade had already been established around the antidepressant, with many abusers giving it the name on the street of TMF, or Total Mind... can we say that one? No? Um, Total Mind... Fornication, hopefully the viewers at home get that one. But it also goes by Rob Zombie, Headbang, or Galaxy Quest in various other circles around the country. Especially rural areas already cut off from a lot of urban drug centers have been heavily affected as users were able to stockpile their prescriptions or from *misplaced*— and I use that word very lightly—or unaccounted for crates of the stuff. The drug gets its pleasant name and reputation from a case earlier this year in South Florida that mirrored the famous case of the bath salts cannibal. Local drug runner Rodrigo Velasquez was found on top of the mother of his own child with parts of her face hanging from between his teeth when police arrived at the scene with reports of violent screams from next-door neighbors. Luckily, the child had been staying with his grandparents for the day. Unfortunately, however, communication was unable to be established with the crazed Velasquez, who was gunned down after he attacked several officers by hand. One victim was reportedly bitten up to a dozen times along the arm and upper torso, with one of the bites tearing a tendon in his shoulder blade.

"There have been various reports like this from around the country, including a college girl in Oregon who ingested up two hundred milligrams of Cataboxil in a spiked beverage at a party and threw herself along with the man who had been seen giving her the drink out of dormitory window on the fifth floor, killing both of them. There have also been an increase in Cataboxil users in drug rehabilitation clinics, with over three thousand abusers in the state of Maine alone. In fact, Maine along with Vermont and New Hampshire are in the top 5 states most affected by the Cataboxil outbreak. Knowing this, it's hard not to draw parallels between the increase in violent crime in the area with the growing drug trade we are seeing in our own backyard."

"So are you saying that this robbery may have been motivated by some kind of drug-induced hallucinations?"

With a quick slide of the thick black frames up the bridge of his nose, Jack Rodgers's beady emerald eyes became visible. Somehow, they seemed to be more lifeless than the silvery reflections that had glossed over his frames moments before.

"Well, it's definitely very easy to think that. Like the case in South Florida, the incident at Mickey's is marked by excessive violence toward police officials. One of the few pieces of information that we do have is that the suspects had been issuing heavy threats at the officers on scene before opening fire. One of the assailants was reportedly making animal like howls and raving loudly about pigs, so the signs of drug abuse are definitely there."

With a final look that certified that Mr. Rodgers was quite pleased with himself for piecing together such an intricate connection, the screen cut back to Ms. Chastain, most of her usually bubbly personality returning to her with each passing second.

"I see the town has practically fallen apart since I left. It's always a shame to see what's happening to the small town in America. We used to think of the suburbs as a place where you could get away from all the crime and violence of the world and settle down into a cozy nest to raise a family. Now it seems like the nest was built on top of a bed of snakes," Olivia mused, wearing a look of smug satisfaction that made Jake Rodgers seem humble in comparison.

"Maybe there are some problems you just can't run away from," Vel said, not looking at her.

Her eyes remained on the screen, the veil of terror that had been draped over her since Olivia's illustrious return to sleepy Loganville's borders seemed to grow thicker, stickier—like a web had been spun over her and the patrons while they sat distracted by the holistic glow of the television and the spider was slowly making its way up the support string, fangs bared, ready to feast upon the day's writhing catch…

Vel's skin squirmed on top of her bones. She felt like Geena Davis in that old horror movie with Jeff Goldblum in the 'eighties. It seemed like ages ago when she saw that movie as part of a double feature with the remake of *The Blob*. Jack Funko had taken her, and after the first half of the second feature (she couldn't remember which had played first), his shining eyes and whispers of everlasting devotion broke down her resolve and the underwire of her bra as he pushed his greasy hands up and heavily onto her breast, groping and pulling like he thought it was a water balloon you're ready to toss at your friend's crotch during a warm summer day. He had even said that she looked like Geena Davis, with her curly auburn locks and emeralds for eyes; and the thoughts of a life like hers had nearly driven her over the edge then and there, but his sloppy kisses filling her cheeks with drool slowly brought her back down into the less-picturesque reality of her own mundane life.

She hadn't thought of Geena Davis in the longest time. The rest of the world seemed to have the same prerogative, as Vel was fairly certain that her absence wasn't based on an early retirement, unless you counted a forced one. The world had just forgotten about her, just like it seemed to have done with poor Vel Veshkin.

Lacey Chastain's long diatribe on the destroyed plant life left in the meteor's wake, including mile-long stretches of forest and farmland and fires that were spreading further and further across the greater Somerset area, slowly drifted off into an uncomfortable silence. Her eyes rolled sideways, looking hard at something off camera. Every feature seemed to be tense with exasperation, her bottom lip hanging limp and dull as if someone had just told her that the early morning vomit sessions weren't caused by all the nights spent face-first in a bottle of Smirnoff.

"This is just in, ladies and gentlemen, we seem to have a break in the story about Mickey's Bar. Yes, I am receiving word that the channel 7 news copter is capturing live footage of a chase between local officers and the suspects. We will now cut live to the chase as it is taking place."

Static burst across the screen in an explosion of fuzz and white noise before cutting to the frantic scene of madness being captured by the camera hanging from the sky. A large brown van, the bumper covered in rust and Legalize It! bumper stickers, was peeling down a highway surrounded by an ocean of firs. The road curved in a serpentine pattern around the small mountain and was spotted by a growing mass of red and blue lights, moving through the darkness like a school of illuminated fish in the darkest pits of the sea where even the sun's light cannot reach. A large spotlight from another helicopter, most likely operated by one of the brothers in blue to the officers below, struggled to remain on the van as it curved and careened through the narrow pathways.

A spotlight, much like the one suspended in the cold mountain air several miles away, burned into existence with a heavy click and a small sizzle inside the stage in the back of her mind. The pale beam fell over Gloria's porcelain skin, giving her a haunting glow, like a ghost from the old movies. Lifting her leg up almost parallel to her body, she began to twirl around herself, the toes of her shoes squeaking against the dusty wood floor. With a giggle that seemed to come from a girl thirty years younger, she fell forward and caught herself with her extended leg, before springing off and landing in a shapely pirouette.

Are you ready, Vel? Are you ready for my big show? I do hope you pay attention, maybe even take some notes. You could use all the help you can get.

"The suspects are fleeing in a 1996 Toyota Previa down Highway 60 just north of Loganville. Again, we report to all our viewers heading to work in these early hours of the morning to please travel with utmost caution if taking any highways or long open roads near the Loganville-Merryton area," Lacey Chastain said, concern finding its way into her dreary cadence. Her hand quickly shot up to her ear, hovering gently above the small plastic earpiece there, feeding her head with voices of a much different variety than the ones that currently plagued Vel Veshkin. "We're now getting official word from authorities that the vehicle is registered to one Tyler Rosenthal from Loganville. Our sources confirm that Mr. Rosenthal is a well-known narcotics dealer who has been brought in on drug charges before, including possession, intent to sell, and unregistered firearms that were found in abundance on his premises during his arrest last fall."

Vel's heart sunk deep down in the pit of her intestines, which began wrapping themselves around it like a boa constrictor as she remembered that Matt had told her that Tyler had planned to accompany him on his "business trip" up into the good-natured land of Canada, his forlorn hesitation at the end of their last encounter clicking into place like a puzzle piece that had been turned right side up. Suddenly, she felt the need to run to the bathroom and vomit violently. Actually, she had felt that way for the past few minutes; maybe it was the fact that her heart was sitting right next to her stomach that finally made her realize it.

The program quickly cut to an earlier broadcast, the rotted lawn spotted with weeds and burs with the small cracked side path leading up to Tyler's place filling the screen. A small side path, most of the concrete cracked and crumbling into formless shapes beneath the toes of many comings and goings, led up to the equally malformed step beneath a flimsy screen door. It looked like the type of doors you would see on the front of a trailer, or smaller recreational vehicles. It crashed open suddenly, giving a squeal of protest as it slammed into the yellow, rusted stripping; and out came Tyler in his usual greasy wifebeater and chain, this extravagant piece bearing the emblem of the Los Angeles Clippers—which Vel only knew because their name was also written in large golden letters in the center of the basketball with streaks that were meant to give the impression of forced direction behind it. He was being led by two rather burly officers, one sporting a mustache that seemed like something worn by a weekly guest star on *CHIPs* in the 'eighties. Their large arms had Tyler's restrained behind his back and his shoulders contorted and writhed in an attempt to break loose of their ironlike grip.

As they led him forward out onto the lawn, several more officers began to file out of the house, carrying large packages of marijuana wrapped in Saran wrap and vacuum sealed shut; others came out with firearms that seemed to be taken directly from the latest Arnold Schwartzeneggar film; and still more came out with a girl in a state of undress, her lipstick smeared and a nail file clutched within her fingers, swinging wildly at anybody that dared to approach her, along with other men that looked almost identical to Tyler—save for the fact that their skin bore the dark complexion that Tyler so desperately believed his bore too.

Tyler's mouth was moving rapidly, engaged in a fiery rant that, even without the audio—which had been muted to prevent it from interrupting the drawl of Lacey Chastain—clearly contained enough expletives to require his mouth to turn into a mishmash of pixels on more than one occasion. The words were apparently more than enough to rile up the policemen around him as looks of rage sprang up on their faces, spittle flying from their mouths like comet streaks. They slammed him down on the hood of a nearby cop car, the picture freezing on Tyler's face scrunched up in pain, his teeth grinding together harder than gears.

"Mr. Rosenthal was tried and convicted, but only for petty possession charges and was sentenced to ninety days' community service by the judge after heavy legislation from his family legal team provided by his father, Phillip Rosenthal, Maine senator, notorious for pushing through a tax cut for the wealthy top 15 percentile, who is up for reelection later this year. A story like this is certainly not going to help his chances if it is confirmed that it is indeed Tyler Rosenthal behind the wheel and connections are made between him and the murder at Mickey's Bar and Grill."

"The connection seems almost certain at this point, Lacey. I mean, most innocent men don't run from the cops, especially not in a high-speed pursuit down a highway in the early-morning hours. While Mr. Rosenthal's car very well could've been stolen, with his past charges, I think it's pretty safe to say that the workers at Senator Rosenthal's political headquarters are certainly praying for grand theft auto at this point," Jake Rodgers added, his self-righteous grin capable of making the wallpaper cringe.

"Well, let's certainly hope so for the senator's sake. We now go live to our correspondent in SkyCam 2, Marty Flemen, who is currently traveling down Highway 60 behind local authorities. Now, Marty, can you tell us a little bit about what we're seeing down there?"

The screen cut back to the sea of green pines, the stars barely visible under the shadow of night any more with the first few rays of sunlight creeping over the horizon, like spirits watching over the disastrous scene below. The van curved around a sharp bend, tearing right through a yellow sign indicating the road ahead was only about to grow more harrowing in the upcoming miles.

"Certain... certainly, Lacey, we've been following the chase for several miles now, heading up Highway 39 first before the merge onto Sixty just a couple minutes ago. It looks like they're... and yes, they just exited off onto the Matheson Expressway, cutting off a Ford Pinto and bringing several polices cruisers to a stop as the road narrows out around the exit there. Luckily, it appears nobody has been injured and more officers, some from counties as far out as Cumberland as you can see on sides of several of them down there, joining in the chase as it tears through their unsuspecting counties...

"Officers got lucky in these early-morning hours with the fact that the roads have been relatively empty for most of the chase. There was some construction during the final stretches of Highway 39 near Tuskegee, but the suspect promptly turned off not much later when the road turned hazardous. But of course, that luck goes both ways with the suspects now having a mostly straight shot to build speed and elude the police. However, the cruisers should be powerful enough to gain on them, especially as the road continues up toward Mount Chillian and the surrounding valleys. In some of the longer—

"Oh! We're getting some action down there, Lacey! It appears the suspect, Tyler Rosenthal, is leaning out of the *passenger* side window, firing at the approaching police cruisers with a type of small-caliber submachine gun. Not only does this indeed confirm that Mr. Rosenthal is still in possession of his vehicle and a very damning piece of evidence, but it also indicates that there are at least one or more accomplices as someone else is clearly driving the getaway vehicle. Oh my… Mr. Rosenthal is now almost completely out of the passenger window, sitting precariously on the edge of the window. You don't see that too often, do you?

"Oh! And with a quick turn, Mr. Rosenthal is almost thrown completely out of the Toyota but appears to have been caught by a hand from inside the vehicle. We can't exactly make out if it is the driver's hand, although it certainly seems to be coming from the back of the vehicle. However, the tinting is making any clear sight into the vehicle nearly impossible. All right, it seems like the suspect has been stabilized and is making his way back in through the window, firing several more shots here on his way back in and… and Jesus Christ, it appears to have struck one of the drivers of the cruisers as it just veered off suddenly into the bumpers. We've lost sight of them in the feed, but it appears that the vehicle is now smoking, and there are no signs of movement that we can yet make out. Just when it looked like this morning couldn't get any crazier, it seems that the injury count is still rising."

As Tyler's body fell awkwardly back inside the van, the picture shrunk into a small corner of the screen, the rest being filled by Lacey, who had managed to sneak some eye shadow around the bags that had formed there—a corpse that was slowly turning back into a human being.

"As you've seen, folks, the footage clearly indicates that Senator Rosenthal's son is now the prime suspect in the Mickey's Bar and Grill slayings. This is obviously big news for the senator's camp and will severely hurt his poll numbers come November," Lacey said, practically singing. Her voice was clearly following the example set by the rest of her rejuvenation. Then again, what news reporter wouldn't be exalted by the fact that the story of the year had been dropped into their lap before the sun had even bothered to rise.

"This is baaaaaaaaad news for the Republicans indeed. Senator Rosenthal was the front-runner to win in the primary earlier this year, with Daniels following closely behind for the Democrats, and Jack Moongood for the Tea Party gaining a fair amount of independent voters to shake things up, as I'm sure you recall. It certainly seems like it's time for a change, Lacey. I mean, first we have this drastic increase in crime in the area, only to see it peaked off by a spree of reckless violence and endangerment by our state senator's own son? The man can't even seem to stop crime in his own household, let alone the state he's in charge of," Jack Rodgers said through a grin so wide Vel was sure his head was about to snap back entirely up his own ass. "The thoughts and prayers of all of us here at channel 6 go out to the family and friends of Mr. Caplin, may he rest in peace, and of course, Sheriff Nottingull, who we only hope can make a complete recovery and testify against his attackers personally. And I want all of you to be thinking of their faces…"

With a furious shaking of his hand toward the side of the screen, it cut again to a photo of Greg Caplin and the sheriff together at a type of small family party, one that appeared to be for a small child with the large amounts of balloons, party hats, and those small, curled-up ribbons you blow into to make that annoying whistle that was enjoyed and loathed by adults and children everywhere respectively. It seemed to Vel that the sheriff didn't seem all that pleased to have Caplin's long tendrils around him, his face that was usually as revealing as a woman's bathing suit from the late nineteenth century bearing a grimace that spoke a little too honestly about the sheriff's actual feelings relating to his brother-in-law. Their wives sat on lawn chairs in the background, lime-green daiquiris with crazy straws in their hands, faces hidden by exuberant shades, shoulders squared firmly away from the children leaping with electricity in their eyes and fire in their open mouths behind them. The picture, supposed to be of a happier time in the men's lives, somehow made her sadder than the sight of the blood pooling in the parking lot.

"I want you all to be thinking of these faces when you go back into the voting booth in November. For too long, we've had issues with gun control in these isolated sections of the country, and it's time to take a look at ourselves and do something about it. These numbers will show you what I'm talking about. Phil, can I get the slide up on screen please?"

The still life of the broken American Dream was taken off the screen, the spirits in Vel's chest rising with its departure. An infographic devoted to gun control had taken its place, the two deaths reduced to kindling to stoke a bonfire that had been raging for years, almost indistinguishable in the rising flames. The small upper-left corner was still devoted to Tyler and friends' wild ride through the forest. Vel was almost afraid to look at it, knowing all too well what was coming next. Gloria had told it true; she knew it. And a viper with poison dripping from her fangs lay in wait behind her. Still, just like telling yourself something is going to hurt before you actually hit the ground does nothing to lessen the fall. Knowing that the small world she had built for herself—her lie, her fantasy—was about to fall apart did nothing to prepare her.

"And the numbers have only increased from last fall. I don't understand how some people could be expected to keep something that's essentially a ticking time bomb around them and their children. I'm not a father myself, but I can't imagine anything more—"

"I hate to cut you off there, Jake, but as some of you can see on the corner of the your television, there is a breaking development in the chase as we now have confirmation of a second accomplice, *other* than the driver, involved in the shooting and subsequent chase. Can we get it full screen again? Thank you. Now that we're closer, you can clearly see that a third person had thrown open the trunk and is now firing shots from what looks to be a type of heavy-duty riot shotgun, already destroying the tires of one of the seven police cruisers still in pursuit, a dozen more following several miles behind waiting to overtake should the chase continue much longer. The cruiser seems to have come to a stable stop in the middle of the expressway as the van hits another corner and—*oh*, a cruiser has slammed into the back wheel and knocked the Toyota into a median! They lost control for a minute, but… it seems they have regained control and are firing more shots at the police as they clump up behind them. We now have a better look at our gunman as well, and we have analysts trying to figure out who he is as we speak."

Vel didn't need to wait for the analysts as she recognized the man behind the gun immediately, the rapid beating of her heart her greatest clue and biggest regret. His visage was something terrifying, a monster draped in darkness and blood. Drunk on rage, he howled through the pixels as he fired into the peacekeepers in front of him. Still, Vel's attraction burned brighter than it ever had. It felt like home after an extremely long day of school, capped off by an unsupervised wait at the bus stop where the other kids took turns making fun of the fact that her clothes looked like something out of a moth supermarket. As much as she feared Matt Métier in that moment of his unfathomable fury, when she looked at his pale blue eyes and tussled brown locks, she couldn't deny the part of her that wanted to be right there next to him, immortalized on the screen.

"Oh my, oh my goodness! Sweet Mary and Joseph, did you see that? It appears that the accomplice has thrown some kind of large gray cylindrical object out of the back of the van. Did it look like a keg to anyone else? I'm pretty sure it was a keg. Yes, like a beer keg you'd rent from a liquor store. Well, I don't know, Phil, maybe they got it from the bar, how am I supposed to know?"

"Marty! Marty, can you describe what you're seeing for all of us here in the studio? What's going on out there?"

"Right. Right. Well, just moments ago, the man from the back of the van threw what in this reporter's opinion appeared to be a beer keg out of the back of the getaway vehicle. Now, it's very dark out here, but the keg seemed to have landed in the windshield of one of the police cruisers and sent it spinning out and into one or two of the officers around him. All I know for sure, Lacey, is that there's a lot less spinning red and blue lights on the highway as the wake of chaos and destruction left in these criminals' wake seems to grow larger still."

In the small diner buried in the woods just outside Lake Tecumseh, the silence was as thick as molasses, sticking in people's throats like a bad cough—something that wanted out of ya but clung to every fiber of your being like a foul-tasting mucus. Vel knew what was coming and wished desperately for another meteor to fall out of the sky and crush this useless speck of mortar and grease into a puddle in the earth—along with its sexist regulars, Olivia Jarvis and Vel herself—so the shame wouldn't be able to slowly rot her body from the inside out.

The sermon that held their attention continued unabated by Vel's internal longing for it to simply disappear from this plane of existence, and then Lacey Chastain's bright, bubbly face returned again, nearly identical to the one you would find on the billboards spotting the Interstate—which now transported a certain rusted Toyota—wearing a smile that could make Charles Manson grimace in its inauthenticity.

"We are now getting word that the man seen in the back of the van is one Matt Métier—who, as it turns out, is an employee of Mickey's and has moved up as the lead suspect in the murder case of Gregory Caplin. Mr. Métier has a criminal record of his own, one mostly spotted by a few minor cases of public indecency. This is certainly a big step up in the crime world for him, it seems," she said behind a sneer.

"Well, let me tell you, Lacey, I'm sure the Republicans are going to be looking to spin this anyway they can. I mean, just this year alone…"

Jake Rodgers's voice trailed off into the nether. The world seemed spacious, empty. Vel could feel those eyes behind her, clawing through flesh and bone of her back, looking to tear into the tough, juicy flesh of the heart. It wanted a good meal, one worth its time. Still, the huntress sat in silence, waiting for the jackrabbit to turn and face its attacker in a last stand of misplaced bravery.

Vel decided then and there that she wasn't going to provide her with the satisfaction. She would cling to the scraps of her pride even as the ship pulled her down beneath the waves.

However, out of the corner of her eye, she saw poor, trembling Mrs. Jordan who had been eavesdropping on the sword fight hidden beneath pleasantries, much like she did every other conversation that floated past her booth on the edge of the world. Her shaking fingers were working their way into her small red bag, pushing past the steel clasps and finding the old Nokia within. The thing looked like it had been made around the same time Vel had been getting felt up beneath a fifty-foot Geena Davis, but she figured it could still carry a call well enough. Vel was pretty certain as to who was the intended recipient of that call and knew that when the lights pulled up outside of the diner, she would inevitably have to face those smoldering emeralds once more anyway. So she might as well get it out of the way now.

But before she could muster the courage, she heard the familiar tinkle of the bell hung above the flimsy Plastiglass door and turned to find the booth as empty as ghost town, a thin pile of bills and change stacked on top of a small piece of stationary with green vines entangled across the top of the page. There was the squeal of tires and two bright-red eyes that appeared outside, clumps of rocks flying back at the window as the luxury sedan, a BMW from the look of the bumper, peeled out of the gravel drive and back onto the old farm road.

Looking down at the note, she saw several singles that when pushed aside revealed a crisp portrait of Benjamin Franklin, looking back at her with a smug satisfaction. Vel checked the dishes on the table and saw a half-empty cup of coffee and a small plate with sugar packets torn apart hastily, the remains of the package buried beneath piles of its lost contents. Written on the stationary in penmanship that would make a historian unbunch parts of his pants was a small note that Vel's eyes scanned before her mind had the better judgment to stop them.

> Dear Vel,
>
> It looks like you and Matt will be unable to attend the party this weekend after all. Well, it certainly was quite a treat to see you again. It looks like you're going to be needing this more than I will in the upcoming days. Besides, I had already considered my trip back an act of charity.
>
> Forever yours,
> Olivia Jarvis

Vel let the note fall gently back to the table, a corner swinging onto a wet spot and turning into a gray mush almost instantaneously. It had been nearly a quarter of a century now since she had escaped from high school—from *them*—and here they had found a way to rub in her face that she was not invited to a party one final time. The stage in the back of her mind fell to shadows, the spotlight cut off sharply, then Gloria that lay in wait there turning into a morphing shadow, her thin form becoming something twisted and inhuman. The laugh that came from the shadows certainly didn't sound human either.

Vel's attention was snapped back to the glowing mass of electrons behind her by an audible gasp that swept across the room. Cries of "Damn right!" and "It's about time!" came from some of the more alert truckers, while many and most sat unconcerned with the world outside of the plate of bacon and eggs in front of them.

On the television set, the fuzzy video feed had reclaimed its full-screen status, even though the picture was mostly obscured behind thick smoke. As the gales whipped it up and around, you could the see brown form of the van wrapped around another thick brown mass, hardly able to tell where the painted steel ended and the supple bark began. Tyler had already been pulled from the passenger side of the wreckage, limping on a leg that seemed to be more blood than pants and was quickly slammed face-first onto the hood of one of the nearby cruisers. He let loose a howl of anguish that made noise despite its silence, but it was quickly dwarfed by Lacey Chastain's chipper enthusiasm.

"And just like that, it would appear that the madness is over, ladies and gentlemen. We can see the officers are rounding up all the suspects from the vehicle now after running it off the road just moments earlier. We've already seen them apprehend Senator Rosenthal's son, Tyler Rosenthal, and now it appears… Yes, it appears that Matt Métier, former employee of the victim, Gregory Caplin, is being pulled from the wreckage now. He appears to be bleeding profusely from the forehead. It could be that he is severely injured… well, that's certainly not the case. Mr. Métier now seems to be attacking the officers but is quickly brought down by one of the officer's stun guns. Oh, boy, they really thrash around quite a bit, don't they? Might want to put up a warning if you show that clip again, and what's happening here… Oh, and we've got our first look at the driver. It appears to be an older gentleman. Already our experts are trying to get word on his identity."

"Well, I can tell you one thing, Lacey, he certainly does have a good amount of skill behind the wheel."

"I don't know if that's exactly appropriate to be talked about right now, Jake. Well, we've had a quite a start to our day here in Loganville, and with the Manahen comet striking down in Castle Rock earlier this week, the Somerset area has seen its fair share of tragedy over the past few days. Hopefully, a sense of normalcy will return, and we can finish off the week in a relatively quiet fashion. It doesn't seem like there's much else that could happen that would be a bigger headline at this point."

"Not unless World War III broke out… God forbid."

"I think we could all use some coffee here in the newsroom after the stressful events of the morning. Stay tuned to channel 7 as we'll be having round-the-clock coverage of the Mickey's shooting and how it will affect Senator Rosenthal's chances in the polls later this year, along with the ongoing relief efforts being provided to the areas of Castle Rock and Fair Oaks still affected by the forest fires caused by the Manahen comet. Speaking of which, we will now go live to our Fair Oaks correspondent…"

Old Ms. Jordan tugged gently on Vel's sleeve, her crinkled-paper skin cold to the touch. Vel managed to turn her head toward her without the world falling out from under her.

"I just wanted to tell you, dear," she said, slipping her hand around Vel's clenched fist, "the police sent someone over. They said he'd be here soon. I'm sure everything is going to be okay."

"Men," she added, "you can't ever trust 'em. That's why I got rid of mine."

Despite Ms. Jordan's sagely words of comfort (which would have possessed a lot more comfort if Vel wasn't certain that Old Ms. Jordan was a widow) and the fact that the danger had left the small diner in the middle of the woods, Vel's hairs still stood on end, apparently possessing some kind of foreknowledge that she did not. She supposed it might have something to do with the fact she had remembered about the Ol' Beezel's Place murders during the chase, something she had made herself forget after the thought of it kept her awake on the nights that were particularly dark—something Gloria and Olivia had told her over and over again in the gym locker room even though Vel had screamed for them to stop.

They had found several bullet holes in poor Susan's chest, and many believed that it closed the book on a simple case of domestic violence gone horribly wrong, even though a gun hadn't been recovered from the crime scene and all attempts to find one nearby turned up just a fruitless as the original hunt for the runaway lovers. However, after a coroner's examination revealed that some of the bullets were made premortem and others postmortem, others believed that Susan's boyfriend was nuttier than a squirrel in a straight jacket. That was until they cut poor Susan wide open and found the missing handgun, matching prints and shells and everything, deep within her small intestine.

But that was nothing to think about now. It was just an urban legend from the past, a nightmare from her childhood.

There were things happening now that were far more terrifying, like explaining to the police why she had lied about dating the most wanted man in the county.

Veronica shivered before slamming the window pane shut. The smell of crisp morning air had always been pleasant to her. It reminded her of waking up early and heading to track practices, usually before the sun had risen and the sky was nothing more than a pale blue shade. It reminded her of being surrounded by people, many whom she was proud to be able to call her friends, many more acquaintances, and plenty of boys she knew would gladly trade their athletic scholarship for a drunken night spent with her between the sheets of some younger brother's bed, with a crowd of milling peers downstairs drunkenly offering high-fives and confirmations of masculinity upon hearing of the conquest that had taken place just above their heads. That was the more important part, of course. Sure, the sex itself would be great; it always was with her, she made sure of that. But what was the point if no one knew you had it?

Veronica took no pride in being the dream girl of the many members of the opposite sex in the school, especially when you considered that most of those dreams were the ones that involved quietly and ritualistically changing the top sheets in the morning. She knew that it may seem quite the opposite to many of her peers, most notably the plenty of other girls who wished for that very attention while condemning it to their friends—who, being just as fake and hypocritical, would all squawk in agreement. She knew better than to worry about the jealousies of the have-nots of the world.

What Veronica did pride herself in was the status that this attention gave her. There were other aspects to it, of course, but Veronica would be stupid or willfully ignorant to not see that most of her prestige was not due in part to the fact that she was, well, for lack of a more humble word, hot. There was no reason beating around the bush. Examining her reflection in the large boudoir mirror, she noted her petite nose with the small curved tip, which many boys would tell her looked like something Lola Bunny would have, smiling like an idiot as they undressed her, each thinking they were the first to come up with such a witty observation, without realizing how odd it was to compare a girl to your cartoon rabbit childhood crush. And Veronica would laugh each time, because that's what came with the territory.

Her eyes were a deep shade of hazel that she thought looked like the bark on a pine tree in the summer when it's coated in the type of thick sap that makes your fingers stick together for hours after touching it. Her skin, while freckled too heavily for her taste in some places, was mostly left unblemished. She could probably count the number of zits she had gotten in her life on her two hands. Her lips were full and managed to walk that thin line between bimbo and high class that was becoming harder to distinguish, especially in the more recent *Cosmo* she had been getting. Veronica, while not lacking in experience (although, she figured, less experienced than many of her contemptuous peers would like to suspect), was certainly no expert on sex; but even she was starting to get suspicious that somehow they managed to find hundreds of foolproof, earth-shattering orgasm techniques to please a man every single month, especially when those techniques involved rubbing chili powder in your palms "for that added spice in the bedroom."

After practice, when the team had retreated into the steamy sanctuary of the shower room, where even the most socially taboo topics became thoughtless gossip, Stacey Keeling had told everyone about a trick her cousin had told her about, something about shellfish being the most natural aphrodisiac. So she had planned on eating out at the fancy French restaurant Le Chauvre out in Burlington right before stopping over at Hank Dillham's house for his birthday, planning a night of heated, passionate lovemaking more like something you'd see on *Gossip Girl* or *Pretty Little Liars* and less like *Skins*. Veronica had found that bit of naïveté amusing—that one could turn the act of screwing into anything close to resembling what you read in those gushy tween romance novels. It was a means to an end, nothing more—a way to pound out a few seconds of uncorrupted bliss, to feel needed for several seconds of huffing and grunting, even if it only was as a place for some hormonal man-child to relieve himself. She usually found that there were other perks to spreading her legs as well: invitations to the best parties, alcohol whenever she felt so inclined. These ideals wouldn't earn her any modern feminism awards, but she had begun to notice that most modern feminists—the ones who hated men the most—were the ones that hadn't been able to land one in the first place.

Still, naive, young Stacey had filled up on an entire tray of oysters imported directly from the shores of Brittany and soon found herself alone with Hank in his bedroom, the large Steelers poster covering the entire back wall in a sickly shade of yellow and black. When Veronica had spent the night lying beneath that poster, her mind millions of miles away as the slobbering drunk Hank tried his best to keep his manhood from going limp every couple of seconds—an incident which she had never told Stacey (but the thought had crossed her mind, because seeing the crushed look on Stacey's face almost would've made the night worth it—well, other than getting to ride in his father's souped-up Spyder GTX90)—she had almost thrown up; and Hank was doing his part to only make the matters worse, that horrible smell of liquor that seemed to radiate off his body. It reminded her too much of nights she had spent many more nights trying to forget—ones that always started with that horrible squeaking of her bedroom door.

Slutty Stacey and her oysters, that's what she was thinking about.

When Stacey finally worked her way down to the small steel trap that would loose Hank's small, floppy beast onto the world and started giving lucky young Hank a bit of "dome"—as many of the boys in her grade had started calling it (Veronica wasn't fond of calling it dome; it sounded unpleasant in the ear and made the whole thing seem sillier than it already was; she supposed the boys liked how short but powerful it seemed with that hard *o*)—she was soon greeted by a chorus of soft moans, not atypical for a boy caught in the fervor of a good dick-sucking. Even when he planted his hand on top of her hand, while not entirely desirable, it was a normal enough occurrence in the occupation of oral sex that Stacey had continued, unfazed.

It was only when that same hand clamped down hard around her skull, squeezing so tight that she was sure her brains would squeeze out of her nostrils like Play-Doh, that she realized something was going wrong with her genius technique. With a quick yank that nearly ripped her head from her shoulders, Hank tossed her aside, standing up in a howl of agony that Kelly swore she could hear six blocks over the day after. Dazed by her forceful make-out session with the floor, it took Stacey a moment to look at what had turned an exciting night of unrequited passion into something out of a raunchy sex comedy.

She almost wretched when she saw his penis, still erect, beet red and bloody like raw meat. Patches of skin had broken out into blisters and torn into pus-ridden craters. The head had gone from a bruise-colored purple to a dark scarlet, looking like a bloodshot eye. It turned out Hank was deathly allergic to all shellfish, and Stacey's unmentioned trip to Le Chouvre required a trip to the emergency room and a skin graft. Hank had not been pleased at the sight of his ruined manhood hanging before him, limp *and* monstrous, and turned back into the unevolved ape that any man becomes when it is threatened, bringing the back of his hand heavy across her face and bringing her to the hospital with him with two black eyes and several missing teeth.

He quickly transferred schools after that, someplace several states over so no one would know him as the guy with the "burnt oyster dick" anymore. Stacey was affectionately named Poison Ivy by many of the girls who laughed off the incident or chalked it up to some kind of female empowerment, and while many boys gave her weird looks in the hall for the rest of the year, her battered face quickly reeled in sympathy from many boys caught up in their misguided chivalry. However, locker-room gossip revealed that when of one of these white knights had successfully rescued the damsel back to his keep, she had screamed at the top of her lungs when she saw his dick for the first time, slinking down and cowering in the corner, swearing it looked just as awful as Hank's rotting meat had.

Veronica had never been too fond of the male sex organ. She always thought they looked like some kind of lumpy angry animal. Even when erect, they looked like those fish that floated through large aquariums mouth permanently agape. She always wanted to laugh but knew that was the worst sin that any girl could commit. That was one of the basics. She remembered her first time seeing one of the boys in her classes' penis in eighth grade, sneaking away on an overnight field trip into Tim Stedder's hotel room, dashing into the bathroom to get away from his pals who were shooting elbows into each other's sides in between a game of black Jack Daniels. She had wanted to laugh very hard then but knew that if she didn't stifle it, her chances of any boy showing interest in her for the rest of the year would disappear as fast as his hairless erection; and in eighth grade, when having a boyfriend was an elite status that separated you from the rest of your sexually inactive peers, that simply was not an option.

When Veronica had pulled down her cotton panties for her own turn of this advanced game of show-and-tell, she was able to laugh as Tim's hand flailed awkwardly high, just below her belly button, slapping against her groin like a fish out of water, his confusion and embarrassment growing by the second. When he finally admitted defeat and looked down, his shocked face sent Veronica's giggle into full-blown fits of laughter. Apparently, Tim had only been expecting a small slit, like a coin slot, possibly with "25c" written above it. (He was also expecting a bush, like a Serbian, but Maria's older sister had been quick to share her secrets of the bikini wax with any girl who was willing to listen). The sight of her labia poking out from her lips and dripping wet made him question everything he thought he had known about the female form. Instinct took over from there, things progressing further than Veronica originally would have liked. But while awkward, stiff, and uncomfortable, it still felt amazing, like it was filling this deep hole inside of her—not just the one between her legs. There had been some slight confusion over the lack of blood, but he was so eager and so in doubt about his own knowledge of the female reproductive system that it was thrown aside quicker than the condom wrapper.

 The phone rang again, drawing Veronica from her genial memories, shattering the earthly silence that morning held, the kind that seemed too sacred to break so you kept your mouth closed and enjoy the cries of birds and the drips of dew. Veronica often found that she enjoyed the deep pockets of silence more than her friends' incessant chattering; but like many of her less desirable qualities, she kept it hidden behind the glass curtain that was her personality, knowing they would never notice the way her eyes twitched when they asked her the same tired questions about her night before she even had a chance to finish her coffee. It was a perk that her beauty allowed her. People noticed you, but they never really *saw* you. They never saw the ache behind each smile or the high note of insecurity that would squeak out with every dismissive comment, desperately hoping to draw attention away from her own shortcomings—small as they might be, of course.

 The hopeless wail of the telephone was ended by a quick click, followed by her father's voice, cautious as to whether the caller would fall into the "condolences" or "shit-eating reporter" category. Fortunately, when his icy tone melted to a low whisper, one naked enough that you could feel the pain it held, she knew it must be the former. Hearing that weakness in her father almost made her sick, especially as she sat here, prepared to keep things at school exactly as they had been before, despite her brother's best efforts to destroy the status she had spent the last five years of her life working tirelessly to obtain. Still, part of her deep down, behind the glass curtain and the shadows of its rafters, felt a deep pity for her father and mother—whose gentle sobs could still be heard if you put your ear close enough to the rattling radiator in the floor—and even for her brother. Although there was a much deeper part of her that felt a satisfaction that was near indescribable, one that to admit its existence would be the ultimate defeat, the ultimate destruction of her being.

Her father's voice trailed off down the hallway, his shuffling feet on the stairwell startling her enough to check her bedroom door. The small lock on the knob, cast in the shape of a small rose that was Veronica's sole motivation in making the room her own when the Métiers moved into their new place some thirteen years ago, was pressed firmly down and been that way since they had received the first phone call that shattered the errant peace of the morning with the news that lay in wait on the other end. The first had been innocent enough, from what her father told her of it after the fact. The police had called, asking for any information from Matt as he had been supposed to be working the night shift at Mickey's where his boss was found murdered. When George Métier told the officer that Matt hadn't lived there for years now, there was a long pause, pierced by the shuffling of paper and ended by a brisk dismissal when he began to question what news they had on his son's whereabouts.

The second call, which came roughly around twenty minutes after the first, was to inform them that Matthew had been named the prime suspect in the murder of Gregory Caplin and that any sightings of Matthew or attempts by him to return home should be reported to the police immediately. They also mentioned how he was most likely armed and dangerous and not to believe that just because he was family, he wouldn't do something to harm them if it meant "keeping his skinny, pretty-boy ass out of jail." The thought sent chills down the back of Veronica's neck and caused her heart to leap up into the bottom of her throat in fear, fear that was all too sickeningly real to her.

While her mother broke down in sobs of vicious tears that seemed ready to tear her body apart with each heave, Veronica had retreated into the sanctuary of her room, shutting the door with the rose-shaped knob and clicking the lock into place almost immediately. The small vines covering the trim that were themselves covered with small rose buds—painted there by Veronica herself in her younger, more artistically inclined days—seemed to grow over the edges and seal it shut like an enchanted panic room.

Examining herself in the mirror again, she had distracted herself for most of the morning by planning out how she would look while walking into the lion's den that was referred to as high school, if you survived long enough to graduate from it. She knew it was a shallow pursuit, but those were the ones that often got you the most in life. Swim too deep, and you often found yourself struggling for air, hoping for someone to pull you back up, but why would anyone take the risk of drowning themselves? Of course, staying in the lighter waters ran the risk of becoming a nameless speck in the giant school of fish that moved a single, unabated entity—your identity only a hollow copy of something greater than yourself. Luckily, Veronica liked to think of herself as pretty practiced swimmer and a pretty big fish.

Arching her back, she looked at her small yet perky breasts, keeping up the silent hope that every young girl had: that they might have grown just a bit bigger over the night. It was hard to tell when her nightshirt was wrinkled and twisted into a shapeless mess that made it hard to tell where her body ended and fabric began. Smoothing it out over her flat tummy, she thought of the doorknob turning, the brass crying out in a rusted squeak in the night, and suddenly felt very dirty. She stopped herself and looked back out the window as the sun finally peaked through the clouds, shafts of light falling onto the world for the first time of the day. That seemed to calm her again and refocused her on the task at hand.

Opening the Clinique makeup bag that her mother had gotten for her last Christmas when she insisted that her old one, despite being bought that same year, was missing colors that were essential to the tone of her skin and would be the downfall of her entire social career—which while certainly dramatic, held some credence to it—

she found the shade of rouge she was looking for and set it on top of the dresser. She liked to think it was this bag's shade of amber overdrive that had gotten Billy Sorkin into going down on her at his own girlfriend's graduation party later that year. Looking back up at the mirror and catching sight of the sinking bags around her eyes, she reached down for her toner and began to apply it just above the high rises of her cheek bones.

Knowing that her brother's late-night escapades would be the talk of the town for most of the day to come, she decided to leave some of the dark bags visible, so it was clear that she had spent many hours awake, wondering about her dear, older brother and his ultimate fate in the universal scheme of things. She also knew there would be plenty of people who would find it tasteless to come in with a heavy coat of makeup in light of such a family tragedy, especially the have-nots who loved to tear down anything that might make them seem morally superior to make up for their own blandness. She knew that little troglodyte Gwen would have something to say about it either way. She liked to play the part of the rebellious girl who was seemingly immune to the criticisms directed toward her because of how little she cared. But it was easy to tell that her mother's reputation was always on the back of her mind, as it very well should be. When a woman like the Prophet of Loganville is your mother, that was something you had to live down for the rest of your days, no matter if you had a say in your birth or not.

This wasn't a world where morals get you to the top. There was only your status, and that was passed down by factors that no one person can control. Yes, you could make your status better; Veronica knew this from firsthand experience. But there was no erasing the unpleasant memories that stuck to your name. Just recently, Veronica had walked passed a news story her father was watching about how the remaining family members of Hitler had decided to end their family line for the sake of the world. Her mother had scoffed and laughed it off as an extreme attempt to save face, but Veronica found nobility in it. They had accepted the lot they had given and played it to its only proper conclusion, something Gwen could take note of.

The clouds grew darker and thicker, the light that had broken through disappearing into the cracks, leaving the world covered in an icy blackness. A fog had covered the ground, turning the town into something out of an old movie, where you expected the monster to suddenly appear out of the mist, bloody and frantic and wild.

There came the heavy footfalls of someone running up the stairs, a combination of stampeding elephants and roaring thunder and a slam as the cordless phone was put back into its receiver on top of the cabinet just outside her door.

"Veronica, dear, your mother and I are heading down the police station. Your br—your brother is in… custody there, and we're going to try and post a bail, although the lawyer doesn't think they'll let us. Are you… going to be fine getting to school by yourself?" her father's voice said, or a hollow imitation of it. At this point, she couldn't be sure.

"Yes, Dad, I'll be fine."

"That's my girl," George Métier shouted before heading back to the stairwell, not thinking to ask if her coolness regarding transportation to school also extended into being fine with the entire situation, but questions like that had never been his strong suit.

Veronica sighed as the heavy front door slammed shut, taking solace in the silence once more and the fact that, as terrible a morning it had been, at least it was probably more interesting than anything in the have-nots' lives—especially boring, old Gwen.

She was having a hard time washing all the blood off. At least, she thought that it was blood. It was too black and crusty to be entirely sure. When she realized that she was silently hoping it would be blood, the strangeness of the entire situation really set in. The past few hours had passed in a haze eternal, like a drug trip in one of those old exploitation movies that only played for a week in the small Alamo Theater over in Merryton. Gwen could hardly remember it all, and when she was able to fill in the brief flashes that had plagued her the entire walk home, the explanations only made it seem more and more like some kind of horrible dream—a nightmare that no one had told was supposed to remain in the confinements of the psyche, hidden away during waking hours.

The cold white plaster walls of her room had never seemed more confining as she paced back and forth, her fingernails digging into the fabrics of her hoodie as she tried to pull the muck up from the threads. The lone cross that hung from the wall had fallen slightly askew earlier in the week, Jesus's limp hand pointing down through the floorboards without much enthusiasm, which Gwen could easily forgive due to his situation. She found it mildly ironic people choose to depict their savior in his moment of greatest agony—almost as if Jesus himself was forced to relive it for all eternity, but she also supposed she wasn't the first teenager to come across a thought like it. With a sigh that seemed to signal her defeat, she collapsed onto the bed, her arms sore and her legs aching, with a dull heat burning in her upper thighs, like someone had started a bonfire underneath her. The bed shook heavily, the floorboards producing a symphony of squeaks that caused her muscles, already drained, to tense back up—the image of her mother coming up the stairs, her eyes thin and hard with her Bible clutched between her bony white fingers and her leather belt with the metal crosses buried in the leather limp at her side. Even her breath grew silent as she lay in wait for any noise that might signal her mother's inconvenient arrival into her prison cell.

When the door remained eerily still, Gwen finally allowed herself to sit up and begin the process of removing her blood-splattered clothes. Taking off her hoodie and shirt and moving to her meager closet—which hung open as it often did, a habit from when she was a girl and believed that closing the door only made it easier for the monsters to slip through (and even if closing the door didn't make a difference, at least she would be able to see her attacker and dart beneath the holy protection of her bedsheets)—she pushed through the collection of sweaters and tops that her mother deemed appropriate. Anything that suggested her breasts had grown from when she was twelve or anything that clung too tightly to her rear end were out of the question, as was anything that dared to have straps instead of sleeves, like the Lord intended. To wear them and tempt men with her sinful lumps of flesh was one of the ultimate offenses against

God, which seemed weird when you compared it to something like murder or even hating your fellow man; but Gwen had learned to swallow those questions lest she wanted to swallow blood for the rest of the night.

She slipped on an old white tee that she had bought from Hollister back in her more rebellious days, removing all the rhinestones that spelled the store's name across the chest—something her mother, the voice of God, would've seen as an open invitation to all the men around her. Still, she had felt proud wearing them for the few hours spent traveling home from Oak Parks Mall, especially enjoying the way the sun reflected off the small stones, giving the illusion that their worth was more than a couple weekends of chores for elderly neighbors. It felt silly now, to take joy in such a trivial thing as dollar-store gems, but what was the difference between the fake and the real thing if they look as pretty?

Her whole world seemed to be covered in those tacky rhinestones now. The sick feeling in her stomach seemed to have finally passed, but not her own mild disgust at her complete infatuation with the mysterious boy who seemed to be more interested in his chipped old guitar than her. But feelings being the terrible disease that they were, there was nothing she could do but live with it at this point.

Shimmying out of her jeans with a wiggle, she nearly gasped when she saw the blood that covered her midsection, a large collection that had dripped down her legs in her hurried rush to get home following the night's altercations. The stain had seeped and pooled around her groin, giving the illusion that her own red flower had decided to bloom in the night. She supposed that was a good thing, as far as her mother's suspicions were concerned. There would be no difficult-to-answer questions about her late-night escapades.

You could just a call it a date, you know? It doesn't taste like poison.

Pulling her underwear off, she checked herself to make sure that none of it remained on her skin, or any of her more private areas, even going so far as to let a few fingers slide inside herself—a small moan escaping as she did so and Range's face leaping into her mind as quick as he had rushed the writhing hand in the ground in the night.

Falling back onto the bed, she let the memory overtake her, willing her fingers to stop their rhythmic intrusion but finding herself unable to stop. She suddenly saw it all again in front of her, the sifting dirt, the crumbling paper flesh over yellow rotting bone and tendon. Still, Range's face was there too, his blond locks pressed hard against his face clinging for dear life as he forcibly yet gently placed his guitar into Gwen's arms. Throwing his legs over the dirty tombstone before him like it was hurdle on a track field, he slid down into the dirty grass of the cemetery, his feet landing with a soft clomp in the hardened dirt. His feet pounding down the small embankment toward the grave, he swung quickly to the right to grab hold of the shovel there, leaned up against the shining new tombstone that had yet to be engraved with its first and only owner's name. She could see it now just as clearly as she had then, the wiry muscles in his forearm tensing as his hand wrapped around the metal bolts just beneath the spade. Thinking of it sent deep chills down her spine and caused her muscles to clench around her fingers, spiraling what little control she had left into the primitive abyss that was her libido. Even the thought of her mother brought to her door by the voice of God himself, bursting through the splintered wood frame to see her splayed on the bed, hands exploring her own sin with piles of bloody clothes strewn about the plain white shag carpet didn't seem to give her any caution.

By the time he had turned toward the grave, the top of a skull had begun to tear its way through the dirt, like an animal wringing flesh from its prey. With violent shakes and thrashes that would have broken any neck that was still held by muscle and spinal fluid, the dirt slid away around it, revealing tufts of thin stringy hair that had long turned white and frayed into something that looked more like spiderwebs. In moments, its whole head was free, its teeth framed by lips that had begun to fall away from the skull, the lower half drooping almost entirely beneath the chalk-white chin. Another howl sprang forth from its throat, chunks of dirt spewing forth like vomit. The wheeze of air flying through passageways it had not reached in decades became a whistle almost as loud and shrill as the creature's cry.

A quick smash of the spade against the top of Maria Lemtrobe's open skull, a sickening crack, like a baseball bat shattering on contact with a fastball, brought with it an eerie silence. It was shattered quickly by a low rasp as the dead woman's lungs pulled in air again, her fingers still struggling to find a hold strong enough to pull herself up. Gwen found herself in a similar situation now, trying desperately to pull her head above the mountain of lust that she found herself buried—no, *suffocated*—beneath. And it was hard not to feel a pang of sympathy for the woman the creature had once been, her auburn locks turned to brittle tufts of straw and her face falling into disarray as easily as a building turns derelict.

A chunk of earth gave away, causing most of it to collapse beneath the flailing arm of the thing rising from beneath it. With a rush of momentum and the leverage provided, the hand managed to free itself and the bony arm that held it from its prison cell of dirt and wrap tightly around Range's ankle, coiling beneath the joint like a series of small white snakes. He let out a small gasp as he was dragged off his feet and tumbled onto the hard earth below, a heavy thud signaling his impact. His elbow slammed down awkwardly, the vibration from it knocking the spade from his grasp and sending it bouncing across the row of tombstones and down the small embankment to the edge of the fence, where its steel clinked lightly against the links, like pale imitations of the heavy brass behemoths across the street. The creature let out another scream of displeasure, victory, or some emotion understood only by the deceased, which brought every hair on Gwen's body to a horrified attention. It began to yank heavily on Range's leg, tearing through the denim jeans and allowing him a moment of respite to try and pull himself from its bony clutches, but the digits snapped down into his bare flesh mere seconds after being freed.

Before she had realized that she was moving, Gwen was sprinting toward the base of the tangled fence, scooping up the crusty shovel and back toward the horrible thing in the ground despite every natural instinct willing her away. Still, the sight of Range's wide eyes as he was being dragged toward the widening pit kept the fear at bay, if only for a moment, as she began climbing back up the small crest of land. As Gwen started running toward the struggling Range, she felt her foot snag on a divot in the ground and instinctively pulled up sharply. When her foot did not come free, she found herself tumbling forward, the curvature of the hill coming up to meet her.

She threw her hands out to stop her descent but was unable to recover in time, landing on the side of her wrist and twisting into a painful roll, the shovel knocked loose from her trembling fingers. Groaning, she managed to push herself up enough to see Range send a quick kick into the creature's open mouth, the sole of his heavy work boots jamming the creature's maw and keeping it from closing around his foot. With a violent twist of his ankle, there came a horrible snap as the thing that was once Maria Lemtrobe's head slumped awkwardly to its shoulders, its teeth still clacking and foaming with a sick green sludge like a rabid animal where Range's foot had been only moments before. Somehow, its fingers still clung tight to his pant leg, the rotting green skin almost becoming indistinguishable from the grass-stained jeans jutting between the joints in its exposed bone.

Back in her cold cell, watching it all play out again, she felt her own knuckles slide completely inside her and stifled a moan by biting down on the thumb of her free hand.

Range had turned to her then, his face awash with a concern that caused a blender to start on her stomach, turning the butterflies there to a nauseating bile. There was still a confidence there, though, one that seemed to not only be placed in himself but in her as well, as if he knew what was going to happen—like he knew that she would be able to rescue him. Seeing it again now, she almost felt herself tip over the edge into the rushing ocean beneath her and welcomed it despite all her previous reservations. She only made a point to stop the writhing of her hips as she could hear the wire frame of the bed cry out in a jolt of surprise with each wanton thrust.

She saw herself again, rising up from the ground by placing her scraped, bloody palms against the dirt and charging forward, so quickly that if she hadn't caught herself with her hands again, she would've fallen forward. The shovel that had fallen just out of Range's grasp was in her hand before even she knew what she was doing, and like instinct, she raised it over her head and brought it down hard, overly confident in her own aim as it crashed down on the creature's shoulder, splitting the bones and flesh into gangling tendons. A lower, more guttural cry rose from its mangled windpipe, the bubble of some kind of mucus bursting from the porous remains. The arm that gripped Range in place fell from the body with only a thin string of muscle keeping it from collapsing into the dirt below. However, the fingers remained constant in their vigilance, never releasing their iron grip around Range's ankles, as he slid backward up the embankment, bringing his leg down hard with each push to no avail.

"Hit it in the head!"

She heard the words ring in her ear like bells, sounding prettier than the verses of a thousand sonnets written by lonely hearts or the glowing chorus of ten thousand monks raising their exaltations of glory to the heavens. As the spade fell upon and cracked the demon's skull, wrenching the head from the meager remains of its neck—Gwen felt herself fall into total ecstasy, each wave of the mind-blurring tingles that wracked her body coming in tandem with each fall of the shovel.

Crack.

Crack.

Crack.

With a final heavy smash, the job was done, the shovel wobbling slightly in the night air, protruding from the bloodied mush that used to resemble a human skull. For a few brief moments, she felt cold, seeing the black blood on her fingertips and her clothes, feeling the splinters that had wormed their way under her skin; but then she had looked at him, and he had smiled at her. She kept that image there as the pleasure left her, the rosy hue around it receding with the tide.

A final sigh escaped her, falling on the air like a cold winter breeze, bringing dreaded reality back with it. She sat up and felt the dampness of the sheets against her thigh and fought off a quick wave of postlust disgust before moving back over to her closet and grabbing a fresh pair of plain white panties with the red ribbon from the drawer inside. She realized then that she had never changed out of the bloodstained underwear from earlier that night and felt a horrible cringe in her lower extremities. It was far past the point of concern now; she thought as she slipped on a new pair, shimmying into them quickly. The clock said it was nearing six thirty, and her mother would be making her rounds soon, waking first her aunt with her daily serving of oatmeal and grief pills before checking on the prisoner.

Her legs still felt wobbly, but she managed to wrangle them into a pair of denim jeans. She almost absentmindedly grabbed one of the sweatshirts she had taken from the lacrosse game all those years ago but decided that she would rather spend the day without wondering whether or not a sweat stain was hers or one of Bobby Sloth's teammates and reached for one that her aunt had bought her. It didn't fit as well as it used to (it was from before she had taken her place at her mother's right hand); but like many of the clothes that her aunt had gotten for her in the time before she joined the Holy Church of Peggy Sinais, she still liked the way it looked. Slipping it on, she thought about Range's face again, the one he wore right before they parted ways, covered in blood and muck. There was something different about it, or maybe it was just the way she saw it, but it looked like something had clicked into place. It almost seemed like he felt the same way about her that she felt about him, as an insane a thought as that might be.

The insane thoughts stayed with her for most of the morning as when she was finishing up her paltry offering of toast and a single egg. She even found herself genuinely excited about going to school that day. She kept expecting her mother to say something, to grill her on her whereabouts that night, or even to proclaim, as she usually did, that the world was ending; but she was oddly silent, sending spiteful looks at her aunt for a change, as she listlessly spooned at her oatmeal, circling the crumbled-up pills that floated like drowning refugees inside of it.

———◈———

Questro misero modo, tegnon l'anime triste di coloro, che visser sanza 'nfamia e sanza lodo. Mischiante sono a quel cattivo coro, de li angeli che non furon ribelli, ne' fur fedeli a Dio, ma per se' fuoro. Caccianli i ciel per non esser men belli, ne' lo profundo inferno li riceve, ch'alcuna gloria i rei avrebber d'elli.

Do you recognize that? No? I'm sure you read it in high school, just probably not in its native Italian. You'd be surprised how much time you have to study in mental institutions. Then again, you really couldn't do much of anything else. And that's if the pills didn't make you too numb to even read. It's from Dante, from an early canto in the *Inferno*. It's the guide and poet Virgil's descriptions of the sinners in the very first circle of hell. Basically, it translates to,

These miserable people who lived their lives neither drenched in debauchery nor with faith in God, but for themselves. They lived without glory or praise, forever unhappy with their lives, they will be exulted by neither Satan nor God.

There's such a sadness to that verse that I feel gets ignored for the torments described later on as Dante dives deeper into hell. I mean, these people are plagued by hornets and wind, their face bloody, maggots eating away at their feet, forced to follow a flag on a death march to the ends of eternity just because you decided your own pursuits were nobler than that of God or country. Or you spend your life so entrenched in foul misery, unable to find happiness in the dreary gloom of your own life, so now you must spend the rest of time trapped in the same horrible state of hopelessness.

I've always found the first circle of hell to actually be the most tragic. Here you have hundreds and thousands of wailing souls, some whose only crime was being born before the concept of a singular God had even been thought of. Think about that. You spent your whole life treating others with empathy and respect, only to wind up in a pit of fire and wind because a God whose name you've never heard had yet to make himself known to you or your people. Seems like quite the shitty break. I mean, even the greatest of ancient minds were down there—Socrates, Aristotle, Homer—all because they believed in something that people had believed in for thousands of years before them. Even children who died before they could have a priest sprinkle water on their foreheads are stuck forever in limbo, cursed with a short but eternal existence.

That shit's pretty fucked up, if you ask me. It cool if I smoke in front of you? Is there an ashtray somewhere… oh, thanks, sweetie. Tried to quit a couple times now, but I always seem to end up with one of the little bastards between my fingers.

So I guess you're gonna wanna hear about Judgment Day now, aren't ya? Wasn't that what all the papers were calling it? I didn't get much news inside the hospital. They barely had any books for me to read until I petitioned the board directly, citing cases of cruel and unusual punishment since there was no proof that I had even done anything wrong, other than surviving the end of the world, but they must've passed a law against that before my time. One of the doctors I spoke with, I think his name was Marcelli, the one who wrote that dissertation on post-traumatic stress in natural disasters survivors—I think it was published in some kind of psychology journal, not like I ever received a copy of it—he told me that he'd been there, flying overhead in Denang when they dropped napalm down like a crop duster, clearing the pests out of a field, and that, after the things he saw in Loganville, given the chance to see what happened there or the fires of Denang again over and over for the rest of his life, he'd choose Denang every time. Hmm? Would I classify what happened there as a natural disaster? Probably. But then again, you could probably classify a lot more things as natural disasters if you took human nature into account.

That was the thing that seemed the oddest about the whole media sensation it became. I spent months isolated from the general public, but even I knew that it was one of the biggest news stories since 9/11 with a death toll that almost pushed it into the record books as the most deadly attack on US soil. There were cameramen outside my windows day and night. They had to start keeping orderlies outside in thirty-degree weather just to make sure paparazzi weren't huddling in bushes with thermos hidden between their legs like tails, the rats that they are. One of them managed to get a shot of me washing up in the communal showers. Snuck in with the laundry cart and waited there for an entire night, all just to get a photo that ended up being too blurry to see anything other than maybe a foot or part of my backside, and not the part that would pay out.

Anyways, one of the times I was being transferred, they put me up in a motel 6 just outside of Portsmouth, and I saw this story on the news. I was so desperate for some connection to the events that had been going on in my absence from the world that I even sat through several minutes of Fox News. There was a story about a village in Africa, Sudan, I think, that had been completely decimated by one of those people's armies. You know, the kind that fights by arming children? The only survivors were so badly disfigured that most of them didn't even look human anymore. All of them, even a girl as young as twelve, had been raped by over fifty men; they didn't bother to test the dead ones. Afterward, they razed the place to the ground and moved on to the next town. As of the time of the report, they were still on the path there with no signs of government intervention or last-minute change of hearts slowing them down. The newscasters talked about the story for maybe two minutes, maybe three, before switching to a story about a new tax on sugary snacks in Rhode Island. These terrible, horrific things were happening all over the world all the time, and most people couldn't care in the slightest. It was only when it happened in their backyards, with the possibility of affecting their lives and the lives of their loved ones, that they managed to give a shit. I guess you can't blame them for feeling that way. Most of them don't want to think things like that are real. I've done my best to forget them; why shouldn't they?

Yet here we are, bringing it all up again. I suppose I should stop rambling and get back to telling you what you came here for. Guess I can't really put it off any longer. I guess I'm not sure what to tell people anymore. I go back and analyze every detail of that morning, trying to piece together the moment when everything fell apart, but nothing stands out. There's no simple solution that magically explains all the death and misery—something that can be easily avoided next time by sticking a Post-It note to your head. The glue on those things never really lasts, especially under pressure.

For as abnormal of a start that it had, the morning seemed to pass just like all the others. The clouds were bunched tightly together like fake cotton snow in a mall Christmas display, the sun slipping through the horizon almost like a giant was trying to keep its eyes open. There was a heavy fog that covered the ground and gave everything a feeling of dampness as if the ocean had risen up and swept two hundred miles across the country to crash over the town in the night. My mother came and woke us up for prayer in the small chapel in the living room. She decorated it with paintings of the Apostle Paul and John the Baptist—you know, that famous one of him holding the cross and pointing toward the sky? I always thought it looked like he had just gotten away with a murder—one that even God couldn't see. I mentioned it to Mother back before I knew better and ended up with several hits from the switch before being sent to my room for two days.

Mother then began to make breakfast while my aunt sat at the kitchen table, reading through the Book of Revelations for the umpteenth time. At the time, I really didn't think anything of it, but the more I look back on it and the way she was acting… Don't get me wrong; she was always a troubled woman, my aunt. The creature my mother twisted her into was something else entirely, but you could always see the woman she used to be underneath her molded clay exterior. That morning, she was more like Gena Sinais than she had been for years.

Most of the reports leave her completely out of it. The name Judgment Day was coined by journalists who specifically knew about my mother before the events of October 17 took place. I wouldn't necessarily call it a smear campaign, because nothing they reported was actually falsified in any way. It may have painted her in a negative light in the weeks following, but my mother made her bed many years ago, and it was time for her to lay in it. And yes, I do tell myself that at night, in case you were wondering. It's become something of a nightly prayer, and if God appreciates irony, he's definitely laughing about that one.

Unlike her sister, however, Gena was unashamed of her baser temptations—for a time, at least. I think it stemmed from the age difference between the two of them. My grandfather was the religious nut in the household back then, and while my mother never spoke about it, with the media blitz that followed, I learned more about her time as a child than I ever had from her very own lips.

Deacon Roger Sinais found religion after his time in the war, although not immediately after apparently, as my grandmother, Eliza—whom he did the duty of marrying shortly after—produced a daughter for him several months after his appointment. Margaret Annabelle Sinais was born happy and healthy, and all accounts of the time spent in their first home in Northern Pennsylvania are only positive from the neighbors and clergy, save for a few whisperings about Roger's unruly temper and his unusual involvement in Shaker revivals on the town's outskirts.

Shortly after a forest fire burned down the local archdiocese, my grandfather relocated his small family to the town of Loganville, taking up sermon duties at a small local congregation of Catholics known for their strong conservative views, even for Cold War America. This is where the odd reports of my family really start to come to prominence in the archives. As ashamed as I am to say, it really started when Roger was arrested—along with several other famous members of the congregation, some of them even holding positions in local government—for burning a cross outside the house of a local African American family. Charges were pressed but ultimately dismissed, mostly due to pulled strings and political favors, although most of their careers ended up petering out soon after. Besides, people weren't too excited to stir up a huge controversy over a little old Black family that lived out past the Interstate. People originally feared, there might be a local chapter of a certain famous hooded organization, but the idea of one this far north was quickly brushed under the table.

I wish that was the only instance of my grandfather's run-ins with the law, but it was only the first of many. His most famous was probably the effigy-burning of Kennedy in town square—who, he claimed, despite naming himself a Catholic, was destroying the holy institution of the presidency and turning the White House into a place filled with sexual debauchery and unholy rituals. He was also completely smashed at the time and set fire to several cars downtown with his supporters before he was brought in. Several officers wanted him to report to Calm Lake Mental Hospital for a psych evaluation, but my grandmother posted his bail and had him back home before anybody could sign anything official. Over the years, there were several reports of abuse in the Sinais' household—neighbors whispering about Eliza's bruises, young Margaret's complete and total silence around strangers. People began speaking about the deacon and his wild ravings, and as the times began to change, he and his dwindling supporters found themselves in a world that was beginning to tire of their constant damnation of its every little facet. By this time, Gena Malachi Sinais was born to the couple, several years before Peggy graduated from the St. Ignatius School for Girls in the nearby town of Oldbrook.

It was about two or three years after that, Roger Sinais got behind the wheel of his Ford after drinking a bottle and half of Jameson and wrapped himself around a tree near Catalano Boulevard. The funeral was fairly well attended by the community, although there were several reports of people breaking out renditions of Hallelujah with a bit more enthusiasm than was customary at funerals, many of the participants being members of the African American community that were asked to leave shortly after the song started. After that, the family passed into a state of blissful anonymity for several years, with most people forgetting about the deacon and his offspring that lived in the small, plain white flat buried in the neck of the small forest preserve near the edge of town. Gena grew up relatively undisturbed. My grandmother was made of kinder stuff than the rest of the family and treated her well. My aunt used to tell me stories about my mother and her when she came over to visit when I was little, back before she and my mother became one inseparable entity.

My mother went off to train at a seminary in Northern Maine, hoping to enter the church as soon as she could, as a sister to God himself. She returned after several months, declaring the place to be a "bed of serpents" and a "perversion to all of God's teachings." Mostly, she felt their beliefs adhered too strongly to the newer, trendier split-offs of Christianity and were only a shade of the true Catholic spirit. They were leading us to Judgment Day, she declared, and started studying on her own, in her room in the attic, while Gena and my grandmother continued their happy existence, unaware of our supposedly impending damnation.

Gena met her husband, Gregory Merchant, in high school; and they were often a cause of dissension in the house as Margaret would often walk in on the two, um, lying together as one, while still unmarried, and begin to angrily recite psalms at the top of her lungs, waking up their mother and condemning them in front of the eyes of God while they awkwardly shuffled into their underwear. My grandmother was certainly upset about the whole situation, but she lacked the religious conviction that my mother seemed to inherit directly from my grandfather—although it had less to do with genetics and more to do with bruises, long concealed and healed underneath foundation.

This continued for about a year, before Gregory finally got angry enough with Margaret's nightly intrusions that he snapped and told her to mind her own goddamn business and to just "finger herself like a normal person." Greg told me that story himself when I went to visit them at their house when I was around five or six. He was quite inebriated at the time and didn't realize it wasn't the best story for a child, but I enjoyed it all the same. I couldn't tell you how they got me out of my mother's fingertips, let alone her sight, for a weekend, but it's something I still think of fondly.

The backyard pool sat right near the edge of a large drop-off to the ocean; the waves crashing against the cliff side always gave you the feeling that you were swimming in the ocean as well. Even though it was cloudy every day, I still go to it in my mind when I need to get away from everything. I spent quite a lot of my time in the mental hospital there, days at a time even. Daily, more days than not, I imagine they were right to keep me here…

Right, yes, we were talking about a seventeen-year-old Greg telling my mother off, weren't we? Well, as valiant an effort as it was, it was only met by a look of scorn so intense he told me that he was convinced that he had wet himself just by looking directly into those eyes. They seemed to glow with an intensity that seemed inherently... righteous and shook him right to his core. She pulled the rosary beads from her belt and brought them hard across his face, buried in her palm, and began to swing savagely at his head, like she was trying to bash his skull in with them. Luckily, Gena and my grandmother were able to pull her off of him, but he didn't come around to the house much after that. His retellings of this story at the local bars were the building blocks of my mother's legacy, and I try not to blame him for that, as even he couldn't see the monster that she would become: a local boogeyman that mothers warned their children about while straightening their clothes before school.

Shortly after Gena turned eighteen, she and Greg got married in Roger's old church, with one of the surviving members of his congregation the one to read them their vows. They quickly moved down to Virginia, right along the shoreline, while Greg started his own business of boat rentals out on the local marina.

It was about nine years later when Greg died. Aunt Gena found him floating facedown in the pool after he arrived home late from a holiday party at the office. He was quite inebriated when he did get home... that was his greatest flaw really. No child really understands the effects of alcohol, but even when I was young and Greg and Gena came over for the usual yearly family milestones—Christmas, Thanksgiving, birthdays, and the like— I always noticed a change in Greg when it got dark out. My mother told me that it was at night when the demons in men's hearts were given free rein over their earthly confines and that Greg liked to indulge in a drink that would only fuel that demon's fire. It was the same vice that claimed my grandfather, she said, something that would be the doom and ruin of all men and the godly women around them. When I asked if women had this same demon inside them, she responded only with a look that indicated there would be a late-night sabbatical to the chapel to see Father Switch.

Well, when Greg got home from this Christmas party, Gena was asleep in the bed; and finding himself unable to relieve the built-up tension with his own sabbatical to the church located between his wife's legs, he settled for a glass of brandy and a soak in the early-morning air. Unfortunately, his drowsiness took advantage of his intoxication and convinced him a few minutes of drooped eyelids couldn't hurt anyone and carried him down beneath the shifting water. When Aunt Gena found him, she never actually phoned the police. The neighbors called, believing there had been break-in because all they could hear were her screams down the whole block.

The funeral was fairly uneventful, as I recall, but I was still very young at the time. I remember because I wasn't particularly sad about the whole thing. It sounds heartless, looking back on it, but most kids my age don't fully understand the ramifications behind death enough to be truly impacted by it. At least that's what I tell myself, I guess. It's weird to think the only positive male role model in my life vanished so quickly, and I couldn't even be bothered to be sad. I thought he was going to a better place—up to heaven, with God and Jesus and all the angels, and Greg would show them the same tricks he had shown me, like being able to know what card they pulled without seeing it. I told my aunt this, and she smiled, even though her eyes were runny with tears; she even laughed. My mother overheard and told me that God wouldn't be impressed as his omnipotence was better than any trick. I replied that maybe he was just laughing to be nice, but a quick squeezing of my fingers shut me up pretty quickly.

"Besides," my mother said, "Greg's probably down in hell, sharing a drink with our father."

To this day, I don't know how my aunt just stood there and listened to that, let it wash over her, and continued to smile with a horrible silence that broke my heart. I kept expecting her to tell my mother that she was wrong, that Greg couldn't be in hell. There was no way that God would put someone like Greg in hell, but that awful silence just stretched into the edges of eternity. Part of me hated her for it. Part of me still hates her for it. But in the many years that's passed and after all I've experienced, after all the lies about That Day and the people I watched die, I think she had a strength that I might never know. And maybe I hate her for that.

The life insurance settlement wasn't enough to afford the rent on the house in Virginia very long, especially since the business defaulted into the hands of several of Greg's business partners, who offered support in crowded, bustling places but answered private calls with excuses or quick dismissals to their voice mails. My grandmother had passed away several years earlier due to heart complications, so the only person my aunt could really turn to was my mother. Unfortunately for her, this seemed to be her ultimate undoing. Her safety net was more of a rabbit trap.

When my aunt first moved in, she started attending therapy at a psychiatrist down in Hartford to cope with grief; but my mother's late-night prayer sessions proved to be a more rewarding outlet, it seemed—at least a more immediate one. Mother had to clear room in her chapel for her sister to stay, and while she didn't say it with a grin, she happily quoted Leviticus's views on hospitality while helping her get her meager belongings tucked away. Despite my mother's grumbling about seeing a man who "probably got his doctorate from Satan," things settled into an odd normalcy—although there was enough tension in each silent dinner you were expecting it all to explode at any moment. Every small glance that carried disfavor also carried a lit match over a powder keg. Then one day, several months after she moved in, right around the time of that huge pileup on Interstate 90, my aunt woke up screaming in horrible agony—I mean, absolutely howling at the top of her lungs. Her eyes rolled back into her skull, and all you could see were the bloodshot whites, teeth grit and covered in foaming drool. I ran out of the room as soon as I saw her. Mother simply gave her a switch to bite down on from the closet and waited until the fit ran its course. The two of them didn't come out of that room for what seemed like an eternity and a half, but when my mother finally did emerge, she was as calm as if she had been doing a quick load of laundry and instructed me to call the police and have them send an ambulance to the house.

All tests came back negative for any type of seizure, or preexisting form of epilepsy, along with tests for some kind of tumor or growth that could be pressing up against the frontal lobe of the brain. As far as medical science was concerned, my aunt was simply experiencing the results of extreme stress and anxiety on the human body. And yet the seizures kept happening. Every few months, I would hear my aunt's screams bellowing from the chapel, followed by my mother's rapidly shuffling feet. They prescribed a month's supply of Dermoxitil, a depressant used in patients with bad cases of PTSD. When my aunt was on those pills, she could barely answer you with anything more than a grunt or a motion of her head that could be interpreted as a nod or a shake, some days more easily than others. Some days, my aunt wouldn't want to take them, saying that she would rather live in a clear head of grief than a clouded one of bliss; but for the first time in her life, my mother had decided that the doctor's word was the highest in the land, almost as if God had come down and spoken directly through his mouth, making every word a gospel, and insisted that she stick to her weekly routine. When my aunt insisted further, she would crush them up and hide it in her breakfast, usually in bowls of thick oatmeal where you couldn't taste the powder…

They found a whole case of those pills in the basement during the cleanup. Did you hear about that? Direct from the pharmacy. Apparently, one of the pharmacists' father had been part of my grandfather's late-night congregation and cut my mother a deal under the table for cheaper than market price. Cutting out the taxes received by the pharmaceutical company, he himself was making quite a bit more on each week's paycheck. At first, I didn't want to think why they were down there. I knew why they were, but I never wanted to say it…

And today won't be any different. I'm afraid.

Now, where was I? Oh, right, breakfast—that last breakfast. It's weird, looking back on it, knowing that it was the last time I was at that table, going through the motions that I put myself through every day, strangely content with the ritual. My aunt sat in silence, face buried in her Bible, but she kept casting glances at me from time to time without ever speaking. Part of me wanted to ask her what the problem was, to start yet another confrontation in the hopes of some kind of angst-ridden validation, but I held my tongue. I found myself in an odd state of zen, even though I knew I shouldn't have been. I had been covered in someone else's... something else's blood an hour ago. Even if it was just shock, I wanted that feeling to last forever.

My mother seemed to pick up on this and began asking me questions about my studies the night before, which I answered diligently to the best of my ability, despite the fact that more than half of the homework in my bag wouldn't actually be completed until homeroom that day. I slipped up when she quizzed me about the Bible passages I was supposed to read that night—something from Ezekiel related to one of his visions in the temple. She brought me into the chapel and led me in several good prayers along Father Switch, killing any sense of complacency I may have made before I had even started my day.

I was led back to the table, and as I sat down, my aunt turned to my mother and said, "You shouldn't do that to her, you know?"

The sound of her voice alone was unexpected enough to startle me out of my chair, let alone the bold tenacity of her statement. My mother let the question hang there, deflating like a day-old balloon, her silence heavier and more absolute than any rebuttal. She simply told my aunt that they would speak in private after I left for school, went back to the counter, and continued making breakfast as if she hadn't heard. She served my aunt an extra large portion of oatmeal that morning, but I only noticed it as I came back down from my room, backpack in hand, more adamant to face the cold autumn breeze than the cruel words of the prophet.

As I slipped out the back door, I felt a hand catch mine; and I turned to tell my mother off, ready to say everything I had ever wanted to her, inspired by my late-night adventures, only to be greeted by the sorrowful gaze of my aunt. She looked as if she had aged half a century in a night. The bags beneath her eyes could fit enough luggage for a month-long vacation. I went to leave again, expecting nothing more than a stern follow-up from the prophet's shadow; but instead, she hugged me, so tight that I wasn't sure she planned on letting go. But she did, and she told me she loved me, which I hadn't heard her say... in so long I couldn't even tell you the last time before that. Maybe since when Greg was still alive? I didn't know what to say for a while. I only stared at her with that same stupid look of defiance that I had practiced in the mirror so many times that it seemed to have stuck that way. I told her thanks and left her there. I replay that moment in my head every night, like a bug that endlessly torments me, always just out of reach.

She called after me. "Be careful," she said. "Be careful with him…"

The verdant rush of pine trees blurred and bled into a trail of red neon as the small minivan's curved frame rolled down the gravel road through the early-morning fog. Billy's eyelids felt heavy and never stayed open for long; it was only the tapping of his face against the glass that kept him awake. Every shake and bump of the road would send his forehead into the glass with a small thunk that soon gained a rhythm that was frustratingly hypnotic. His dreams still danced before his eyes, dreams of bloodied swords and shadows that moved beneath the darkness only to meet his holy blade. Any normal man would've been slain, but not when they were the chosen one, whose sword glowed with a fiery strength born from a purpose most noble. If a demon was so much dare to look upon his visage in that world, one swing of his blade and it would be dashed to a pile of soot, blood, and brimstone at his feet, its laughter ringing in his ears.

Then he awoke again from the small thump of the window and found himself sucked back into the horrifying mediocrity that entailed the real world. The voices on the radio droned on, talking about some recent news story that his mother had attempted to fill him in on over breakfast that morning, but every word had passed right through the dream-addled miasma and out the other side. That was until he heard the name of those involved. His interest was piqued as high as any distracted teenager's interest in the news could rise.

"You sure you're up and ready for school, honey?" his mother asked, her voice distracted as she tried to divide her glances between her son and the road. "You've been asleep the whole car ride, and the bags under your eyes look like they're from Sam's Club. Were you up late doing homework?"

"No, Mom."

"But all your homework is done and ready to be turned in, isn't it?"

"Yes, Mom."

"Well, good."

For a moment, Billy thought his mother might actually broach the subject of his insomnia, but soon, the gentle rumble of the wheel axles became the only discernible sound. The constant noise soon became a sweet lullaby, a gentle drone that, coupled with the vibration of the car frame, lulled him back into the wisps of his dreams.

He was not in the midst of battle for long, for now he beheld a brilliant throne room with high arching walls that bent into curving pillars and flying buttresses that supported a grand mosaic on the ceiling of men and beasts locked in their eternal struggle. Its floors stretched almost as wide as the horizon would carry them, tiled in a style that seemed reminiscent of a chess board. Court retainers stood at either end, their faces beaming with both pride for their conquering hero and spite for their better who had taken another step up the rungs of a ladder that was out of their own reach. Still, he smiled at all of them as a true chivalrous knight is meant to do, twisting his hand back and forth, like a beauty pageant contestant sure of her own victory. And why shouldn't he be? He alone destroyed the demons that marched on the castle's gates. He alone was the kingdom's beacon of light who, by his own destiny, was able to lead the kingdom from the darkness that enveloped it. And today was finally to be his reward, his recognition for his years of patience and due diligence, hard work that was never awarded with a word of praise or devotion from even his family.

Yet here he was, standing before the throne, the princess lying in wait at the end of the hall, the rose-colored light from the windows splaying down upon her shining face and bosom. Her golden locks fell down to her waist, wrapped in fine silks and a gown that gave form to her splendid figure as well as any scarf of cloth could. The effect on him was noticeable as he often had to widen his steps to accommodate for the discomfort in his tights. As he stepped closer, he watched with adamant attention as the princess's fingers traced the curves of her body, her eyes half closed in lust as he moved toward her and the throne. The tip of his steel foot cuffs smacked against the small stairs of the great hall, sending sorrowful echoes reverberating through the spacious surroundings, like it was the throat of some mighty beast. When he reached the apex of the small set of steps, he knelt down before her, as the echoes continued in the rafters, rising to a dull roar, like waves crashing through a cliff-side cavern. He unsheathed the blade at his hip, almost needing to shield his eyes from its magnificent glow, as bright as the morning sun and just as powerful as every god that had borne its image. Setting it down at his side, its shine was diminished and absorbed by the dark marble; but his eyes were lost within the creamy sea of milky skin that moved ever toward him, her hips twisting like the serpents he had slain on the mountainside earlier that day.

She stopped before him, her hazy green eyes entwined with his own, even though she stood tall over his kneeling form. William went to rise, but her slim yet powerful hands stopped him, the fingers wrapping themselves around his shoulder guards like they were part of the intricate patterns carved within them at their creation. Smiling wickedly, she pulled him forward, into her navel, where he inhaled her mind-numbing aroma, letting the fragrance take residence within him. He could feel her grip inside him now, pulling at the neurons in his mind, taking control of every inch of his body, relaxing every muscle with exalted bliss. Still, the roar of the hall grew louder, the smell of charcoal becoming ever more apparent.

William tried to look up, but his head was pushed down lower until he found himself in the fold of her legs, the tip of his nose burrowing into her womanhood. He heard—nay, felt—her moan of satisfaction and let his worries fall to his side like the tempered steel beside him. However, the roar did not cease and started to shake the rafters and flying buttresses as if a tremor had taken hold of the ground. The stained glass windows began to tremble and rattle with the stonewalls of the great hall, becoming more and more violent as the rush of noise grew even more intense, until the window at the northwestern-most corner of the hall shattered and sent chunks of captured rainbow spiraling through the air and onto the tiles below. A horrifying light burst through, one so bright it seemed to darken the rest of the room in comparison, that horrible roar following close behind it like thunder. Before he could even stand and right himself, the curling wisps of smoke began to twist their way around the remains of shattered glass, filing into the hall and collecting amidst the heavenly clouds above, becoming almost indistinguishable from the actual thing. The bright neon-red flames came last in that train of misery, pouring through the gap in a torrent that was like a wild river of death incarnate. The fire's light danced across the ceiling and breathed life into the angels and satyrs above, a sick inversion of the bodies writhing in agony below.

He turned back to the princess, his eyes wide and his mouth dry and tasting of sulfur. His tongue felt so swollen that it seemed to be clogging his throat, keeping what little oxygen remained from his lungs. Reaching for her, he tried to speak, tried desperately to form words but instead coughed and wheezed while collapsing to his knees at her feet. His mailed hand reached out desperately at his side, feeling for the familiar glowing steel. It was dim beneath the veil of putrid smoke, but it was there.

The flames leaped closer, propelled by an unseen force, one that William refused to believe could be true, although this did little to halt its rapid encroachment toward the throne. A rush of wind sent the flames twisting into savage shapes and only rushed them forward, licking at the pillars of marble and turning the bases to a sickly black. He threw his hand around aimlessly, hoping, praying for the ring of steel on steel. Finally, he heard the clink on his lobstered gauntlet and opened his fingers wide, only to feel the steel slip through and melt in the intense heat, running like molten honey through his fingers, its dazzling light paling in comparison to the true fire that had engulfed them.

Hope left him, and a crippling fear remained. Cautiously, he turned back toward the hall, only to find that the inferno had calmed, with a few small fires still raging at the foot of overturned lanterns and beneath melted torches. Somehow, this calm inspired him enough to find his footing, but another large tear of wind almost threw him back down. It was strong enough to force him back, his boots scraping against the warm tile, like a dying animal.

There was an earth-shattering crash that caused the roof to fold in on itself, the oil-crafted sky falling into the fires beneath. The southwest pillar gave way, the bottom stone finally relenting to the flames and sending the stones down onto the still-screaming bodies, burying them beneath rubble and shattered angels. A terrible snout—led by two gaping nostrils that gave residence to twin trails of smoke and a maw that shut uneven on its right side due to its large, gnarled fangs—made its way through the open portmanteau. The remaining stones held the monster at bay beyond its high cheekbones, but his dark-maroon eyes pierced through the haze, like Mars on a summer solstice. After several seconds of terrifying reprieve, where the only sounds that could be heard was the gentle crackle of the flames and the strained breaths of the giant behemoth, it opened its jaw wide—exposing a raw, bloody throat, with chunks of bone and crisped flesh stuck between its teeth. And a roar of flames came forth again, filling the back of the room and rushing forward as fast as an echo.

With barely enough time to think, William whirled about and looked down at his love, his shielded hands reaching down toward hers and gathering them up.

"Get behind—" he started but was cut off by the chill of iron and the taste of copper.

His eyes looked but refused to see the dagger protruding from his jugular, still tight in the dainty fingers before him. Her emerald eyes seemed to laugh, and her lips twisted into a foul smile that poisoned the air more than the heavy smoke. Again, he tried to speak, but a bubble of blood stopped him, drowning the words at the bottom of the well that was his throat. The fire enveloped them both alike, boiling the blood in his throat and congealing it into a sticky tar that sealed the screams in his lungs. The princess's lips cracked and then fell away in rush of dead skin and burning, curling flesh. Her eyes melted into a green pus, and her blond hair shriveled into gray ash; but that horrible smile remained, plastered to her skull. Somehow, she managed to laugh, loud and hard, as their bodies became nothing more than blackened, smoking bones melting into the ear-deafening roar that had grown so loud and so savage that he was certain that it was the last horrible sound he would ever hear…

Until it shook him awake just in time to catch himself as the van screeched to a halt, inches away from the bumper of the Prius in front of them. His mother pulled off the horn before laying into it several more times, just to make sure that the driver in front of her knew full well about her disapproval of the situation.

"God bless it, can you believe some people? How they were able to walk out of a DMV with a license, I'll never know," his mother said, collecting herself and straightening the messy lump of auburn curls that had once been called a hairstyle.

The Prius remained motionless, a steady stream of exhaust rising from the tailpipe that Billy followed up as it disappeared amidst the unbroken gray above, swearing that he could still feel the heat on his skin, boiling him from the inside out. It felt like his skin was moving—no, bubbling—turning into a sickening mess of pulpy flesh and blackened blood, fusing muscle and skin and shattering bone. The feeling passed after a moment, but the hairs on the back of his neck stood at alert, aware of some danger that he himself seemed oblivious to, although he had wrestled with that feeling for the past few days.

After the meteor impact over in Castle Rock, everyone in town had been tense. I mean, it wasn't exactly a normal occurrence, and it seemed like people weren't quite sure how to react. There had been riots and looting initially for the first couple of hours. Everyone was convinced that their homes would soon be reduced to a steaming pile of cinders after the fires had started and spread through the northwestern part of town, burning down the community center, a grade school, and several large local businesses—including a logging company that had been working near the actual impact site. And of course, there was the actual church that it crashed into directly, taking the life of some poor young woman that had come seeking guidance and got an answer that probably only confused her more for the few seconds that her mind had to analyze it. There was also the robbery that had been the talk of the table at breakfast that morning. The story had been plastered over every local news channel that morning, and his father had insisted on watching all of them, desperate for any more information that he could get.

"This country gets worse every day, I tell ya, crazies shooting the man decent enough to provide them with a living wage and killing cops for trying to stop it. Not to mention in the same week, a bloody comet comes and wipes half a town off the map. People are going insane nowadays, although I think I'm starting to see why," his father had said, his glasses nearly falling off his nose as his gaze alternated between the glowing screen and the small newspaper in front of him.

"It's that damn information overload I've been telling you about, Nadia. Today people are being bombarded left and right with story after story—of course, all of them modern-day Shakespearean tragedies because those are the ones that generate the most clicks, or 'likes,' or whatever the kids wanna call their signs of approval these days, and people can't handle it anymore. How many times can you hear about children being blown to pieces by machines meant to defend your so-called freedom? How many times can you hear about a mother who decided it would be easier to kill her child than to raise it, before you just… snap? I'm telling you, it's becoming easier every day."

"Guess we're lucky you haven't snapped yet then, Dad," Billy had said, his daring bolstered by the confidence that if his father had paid enough attention to actually hear what he said, he wouldn't get a response anyway.

It was rare to even get a spared glance from him when he went on one of his daily diatribes, answering all the world's problems by unraveling them out in front of him again, although there never seemed to be any tangible solutions to be found at the end of the string—only a smug sense of self-satisfaction. But that was enough for Gerald Bosk, for he valued the simple pleasures in life. Well, at least, that was what he said, but his brand-new Dyna Wide Glide sitting in the garage next to his Prestigo golf clubs and crate of imported Dal Forno put up quite a different argument, that, like Billy's own, was swiftly ignored.

Gwen often ranted to him about her mother, the Prophet of Loganville; and despite his best efforts, he had heard the stories. It was hard not to, growing up, when it was on every one of your peers' lips, the spoonfuls dropped in their ears by their parents' after-party ramblings and whispered spite dripping down their lobes. He had heard about her hate-filled condemnations of those around her and almost laughed when he realized that they sounded very similar to his father's "told-ya-so's" that came guaranteed with each glass of brandy. Seeing his father without a glass of liquor in his hand was a rare and strange sight. When you did catch a rare glimpse of his bare hand, you had to strain yourself to figure out the special occasion that would denote its absence.

He had told Gwen of these similarities, expecting the revelation to be the catalyst that would finally make Gwen aware of their deep understanding, the strong connection between them. Instead, she had replied like most of the girls in his life had, telling him that it wasn't the same and that he didn't actually know what he was talking about. She was thankful for his support, of course. They were always gracious about his support because otherwise, they might lose it, which they didn't want. They just didn't want him.

However, this morning would be different because it wasn't just anyone that had committed one of the worst crimes in recent Loganville history; it was none other than one Matt Métier—the Queen Bitch of Loganville High's fuck-up of a brother, the guy who had settled for life as a bar hand. As soon as the name had flashed across the screen, the fall gloom that had been with him since his eyes opened to a window pane spotted in raindrops and fog evaporated just as quickly as it had settled; and Billy Bosk found himself almost excited for the school day ahead of him, which was a rare occurrence indeed.

Billy didn't like to consider himself someone who carried a grudge, but it was hard not to think of Veronica Métier without his blood pressure rising. Even though he didn't like to admit it, he had, at one point, early on in his freshman year, counted himself among the misguided collection of Veronica's many admirers. On the rare occasion that he was invited to one of the larger social gatherings on the weekends, he would often run into Veronica and strike up sloppy conversations filled with bad drunken innuendo, surprised to hear laughter as a response instead of soul-shattering silence. However, about halfway through the school year, when he turned one of these horrible miscalculations of hotness leagues into an awkward invitation to a movie that weekend, the laughter he received was not as empowering as it once had been. It especially didn't help to watch her walk over to a group of seniors he recognized from one of his study halls and encourage a rousing bit of laughter from them, glossy eyes and slimy fingers twisted in his direction.

After that, it had been easier to see past her looks, to observe the dark creature that she really was. These observations he shared with Gwen were the ones that brought the most smiles to her face, and today, when eyes and whispers would follow behind Veronica closer than her shadow, seemed like a day that would have the two of them smiling all the way through.

"It sounded like you were up pretty late last night, sweetie. You wouldn't be having any trouble sleeping, would you? My grandmother used to give us NyQuil whenever we couldn't sleep. That way, it would keep you feeling healthy and keep you quiet too, which were two of your grandmother's favorite things, so she always considered it a win-win," his mother rambled, sparing occasional glances at her son when the early-morning traffic allowed. They were moving at a steadier pace now, one that seemed to pacify his mother's badly concealed road rage.

"No, Mom, like I said earlier, I was just up late, doing homework," he said, trying to keep his voice from shaking.

In earnest, he had spent most of the night tossing and turning beneath sheets, replays of the most embarrassing moments of his life projected on the canvas sheet that his eyelids became in the darkness. Asking out Veronica had become one of the greatest hits, a regular box office smash. Even if he did sleep, these thoughts would lead only to nightmares far worse—ones that found him cold and alone in an echoing pit of black, or others that started off happy enough, as the one this morning had, only to spiral into a disturbing climax that left him craving the dark pit.

If he did dream, his mornings only became harder, as his body seemed to weigh several tons more and require all his effort to even raise the strength to throw his feet out of bed. His dad would come to the small, plain white pinewood door and pound loudly, his Class of '82 ring cracking against the notch it had made throughout the years of similar abuse. He would remind Billy that if he didn't get up soon, his grades would suffer and any aspirations of going to a good college where he could make enough money to live an actually happy and healthy life would fly right out the window while he wasted away—which, of course, completely removed all the stress from his body like the flip of a light switch.

"It seems like you've been staying up pretty late for a while now, honey. You're sure everything's okay?"

Part of him ached to tell her exactly about the seemingly immovable cloud that hung over him, but he couldn't find the words that seemed to fit properly. Every description felt wrong, like he was cheating it or giving up and admitting it out loud; even if it was quieter than whisper in a dark room, it would fell like defeat. Hearing it out loud from his own mouth would be a confirmation of his own worthlessness that he wasn't sure he could bear. While he stayed quiet, it wasn't real. It was just dark thoughts every teenager had, and they would fade away, like coarse sand making the fingers cut and raw as it slides through.

"Everything's fine, Mom, I swear," he added, although he wasn't sure if it was for her or himself.

His eyes met his mother's in the rearview mirror, and despite his growing desire to look away, their shaking concern filled him with a guilt that stung like bad heartburn eating away at the bottom of his diaphragm. They seemed to pierce right through his hastily constructed facade of disinterest, deep down into the parts of his psyche that he refused to believe existed anymore—fears and doubts that should have left a child years ago but clung to his insides, refusing to let go; deep-rooted voices that whispered malicious biting remarks that weighed down any lighthearted thought of progress with malicious undertones; voices that all sounded like one terrible, tremendous voice, dampened by the crinkling sections of the morning paper…

"Mom! Watch out!"

A squeal erupted from beneath the car, and for a moment, Billy was sure a creature had found its way underneath the tires in their shared distraction. And yet nothing but smoke rose up from beneath the car as it twisted to halt, his mother's fingers straining to the bone to maintain control over the two-ton behemoth. The front end turned sharply to the left, the tires hopping over the small median and cutting into the far end of the left turn lane, the right headlight grazing past the Tacoma's taillight, their hazy halogen glows mixing into a sick cocktail with the early morning fog. The Taurus behind them, who was apparently planning on hopping the median to save an entire two seconds on his morning commute, slid to a halt several inches from the glass on his mother's side, the lights pouring in like a shady police interrogation room. The driver promptly laid on his horn and rolled his window down to ensure that they saw the entirety of his raised middle finger before pulling out and around the trembling family, keeping his finger aimed directly at them as his car rocked over the small median and into the cool yellow lines of the empty turn lane.

"All right. What in the name of God is going on with all this frankenfurten traffic?"

His mother often liked to replace the word *fuck* with random, nonsensical words that also began with the letter *F*. It started as a way to protect her precious William from hearing such filth during angry outbursts but had become her own way of dealing with her distaste for the word. It was one of the many reasons he didn't like having friends around his mother.

The car rolled slowly around the trail of parked cars, like a hearse moving into position at the front of its pack of followers. They passed many cars he recognized—the Dunnigans' CR-V with their family stick figures in the rear window (which was also considerate enough to include a dog and parrot for their furrier family members); the Houlihans' Escape; the Hickams' C-Class in its usual position at the head of the flock. The makeshift parking lot stood in front of the tall white steeple, with skylights revealing the dark-red brass of the bells behind it, like some kind of diseased heart. A growing collection of people were gathered under the large stone arches, decorated across the top with the tale of Jesus's resurrection, starting with the crucifixion on the left pillar and ending with the shocked crowd of onlookers as he rose from his tomb atop the obelisk to the right. He recognized a few of the faces in the crowd, but the commotion was making it hard to tell just what exactly was drawing them.

"Is there some kind of special mass going on today? Maybe for the poor sheriff's family? Doesn't it seem a bit early for that, though? Don't you think it's a bit early for something like that, Billy?"

"Yes, Mom," he said, wishing he had another answer but relishing the silence that came after.

Until he realized that the silence was simply masking his mother's fears, fears that echoed his own growing apprehension—fears that were only confirmed when they saw Mrs. Hickam stumbling hysterically through the crowd, her usual perfectly styled coif of a hairstyle limp and wild, resembling more of a bird nest than someone's hair. Her face was covered in dark soot and a sharp crimson that seemed to gleam in the sheen of the fog, a deep red that turned his stomach into a twisting pit of worms.

As the minivan pulled down the street and round the next corner, barely breaking five miles per hour, and rolled out of sight of the church, the whole scene seemed to sink out of reality, back into the miasma of his dreams. That is, until they heard the whistle of the ambulance and saw the burning red-and-white strobing lights reflected in the fog, like demon fire coming from the center of a tower of smoke.

Bruce shifted his weight in the cold plastic chair, the flimsy steel legs giving a screech of protest against the plaster tiles. The slow tick of the clock on the wall behind him, a simple black-and-white wall piece that reminded him of the type he used to stare at longingly in middle school, continued undisturbed by the frantic madness taking place just beneath it. Each tick was like a knife across his eardrum, sharp and piercing deep within his own psyche. Every one felt like it would be the last he would hear before some red-eyed doctor came to tell him the bad news. Yet the next second would come just like the one before it, completely unaware and unconcerned with Bruce's shoddy premonitions of grief. Every now and then, he would feel the acute strain on the side of his eye; and he knew it was twitching again, a regular occurrence under situations of extreme stress, like the one he found himself in.

It was hard work, waiting for someone to die.

He buried his face in his palms again, feeling like an ostrich making a futile attempt to bury its head in cement, but gave him a moment free from the blinding lights of the waiting room that seemed more at place back in the interrogation room, beating down on the sweating foreheads of nervous felons instead the heads of concerned friends and family. The LEDs flickered regularly, almost like they were on set intervals, and Bruce began to wonder if the hospital was intentionally trying to incite mental breakdowns to give themselves a little extra business.

The broad steel doors that led down the hallway to the operating room swung open regularly, sending a ripple of turned heads through the growing crowd. There were several small families sitting across from Bruce that he recognized as various nieces and nephews of the sheriff; a brother and his wife; as well as the sister-in-law of his brother that had passed away several years ago after a drug overdose. The sister-in-law looked close to an overdose herself, her eyes sunken and lips cracked and yellow, but at least she was in the best possible place for it. The track marks in the creases of her elbows were deep and dark circles, one of them scabbed red from being freshly torn open, probably just the night before while the sheriff was busy getting part of his skull and most of his shoulder blown off by the spray from a shotgun shell. How she had convinced the sheriff to look the other way so often, Bruce would never know, although he suspected John's devotion to his brother made him do a lot of things he regretted.

There were others there as well he didn't recognize, if only because they looked so terrible and sickly that they barely resembled anything human. All of them were trembling, clutching their stomachs and groaning, and Bruce thought it might be stomach flu until he saw the horrible gashes and cuts that marked each and every one of them. Their eyes were wide, with dark circles turning them into sinking pits, like those found in bare skulls; and their gazes drifted listlessly across the room, straying from person to person with a curiosity that set Bruce on edge.

Bruce shook his head, hoping to loosen up the clutter there: the visions of dark blood trickling through cracks and anemic wheezes of someone struggling to catch their breath when there was none to grab onto.

You should've been there. Said screw all with his concerns and been his backup. Maybe then he'd…

Another quick shake stopped the trail of thoughts before it led him someplace too dark to find his way back easily.

The door to the operating room hallway swung open quickly, and a man in a bloodied coat walked through briskly, his eyes focused and harder than diamond. They drifted over the circus that had been set up in his waiting room in the early-morning hours, complete with tumbling children and the curious gaze of vultures with cameras around their necks, and found their target in a secluded corner near the sliding doors that read "Emergency Room" in bright-red letters. He moved as stealthily as anyone covered in a good pints' worth of blood could move through a crowd of people, drawing eyes with him as he went; but any questions that came at him seemed to bounce right off and fall deflated in the asker's lap. He approached the woman and her children tepidly, crouching to his knees so that he was level with them in their similarly flimsy chairs, and waited for their gazes to meet his before he began.

"Mrs. Nottingull, thank you very much for waiting so patiently. If you'd like to come with me, I can fill you in on what's happening with your husband, if you're able," he said, his voice raspy but unreadable.

"Is he okay? Can you just tell me if my husband is okay?" she said with an air of franticness that seemed to be losing what little restraint it had.

Her eyes were a shade of crimson that would've caused many to think that she herself belonged in a sick bed, but the streaks of dampness down her face provided a better diagnosis. The children at her side—a boy of three years with curly blond hair and fat cheeks and a brunette girl of five with bright hazel eyes like her father—moved around awkwardly and confusedly, their own eyes dry and searching.

"Is Daddy back there, Mommy?" the girl asked excitedly, her face breaking into a sunrise of smiles.

The boy's sentiments didn't seem to match his sister's, and he quickly buried his face in the creases of his mother's burly sweater.

"Yes, sweetie, Daddy's back there," Ms. Nottingull assured, wearing a harlequin smile. When she turned back to the stooped doctor, her face melted back into one plagued by dark demons, her eyes seeming to sag into her cheeks with a sigh that seemed to stretch into the finites of eternity. "Is my husband all right, doctor? I'd like to be able to tell my kids that, at least, before we go back there to… see him."

The crowd of eyes halted their frenetic buzzing and centered on the pair, their interest making the air feel barbarous and toxic. Bruce let his fingers dig into the edges of his chair, his fingernails slowly pulling up and collecting pieces of loose plastic. It took all he had not to jump up and scream at all of them for their insensitive prerogatives—until he realized he was just as selfish as the lot of them, his gaze locked intently on the doctor's sweat-filled brow.

"He's stable… for now, although we're passing through the eye of the storm. There's still a lot we can't be sure of," he trailed off briskly, taking note of the collective sigh that rose like steam from the crowded room. "Ms. Nottingull, I really think it would be best for you and your children if we discussed this down the hall. I can give you a more thorough update on his condition and ask you some questions that would be answered easier without the live studio audience awe seem to have drawn. Besides, that way, you'd actually be able to see your husband as we discuss what our next action should be."

"What do you mean—?"

A stray cough silenced her final, agitated protest, her overwrought face making eye contact with several uncomfortable sympathizers before settling on Bruce's own, sending a twang of guilt and a wave of goose bumps over the ridges of his flesh. Her eyes seemed to sift through the contents of his soul but never flinched or gave any indication of the results of this probing. They seemed to be focused on something far off, dull and dimmed to the world passing by in front of them—a silent mask of defiance to the hell that it had become without so much as a warning. Bruce felt he could relate to her on that level, although he doubted she would've liked to hear it from him.

After several tense moments in which Bruce feared she would break down in the middle of the buzzing waiting room while looking at him, her attention snapped back to the doctor with the wrinkled khakis and frayed dockers.

"All right, Doctor, I understand. Come on, kids, we're gonna go check on Daddy," she said, her warm stare showing no signs of the haunted one that had faded, an apparition you see out of the corner of your eye but disappears when you attempt to look at it directly.

Shifting forward uncomfortably, Bruce planned on following after them, but a biting sense of trepidation held him back. Even though it had only been for a few seconds, the look Mrs. Nottingull had given him had been disconcerting enough to set his stomach bubbling. The doctor turned quickly and ushered the small family toward the double doors, Nora Nottingull prudently grabbing her daughter's outstretched hand and scooping her young son up into the cradle of her forearm, his face plagued by hesitations and misgivings that even his mother's gentle whispers couldn't calm. Eventually, the dam of newfound bravery shattered beneath the crushing weight of the unknown that awaited him beyond the long hallway; and he broke out into a series of long cries, his eyes and chubby cheeks shutting tightly until only tears could escape.

The doctor's face seemed to grow even more strained with this new stimuli, but he wore his practiced smile of bedside manner all the same, rushing the nuclear trio past the tan doors, a wail escaping back into the room before the door slowly slid and clicked into its airtight seal. The cry seemed to echo much longer than it should have, thick in the air like rain on a cloudy day, sticking to Bruce's skin as if it were condensation from the chills he felt passing through his body. He shook his head and dug his fingers deep into his ear canal, his finger bringing back a waxy souvenir in the process; but the cry continued unabated, mingling with the buzz of the overhead lights until the two became practically indistinguishable. Even slipping his cupped palms over his head didn't provide any relief, as he heard it rattling around in his cavernous skull, like loose baggage in a spacious trunk on a curving road.

Falling back in his chair, Bruce tried to close his eyes but only found more visions of blood, moans, and closed doors. His eyes shot open abruptly, and he quickly mourned for his nights of restful sleep, as he knew he would not be seeing them anytime soon. Several minutes passed in silence, Bruce struggling to focus on the tiled floor in front of him, the black-and-white spaces mixing into a dark whirlpool that seemed to hypnotize him as the seconds trailed off into the shapeless eternity the day had become.

"Holy shit, Bruce, there you are!"

He snapped up quickly, his ears pricked and his mind firing and sparking to determine where the voice came from. Asworth appeared in front of him then, coming from the side of his peripheral fast enough to make him jump back in his sight and exhale sharply.

"Sorry there, pal, didn't mean to spook you. I've been wandering all over the damn place, trying to find ya. I went by the cafeteria and the intensive care room twice before finally making my way over here. Never did I think they would have kept Sergeant Hulk cooped up in the waiting room this whole time. I figured you would've kicked the doors down to the operating room if they tried to keep your ass out, but I guess in light of the… uh, situation, you've managed to restrain yourself better than the rest of us have. Can't say I'm surprised about that either, really," he said, his eyes on the ground and his voice shaky and hoarse.

"Jesse… you were with him, weren't you? I mean, you were there when it happened, right?"

Asworth lifted his gaze long enough to meet Bruce's but dropped back to the floor quickly after, his mouth open and struggling to unstick the words from the roof of his mouth. It was then Bruce noticed his uniform, torn and bloodied with deep-set stains of crimson that ran from his chest and down to the cuffs of his pants. In some areas, the splotches were so thick that it weighed down the fabric and glistened in the light, deep lakes covering the barren teal landscape.

"Dammit, Bruce, I tried to do something, but… it was so fast. They always tell you it is. So fast you have to react on instinct alone, but I didn't think it'd be like *that*. The sheriff was calming them down, doing the same thing we've done maybe a thousand times before, in training and on the street, and then all of a sudden all you hear is this roar, so loud your ears don't stop ringing for minutes afterward, even as far back as we were. And the sheriff, he was there in front of me, and then he was gone in a flash of red. Took me a moment to realize he was on the ground and hadn't been blown clean to bits, but when I did realize it, I was too damn worried about my own ass to do anything about it.

"I felt it, Bruce. I felt the bullet whizz right by my fucking face. I heard it pass my ear like it was goddamn housefly buzzing too close. Then came the warm splash on my face, and that horrible way it trickles down… I… I thought I was dead, Bruce. I really did. I collapsed on my knees and waited for the darkness, but when the ringing finally stopped and I realized I was still sitting like that, kneeling in a bar parking lot, like some kind of fag, I threw myself against the back of the squad car and called for the ambulance, but I couldn't tell you how many minutes had passed. And the sheriff… he'd lost so much blood by then. I even saw it pooling underneath my feet behind the car. We're supposed to act by instinct, but what kind of instinct is that, where I just lay there and waited for death? I always thought… it'd be different… I'd be different. Goddammit, what the hell is wrong with me? What the hell is wrong with me, Bruce?"

Asworth's voice, despite its trembling, was growing louder, and the chorus of squeaking chairs behind him seemed intent on following his cue. He turned quickly and saw the waiting room watching them with concerned yet venomous glares. Mr. Habcock, the sheriff's longtime bowling partner, was giving him a look that suggested he would very much like to confirm the panicked officer's suspicions, and Georgina Lemon seemed ready to rally the people around her to a similar cause. Even the sheriff's sister seemed to manage to find enough energy for spite, her body more lithe and alert than he had ever seen it. The situation only worsened when Asworth broke out into a long, dreadful sob that rocked his whole body and sent his head into his hands. His long, tenuous fingers began pulling at his dark curls, moving between the wiry locks and coming back coated with that same sticky crimson stain that covered the rest of his body. Bruce felt a horrible pang of guilt for the weeping man before him then, strong enough to pacify the worms in his stomach—although the screech of a chair flying across the room was confirmation enough that the rabid mob behind him did not share his sentiments.

Bruce whirled around and saw Habcock walking across the room, his loafers clacking against the floor as fast as the beating of Bruce's manic heart. The scowling man darted around a small wooden table covered in ratty, old magazines strewn about lazily, and his leg collided with its wooden counterpart and sent the stacks spiraling to the ground beneath his feet—which crushed and tore through the pages, completely unaware of their presence. Fortunately, he was cut off by a large group of folks in white coats, several doctors Bruce recognized and several others he recognized as nurses from his many trips here during his years on the force. Many wore scrubs underneath their heavy autumn coats, and they pushed stretchers piled full of black medical bags and other loose equipment, including a defibrillator and gurney for morphine and any other fluids. They pushed through the group like a somber parade of melancholy, fitting all too well with the downcast lot that filled the room, and right out the automatic doors and into several waiting ambulances.

They loaded the stretchers into the back and climbed inside, the last doctor—whom Bruce believed to be named Gurlokovich—slamming his hand on the back of the door twice before swinging his leg over the back.

"All right, Jimmy, off to Saint Roma's Catholic, and ignore any and all stoplights, got it? You get us there before eight, and I'll buy all of you lunch today," he said before the door cut him off, the taillights of the ambulance glowing red hot and the engine screaming to life like a newborn.

Taking his chance, Bruce grabbed Asworth by the shoulders and spun him around the corner of the waiting room, out of sight of the masses and visible only to the abandoned information booth in the corner of the room. The maneuver seemed to catch the despondent officer off guard, his face quickly souring and turning vengeful while his hands quickly seized Bruce's arms and tried fruitlessly to push him off. The response quickly passed, and his chin crumbled back into his chest with another fit of heavy, body-shaking sobs.

"Get ahold of yourself, officer. Hey! You hear me? I need you to get ahold of yourself. I'm not asking you to forget what happened, and I'm not asking you to get over it right this goddamn second, but I am asking you to suck it up and act like you deserve that badge on your chest, at least in front of all those people out there. You got me? As soon as everybody gets word on the sheriff and this whole mess gets sorted out, you can quit the force and go make margaritas for octogenarians down in Cabo for all the shits I give, but until that happens, you need to do your damn job and help me keep the peace, you got that? Hm? There's a lot of angry, confused people out there, but most of all, they're scared, scared because their town sheriff, the man elected to protect them, just got part of his skull splattered all over a parking lot just down the street from where a lot of them live. And I can't blame 'em for that. But there's nothing more dangerous than a crowd of scared people looking for someone to blame. And right now, you spouting off about how it's your fault that John got shot in the face by some lunatic who's seen one too many bad movies isn't doing anything but kicking a hornet's nest, all right? If you wanna needlessly blame yourself, go ahead. You're as good a candidate as any. But don't give them a reason to hate the thing you represent, because if that happens, this powder keg is gonna blow up in our faces, and we're not gonna be able to do a damn thing about it. A group of terrified people is just as dangerous as a group of lunatics with guns. In fact, they often end being the same thing, and I'd like to deal with only one of 'em at a time, if possible. Besides, your reflexes seem fine to me," Bruce said while pulling away, nodding toward the vicelike grip Asworth had on his forearms.

When he pulled away, his skin was red and raw and ached something horrible, but he kept his demeanor imposing.

"It was that kid, Bruce, the senator's son. That goddamn sonuvabitch shot him point-blank, didn't hesitate or nothing, even celebrated afterward, whooping and hollering like he was possessed or drunk or high or… *something*," Asworth mumbled, distant and unfocused, his mind millions from its fleshy shell. "It's *him* they should be blaming."

"I'm sure plenty of them do, but we need to defuse the situation, not just redirect it somewhere else. Either way, the boy's in our custody, and if this crowd starts begging for his blood, they're gonna turn on us for not giving it to 'em. Besides, just a minute ago, you were ready and willing to take the blame yourself. What's changed your mind?"

Asworth's gaze met Bruce's briefly, a spark of anger passing between them; but with a quick grinding of his teeth, his eyes dropped down to the floor, defeated.

"Listen, Asworth. Jesse, we were at the academy together. Hell, we even went to high school together for a couple of years. I was moving out when you were moving in, but our circles crossed a couple of times. I remember seeing you jump off Rick Berringer's garage into an inflatable pool and break your damn coccyx. You've got courage. You're also pretty dumb and misplace it a lot of times, but there's no denying it. You've been in fights with junkies twice your size and didn't back down. You've even smashed a couple noses on the force back when they brought you in for those bar fights a couple years back. I've heard you tell the stories, even when some of the faces behind those broken noses are staring right at yours. Now you're gonna break down on me just because some punk kid took a couple cheap shots at you? I thought you were pretty resilient, but I guess I was wrong. Maybe you are just stupid."

The guilt seeped into his features quickly, weighing his head down and causing the torrents of tears to dam themselves in his puffy, red eyes. Several drops of blood were dripping from his sleeves, his uniform still damp and matted. The drops broke across the floor in small bursts, seeping into the cracks of the tiles, and Bruce was suddenly reminded of red wine stains setting into a dirty shag carpet, mixing with the yellow stains of nicotine into a dirty maroon.

"I'm sorry, Bruce. I'm… sorry you had to see that," Asworth murmured, shoving his dirty fingers into the corners of his eyes and wiping the glistening tears from his chaffed skin.

Bruce was speechless at first, lost in his drunken trance, his mind a dark tunnel that seemed to be filled with dead ends. After an incredulous look from the shamed officer, Bruce managed to find control of his tongue.

"It's no problem, Asworth. You can thank me by straightening up and showing me to the sheriff's room. I heard the doctor mention he's in stable condition, and I want to get a more thorough report from him."

Bruce managed to keep his voice steady and professional, his face still as corpse. Asworth nodded, his beady eyes smaller than usual and filled with contempt, which Bruce wasn't sure was meant for him or not. He started off toward the door, briskly passing by Bruce's side when he quickly grabbed his shoulder.

"And don't you worry about any of the boys on the force hearing about our little chat here. I've got a talent for keeping private things private."

A ghost of a grin passed over the officer's face, but the reminder of his wounded ego quickly soured it again. He ambled quickly across the waiting room, sparing a quick look at the collection of people whose attention was held by the parade of ambulances outside. In fact, there was a growing commotion centered around the sliding doors, the crowd circling around the entrance turning to each other and fighting for a clear look. Bruce made a mental note to come back and check the situation, defusing it if necessary, after he had quickly checked on John.

The trek was a long one, as the operating room and subsequent patient rooms were on the opposite side of the hospital. Asworth led with Bruce following closely behind, purposefully slowing his stride to hide any kind of impatience. They passed the children's wing first, with Bruce giving a quick wave to the nurses and a passing child rolling an IV stand and holding a ratty teddy bear. He tried to talk to the child, but he walked right by as if Bruce wasn't even there. The rehabilitation center was next, bustling and overcrowded as it had been the past few months with the growing pharmaceutical trade on the street. The new drug that John had mentioned earlier had not gone unnoticed on Bruce's patrols, with a good quarter of the arrests coming from his own squad car. Often, he drove alone, unless assigned to a violent offense that required backup, but that was based more off of a personal preference than any dismissal on account of the other officers. A lot of them would have loved to go out on patrols with Bruce, despite their personal misgivings, equating it as a chance for a promotion based on Bruce's own rapid ascension of the local precinct ranks. Asworth himself had mentioned it during the last function several members of the force had attended, one of the many charity benefits that seemed to deepen the pockets of the organizers more than it did of any actual charitable organizations, even offering a slice of his paycheck for the opportunity, which Bruce flatly denied.

They came upon the outpatient rooms next, passing a bed with an old man who looked like he could float away if the air conditioner was set too high. He was surrounded by several grieving family members, including a young woman Bruce recognized from one such benefit, her makeup a messy smear of rouge and mascara. The man beside her seemed more reserved; in fact, he almost looked worse than the man lying in the bed, his gaunt face tipping lazily from side to side. Bruce felt his chest cave in briefly but hardened his resolve and pushed forward after Asworth into the inpatient wing. They rounded a corner and passed another information booth, although this one was manned by a male nurse in dirty scrubs who mouthed a word of protest before spying Asworth's uniform and quickly swallowing it.

As they turned the final corner, they spied the sheriff's family gathered around the doctor from the waiting room. Mrs. Nottingull's hand was over her mouth, holding in muffled cries of anguish. The little girl at her side was in the same condition as her mother, although not managing it nearly as well, her loud cries audible down the length of the hallway. The smell of antiseptics and sickness made Bruce audibly gag and freeze in his tracks, his legs turning to jelly and his feet to stone. He bent over, placing his hand on the bumpy, plaster wall for support as he thought his breakfast was going to come roaring back up in a brilliant escape attempt. Asworth turned and approached him, but Bruce quickly waved him away, hoping with all his might that the sheriff's family was distracted enough to be completely unaware of his presence.

When he finally righted himself, he saw that this was the case and moved back to the information booth to find a trash can to spit in, to clear the acid flavor from his mouth. When he returned to the glass window that showed into the sheriff's room, Asworth was waiting for him and Mrs. Nottingull and her children had taken seats on the wall opposite, the disgruntled doctor nowhere to be seen. Mrs. Nottingull's face was in her hand, her other arm still wrapped tightly around her son. The boy still seemed unfazed by the scene in front of him, heedless and oblivious to the implications of his mother's behavior.

Bruce inhaled deeply, his eyelid fluttering and flirting with the idea of shutting themselves tightly. Fortunately, he found that he was stronger than his own intrusive thoughts and gazed upon the man in the room through the window. The sight almost sent him right back to the information booth trash, but he held his ground and stood firm.

"The doctor said he's stable now, but the shell tore off a good part of the right side of his face. He's completely lost the use of his right eye, and his hair… well, let's just say there's not enough skin left for it to grow from. Most of his skull is still visible, and they're looking for possible skin graft locations to try and repair some of the damage, but they don't know if his body will accept it in his weakened state. There's nerve damage everywhere on the right side of his body. The doctor said that one of the balls made contact with his spinal column and cracked it. Not enough to completely sever it, but deep enough where, if he does regain consciousness, most bodily functions will become a chore. Most of his teeth are gone, as well as part of his tongue, so speech will likely be impossible without some kind of therapist, and even then... They're not even really sure if he's gonna wake up. They have him stabilized now, sure, but they were forced to induce the coma when his vitals started failing, and with his condition, even if he does survive the necessary operations, getting him out of it is going to be considered something of a medical miracle."

"What happened to his..." Bruce stopped himself, turning to check if John's children had begun to pay any attention to the men near the window talking casually about their father's slow demise. Fortunately, the girl's face was buried in her mother's dress pants, and the boy's attention was held by the vending machine across the room. Lowering his voice, Bruce turned back to Asworth, "What happened to his goddamn arm?"

"They were able to salvage enough of his shoulder from the surrounding tissue to reconstruct most of the shoulder blade, but... the joint was completely shattered. The ball socket of the humerus was shattered, and the scapula couldn't even be found. Most of the nerves were gone, and if he even had any movement in it, he never would have been able to have any kind of control over it. It was a piece of dead flesh, and in the hopes of stabilizing his vitals, they removed the arm. Supposedly, the doctor said, it helped bring the bleeding and heart palpitations down to a more manageable level, but the guy seems like he's covering his own ass on that one," Asworth paused, looking around for a sight of the doctor with the dirty khakis but quickly finding that his scapegoat was nowhere to be found.

"I'm sorry, Bruce. I really am. Every time I replay it, I keep thinking, 'You could've stopped the guy. You could've saved him.' If I had been quicker, Bruce, if I had just been—"

"Not here. Don't you dare do that here."

The coldness in Bruce's voice silenced Asworth's stuttering and caused the man with the bruised ego to back away slowly, almost stumbling over his own feet. Any other time, any other situation, and he would've added some kind of pacification, but his mind was completely lost to its own shadows—the darkest ones he had spent his time in the waiting room trying so desperately to deny, and now they were staring him in the face and laughing at him.

The hall fell silent, save for the whirrs and beeps of the medical equipment beyond the glass, a silence so heavy it truly felt like an absence of sound. Everything sounded distant and echoed longer than it rationally should have. It was like someone had ripped open another dimension between him and the one he currently inhabited. Bruce found himself digging for some hidden reserve of strength, something he had always convinced himself he had, a possession buried underneath all the self-doubt and feelings of inadequacies he had battled with since he was young. When he found nothing but those very same insecurities, his fear got the better of him and he lashed out angrily against the dirty pane of glass, his fist slamming into it and rattling it violently. When it settled, Bruce had a hard time looking at anything other than the white splotches of dirt and dust on the pane that had seemed nearly invisible before.

When the hum of the vibrating glass finally disappeared into the net of silence, Bruce felt horribly alone, more so than he had felt in years. He had seen the crack in his usually tough veneer. More so, he had shown it to someone else, someone on the force, a sin he considered to be one of the most heinous in his moral code, one he had developed in his years of isolation and abuse—the same code that kept his hands steady when he heard the slurs behind his back, the same rules that held his lips firmly shut when the whispers about affirmative action being his saving grace and sole contribution to his promotion; it was what kept that young outcast, bullied for things forever beyond his control, from ever becoming a victim.

Yet here he stood, feeling pretty damn victimized, and by a callous rich punk who never got enough attention from Daddy in his all-too-comfortable childhood—the same type of kid that spent their time on the schoolyard by making sure Bruce knew just how different and out of place he was: the quiet, token Black boy who spent most of his free time buried in his schoolbooks than conversing with his classmates. They would often remind him that the only reason he got invited anywhere was because of the color of his skin, and it was for that same reason why true acceptance would always be just out of his reach.

Ah, his burned skin pigment—his supposed gift and apparent curse. He had never given much thought to it until the other kids started to mention it to him. It wasn't just from angry confrontations with bitter, bruised children either. It seeped into every one of his relationships, even in the most well-meaning ones, where they would find offense for him in places where he would have never thought to notice them or relate things to him that were supposedly appealing to him, like a new rap song from some artist that spelled their name with dollar signs or the release of some high-profile athlete's new line of shoes—all because of assumptions that his interests were based solely off of his skin color. Despite what he was told by his father, Bruce didn't see his skin as a reflection or contribution to his identity whatsoever.

Bruce quickly learned to shrug these instances off as an inevitable annoyance of the world, but it wasn't until high school that he found himself truly troubled by his own crisis of self—although his skin tone was not the shade contributing to that shadow of his soul.

"Bruce."

The word, despite being one so familiar and routine, took him by surprise, his eyes widening and his balance faltering. He saw her reflection in the glass, her blond curls wrapping around her slender shoulders and folding into the neck of her cherry sweater. Her eyes were raw and red as her sweater but shining from the presence of tears that had been wiped onto the meager clump of tissues in her fingers. Bruce examined her nails and saw that there was a flaking coat of green that covered maybe half of her stubby digits.

"Sarah. Sorry for not saying something sooner. I must not have seen you get up," Bruce managed, nodding toward the lone chair of knitted wool at the end of the hall, which now seated the sheriff's children—the young girl cradling her absentminded brother in her tiny arms, wiping her eyes on his shirt. He gave them a quick wave of his hand and his best attempt at a smile, although from their expressions, it seemed to come out as more of a grimace.

He quickly turned his gruesome, sagging face back to Sarah. "How are they holding up?"

"Carter's fine. He doesn't understand enough to really be affected. I imagine when it comes bedtime and his father's not there to tuck him in and read him a story, there will come some... hard questions, but until then, he's blissfully unaware," Sarah said, most of it coming out like a heavy, exasperated sigh.

"If only we could be so lucky."

A ghost of a smile passed over her face, but much like a real ghost, it didn't leave much evidence of its arrival, and her sorrowful countenance returned quickly. She sniffled and gave a sharp intake of breath, but Bruce was the only one who managed a dishonest chuckle.

"Becca, on the other hand, is... devastated, to say the least. I'm worried about her, but she's shut herself up pretty tightly and thrown away the key, it seems. She's barely answered me since we got here. Most of the time, she just nods at what I say, and the other times, she acts like she hasn't even heard what I said. She hasn't stopped crying long enough to sleep, but I'm hoping she'll tire out soon enough, and that might give her some relief, however momentary," Sarah said, her eyes glazing over and disappearing into the infinite reflection of the glass.

"And how are you doing, Sarah?"

Bruce regretted the words quickly when she turned to face him, her face hard and bitter like a winter wind. The bags under her eyes sunk deep into the pockets of her flesh, pulling the rest of the skin around her face taut and making deep lines where there hadn't been any days before. She looked like she had aged twenty years in several hours.

"How do you think I'm doing, Bruce? How does it look like I'm doing? My husband's missing half of his goddamn face and may never wake up again. My brother was murdered by a disgruntled employee, shot in the head with a bullet so large my mother won't be able to see him during the funeral. The television's been showing my husband's possible death on repeat for three hours, and my daughter's seen it countless times before I walked in on her watching it. Half of the town is talking about it, and the other half is in the waiting room, waiting to talk to me to 'see how I'm holding up.'

"Well, you wanna know how I'm holding up, Bruce? Huh? Do ya? I'm holding up pretty damn badly, Bruce. In fact, one could even say, I'm falling the fuck apart. I wanna lay in a dark room and pull my hair out by the roots. I want to bash my head against a wall until either the wall or my head turn to dust. I wanna feel like I can do something, instead of sitting around here, balling like some weak-willed tart who can't imagine functioning without her husband.

"When I lay down in bed for the night, he came in and kissed me good night, telling me not to wait up as he was expecting another late night. And when I woke up to an empty bed, I didn't give it much of a second thought. It was still dark out, maybe a few slivers of light breaking through the tree in the front yard but not enough to really call it day. I turned on the television without even looking at it. I like it as noise in the background while I fix breakfast and lunch for the kids. I even started cooking John his usual plate of eggs, always sunny-side up on Thursdays, with a couple slices of bacon. I suppose they're ice cold now, unsalvageable."

She choked up and turned away to hide her shameful tears but dismissed his attempts at comfort with a stiff finger and found solace in her clump of Kleenex.

"I didn't really hear what they were saying until I heard Becca screaming. She came running over and buried her face in my nightgown, and I looked up at the screen… And there he was, lying on his back in the parking lot of my brother's shitty bar. They blurred out the worst bits, most of his face, due to the damage. But I knew it was him. I could tell by the coffee stain on the lapel. Those horribly tacky shoes his grandfather gave him, the stubborn old ass. They showed a couple pictures of him next, mostly from old newspapers and his portrait for the force, even a few of me in some stupid green dress we wore to one of the hundreds of stupid, self-aggrandizing balls the vapid shrews of this town love to throw to feel better about their own callousness. I expect to have to go to another in John's honor before the month is done.

"You know what the worst part is, Bruce? They showed that stupid wretch's face more than they showed his, Bruce. They ran a whole fucking biography on the son of a bitch, talking about his childhood, his dad's election, what schools the little shit got thrown out of. They gave fifteen minutes to my husband, the man who kept them safe for nearly twenty years, and more than two hours to the dropout drug addict that shot him down in cold blood. I must've missed the minute they gave to my brother, although they had quite a bit to say about that Métier boy, as well…

"I'll never forget those faces 'til the day I die. I swear it. They're there when I close my eyes. They're there when my eyes are wide open. I even see them when I look at my children, for Christ's sake. The worst part is that, I want it that way. I'm glad that I can't forget what they've taken from me. And when I see it taken from them, their shallow, pathetic excuses for human life, my retribution will be like an enlightenment. Their faces, in that moment, will take the place of the ones I saw this morning. And I'll smile thinking of them before the nightmares take me."

Sarah's voice remained steady, never wavering, even though Bruce suspected her to break down into a million fleshy pieces at any moment. Her visage remained stony and removed, inaccessible to the sterilized world that surrounded it. Bruce opened his mouth to say something but quickly thought better of it and let his mouth hang there like some kind of dog in a hot car. Instead, he tentatively extended his hand, struggling to make sure it wasn't trembling, reaching for her far shoulder. Despite her vacant stare, her hand shot up quickly and swatted his meaty palm aside, lips curled in a bitter sneer.

"Some part of me still expects him to come home, despite everything that's happened, that he'll just wake up, throw off the blankets, and smile at me like he used to. When I went to sleep, he was fine—vibrant, hungry enough to eat two plates of dinner, enamored with some show the kids were watching, *alive*. When I woke up, he was like this—dead to the world, for all intents and purposes, a shell of the great man he used to be, one that will never possess a tenth of who he truly was, a husk. How could so much change in what feels like an instant? For a few blissful minutes, when I was still half asleep, I even thought everything was fine, that nothing had changed.

"I expected him home. I expected him crawling in bed, smelling of your obnoxious cologne, but I expected him home and safe."

The worms in the pit of Bruce's stomach seemed to combust spontaneously and fly up his esophagus as he choked down his breakfast. He waited several moments in a silence that made the hallway seem miles long, unsure if he had heard her correctly or if his own dark dreams had burst from his troubled head, crawling through his ear canal and birthing themselves into this hideous new world. What he had thought was reality mere moments ago turned out to be nothing but a fantasy, and his nightmares were the only real truth.

"What… what are you talking about, Sarah? Don't tell me you're also upset about John and I riding together so often, because I get enough of that from the guys at work, and I don't think this is the time—"

"Don't treat me like I'm an idiot, Bruce. If there's one thing I don't need right now, it's to be patronized by my husband's little fuck toy. Did you honestly think I didn't know?" she said, her eyes weighing him through the honest reflection of the glass.

Noticing his wide eyes and trembling lip, she scoffed and managed a small, gravely chuckle that would've rivaled Clint Eastwood in gruffness.

"Jesus Christ. You thought nobody knew, didn't you? Dear God, are you dense? And here I thought my husband enjoyed you for your intelligence, but it seems he was just interested in dark skin and a tight ass. Figures."

Bruce found his knees weak, transparent even—like he was floating on some type of wind current that was pulling him away from the wreck that was engulfing his paltry but contented life.

"I don't… I don't know what you're going on about, Sarah, but I think you need to lie down before you do anything else. Your mind's obviously not handling the stress very well," Bruce said, trying his best to look imposing, his voice a cadence deeper than usual, but it only made his accuser break into another spasm of hoarse laughter.

"I'll admit, you put on a good show, but you haven't been able to fool me about which team your bat swings for a single day. You think I don't notice the way you look at him when you two talk? You think I don't notice the way he talks about *you*? The way his eyes drift off into places I haven't been able to take them since before we were married. The fact that on the rare occasion John does perform his husbandly duties, he takes me from behind, grunting like some kind of injured animal caught in a trap. I'm not a moron, Bruce. Most people in this town may be, but I'm not."

Her expression remained cold yet bristling with satisfaction at her newfound control. She was actively enjoying every second of her condemnation.

"Listen, Sarah, you're confused. You don't know what you're saying. You're in mourning, and grief can make people think crazy, ridiculous things, even make them act on suspicions that were dismissed as batshit insane before. And let me tell you that what you're suggesting definitely falls into that category," Bruce reasoned, hoping to dodge the flaming wreckage that was about to crush him.

"Let's get one thing straight, Bruce, before we continue. I loved my husband. I loved him more than life itself at one young and foolish part of it, but this grief is not for him. Personally, I hope the bastard never wakes up, but unfortunately, things aren't that simple, and my poor, loving husband is clinging to thin, fraying strings of his life like a cockroach. My brother, despite being a class A prick, was family and most of these tears have been for him, but if you tell me that I'm too distraught or too frail to know what I'm talking about again, this conversation is over, and everyone will hear about the sheriff and your late-night ride-alongs. I swear to God, Bruce, if you deny me one more time, I will tell Officer Asslick over there about my 'suspicions' as soon as he gets back from shuffling his feet in front of the vending machine, and we'll see just how crazy he thinks they are. How does that sound?"

She received her answer from the depths of Bruce's silence.

"That's better, although part of me, a very large part, in fact, would absolutely revel in hearing you admit it. Call it closure, or smugness, if you must, but I need to hear it from your own cock-sucking lips."

Bruce took the comment in stride. It was one he endured throughout most of his high school career until he dispelled the rumor with an arrangement from one of his close friends, agreeing to tell everyone that the other had taken their virginity so that their own actual preferences could remain… private. Still, it took all his will to stare his attacker head-on and muster a curt nod.

"And if I could take it back…" the words caught in his throat, weighing more than he ever thought they would, "I would, but what does telling everyone now accomplish? All you're doing is tarnishing your husband's legacy, and if that truly means nothing to you anymore, think about your kids. It might mean nothing to them now, but you're gonna curse them with that burden? Make them resent their father as much as you do? I understand that you're upset. You feel betrayed, cast aside. I get it. We've all been there at some—"

She slapped him hard, too fast for him to react with anything but shock. The shame came later, like a bad aftertaste that sits in the back of your mouth—a liquor that's horrible taste wasn't worth the miserable buzz.

"Don't you dare to presume you know what I'm going through, you sick fuck. You've never given your life to someone, your trust and your entire being to someone, only to have them throw it aside like it was a bad birthday gift. To be strung along by someone that… pitied you, used you for their own lurid agenda. You have no idea what I had to put up with. The rumors I had to put up with from all the onlookers, the questions from my family, from the other ass-kissers on the force confused about why John never seemed to want to ride with anyone else, from the stuck-up bitches at every social event, making light jokes about my greatest shame like it was nothing to them. Even getting my hair done would raise a flurry of questions about whether or not our sex life had recovered from the tailspin, prodding me with questions inspired by their own husband's hearsay. I deflected them with lies and half truths, screaming inside myself, wishing I had someone to talk to about the self-loathing that comes with finding out that your whole life has been someone else's charade—someone to tell me that, despite the fact that every loving embrace and tender word had simply been a facade, I still mattered.

"I thought about killing myself, you know, taking a razor blade and heading into the bathtub and slicing right down to the bone. Give him the rest of me, even if he never really wanted it. Put that on his conscience, if he even had the remains of one left. At least, then, it would feel like my entire life hadn't been for nothing," her voice trailed off to a whisper, her glossy eyes turning back to the corner chair, taking in the sight of her children asleep in each other's arms, like water in a desert.

"If it wasn't for them, I would've done it. I couldn't bear the idea of them walking in to find me instead of him, let alone the thought of them growing up without me. A naive part of me even feared the thought of you raising them, although, let's be honest, there wasn't a snowman's chance in hell of that happening. Even if that spineless bastard's balls got big enough to remarry, it certainly wouldn't be to some faggot. Too many questions would be asked. Too many suspicions would be confirmed. This town would tear you apart and bury you deep down with the rest of its mistakes without even a second thought or a question of conscience.

"But now it's him who's lying there, at death's door and me who's standing here with you, which leads us back to what's going to happen now that we're both aware of what the other one knows and where they stand. Obviously, you want your precious little tryst to remain private. Otherwise, it will raise a lot of very obvious, detrimental questions about your rapid advancement in the precinct. I, on the other hand, would love nothing more than to expose you for the queer piece of shit that you are, but there are factors at play that make doing so difficult. Fortunately for you, Bruce, my husband is still clinging to his wretched excuse for a life, and that complicates things. Despite my husband's treatment of me in the past, I'd get eaten alive if I left him now, no matter what the reason. My husband's injuries have bought him a clean slate in the eyes of this town, and I'm not gonna risk my own self-destruction just to spite my husband's new screw.

"However, if my precious husband has enough good sense to die, I will collect a very healthy life insurance policy, along with a settlement from the senator, I'm sure. I'll be a widow, the most pitiable creature you can find on this planet, and you will have nothing except the lies you've lived for all these years. And lying has never been your strong suit. So I would pray for my husband, Bruce, and make sure you pray loudly, because he's your only protection from the wolves out there."

She turned on her heel and started back toward the softly stirring children, leaving Bruce to his thoughts, which had begun to eat him alive.

Yet halfway through her stride, she turned back and caught his gaze with her own and pulled him in against his overwhelming desire to keep focused on the terrible tile work that matched those of in the waiting room—his own personal purgatory.

"When I told you that I'd see those two gun-crazed bastards that did this every night before I fall asleep? Do you know how I know? How I'm so sure? Because for the past three years, your face has already been there."

With that, she floated back to her chair as if in a dream, leaving Bruce's tongue twisted and obstructing his throat, suffocating him. He was horribly aware of the beeping of the EKG in the other room, his body numb to everything else except for his own ragged breaths. Bruce tried to steady his fists but, for the first time in a long time, found himself unable to do so, his body no longer feeling like his own.

The hum and rattle of the heat coming from the vents kept a gentle buzz of electricity in the air of fourth-period math with Mrs. Bell—a class that was generally used as mature version of nap time by most of the students, her stilted and monotone cadence melting into a drone of white noise. Gwen felt bags of iron hanging beneath her eyes but still found them unable to close without resistance; and even then, it wasn't long before they were open again, darting about the room to make sure the dream hadn't ended.

She still wasn't entirely convinced she hadn't just fallen asleep early last night before sneaking out and everything around her wasn't some elaborate recreation of her life plagued by her oncoming psychotic breakdown. Her hands still felt sticky despite how many times she had run them under the water before leaving the house that morning, a peculiar act her mother had inquired about; but Gwen had dodged with a brisk deflection, inquiring about the scripture her mother had recited in the chapel that morning. The holy prophet had swallowed it for the time being, knowing it to be an outright dismissal of her question, although Gwen was expecting to pay some kind of penance when she got home. Another part of her was already thinking of a way to circumvent this given punishment without her mother's knowledge, inspired by her newfound disbelief in reality.

It had to be a dream. She had practically floated into school, disgustingly *eager* to be there on the off chance that he would see his face amidst the crowded halls, even though she had only caught glances of him several times before last night. It was strange, feeling this excited about something again.

Oh, and let's not forget that she had seen a corpse pull itself from its own grave and attempt to devour Range's leg, which had definitely been strange, as well. In fact, her whole complacency about the whole situation seemed to only confirm her suspicions regarding the authenticity of her reality. She was simply dreaming, curled in her stiff, itchy blankets, getting tangled and uncomfortable and falling prey to her own fucked-up subconscious. Given her living situation the past entirety of her existence, there was no way her subconscious wouldn't be ruined beyond repair. It had to be a dream.

There was no way she would feel this way, this good, after what happened—or in general, over something as asinine as a boy, and a really odd one at that. Sure, he was something to look at. Even now her muscles tense just thinking of him, but there was no denying that he gave off troubling vibes. Somehow, it didn't seem to matter, and she found herself completely and terrifying smitten with someone she barely knew. The very idea of him, his very essence, seemed to fill her with a painful kind of hope, to fill this part of her that she never thought could be filled—a piece wedging itself into place at the edge of a puzzle, uncomfortable only in its unfamiliarity.

Stacey's sharp jab to her shoulder blade with her pencil snapped her out of her fantasies and excuse-making and down into the horrifying realization that all this was truly real. A thin square of folded notebook paper followed over her throbbing shoulder, plopping lightly on her notebook, sliding over her messy attempts at figuring out the logarithmic variable of z. With a quick glance to see Mrs. Bell's dour face nearly buried in the blackboard, Gwen snatched it and cradled it into her lap, working at its corners to get at the nougat of necessary class-time gossip inside.

"You look tired!" it read, a bright-red winking smiley face staring into her soul.

Gwen felt her face redden despite herself and kept her head down in hopes of preserving her dignity.

Grabbing her own pencil from the small rut at the top of the plywood desk, Gwen quickly scribbled back a short reply, hoping to end the conversation with an air of nonchalance.

"It was a long night," it read, smiley-less.

Bending her arm beneath her seat, she managed a quick flick that landed in Stacey's own notebook from the sound of scraping paper. Within moments, the paper carrier pigeon came flying back to her desk, grazing her ear.

"Is that some kind of dick pun?" Another damned winking smiley.

"Umm, no," Gwen replied, her toss missing the desk entirely and landing at Stacey's feet.

Gwen tried to tell herself that it wasn't because her hand was shaking, but her face suddenly felt a thousand degrees warmer.

"So did you two hook up at all?"

"Nope."

"Well, that's lame." A frowny face this time, with *lame* underlined several times to highlight its importance with an, oh, so subtle emphasis.

"If you say so. We just had a good time."

Gwen switched tactics, hoping that her inclusion of a smiley would placate her friend for the time being or, by its inclusion, convince her friend that something had gone horribly wrong with her and to call the nearest mental hospital.

The next message bounced off the back of her head, sending her hand to swat at it and grasp only her own hair. She turned and gave her friend a dark look, hoping it would hide her blushing cheeks, but the laughing sneer she got as a response didn't give her high hopes. Grabbing the small square from the top of Stacey's desk, Gwen gave her another quick death stare before turning back to Mrs. Bell, making sure her lesson on logarithmic division was undisturbed by their nearly silent communication before unfolding its message.

"You lying slut!" A smiley face with a large X for its eyes, mimicking a squeal of delight. Well, so far, her plan was working just perfectly.

"I swear, we didn't."

"Oh, come on, Gwennie. You know you can tell me." This smiley was plain and pretty mild mannered compared to his brethren. Still, his stupid grin pissed her off.

"I can tell you, we didn't do anything."

Stacey broke out in a small fit of coughing, with a clean rip of notebook paper muffled underneath. After a few seconds of rabid scribbling, a new unblemished square bounced off her pencil and sent it spiraling to a corner of her desk.

"So you're saying you just sucked his cock?"

Gwen twirled around quick enough to give her a stronger stink eye, increasing Stacey's stifled laughter and making her snort loud enough to draw the attention of Ryan McCaffrey and Jenny Slate behind them. McCaffrey shared an exasperated look with Stacey, whispering something to her that resulted in a swift kick to his shin beneath his desk. He cried out in pain, loud enough to draw Mrs. Bell's attention away from the chalkboard and to their isolated corner in the back of the classroom.

"Something the matter, Ryan?"

"No, Mrs. Bell, I just jerked myself too violently, and I injured myself."

This triggered a series of sniggers from several people nearby, mostly other members of the football time who had used the joke plenty of times before, each thinking they were more original than the last.

"You jerked yourself?"

"My leg, I mean, banged it on the leg of the desk. They really oughta make these things wider, you know, Mrs. Bell? I'm sure some of the larger students have a hard time fitting into them," Ryan said confidently, his look shifting to Stacey, who had turned to face her victim with a wide smile on her face, which quickly soured after he finished.

She sent another small jab with her pointed Abercrombie moccasins into his shinbone. Ryan cried out again, louder this time, cutting a curse word short as his head cleared and he remembered Mrs. Bell's presence.

"I see your point. Maybe we'll have to tell Coach Rutley to give you some extra sprints to burn off the calories."

A more resounding chorus of laughter erupted from the room, eager to share in the shaming of their own when instigated by the person who usually put an end to anything of the sort. Gwen even found herself laughing, even though she didn't find the remark especially witty or even particularly funny. It simply felt natural, or right, like she was in on some greater shared secret that went unspoken. It was something she hadn't really experienced before but felt nostalgic for all the same.

The laughter was silenced by a sharp rap on the door. The fist, draped in crystals by the frosted glass, pounded heavily against it, shaking it in its frame and making a rattle loud enough that Gwen was sure it was going to smash right through. Her breath caught in her throat, flashes of the creature's pale, haggard skin coming with each crack of the wood, getting louder and louder to the point where it looked like it was going to explode in a maelstrom of splinters and shards of glass. Gwen covered her ears with her hands, hoping the ghastly rattling would stop, but it only grew louder, to the point that everything was one gruesome wail, a wave of sorrow and desperation that seeped pain into everything it touched.

The bubbling cacophony imploded into a vacuum of noise, Gwen suddenly aware of her own heavy breathing and wanting desperately to wake before this dream turned even more foreboding than it already had. The door to the hallway creaked open slowly, every inch tightening and tensing her muscles. Finally, a greasy skull poked its way in through the modest opening, so quickly that its horn-rimmed glasses nearly flew from its sloped ears.

"Mrs. Bell, I need you to turn on the television and turn to channel 9," Principal Macklin said, pushing his glasses higher to the bridge of his bulbous nose.

"What? Why? I wasn't told about this," she rebuked, erasing her most recent series of equations before turning to face the squat man with her broad arms poised at her hips.

"It's an emergency, Regina. I don't have time to explain. I just need you to do it. I've got at least two dozen other classrooms to stop in," he said, already disappearing back through the strange portal he seemed to arrive in, as a herald of something unusual in the never-ending gray of the mundane that most school days became.

"But I'm in the middle of a lesson!" Mrs. Bell protested, slamming the eraser into the steel shelf at the bottom of the chalkboard, a curtain of chalk dust rising around her.

"Just do it!" Macklin said, reappearing in the doorway like a demon, his eyes wild and bulging.

His face was beet red, his cheeks flushed, and the veins in his neck bulging with an undeterminable rage that didn't fit well with his usually jovial features. Just as swiftly as he appeared, he was gone, back into the buzzing glow of the hallway, the clacking of his cheap shoes sounding off the freshly shined linoleum. The large wooden door at the front of the room, decorated with posters of giraffes counting apples and cats inspirationally hanging from branches, had truly become a door to the extraordinary.

Still looking like she had been bitten and petrified by some kind of unseen insect, Mrs. Bell shuffled uncomfortably over to the television set suspended in the opposite corner of the room. Stretching on her toes, she brought the old monstrosity of technology back to life and shifted it away from the glare of the windows.

"All right, let's see what's so damn important that it had to interrupt me teaching his damn students," Mrs. Bell mumbled, the swears softer than the rest to preserve some sense of decorum in front of her onlooking audience of the continually unimpressed, also known as teenagers.

Gwen's heart rate had slowed back to its natural rhythm, but the hairs on her arms still stood at attention, radars tuned to any slight disturbance that would signal the coming of whatever terror she sensed was lingering just on the day's horizon.

The screen remained a dark mirror, showing the curious audience their own craned necks and inquisitive glares. A flash of static burst across the dingy glass canvas, sending Gwen jumping in her seat and her hands to the steel bars that made up the frame of her desk, her fingers wrapping around it like pythons. This incited a round of giggling from behind her, but she barely noticed it, her attention lost to the torrential waves of fuzz.

Eventually, a colored picture slowly burned its way onto the shaded screen, the channel 9 news logo appearing in the bottom-right corner and the familiar and oddly comforting yellow ticker slowing drifting across the bottom. A relatively attractive young woman with a petite nose and eyes that carried bags crudely covered by a poorly matched cover was speaking frantically and waving her arms wildly at a throbbing mass of people behind her. A lot of her makeup looked streaked and smudged, moved by sweat and tears and passing hands. Unfortunately, the sound was still miles behind the picture, the speakers grumbling to a reluctant start.

"Oh, shit! I hope it's about those dudes who robbed that bar last night and lit up, like, half the police force. Those guys were gangsta as fuck! I didn't think we had trapped motherfuckers like that around this shithole," Bryan Fuller whispered excitedly from several desks back, several intermingling voices muttering their agreement.

However, the banner above the ticker seemed to be telling a different story entirely.

Missing Girl Found! it declared with a modest enthusiasm, but the looks on everyone's faces indicated that celebration was the last thing on anyone's mind. In fact, it looked more like a bomb had gone off, or as if someone had shot up a school… Gwen's heart decided to leap into her throat, apparently planning a suicide with or without her consent. Ashamedly, her mind conjured an image of Range with a high-caliber weapon, stalking the halls and whistling his dark tune for her; but she angrily shook the thought away, wanting to slap herself for being so foolish. The shifting crowd revealed a sign that bore a giant cross in its center above its heart, the words *Roma* and *Catholic* briefly visible, and setting most of Gwen's fears to an anxious rest.

The sound kicked in sharply, the reporter's rapid ramblings coming off as some kind of strange performance art or an alien language heard through a short wave radio, almost entirely unintelligible until she slowed to a long breath and managed to calm herself.

"The scene here is still wild and disorganized with many concerned citizens showing up to see the girl, many of which are already declaring her to be some kind of divine miracle, and so far no one has been critically injured although several fights broke out earlier for room inside the church, with the small police presence here doing its best to keep everyone orderly but struggling due to a lack of leadership following last night's shooting of town sheriff, Johnathon Nottingull."

There was a scream followed by a tremor that shook the camera, and the resulting picture became a jumbled mess of legs and the leaf-strewn lawn. The slow crunch of dead leaves and static followed as the camera readjusted, trying to find its center of focus on the young girl's blouse and zooming in close enough to examine each individual crater and pore in her skin. It pulled back, framing her in the center of a tangled mess of writhing bodies and limbs, several officers struggling fruitlessly to pry people apart while also deflecting blows that were directed at their own faces, with several returning some of their own and eventually joining in the chaos.

The young girl holding a microphone that seemed larger than the total volume of her head, its soft mesh cover twisted and mangled out of its usual spherical shape, was panting heavily—which didn't help glamorize the ruffled collar of her blouse torn and dangling limply from her shoulder and exposing a gratuitous amount of skin and a lacy turquoise bra strap. Gwen would've had an easier time believing that she was a lonely housewife waiting on a well-endowed pizza boy instead of a reporter getting ready to deliver news that had seemingly shook the foundation of an entire congregation.

"As you can see, it's a very dangerous atmosphere here right now, Ryan. People are tense, scared, and teetering on the edge of full-blown madness, a riot simmering beneath the surface, ready to go off like an unstable stockpile of powder kegs. For those of you just joining us, I'm Lacey Chabert for channel 9 news, and I'll do my best to summarize exactly what we know so far. Most of this information has not yet been confirmed by the police department, with the shooting of Sheriff Nottingull leaving no de facto leader in place to issue any such kind of update or confirmation about the situation and its state going forward. All that we know has been gathered from members of the congregation here at St. Roma's Catholic Church at the cross section of Elm Street and Crystal Boulevard near the center of town.

"Father Jeffrey Jones, head of the diocese here at Saint Roma, while preparing for a sermon this morning, heard strange noises coming from the basement of the church and went to investigate, along with the local head of the Home Owners' Association, Gloria Hickam, who was there planning an upcoming fund-raiser for the Frannie Peabody Association to be held there later this month. In one of the boiler rooms at approximately 7:30 a.m., they stumbled upon the emaciated and ravaged body of Sarah Marsden, whose remains had been missing since last Saturday when they were stolen from a local cemetery by a groundskeeper there, Marshall Meers, whose whereabouts are still unknown.

"However, when Father Jones and Mrs. Hickam stumbled upon the body, they were surprised to see that not only was Mrs. Marsden breathing but was fully animated and seemingly conscious. Those following the story will know that Sarah Marsden was murdered by her boyfriend, Clark Porter, several weeks ago in a trial that managed to capture the attention of the entire state due to its particularly brutal details. The couple were seen going to a concert earlier in the night, where several friends reported seeing them arguing but were unable to hear most of what the argument was about. After returning home, the argument seemingly continued, with neighbors reporting hearing lots of shouting and objects slamming, but this had apparently been a regular occurrence with the couple, and neither witnesses reported anything to the police. Sarah Marsden was found the next day in their apartment, having received numerous injuries, mostly to the head, with a hammer, while Mr. Porter was nowhere to be found. He was arrested later that day at a known associate's, reportedly packing a large suitcase filled with his life savings in cash and several pounds of illegal narcotics. As of this morning, Mr. Porter remains in custody at Charleston Correctional until his trial later this year.

"So far, several medical professionals have arrived and tried to remove Ms. Marsden from the premise, hoping to treat her and examine her further in the pursuit of attempting to explain this medical mystery that has completely baffled every doctor that has gotten a chance to look at the young woman."

The program cut quickly to the haggard and stubbled face of a man in scrubs, a surgical mask hanging limply from one ear. A dark sludge stuck out against the bright green fabric, looking like sewage made of some kind bodily fluids that Gwen didn't dare attempt to identify. A banner identified him as Dr. Jacob Marcus, before quickly pasting the words "Dead Woman Found Alive" over it for anyone who was too disinterested to be paying attention to the smaller, tedious details.

"It defies pretty much everything we know about medical science. Her pulse is virtually nonexistent. The heart muscles move just enough to circulate blood to the limbs and brain, tensing and relaxing, like some kind of electric shock is continuously passing through it. Her spinal column is still completely shattered like the previous autopsy confirmed. Part of the brain stem is even exposed, and through soft, accidental contact during the examination, we were able to get the only physical response from her. Every other part of her body seems to be under her control but immune from any kind of sensory responses from the central nervous system. During our attempts to restrain the patient, she received several injuries, such as breaking the digits on her left hand, but exhibited no signs of pain or even acknowledgment of her injuries."

"Now, Doctor, you said you attempted to restrain Ms. Marsden," Lacey Chabert of channel 9 news interrupted from off camera, "what exactly do you mean by that?"

Dr. Marcus paused for a moment, his mouth opening without a sound to accompany it.

"The patient is... resistant to our attempts to help her. Father Jones and Mrs. Hickam were attacked by the poor girl when they found her, both receiving several serious injuries. Mrs. Hickam has been moved back to Saint Jude's Memorial for proper care and sterilization of the wound."

"Sterilization?"

"Yes, one of her injuries resulted from the patient's bite, and although many people wouldn't think it, the human mouth is one of the greatest hosts to bacteria and leads to most wounds getting infected within the first couple hours. Father Jones insisted that he was fine but is currently being treated in the church rectory to make sure."

"What do you think is causing her to behave this way, Doctor?"

"Well, it's obvious from our cursory examination that her injuries are severe, obviously, since they were enough to have her declared dead several weeks ago. She seems to have received several fractures and cuts that would normally render a normal human being unconscious, so it leads me to believe that she is purely running on adrenaline and is suffering a kind of 'adrenaline high,' if you will. Her mind has completely shut down, and her survival instincts have been peaked for so long, in conjuncture with the brain injuries received, her id seems to have completely taken over. Right now, she is little more than a frenzied animal, not that she shouldn't be treated with the utmost respect and care. However, it's safe to say that all reason and logic are concepts completely out of her reach."

The scene returned quickly to Lacey Chabert's bedraggled face, looking off screen at something that was causing her eyes to glisten and flutter. A quick whistle and hand prompt, barely concealed by the corner of the frame, brought her attention back to the camera, although every now and then, her eyes would dart back to the obscured scene, with more worry sagging into her features every time.

"That was a report from local cardiologist and head of the Medical Science Division at Saint Jude's Memorial, Dr. Jacob Marcus, who was by no means able to accurately and precisely diagnose the patient with complete scientific certainty but was able to provide a medical look into what many believe and are claiming to be an act of God."

A small woman with cheeks wider than the pixie cut she wore and a dress that was wide enough to cover her excessive girth and still reach the ground took over the screen.

"Now, listen here, Lacey, I've seen that poor woman, and I can tell you with 100 percent certainty that this was an act of our Lord and Savior Jesus Christ. She is a modern-day Lazarus, meant to bring us a message from our Father who art in heaven. I don't know how anybody could look at her and see anything different, especially these doctors who always claim to be so intelligent yet can't figure out something as simple as a miracle."

The irate woman was cut off before the rest of her rant continued into its illogical conclusions, and Gwen feared her own mother would appear next to continue the agitated sermon, but her fears were allayed when an older gentleman whom Gwen recognized from the thrift store in the few haunted blocks of the downtown shopping district took her place. He was often in there, working the front counter from ten to nine, eager to discuss his new finds and long-held trinkets and treasures with anyone who would listen. Every time he made a sale, he would grin at the small picture of his wife stationed next to the register.

"It's the end-times, that's what it is. People around here are saying it's a message from God, but they're only half right. It's a warning, that's what it is. Revelations foretold all this, and I plan on enduring the worst of it from my living room with my shotgun and a cold beer."

The man's wrinkled jaw curled up into a whispered grumble as he turned, the scene switching as the back of his plaid jacket came into view, green-and-red stripes blurring into one. A younger woman replaced him, her hair up in a style that looked at home in the back few pages of a *Cosmopolitan*, a smear of makeup splattered across her face and a look of concern that seemed as disingenuous as the chest stretching out her sweater.

"A lot of people are speculating on what happened to that poor, emotionally and physically abused woman, but all I can think about is how horrible her experience must have been. To have been vandalized by that a brute of a man of hers then to be buried prematurely like an unwanted family pet, only to then be kidnapped by that sick pervert Meers. I'm just glad her nightmare is finally over, and she can attempt to rebuild the pieces of her life. I'm just so grateful, the wonderful and immaculate Gloria Hickam, whom I have the honor of being dear friends with, was able to end this woman's suffering at the cost of her own safety and well-being, and I will be sending all my prayers to her and Ms. Marsden."

Her thin veneer of a smile ended just before the camera cut away, a look of disgust freezing on the screen before the transition to a dark new background that was dirty enough to smell through the screen. Ratty towels hung from rust-encrusted pipes that stretched through the dark recesses of the ceiling into the far abyss, dark spots dripping from the rickety holes onto a gathering of people crammed in between the walls. The light from the camera infinitely brighter than the measly 60-watt bulbs that hung limply from the rotting ceiling penetrated deep into the darkness but was blocked by the squirming mass of confused people desperately trying to squeeze into a doorway that would adequately hold two mid-sized people side by side but was currently occupied by what seemed like more than two dozen. The young reporter, looking like she had been drenched by a freak rainstorm on her trip down into the bowels of the church, wiped a quick line of sweat from her brow and tried in vain to fan herself, an extra button on her blouse undone and revealing a small crucifix dangling just beneath her clavicle.

Following an unseen signal, she nodded and went into another speech, preparing viewers for the graphicness of the footage that was promised to follow. There were excited whispers from the anxious room of pent-up teenagers lurking just behind Gwen's line of sight.

She could feel the tension in the room, like a static charge before a summer storm, and the ones this late into autumn tended to be the worst of the year. Gwen turned and saw Ryan McCaffrey leaning over the sidebar of his desk with it digging into his side, talking to Bryan Fuller eagerly with fingers pointing at the screen and going back to their chests in a mock imitation of a large pair of tits, before giggling like girls that had yet to grow their own. Behind them, Mallory Green had become disinterested in the program and was checking her phone with the screen beneath the top of her desk, buried in a massive fold in her skirt but was growing frustrated by its lack of signal.

"Now that we have given enough time for our more squeamish viewers to properly leave the room, we will now attempt to get footage of Ms. Marsden with special permission from Dr. Marcus and Deacon Knopner, speaking on behalf of Father Jones."

An unbreakable curtain of people had gathered round the perimeter of the room, blocking all sight of the main attraction of this modern-day freak show, camera flashes and digital shutter clicks sounding like gunfire in a war zone. Flashing her media badge with a smile that thinly veiled her contempt for the flapping heads that blocked her career-making shot, Lacey Chabert gently pushed through the enraptured onlookers, pausing just before the inner ring and taking a breath deep enough to be noticeable before turning to face her own dark reflection in the camera lens with a bright smile.

"Again, we warn our younger and more squeamish viewers to look away as Ms. Marsden's appearance is reportedly graphic. And now, channel 9 will show you your first glimpse of what some people are already calling the greatest medical breakthrough of the twenty-first century."

Lacey waved aside the final gawking stragglers, some turning angrily before seeing her laminated badge and large, obviously expensive camera and moving aside with a difficult groan or sideways glance that channeled strings of curse words left unsaid. The camera pushed through, first coming upon a lone stonewall, blank and bare save for a calendar dated December 1989 and several small pamphlets hanging askew from colorful thumbtacks. Gwen's heart felt ready to explode, her pulse going so fast that it was hard to distinguish each beat from the following three.

And with a slow pan, Sarah Marsden came into view in all her horrible, deteriorating glory. She swung an arm at an aide trying to wrangle her into a submission, who didn't appear to be making any progress, her skin hanging loose and limp from her bones, torn and twisted in fleshy knots. Its tone was a murky gray that looked like a bog, specked with flecks of green rot and decay and yellowed around the edges of large patches of missing skin. Bones poked through her forearm, and her bicep was exposed beneath a tear on her right arm, the muscle looking like a pile of shredded pink lumps. Several of her fingers, including her left thumb, were missing; and one of her ring fingers was hanging by a thread of skin and sinew, the ends of the joints clacking against each other to the beat of some sick macabre dance. The dress she had been buried in was torn down the right shoulder, the white lace stained by the thick sludge coming from the wounds in her chest. One of her breasts was exposed, torn down the same line as the dress and flopping lazily over the shredded fabric, scrunched into a shape like a hideous worm. Behind it, her breastplate shone white and seemed to gleam beneath the swinging overhead light. The bottom of the dress was almost completely shredded, looking more like an upturned parasol than what was once considered a piece of Sunday best, and her legs were exposed beneath panties soaked black with the same sludge that coated the rest of her body. It was a wonder how she was even managing to stand upright on the stalks that her legs had become. Half of the bones jutted out of place, like nails pounded through a flimsy two-by-four, and each of her bloody stalks looked more like a *z* than a straight line. Her stance reminded Gwen of a flamingo trying to keep itself above the water line and hunt for fish.

Her face was the worst of all, a moving mockery to everything humans thought they knew about life and its infinite cessation called death. Gwen felt that just looking at it at sent her into the frays of total madness, scraping along a sparking roller coaster teetering dangerously close to the edge of a dark mountainous pit of insanity. The lower half of her face—including her lips, her cheeks, and all the skin around her jaw—had completely fallen away and hung at the sides of her neck like a tangled scarf. Her eyes were dark and glassy, reflecting no light and darting wildly in their sockets in what appeared to be means to an escape from the confines of her skull. The one on the left had completely filled with blood, the dark substance falling down the remains of her cheeks and onto the pale bones, like rust on a battered steel shed. The bridge of her nose was cracked and bent close to her bloody eye, both seemingly resulting from the same savage blow. The rest of her nose seemed to be excreting that same brown sludge from its nostrils, falling down into her open gullet through the teeth and out the opening of the jaw below, pattering to the floor like raindrops. Even though most of the lower half of her face was gone, her tongue still flopped in its cage, slithering like a cornered snake and lashing out at its attackers from beneath its pearly bars. Enough muscle remained tied to the corners of her mouth to move the jaw open and shut, although it was slow and labored enough to pose little threat to the two EMPs trying to gain control of her arms.

There was an audible gasp, and Gwen was yanked back from the dreary crypt into her classroom where panicked whispers began to spring up like crickets at twilight on crisp summer nights.

"What in the fuck is that thing?" Greg Hines said from the front corner, jumping out of his seat and moving toward the wall, with one hand tentatively resting on his desk for support in case his trembling legs gave way.

"Oh my god... that poor woman," Katie Marker said from Gwen's peripherals.

"Fuck that! That thing isn't a woman!" Bryan Fuller shouted, slamming his fist on his desk and jumping to his feet.

His hands also remained on the sides of his desk, although with how strong they were digging into the pinewood, Gwen was sure it was going to shatter into a million pieces. His face was contorted with rage, veins rising from the smooth skin around his temples.

"Well, what the fuck is she then, Mr. I-Got-a-D-in-Chemistry?" Stacey said, baring her disgust with Bryan's callousness on her sleeve.

Gwen knew exactly what she was; she had killed one just like her just several hours earlier.

"I think I'm gonna be sick," Greg said, backing further into the corner and sliding off the old lamp light projector and onto the ground.

"We're gonna need you to stay back, miss! She's most likely infectious and rabid as a dog…" said a voice from the horror show hanging suspended in the corner of the room.

"She looks pretty distracted to me," Lacey Chabert's lucid voice came through and recaptured everyone's misplaced focus.

The camera remained frozen on that horrible face, its haunting glare unavoidable in its awfulness, dragging you in and hypnotizing you with its stern defiance to necropsy. Gwen could feel those eyes boring into her and her alone, contorting through the static and squeezing itself through the screen to see her face-to-face—to weigh her very being, turning it over and examining it like one would check the tenderness of roasting meat.

"Does she recognize the camera?"

"It seems to be pacifying her, at least."

"Maybe she's coming to her senses. I'm gonna try and talk to her. Get an exclusive channel 9 scoop from the woman who defied the man who killed her and even death itself by staying in the land of the living," Lacey mused confidently from off camera.

Gwen's eyes were still ensnared by Sarah Marsden's empty but powerful glare, looking for answers or reason and pulling up only inky darkness that seemed to cling to the very air like molasses. Slowly, Lacey Chabert's brown hair with the blond roots showing came into view, her hands tensely and tepidly testing the space in front of the decaying, walking carcass. Her arm floated out in front of her, reaching gingerly for Sarah Marsden's sagging and stretching skin, almost like she expected to tug on it like a child would her mother's dress.

As the camera panned to accommodate Lacey's growing presence in the frame, whatever spell that seemed to hold Sarah Marsden's complacency was broken, along with her hold over Gwen—who jumped to her feet in a vain, futile attempt to stop the wayward reporter despite the shining screen that separated them. A screeching roar came from the exposed throat of the ragged woman, her uvula and other muscles shaking with a terrible force as her head reared back and snapped forward with frightening, unfathomable speed.

Her jaw clamped down on Lacey's fingers and cut right through them, with some falling down her gaping gullet and the rest falling to the dirty floor like spilled fries. Blood began to pour from the wound and onto one of the aides, who released his grip on Marsden's arm and fell back against the wall, trying to wipe his face clean enough to regain his sense of vision. In this time, Lacey had begun to scream herself, parroting and joining Marsden's wail in a horrible symphony. The other EMT ran over to help his partner but was met by Sarah Marsden's bony appendage, which flew into his neck, the broken bones piercing the exposed flesh and bringing forth a river of blood with each haggard breath that came through the muffled audio. The shocked and bloody man fell backward into the camera, shattering the lens and sending it to the floor where it crackled and scraped loudly before sliding to a halt at the opposite wall.

From this new viewpoint, the scurrying of feet could be seen, with the large clogged artery of people trying desperately to reverse its flow, screams and begged mercy flying from their unseen mouths. Lacey Chabert fell back over her own high heels, her one good hand wrapped around the stump of the other, tears and blood covering her face as she whimpered and backpedaled away from the creature offscreen. She managed one final, soul-shattering scream as the lithesome, wriggling body of Sarah Marsden pounced on her, collapsing on top of her in a flurry of blood and gurgles, its foot with the heel exposed flying back into the camera and ending the feed in a hail of static.

The classroom erupted in a fury of screams and exacerbated shouting, with Bryan Fuller angrily tipping over his desk and moving to the head of the classroom, where he was met by a furious Mrs. Bell. Her eyes were set and determined, seemingly immune to the panic in the air, which was spreading through a group that had previously thought themselves immune and invincible. The illusion had been shattered by a tiny screen hanging from a ceiling, delivering its grim treatise with no more aplomb than it would the weekly cafeteria schedule.

"Now, would everybody just calm down and get back to their desks!" she said, struggling against Bryan Fuller's presence, who was still deciding whether or not his own safety warranted assaulting a teacher.

"Are you insane? There's no way I'm staying here and waiting to die with a bunch of faggots like you guys!"

"Hey, speak for yourself, asshole!"

"Oh, fuck off, Kyle, like covering up your love of dicks really matters now, you stupid fuck."

"Why are you freaking out so much? Some crazy woman attacks someone on the television, and all of a sudden your vag is bigger than mine," Stacey said from behind Gwen, smirking at her own lewdness.

"Yeah, bro, it's just some crazy bitch on TV. They got cops there, it's not like she's gonna come running all the way over here for you, unless you're her other boyfriend or something. She definitely looked your type, man," Ryan said, eliciting giggles from Stacey, who briefly fell back against his shoulder before catching Gwen's eyes and seeing that her own fear easily exceeded Bryan Fuller's manic hysteria.

"Are you guys serious right now? Are you really that dumb?" Bryan said in a fit of mad laughter that was more frightening in its authenticity than it was amusing.

When only silence answered him, his laughter became a booming chorus that filled the hollow plaster walls like it was a cave twice its size, ominous in its vastness.

"That chick is a fucking zombie, man! What? You see the thing in real life, and all of a sudden, you guys are too retarded to understand something you've known since you were too small to shit properly? How can you guys be such goddamn retards not to see it?"

"Zombies aren't real, you idiot!" Stacey said, crossing her arms and settling down on the edge of her desk, concern growing in her face as she tasted the words in the air and discovered that they couldn't persuade her from the truth she knew deep down.

Gwen wanted to believe it too, but she had known it since the minute she saw the woman, from the moment the report had come on; from the second she had sat down in her desk this morning, she had known the truth. It was one she had faced the night before in all its impossibility, but she had come out relatively unscathed on the other side. Her resolve was to do the same today, but first she had to find Range; he would know what to do. She just had to get to him, even if it meant shoving Mrs. Bell over herself.

"I know what I saw, and what I saw was a goddamn zombie, like the ones from the movies you've all fucking seen probably a thousand times by now. And after what we saw on that screen, there's about to be a lot more of 'em, and I'm not waiting here to be food for one of them," Bryan insisted, walking forward, ready to step around or through Mrs. Bell, if necessary, only to be pushed back and almost knocked to the ground.

"You will sit down until I tell you, you can leave. Is that clear, Mr. Fuller?"

Bryan looked at her like she had cut his manhood off in front of all of them and dangled it around like a cat toy, his face the color of Mars and his fists clenched in balls so tight it was impossible to tell where fingers and palms ended.

"Get out of my way, you stupid *bitch*," he countered through gritted teeth, the muscles in his mouth barely moving due to how tightly drawn they were.

Like a cherub waving incense and playing a song proclaiming glory to God, the fire alarm broke out in a series of flashing lights and siren bursts that pierced the tension and let it deflate harmlessly to the floor. Gwen managed to quickly scan the windows for any signs of Range and his guitar outside, almost convincing herself she heard that melody of his rising through the cacophony but knew it was her own mind attempting to reassure her.

"All right, everyone, you've heard the alarm, and you know the drill. We just ran it two months ago. Since he's so eager to leave, Bryan here will lead everyone in a single-file line down the hallway, through the science department and the gymnasium to the southwest entrance where they will gather outside and wait for word from the principal for dismissal. Is that clear?"

There was a weak answer of yeses from the room, although many faces were downtrodden, unable to shake the shock from their bones. Stacey looked at Gwen, the worry in her frame almost palpable; but Gwen managed a quick, self-assured smile that Stacey did her best to mirror.

"I said, 'Is that clear?'" Mrs. Bell reiterated, her gaze squared solely on Bryan.

The room managed a louder response, with even Bryan shouting, "Yes, ma'am," in a desperate act of appeasement, his own face starting to harden and sweat.

"All right then, Bryan, would you please start into the hallway, and then I want each of the aisles to follow behind, starting with Jimmy and ending with Greg."

"Why don't I get to go first? I'm closest to the door!"

The outburst triggered other arguments of a similar nature, everyone presuming their own life of more value than their counterparts. Gwen remained silent, although her patience was slowly waning into agitation as she checked the windows for signs of Range again.

"Fine then, Greg, you can go first! Now, if anyone holds us up again, I'll lock the door, and none of us will go anywhere, how does that sound?" Mrs. Bell said, practically frothing at the mouth.

Without waiting for further confirmation, Greg practically sprinted through the door with Bryan following close behind and the rest of the first row consisting of Nancy, Glen, Tina, and Rod behind him. The second row followed suit, along with the third; and finally, Gwen found herself hurriedly pacing down the hallway, past rows of lockers that had been hastily ransacked, papers and notebooks spilling out of the steel frames and onto the floor below. It reminded her of every last day of school she had ever had, foolishly believing herself to be free and contented, sorting through half-remembered supplies, throwing most into the trash or on the floor and saving some just to throw them away the next year. The line continued ceaselessly over the stacks of loose papers and continued down the hall and around the corner, into the science department and out of sight.

"Do you think Bryan knew what he was talking about in there? About... *them* spreading and making their way across town?" Stacey whispered from over her shoulder, her voice timid and wavering.

"Well, going from previous experiences, I'd say that Bryan definitely doesn't know what he's talking about," Gwen reassured, hoping to ease her friend's unease, as the terrible feelings that seemed to have sunk their claws deep into the back of her neck showed no sign of loosening.

Stacey replied by placing her hand gently on Gwen's shoulder and squeezing, something that caused her to tense and almost throw the hand off of her based on every instinct she had ever known—prayers and psalms repeating in her head like code while flashes of her mother's switch dug their way into her skull. The warmth of her touch was odd and the comfort it provided foreign yet intoxicating in its simplicity. Gwen placed her own hand over top and squeezed, following an instinct far greater than the ones her mother had beaten into her. She wanted to hug Stacey then and squeeze until she was sore, but she resisted the temptation, as there wasn't time to waste on fleeting bonds of friendship.

When they rounded the corner, another line came into view, snaking ahead into the double doors on the opposite side of Gwen's own line. She recognized several faces amidst the shuffling bodies, but none of them were Range, or anyone that would know where he was. In fact, she didn't know anyone who would know where he was, as she had never really seen him talking to anyone—at least not in the school. She had seen him once at the library speaking with one of the librarians there, but she had been there with Bobby Sloth at the time—that fleeting glance only coming to her now after she actually had a name to match the face. She had also seen him outside of that bar on the outskirts of town talking to some of the regulars, the same one from the shootout earlier that morning; but she had been in the car with her mother, so approaching him was something she never dared consider. She supposed those would be good places to look once she finally escaped from the bureaucratic hell she found herself in.

There was backup at the doors leading to the gymnasium, and the lines had all but come to a halt, several students trickling through with each passing minute. The students stood quiet and huddled over, staring at the ground or off into landscapes unseen, their eyes glazed and defeated. They moved like prisoners waiting to be executed, like lambs being patiently led to the slaughter. Gwen wanted to scream at all of them, to rile them up and get them furious, but she knew it would do no good. They hadn't listened to her before; they would hardly start now, when their very lives were at stake.

"Gwen! Hey, Gwen!"

She turned fast enough to startle Stacey, hoping that the voice was flowing from Range's silver laced throat, but was met only by Billy's eager smile and sigh of relief.

"Oh, hi, Billy, are you all right?" Gwen said, hiding her disappointment.

Slowly, her lucidity seemed to be returning, the shock giving way beneath the weight of the realization that all this was real—a nightmare that had trickled into reality, like rot seeping into the rafters. Her lack of sleep had been catching up with her, but Sarah Marsden's performance on the television seemed to unearth a hidden cache of adrenaline that was pumping through her veins like a drug.

"I'm fine, but that's not important. How are you doing? Are you hurt?" he fretted, grabbing her forearms and looking her over like a product passing inspection at the end of an assembly line.

Gwen gave him a quizzical look, confounded by his sudden rashness; but he seemed to look right past it, wheeling her around to where she could no longer follow his glare. Shaking free from his grip, Gwen turned back to Billy, straightening her wrinkled and scrunched-up sleeves.

"I said I'm fine, Billy."

"You must be terrified from what happened on the television, though, the way that woman attacked those innocent people. She chewed that reporter's fingers off," Billy said, his voice trailing into a whisper and his eyes scanning the slowly moving lines for those keeping keen interest in their conversation.

Everyone seemed much more interested in making it through the doors into the gymnasium or the patterns of the tiles on the floor than in what Billy was going on about, although Gwen could definitely understand their sentiment.

"Listen, have you seen Range anywhere around here today?"

"Range? Why are you looking for him? Does he have something to do with this?" Billy said, his voice rising louder than it should have, causing Bryan Fuller—hovering just before the gym doors—to turn back and accost them across the divide.

"Have you seen him or not?"

He looked like she had slapped him clean across the cheek.

"No, I haven't," he said, his pride wounded.

Gwen felt a twang of regret for her callousness, but the situation was too dire for misconceived affections.

Billy filed into line behind her, wedging himself in front of Stacey, who hardly seemed to notice as her focus seemed devoted to chewing her fingernails. Her eyes were staring past the gymnasium, and Gwen knew that fear had wormed its way into her head and seized the controls. They passed beneath the rectangular arch into the cavernous space of the gym, the thuds of feet reverberating off the walls and filling the room. Gwen noticed a girl in the corner, sinking into the padded backboards with her head in her hands, hysterical with tears. Several of her friends had gathered around her, on their knees, waving their hands in front of distant, broken eyes, as she rocked back and forth, immune to their appeals of safety.

As they passed the half-court line, Bryan Fuller spared another look back at the three of them, making no effort to conceal his malice or his suspicions. Gwen met his gaze and held it like a rapier locked against her own, looking away only after Bryan's head drifted back to the slowly moving procession before him. Despite being prepared to dole out a well-deserved middle finger, Bryan did not turn back a third time before passing silently through the double doors into the blinding light of the new world that lay outside the tall walls of the gym. The arctic chill that whistled from the doors as they swung to and fro only heightened her concerns, a shiver crawling up her spine.

The manic girl in the corner gave a piercing shriek as one of her friends put their arms around her shoulder, causing the rest of the room to jump and turn in her direction, only to counter with a volley of curses and harassment when the culprit was discovered. This final outburst was apparently too much for most of her friends, who waved their hands in an animated display of frustration, as if trying to justify their desertion to their captive audience or, more likely, to themselves.

"I really was hoping you weren't going to show up today."

Gwen knew who it was before she finished turning, but it still didn't prepare her for the burning of her cheeks and the rapid stutter in her heartbeat when she saw Range's distraught yet bewitching face across from hers. She chastised herself for thinking of something as foolish as romance when society, as she knew it, was crumbling around her; but she supposed involuntary reactions could be excused, at least for the sake of the issue not preoccupying her.

"What do you mean?" she said, quickly checking the gym for a sign of Bryan's sharp-red buzz cut.

"Well, after what happened last night, I figured you would stay home and prepare," he said, almost absentmindedly, his eyes searching for something as well; but of what, Gwen couldn't be certain. It didn't allay her own misgivings very much, though.

"Prepare? Prepare for what?"

"And what exactly happened last night?" Billy inquired from behind them, weaseling his palms between their shoulders and sliding his own head through like a mouse through a knothole. "Are you saying... are you saying you knew this was going to happen?"

Gwen suddenly found herself feeling very sick and starting to wonder if Bryan's suspicions weren't entirely off base. Maybe these feelings had clouded her judgment more than she originally allowed, blurring the truth beneath a cloudy sense of the exotic.

"I'm sorry, I thought I made that clearer than I did last night."

"Well, you could've taken a couple extra minutes to explain that part a bit better."

"I'm not the best when it comes to conversation."

"Yeah, I've noticed."

He studied her then, less scrutiny and more like he was seeing past her walls and barbed wire, the ones she put up every morning when she realized that the room she was in was still her own—the ones she had needed to retain her sanity on those long weekends away from school, her only lessons coming from the hunger of a fast and the wisdom of repentance for sins she didn't fully understand, to withstand talk of the world ending in blood and pain, visions that seemed all too familiar now. She wanted to pull away from that look, even though she had her doubts that she could, but she did not. In fact, with acceptance came a resolve to show him everything—her flaws standing in equal measure beside the good—despite the foolishness that accompanied it.

"I didn't have anything to do with it, Gwen. I swear. I know it's probably hard to trust me, especially now, with everything that's happening, but I need you to. We can't survive this if we don't trust either completely."

"And why should I trust you? You seem to know more than anyone else about it, but you haven't explained any of it to me. You asked me to the graveyard to show me one of these things then ran off before telling me any more about it or what it meant. What was the point of all that?"

"I wanted you to be prepared. I was going to tell you more, but I wasn't sure quite how to explain it. I also wasn't expecting things to be escalating as quickly as they are."

"What do I have to do with it in the first place, huh? Why do you want to help me so badly?"

"Because the thought of you dying was too painful, at least with me doing nothing to prevent it, so here I am."

He didn't look at her when he said it, not even when she finally turned to face him, her eyes hungry for a sign of sincerity, but she knew it was only because it was difficult for him to do so. Still, she hadn't been afraid of his inquisition; he shouldn't shy away from her own.

"I don't need you to save me. I'm not a damsel in distress. Let's not forget who saved who last night."

"You found me out," he said, a rare smile cracking through his somber veneer. "I actually came here for your protection. I'd be dead within minutes without you. I really hope you kept that shovel."

She smiled despite herself, even stifled a brief chuckle, before crossing her arms in a hapless attempt to catch the laughter in her diaphragm and silence it. She turned back toward the exit, which was growing larger with each slowly realized step toward its promised salvation.

"Everyone needs saving now and then, and with what's coming, it's gonna happen a lot more now than it is then. Even if I just end up standing useless by your side as you fight your way to the edge of town, it'd be worth it just to see you cross that border safely," he continued, his grin becoming transparent, a shade of the true face behind it.

He was struggling with something much darker than he was letting on, and Gwen wasn't planning on letting him off the hook for his insistence on keeping up with his mysterious loner charade, but she *did* trust him enough to believe there was a suitable reason behind it.

"So if you didn't expect me to show up to school today, why are you here?" she said, attempting to inject her voice with amicability but coming off overly cheerful.

"Well, I went looking for you at your house first," he said, at least pretending not to notice. When he saw the look of exasperation on her face, he began to laugh, her slap to the arm only sending him into further hysterics. "Don't worry. I didn't knock on the door and introduce myself. I did look through several windows 'til I found what I suspect was your room, but no one saw me."

Gwen wanted to protest but knew his intentions, especially in light of the situation, outweighed her own discomfort with the situation.

"How did you even figure out where I live?"

"Well, after you told me those stories about your mother, it wasn't really hard to find it by just asking around about the Prophet of Loganville's house," he said, still smiling that cute, damnable smile of his.

"Oh, right," Gwen said, disappearing into her own thoughts.

For the first time that morning, she found herself wondering what her mother and aunt were doing after Lacey Chabert's report that morning. She felt something teetering between concern and schadenfreude, but there was something else gnawing at her as well. Deep down, there was a part of her that was starting to question her own rebellion now, when the Prophet of Loganville seemed to be finding her validation in the horrors that awaited them beyond the double doors. The thought that the destruction and horror she had been bombarded with, in the form of self-righteous sermons and smug warnings since before she could even retain memories, images of all-engulfing flames and screaming innocents that haunted her darkest dreams—even if she'd never dare admit that her mother's wild ravings actually affected her—may very well exist just behind the threshold sent shivers through her skin and slowed her step considerably.

Noticing her discomfort, Range gave a small yet sharp, "Hey," to grab her attention.

"Don't worry. It's not as bad as you're thinking. Just remember, the hardest part always seems to be the easiest in retrospect."

Before she had time to steel herself, they were crossing over the clacking steel door stops, her muscles tensing to flashes of her mother's mosaics of demons and brimstone that decorated her family mantle where children usually found pictures of their own innocent faces.

Instead, she was greeted by a gray, dreary fall day, a light mist rising from between the blades of grass—no beasts, no fire, no death raining from the sky—just an impatient collection of peers gathering in disjointed circles by homeroom, the whispers going full force as everyone tried to find reason in the chaos. The breeze caught her off guard at first, instinctively pulling the sleeves of her hoodie down to her wrists to combat the chills. She paused briefly to collect herself and stop her trembling, taking a breath so deep she thought the bottom of her lungs had fallen away beneath her.

"You know, it's not as difficult as you make it out to be."

"What is?"

"Trusting you," she said, basking in the stupid grin that passed over his face for the briefest of moments.

Hurriedly, she led the small group over to Mrs. Bell's slowly expanding circle, mitigating themselves to the back, with Billy casting nervous glances back at Mrs. Bell, who hardly even noticed his existence. Stacey seemed to be returning to her normal self, returning waves with ones of her own—small, timid ones—with her hands buried in her sides, even managing a smile or a "hi" or two. Ryan even pushed through the crowd to join them, sharing odd looks with Range and Billy before lightly joking with Stacey and getting gleeful spurts of laughter in return.

"So what's our next move here?" Gwen said, scanning the horizon for a sign of rescue vehicles or a trail of concerned parents but was met only with a soupy fog that obscured everything past the edge of the football field. It was like the world had condensed itself, its edges fading into a white, swirling infinity.

"Mrs. Purnis said we were supposed to wait out front until the principal dismissed us."

"I'm not just gonna wait here all day. What if those things from the church start making their way over here? They could have every street covered with those bastards in a matter of hours. As much of a dipshit Bryan is, he did have a point," Ryan added, turning away from Stacey, who had wrapped herself around his waist.

"There's not that many of them—not yet, at least. Those bitten usually don't turn for at least a half hour. Those more resistant to the effects can last up to several hours, but I imagine it's a pretty rare occurrence," Range lectured self-assuredly.

"And just how would you know all that, freak?"

Bryan's hands were coiled in the folds of Range's collar before either of them seemed to realize what was happening. He backed their conjoined bodies up onto the central walkway that cut through the front lawn like a river of cement.

"You seem to know quite a lot about this whole thing. If I didn't know any better, I'd be inclined to think that you had something to do with it."

Range kept his face stiff, unmoving, almost statuesque, while Bryan's seemed to have gone through a rapid devolution two times over.

"I guess I just watch a lot of bad horror movies," he proclaimed, a smug smile on his face.

Bryan let out a grunt of rage and shoved Range back hard before grabbing his collar and pulling it back to him, the fabric tearing at the seams with a loud rip that drew the attention of many of the ever-growing circles.

"Don't you smart-ass me, you autistic faggot."

"Leave him alone, Bryan," Gwen interjected, reaching for Bryan's forearms before being violently thrown back by a halfhearted shove.

Range seemed to rile at this and tried to shake loose from Bryan's vice grip, only to have it tighten and reel him in until they were practically breathing down each other's throats.

"Don't defend him. With what he knows, he's probably some kind of scientist working with the government on some kind of biological weapon, you know, a guy who looks our age but is actually some Ivy League fuck sent her to spy on us, testing it on the town while he reports back to them every week. It would explain why everybody always sees him walking around random spots, being weird and carrying around that stupid fucking guitar of his, but he never seems to know anybody or be going anywhere. What have you got to say about that, you fucking freak? Planning to kill us all in your sick experiment or something?"

Range somehow uttered a stiff laugh. "I guess we've both seen too many movies, huh?"

Bryan's arm pulled back, ready to slam it into Range's teeth and send them flying all over the concrete and dead grass; but Gwen managed to catch it, stopping him for a fleeting second.

"Stop it! He was with me last night, and we saw one of those things rising up from its grave. He's been watching it happen every night for weeks now. That's why he knows so much, not because he's a fucking spy. We even managed to kill the one from last night because he knew how to deal with it."

"What else did you guys end up doing last night?" Billy interrupted, receiving only silence and a slap on the shoulder from Stacey.

"Oh, come on, Bryan, they're not worth it—not right now, anyways. They're just a couple of freaks trying to stave off their lonely futures with each other's unpleasant company. If they wanna run off and pray or fuck or whatever it is religious nuts do when they think it's the end of the world, then why stop them?" Veronica Métier said, stepping forward behind Bryan, her arms tight against her North Face jacket and the knees above her Ugg boots shivering in the winter chill that snuck in on late autumn mornings.

Even with all those layers, she still seemed naked without cronies behind her.

"If what you're saying is going to happen actually happens and everyone starts dying, these two will be the bodies at the very bottom of the pile. They won't last an hour. Gwen's always thought she's better than everyone else. It's time for her to get a harsh reality check that only natural selection can provide."

"Thanks for the vote of confidence, Veronica," Gwen said, restraining herself from using the string of obscenities she had prepared. "Now, if you'd like to just stay out of this, we'd all really appreciate it."

Bryan looked back at Veronica and smiled, his grin curling up the side of his face like it was splitting in two. "You do make a good point, Veronica."

He leaned in closer to Range, almost as if he planned to sniff him like a wolf identifies its challenger, asserting its dominance while testing the opponent's will. "And here I thought her mouth was only good for sucking dick," he said, just out of Veronica's earshot.

Range's eyes narrowed, and his body seemed to go rigid like a board, but he didn't move.

"You know I'm right. Gwen's been trying to cover up the fact that her mother's the embarrassment of the whole town for years now by acting like she's better than everyone else. Now she's finally found the King of the Hipsters to help her convince herself that her acting like a bitch 24-7 is entirely justified. They've just made a pathetic game out of it, like the weirdos they are."

Veronica set her sights on Gwen, boring into her and attempting to pull her guts out by the root. She felt a fire in the pit of her stomach and was sure that Veronica had developed some kind of pyrokinesis and was attempting to broil Gwen from the inside out, but in the end, it was just the deep-set desire to plant her fist in the center of Veronica's pompous smile.

"I don't know. I still think the fucker's got something to do with it. The things he says… they may be fucking weird, but I know what I saw on that screen. He's probably on his way to some evac site now, helicopter waiting, ready to drop a nuke on this whole goddamn town and wipe it from the record books." Bryan allowed his demented stare to waver, shifting his squinting eyes to give Gwen a quick once-over. "The guy even broke himself off a nice piece of ass to take with him in the process. Doesn't seem like a bad job to me. Get paid to doom an entire town, and you get to fuck the town crazy's slut of a daughter as a consolation prize. Can't say I wouldn't—"

He was cut short by Range's palm heel mashing into his jaw, slamming his teeth together in a sharp crack. Blood began spurting from his lips in wide arcs, mingling with spit and mucus as his head traveled with the momentum, jerking back violently. His body was carried with it, nearly collapsing back onto itself before his feet slid to a stop, his high-top Nikes tearing up tufts of grass and dirt. Without hesitation, he lashed out in a fit of rage, his fist catching Range in the forehead and sending him sprawling onto the sidewalk, where his cheek colluded with the concrete in a sandpaper kiss.

Range turned himself over quickly, catching a fall stomp of Bryan's heel heading directly for his chest with his hands. After a brief struggle, he tossed his foot to the side, throwing Bryan off balance and sending a kick of his own squarely into the center of his crotch. There was a heavy grunt, followed by rush of breath and an airy wheeze as Bryan fell to his knees, his hands forming a protective cover for his groin.

"Gah, you crushed my fucking balls, you dirty cocksucker. As soon as I can stand, I'm gonna rip your dick clean off and shove it down your damn throat!" Bryan shouted, making sure that anyone that wasn't aware of the altercation was now a front-row attendee— the separate contained circles merging into one larger organism that formed a new ring for the fighters buried in its center.

When he finished, Range brought a haymaker down across his earlobe, turning his head on a pivot and sending him into the grass. Several teachers began moving through the crowd, silent sentinels thrown out of their element and into the uncomfortable position of equality with their charges, even though many of them towered above the sea of heads, like bleak brigantines pushing through the waves.

Bryan spat, turning the grass around him a sickly hue of red as he pushed himself back to his feet, stopping for a breath on one knee. Billy, in a delayed gesture of bravery, ran up beside Range, grabbing his shoulder in a feeble show of support. The act caused Range to almost turn and hit him, believing that one of Bryan's cronies had decided to join the confrontation; but other than several struggling teachers, no one showed any interest in aiding either of the bruised boys. Half of them had their faces obscured behind a phone screen, whispering to each other and pointing at things seen through the screens and declaring their allegiance to various video upload sites, followed by complaints that their service wouldn't allow them to upload or send anything, a gripe that had been echoing around the school all morning. Nevertheless, they kept on watching from behind their handheld screens—the thought of stopping the insane gladiatorial spectacle that had broken out in front of them never once crossing their fear-rattled minds. They had been given a distraction from the terror of the morning and seemed all too grateful for it, delighting in the ridiculous, if easily digested, drama that made up their high school existence. It was something normal to grab onto in the torrid rapids of the unknown that lay ahead of them.

Like a panicked animal, Bryan worked his way into the back pocket of his jeans, sliding a small object from its confines and concealing it in his hand. As he rose to his feet, almost stumbling, he snapped the switchblade open with a sharp flick of his wrist, grinning like a jackal baring its fangs. His stupid and bloody grin and drunken swagger denoted that he believed him the first man to ever use such a complicated display of intimidation.

Billy stepped back and congealed with the crowd as soon as he saw the glint of the blade, the severity of the situation finally settling into many of the faces that formed the curtain around them. Range stood steady as stone, hardly moving a muscle or stealing a breath. Fear shone in his eyes like a watery veil, but he didn't flinch, keeping his gaze on the edge of the blade as Bryan angled it toward him, testing the space between them.

"You better know how to use that," Range insisted, spreading his legs just enough to find a surer balance.

Bryan's answer was only a haughty grunt, displeased by his opponent's response to his trump card. Gwen started to inch forward, closest to Bryan's waving arm, the blade always facing Range as its handler fidgeted and twisted his stance. Keeping her hands ready at her side, she took another step forward, not realizing the grass had ended a step back, her foot crashing down loudly on the concrete path. Bryan turned as quickly as wild beast, jabbing the point toward her face and halting her in her tracks, her courage failing in the shadow of death.

With a wave of his hand, Range brought Bryan's rabid attention back toward him, the saliva and blood falling from his lips looking like the foaming mouth of an infected dog while waving away Gwen's attempts at rescue.

"Great. Are you happy with what you started, Gwen? The whole town's in a state of emergency, and you got your psycho spaz of a boyfriend scaring and beating people," Veronica said, animated hands waving at Bryan, ignorant to the monster she had helped create.

"Oh, fuck off, Veronica," Gwen shouted, unable to contain herself any further.

Her nails were making deep-red indentations in her palm, but it was all that was keeping her feet from crushing Veronica's smug face beneath the heel.

"Who are you, of all people, to judge me? To call me a bitch when your whole identity is based around your false sense of superiority and your ability to take as many dicks as humanly possible in your gaping vag!"

Several snickers drifted up from the crowd, nervous titters that seemed to be due more to obligation of hearing a reference to sexual intercourse than actually finding the hurried and awkward comeback entertaining.

"Very cute, Gwen, how intellectual of you to insinuate that I have a loose vagina. It's like your trying to help prove my point for me. Here you are, thinking you're above all of us, and you use the same crass insults as a toddler who just learned how to swear. I'd almost be able to forgive you for you psycho mother if it wasn't for that."

Bryan let his eyes drift back to the brewing storm behind him, only briefly, fully aware of the threat in front of him.

"Your girl looks like she's in trouble over there," he said, but Range ignored the bait and kept his gaze steady on the shining steel between them.

"Oh, how gracious of you, Madame Métier. Thank you for being so forgiving of my transgressions against you. Then again, I can kinda see why you'd need to be easy on me for my mother, considering your own brother is a murderer who killed two men last night and will spend the rest of his life rotting in prison where he belongs."

The verbal blow struck her and caught her off guard, her cheeks reddening, her eyes darting side to side, while sharp whispers rose on the wind. Her eyes seemed to sink deep into her skull, the eye shadow making the bags underneath look like bottomless caverns. The sudden flash of vulnerability brought forth a hint of regret in Gwen's mouth, but she swallowed it back down and continued unabated.

"What's it like, Veronica? Huh? Go ahead, and tell everyone what it's like. What it's like to be the family of the local pariah. Tell them what it's like to be me. Go on, since you seem to be such a good judge of a character to know me. Well, let me know that if you didn't know what it's like to be me, I guarantee, you will, soon enough. People aren't going to forget about the sister of the guy who shot the sheriff over a couple thousand dollars. And when it comes, when you truly understand what it's like, I'll be there, standing where you are now, where you've *always* stood, and I'll play the part just as well as you did.

"I know, Veronica, I already know why you hate me. You weren't lying when you said that it wasn't because of my mother. It's because I know the truth, the truth about you. The truth is, you're not like your brother. No. You're not some heartless beast like him, but neither are you a saint among us, a celebrity for us to worship. You're average, as plain as they come. Yes, you have your looks now, and you use them as best you can, but when those fade, what will you have? Will *your* so-called friends still be there when there's nothing to interest them anymore? Something tells me they won't, and you know that. No, the truth is, you're horribly ordinary, and no matter how you try to disguise it with disdain for me, it'll never not be the truth."

Bryan looked back again, laughing to himself, the only one laughing for miles, the sound echoing through the mist like an insane howl. Range took the opportunity to slide his foot forward but was cut short by a quick jab of the switchblade when Bryan's attention returned. He wiggled his finger and tsked, reveling in his control, like a pig in the sty. Veronica, however, looked ready to shatter into pieces, her lower lip trembling and her eyes fighting tears. The clacking of her knees turned almost rhythmic, distractingly so.

"Close, Gwen, although you really are adamant about helping me prove my point, aren't you? The reason I despise you… is because you're a goddamn hypocrite. You pride yourself on denying your own flaws and projecting them onto everyone else. I may be a raging bitch when I wanna be, and I may enjoy fucking more than your average teenage girl, but at least I have enough self-awareness to be upfront about who I am without condemning others. I've heard your rants, Gwen. We've all heard them. When you're walking through the hallway, loudly blasting your opinion to whatever "yes" machine will listen to you at the time, condemning everyone for the very feelings you bury beneath your holier-than-thou persona. It's funny, Gwen, how much you claim to hate your mother, when in fact, you're almost just like her. All you need is to have a whiney freak of a kid out of wedlock, and then the transformation will be complete." She nodded her head toward Range, "I see you've already got a candidate lined up."

Gwen punched Veronica right beneath her rib cage, burying her knuckles into her stomach and twisting, feeling the skin beneath the shirt tighten against her own. A whoof of air flew out of her as she doubled over, her mouth hanging open and her eyes slammed shut. She managed to recover quicker than Gwen had anticipated and sent a half-curled fist of her own into Gwen's chin. She bit down hard and tasted iron on her tongue but forgot it quickly as Veronica seized a handful of her hair and begun to pull like she was competing in a tug of war against a five-man team. The world disappeared behind a million sharp needles as her vision blurred into the pain. It felt like her head was filling with static.

Hoots and hollers followed, with cries of "Catfight" being in large supply as the girls ended up falling on top of each other, with Gwen managing to pin Veronica underneath her despite the grip she had on her hair. With a struggle and quick yank of her neck, she pulled free, losing several clumps and strands in the process, but was so consumed by anger and, strangest of all, guilt that she hardly seemed to notice and slammed her fists down on Veronica's chest. She cried out in pain and pushed Gwen off of her with her knees, her hand then moving up to massage the area with a hoarse groaning.

When Gwen was able to get back on her feet, Veronica started to backpedal through the grass on her rear, tears welling behind her eyes that bore a bitterness in their defeat. Gwen let herself relax, the pain that she had pushed below coming back up tenfold and turning her breaths into shards of glass down her throat.

Bryan shifted his weight, keeping Range in his peripherals while he looked down the concrete walkway shaded beneath the haunted shadow of the gymnasium, the windows at the top bearing witness to the crimes below and the doors serving as the perfect toothsome smile.

"It looks like your girl is pretty brave. Let's see if you are," he said, wiping sweat from his brow with his free hand.

He prodded at Range with the switchblade, gently at first and then more aggressively, all while keeping his feet planted firmly opposite Range's own. Even though her vision still seemed foggy and obscured, like she was looking through sugar glass, Gwen thought of making another attempt to grab the blade while Bryan was unaware, but she remembered the paralyzing touch of fear from her first advance and remained still.

The idea proved tactful as Mr. Jonas finally shoved his way through the knot of students and into the makeshift gladiatorial arena that had formed, shouting angrily at anyone foolish enough to find themselves in his way.

"What in God's name is going on here?" he said, disappointment dripping from his stare.

Ashamed, Gwen turned away and back toward the standoff, unable to explain herself to him without feeling as if she was admitting to some terrible crime.

Met with nothing but silence from Gwen and cries of blood from a crowd that had been stricken dumb from the sight of it on a blurry television screen just moments before, Mr. Jonas bitterly pushed Gwen aside and forced himself between the two. Bryan—ignorant to the world around him and his mind drenched in bloodlust—charged forward, bringing the blade up in a wide slash. Dragged aside by Mr. Jonas's pull on their shoulders, the arc of the blade went wide and ended deep inside his rib cage. Sliding through a gap between ribs, the blade was buried to the hilt in Mr. Jonas's chest—a spray of blood leaking from the tear in his blue-collared shirt and dark-maroon tie, which soon became invisible amidst the growing stain.

The screams came again—one of them surprising Gwen by coming from her own mouth—a chorus growing in crescendo along with the torrent of blood from the wound. Mr. Jonas's hands went limp around the boys' shoulders and straight to the hilt protruding from his sternum, Bryan pulling his empty hand back drunkenly, mouthing, "No," to himself over and over. Range had fallen from the awkward yank of his shoulder but was slowly rising and moving toward the staggering teacher. Mr. Jonas had begun to dazedly remove his jacket, the sleeves getting stuck on his stiff arm movements. Range reached him just as he collapsed backward, his eyes rolling up to his head, while Range tried desperately to stop the bleeding with his hands coiling around the exposed blade. Gwen ran over to them, looking first at Range for some sign of what to do; but his attention was buried completely and calmly in the amassing puddle of blood on top of Mr. Jonas's shirt. When the convulsions started, Range's hands came up from the wound in defeat, the bleeding becoming unmanageable.

His eyes wide with fear, and sporting a face spotted with dried blood and coated in a sheen of sweat, Bryan retreated into the terrified circle—which had begun to collapse in on itself, its shape morphing and crumbling like snow in an avalanche. Stacey, who stood in his way, made a feeble attempt to grab him, but he shoved her to the ground almost instinctually. He soon disappeared from sight, his head, although easier to spot than most with his fire-red hair, was awash in an ocean of migrating bodies as the students began to flee from the scene in disorganized terror. Veronica seemed to have disappeared as well, sinking into the madness behind her and becoming one with writhing masses. Stacey tried to stand, but the crowd had already started to work their way through this new opening, unconcerned feet falling on top of her legs. She called Gwen's name, who barely registered it as she watched Mr. Jonas's life drain from his body.

As if the earth was shaking and cracks were tearing them apart, the crowd of frightened students pushed and shoved against each other, fighting their way out of the entrapment they had made for themselves, reality sinking in and spoiling their illusion of invulnerability. Fear turned them blissfully unaware; flirting with madness and dancing on the fringes of derangement, they rushed forward like a stampede of cattle.

Ryan McCaffrey was trying to fight through the people pouring in around him in an effort to reach Stacey and get her back on her feet, yet he too was knocked to the ground by an unwarranted elbow that seemed to render him unconscious. The gap widened in his absence, even the people next to him unaware of his disappearance beneath their shoes, charging forward in their struggle for escape.

Stacey cried out again, hoarse and with an urgency that came only with the foreknowledge of certain death, and finally got Gwen's attention—who turned just in time to see her friend reach out for her one final time, her eyes red from tears and shaking with unmitigated terror, her fingers trembling with helplessness. Before Gwen could react, a fleeing student's shoe collided with the top of Stacey's skull and knocked it back into dirt, her eyes rolling up into her skull before fluttering shut. Another student, blissfully unaware of anything that wasn't directly in front of him, brought his boot with heavy brown soles down on top of the limp girl's head and drove it deeper into the ground with a sickening crunch, pink matter spilling out onto the lawn.

"Oh, God, no..." Gwen moaned, feeling her breakfast come up violently.

More feet and pounding soles continued unabated over Stacey's twitching form, her body becoming unidentifiable between the forest of legs that swallowed her and Ryan. The slight rise in the rampaging crowd as they frantically charged over the spot where their bodies lay was the only indication that they had even been there.

Before she could even finish vomiting, Range began pulling her up by her diaphragm, wrapping his arm around her stomach and dragging her to her feet. She fought him and cursed him, but he held her firm and started toward a gap in the struggling mass, which had begun to dissipate near the street as more people began filing out. She cried out desperately for Stacey, even reached back to her, unable to get that final look of fear out of her mind, but found it playing on a seemingly infinite loop, over and over again in her mind.

After several labored steps, Range whirled her around and placed his hands heavy on her cheeks and brought her face level with his own. She tried to fight him off, still wanting to throw herself under the crowd that had stolen her friend from her—her only friend—and drag her back out, even though she already knew the terrible fate that had befallen her. But he held her tight and shouted over the explosion of insanity that had started with Mr. Jonas's demise.

"Gwen! Gwen! Gwen! I need you to calm down! There's nothing we can do for them now! We have to go! Do you hear me? We have to get out of here now!"

"Let. Us. The. Fuck. Out. Of. Here!" Tyler hollered, shaking the iron bars with each syllable before slamming them once more in frustration and falling back on the lone white bench in the tiny square box of a cell.

The chain links that held the thin whiteboard to the wall shook and rattled, stealing the rare moment of silence that Matt Métier had been so desperately anticipating right out of his hands. Since they arrived at the police station, they had been harassed and beaten in turn by every officer in the precinct, most of them gathering around outside of the cell, like children at a zoo, throwing barbed insults and premonitions about their judicial future until the lot of them were called off on some urgent phone call that sent them all scrambling like roaches. The silence had only been momentary, though, as Tyler kept shouting back despite the fact no one was there except for one geriatric, out-of-shape officer who was probably of more use in his chair than out in a squad car.

Matt's head ached tremendously and spun like an axis that had come loose of its mooring and was wildly out of control. There were several times when he thought he was going to throw up, a feeling of nausea that he couldn't shake permeating his every breath. Each passing second had become agony, an agony that showed no sign of reprieve due to his current situation.

His thoughts about his imprisonment had disappeared into the nether, lost amidst a violet haze that made them unintelligible whispers, voices heard beneath the water's surface. It felt like his skin was crawling, his bones fighting a losing battle to keep the two attached. Sweat was forming on his brow, so he focused on that—feeling as the drops slid down the curvature of his skull, following their trail and trying to predict where they'd go next. But soon, the twists and turns formed patterns, ones he recognized as the sweet curves of a woman's hips and her breasts; and soon, he could feel her skin beneath his fingertips. The way it tugged against his own, almost like it was trying to cling to him and never let go and form a perfect, inseparable piece of flesh. He felt himself stiffen down there and shifted his weight, struggling to discomfort himself in a futile attempt to soften the coming storm.

The urge was on him now, pulling hard on his strings and twisting them into tangled knots that made the pulling of one impossible without yanking all the others out of place. The room felt a thousand degrees, his blood boiling in his arteries, steam rising in his lungs. He heard the steady beating of the air conditioner but couldn't feel the breeze. His head drifted up and saw that it was above him, pointing at Tyler, who was getting back on his feet for another round at the cell bars.

"Hey, ass clowns! You cracker-ass pieces of dick cheese, better let us up out of here before I start getting real angry! This here is some discrimination-ass bullshit, and I, as a citizen of this great country of A. Mer. Ee. Ca, will not be treated this way, you feel me? Now, somebody get off their lazy, fat, dick-taking asses and let me the fuck out!"

Tyler kicked the lock with his heavy boot, the leather sole cracking hard against the steel and shaking it like it was possessed. He repeated this brilliant tactic several more times, each with more of a head start than the last, as if he expected the bars to fall away beneath the might of his Timberland high-tops. His mouth went open in a gasp of pain as he reached down, seizing the bloody bandage around his other leg as the dark crimson stains began to darken.

"Oh, would you give it a rest already, Tyler. For Christ's sake, we've been in this damn cell for two hours, and I already wanna stick a shiv in ya. I figured it would take at least twice as long, but you've always exceeded expectations, haven't you?" Frank said, slouched in the corner of the cell, his bald head shining next to the bright silver of the toilet seat.

"Man, fuck you, Frog. If you don't like it, you can hop your bitch ass right on out of here and go eat some more flies out of that boss of yours' ass," Tyler said, facing Frank only for a moment before standing shakily on his bad leg and falling forward to rest his face between the bars of the cell and straining to see around the empty precinct they found themselves in. "Besides, it's your own fucking fault we're in the joint in the first place, so don't be trying to make me seem like the dick here."

"How the hell is it my fault?" Frog said, exasperated, looking to Matt for answers and finding only more questions in his friend's blank expression.

"You're the one who crashed the van into that bitch-ass tree."

"Only because I had to swerve just to keep your dumb ass from falling out the damn window!" Frank said, finding his temper steeled by the thought that his situation couldn't possibly get any worse. "In fact, it seems like all our problems were caused by you taking potshots at the fucking police like a toddler with a tommy gun!"

"Dat ain't true, boy, that was me improvising and handling shit like a muthafucking boss after you couldn't get your old, wrinkly white ass inside that safe because you 'retired' so long ago the safes were probably made out of dino skeletons or some shit," Tyler said, barely acknowledging his accused in the corner, his attention honed on the steel bars as if they would suddenly break apart via telekinesis if he concentrated hard enough.

Frank fumbled for words as a response failed him, his face growing increasingly red with each second lacking a valid self-defense. The words had made a horrifying amount of sense, and the weight of responsibility for their present incarceration grew heavy on his shoulders, as most things that weren't his fault usually did. Soon, his anger began to turn on him, picking at the weakest supports of his mental state and trying to tear them down.

"You make it seem like it was all my plan or something. Like it was me, driving up to *you* when you get off your shitty jobs and recruiting you for this… suicide mission! 'Cause that's what this was. I hope you know that. The whole plan was doomed to fail from its conception, which I imagine involved a bottle of cheap whiskey and quite a few rips from the bong, am I right? I am, aren't I? I'm starting to think you guys knew that the whole time and only brought me along so you'd have somebody to blame."

Frank seemed to slouch further into himself, his shoulder slinking above his forlorn head, which had drooped like a flower with a dying stem.

"My life is ruined. I didn't have much of one, I know that more than anybody. But what I did have… the little dignity I managed to keep after seventeen years of doing whatever that snidely bastard Klunesberg asked of me… my small apartment with the fan that doesn't work no matter how many times you click it and the sink that always smells like there's food caught in the disposal… the stupid parrot, Eumaeus, always calling for food at four in the morning, like a set alarm. There'll be no one to feed him now, I suppose… and the way Mrs. Germer next door would smile at me like I was an actual person and not just someone there to do something for her… it's all gone now. It's all gone."

Frank licked his cracked lips and looked down at his hands, following the wrinkles like a map that traced every mistake in permanent marker across his skin. He had many regrets in his life, even though everyone told him that there were none worth having. Still, inevitably, his timidness found a way to hold him back from his own desires. And now, here he was, rotting away to dust inside a cell, away from the world he had longed so desperately to be a part of but always found himself stumbling beneath—a stepping-stone for others, shoved down whenever he had tried to pull himself up. Except now, he could sink no further into the muck and grime that had pervaded so much of his life."

"Jesus Christ, Frankie, your life is depressing."

"Tyler!" Matt said, his rage acting as strong enough blinders to keep the urge at bay for the time being.

"What? All I'm saying is this nigga's here trying to be all melodramatic and send us on some guilt trip, when none of this shit is gonna matter by the end of the day anyway. I guarantee ya'll that Pops is on his way down to this shithole now and is gonna have a few things to say to whatever piece of bacon they got in charge around here. Ya know, now that the other sheriff is currently eating his meals through a bendy straw, nukkah!" He threw his arm up for a fist bump but found himself left hanging by his cellmates, both of which couldn't stomach to even look at him.

"Man, fuck ya'll, I'm here, being the only nigguh trying to raise everyone's spirits while ya'll pussies are moping and crying about how sad you is to be in jail. Man, who gives a fuck? Anybody knows a nigguh ain't hard unless he's served a couple stints in the joint. When we get out of here, everybody gonna be treating us with that kind of respect you can't buy, dawg! Some hardcore OG shit, homie! When I get out and we head down to Merrilville to pick up some of that good rock from the burbs, Boozie and Kwon ain't gonna believe this ish, I'm tellin' you, fam! I'm tellin' you! Mothafuckas like them shit their pants around mothafuckas like us. They gonna be all like, 'Whoa, T-Dawg, Tyga Killa, we been hearing some crazy shit on news about you lighting up some 5-0 outside a bar?' And we gonna be like, 'Fam, you know a real gangsta goes hard like that all day, hoe!' And these mofos, they gonna try and give me bullshit before they fall in line to ride dis dick like everyone else! And all the bitches that 'bout to be blowing up my phone! Fuck, man, I can taste all that sweet pussay already, nigguh, you feel me? I'm telling you, the life of a real OG, that's the life for me, and that's what we about to be livin', fam! So perk the fuck up!"

Tyler continued waxing poetic about his newfound status, despite the fact—the very apparent fact—that his audience was elsewhere, lost in their own respective prisons, ones smaller and darker than the blanched white cell that held their bodies.

Frank was burying himself beneath his despair, finding solace in their hopelessness, as it meant that there was no longer a need to lie about a future he had stopped believing in many years ago. He felt lighter through this revelation, less tethered to the idea that his happiness was dependent on his accomplishments. The moment did not last long, fleeting past his consciousness like a hummingbird fluttering past a window, but it was a meager comfort in a time when comforts were going to be few and far between.

Matt, meanwhile, was suffering through his own personal purgatory, drifting on the thin plane between the waking world and the subconscious. The world seemed incredibly small and suffocating, his chest heavier than stone, each breath a labor that sent sweat trickling down the curve of his back. Spasms rattled his arms and legs, mild ones more often than not; but every once in a while, his leg would kick out of his control, just subtle enough for his companions to believe it a sign of passing anxiousness. They were partially correct, although calling the urge "anxiousness" was liking calling a twenty-car pileup a fender bender. Every muscle in his body tightened and ached, desperate for release that he knew could only come one way. He glanced over to the toilet next to Frank's wrinkled dome and thought of throwing him aside, throwing down his pants and finishing himself off right into the bowl, letting his body melt into the water below. The thought passed quickly, Matt managing to suppress it, despite protests from the urge in the form of past encounters with bouncing, slippery flesh playing before his clenched eyes.

An old nun, dead on the floor, tits saggin', blood drippin' from between her legs.

The technique imparted to him by his psychiatrist all those years ago seemed futile now, no more impactful in stopping the urge than a single board is in stopping a breaking dam. Whatever horrifying images he could think of were replaced in seconds with a thousand more that awoke the hunger deep in the bowels of his soul, the dark part he convinced himself didn't exist, even when indulging in its tainted pleasures.

Blood stickin' to her gray pubes, soakin' through her wrinkled lips.

It was a drug he told himself he would quit, except quitting would require removing a piece of himself—a pound of flesh in exchange for life undisturbed. A fair price it seemed, until the time came to collect.

Teeth broken, guts spilling on the floor, tits saggin', blood dripping from between her legs, but she wants you. Yes, she still wants you. She could be yours.

Matt nearly vomited then and there, the bile backing its way down his throat slowly, ready for any slight invitation to leap back up. He brought his hands to his face and ran them through his hair, his fingers getting caught in the greasy tangles. Struggling to catch his breath even though it felt like his head was going to implode in a red haze, he noticed something acrid on his lips, sticky and syrupy. Looking into his open palms, he saw them covered in blood—a mix of his own from cuts received jumping out the window, Tyler's from his open wound before the paramedics hastily bandaged it without administering any kind of painkillers, and Greg Caplin's brains. He had placed his hands in the giant puddle of them when dragging Tyler back into the bar.

In Caplin, Matt found an eye in the storm, the urge held at bay by something much more foreign and hard to place. It wasn't guilt, per se; he still felt plenty of justification and divine right in his sentence of that piece of shit. But there was a feeling that something was off, something wasn't as it had been. It was an empty feeling, a hollowness that didn't feel much like happiness, and it didn't feel much like sadness—but a cocktail that seemed to leave only the worst flavors of its base ingredients, the sick stomach that came with sadness and the bad aftertaste that came with most forms of cheap happiness.

"It really would be the best time to drop my follow-up mixtape. That shit's bought to be straight fire, son. Everybody's mixtape right when they get out the joint is some of the hardest shit out there. You know motherfuckers be hungry, you can feel that shit. Just look at Gucci's tapes, proof right there. Now, I know what you gonna say, that my bars ain't that good on the timing, and my metaphors need work, but that shit don't matter in rap nowadays. It's all about how hard you come off. I mean look at Raff. That motherfucker got a record deal, and I'm pretty sure that nigga's retarded."

"Oh, Jesus Christ, Tyler will you just shut the hell up! It's bad enough in here without having to listen to your bullshit all day. I just want a minute of peace and quiet, unless that's too much to ask from an infant like you," Frank said, shaking with a rage that took Tyler off guard if only for the fact that it was something he hadn't seen from Frank in their few times drinking together at Mickey's over the years.

"Motherfucker, who you calling an infant? You're the one over there moping in time-out! You know, I oughta have my dad leave your ungrateful ass in here, with your punk-ass bitching and moaning. 'Oh, look at me, I'm Frank the Frog, nobody takes me seriously because I'm such a little bitch, wah, wah, wah.' Hopefully they got a titty to suck on nearby so you can get your nap in."

"This is exactly what I'm talking about. Anyone calls you out on your damn childishness, and you freak out and go on some nonsensical spree of vulgarity that doesn't even make sense half the time."

"What doesn't make sense, nigguh? You a baby who sucks on titties, I thought that was pretty clear."

Frank hopped from his corner and threw his body into Tyler's, catching him in the gut and knocking the wind out of him. They collapsed against the bars, Tyler bringing his fists down on Frank's back, each hit causing a tremor and grunt. Eventually, he was able to throw Frank over and onto the bench where he began trying to wrestle Frank's flailing blows into submission but was brought to the ground by a swift kick to his bandaged leg, the toe of Frank's shoe digging into the wound and tearing the shallow scab that had formed. Tyler squealed in pain, his teeth clenching as he went down and his hands digging into Frank's throat as he dragged him down with him, like a sinking ship pulling down its uncommitted captain.

Matt heard none of this, and all of it, his mind struggling between the voyeuristic images of his id and the strange sense of guilt that was nagging at him. He started to suspect it was a guilt tied to the urge itself, one he suspected he knew the cause of: a memory ingrained in the deepest chasms of his mind that he tried the rest of his life to erase. However, it was impossible to fix the damage of something that you believed never happened, especially when the person you injured would keep that memory for the rest of their life, whether they wanted to or not. He shook his head, believing it would clear his thoughts, but it only seemed to make them louder.

A rustling from behind him was what silenced them, a noise so quiet that at first he believed it merely to be another attempt by the urge to draw him into its red velvet curtains; but it persisted, growing louder and wilder, as if something was thrashing against the wall behind him. When he felt the wall tremble, he knew that it was not a trick of his mind but the presence of someone in the cell adjacent to their own.

"Shh!" Matt said, rising to his feet due in part to some long-buried primal instinct that seemed to have awakened within him.

Frank and Tyler continued to struggle awkwardly on the floor, occasionally sending cheap, rapid jabs into each other's sternums, grunts and groans forming an off-kilter rhythm. The heavy rustling and shaking of the wall against Matt's back seemed to come in bursts, like whatever was behind them was spasming violently, thrashing against the cold bricks. So low at first that Matt believed it to be his own breath, a moan joined the muted symphony, low and guttural. Phlegm could be heard rattling inside the throat from which it originated, thick and suffocating from the way it seemed to turn the moan into something completely alien. Matt could hear the outlines of words, bitter mutterings that floated between groan, a message that was struggling to find clarity and comprehension in its own whispered rambling. Matt thought he could make out the word *death* before Frank was thrown back into the bars of the cell, the clang pulling Matt from his focus and setting his built-up tension loose.

"Would the two of you just shut the fuck up for two seconds?" Matt hissed.

The two fell into an impromptu cease-fire to look at him, their curiosity and the desperation of their situation taking precedence over their respective grievances with the other.

"Can you guys hear that?"

Frank and Tyler's bodies fell away from each other, untangling and sending Frank falling onto his ass as he pulled a leg loose from Tyler's side. Annoyed, he sent a final thrust of his foot into Tyler's crotch, causing him to groan in unison with whatever it was that lay in the cell beside theirs. Frank stood and dusted off part of his Levi's spotted with dirt, before approaching the spot where Matt lay with his ear to the wall. Tyler eventually managed to stand and join them, punching Frank quickly in the kidney in a form of inelegant retaliation.

Now that the station had fallen back into its uncomfortable and almost unnatural silence, he could hear the baying of whatever creature was beyond the bricks that separated them in all its unearthly glory. It seemed several octaves too low for anything human, coming off more as a haunted growl than a moan of displeasure; but the emotion behind it gave it a sick sense of familiarity that sent chills through Matt's body, cooling the fire that had been there moments before. The images remained, the urge not conceding to something as paltry as terror, but felt wrong as the moans of the sensual had replaced by something that felt more at home in old monster movies Matt used to catch on TV late at night, staying up in front of the glowing screen in his room well past the midnight hours of his bedtime, waiting for the dirty movies that began playing in the early-morning hours. For just a flash, his mind reached for the image of the bloody nun but pulled back at the thought of that wail coming from her chapped, decaying lips.

"Oh, God, help me."

The voice, unexpected in its humanity and its implication, caused the three of them to jump back from the wall to which they all clung, exchanging glances that shared thoughts they felt too foolish, or childish, to speak aloud.

"What the fuck was that?" Tyler said, his voice low, the color draining from his face like a leak had sprung underneath his chin.

He looked to Matt as if he was expecting an answer to the question, which seemed to spark a fearlessness in Matt, although he couldn't be sure if it was due to concern for the person in the next cell or disdain at his own friend's timidness.

"Hello? Is somebody in there?"

They all waited with bated breath for a response but found none other than another heavy groan that seemed to sink into their very bones and rattle the foundation. Frank's face went blank, his thoughts twisting around a connection that he knew was there. It slipped between his fingers like sand, traces of it sticking to his skin as a subtle irritation.

"I know I've heard that sound before, but I can't place where…" Frank said, muttering to himself, hoping his voice would absentmindedly lead him to his conclusion, but he trailed off before reaching anything other than more questions.

The groan echoed through the rafters of the abandoned station, reverberating down hallways of framed commendations and into cold steel rooms with cold steel chairs and cold steel tables, reflecting everything but comfort. Before the echo trailed off completely into the nether, another began in its place, even louder than before, more base in its primality. It sounded like an injured grizzly, or some kind of dying caribou—a beast twice the size of any human, with an unchecked ferociousness that dripped beneath its tones.

"Oh, God, it hurts. It really hurts."

The voice came through again, clarity found in its increase in volume, the intonation clearer and sturdier. Matt pressed his head back against the wall, hoping to hear more of whatever was in that cell but only heard more of that terrible groan, along with the occasional rumble of the wall. Tyler went to the bars of the cell, hoping to see around the corner and into the bars of the cell adjacent but was struggling to even see past the edges of their own.

"Hey, buddy, can you hear us? What's going on over there?" Matt said, his mouth so close to the wall he could taste the years of fingerprints and sweat on his lips, nearly making him gag.

After nothing but silence came once more, he pounded heavily on the wall, like knocking on the bathroom door of a friend passed out inside, an act he'd done many times before and gave a sense of comfort and familiarity to the whole situation.

"Is everything all right in there, man? Do you need us to get someone? Do you need help? Are you sick?"

"Oh my god, my insides… they're burning. They're twisting… and burning. Why won't they stop burning? It hurts. It hurts. It hurts!"

Tyler pulled back from the bars, flecks of paint falling beside his face. He brought his hand, wrapped in the lengths of his sleeve, to his mouth as a type of makeshift quarantine mask and wheeled back to the bench, sliding as far back as he could.

"What the fuck is this shit, man? They got a bunch of sick niggas up here? Probably got fucking swine flu or measles or gonorrhea or some other deadly shit like that and they just threw us next to him? What in the actual fuck, man? You know Pops is gonna sue this place to oblivion for this shit."

"Are you kidding? This could be our way out, and without having to wait on your dad to throw a tantrum to his political connections," Matt said, softly trying to contain his excitement.

"What do you mean?" Frank said tentatively.

"There's one guard still here. You both saw him roaming around after the rest of them left, the fat fuck with the thermos and the pants with the tears in the leg? If we can get his attention long enough to tell him, that poor bastard in the next cell is dying, we can get him close enough to grab him through the bars, with enough leverage to get him in a headlock and get the keys so we can let ourselves out of here while all those cops are off dealing with whatever bullshit call that's got them held up right now," Matt explained with relish, his mind jumping from bullet point to bullet point, looking for any obvious flaws that would worsen their already-desperate situation.

When none presented themselves, he began to slam on the bars much like Tyler had, only with an added fervor that came with a plan, however scattershot it may be.

"Hey! Officer! We need help over here! This guy's in trouble!"

Tyler soon joined in, throwing his weight against the bars and hollering like a chained dog. Frank, reluctantly at first, added his own voice to the mix, before finding resolve in the possibility of spending the rest of his life someplace other than a small windowless room.

"Ohhhhh, ohhhhhh. My stomach… it's burning. I think it's… dissolving itself. Ugh, I can feel it… shrinking, burning, tearing itself apart…"

Matt almost stopped himself after hearing the stranger's cries, his message sounding horribly sincere, something conjured up by the deepest, most primal horror brought about only by the certainty of death.

Matt had heard it before, even experienced it several times in some of his less-than-legal jobs he had undertaken, staring down the barrel of a sawed-off, with eyes behind it that barely seemed to see him. Instead, the meth head behind the trigger had met his own untimely end that night, focusing too long on Matt, even running the dual chambers of the sawed-off down his cheek like a lover's playful touch. While he was doing so, his friend Reg, having slipped outside for a cigarette before the tweaker had worked up the nerve for his makeshift robbery, unloaded a slug into his skull and sent his brains all over Matt's face, bits of cranium stealing his vision and clogging his nostrils with that horrible copper smell. For several seconds, Matt thought it had been his own head that had exploded and, in what felt like an eternity, drifted into the terror that came with the realization of one's death.

The darkness was pure and murky, suffocating like nothing else he had experienced, a fear that was absolute and irresolute. The voice hidden in the shadows of his subconscious slipped from their confines and enveloped him completely, their usual gentle whispers turning into harsh, indignant abuse that was impossible to ignore because it had become the entirety of his existence. When Reg slapped him on the back, laughing, he awoke from this spell—as terrified as he had been the first time he had come sliding down into this horrible world, unsure if this was reality or if the darkness in his head was.

"Hey! Officer! Officer! You need to get over here now! It sounds like this guy's dying down here!" Matt said, shouting away his convoluted thoughts.

The plan before them required all his focus; it might be the only chance they got before they found themselves separated, bound for different prisons, their chances of escape diminishing with each mile apart from the other. Matt didn't know if they planned on splitting them up, but he suspected it was their intention. When they arrived, there had been preparations made for three different prisoner transports, each heading for a prison that seemed to stretch to the very farthest borders of the county. It seemed that even if they weren't able to have Tyler, they were going to take Matt and Frank as sacrificial lambs in his place. They were already guilty of other crimes from that night, and the cops weren't about to completely suffer this injustice no matter how many fingers were greased under the desk.

"Hey, Officer Piggy! Oink, oink, motherfucker! You as deaf as you is fat or something? Can't you hear we got a nigga dying over here? Hello? Oink, oink, oink, oinkity oink, oink, oinkity oink."

Tyler cupped his mouth and sent his sophomoric shouting further down the hall, the twisted sounds of the animal echoing through the corridors and becoming sickeningly distorted. Matt shushed him, whacking his arm with the back of his hand.

"Come on, cut the pig shit. We want them to believe us, not to think that we're messing with them some more."

"I'm just trying to communicate via their native tongue. Most niggas would consider that a sign of courtesy, but leave it to cop to get all offended over nothing, but fine."

They shouted louder, their voice going hoarse with thirst and making their words crack and run dry, slamming their bodies into the bars as the groaning crescendoed into a wave that washed over the small nook of cells. Soon, it grew so loud that Matt was having a hard time hearing his own shouting through the steady droning of it and saved his breath, suddenly aware of just how off-kilter the moaning really was. Its frequencies seemed to be dipping down into sublevels that no human should have been able to reach, along with octaves that seemed to contain voices crying in a chorus of disdain that added to its noxious lament.

"Oh, I can feel them mashing together… My stomach… lower… so tight. The pressure there… crushing themselves together. There's something wrong. Oh, God, there's something wrong. The pain… somebody stop it… for the love of God, somebody make it stop."

There was coughing, so heavy that it seemed to shake the bars on every cell in the corridor. The whole building seemed to tremble on its foundations from the hacks and wheezes of the moribund patient. There was a sudden rushing gurgle, followed by a sickening plop, and Matt knew the man had vomitted, a sound that was all too familiar in his line of work.

"Ohhhhhh, no. No. No. No. No. No. No. That's not supposed to…"

The wet gurgle of vomit cut him off again, but the silence seemed to spread like a disease, stopping Matt and Frank to share a look of concern, while Tyler continued bashing the bars as if the words' haunting meaning had completely passed by him.

"Hey, Matt, I think he's actually hurt pretty bad. Maybe we should rethink this plan of yours," Frank said, rubbing the back of his head, his finger circling his bald spot like water round a drain.

"We don't have time for that, Frank. As soon as those cops get back from that church fund-raiser or whatever the hell they were running off to, we're gonna be separated, and you and me are gonna lose the only chance we've got of escaping. Hell, we'll probably lose each other too, and then getting out will be entirely up to you, with no help or assistance from anyone but yourself. If that's how you want it to be, then go ahead and be my guest and remain silent, if that helps your conscience, but I'm getting us out of here," Matt said, shouting once more for the officer down the hall, the lack of enthusiasm in his voice noticeable even to him.

"But if we incapacitate the guard by any means necessary, like you're talking, especially if it means what I'm assuming you mean, then nobody's gonna come and help that guy. He could *die*, Matt," Frank said, testing for a reaction. When the expected one didn't come and was replaced one of silent, bitter acceptance, his lips curled up in disgust. "So now we sentence some poor innocent bastard to death as well? How many more people gotta die before this whole thing is done, Matt? Just one more, right? Just one more won't matter? Well, fuck that, this one matters."

"You're being ridiculous, Frank. You don't know anything about that guy over there. The guy could be some poor bastard about to be sent up for forty-five to life and would welcome to the idea of an early death, no matter how painful."

The man wailed horribly, almost intentionally trying to derail Matt's already-flimsy argument. He could hear the wavering of his voice, his own conviction falling short when said aloud. At this point, he wasn't sure whom he was trying to convince, or why he was trying to convince anyone, when two-thirds of them was all that was needed to make the half-assed plan a reality.

"Hell, the guy could be some horrible serial killer on his way to death row. The guy could have it coming, for all we know."

"Oh, well, how noble of you, the man who just killed his boss in cold blood less than twenty-four hours ago, to pass on the sentence."

Matt wanted to lash out at him then, in that moment. He even played with the idea of pounding his fists into his face until they were bloody and twisting into a pile of red mush, but it passed, just as fleeting a thought as those sent by the urge. He allowed himself a breath, a slow one, in, then out, letting his anger bubble just beneath the surface of his skin, simmering and boiling his blood and turning it into a turgid froth. Frank noted this but kept his eyes, heavy and accusing, centered right on Matt's, his intensity like static that clung to the air.

"That was justified, and you know it," Matt said, hoping it would sound more convincing out loud than it did in his head.

He could feel the doubt creeping into the fibers of his being and knew that if he let them in, it would be the end of the plan and of himself, forever lost to a darkness that he had skirted along the edge of for years now. Holding it at bay, the guilt and the blame, required work, denial to the point where you can't find any aspect of yourself that wasn't tainted and you felt more like a husk going through preset motions, stymied by your own fear of where going forward might lead you. And when you're about to lose your balance and tumble into the dark pit below, standing still can be your only option. The fear was there now that this was the turning point, where things had spiraled completely out of control; but the plan, the great and infallible plan, gave him purpose and kept his thoughts pure. Using this as armor, he met Frank's gaze openly, letting him disappoint himself by finding only a mute resolve in his face.

"Yes, I'd say it was, that's true," Frank sighed, his eyes closing tightly in defeat. "I suppose I believed that as soon as I agreed to come along with the two of you. I may not agree with the extreme measures taken, but I can't hold you at fault for them. Even the police officers, as fucked as it sounds, self-defense and all that. But that man next door… he's just like us, Matt. He could be in there for the exact same reasons we are. To condemn him like that… I'd feel like we were sentencing ourselves to the same fate."

The words floated between them for a while, occupying the air with their weight, making Matt's breaths laborious, forced, tighter than they should've been. He tried to picture that man in the other cell, tried to see him as clearly as he was seeing Frank's wrinkled features in front of him, his eyes soliciting reason and empathy that was currently failing his two counterparts. Matt tried to see his face, to concoct some kind of empathetic back story to give pause to his plan, but he found nothing but cold indifference inside him. Soon, his thoughts began to turn against him, contorting the man into various forms, feminine and warm to the touch, their fingers up his back so real his knees practically buckled out from under him as they were trembling so hard. Shaking off Frank's gaze, he fueled that passion back into his resolve toward the plan (*bloody nun, broken knees, floppy, lifeless legs with blood spilling out all over*), feeling empowered by it, sure in its righteousness.

Tentatively, unsure of how Frank would handle the betrayal, Matt turned back to the bars and joined Tyler in shouting for the guard, the beast in the cave at the end of the hall that could be their salvation or their damnation depending on how they played it. Matt now had to factor in the possibility of resistance from Frank, an attempt to thwart their efforts at escape due to a misguided adherence to medieval ideas of morality that would end in their forced repentance for sins that held less weight on his soul than ones committed years before.

Surprisingly, it was Tyler who found the middle ground.

"Don't you worry, Frankie," he said, sounding frighteningly like the stern politician that raised him and remained their only legitimate hope for liberation. "Before we get out of here, we'll call the hospital and have 'em send an ambulance over for our poor friend in the next cell."

"So you want us to call the cops as we're escaping and have them send more men down to the place we're escaping from?" Frank asked, bewildered, but Tyler laughed off his concern.

"We're gonna be long gone by then, Frankie," he said, still using his more dignified tone. "We'll call on our way out the door as an anonymous tip from a concerned citizen. That way, we get out of here, and your boyfriend next door gets to live another day for you to give his ass a nice licking."

And with a heavy cackle, the formal Tyler disappeared back underneath the boorish slob that wielded him.

"When the cops get here, they're gonna see we escaped and start looking for us right after, especially if they find another dead cop."

"Hey, you're the one who wants to help save that guy's life, not us. No matter how you feel about the whole thing, Matty and I and are getting out of this bitch. If you want to get help for that nigga next door, then by all means, be my guest, motherfucker, but we're outtie, you got it?" Tyler said, turning back to his duties of banging on their cage like an irate baboon adjusting to his new life as an exhibit at the zoo.

After this, Frank relented, unable to conjure up a plan that was any better, but stood by in quiet protest as Matt and Tyler continued their attempts at alerting the guard to their neighbor's ever-worsening predicament. They went on shouting for several minutes before frustration started to set in, the hopelessness of the plan starting to bear its ugliness. Their throats, hoarse and raw, were starting to fail them, their voices cracking and dying within them. Matt was starting to notice his thoughts straying again, lingering in places they shouldn't, and felt that control was slipping through his sore and bloody fingers. He opened his mouth to shout but felt only a burning pain at the bottom of it, stinging deeply like his throat was relentlessly chastising him for its misuse. Stumbling backward, his leg collided with the chain that held the plywood bench to the wall and shattered the levee that was keeping his anxiety at bay.

With a roar, he slammed his foot down on the edge of the bench, hard, so hard that the mooring holding the chain in place came free from brick that held it, dust tumbling out from the pocket of space left behind. Several more heavy drops of his leg, along with one or two awkward attempts at assistance from Tyler, the board clattered to the floor, its chains falling slack at its side. Wasting no time, Matt grabbed the flimsy piece of wood and, in one swift motion, threw it and himself into the bars of the cell. The rattling that resulted from this was more intense than any of them anticipated and caused Frank to cover his ears with cupped palms. It was as if a thousand banshees had gathered together in an attempt to recreate Barbara Streisand's discography.

Before the steel bars went completely silent, the opening and slamming of a heavy door off in the distance could be heard, accompanied by the shuffling of feet, hurried but not running, agitated but not angry. Matt had wanted him angry. It would've made him impulsive, more prone to rash, foolish decision-making. Now, instead, he was the one that was riled up, panting and sweating like a whore in church.

Old nun, tits sagging, blood dripping from between her legs.

The footsteps grew louder, less echoed, more uniform in their pace and steady in their rhythm. Tyler looked at him, his eyes searching for approval, which Matt gave with a curt nod. He looked back at Frank, who returned his gaze but merely stared at him transfixed like he was under some kind of spell. Something had spooked him, but Matt couldn't be sure if it was the arrival of the officer or related to the dying man next door, who had picked up the charge of moaning in agony again, almost as if he understood their plan and knew his part to play in the imprudent production.

"Just what are you shitheads up to now?"

The officer's head finally appeared around the corner, approaching the cell with slow saunter and gait that implied that his arrival here was due in part to his own boredom with guarding a mostly empty building and a couple of prisoners that were already trapped like bugs in a roach motel, waiting to be collected and pried from their sticky tombs. He wore a grin that showed he was here solely for his own amusement and relinquished no concern for the moaning of the prisoner in the far cell.

"Now, I'm trying to get some sleep in the other room before I've got to start my second shift out in the car, and right as I'm about to slip off into the blissful fields of dreamland, filled with beer by the tap and women with biggest tits you'd ever seen, when I hear, pounding in my head like a goddamn jackhammer, this unholy rattling from down in this shithole like somebody done woke up the devil himself," he said, his feigned anger causing the jowls of fat around his chin to wobble and shake as if an earthquake had passed through them.

Sweat was pouring down his wide forehead, over the thick bridge of his nose, and down onto his strained uniform, the top button left open to make room for the bulge of his chest. It'd probably never been buttoned in all its history with its chubby wearer. His name tag beneath the small badge, tucked between two rolls of fat, read, "Officer McCulley." An Irish name for an Irish face. Matt had to try not to smirk, picturing him in his plainclothes, loose sweats and a sports jersey representing whatever team was on a popular winning streak, more often than not the Patriots or the Yankees, spitting up beer with loud guffaws to the terrible edited-for-TV movie playing in the bar at 1:00 a.m., the sound so inaudible he was reading the black letterbox of closed captioning.

"Well, pardon me, sir, but you have to understand, we were—" Matt began before a crack of the officer's baton against his fingers curled around the bars of the cell, feeling a white-hot pain shoot out from them like fiery tendrils. Matt pulled back, hooting, and started to shake them loose, listening for cracks and feeling for any splinted joints.

"What the fuck did you faggots do to my pretty little jail cell? Knocked the damn bench clean off the wall. You know how long its gonna take me to fix that? Well, not me, of course, but you know long its gonna take Hoo-Li-Oh the janitor to fix that? Probably the rest of the goddamn day. Are you happy about that? Taking up the rest of Hoo-Li-Oh's day? I bet you sick fucks are. I bet you're real proud of yourselves, shooting our poor sheriff in damn head and then coming back and smashing up the nice little room we gave you free of charge? Well, ain't you some of the most ungrateful sacks of shit I've ever seen? But I'll tell you something, boys, just between you and me," Officer McCulley said, leaning in close to the cell as his voice dropped to whisper.

Matt quickly looked at Tyler as a sort of impromptu signal, hoping to take advantage of the officer's close proximity to the cell bars, but Tyler's eyes were hard lined on the baton in the officer's fist, ignorant to Matt's suggestions.

"I didn't even like that faggot of a sheriff. In fact, I'm almost glad you little shits shot him, always looking down on the rest of us while he himself was bumming some nigger in the back of some squad car."

"What the fuck?" Tyler said before a quick whack of the baton against his fingers sent him back, howling in pain. "You racist-ass motherfucker…"

"Ha! You're one to talk. For a senator's son, you try really hard to convince people you're not just some scared white boy tucked between Daddy's legs. I bet you even thought Daddy was gonna come down here, wave his big dick around, and save your ass from getting rammed by a real nigger in federal penitentiary. And in the past, that might've even been the case. Sheriff Nottingull, he liked him some dicks and would've gladly slurped on your daddy's to save this sorry department. But you killed him, boy, and you got the board to suddenly grow some hair on their peaches and take a stand against Senator Rosenthal in light of this viscous attack on the justice department."

"What're you trying to say, piggy? I can't understand your words through all that fat."

The officer smashed the nightstick against the bars again, the loud clack startling Tyler enough for him to fall onto his backside. This brought a heavy shriek of laughter from McCulley.

"It means you're gonna rot in here, boy, either for the rest of your life or 'til they get sick of ya and send you on up for the lethal injection, although personally, I wish they'd do it the old-fashioned way, with a tree branch and a noose, just like those niggers you love to emulate so much. Ain't nobody who's gonna be able to get you out of this one, not even your big-shot daddy."

Laughing harder, McCulley slapped the steel with his baton again, in a quick triplet that made Matt's ears ring. He tried to look at Tyler again, hoping this time, his attention would be keen enough to pick up on his signal. However, Tyler's head was hung low, practically buried in the dirt, his face indiscernible. Matt felt a tinge of sadness for his forlorn friend but not enough to distract him from their attempts at freedom, as it just jumped up quickly in priority.

Craning his head to peer into the cell, McCulley chuckled.

"Why'd you idiots break down the damn bench in the first place? I knew you guys wanted to see me, but I didn't think you were that desperate to see another man after only a couple hours in here. You guys get tired of fucking each other already? Needed somebody new to think about, that it? Or let me guess, you broke the bench during all that fucking and needed me to bring you guys a new one, that's it, isn't it? Now, let me ask you, since I probably won't have another chance to before they beat your asses senseless and send you up to state—which one of ya'll is the bitch? You know, the one who takes it? With the sheriff, it was pretty obvious he was the giver, since he was always giving that nigger his everything. But with ya'll, it's a little bit harder to figure out. Hold on now, don't tell me, you gotta let me guess first. Don't try and ruin all the fun now. Let me see, let me see. Okay, I'm gonna say that *he*," he pointed his thick sausage of a finger at Matt, "sticks his fist up *your* asshole," he said, turning his finger to Tyler. "While this one watches in the corner and jacks off like that ugly thing from Lord of the Rings, am I right? Oh, come on, you gotta tell me, now that I guessed!"

The slur in his speech became more apparent, the sway in his steps more exaggerated, the foundation of his courage ripe on his breath, spraying forth from his false fangs like venom as his laughter filled the small corridor. Lifting his head higher, he brought his vitriolic gaze down on Frank, his beady eyes twitching in their meaty sockets.

"Hey, you, the little guy in the back! Don't I know you from somewhere?"

Frank replied by retreating further into the tight confines of the corner, his shoulders shrinking like a cornered animal.

"You look awful familiar, you know that? Not enough to remember a name, but with a mug as hideous as yours, I probably couldn't forget ya if I tried."

McCulley laughed, pulling out a small silver flask from his front pocket, ingrained with the Irish flag, his national pride displayed for all to see—not just by his flask, but his enthusiastic downing of what he considered his national beverage.

McCulley was the bane of many an Irish American, a man clinging to ideals adored by the same people that claimed to possess an Irish ancestor on Saint Patrick's Day, using remnants of stereotypes meant to paint their race as lazy and uncivilized from all those turgid years ago. Finishing its contents, he let the flask drop lazily to his side, not bothering to fix the cap, letting several amber drops hit the dirty concrete floor.

Suddenly, his eyes opened wide, and he nearly choked on the liqueur still collected in the back of his throat, hacking up most of the brown liquid onto the floor and coughing in fits afterward with horrible wheezes that almost sounded worse than the wailing man's.

"Excuse me, boys, got a little tickle in my throat."

As he finished, a realization struck him, one so enlightening that it seemed like some spirit had smacked him hard across the face.

"In fact," he said, continuing with a sly smile that showed too much of his bloodred gums, "you could say I've got a frog stuck in there."

He cackled then, enraptured by his own profound wit, holding his massive belly as it shook. Frank seemed to shrink inside himself and disappeared into the shadows at the back of the cell. Matt wanted to throw himself against the cell door once more but restrained himself, the plan replaying itself on a loop in his head like an emergency broadcast message.

"I knew I recognized you, you sonuvabitch! Why you crouching back there? Come on, let me get a good look at ya! It's been awhile since I seen you last. Klunesberg usually doesn't let his pet Frog out of the cage, I know. I think the last time I saw you was when he had you go around to all the boys' homes and install that new heating system he was bragging about free of charge. It was real nice of you to do all that work out of the bottom of your heart there, Frog. The boys and I were real grateful. We even bought Klunesberg a beer afterward. You should have heard the stories he told about you, some of the funniest shit I've ever heard right there. About how he kept you working extra hours specifically on days you requested off, just waiting to see if you'd say anything about it. Of course, you wouldn't. You'd even still bend over backward to do everything he wanted. He even told us about how he was the one that gave you that perfect little nickname of yours. Said you owed him more than your own mother because he was the one that gave you the name that actually fit you. Me? I suggested we change it to 'Giant Pussy,' but that prissy boss of yours said it was too 'lowbrow,' or some horseshit like that. I will admit that boss of yours does like to act like a stuck-up prick from time to time, but we all have our vices, don't we?

"You know, I don't think I ever expected to see you behind these bars. I really didn't. A lot of the guys liked to think you'd just finally snap one day and go on some kind of killing spree like one of those crazy snipers or whatnot, but me? To be honest, I never thought you had the balls. And yet here you are, finally found your way out of one cage and right back into another one. Klunesberg'll just be tickled to hear that, I tell you, he will be."

The cop laughed again, wiping beads of sweat and tears from underneath his eyes, the salt causing him to blink heavily. He stumbled backward ever slightly, enough for him to have to haphazardly catch his balance. Hoping to alert Tyler to this show of weakness, Matt was met with a shapeless being of white and soon realized that Tyler had thrown the massive hood of his sweatshirt over his head, the clean white of the hood almost glowing in ethereal light. Discouraged and desperate, Matt turned to Frank and studied him closely, watching for any sign of life behind his glassy eyes; but they were pale and empty, drifting across the floor of the cell to the far wall next to the dying man. McCulley seemed insulted by this and tried to play the insult off with more of his stilted humor.

"Oh, come on now, Froggy, you don't wanna talk to me? You don't wanna say 'good morning' to your old friend McCulley? Come on now, don't make me beg," he said, slowly approaching the door. "It'd be very rude of you to not at least say 'hello,' Frog. Is that too tough for you? What say we meet in the middle and you give me a nice healthy 'ribbit'?"

"How about 'oink, oink,' motherfucker?"

Without warning, Tyler had leaped up like a wild cat from tall grass, pouncing on its unsuspecting prey and grabbing McCulley's upturned collar through the thick steel bars and pulling him close. Caught off guard himself, Matt wasn't sure how to react and spent several seconds standing still as stone, the plan suddenly seeming far worse now that it had in practice, almost insultingly so. Part of him wanted to remain there, a silent observer, disapproval shown in his placidity, pulling his name from such a misguided project; but he knew that he couldn't—not now, when no other option, however reasonable, had presented itself.

Charging forward, his foot connected with the disassembled bench and brought his momentum to a screeching halt and him face-first into the cold steel and warm flesh of McCulley's extended gut pouring through the bars. This blow knocked McCulley from his feet and sent him sprawling backward over his thick, stubby legs. Tyler's grip remained strong, however, and held him suspended in the air, the collar straining against its own fibers, tears already sprouting beneath the seams. In a matter of moments, it was over, the loose flap of cotton in Tyler's clenched fist and McCulley's ass spread across the crisp concrete, the cracks spreading from its epicenter as if the impact from his fat ass had been their cause.

Tyler cursed savagely, whipping the collar to the ground and throwing his whole body into the door of the cell in a final, frenzied attempt at freedom. Matt was struggling to recollect his thoughts after his fall had scattered them around the room. He heard his neck crack as he stood, the muscles tightening and seizing up like a fit.

Meanwhile, McCulley, in a craze brought upon by his brief but closest dance with death, pulled the revolver from his waist and waved it wildly at the duo, his finger hovering too close to the trigger and his thumb practically embedded to the hammer.

"You sons of bitches get back! You hear me? Get the hell back before I blow your brains all over the wall like you did that pillow-biting sheriff!"

Catching his breath with animated effort, the officer patted himself down as if he was checking that none of his body had been pulled off in the tussle. Holding the gun out in front of him, like a child with a pointed stick, he maneuvered back onto his feet, pushing off his meaty claws and stumbling to an awkward truce with gravity. Tyler took a quick swing at the revolver's dangling barrel, but it was jerked away quickly by a frantic reflex that caused the thing to go off into the ceiling. The noise deafened Matt heavily, the hollow ringing becoming all that he knew for the next minute. When he was finally able to open his eyes and regain some semblance of intelligence, he saw McCulley waving the gun back and forth between the three of them, hovering the barrel at their skulls for a couple seconds, driveling away about something that was still obscured by the dead ringing in his ear canal. Fortunately, or unfortunately, his hearing returned to him soon, bringing his words back into painful audibility.

"You stupid fucks knew anything, you'd know not to fuck with an officer when he's the only one to vouch for what happened to ya when the rest of those idiots are away. Do you have any idea how fucking easy it would be to shoot the lot of ya—point-blank, right in the center of your temple like one of those Hindu bastards—without anybody giving a flying *fuck*? Huh? Do ya? Hell, you stupid bastards already gave me a pretty damn good excuse. Self-defense has been a cop's best friends for centuries, and you faggots practically wrote me a blank check to waste your dumb asses. The only question is—

which one of you parasites do I get rid of first? Huh? Do I have any volunteers, any noble souls that can't bear to watch their lovers die? No? What about you?"

He pointed the gun square at Tyler, slapping the tip of his nose with the red-hot barrel, smoke still curling out of the end.

"I can't wait to show your daddy your bloody corpse, so much so I think I should do you first, especially since you were the eager beaver who wanted out so bad he couldn't wait to the transfer before we fucked him up."

McCulley slammed the butt of the gun into Tyler's chin, the force cracking his face against the bars before falling to the floor with a groan of pain.

"Does that sound good to you, punk? You can finally die, like all those niggers you love to play as so much."

"Nah, fuck that," Tyler said, through the tears and blood clogging his throat, "kill Matty, this whole thing was his idea."

Before Matt had a chance to respond to Tyler's inspiring display of bravery, the man in the cell at the end of the short stretch of cells began to howl, having lulled into a tenuous silence while they were distracted by McCulley's idle threats. The sound caused the panicked officer to turn wildly in its direction, almost firing off several rounds into the shadowy abyss that had been created by his previous shot, destroying one of the flickering fluorescents at the end of the hallway. The bellowing grew louder, more monotonous and uniform, stiff with a sorrow twisted by rage. It was like swallowing a cocktail of all the worst emotions a man possessed, distilled into some abject horror, putrid and repugnant in taste.

Soon, the arduous wail was so loud that it seemed to drain all the air out of the room—a cacophonous vacuum, suffocating in its totality. Life's frivolity contained and summarized in that one unearthly moan that made the lights tremor and shake, shadows darting around the room like freed demons. Sediment began to loosen and fall down, like ash from a ruptured mountain, dirt and dust blurring into a fog that permeated the room, making it closer resemble a boggy marsh atop a swamp than a cell of steel and brick and mortar.

McCulley's form disappeared beneath this moldered veil, lost to their sights, the glint of his revolver's hammer occasionally reflecting the two lights above that were still clinging to their short, busy lives. Almost on cue, the glass tube closest to the far cell shattered and rained shards down on the officer's exposed head, causing him to skitter backward, wildly thrashing above his head in a ragged, drunken attempt at safety.

The clamor showed no signs of stopping—the wall's slight trembling turning into a steady sway, the bricks rattling against each other, cracking and splintering like veins opening under the skin. Matt covered his ears, but this provided no relief; it merely gave the roar a hollow tint, a ringing it did not have before. But that seemed to allow his sense to gather and reform themselves into something close to functioning. He searched for Tyler, but the dust from the ceiling was stinging his eyes and shrouding the space inches in front of his own face, like he had thrown a white, translucent cloak around his head. Somehow, against the sparkle of the polished steel toilet bowl, he was able to make out Frank's fearful look, dismay seeping out of every pore. His lips were engaged in some kind of silent prayer—at least that was what Matt assumed it was, at first, but there seemed to be no rhythm or reason to his words.

And just as suddenly as it had come, like a summer storm, it was over, silence descending on the room like an iron curtain, gravity feeling ten times stronger than it had before. There was a whistle of wind from the newly formed cracks in the ceiling and walls and a steady stream of coughing coming from just beneath Matt's right leg, which he assumed to be Tyler, and a quick kick of his foot and a curse of pain confirmed this suspicion. He felt guilty for a moment before remembering his previous declaration and decided to kick him once more, albeit slightly gentler.

"Why couldn't he have done that earlier? Would've saved us a lot of screaming," Matt said, practically thinking aloud.

Part of him wanted to hear his own voice, just to reassure himself that the moaning had stopped and he hadn't just gone completely deaf. Part of him knew this test was silly, as he could hear the wind and Frank's ramblings, which had finally become discernible.

"I swear I did, I knew I heard it but didn't think… no, I didn't make the connection. Couldn't be the same… no… it's just a coincidence… Yes, just a coincidence, that's what it is. This isn't my fault. This isn't my fault."

"Frank, what the hell are you going on about over there?"

Frank continued on mumbling himself, oblivious to Matt and the world he inhabited, chained to a thought that was pulling him along faster than he was able to process. There was a heavy groan, and Matt tensed, believing that the man in the far cell was preparing an encore; but it was only Officer McCulley attempting to rise from a pile of dirt and rubble, buried in chunks of plaster ceiling tile—a series of rapid clacks as he hopped to his feet, surprisingly graceful for someone of his girth but ruining the mystique by nearly tipping right back over after waving his gun like a madman.

"What the hell are you assholes trying to do? Blow us all up with some kind of smart bomb, is that it? Planted some shitty homemade C4 to an old wristwatch in the far cell and blow this place to Kingdom Come, huh? Well, not on McCulley's watch, you're not! Ya'll should'a paid more attention in chemistry because that weak shit barely shook the bones of this old bitch!" he exclaimed, smacking the tip of his barrel against the wall.

As the dust cleared, Tyler became visible, curled in a ball on the floor, clutching his stomach in a puddle of his own blood still pouring from his nose like an unstopped drain.

"That doesn't even make any sense, you stupid motherfucker! First, how would we have gotten down into that cell when you and your pig friends locked us up in this one? And second, why the fuck would we blow up the building we're trying to escape from while we're still in it? And you're calling us the stupid ones, damn!"

McCulley kicked the bars of the cell with his stubby legs, striking close to Tyler's exposed head and sending him cowering back into his chest.

"Quiet, boy! I don't need no lip from a wanna-be nigger about intelligence."

"There's a man down there dying, Officer. That's what we were trying to tell you earlier, why we called you down here," Matt said, clinging to some small semblance of hope in his plan, relying on the idea that carrying the dying man out of his cell might distract the bloated officer enough for them to make a better grab at his keys.

Still, with Tyler indisposed and Frank practically catatonic, his chances of getting them on his own were drastically lower.

"But it's exactly the same… why would it sound the same? Not just close, but it sounded exactly like it. Did it follow? No, no, couldn't have. Couldn't have. It was there… in the darkness. When I left, it was still in that darkness."

Frank's rambling became like a soundtrack in Matt's head, watching McCulley's face as he considered the information Matt had presented him. Finally, after what seemed like eons of deliberation, he hocked and spat on the floor with a boisterous chuckle.

"Sure as shit, there is. Do you idiots really think I'm dumb enough to believe a story as stupid as that bullshit? I oughta shoot the lot of you right now for even trying something so clichéd. The 'there's a sick guy in the cell' routine? Really? You think I haven't had that shit pulled on me in my twenty-five years on the force? You dense pieces of shit."

As if part of a protest of mockery, the moaning from down the hall started up again, less like a tremor but just as ethereal and distorted. The color drained from McCulley's face as he peered into the dark end of the hall, his glistening eyes darting from corner to corner.

"What in the fuck?" he said, his revolver nearly shaking out of his fingers.

"It's the same. I know it now. I knew I heard it before. I heard that same voice coming from down in the church basement, the breathing behind the shadows," Frank said, gasping as if his heart had suddenly given out.

Matt turned toward him in concern and confusion, his friend's exasperated conclusion falling on ears too muddled to understand their significance. Frank's gaze met his and supplanted his fears in Matt, who was starting to think there were worse fates at stake here than simply being transferred to another cell made of steel bars.

"Hey! You down there! In the cell at the end of the hall! What seems to be the problem, huh? Can you hear me all the way down there? Can you understand the words I am trying to say to you, son?" McCulley took several trepidatious steps forward, pulling the small black nub of a flashlight from his belt and shining it into the shade.

The man answered with another groan, one loud enough for Matt to study, closer than he had before now that he was focusing on the noise instead of attempting to shut it out. The frequency seemed to be split into octaves, some lower than Matt had ever heard from a human before and others so high that the note was partially drifting into the realm of inaudibility, like there were multiple voices crying out in a tandem agony shared between their very souls.

As McCulley moved out of view from the confines of their cell, Matt shifted forward while staying crouched low to the ground, sensing danger—like one predator encountering another, stronger than himself, in the wild. Tyler had managed to push his weight onto his shoulder and was looking out into the passage, watching the man's blubber slip past their view.

"Something really strange is happening here," Matt confided, taking a long, low step toward Tyler.

"Tell me about it. What the fuck is this racist Irish bastard doing up here in fuckin' Maine? Cracker must be miles away from the sheep farm he grew up in," Tyler mused, righting himself into a sitting position.

"Not just that, everything—the fact that this drunk fat ass is the only cop here guarding a cell of cop killers on the middle of a Wednesday morning, that tremor just a minute ago. And pretty much everything about that man down there is not normal. I've never heard anyone make a sound like that before, not even a dying one."

"Maybe that nigga's got Ebola or something like that?"

"Yeah, I'm sure that's what he's got."

"Wait, you serious? Does that mean we're gonna catch that shit? What the *fuck*, fam. This day just keeps getting worse and worse, I'm telling you."

"Would you stupid assholes shut up?" McCulley shouted, turning his beam on them and blinding them temporarily. He grumbled to himself as he went back to his daunting task, slowing to a stop when he reached the cell's door and illuminating the interior. "Sir? I need you to respond in there, sir. Sir? Sir! Are you still alive in there or what? Oh, Jesus Christ!"

There was a crack as the flashlight tumbled and bounced against the floor, the beam spinning around the short passage, a strobe light constantly shifting the world between light and dark. There was shuffling, heavy yet quick, and the clang of bars, and Matt's heart sunk into his stomach. He suddenly felt very trapped in his cell; when before he was merely contained, unable to leave, kept from his freedom, now he had become suddenly aware of the inescapability of his ten-by-twelve cell.

"Hey! What's going on down there? McCulley? Can you hear us, you fat fuck?" Matt said, slamming against the cell door, hoping against all rules of logic and the universe that they would snap free and fall away at his touch, but reality reared her enigmatic and uncaring head and held the bars in place.

"I said, shut up!" came the response from the dark cavern that had enveloped the cop. The flashlight had slowed to a shaky stop, rolling back and forth alongside its ribbed casing. "I just didn't expect so much… blood, that's all. This poor drunk must've cut himself while no one was looking."

"Nah, that nigga was throwing up. That wasn't some pansy-ass suicide bullshit."

"Do I need to come back there and shoot you stupid bastards before I can get a little peace and quiet? Hmm? Is that too much?"

McCulley stood, righting himself and shrugging his shoulders, cracking his back in the process. He winced in pain but continued over to his fallen flashlight and scooped it up and brought it across Matt, Tyler, and Frank's face once more, chuckling menacingly as he did so.

"You boys seem to just love tempting me."

He lifted his revolver again and took aim at the spot between Matt's eyes; he could feel its presence. It carried a weight, while invisible, that was impossible to shake, no matter how much you steeled yourself or how many times you found yourself on the wrong end of its volatile gaze. If you stared hard enough, you'd swear you could see the shell on the other side, mocking you, boring into you before it's even fired, like a miner chipping away at the spot beneath his drill.

With another hefty laugh, he dropped the iron banshee to his side and waddled back to the far cell, shoving the light into the fleshy fold of his chin as he fumbled for his keys. Going through the small yet overpopulated ring, he eventually found the one that belonged to the rusted lock in front of him and twisted it into place. With a retched screeching, the cell door slid open, several small but generous sparks flying from the scrape of metal on crusty stone. Shielded by shadows, McCulley looked like some kind of grinning demon as he moved into the cell, his rosy-red cheeks turning a shade of crimson, the torch he clutched giving his shadow a bulk that suited his large, overburdened features.

There was a sharp rap against the bricked wall that echoed down the cramped hallway.

"Sir, now I'm only gonna ask you a few more times before I assume that you're food for the maggots. Can you hear me? Can you understand anything that I am saying? Or are you just as retarded as those fuckwits down the hall?"

That horrible booming groan was his reply, not loud enough to turn the precinct back into the fun house room with shifting floors, but enough to make the following silence seem empty and strained.

"Oh, God, it hurts so much. It feels like my intestines are… eating themselves. I can feel them twisting around," the dying man's voice drifted over the silence like a haunted melody carried by the wind, so soft that Matt was surprised he heard it but so all-encompassing that he couldn't explain why he could not. Another groan followed, this one bringing every hair on Matt's body to a rigorous standing.

"All right, sir, all right. I need you to stop screaming and hollering like that, you hear? You need to pull yourself together for me, you underst—" McCulley's reassurances were cut off by the sound of a slick slide and plop, along with a horrible tearing, like a thick stack of shirts being pulled apart, the seams giving a sick, taunt resistance.

"Oh, Sweet Mary, Mother of God, your hand. Why'd it… ? Why'd your hand come off like that? What's the matter with you, boy, you got some kind of leprosy or something? Are you telling me we got a goddamn leper in this stupid backwater police station? Answer me, goddammit! Answer me!"

Matt tried to piece together everything he was hearing next door but felt a strange disconnect from his own body as the words started to untangle themselves from the knots in which they entered. His skin suddenly felt like a rebel trying to escape its own body, tearing itself loose from his rotting bones and sliding to find a new host, one that would openly accept its wanton desires. Despite his confusion and his terrible foreboding about what lay at the end of the hall, be it disease or something far, far worse, the urge still had its dark digits embedded deep with the wrinkles of his brain, its hold suffocating him and disorienting him from the world.

Still, it was impossible to ignore the pounding against the wall as McCulley threw the dying man against the wall, shouting at him for vague answers to questions he wasn't even sure of.

"What in the fuck are you doing, you sack of shit? Look at me! You hear me? Pull that ugly head out of your hands, and look at— what the fuck? Are you… chewing on it? Did you chew it off? Put your hands up, you crazy bastard! I mean, put your hand up, or… you know what I mean! Just get those arms up where I can see them, and don't try—Agh!"

A shot went off, so sudden that Matt dropped to the floor practically by instinct, Tyler following suit, while Frank remained steady, calm only in his removal from this plane of existence. Matt grabbed the wrist of his jacket and yanked him to the ground, a position he went into easily and without question, even in his eyes. They heard a struggle and saw the shaking of the wall, with its puffs of dislocated sediment signaling the hidden blows. McCulley was grunting, and there was nothing but a groan from the dying man, along with a sound that was halfway between a growl and a wail, static and bitter.

Several more shots went off, the trio ducking like students crammed underneath desks in fear of some kind of nuclear retaliation, their nerves tuned to react at any perceived danger, however harmless it may seem. There was a booming yell that came before a heavy crash, the flashlight rolling out into the hallway in crazed and wild circles. The cell was thrown into madness, screeching and grunts and groans as the morbid soundtrack, with flashing bouts of blindness that made keeping your eyes open a challenge, no matter how fearful you were of closing them.

"Ah! Get off me, you psychotic sonuvabitch! As soon as I get this thing reloaded, I'm gonna blow your brains clear across the room. Ow! Ow! Oww! What the hell are you doing? Stop biting me, you crazy fuck! Stop it! Oh, fuck, you're pulling my skin off, you bastard! What the hell's the matter with—Ah! Ahhhhhhh—"

McCulley's watery voice descended into one continuous scream, the howl of a dying animal that knows its doom but is unable to accept it. He cried out several more times, bemoaning his attacker and praying for help. He even turned to offering pleasantries to the crouched trio, giving his apologies, desperate to strike some kind of deal despite knowing full well that even if they were foolhardy enough to accept, they were powerless to act.

"Oh, get your hands out of there! Get your hands out of me! Oh, God, you're pulling it all out, why are… why are you pulling it all out? Why… why are you pulling them all—"

His voice stopped and spiraled into a crunchy rattle, the phlegm and blood sticking to his final sigh. The silence, although originally a gift, showed its blackened insides when they were able to hear the mashing of teeth into meat, the squishing and gnawing of a full mouth chewing something long and stringy. However, the worst part was not the sounds that filled the room but the absences, like the fact that Matt could no longer hear any breathing coming from the far end of the hall.

The flashlight, cracked and splintered, was flickering steadily, fighting a losing battle against its own slow, drawn-out death. After a few tense seconds, it finally gave up and let the passageway fall into darkness, the only light now coming from the fluorescent at the other end of the short stretch of hallway.

For what felt like the passing of eons, nobody spoke—the air charged and thick with the smell of blood, sweat, and excrement (which seemed to be permeating from somewhere near Tyler's sagging drawers). The only sounds that could be heard was the futile struggle of the flashlight in preserving its meager light, clicking and buzzing like some kind of dying insect, and the sound of whatever was in the far cell feasting—the sound of chewing and gnashing, of tearing and slobbering—whatever it was, taking long, stringy bites, harshly yanking on sinews. A growing pool of blood was forming underneath the bars of the cell, spreading outward like a replicating virus and collecting beneath the cradle of the flashlight. The red syrup-like substance soon grew high enough to pour over the light's protector and turned its final flashes a bright, startling crimson—an emergency light going off as some kind of belated warning—before the viscous liquid snuffed it out completely in a fiery sizzle.

After many tense minutes, Matt finally seemed to find enough courage to stand, pushing himself off the cold concrete and taking note of the dark abyss at every opportunity. When on his feet, he spent several moments peering into that darkness, scanning for any sign of movement or danger, his muscles painfully tense, his skin clammy and cold with a layer of perspiration that filled his mouth with the taste of salt and copper. As his gaze fell deeply into the hypnotizing pull of that total blackness, that complete absence of light, he half-expected to see his own demonically grinning features staring back at him, blood dripping from his mouth and down his toned, naked body, erect and feverous. The squishing, sloppy crescendo from the far cell was feeding the urge; and soon it was impossible to see that unknown assailant as anything other than that nun, blood seeping between her bruised and sliced-up legs, to the point where he was entirely convinced that it *was* her that had bestowed whatever horrible fate on Officer McCulley.

The hairs on Matt's arms were rigid and at attention, pulled toward the dark, like some kind of weird form of divination. He knew that whatever waited for him down there would spell their doom and understood his earlier apprehension about the cramped cell and its lack of any form of escape should they find themselves under assault from the demented form next door. Matt pictured her smiling—her toothless, mocking grin tearing into him before they even touched, her long, slimy tongue circling her cracked lips in a mockery of Matt's own sacred ritual. His thoughts were upturned by the horrible moan of that creature rising again, sending Matt staggering back in fear of his own inescapable destiny, one that he had been dreaming of for so long now that it had become an unmovable landmark at the edge of existence. His body trembled with anticipation, ready to transcend his own tainted flesh and embrace the darkness beneath it, hoping to find some form of purity beneath the dark corruption he felt nagging and clawing at his skin. The dancing corpse of the nun began her striptease in his mind, degrading rapidly before his eyes, removing large gray chunks of flesh instead of lingerie. Digging her long nails into the skin around her groin, she uprooted a large chunk of fat and tore vertically like string cheese—exposing the shiny, wet bone underneath, flecks of muscle and sinew clinging to the corners and connections.

Matt felt like throwing up but knew that wouldn't add anything to their situation, especially when Frank was still dead to the world and Tyler was cowering in his own excrement, whispering affirmations to himself. The shuffling of feet could be heard coming from the far cell, slow and monotonous, like they were being dragged across the floor with every effort their host had, the leather of its shoes scraping along the cement. The macabre burlesque show continued, projected on his eyelids for him, courtesy of the urge, to be seen and enjoyed every time he closed his eyes to regain composure, think, or even blink. The nun was cackling, but he could not hear the laughter. It was the only thing keeping his sanity intact and dividing the already-lurid lines between reality and his own sick fantasies. With closed eyes, he saw her wink at him and blow a kiss, inadvertently throwing her lips at him from across the room.

Shivering, Matt decided to move toward the cell door again, occupying his body with some task, however futile, to keep his mind from its own dark intentions. He worked at the door, hoping against his own logic that it would come loose this final time, believing that all the previous attempts might've loosened its bearings and this one final push would be the one to finally conquer it. Alas, it seems reality decided it would be unyielding in this instance, despite the madness all around him; and the door held firm, his violent shaking doing nothing but adding accompaniment to the rhythmic shuffle of feet from the cell at the end of the hall.

Every few tries, he would poke his head up and stare into the darkness, searching and sifting through it for any sign of their attacker, but all that he could see was blackness. However, on the fifth or sixth time looking down into those shadows, he saw them split and move and knew that there was something lurking behind their curtain. His breath caught in his throat and nudged Tyler with his foot, hoping to rouse him and get back his virulent personality, however double-edged that sword ended up being; but Tyler merely swatted the intruder away like he would a fly, hardly pulling his head from the floor to look at it.

Finding no help there, Matt went to whisper Frank's name but was cut off by the howl of that foul creature, its rancid "breath" mingling with the air and turning it just as rotten. It smelled like a mixture of bad meat and some kind of wet animal, with a dash of copper and the worst-smelling shit that Matt could imagine, although he couldn't be entirely sure that wasn't coming from their own cell.

A flash of white appeared in the darkness, the creature's maw appearing before the rest of it, the bottom row of its jaw hanging loose and flapping untethered from the muscles that usually held it. It stretched longer than it should, like a snake that had unhinged itself to eat but couldn't fit all the pieces back into place. The rest of its face appeared next—its long, scraggly red beard framing its horrible mouth and its gray, dead eyes appearing above it, bright in a way that didn't betray life but some perverted extension of it, a twinkling behind the glossiness of death. Its skin was torn in log shreds down his cheek as if it had been clawing at its own face, gripped and rattled with pain.

A stub of a hand appeared beneath him, its edges uneven and misshapen, chunks and pieces seemingly torn and still hanging loose from its end, like strips of bandages from a mummy in one of those old movies they played on television when all the kids had gone to sleep and the people who remembered when color film wasn't even an option tuned in. It wasn't long before the rest of him came into view, in all his terrible glory. His pants sagged low and deep, and the remnants of a belt hung through the loops, the loose strap of leather chewed through to the steel buckle near his gut. Hiking boots were strapped to his feet, but his ankle had broken sometime during his escape from his cell; and his left boot bent at an uncomfortable angle, probably the entire ninety degrees possible to bend without coming loose.

Somehow, he continued undeterred in his incentive, reaching out for Matt with his stump of an arm as soon as their eyes connected. A chill went over him when he met those eyes, so cold that they seemed to freeze him in place, rooting him to the ground beneath his feet. The thing that was once a man shimmied forward, his shoulder against the wall as he made his way down the darkened passageway, its ferocity slow but wild. Foam was forming at the edges of his mouth, a nauseous combination of green and crimson bubbles mixing in his bloody gullet.

Matt felt the need to void his stomach again. He was certain, though, that if he did, the creature would grab his head and pull it free of his shoulders while he was crouched over on the floor and instead decided to back slowly into the farthest reaches of their own cramped quarters. Frank, now aware of their danger and coming back to his fried senses, was doing the same, reaching down and pulling on Tyler's shoulder, indicating that he should follow suit. It took a Tyler a moment to realize as his eyes adjusted to the light, however minimal; and when he saw that horrible stub grace the bars near his ankle, he scurried to his feet, like a panicked crab fleeing back to the ocean, as he scuttled into the shadows between the two of them, pressing himself flat against the mortar.

The thing was now at the bars of the cell, swinging its jaw to and fro with rapid twists of its neck, moving statically, almost as if there was a frame removed from the way the light of his movements was hitting Matt's eyes. Pushing the long, decrepit finger that it still possessed through the bars, it swung at them like a cat batting at its prey, toying with it but desperate to feel their flesh giving way beneath its swing, nature compelling it just as much as it compelled any predator to feast on its prey.

A groan was still coming from its open throat, the long distortion of it giving it a deep rumble that Matt could feel from across the room. He could smell it as well, the toxic odor hitting him like a thunderous wave and nearly knocking him unconscious with its putridness. Tyler was screaming, shouting every one of the many obscenities he knew at it, hurling insults and insinuating that it wasn't particularly well endowed and that it enjoyed the company of other men—all of which, surprisingly, did nothing to slow it. It hardly seemed to even take note that Tyler was speaking, now attempting to shove its twisted skull between the bars. Its pale, saggy flesh was being pulled back and torn by the pressure of the bars, stretched tight against its bones. Clots burst beneath his broken jaw, pouring slick black blood down his throat and turning his growls to syrupy gurgles.

Taking another step back from the paralyzing sight before him, Matt nearly tripped over the dislodged bench; and feeling a surge of daring, he scooped it into his hands, unsteadily trying to find a good balance for it. Letting it slide into a good fit, he charged forward and whacked it against the steel, cracking the creature's arm at the elbow and sending it into a ravenous fit of howling as it struggled against the heavy wood panel. The board was shaking heavily and came free of Matt's grip, and as the reality of his makeshift plan sank in, he quickly decided to back off, holding the bench in place with his foot as he hopped back into the recesses of the cell. He was nearly thrown back as the creature pulled its arm back and threw its body against the bars, the bench falling and clattering against the concrete.

Almost as if it was celebrating its own victory, the creature reared back its loose and flopping jaw and let loose a horrible roar, much like the one that alerted McCulley to its presence in the first place, shaking the entire precinct and causing Matt's stomach to turn over itself. Frank was sinking into his knees in defeat, as Tyler had done many minutes ago, and Matt finally lost to the hopelessness of their situation and readied for the fate that he had accepted long ago, after the darkness had defeated him, destroyed every reputable part of him on that night, the night the urge had finally won out over his conscience. Slowly, bitterly, he sunk into himself and let that roar become all that he knew…

But before the creature could finish its grisly celebration, his head was torn to bits and scattered over the side of the cell and the hallway by the loud ring of a gunshot, its body falling to the ground in a slump immediately afterward, so fast it seemed almost cartoonish.

For a moment, none of them spoke, dumbstruck at their reversal of fortune, waiting to see if some far-worse evil had presented itself, not allowing themselves any optimism, however cautious. Their fears proved unfounded when another cop—in full, straightened uniform and jet-black skin, holding his gun high in front of him but still close to his chest—moved toward the still body that lay on the blood-coated floor. With a sharp kick from his polished black shoes, the officer checked the gnarled corpse for any stray twitch or flicker of movement. When he was satisfied with its prolonged, uncomfortable silence, he turned his attention toward the three of them, squinting and straining to make out their form in the shadowy corners of their cell.

"Is everybody okay in there?" he asked, making a quick inspection of the other empty cells and the viscous puddle that was still surging forward unabated.

"Yes, we-we're fine," Matt stammered, and Frank and Tyler gave similar affirmations.

With a curt nod, so quick that it seemed like he had been impatiently waiting for their answers based entirely on the protocol behind it—which, Matt assented, given their imprisonment, made sense—the stiff officer started to move forward, before stopping awkwardly and turning back to them.

"Don't you guys go anywhere now," he said, clearly pleased with himself.

"Wasn't planning on it," Matt said bitterly.

The officer continued on into the far cell, stepping lightly over the wads of hair and brain of the cell's previous occupant. His shoes made splashes in the deep puddle of crimson as he entered it, exhaling sharply as he entered.

"What the fuck happened in here?"

"Your guess is as good as ours."

He went silent for a while, long enough where Matt's irrationality got the better of him, and he started to suspect that their savior had dropped dead himself inside that cursed place. Before he could call out, he reappeared, aiming his gun square down the hallway, giving it one final assessment, before holstering his weapon at his side and turning to face the only living occupants of the cell block.

"So you're telling me you guys have no idea what went on in that cell over there?"

"Well, we heard, but as you could probably figure out, our view was slightly obscured, so it'd mostly just be guessing on our parts."

"Did our friend here…" the cop sent another kick into the creature's limp limb, "give any reason for attacking Officer McCulley? Did he say anything beforehand? Shout anything out, manifesto-style?"

"He shouted something out, all right!" Tyler said, his voice shaky as he was finding his words for the first time after his brush with certain death. "But I sure as shit couldn't tell you what he was talking about!"

"He was moaning, screaming about his stomach. It sounded like he was throwing up or something," Matt almost told him about being used to the sound as a bartender.

But from the look of actual concern and passiveness on the cop's face, it seemed, by some divine grace, the officer didn't recognize them, and he aimed to keep it that way.

Leaning back so that he could stare into the darkened cell with his flashlight, the officer nodded grimly.

"He definitely threw something up, all right. From the looks of it, the guy threw up half his guts."

"That much?"

"No, literally half of his guts, intestines and such, they're sitting in a wet pile at the foot of the bench," he said, motioning with the flashlight to the unseen horror—an image Matt could only fathom as some kind of panel from an old horror comic he used to filch from the corner store as a kid.

"Some of those might be McCulley's," Matt added, remembering the officer's grim final words.

An incredulous look decorated the officer's face as he checked back into the cell, only to fade into one of morose resignation as he spied what Matt was referring to.

"It seems you would be correct."

Taking a step back, the officer began to look over the dead man's body, examining the stretch of his jaw with his small finger, twisting its inverted joints in a futile attempt to understand how the man had managed to be standing before the bullet had taken off the top of his skull. His foot squelched softly against a piece of pink matter, but he remained steady and calm, disturbingly so, as he got back on his feet.

"What do you think was wrong with him?" he said, more to himself than anything, his thoughts slipping loose from their bonds and into the real world.

The heavy silence was interrupted by a scoff from Tyler.

"Shit, are ya'll serious? That motherfucker's a goddamn zombie. Ya'll ever seen a movie before? Dead, infected motherfuckers rising from the ground and biting other motherfuckers so they turn into zombies too? Shit ain't rocket science. Damn, ya'll niggas is stupid."

"What did he just say?" the cop said, shining his bright beam on Tyler, the disparity only highlighting the dark tones of the officer's skin.

"Sorry. Ignore him. He's just a little traumatized by the whole getting attacked thing and doesn't know what he's saying," Matt said, as fast as his mind would let him.

The officer's face darkened, like storm clouds had formed above his brow, dark and furious, as he brought the flashlight across all three of their faces. Tense seconds ticked by in strained silence, the officer studying their faces like a book, his eyes burrowing into them, sifting through the contents, looking for an answer that he already knew.

"Who are you guys? What are you doing in here?"

Tyler opened his mouth to speak but thought better of it after a quick dismissal by Matt, who attempted to strangle him with his gaze. Frank remained silent, almost as if he didn't know the cop was there or had even arrived to rescue them from their fate. His mouth was moving, working out secrets, hidden plans and dilemmas that only he knew of, but Matt couldn't hear them well enough to even try and piece them together.

"You're the guys who robbed the bar on Twenty-Ninth, the ones who shot the sheriff."

"Allegedly, homie, but I didn't shoot the deputy, nigguh," Tyler said, stifling a thick laugh.

Never in his life had Matt wanted to wring someone's neck out as much as he did in that moment; his knuckles were white and digging into his thighs in an attempt to hold themselves back.

The uncomfortable silence that followed was thicker than any before it; the very air in the room seemed to take on a different feel as if the whole world had shifted in a violently different cosmic rotation. It fermented and grew stale, made worse by the overwhelming noxiousness of the fresh corpses that had taken residence in the cell block. No one moved. Tyler had long fallen silent after chuckling at his own bit of sarcastic wit and was now watching the officer behind the bars, hunched over and breathing heavily in a silent resignation that gave him a zenlike wisdom that was oddly befitting him.

In a flash, the cop flipped open the buckle above his holster and pulled loose his .38 special, taking fast aim at Tyler's forehead. There were no words spoken, and the veil of silence remained untarnished—a silver veneer that gave the whole scene a holy feeling, retribution in its purest and most logical form. It was sickeningly simplistic, disturbingly basic, and horrifyingly human. Matt's first instinct was to shove his friends aside, even of throwing himself in the bullet's path; but he knew this to be an empty, hollow gesture based solely on what heroes in cheesy movies told him to do. And the action would prove as futile as trying to ram the door again, because even if he managed to spare his friends' life with his quick reflexes, the cop would only fire the remaining five rounds into him soon after. Instead, he remained steady, preparing for his own end, taking solace in the unexpected tranquility of it—especially after believing himself doomed to that grisly yet not undeserved demise just moments ago. Part of his calm demeanor came from his inability to believe in an ultimate fate other than the one he preordained years ago, at the hand of the demon that lurked within the cellar of his being.

"Now, why don't we all just take a deep breath and relax. Now, Officer…" he squinted to make out the name beneath the badge, on the small clipped-on placard, "Vincini. Obviously, we were put in here for our questionably legal actions and accept whatever punishment that a court of law determines fair, but I think in light of the recent situation, we could possibly just put our past actions behind us and move forward as allies? We could help you. We'd definitely be a hell of a lot more helpful breathing, than not, because if what my retarded friend here said… about what that guy… is, then you're just gonna have to use another three bullets to put us down again. And after taking out our friend there, I don't think your old revolver's got enough bullets left for that."

The officer seemed to consider this, taking a brief moment to inspect that rotting body at his feet, the blood engulfing the soles of his shoes, like cliff sides on a beach after a battle. Seemingly mollified, Matt dared to step forward but thought better of it, not willing to relinquish any reason for the man to shoot them on the spot, even resorting to Tyler's puerile fantasies, hoping to appeal to the officer's most illogical fears in the face of something truly irrational. This seemed to pay off as the cop's shoulder slouched, and the gun dropped away from the top of Tyler's skull.

"Come on, you know it makes sense. There's gotta be a reason why the cops aren't back yet, and something tells me it relates to whatever happened to that poor bastard at your feet. Faced with something as big as that, in the bigger picture, does what we did really even matter? I mean—"

At that, the officer stiffened, and the gun snapped back to its previous position, the muscles in his arm going rigid. He clicked the hammer back and switched his sights to Matt, procedurally but brimming with a concealed fury.

"Whoa! Whoa! Hold up and think about what you're doing, man," Matt reasoned, his grip on the situation slipping to the point where it had spiraled completely out of his reach.

"It does matter! It does!" the officer said, his voice expressing the emotion his body dared not show. "Don't you dare say that it doesn't matter, that he doesn't matter…"

The cop's face was passive, emotionless and blank, showing no hint of his intentions beyond that of the raised gun. His eyes, however, seemed to betray the battle raging behind them, his pupils wavering and watering without pause. Accepting his fate, Matt took a final swallow of air, shut his eyes tight, and waited for death to come—almost drawing pleasure from it, the sour taste of guilt fresh and thick in his throat. Darkness seemed as natural a home as any for him.

The officer gave a heavy sigh, so long that he was certain that he had pushed out all the air in his body and had nothing left to sustain him. Slowly, struggling the entire way down, the cop lowered his gun, reholstering it with such bitter shame that Matt almost felt guilty for not falling dead right then and there.

In what seemed like one incomprehensible movement, the wary cop pulled the ring of keys from his belt and threw them into the lock at the front of the cell, twisting until there was a sharp click that shook the air. Sliding the door to the side, he motioned them out, the three not waiting for a second invitation and quickly following his silent instruction. Out of their cells, they quickly examined the scene in closer detail, looking down at the dead man's twisted body, his long, warped jawline forever locked in an anatomically distorted scream that still seemed to ring within their ears. The pool of blood seemed larger now that they were staring down at it, covering the expanse of the hallway, steadily trickling from the open cell at the end, in which none of them expressed an interest in inspecting closer.

When they finally turned their attention on their savior, none of them knew exactly what to do. Part of Matt wanted to unapologetically take advantage of the stranger's extraordinarily loud conscience, taking the gun and leaving him here for dead—as the three of them, however ragged, might still be able to overpower the lithe young man. As if he sensed these thoughts, the cop put his hand back on his revolver, staring dead into his eyes, like he was willing him to do it, begging for the excuse he had prayed for.

"So are we gonna agree to a truce or just do this right here in this bloody-ass hallway?" Officer Vincini said, letting his gaze drift between the three of them, intimidating them and seeking acceptance in the same gesture.

"You've got my word," Frank said quickly, adjusting well to his new surroundings.

Any sign that he had been near catatonic just minutes ago seemed to have faded, and all that remained was that same timidness that had always plagued him.

Officer Vincini nodded briskly at this, as good of a word as he was going to give.

"Aye, I'm with Frog," Tyler said, unexpectedly. There was a tiredness in his voice, his posture still doubled over itself, his hands clutching tightly at his injured leg. "I ain't got no beef with ya, homie."

The officer bristled at this treaty, struggling to swallow the thing he himself had suggested, before giving a nod of assent that couldn't seem more pained than if he had a broken neck. Finally, he turned his sights back on Matt, still just as deadly, despite the fact that a gun was no longer held between them. He studied this officer, looked at the deep lines in caramel skin, the small scar that ran beneath his earlobe, finding no weakness to exploit or anything to turn in his favor in a fight. Accepting his own logic and swallowing his own self-made poison just as the cop did before him, he gave a sardonic smile and waved his hand down the hall.

"Lead the way, Officer."

With a check of sincerity, a probing moment of trust, the cop turned to start down the small hallway into the precinct before facing them again.

"Call me Bruce."

"Nigga, I'll call you whatever you want, just get us the hell out of here. Shiet."

Bruce looked at him incredulously before turning back to Matt. "Man, does this guy want me to shoot him?"

"Like I said earlier, it's better to just ignore him. Now, do you guys have some kind armory here, or do you all just keep those little revolvers of yours in your purses?"

"There's an armory on the other side of the building, near the locker room and the stairs leading up the second floor. Unfortunately, it's been pretty much cleaned out. I checked on the way over," Bruce said, pretending that he hadn't heard the second part of Matt's inquiry.

"Cleaned out? Who the hell cleaned it out?"

"They didn't tell you guys anything before they left you here, did they? A riot broke out down at Saint Roma's. Couldn't tell you what started it or what that many people were doing out there on a Wednesday morning, but when the other officers stationed at the hospital to check on the sheriff's… condition…" A chill seemed to pass through Bruce's body, but it passed so quickly that if Matt hadn't been watching him with his full attention, he wouldn't have noticed it. "When we got word from our guys at the church, there were reports of officers down, fires, all sorts of things you don't ever expect to hear over your radio in a town with less than fifteen thousand people in it. Asworth and Roeg decided to head straight there, while I came back here, grabbing as much ammunition as I could, but everything was like you see now by the time I got here. I stopped in the armory and managed to grab a couple .38 rounds before I heard that… thing growling and thought some kind of fox had gotten in or something. It really wouldn't seem that strange at this point in the day. In fact, it'd probably be more normal than what actually happened back there."

"And there's no other place you guys have any other weapons? Police armor? Batons? Fucking anything?" Matt was starting to romanticize the idea of returning to his cell.

"I do," Tyler said, drawing everyone's attention with the flippant manner in which it was said.

"And how the hell would you know where weapons are in a police station?" Matt asked mockingly.

"And try to say it with as few slurs as possible," Bruce added.

Tyler smiled devilishly. "'Coz I'm the one who brought 'em in here," he said, smugness drizzled over the words.

He shuffled forward down the hall, insisting the others follow him based on the cocksure demeanor he carried. "Bitch," he added as he passed Bruce, the flinch in his face as he contained himself going unnoticed by the limping thug.

As Matt approached him, he gave the upright officer a pat on the shoulder, a smile inviting him to share in the reverie of the harmless quip. They moved forward in silence, Bruce waiting until Frank passed him as well before taking his spot at the rear, his hand hovering above the revolver at his hip, the small strap of leather that held it already untethered.

They moved into the central office of the precinct, the rows of desks neat but spotted with overturned trays of papers and upturned drawers that stood as evidence of a hasty and frantic departure. Several computer monitors were still displaying screensavers, amorphic waves of light undulating to unheard celestial beats, a light psychedelic treat for anyone who got distracted from their tedious filings. The front door stood open—or, at least, one side of it—its heavy metal handle clacking in the wind as the door bounced against the glass wall that contained it. Leaves had been blown in and strewn across the floor, giving the room a feeling of longtime abandonment despite the fact that just hours earlier, it had been a bustling hub for the tax-paid protectors of the city, lives passing in and out, many of which were now in the thick of some kind of riot going on downtown. One that was most assuredly spurred on by the effects of whatever disease the man in the far cell had inflicted. Many of them would probably never come back through those doors, their work forever half complete, their personal belongings left in this ruin of the modern age, anthropological marvels for future generations to piece together how earlier humans enacted their own contemporary version of justice on each other.

Lost in thought, Matt didn't realize how long they had been waiting stationary in the center of the room, their self-appointed guide scanning the stretches of its corners as if he had suddenly awoken from an afternoon nap and was checking if the sun had set yet.

"Why have we stopped?" Frank asked from behind them.

"Yeah, what are we waiting for?"

"Which way are we even heading right now?"

"How the fuck would I know? I was just getting out of the stankin'-ass hallway," Tyler announced, plopping himself in a nearby chair and massaging his bandaged leg.

"What are you… I thought you were leading us to where the weapons are?"

"What? Why the fuck would you think something like that?"

"Well, gee, T-Dawg, I don't know… Maybe it has something to do with you… and this is just a guess… declaring that you knew where the weapons were."

"Ohhhhhhhhh. Ohhhhhhhhhh. Okay, okay, I think I can see the confusion there. What I meant was, I know where the guns is, but I don't know where the guns *is*."

Bruce gave Matt an exasperated look. "What the hell is he talking about?"

"Ugh, damn, ya'll motherfuckers really are dumb as shit, ain't you? Listen up, retards, I had a bag when we got brought in here. In this bag, Gucci label, by the way, I have a metric shit ton of guns and ammo in there. Along with a couple choice explosives, some body armor, I think I managed to squeeze a couple knives in there for the extra badass factor, you know? All that shit is in impound right now. All we have to do is get there, but I obviously wouldn't know the fucking way there, otherwise, I'd be there already."

Bruce didn't wait for Tyler to finish his rant, moving around him to the hall opposite the cell block as soon as he heard the word *impound*. Stopping behind a desk and throwing open several drawers, he found a hidden ring of keys, a paper label with "Spare" written in Sharpie taped clumsily around it. He quickly started down the left passage and stopped at the first door on the right, the words "Impound/Evidence" written on the frosted glass, with the head of the department's name slid into a placard underneath. Matt and Frank filed in behind him as he opened it, Tyler still groggily lifting himself for his rolling chair in the main hall.

As they entered, they were hit with a strong cornucopia of aromas, many pleasing and many more foul, mixing with the sterile burn of the cleaning supplies that had been used in excess in the cramped room. Matt noticed the smell of lilac amidst the others and was reminded of Veronica and wondered if she was okay or if the riot had reached the Métier home as well. Part of him wondered how she had received the news of his incarceration, whether she had found shame in it or if it had brought her some kind of peace, however minor a sentiment it was.

"Which bag is it?" Bruce said, moving haughtily about the room.

His impatience was mounting, Matt could tell, a steady coating of sweat on his face that seemed out of place in a room blistered by the cold autumn breezes.

"That one there, with the black polyester handles," Tyler said, entering the room with a grimace of pain on his face and shutting the door behind him. He quickly threw his weight against the table, taking the pressure off his leg and sighing with a tepid relief.

Spying it near the top ledge beneath a small, dimly lit, dirt-stained window—Bruce reached up and pulled it free of its high shelf, slamming it down on the table in the center of the room, struggling with its weight enough that Matt had to lend a hand just to carry it to its destination. He reached up to the zipper at the front and unzipped their prize, exposing the destructive treasure trove within. Barrels and muzzles sprung up with a frightening quickness that caused them all to stumble back, their nerves already nearly frayed.

Bruce pulled loose a large assault rifle that Matt didn't recognize, but from a quick inspection, it appeared to be army grade. There was even a hunting scope on, the glass marked with the standard issue sights, which Bruce tested with a reserved glee. Tyler reached in and retrieved a classic-style .357 and tossed it to Frank, along with pulling out a large Desert Eagle revolver that he slipped into the back of his shorts.

Matt looked down into the bag and saw that there were still at least three or four more large firearms in the bag, along with several other shadows he couldn't distinguish.

"Why the hell did you have so many guns on you when we were arrested?"

"I like to be safe, rather than sorry, plus that shit shows up on the news, and I always want motherfuckers to know this nigga be packin'."

Bruce grunted but kept himself silent. Tyler dipped his hand back into the bag and carried out a handful of grenades clutched in his fingers, looking them over like eggs at the supermarket before plopping them back inside their cloth container. Finally, he pulled out the Remington he had used back at Caplin's and another model that was close to its exact twin and handed it to Matt. He gave his a quick cock to clear the barrel and loaded in a fresh slug from the duffel bag, handing several to Matt, who did the same.

"You know, I do believe those bags of weed up there were in my bag as well."

"Nice try," Bruce said with a ghost of a grin. "Stuff's dated February 13."

Tyler accepted this defeat with a quiet grace, rubbing his fingers over his mess of stubble before seizing the bag by its strap and throwing it over his shoulder. Inside, you could hear the sliding and crashing of the firearms tumbling against one another, a squeamish look passing over Tyler's face as he heard the sound of the slow cock of an automatic rifle, followed by the click of its release seconds later.

"So what's the plan here?" Matt demanded, staring at his companions and finding subtle faults with all of them.

Frank was still dead to the world, less a vegetable than he had been when they found themselves attacked; but the several times Matt had tried to get his attention, he had been met with paltry success, with Frank giving only gruff nods or brisk grunts as answers. His limbs were constantly trembling, twitching, randomly flinching at invisible terrors, his eyes animated but wasted on things that didn't exist on this plane of existence.

Tyler was more nonchalant, calm, and collected in that way he could be when his privileged upbringing was fresh in his mind, fuel for the god complex he exercised on himself. Matt knew from his own experiences with Tyler that this would make him damn nigh invincible in the face of any viable threat, one that he could actually wrap his consciousness around, unlike their foe in the cell. However, the drawback was his unpredictability, his mind playing by rules that had never been shared with anyone else and that were willing to be changed without warning to better his own situation.

And while trust in Tyler was hard to place due to his questionable ethics, especially with the threat of death bearing down on them, trusting Bruce was something Matt couldn't bring himself to do. While Bruce would surely need them if things were as bad as he said, Matt reasoned that the three of them didn't necessarily need the officer tagging along, weighing them down with his burden of perceived justice. The weight of the shotgun in his hands felt heavy, and the thought of turning it on their would-be savior seemed cathartic—within reason, almost righteous. But something, some part of him that he hadn't touched on in years, stopped his hand. Besides, Bruce had risked his own life to save them, knowing full well they might've overpowered him and stripped him of his weapons. Justice aside, they did have an obligation to him, despite their perceived slights against each other. Matt could still see the intensity in Bruce's eyes when he looked at Tyler, the one he sported when aiming down the sights of his clunky revolver.

"Say, why do you carry that old thing around anyway?" Matt said, bridging the awkward silence with a stilted attempt at small talk. "Cops haven't carried those things around for decades."

In a motion that seemed to turn the world further upside down than it already was—Bruce smiled gently, looking down at the small piece in his hands, his fingers caressing the wooden pommel, the oak handle smoothed to the dazzling shine, the chambers rusted and squeaking but working in a shaky tandem that Bruce treated like a kind of luck, one that didn't dangle uselessly from around your neck but from the tips of your fingers.

"You're right. It was a special request. Honestly, it's pretty stupid, now that I'm really thinking about it," he mused, looking at the gun like he was getting ready to capture its portrait. "It's the kind you used to see on all those old-cop serials—*Columbo*, *Magnum, PI*— all those cheesy old guys with mustaches thicker than their Boston accents and knuckles tougher than brass. I used to watch them when I was a kid, my father at my side before the cancer took him, and I used to think to myself, 'You know, these guys are all either arrogant jerks whom no one would ever want to be around or these total dorks the television writers love telling you are super cool cats who could bag any woman than crossed their paths, but behind all of it, when it finally came down to the final confrontation, there was always them and that gun standing between the criminals,' a clear distinction between the right and the wrong. The face behind it may change, but their sense of right never did. I used to run around the lawn, shooting invisible baddies with my finger, cocking my thumb back in that surefire, cocky way they always loved to do. It made me think that no matter how I turned out, as long as I could carry that gun, it would give my life some kind of purpose—a noble one, one that, when it came down to it, just me, them and the gun between us, no one could really deny. And then they got rid of it, like you said," he sighed, "switched to the more reliable semiautomatics, reloaded with a quick clip in, quick clip out, instead of dropping bullets like coins in a well. Part of me thought of moving on, forgetting my stupid flights of fancy and kid games I used to play, but I couldn't shake that feeling. Couldn't get rid of that sense of right and wrong those shows used to give me, however fabricated. So I applied to the academy, made it to the top of my class, and decided to use that as leverage in an attempt at a special request from my CO. I asked the sheriff with a formal letter—pleaded, really—to let me use that Colt .38 Special, slow, pain-in-the-ass reload and all. He looked me over, asked me if I had some kind of death wish, putting myself at an obvious disadvantage in the line of fire, but I gave him the same spiel I just gave you, and he stared at me for a while, neither of us speaking. I thought he was gonna tell me to get the hell out of his office and find another job that would meet my high and mighty requests, but he simply stamped the letter and shook my hand, welcoming me aboard and saying he looked forward to seeing me on the beat. That was the first time we spoke, actually."

A strange smile passed over his face then, brusque and laden with a sadness that Matt couldn't understand—one that seemed monumental and ineffectual at the same time, something paralyzing but catalytic as well, a genuine warmth that shone behind a self-imposed coldness. Matt shared a look with Tyler, who simply shrugged, his hand sliding near the trigger in case the bout of sentimentality turned against them. This moment passed without mention, and soon, the air of the room returned to its charged sense of foreboding doom.

"While that's cool and all, dawg, you sure you don't want an Uzi or something? You know, something with a little more firepower than your BB gun? It's no trouble, I think I got like two or three in here. Even a little sawed-off or something would be better. I think I even had an M79 I bought off some guy in Thailand somewhere in here… I don't know, maybe one of your pi—cop friends came and took it, 'cuz I'm not seeing it," Tyler said, shifting through the large bag at his shoulder.

Bruce waved this offer aside and shook his head just to clarify.

"Are you sure? Even another pistol or something? Dual wielding a couple Desert Eagles, popping caps sideways, like one hard-ass ni… dude."

"Thanks, but no, thanks," Bruce said, a hint of a smile on his lips, reviling in Tyler's obvious discomfort. "Now," he added, moving to the other side of the room and pulling a large black frame off the wall so quick that Matt could not identify it, "about that plan you were asking about…"

He slammed the frame down on the table between them, the glass inside it flexing and shattering, the shards collecting in the center. With a quick shake and turning over, there was a clear and easy-to-read map of Loganville lying before them, its streets and boulevards marked with a red highlight that seemed deviously ominous. Bruce slammed his finger down near the bottom-left corner.

"This is where we are," he said. He dragged his finger further southwest, circling a small road extending to the frayed edge of the map. "This is the nearest exit to town. Last thing I heard over the radio, an accident has the whole route closed off, with reports being of mob activity already having reached there."

"So what you're saying is sick people, just like our friend in the cell back, are already swarming the place?"

Bruce nodded. "Crazy ones as well, caught up in whatever mentality is turning everyone into rabid dogs."

"Ya'll are talking about the zombies, right?" Tyler said, slouching onto the table with his chest.

"Would you shut up about that zombie bullshit?"

"What the hell? You were supporting me just a couple minutes ago, cock gobbler," Tyler said haughtily.

Bruce flinched at the bitterness contained in the final slur, but it went unnoticed by the others in the room.

"I wasn't being serious. I was just saying anything I could to get us out of that cell alive."

Bruce's eyes seemed to glisten at this, but he remained silent.

"So how do you explain what's goin' on in this shithole, huh, Stephen Hawkman? We got motherfuckers pulling guts out of other motherfucker's bodies, puttin' 'em away like a bunch of high-ass niggas with munchies, and you're gonna tell me that those fuckers ain't zombies?"

Matt opened his mouth to speak, expecting some form of obvious logic to come to him and do the talking for him; but he found himself answerless, his mind straying to the dark reaches of the impossible for explanations.

"If it was zombies, why haven't we heard from our good friend McCulley? Shouldn't he have gotten up already and come to stuff his fat face with our innards by now?"

"Nigga, I don't know how long it takes or how that shit works. This motherfucker just knows a dog when he sees a dog, a cat when he sees a goddamn cat, and a zombie when I see a fucking zombie. That guy down there had a jaw that looked like something out of the *Exorcist*, and ya'll assholes think it's just some nigga who escaped from the sick ward. What do you think, he ate some bad enchiladas, caught a little food poisoning, and threw up half of his fucking guts or something?"

Matt started to debate this but found himself interrupted by Frank's shrill voice, of all things.

"I agree with Tyler on this one."

"You what?"

"I agree with Tyler. He has a point, and that thing down there… I heard something like it before, at the church, when you picked me up. I thought it was my imagination at the time… until I heard it again in that cramped cell. Nothing human could make that noise, so filled with despair and pain. I've been thinking about it nonstop since we heard it, trying to find an explanation other than the one Tyler's going on about, but there really isn't one, Matt, especially if what Bruce is saying about Saint Roma's is true."

Frank turned to Bruce for support, which he gave in the form of a small nod, a confirmation to Matt's worst fears: he was losing control of the group.

"You can't be telling me you believe in this horseshit too, right, Bruce?"

He didn't answer, not for a long time that seemed like several decades passing in an instant, but finally gave a sigh that seemed to convey the weight of his words before he spoke them.

"Unfortunately, since I can't give any better explanation than Tyler's, I have to say that I do, although I will readily accept another more plausible one when it presents itself. Those things... the way they move... the noises they make. Whatever those creatures are, they definitely don't seem human."

Swallowing more than just saliva, Matt looked amidst the members of his ragtag group, unsure of his own convictions in the face of something truly demonic. Before, when counting their weaknesses, he had purposefully avoided his own—the way his flesh was slowly roasting, the bones underneath fighting against him, desperate for the feel of flesh pounding against them. Matt's disposition was not that he didn't believe in monsters but only those that were real, the ones that moved beneath the shadows in one's own soul, patiently waiting for their chance to strike out at the world just out of their reach of spindly fingertips—the type of monster he had become all too familiar with in his life. To have something so tangible, so simplistic and easy to digest as evil, he felt himself wary about throwing the world into black and white, unsure on which side he would fall.

"Fine," he finally relented, running his hand through the tangles of his messy hair, "I'll mimic Bruce's sentiment in that I'll accept this theory until a more rational one presents itself. Now, what is our plan now that we're we taking into account these creatures supposedly roaming the town?"

Bruce pointed to a large black dot near the center of the map, a large squared-off mark of blue amidst a sea of green trees that spotted the upper-left corner.

"This here is the church, Saint Roma, that the riot started at. If our reports are accurate, there should also be a fairly large mass of creatures like the ones in that cell. And by large, I mean most of the town and most of the police were gathered around this place right when this whole thing started. With how large the mob was, and the police doing their best to keep everyone contained, I think it's safe to assume most of them are dead or... *risen*, for lack of a better term. By now, a lot of those things probably have already started to spread out into nearby streets and cul-de-sacs in the area around here and... here. What I'm proposing is, we pass through the woods nearby here, and we can use the trees as cover when needed and slip through mostly unseen, with enough underbrush to cover up any excess noise and movement."

"And go where?"

"We'd pass straight through, coming off on the southeast end of the church with a fence between us and whatever creatures are still lurking the grounds. Probably won't hold off too many of them but enough for us to slip by into the center of town, and from there, we can move to the next nearest road out. Probably, the old highway near the O'Dea farm would be our best bet."

"Why don't we just continue pushing north through the woods into a nearby town? Something like New Haven or Castle Rock?"

"Too risky. It would take us well into the night to make it to any town. The nearest is probably at least thirty miles if you were to travel directly through the forest. We'd never make it there before nightfall, and I don't wanna take my chances at night in the pitch-black woods with those things."

"Man, what the fuck? They're fucking zombies! Did we not all just agree on this? Why are people so damn opposed to using that word? Say it with me now, ya'll, Zom. Bee. I swear to God, every fucking movie with zombies coming and biting people's faces off, and every nigga acts like all of a sudden, there hasn't been a thousand and one movies with the fuckers, that explains exactly what the fuck is going on. Nah, they call 'em creatures, things, or fucking walkers, whatever that shit means, but never just call 'em what they is. They're goddamn zombies—back from the dead, wants to eat your brains, zombies. Acting like they're something different don't make them different, shiet," Tyler said, slouching back into his chair in a mild disgust.

"Since when do zombies actually eat brains? That's just some bullshit from cartoons."

"Nigga, how have you never seen *Return of the Living Dead*? Did your mamma keep the TV locked up when you were a dumb-ass kid?"

"Enough. If you're that adamant on the terminology, then I think if we head for the old highway, we'd encounter less *zombies* and have a better chance of grabbing a still-working vehicle that can get us easily to the next town, where we can find help."

"And what happens when we get there?" Matt said tentatively.

Bruce gave him a hard look, not reproachful but bordering on distaste. "We'll figure that out when we get there."

Matt wanted to protest but knew this to be the most concrete and firm answer that he could expect in the situation, especially one that would keep their meager group together long enough to even make it to that point. Despite a frustration to find his leadership pulled out from under him, he gave Bruce a respectful nod, already setting to work on their possibilities of escape should their friend's conscience get the better of them once they've escaped whatever madness they found themselves in now.

Frank and Tyler quickly agreed to this plan, thinking that any strategy that got them out of the foul-smelling and musty police station as an acceptable one. Frank readied his small pistol, checking the sights and testing the weight before sliding it down the back of his bloodstained jeans. Matt followed suit with his Remington, loading as many shells as it could carry and stuffing the other twenty or so into the chest pocket of his flannel. Checking his leg, Tyler remained at the table, his gun held upward, looking like a lost child soldier, his youthful features turning him into an absurd spectacle. Bruce checked the wheel of his revolver and started for the door, turning once he reached it to survey the team that he had assembled.

Matt felt his pride stiffen at this but swallowed it, the taste of breath in his lungs reminding him just how much they owed this overly self-righteous gentleman. It was in their best interest to placate their sanctimonious savior as much as possible—at least while there were still others, possible thousands of others, that still wished them harm.

Besides, who was to say that Bruce wouldn't meet an untimely demise somewhere along the way? Even at the very end, several steps away from the door of their salvation, his brains leaking on the pavement much like his beloved sheriff. Matt smiled at this thought with little guilt and started toward the door before spying the map on the table. Hastily, he put his shotgun aside and reached for the frame, pulling the thin paper out from its mangled insides. It took some shaking, louder than he would've liked; but it reminded him of wind chimes on a sunny day, blowing against the boards of his home, one he doubted ever seeing again.

After he had gathered the map into his pockets, Bruce gave him another one of his stubbornly curt nods and started to turn the long doorknob, when the frosted glass above it imploded inward in a flurry of glass and dark blood. A gray and slimy hand burst through and wrapped itself around his throat, its pale skin clashing against his dark chestnut tones. The fingers tightened, and the breath went out of him, so loud that Matt could hear it escaping across the room.

Despite his earlier fantasies, Matt found himself reaching for the shotgun on the table, moving without thinking. McCulley's fat jowls were jiggling sickeningly from his emaciated face, torn loosely with his cragged teeth showing underneath. He was chomping wildly at the air, like an animal in a trap, and was trying to draw Bruce into range of his bloody maw, dripping with a rotting and acrid saliva.

Matt's finger found the butt of the shotgun, but his fingers clumsily fumbled it and sent it flying across the table to the other side of the room. In that moment, he believed Bruce truly dead, his salvation flying out of his reach, but the sound of thunder snapped him from this dark dream.

McCulley's head exploded in a cloud of pink mist, his fat cheeks slapping against opposite walls and his teeth chattering as they fell to the floor like hail. His arm, previously writhing like a python, went limp and slouched into the crease of the small window. Bruce's hands instantly flew to his throat, gasping for breath like a dog left in a car on a hot summer afternoon. Somehow, he stayed on his feet and looked for his defender, whose gun was still smoking with a trail that was dancing among the fluorescent lights that dotted the ceiling.

Tyler's face held a grin that contained an unexplainable joy, one entrenched in a gleeful madness.

"I told ya'll, niggas. I fucking told you!"

Bruce didn't speak, his hand clutching at his chest, his eyes watering and dealing with some kind of existential crisis that Matt felt guilty for observing, despite the silliness of the sentiment.

"Are you all right?" he asked, hoping to shake his uneasiness.

Breathing heavily, Bruce managed one of his trademark affirmations, "Only mad I wasn't able to shoot that fat, racist fuck myself."

Matt couldn't help but laugh. Tyler seemed to think it was the funniest thing he ever heard, and Frank even chuckled, seemingly despite himself. Bruce motioned for the now-open door, urging them out into the police station's hall, which was now littered with a corpse that had previously sat in the one adjacent. Frank needed no second telling and headed out into the passage, stepping over the large corpse cautiously.

Gathering his shotgun from the other side of the room and slapping Tyler enthusiastically on the shoulder, Matt trailed behind him, asking Bruce once more of his condition before proceeding. Tyler hopped off the table reinvigorated and walked back to the rear of the evidence lockup and scooped up one of the large green vacuum-sealed bags off the top shelf.

Moving to the door, he waved the bag temptingly in front of Bruce's face.

"I'm taking this," he declared forcefully.

And without waiting for an answer or some kind of heartfelt thanks, he followed after his friends, leaving Bruce in the thick silence of the room, alone to his thoughts—which were only of the bullets that had gone past his head, the ones he had been convinced had ended his short, troubled life, the same kind that had passed through Sheriff Nottingham's head earlier that day. Part of him wanted to laugh, the other to scream; but he instead nodded to no one in particular, possibly to himself, and closed the door, heading out of the precinct into the misty autumn day.

The smell of smoke was overpowering, but at a time like this, it was oddly comforting, like a visit from an old friend you distanced yourself from due to their self-destructive tendencies. Vel crushed another butt in her car's ashtray and instantly pulled another from the crumpled pack on the car seat next to her. Igniting it with the car's lighter from the dashboard, she let the tingles of the nicotine wash over her, pretending them some kind of aromatic wave, defusing the stress from her body, wresting it from the vice grip she held onto it with, her thoughts betraying her at every street corner with some new impossibility, but one that took precedence nonetheless, urged on by her own tenacious fretting.

She cracked the window, letting the cloud of smoke billow out like an animal breaking free of its captivity, a dog clawing at the door. The breakneck speed of the wind caught her off guard and sent a fresh batch of chills through her body, despite the heavy jacket she had thrown on before leaving that morning—an experience that felt distant despite having happened only an hour before.

She had awoken to the sound of her alarm, its sweet, dulcet tones sounding like nails on a chalkboard due in part to the message they carried—the one demanding she pull herself from the clinging tendrils of sleep, out from the paradise of her celluloid dreams so like the ones they played on the television, into the harshness of reality, with its drawn shades and large, empty bed. Pulling herself from the tangle of covers had proved easier than it usually did, her body drenched in a hypodermic sweat that seemed to be suffocating her, clinging to her pores. She practically crawled over to the mirror—her ever-present enemy, the shatterer of her self-deceptions, its bleakness matched only by its fanatical dedication to bearing the truth. Staring up into its depths, she saw her own misery face looking back at her:

the crow's feet sinking low beneath her eyes like inescapable pits; her earlobes, far too large, low and floppy like a rabbit's struck with some kind of limpness, something that his wife rabbit would mock him for at her social gatherings; her lips, so thin they were practically nonexistent in the overall scheme of her features, pink and pale and cracked like a lizard's.

After her usual positive morning assessment, she bared her teeth and inspected those too, splotches of creamy white plaque mocking her attempts at cleanliness and the frayed yellow beneath her gums an oversight that bore into her very soul. She tried to imagine a man—a Don Draper, Brad Pitt, or the like—slipping from her fluffy blankets and sneaking himself into a sultry position behind her, sliding his arms under hers and whispering coy flirtations in her ear, praising her imperfections as marks of an unmatched beauty, but it was no use. The whole image seemed wrong, impossibly silly, and demented for her even gathering the gall to imagine such a foolish scenario. Before leaving her mind completely, the image lingered with Matt Métier's head replacing her mysterious, faceless hulk, his eyes pouring over her body, taking it inside him like nourishment, throwing her up on the sink, spreading her legs, and throwing himself into her…

She stopped herself, her hand exploring her nipple, teasing it, wishing the forlorn fantasy into existence, but the recollections of that night, the news program, and her shameful encounters with the police at the diner, casually explaining that her and Matthew had never been involved and that all her talk had been unimpressive lies, not told to protect him, but herself from the embarrassment of the visiting harpy that had pulled itself from the dredges of her past. Just thinking of it again, and they way they stared, the way they shared stray glances with one another during her story, trying not to crack a smile at the pathetic display, hurrying through the procedure, which had wasted their precious time—she began to blush, the crimson shade of her cheeks doing her no favors and making her look like a washed-up starlet, one whose fame had slipped through their fingers, their looks destroyed by all the temptations that came with it, although Vel had received none of this glory or temptation, only the bitterness that usually followed.

Jumping in the shower, she cleaned herself and started her daily routine of attempting to fix the mistakes God had made with her, filling in wrinkles and covering blemishes with heavy patches of foundation, making her eyelashes fuller with heavy applications of eyeliner so thick her eyes felt heavy every time she put it on. Dental strips came next, sitting just beneath her gums, the spiciness of the mint making her eyes water as she poured over her tabloid magazines, attempting to choose a hairstyle from Selena Gomez, Ariana Grande, or one of those other young starlets—hoping that this would be the formula to unlock the beauty she so craved, the one piece that would tie her look together, make her desirable, so much so that she might even find herself in one of these magazines one day, a beacon of hope to girls just like her all around the world.

It was a pipe dream. Her encounter with Gloria Hickam last night had been enough to shatter the illusion she had built for herself, one that hinged on disregarding the truth and living in the edges between it and the lies, skirting the edge of reality, dancing on the lip of fantasy—a technique television had imparted, her lone mentor over all these years. After she was satisfied with the bun she had emulated from something Scarlett Johanssen had worn at a previous year's Oscars, she gratefully turned away from the mirror, slipping back into the pull of her fantasy, the lies easier to swallow now that the truth was squarely behind her.

Groggily, she had moved into her kitchen, pouring cornflakes into a bowl with the last of her milk, turning on the small Panasonic in the corner, the set whirring to life, the channel that it opened to being the one she had wanted already: a program with celebrity lifestyle vignettes for the next hour. Settling into the weary familiarity of it all, she ate in silence, contemplating on nothing in particular as the television poured out news about what stars were eating, who they were wearing, and secret shots of them indulging in scandalous behavior (while only scandalous in the fact that it showed them as anything other than the perfect gods that they were). When they had finished, she went to check her phone on the off chance that she might have received some kind of text or, dare she dream, a phone call from some long-lost acquaintance or one-night stand confessing their forbidden love for her.

She was surprised to instead find nearly a dozen missed calls from her boss, making her wonder if she had misread her schedule for the week. It seemed impossible that he would schedule two shifts so close to each other. She had barely even slept six hours. He might've been mad about the incident with the cops from the night before, but they had parted on good terms. Terry had even made a joke of it, saying she could've just said she was dating him instead of Matt. Vel had found the joke quite funny, but for some reason, Terry seemed in worse spirits afterward.

But then she started listening to the messages, the first asking her to turn on the local news as a "honest to God miracle" was taking place right on the screen, and she got an earful of frightened commentary as Lacey Chabert was violently masticated on live television. Terry, showing an unusual amount of compassion for his usually reserved self, implored her to find shelter, or even to leave town and never come back. The last several messages implied that Terry was making his way toward her house to get her, but the penultimate was filled with heavy breathing and wheezing, the sounds the robust Terry made whenever he moved faster than a slow gait, along with screams for some unseen attacker to get back; and the final was only heavy silence with an odd crinkling in the background, something that sounded like… *chewing*.

Her hands felt clammy and cold, but the rest of her felt hot, even though she was wearing only her bathrobe with the window open to the chill of the wind. At first, she thought it was some kind of cruel joke, even though Terry usually never participated in those; but when she turned to the local news, she was met with a blank screen admitting technical difficulties.

The world seemed to have broken free from its moorings and started down a dangerous spiral into fantasy—something she had dreamed of and hoped for since she could first remember—bathed in the black-and-white glow of the old television, plopped in front of an old daytime soap while her parents were upstairs, immune to her call. Even when her father would come downstairs, he would often walk past her mid explanation of the dastardly actions of John Montgomery and his brood, leaving through the screen door without announcing when he would be back. When he did come home, it would be with a strong antiseptic smell, his breath harder than most drinks; and it would be Vel's turn to ignore him, his hand persistently rubbing her shoulders and back before her mother would come and scold him before luring him back upstairs, a look of grim resignation on her hard face. Vel would slip back into her fantasy then, dreaming of the dashing rogue that would come to free her from her nightmare, answering her inquiries with cheesy declarations of love and quips followed by the giggle of laugh track. She had once read that most laugh tracks that were used where stock tracks from television's conception and that most of the laugh you heard were from people that were long dead, giving every comedy after a feeling of macabre that she couldn't shake, forcing her retreat into the romance and the beautiful people behind it.

Now, here she was, faced with something that seemed completely out of the realms of logic, something fit for the *Twilight Zone* instead of *Melrose Place*; and instead of feeling some kind of elation or grim satisfaction, she only felt hollow, the reality of fantasy far more mediocre than she could've ever imagined.

Her car rattled and creaked, its steel rusted and stiff from the cold. It had taken several tries to get the engine to start, so many that Vel almost presumed she would have to walk—a proposition that filled her with a tightness in her chest and a preemptive soreness in her legs just imaging it.

The roads were strangely deserted, with many cars left in the middle of intersections, doors open wide, its occupants already fled for some unseen reason, although many also sported broken windows and what appeared to be stains of blood from behind the tinted glass of Vel's Mazda. Many of the traffic lights were flashing red, turned into a makeshift stop sign; but Vel went right through them, not encountering another living soul for several blocks to come.

Many of the radio stations were simply playing their regularly scheduled music programs, light happy tunes that clashed with the murky fog that Vel cruised through toward the Hamilton Bridge.

Every now and then, she'd find a local station, only to be met by a blast of hard static, so ear-shattering she had to cover her ears. One she found was actually using its test of the emergency broadcast system as an attempt to send out some kind of pseudo warning to anyone who could hear it.

Vel went to the window and rolled it down by the old crank at the bottom of the door, letting the smoke clear out again but was surprised when more poured back in, this smoke being pitch-black and thick, so thick that one breath made her light heavy and caused her to swerve on the road toward the curb. Her vision shifted, warping as if someone held a pair of kaleidoscope lens to her eyes, and she felt her body start to drift away from her. The two puffs of smoke were mingling and coiling about each other at the gap in the window, before a heavy gust pulled them back outside, snapping loudly against the window. Vel's hands felt miles away from her, stuck to the wheel as if it had become an extension of herself, her skin seemingly melding with the leather. The sunlight seemed stronger than usual, piercing her vision in bright spires, painful to behold in their ferocity, penetrating her fluttering eyelids even when they were slammed shut.

Eventually, the smoke cleared, its rank odor fleeing with it; but its dark tendrils remained outside, filling the sky and pressing themselves against her car, so thick and impenetrable that it appeared to the naked eye as if she had entered another dimension—a tunnel of billowing, putrid smoke that was carrying her someplace on the fringe of their dimension, a *Twilight Zone* for all intents and purposes. The haziness of her head had started to fade, her senses returning in fits, like the wind going from a gentle whisper nestling and nibbling on her ear to the sound of a freight train pounding against her lobe. Her sight was still imperfect, her watery eyes blurring her already-corrupted view, the smoke blocking out the rays of the sun and turning the road into a faux nighttime. Vel had read of dust storms like this and suddenly dreamed herself like Angelina Jolie in that epic of hers she did, clothed in the finest silks and fashions amidst the humid desert air, her beauty unaffected by the harsh, uncaring environment due in part to her luxury and her grace. Vel liked to imagine she'd carry herself the same way, but if her looks barely withstood the tame

Maine summers, she doubted years under a boiling sun would do her any favors.

These thoughts were interrupted by a shadow forming beneath the dark swirl of smoke, one large and commanding of attention in its enormity. Soon, its dark form seemed to cover the entirety of her view; and as her car shot forward against the blackness, her sense returned to her and caused her to swerve sharply and violently into the adjacent lane, her tires bouncing as they passed over the median. The back of the truck came into view as it passed immediately on her right, still and motionless, like the bones of a giant predator. Despite her last-minute intervention, her Mazda scraped against the steel frame, tearing off her side mirror and spraying sparks in a horrible scream of steel against steel. Vel found herself screaming, her terror so paramount that part of her wanted to slam her hands over her ears and wait until the car rolled itself to a stop, to pull away from whatever fate lay before her, refusing to accept that she would meet her end from a stationary vehicle. But she held on, surprising even herself as she steered the car back into her lane and straightened, its tires groaning before falling back into position.

Sighing, she started to laugh, a hearty one meant to celebrate her survival after her brush with death, to convince herself that she had truly escaped its irrefutable clutches, had wrestled her life back from the jaws of oblivion; but it was cut short into a scream as the small black form bounced off her front grill into the windshield.

The impact shattered the glass, sending ripples out from the impact instantly as the black mass slammed against it, crushing it inward. Vel screamed again, expecting the thing to fly forward through the flimsy glass but was shamefully relieved when it continued its trajectory upward over the roof of the car, bouncing heavily, dents sprouting up beneath it as it rolled down the rear window and off the truck, a sick plop following it. Her instincts had already forced her foot down on to the brake, the tires squealing in protest, a pale smoke wafting up from beneath them to combat the thick black blocking her view. The car twisted and turned out of her control, turning sideways so that she was perpendicular to where she had been moments before.

She shook to a sudden stop, the brakes finally finding enough leverage, and let the silence hit her, a punch to the gut that she hadn't been expecting. The severity of her situation seemed to come with it, the pieces of what had happened putting themselves into place with a frightening calmness that didn't match the horrible image that it was forming. Deep down, she knew she had killed that person, that there was no possible way that breath could still be held within their battered lungs, not after hearing each crash of their broken body against the frame of her car. Her breathing was rapid and ragged, drifting dangerously close to hyperventilation; but her composure held, her mind steeled by countless hours of sappy murder mysteries and soap operas.

Still, those weren't based in reality, almost completely the opposite. This was real. A human life had passed out of existence, been silenced forever by a moment of blindness, a preventable lapse in attention. And yet, hadn't she just been thinking about the way reality and fantasy had begun to blend into one indecipherable mess? In this thought, she found resolve, an imitation of every character she had watched on the silver screen in this situation, debating whether or not to open the door and make the scene a reality or keep it in the realm of fantasy, behind the glass screen that separated her and it.

Her conscience (and her thoughts of those starlets, with a gentle kindness behind their strength) eventually convinced her to roll down the window and stretch her head out into the black fog, a compromise with herself to at least make an effort to own up to her mistakes—one that, while heinous, could be easily forgiven in a court of law, most of all, given the circumstances that preempted it.

"Uhm... excuse me? Sir? Miss? Are you all right?"

The shadow of a body remained motionless, an immovable still against the black, billowing backdrop. She got no answer, merely the dreadful familiarity of silence.

"Hey! Excuse me? Are you okay? Ohhhhh, please answer me!"

Her foundation of strength was slipping, and looking at the lifeless husk that lay there, silhouetted against the smoke, she felt the guilt working its way into her system. She started to imagine the daily pleasantries of that person lying there, their foolish hopes and dreams forever crushed beneath the weight of a two-ton steel behemoth. The double-edged sword of her imagination—spurred on by her sepia-toned fantasies, which made it easier to act like so many cold, exacting women—also made it easier to see the person lying back there on the asphalt as just that: person, one whose life was snuffed out by Vel's vapid clumsiness.

She realized escape was still such a pressing concern—one that was pulling at her skirts even now, begging that she pull her head back into the skeleton of her car, roll up the thin pane of glass, and simply drive onward into the darkened horizon.

"Excuse me? Excuse me... um, person? Are you okay? I really don't want to just leave you here, so can you please just say something," she said, her composure faltering on the final words as they came out in a choked sob, the tears welling at the corner of her eyes starting to streak down her cheeks without her letting them.

There was a groan, deep and sonorous, so low that at first, Vel was unaware of its tones, awash in a sea of her own crushing sobs that rattled her chest. When it first reached her ear, she sniffled, resolved to stop her useless crying and inspect the source of that noise with a dry, composed face—one that would impart strength and hope to her accidental victim instead of the fear of a slow, painful demise.

"Hello?" she exclaimed excitedly, her eyes trying to pierce the black shawl that had given birth to this scene of tragedy but being barely able to make out the shadow of the still-inert body. "Are you okay? Can you hear me?"

The groan grew louder, but somehow more distant, its tone more sinister, less part of this world and more a member of those dark dreams that have haunted mankind for years, an escapee from the darkest depths of the collective human psyche. Chills rattled her bones, and she found herself shivering despite the oppressive heat from the smoke, which was starting to whip around the car in a vortex, trapped in a gust of wind that seemed to have the weight of the world behind it. The wind seemed to howl in unison with that poor creature on the road, still struggling to even move itself. The thought of the person lying there on their side haunted her, a stream of blood falling from a gash in their head, groaning as they tried to right themselves, trying to figure out what cruelty had turned their life on its head like this. This image, as imaginary as any childhood monster, was almost enough to get Vel out of her car; but she thought better of it quickly, the sound of that terrible groan growing louder and louder to the point that it was more forceful than the scream of the whipping wind, all-encompassing in its terror, a wavering peak into the jaws of death.

Vel suddenly felt like something was very wrong—well, more wrong than it already was with the town falling into complete chaos overnight. But there was something now urging her forward and away from her victim, her thoughts of selfishness seeming more like ones of survival with each passing moment of that awful scream.

Finally able to take no more, she started to turn the small crank at her foot, and the window began to rise from its resting place. As she did this, her eyes unfocused from her task just for the briefest flash of a second; and she saw that shadow was no longer lying on the ground but standing up straight as if it had never fallen, its form facing her, its features obscured by the thick smoke.

"Oh, thank God!" she said, a rush of air escaping her in what she called relief but didn't feel anything at all like it. "I thought the worst. I'm so sorry about this, I really am. You see, with all the smoke, I didn't see that truck back there, and I swerved and lost control of my car. I know it's asking a lot, but I really hope you can understand."

The shadow did not answer. In fact, it didn't move at all and was just as lifeless as it had been when it was lying on the ground. Now that it was upright, Vel was able to notice how peculiarly short it was, less than half the size of her own vehicle, its tiny body looking like a sliver amidst the clouds.

"Are you okay? Can you speak?"

There was still no answer. Vel started to feel the maliciousness from its stare, even though it was still concealed from view by the smoke.

"Listen, I can give you a ride if you like. I don't know where you're going, but maybe you'll find someone you know at the next town?"

The reply was another groan, one filled with mourning, like a painful cry after a death in the family. Instead of sympathy, Vel felt only fear, the horribly wrong feeling that she should've kept driving from the minute she regained control of her car and not a second sooner, and every one that ticked by now was only digging her grave deeper.

Shambling forward with a lopsided gait, the shadowy figure grew larger, still tiny when compared to its surroundings but enough to convey that it was moving toward her. Vel wanted to call out to it, to invite it into the car; but she remained silent, her mind aware of something she was not and pinching off her words. The shadow kept at its pursuit, the smoke passing against it, its form being bathed in more and more light as it neared her.

Finally, she was able to make out part of its face, to at least look into the eyes of her victim; but when she did, she found that they weren't looking back at her. They were situated on her face, unbroken in their devotion; but there was no life behind their dulled pupils, merely an ocean of inescapable gray. The rest of the smoke seemed to give way at once, revealing the poor creature in all its hideousness—its small broken frame shuffling forward like a puppet that was missing half of its strings, its limbs flopping loosely at his side, the joints broken and twisted, dead things dragged along on the body's demanding vendetta.

The true nature of its small form was soon made clear, sending Vel's hand to her mouth as she felt the sick rush of her breakfast coming back into her throat as she looked on the decayed remains of the child in front of her moving toward her with an otherworldly devotion, consumed by the hatred that lurked just beneath those pale gray slits of ice. She found herself unable to look away from them, almost hypnotized by their dreadfulness, and recognized the look not as one of disgust, or silent retribution, but of unmitigated hunger.

Terror seized her at that point, her muscles lost to its whims as she rolled up the thin glass and turned the key in the ignition, waiting for that sweet rumble of the engine roaring to life. Of course, when faced with certain death, the car did not start, the battery clicking lifelessly beneath her, and Vel was now sure that the world around her really was some inescapable nightmare.

The child reached the back of her car, placing its shattered, bloody skin sack of a hand on the trunk of the car loud enough to cause Vel to scream. Looking into the rear view, its face was brought next to hers, a close-up that displayed all its worst features—including its missing nose, the torn piece of cartilage smushed against its cheek into a bloody pulp. The hole behind it was wide enough to expose everything beneath—with view of the crooked teeth still clinging to the warped jaw, deep-red muscles working against each other, and even straight back into the pearl white of its skull. Its cheeks were torn in long gashes, black clots collecting at their bottom, and what looked like skid marks that ran down the left of his face, leaving its ear flat and the hair matted and torn, revealing more of that sickly white.

Vel screamed again when face-to-face with this monstrosity, this ungodly inversion of innocence. The ghastly creature continued forward, balancing against the back of her car with one swollen, battered hand, while the engine continued to whirr uselessly, fighting every attempt at ignition. After several tries, her persistence paid off and brought the engine into a roar of life, one that caused the vile creature behind her to give one of its own—an animalistic mimicry, like a house cat hissing at an intruder. Instinctively, she slammed her foot down onto the accelerator, but the tires squealed uselessly against the brakes, steam rising from beneath and mingling with its toxic counterpart. It took her a moment to realize her mistake, and in a rushed response, her hand flew to the clutch and pulled it back, grinding the gears of the beaten, old mess of an automobile but one that was well enough used to its abuse that it chugged on regardless, a ray of good luck breaking the skies in a hurricane of misfortune.

The car shot backward, spurred on by the overpowering presence of Vel's foot clamped onto the pedal, and connected with the small demon's body, with enough force to obliterate half of its mangled frame into an even more incomprehensible tangle of parts. The poor cretin's upper half, consisting only of its abdomen—including a partially exposed rib cage, its left arm, and the neck bent at an angle that showed it was nearly broken entirely off from the body—bounced off the back windshield and continued its violent trajectory over the roof before landing into the cracked indentations of the windshield.

Somehow, the child—looking like something completely inhuman at this point, with its head twisted nearly upside down and half of its body gone beneath a bloody mess of loose muscle and cracked, marrow-dripping bones, blood and pus pouring down the cracks and pooling at the end of the hood—tried to worm its way through the splintering glass. Vel thought she was screaming, but her mind was moving so fast, rushing through so many thoughts that she wasn't even sure of that. She thought of failed hopes and dreams that were going to be forever left incomplete, unaccomplished—all the people, however few, that she would never say good-bye to; even a clichéd flash of her life before her eyes, one that consisted mostly of moments that were experienced behind the fogginess of an impenetrable screen; and horrifyingly even in the presence of certain death, the voice of Gloria Hickam—belittling every one of them for the jokes that they were. Soon, her horrible, screeching laughter was all she heard, her final victory finally complete.

Despite all this, Vel's body moved without her consent, slamming the brake and shifting the car into drive. The steel coffin rocketed forward, pressing the writhing monster further into the shattered remains of the glass, his overbearing form making the cracks wider, his flesh pressing through glistening gaps. His teeth gnashed against it, biting at whatever his dead eyes saw in front of them. Quickly, alarmingly, it seemed to realize and come to understand this obstacle preventing it from tearing it into its meal and brought its tiny, clawed hand up high above it, before crashing it down onto the largest shattered indent, the cracks giving way and particles of glass sprinkling through. Its tiny, squat fingers wriggled through like earthworms, the broken bloody nails picking themselves against the shards and tearing themselves loose.

Vel slammed on the brakes again, her thoughts still struggling to catch up to her actions as she remembered her high school physics classes on momentum and how objects in motion usually prefer to stay that way. The force of the sudden stop pulled her forward with it, her forehead slamming into the steering wheel and turning her vision a blinding white. She heard the glass shatter as the creature was pulled forward, its hand coming loose and flying up in the air as the shards ripped it free of the arm behind it. This jerking seemed to be more than the neck, already seemingly held to its body by a mere stretch of skin, could bear; and through her white haze, she heard the tearing of flesh and the crash from its fall.

When she finally regained her vision, it was of that horrible face: half of the skin ripped from its bones, nestled in the windshield's cracked indent. Somehow, its jaws, though half exposed to the elements, were clacking down at the glass in its futile attempts to reach her. Its eyes was still hanging loose from its socket, the red rope looking sickeningly like a red vine that held it to the skull.

Her panic took control of whatever rationality her body had been working on, and she brought her foot up to the glass and kicked it outward, the whole frame of glass falling backward and sending the still crying head through the abyss of foul black smoke. The putrid substance poured in, suffocating her and filling her lungs with fire. The amount that hit her was so concentrated, so heavy that her head—already light from its impact with the hard, plastic wheel—drifted away from her and she found herself falling in and out of consciousness.

Her sense of mind was strong enough that she could feel the car moving beneath her, a gentle unassisted roll forward as her foot hung limp next to the brakes, the gearshift stuck in drive. She tried to lift her hand to reach for it, but a feeble, halfhearted lurch of her arm was all that she managed. The inky blackness around her vision began to fade but was replaced only by the absolute darkness of the smoke. Still, with her awareness returning, she made another attempt at grabbing the gear shift, her legs feeling like dried-out silly putty and passing clumsily over the unseen pedals. The roll gave her a horrible sensation of floating, like she was on a roller coaster about to pass over the lip of the drop, and this image conjured up one of her rolling off the side of the embankment near the bridge, toppling over herself until her car was dashed against the shallow rocks of the river. While horrifying, this thought gave her the push necessary to right herself, pushing her back up in the seat, the familiarity of the pose allowing her muscle memory to locate the pedal. Using a considerable amount of strength to perform a task so simple that it normally didn't require a second thought, she pressed down on the brake, feeling her descent down the mild incline slow but not stopping completely.

Her lessons of momentum turned against her, and she found herself unable to completely stop the two-ton steel beast as it picked up speed down the hill. Unsure of her surroundings and unable to see anything except for the choking fumes of the smoke, Vel was unsure of how close she was to the bridge; but she knew that before her run-in on the road, she had been expecting to see it appear around every corner.

Desperate, she gave one final push of her foot into the pedal; but in her groggy state, her foot slid off and into the carpet beneath, pulling it up and sliding it into the back of the space and trapping her there. This was enough to crush whatever incentive she had and, having considered her fight for survival the limit to what anyone could willingly do, resigned to her fate as deigned by God and the deflated tires of her car.

She was surprised then when the front of the car crashed lightly into another mass of steel, the impact shaking her and sending her limp body forward. Smoke began pouring out of the spot left by the absentee windshield, like a snake uncoiling its disinterested self from its prey discovered to be lifeless, and Vel felt her head clearing almost instantaneously. Oxygen rushed into her lungs, the blood rushing to her head so fast that it made her dizzy—dizzy but conscious.

Fluttering open, her eyes worked to take in the sight before her but found that the smoke, while dispersing, was still a drawn shade that covered most of the world in black. She regained feeling in her legs, although they tingled heavily as if they were asleep. Still, this was enough to shift herself to the door; and after several fumbles for the handle, she opened it and stumbled out to see what her car had run into this time. She tasted blood on her lips, and when she went to inspect, the briefest touch of her nose sent tendrils of pain shooting through her skull, and she knew it must be broken.

Another wonderful addition to that lovely face of yours, my dear. But hey, you're alive. At least one of us should be happy about it.

The smell of the smoke was lost to her, and she was grateful for this as it still filled the air with an alarming intensity, even more so than it had before, although the wind was whipping upward and over whatever large mass lay in front of her. Moving toward it, her fingers cautiously extended to graze it, she felt the coldness of its pipes and axels, two placed side by side, and knew it at once to be an overturned car—not just a sedan or oversized off roader, but the far-reaching underside of an upturned semitruck.

She circled around, going all the way to the far end on her left to find its cargo, the large crate having spilled off its trailer and onto its side several feet away. Its large, bolt action doors read "Great Northern Maine Shipping Co." with a sticker asking, "How's my driving?" plastered right beneath. The irony made Vel want to laugh, but none seemed to come. She couldn't even force a chuckle.

As she rounded the overturned crate, she was met with a sea of cars stretching to the opposite end of the bridge, clustered into both lanes of traffic and spilling over each other like a clogged artery. Several of them were engulfed in flames, high reaching and furious in their destruction of the steel beneath, the epicenter of the pillar of black smoke that was funneling up into the clouds. Vel groaned— all her strength leaving her—as she saw the blockade extended far out into the bridge, all the way to the center, with not a sign of life in sight, only the graveyard of steel coffins, many with unmoving shadows behind their tinted glass. Half of their windows were broken into, their drivers' lifeless bodies slumped over the jagged shards. Something—*or someone*, she thought with a shudder—had torn away most of the dead's flesh. Faces were fragments of their former selves, skulls hollowed out and crushed into bits that were sprinkled around the pink ravaged messes that might have once been considered the epitome of human beauty. Now, most looked like tenderized slabs of rotten meat. Arms were missing beneath the elbow, and someone had been dragged feet first out of the backseat of an old Honda Odyssey; but all that remained of their legs were mangled, bloody nubs, mostly consisting of pearl-white bones, black clots, and tendons that held the green and yellow hue of rot. Vel soon realized that the messy pulps came from the gnashing of come creature's teeth, biting into and pulling loose the blood and bone beneath. It looked like an animal had been through the place, killing and maiming with the reckless abandon found only in nature and war.

In fact, it looked almost exactly like all those static, shaky images of war you saw on television, with a lot more green trees and a wide river, of course; but the destruction and ruinous nature of the landscape seemed better suited for the *News at Nine* than a sleepy town in Nowhere, America. This similarity did nothing to help with her dysphoria, the intelligibility of reality. And the world hidden behind a glowing screen that she'd grown up fantasizing of and finding comfort in was at its peak, and instead of rejoicing in this dream come true, she was finding that old adage about cautiousness and wishes may have been more knowledgeable than she had previously given it credit for. She found herself the star of a show, one of the violent, Sunday-night main events that she usually switched off, too frightened to continue; but this show had no audience—except for herself and the dead.

There was a cry, frightened but brimming with feeling and life; and Vel felt her chest flutter, foolishly letting her hopes rise of finding some other living person, some small connection to the rest of the world. She realized her original assessment that there was no one there except herself had been wrong and that near the center of the bridge, near the giant wall of twisted, flaming metal was a small group of people moving, pressing themselves against the wall of steel, trying at some task that Vel could not make out through the vast distance. Checking the ground before, she hurried forward as much as her sense of balance would allow, the incline increasing as she approached the end of the bridge.

Closer, she saw that two of the people were boosting a third to the top of the pile of wrecked cars, a smaller form than the others, definitely more feminine in shape and seemingly wearing some kind of skirt that they were fighting in the gusts of wind. Eventually, they gave up this futile attempt at modesty, and she threw both hands to the top, dug in, and with a push from the two beneath, found herself over the top of the car, throwing her legs over and landing out of sight on the other side.

At the sight of this, Vel wanted to cup her hands to her mouth and cheer, whistle and hoot, anything to give voice to the joy she felt. In the craziness of the morning, she had thought the world her world as she knew it had come to a screeching, unforgiving halt, one that looked ready to do away with her as well. But now, there was a form of escape; there was other people; there was hope, and the taste of it on her palate was enough to get her soaring. Maybe this was some sick television fantasy, but at least it had a happy ending, like the best of them.

She started moving down the hill toward the end of the overturned semi, rushing to reach the two strangers before they both made their way over the wall; and she found herself stranded without their help or worse, their company. Falling into a fast stride, she squeezed through a line of cars as she saw the second person grab the hand of the woman at the top and pull themselves up, reaching down for the third. Vel knew she had to get their attention or risk losing them behind the steel veil.

"Hey! Wait up!"

Her voice carried over the wind, down the long stretch of concrete, and somehow, miraculously caught the ear of the person climbing the steel wall, the small speck of a face turning in her direction. Throwing her hands up to wave, the person seemed to point her out to his companions. There was a shifting of bodies, and the person hanging from the cars seemed to pause in contemplation, and she could feel their gaze even across the stretch of desolate landscape. Then, with a slow resignation, the person turned back to the wall and started back up to the top, reaching for their companion's outstretched hands.

"Hey! *Hey*! Wait a minute!" Vel was squeezing her way through two cars, finding herself stuck, the frames digging into her stomach, pressing organs where they shouldn't be.

They're going to leave you, darling, but can you really blame them? I mean who could like you, sweetie, except for me, of course? You're like the dog I love to torment.

Fighting her way through the tight spot with her less-than-healthy form made her feel worse than a dozen stood-up dates, and she wished that she had used that gym membership she had gotten from the diner's Secret Santa, surely meant as a subtle dig but holding a shameful truth nonetheless.

"Wait! Please! You can't just leave me—"

Her words were cut short by the sight of the person on the wall's foot slipping, the body falling back down half the ten, or so, feet of piled vehicles. His foot managed to catch on the pipe of an overturned sports car's undercarriage, and there was a sharp crack, like a gunshot going off next to Vel's ears. She saw his foot fall again, the pipe bursting loose and a thick green stream pouring from its ruptured end, out into the middle of the bridge, spreading rapidly to the dancing flames.

In an instant, the world around her disappeared in another flash, much like the blinding white of the one before, except this one was accompanied by such an intense heat that Vel was sure her skin was crisped black and had crumbled away into ash. She was thrown back so violently that she lost track of what was up and what was down, even when she felt something hard and sharp stop her, digging into her back and surely shattering every bone within it. Motionless, she lay as if dead, refusing to believe that she could have survived something like that, at least not without deformities that would make her wish she would have stayed lying there anyway.

What caused her to stir was the feeling of the wind on her face, so fresh and biting in its intensity. Her nerves were sensitive to its touch, receptive to its embrace, tingling at its presence. If her skin had been singed off, there would be no feeling, none except maybe the pain; and while most of her ached so deeply that she wondered how she would even manage to breathe regularly without every second being one of agony, she knew she was alive and well, or as well as anyone who survived an explosion could call themselves.

The thing that finally made her eyes open faster than pulled shutters, however, was the sound of voices, not from in front of her—which, she assumed, despite her loss of direction, was where the small group had been before their bodies were consumed by the inferno—but behind her, approaching from behind the large semi that had, also by some kind of divine miracle, remained intact in the face of the explosion.

Slowly, laboriously, Vel struggled to lift her head from the ground, the sound of crackling flames significantly louder than it had been. She could still feel the heat on her face, another good sign that most of her features were still unmarred by burns or injury. *Don't act like it wouldn't be an improvement, love.* But her nose still felt like someone had pulled it up by the root. With what little strength remained to her, she pushed herself up before falling right back onto her face, her nose turning her vision white with pain again.

Over the roar of the wind and the crackle of the flames, the voices made their way into her ear, tethering her consciousness to the world of the living.

"I'm saying is that sticking in a large group maybe wouldn't have been the worst idea."

"Well, we all value *your* opinion very much, Billy. Thanks for sharing it for the fiftieth time. Next time, let me know when you're gonna give it so I can record it on my phone and listen to it whenever I want."

"Give it a rest, Veronica. Nobody even asked you to follow us."

"Well, unfortunately for me, it's not like there were too many other places to go."

"Aw, your friends all abandoned you, did they? Why didn't you just go with your friend Bryan? You two seemed like you would have made a great team. You guys could just stab anybody that got in your way, whether they're alive or not."

"Fuck off, I had nothing to do with that."

"You had everything to do with that."

"Do you need me to beat the shit out of you again, you skinny bitch?"

"You're skinnier than I am!"

"Trust me, you don't have to tell me."

There was the sound of scuffling feet and blows passing harmlessly through the air, along with the grunts of those trying to keep the girls apart.

"Hey! Hey! We do *not* need this right now! If you guys wanna waste time fighting with each other over some stupid perceived slights, then do it after we make it out of here. Right now, we've got more important things to deal with than each other, but I figured that was common knowledge."

There was an awkward silence then, the voice that had spoken commanding a small authority over the rest, carrying an unwavering confidence that demanded the respect of those around it, not with force but with a compassion that was almost tangible.

"I hate that you're right, but it doesn't change that you are."

"So you two are gonna play nice, like you don't hate each other's guts? At least for a little while?"

Vel heard no answer and assumed a silent affirmation had been given between the two of them. She kept waiting for more voices to join in the play that was taking place, but so far, there had only been the four, and it didn't seem like there would be any more.

"What do you think it was that made that noise? One of those things?" the first voice again, a male, much more timid than the one that had talked down the girls.

"They don't sound like that, stupid."

"I think it has something to do with all the smoke around here."

"You don't think—?"

"Is it coming from the bridge?"

"Only one way to find out."

The footsteps started soon after, growing louder as they came closer, Vel's heartbeat increasing with each and every step. She tried to call out as soon as she heard them but found her throat drier than it had ever been, like someone had gone down the length of it with an ice cream scoop, scraping the skin from its walls. Only a raspy growl came out, the frustration almost driving her to tears.

"Oh my god…"

"Oh, wow, I can't believe… I mean, I can, you see it on the news all the time, but I never thought I'd see something like that up close."

"You've got to be fucking kidding me. We walked all the way here, and we can't even cross?"

"Maybe if we squeeze through that section of cars there, we can reach the exposed support beam there and shimmy across."

"You really are crazy, aren't you? We'd fall like five stories!"

"No, we won't. Look, there's a small ledge around the hole on the right side. If we go one by one, we—"

"There is no way in hell I'm doing that!"

"Well, no one's really asking you to anyway. Like I said, we didn't ask you to follow us," the other girl answered bitterly.

"I think I agree with Veronica on this one."

"At least one of you guys doesn't have some kind of death wish."

"It's the only way across," the first boy insisted, the slight squeak in his voice betraying his young age. "There's too much wreckage in the river. And there's lots of dead in the cars that fell through just underneath the surface. It'll be too hard to see them until they're already on top of you."

"Why do you think any of them survived down there?"

"Half of 'em are moving without all their limbs, and most of their skin missing. Something tells me a little water ain't gonna bother 'em too much."

"What the fuck."

Vel tried to call out to them again, the burn in her throat subsiding and her faculties almost fully returned to her. She was horribly aware of something sharp embedded in her shin, as well as a jagged pain that came with every intake of breath, and her nose was still a constant fire of screaming nerves. Even though she meant to say something concrete, like, "Help!" or even, ambitiously, "Over here!" all that came out was a low groan, punctuated by pauses meant to separate the slur of words. Discouraged, she almost let the pain pull her back under, but the sound of cracking glass and hastened footsteps in her direction provided enough incentive to try again. This call, while louder, was just as much an intelligible mess as the first one, sounding more like a poor imitation of a kind of Slavic language than anything that might resemble English.

"Shhh."

"Don't tell me to shush. I'm just trying to explain why it's dumb to risk our lives on some balancing act—"

"Shut up and listen!" the other girl commanded, a fierceness in her voice that hindered on pure animosity. "Can you guys hear it too?"

Vel nearly burst into tears and tried desperately to build up the strength for another plea to her would-be rescuers, her throat straining at every stiff breath. Finally managing to inhale enough without her shattered rib forcing it all back out, she called out again, this time at least sounding like some kind of message, if still indecipherable.

"It's one of those things, isn't it?" the timid boy said, his voice shaking.

Her heart nearly leaped up into her throat and choked her right then and there, if not for her coughing up a small stream of blood at the back of her throat. She cleared her throat again and nearly vomited.

"I don't think so. They usually don't cough."

"How do you know they don't cough? Maybe you just haven't seen them cough," the timid boy remarked.

"They don't breathe, do they?"

"Good point."

"I'm gonna go check it out."

"Wait, you're gonna what?"

"Are you sure?" the calmer boy, the supposed leader, asked.

"As sure as I'm gonna get."

"Take some kind of weapon with you just in case, a pipe, shard of glass, anything you can use to defend yourself."

"Got it."

Vel heard the distant scrape of metal and felt her muscles tighten, the fear slipping its fingers into her again. Opening her mouth, she tried to speak but found her voice gone. Her throat no longer felt like sandpaper, but still her words seemed caught in her throat, and only a groan came out.

"Be careful, Gwen."

"Yeah, good luck," the other girl said with biting sarcasm.

This quip went unanswered, as only the gentle footfalls of the young girl made her way through the twisting maze of cars, stopping to inspect a broken window or opened door every other step, taking every precaution and no risks. Deathly silent, she moved closer, audible only by the collision of her makeshift weapon against the makeshift walls of their maze and the lovely jingle of broken glass. Vel pushed her head up with her elbows, feeling that same glass dig into her dry, flaky skin. By coincidence alone, she locked eyes with girl, her blond hair flapping against her face and throwing the ends wildly over her features. The eyes were steady, still, and unflinching as they watched her every movement, her absentminded struggle for words.

"Oh, Jesus, are you okay?"

Vel again tried to say something, anything really to impart some modicum of understanding to this girl with the violent green eyes; but all that came out was a squeak, like a mouse, and another low groan. At this sound, the girl brought up the large steel pipe at her side, its ends sharp with torn steel, pried from one of the abandoned mausoleums around them. More defensively than she had before, with her weapon raised, the girl approached, craning her neck to inspect the full length of Vel's body, checking for wounds or any other reason to explain her situation.

"Excuse me, miss? I asked if you were okay? Please tell me you're okay. Please."

Her eyes, while steady, contained a deep fear behind them, a loathing for the part that was coming next if Vel did not answer, doomed to this despicable job by her own choosing. With all the strength her broken body had left, Vel pushed herself from the concrete, aware of the girl's frightened approach.

"Wait! Wait! Wait!" Vel said, her voice breaking through the seal of spit that had been clogging her throat.

The girl, with the pipe held high above her head like some kind of Amazonian you'd see on 'nineties fantasy shows replayed at midnight on sci-fi channels, stopped just short of bringing the jagged end down across Vel's head and dropped it in shock at the sound of her voice. It bounced harmlessly against the ground, the steel ringing out like the final note in some unheard symphony, the end of a grand crescendo that's beauty went forever unheard. Vel almost burst into tears at that joyous sound, better than any song Beyoncé or Mariah Carey's powerful voices could produce, so sweet and refreshing, like she had tasted a forbidden fruit. By the time the girl was kneeling above her, her sobs had morphed into a strange kind of laughter, one that confused Vel herself most of all, even though the baffled look on the young blond's face indicated that her own comprehension wasn't far off.

"Are you okay? What the hell happened here? What happened to *you*?"

"The bri… the bridge," Vel said through a cough, still hacking up half the mucus and phlegm and blood that had cemented her vocal chords, "someone was trying to cross, and they triggered some kind of explosion."

Even though her fingers were trembling, she pointed over to the spot where the wall of cars had stood who knows how long ago, the flames now having engulfed the most of the bridge that still remained, tearing into the sky as if it planned to set that on fire as well.

"Gwen! Gwen! Is everything okay down there?"

"Yeah. Yes! Everything's fine! It was just a woman. It looks like she got injured in the explosion that took out the bridge," the girl shouted, turning her head over her shoulder in the direction of her friends. "What's your name? Can you speak all right? I think Range has some water with him."

The boy she suspected to be Range, his hair as blond as the morning sun against a beet-red sky, came around the trail of cars soon after, a look of concern on his face that didn't seem to fit there but had wormed its way in nonetheless. He rushed over to the two of them and threw his ratty brown backpack on the ground and started digging through it like a mole shifting through dirt, throwing things left and right until he found the clear bottle of glistening water and offered it to her. Upon closer inspection, she saw sticking out of the top of the bag awkwardly, with its large body and long neck exposed, was the top of a guitar, making her wonder how anything else had managed to be squeezed into it.

Vel tried to thank him but felt her voice disappear again into that raspy growl. The two other members of the small group came round next, the timid boy with doubled shoulders and shaggy brown hair and the other girl with straight black hair and emerald eyes, her arms crossed over her ample chest, a familiarity about her that made Vel shiver. As Vel went to take the drink, she almost fell back down and felt the boy Range's hands supporting her.

That handsome angel, she thought, staring at him in the bright light of the afternoon sky, and she soon was sat up against a nearby sedan.

"Whoa! What is that you're giving her?" the black-haired girl asked.

"Water? What else would it be?"

"And why the hell would you do that?"

"Why the hell *wouldn't* I?"

"Because how do we know she's not about to turn into one of those… things?"

"What do you mean?"

"I mean, everybody else is turning into those…"

"Zombies," the blond-haired boy said, with a nonchalance that almost made Vel burst out laughing.

"You can't be serious."

The boy looked at her as if he had never said anything more serious in his life. When her silent plea for sanity went unassisted by the others in her group, who avoided her gaze with awkward stares at the ground, she simply threw her hands up in wild exasperation.

"Fine, how do we know she's not turning into a zombie, like everyone else in the town has?"

"How do we know you're not turning into a zombie? Maybe we shouldn't give you any water either if it's such a big risk," the other girl countered, still holding the water bottle just out of Vel's reach.

Vel wanted to grab it then and there, but the girl with the black hair's eyes were burning into her, following every minor motion, even the beats of her breaths.

"Ha-ha, you all know exactly what I'm talking about. This…" her eyes scanned Vel with a mild disgust, "woman apparently was right next to the explosion that did that!" she said, motioning toward the destroyed bridge and the gaping pit that had been opened in its center. "And she somehow just miraculously survives? Oh, come on, we even heard her groaning like one of those *zombies* before we found her. Who's to say she's not on her way to becoming one of those gross monsters?"

"If we don't give her water, she *will* become one of those monsters!"

Vel felt her neck stiffen, becoming horribly aware of every pain and discomfort in her body, all the aches that felt worse than usual, probing for any sensation of an invader in her body or in her thoughts. Suddenly, every thought felt wrong and not her own, to the point where she needed to close her eyes and inhale deeply to calm herself.

The boy Range was looking at the black-haired girl with annoyance, but he didn't say anything for a while, only opening his mouth as if he was going speak and then closing it briskly as if was only humming something to himself.

"She's right. She could be infected," he said slowly, the words deep and pleasing despite the burden they carried.

"What?" the blond girl said, as if stabbed in the back.

She retracted the bottle as she stood, causing Vel's already-sinking spirit to spiral into absolute dismay. Taking deep breaths, she tried pacify the raging doubts inside her but found her efforts thwarted by Gloria Hickam's delighted cackling.

I like the way this girl thinks. She's got a good head on her shoulders. And what a pair of shoulders she has. That girl would've eaten you alive in school. Maybe now it'll be you who's eating her alive.

She slammed her tightened fist into her side lobe, trying to silence the voice with meaningless self-violence.

"I don't like it any more than you do, but we don't know anything about her, and we all heard the noises she was making," Range explained, his head motioning briefly to the steel pipe at the blond girl's feet.

It was only then that Vel saw the blood on her plain-white gym shoes and began to hyperventilate, unsure herself if at any moment she was going to develop an uncompromising hunger for human flesh. She would've laughed if she didn't believe it so much.

"How can we be sure?" the brown-haired boy asked, leaning in to look at her but turning away sharply when she met his gaze.

"Does she have any bite marks on her?" Range asked.

"Why would that matter?"

"That's usually how it's spread. What I've seen today leads me to believe no different now."

"Well, I'm not checking her out," the black-haired girl said, her lips curling with that same disgust.

I can't say I blame the poor thing.

"I'll do it," the blond girl replied, shooting dirty looks at her and Range, who looked as if she had slapped him, his face dropping in shame and malaise.

Silently, she set the bottle down on the hood of the nearest car and moved back to Vel, crouching until they were face-to-face, her knees cracking loudly in the process.

"Sorry about this," she said as she began, looking her up and down, gentling pulling out her burned arms and tenderly bringing her fingers across the fraying skin.

Vel mouthed a squeal of pain that the girl picked up on nonetheless and quickly moved on to her legs, inhaling sharply at the sight of the large shard of glass jutting from it. Trembling, she went to touch it but recoiled at the last moment, remembering her objective with a face set in determination, almost like she was trying to prove something, or herself.

"She's fine. A couple scrapes, burns, and she's got a huge piece of glass in her leg, but she checks out."

"Check under her clothes."

Vel felt her heart jump in her throat, and a chill went over her, all while Gloria's laughter echoed in the wind. Her face flew past the early stages of blushing into a shade of full scarlet.

"Oh, come off it, Veronica, I'm not—"

"We have to be sure, Gwen. You heard your freak of a boyfriend."

At that, Range started toward the black-haired girl like he was going to move right through her and slam her into the pavement; but he stopped immediately, his momentum almost causing him to fall. The blond girl stayed planted in her spot, her eyes never leaving Veronica's. In silent defeat, she turned back and faced Vel, looking at her with sorrowful eyes that sat perched above heavy bags that pulled at her pretty, if unkempt, face. Vel wanted to tell her that it was all right, that what she was doing was necessary and would put her at ease as much as it would them; but her shame was too great, the thought of those eyes on the body she stared at in the foggy mirror every morning…

Tears tugged at the sides of her eyes, but she restrained them, fighting for a shred of dignity in the situation, one that seemed to be torn from an adaptation of her high school years. When she looked at Veronica, the name ringing in her ears as if it was somehow important, she saw only the face of Gloria Hickam, smiling down at her as she stood a goddess above, relishing in Vel's insignificance.

"I'm so, so sorry," Gwen said finally, unable to hold off any longer.

Her thin and gentle fingers stretched down to the edges of her blouse's fabric, one she had bought because the woman working the dressing rooms had told her it made her look like a Kardashian, but now it only made her feel disgusting as it was peeled from her, the sweat making it stick to the fat she dared not look at. She even would prefer to look at the giant piece of glass protruding from her shin than down at her stomach in that moment.

Looking up, she saw Veronica/Gloria looking on with a sickening glee; but fortunately for her sanity, both of the boys had turned away and were scanning the horizon, neither speaking nor looking at the other. Gwen's eyes were aching, but they continued on in the process of checking every centimeter of her for a wound. It was hard not to picture others from Vel's high school class gathered around, pointing and laughing at the ridiculous scene, throwing mocking gazes and unwrapped tampons at her feet, looking at the shriveled bag of skin that their already-unsightly classmate had become. The chill of the wind was biting into her exposed skin, making her already blemished and burned flesh freckled with goose bumps.

Gwen circled around to the back of her, patting at the fringe of her bra. She made a final inspection over her bare shoulders, before quickly handing Vel back her shirt, helping it back over her head, ignoring the tears as best she could. Vel would've thanked her for that but couldn't find the words.

"Are you satisfied now?" she declared, staring spitefully at Veronica, who seemed nonplussed and disinterested in the whole spectacle she herself had created.

"Check her legs."

"Oh, come off it, Veronica! You'd be able to see the bite mark through her fucking pants! You can see the piece of glass jammed in her leg, can't you?"

"Yeah, that's fine, I guess, not like I know what to look for anyway," she said with a shrug.

Range had whirled around right after Gwen's final assessment and was now moving past Veronica's rigid stance, her gaze following him with a mix of curiosity and revulsion. He knelt down in front of Vel and quickly looked her over, stopping on the flaking skin and impaled leg.

"I'm… sorry about that. I didn't know…" he said abashedly, a brief smile passing through Gwen's lips as he did so. "Can you speak? Can you tell me your name?"

Despite the directness of the question, Vel still found herself unsure as to how to answer. Since that morning, it had felt like she had traveled into another dimension, a *Twilight Zone* that wasn't based on some cruel, ironic punishment, or wrapped around a twisted morality fable, at least one that she understood, but seeped purely in chaos and the surreal. The whole thing felt real and yet not, silly yet deadly serious, as if everything was one big joke that her life hinged upon. She wasn't even sure how she felt about these so-called rescuers of hers, who had come along and offered her water but at the cost of a silent mockery, the type of which she hadn't experienced since high school.

Still, when she looked at Gwen, who was waiting with a look of genuine concern for an answer, wistfully casting glances at the boy beside her with doe eyes that even Vel—as socially awkward as she had been—could recognize as holding a silent significance, she felt no anger, or bitterness, and none when she looked at Range, who, while seemingly uncaring, was more sensible than anything else.

"I… I think… I," she coughed violently in between the words, tasting like caterpillars crawling up her esophagus.

With wild jabs of her finger and her other hand at her throat, she finally drew their attention back to the bottle of water behind them. Almost frantically, Gwen fell backward and grabbed at the bottle, knocking it over in the process and starting a steady spill from the top. She cursed at herself before scooping it up quickly, salvaging more than half of the bottle and holding it up to Vel's mouth. Without even waiting to grab it from her, Vel pressed her lips to the edge and opened her throat wide, taking in as much of the soothing liquid she could. Gwen looked over to see Range still stifling a laugh from her spill, and she swatted at his shoulder angrily, even though her face wore a grin wider than his.

After Vel polished off almost the whole bottle, she sputtered, sending what felt like half of it back up in another spasm of coughing that seemed to rack her whole body. Afterward, though, her throat no longer felt as if there was forest fire going on within it but was now as fresh as if someone had poured mint coolant down it.

"My name is Vel. Vel Veshkin, if you want to be really formal."

"How'd you get out here?" Gwen asked.

She had to take a moment to loom around and regain a sense of her surroundings after the explosion, the large overturned semi lurking high above her head. Only now did she realize how lucky she was that it had not gone up in the explosion with half of the bridge; otherwise, Vel would've been waking up at the bottom of the river, and if she did, it would be as one of those mindless... It still felt odd to call them zombies, as if it was some kind of dark secret that she couldn't admit.

"My car," she said, pointing past the tanker, the group's eyes following the trail with adamant eyes. "I was trying to get over the bridge. I'm not even sure what's going on. When I woke up this morning, well, at eleven, you see, I'm a waitress who works the night shift at Mickey's over on Kennel..."

"You're a waitress? At your age?"

"Shut up, Veronica! Jeez, for someone who's supposedly popular, you have the social skills of a rabid dog," Gwen said, turning on the black-haired vixen as soon as Vel's cheeks started to redden.

Can't blame the girl for asking the tough questions, not like she's the first one, Vel.

When she looked back at Vel, it was with a smile that exuded warmth, radiant, if a little awkwardly forced.

"I'm sorry about that. You should just ignore her. It's what the rest of us do."

"Excuse me! I can't—"

"So you don't know anything about the zombies?" Range interrupted, ignoring Veronica's look of tired exasperation that was boring into the back of his skull.

"No, I mean, I guess not. It's all just so strange. My boss called, he was saying that people were sick or something, like they had a bad kind of bird flu or something exotic like that. Said people were acting crazy and the best thing to do was to stay in my home. Obviously, when I heard the sounds of him being murdered via answering machine, I packed into my car and started heading toward the bridge when I ran into a puff of smoke, and…"

The look of that small child's face, wrapped in mask of hatred and hunger, haunted her and caused a shiver so violent she thought it would rend her body in two.

"I crashed and got out, stumbling around because of the smoke, until I saw people crawling on the bridge. I tried to get their attention, but… they left me here." She heard someone scoff at this and had only one culprit in mind. "Right after, one of the people climbing over must've broke loose a gas line and sent a stream of it into the fire that had already started. I was knocked back here, and the first thing I heard when I woke up was your voices, coming from the woods."

Range remained silent throughout her story, and when she finished, the silence stuck until he stood, stretched, and began to look out at the remains of the bridge, the wind beating the hair against his brow. In the low afternoon light, it was easy to see why Gwen stared at him so. Even now, she looked at him with a longing that was painfully bittersweet, Vel's own one-sided high school gazes coming to mind.

"We've got to try and get across the bridge. If the rest of the town's as bad as you said, as I thought it would be… we don't have much more time to waste. We need to get out before things get worse."

"How do you know the thing isn't global by now? I mean, it's not like this is just some isolated incident. This has got to be happening all over, right?" the brown-haired boy said, having been quiet so long Vel had forgotten that he was there.

At this question, Range seemed to tense up, his eyes darting to the ground unfocused. "It's just here, nowhere else, that's why it's so important that we leave."

"How do you know that?" Gwen asked, her voice strained.

"I told you, he knows more than he was letting on. You do know what the hell's going on here, don't you, freak? You do, don't you?" Veronica demanded, throwing her hands up and stomping her feet like a child in a tantrum.

"It's not something I know for sure, something I was researching back before any of this started. It could just be nonsense, but…" he trailed off, but his eyes kept working, staring intently at the landscape in front of him as though it contained all the answers of the universe.

"But what?" Gwen prodded.

Range turned and opened his mouth as if he meant to answer but stopped himself, unsure if he should proceed or not, as if he was stepping out on ice that might shatter at any moment. Veronica was still staring at him incredulously, her glare probing him for any sign of weakness but seemingly finding none in his pensive gaze. The brown-haired youth had even joined the impromptu circle that had formed, like he was worried that once it closed without him, his place in the group would be just as forfeit.

Vel was still trying to process the idea that zombies—something that had been nothing more than dark dreams of children and the concoctions of low-budget Hollywood sets and bit actors hoping for their big break—were something tangible, a real threat that she may face around any corner, as real as the wolves heard howling at the latest and darkest hours of the night, or as the neighbor seemingly innocuous and transparently pleasant that harbored dismembered bodies in their basement. Except if these kids could be believed, the chances of encountering them were much higher than either of those much more real and frightening possibilities, one that had been ingrained into her psyche since she was a child.

What was she saying? She had even run into one, quite literally, already, seen them face-to-face, stared into their gray, misty eyes and found nothing looking back.

"This theory of yours, as to why all this is happening… was it how you knew to bring me to the graveyard last night? To show me that grave?"

With some mild hesitation, Range eventually gave a grim nod, causing Veronica to wave her hands at this apparent evidence as if it proved some point that she had never really made.

"If this theory relates to why people are rising from the dead and feasting on people like they're walking buffets, I'm assuming it might also have a way to stop them? To stop all this?"

The wind seemed to answer her, kicking up a large clump of leaves and throwing them into the air before carrying them gently, amicably down into their fiery demise at the hands of the inferno raging below. Range seemed incredibly focused on watching their crisp yellow shapes singe and curl in the fingers of the flames, falling into ash before they even reached the ground.

"It might, but I can't be sure going on what I know now."

"What exactly is this theory of yours, genius?" Veronica asked, crossing her arms back into their permanent resting place under her chest. "Chemical weapons left behind by some secret government testing that went on in the 'fifties? Or wait, let me guess! There's an ancient Indian burial ground that's been disturbed somewhere, and you want us to find Chief Kill-Whitey's remains and return them to their proper resting place! Or no, no, no! It's alien brain slugs that have crawled into everyone's brains! I think I remember seeing that one when I was a kid with my brother."

The final word in her long diatribe made Vel's ears perk up, something clicking into place in her mind; but what it clicked where, she couldn't be sure of.

"Well, there was that comet that landed a couple towns over just two nights ago," the brown-haired boy commented quietly.

"Shut up, Billy," Veronica said briskly, although his words seemed to leave her visibly shaken. Perhaps she wasn't expecting her dismissal of the incomprehensible horrors around her to turn into further damning proof of their reality. "That's not really your theory, is it?"

Range shook his head but explained himself no further, leaving them to listen only to the whistle of the wind flitting between the twisted steel remains.

"I can't explain it now without sounding like crazy drunk. I'm missing one important piece of information that ties it all together. Until then, it's all just… wishful thinking."

"How can we test this theory of yours?" Gwen asked. "What's this piece of information you need? I really hope you're not suggesting we get a sample or something."

Range smiled briefly, so much so that it seemed more like a trick of the light than an actual expression of joy.

"No. It's simple enough. Well, it would be, given normal circumstances, but our predicament obviously makes it a tad bit more difficult."

"Just get on with it, Vincent Price," Veronica urged.

"There's a section of the library, the old one that's a couple block north of Main Street, the town history section up on the second floor, in the back of the listening room. That's where I was doing my research before I got… distracted." His eyes shifted uncomfortably to Gwen, before moving back to the ground. "There's a bunch of books up there compiled by one of the librarians that covers the complete history of the town, with newspaper clippings, genealogy trees, stuff like that. He was going over most of it with me at my request, even going so far as to loan me a couple of the books he hadn't finished yet on some of the town's most famous citizens—people like John Raimi, who built the factory that burned down over by Carter's Woods; the schoolteacher that ended up a member of Congress back in the 'sixties; and Jonathan Longwarden, the famous composer from whose great-grandfather we got the original name of the settlement, Wardensville."

"Anything about Roger Sinais?" Gwen asked, almost frantically.

Range shook his head. "He shows up a couple times in a couple of newspaper clippings, more good than bad. The librarian didn't see a reason to make a book on him, though, barely seemed to recognize the name."

At this, Gwen seemed almost relieved, a deep sigh leaving her chest. Vel watched her curiously to try and understand this response before she realized she was staring.

"So what you're suggesting is we travel across town, in the complete opposite direction that we just came, so we can head to the library, a place I wouldn't want to go even if the world *was* ending, just to test some half-assed theory of yours that's so half-assed you can't even explain it to us? Is that correct? That's your plan?" Veronica prodded. "Because it sounds like suicide to me."

"Well, it's either that, or we can try and get across the bridge."

To this rebuttal, Veronica had none of her own and stood in an angry, dismayed silence as Gwen helped Vel to her feet.

"Worst-case scenario, we can hole up there until help arrives," the timid boy, Billy, said. "We can use those heavy oak shelves to barricade the entrances on the first floor and use the second story as a sort of refuge."

"Good thinking, Billy," Gwen said, flashing him a quick smile.

The boy's cheeks instantly flushed, and he turned his head quickly away in shame, a bitterness in his gaze as well that was unmistakable.

Range didn't comment on this new addition to the plan, his mind already set at the task ahead, gathering up the backpack on the ground and throwing it over one shoulder. The neck of the guitar bounced next to his head, almost striking his ear, but he hardly seemed to notice it.

"You might want to take that," he said, motioning toward the steel pipe on the ground.

Gwen nodded and scooped the long steel rod off the gravel, shifting rocks between her fingers. When she lifted it to her side, Vel thought she looked like a child holding a stick, convincing themselves that it was some legendary weapon. The other quickly followed Range's example and scooped up their own meager belongings. Gwen had a similar backpack that seemed equally provisioned, but the other two had nothing but the clothes on their backs and envious looks as they started toward the top of the hill.

Vel shifted into place behind them all, Range silently leading the way on their vigil, their march through death into the unknown wilds before them. She still felt odd and out of place amidst the raging hormones flying around, the thought of zombies still feeling silly in her mind, like a game they were all playing. With an exhilarating rush that was almost more frightening than the creatures that lurked behind the dapper green branches of the pines, their hideousness naked to the daylight, bare for all to see—she thought of running back down that hill and crossing that bridge, escaping town, despite Veronica's prissy Gloria Hickam-esque reluctance to do so. It would be simple, incredibly so. They probably wouldn't even care enough about her to come after her—some battered, delirious woman from beyond their concept of time.

They were already gaining a good distance from her as she stood there, contemplating. She could be off on her own, miles away from this town and all the monsters in it, living and dead—free to start anew, a life only as good as she made it to be. But as she stared hard into the abyss of the bridge and saw the flames lapping at its base and the thrashing waves with dark shapes moving just beneath the surface, she increased the pace of her steps and made sure that she did not fall out of step with the group for the rest of the trek through the woods.

Frank heard the cracking of air and rustle of trees from miles away and knew instantly that some great disaster had taken place down near the highway, somewhere near the MacArthur Bridge that stretched over the river. He swore he could feel the heat bristling at his face as well but knew it to be impossible. That had been nearly an hour ago now, but time had long slipped into the nether, the first casualty in the fall of modern society. Slowly they had passed through the abandoned streets and terraces, their footsteps echoing much farther than they should, as if they were trapped within the confines of the growing fog, which had come in with the clouds. It was so thick and milky that viewing anything further than a block ahead of you became a strain, as much a test of your eyesight as reading one of those charts at the optometrists. Frank thought of the large Coke bottle pair of glasses that his own eye doctor had prescribed just after his forty-fifth birthday, his eyes seemingly waiting for a nice round number to start to sour. Now, they were probably sitting on his nightstand, a thin layer of dust having settled on the lenses. He almost regretted never wearing them now, in the face of this disaster, however unexpected—as if he had missed out on a thousand days of crisper, clearer images of the world around him. But in his life, being able to see clearly the filth, grime, and squalor around him didn't exactly seem beneficial and worth wearing the gaudy frames that made him look like an evil dean from an 'eighties college comedy, or some other stern self-righteous bastard.

They had moved in silence down boulevards many of them recognized, streets that once held bustling faces, faces that held as many smiles as they did secrets—all now left meaningless in the disintegration of the world that gave birth to them. Instead of overhearing excited whispers that contained the juiciest gossip of the denizen of the sleep burg or the louder, more exaggerated banter of those catching up, their performance designed more for the eyes watching them than for the person across from them— the only sound was the howl of the wind and the occasional scream that rose out of the mist from an undeterminable direction, to sink back into the opposite side of it. It was hard to figure out just where any indication of danger might be coming from, even though all their senses had been heightened to the point of hypersensitivity, where even the slightest unexpected scrape or scratch resulted in a chorus of spinning heads and circling feet.

Fortunately, no danger crossed their paths for most of their escape from the station. As soon as they had tasted the fresh, prefrost air that three of them had doubted ever tasting again for many years, if any, they quickly decided to move toward the hospital near the town square and started down Eucalyptus toward Hennigan's hardware store that stood at the five-point intersection nearby. They reached the store, a lone two-story building towering above the others around it, the single culmination of two streets coming together and intertwining into one that continued south into the market district. A low awning bearing the establishment's name hung above the window, black-and-white alternating strips making it seem more like an old barber shop than a hardware store but the cracked window, advertising several of their flagship deals—such as, fifty nails for a dollar, or two table saws for the price of one, a concept that seemed silly now in this new nightmare-like world that they had slipped into.

Seeing the necessity of several of the objects that might be inside the store that looters, or the owner himself, might not have carried off already, Bruce made a resolution to stop and check inside, one that nobody really disagreed with; and if they did, made no point to address it. While Matt stood ready behind him with his shotgun barrel pointed in the shadows of the storefront, Bruce smashed in the glass on the top half of the door, creating a space small enough for his hand to squeeze through and grab the lock on the other side. With a quick twist, the door swung forward in a jolt that caused the gun to jump in Matt's hand like it had been one of those pale-skinned monsters running out of the shadows. Even after waiting several seconds for any responses to their intrusion, none came, the building living up to its dilapidated look.

As they filed into the store, Bruce standing at attention at the door, Tyler snickered casting a low look at him.

"I never thought I'd see the day a pig would be breaking into a place they was looking to loot," he said.

Bruce didn't share the hilarity of the sentiment but did nothing to correct him either. He just stood like a silent sentry, his gaze focused on the impenetrable mist and the creatures he knew lay in wait behind it. When everyone had gathered inside, Bruce shut the flimsy wooden door, its hinges creaking louder than any of them would've liked, but still no attention coming from any unwanted visitors, even living ones. Matt moved quickly down to the lumber station in the back, hoping to grab several two-by-fours, or whatever size they had, knowing that a barricade—while an unpleasant thought considering the implication of the wait associated with it—might be necessary sooner rather than later.

Tyler moved behind the counter and threw his duffel bag on top of it, scooting the steel legs of a nearby stool across the marble floor to give him a seat while he checked the cash register.

"Are you serious?" Bruce chastised upon seeing this.

"Something tells me the owner's not gonna miss it," Tyler said, smiling. "Me, on the other hand, when I get out of this shithole, I'm gonna need a couple bucks. Just enough 'til I can hit up Pops, of course, but damned if I ain't gonna grab a motel and whatever cheap ho is working outside it."

Bruce seemed to pretend he didn't hear any of this and moved back to the section marked Tools in bright-red letters, Tyler watching him going, chuckling to himself all the way.

"Pst, Frog. Pst. Pst!"

Frank turned to face Tyler, who was leaning casually over the counter, his wide grin bordering on maniacal with splashes of blood his face bore.

"Did you see what section he walked down?" he continued. "Seems fitting, am I right, fam?"

Frank gave a forced smile, something that seemed lost on Tyler, who merely laughed and continued on with clearing out the cash register row by row. Shivering, Frank realized how strong the chill was inside this place, striking straight to the bone. The door swung in the wind, slapping against the wall with a heavy smack that nearly made him jump. He moved over to it swiftly and shut it, sliding the bolt closed despite the hole in the glass that stood just above it rendering it a little less than useless.

Stealing a quick glance outside from the large bay window that also bore the store's name in painted red letters, hidden beneath red smears on both sides that looked like crude cave paintings depicting some kind of particularly barbaric hunt, the streets still stood empty, the fog covering every space between the abandoned structures filled with shattered windows, broken doors, and those same red smears, some of them arranged into bleak messages that spoke of death and their own damnation. It was hard to think that just yesterday, the town was undistinguishable from any other small town in the foothills of America; and now it looked as if a human being hadn't passed through here in decades.

The smell had been the worst. Death was everywhere, its rotten musk sinking deep into his chest at every turn and with every breath. He almost prayed that it would be his last just to rid himself of that horrible odor. A mix of rotten meat and curdled milk, staunch copper that stuck to your tongue, a pungent sweetness that was also horribly bitter, like sugar floating on the top of black coffee. The house across the street's door was ripped from its hinges and thrown into the street, half of it slid under a parked car, an old '96 Dodge Caravan, covered in so much blood that he had mistaken it for being red before seeing the chipped white underneath. Looking through the splintered frame, he saw a picturesque living room, one he imagined having himself back when he was still optimistic about his future—one where his wife would sit beside him, commenting on their favorite shows and sharing their views on whatever political scandal was gripping the country that week, while their son or daughter, or maybe even both, kicked their feet in concentration staring down at a torn notebook page of fractions and frayed edges. The green couch that sat unoccupied across the street looked uncannily like the one in his dreams; the lamp shade was more traditional than he would've liked. Maybe his wife would've talked him into it, but they would've agreed on those hardwood floors with the round wool rug in the center of the room.

He sighed, a warmth spreading through him that he hadn't felt in quite some time, mostly due to his own admonition. As the years had passed with promises of the next day being the one to bring the change to his life, he had simply stopped expecting it to come and settled into a normalcy that took the place of comfort—a close substitute, but one without worth, a fool's gold that shone just like the real thing. Was it really so foolish to be tricked by something that felt so similar?

Even though his life had settled into an amiable blur, one spent in devotion to those that would belittle him without a second's hesitation, he could still recall every missed opportunity, every slipped grasp of happiness that had passed through his hesitant fingers for fear of crushing it between them. It all seemed so simple now, to simply shake off the bad, to have lived like he had wanted, to have been sitting on top of that lime green couch's cushions as the world went to hell, his wife and child at his side when whatever horror from beyond human imagination took them. Before he turned away, he noticed the limp gray hand lying across the door's threshold, its bright-blue fingernails curled like a dying spider.

Matt reappeared from the back of the store, carrying a stack of boards of varying shapes and sizes. Most of them were less than a couple feet but looked thick and sturdy and was better than anything they would've gathered from the streets. He looked around quickly before spying Tyler and his large duffel bag that sat next to him on the counter, half of it slouching off the end, the outlines of various firearms poking through the black threads. Tyler was bent over himself, engrossed in whatever project he was working on in his lap.

Hoisting the boards over his shoulder, he dropped them beside the bag, startling Tyler from his work, who nearly dropped the thin object in his hand and its contents all over the floor.

"Hey, fam, what the fuck? I'm trying to roll over here."

"Are you serious? You couldn't wait?" Matt said with a groan, lifting several boards and squeezing them into the duffel bag.

"'Til when, nigguh? This could be the last blunt of my life, and I'm gonna make sure its the fattest blunt that's ever been rolled."

"That stuff's gonna make you slow on the draw, cowboy," Bruce said, emerging from the shadows.

"It's not like the dead move fast. Half of those motherfuckas ain't even got working joints at this point. Besides, the more I chill," he said, putting the wrap to his lips and licking straight across, "the less I miss."

"Can't argue with that logic," Matt said sarcastically.

"I think I can," said Bruce as he moved to the front window of the shop and began to check their surroundings as Frank had done.

Matt followed suit and went to his side, leaving Tyler to his work and Frank to his musings, whose eyes drifted aimlessly about the store, thinking more about long nights slaving over a late Klunesberg tax return or mismanaged balance sheet than he was about the horde that could be approaching from any side.

As his transparent gaze drifted over the scattered shelves, he slowly realized he was fixating on the large framing nail gun, cased in silver plastic that made it look like polished steel. It stood out to him for some reason, the gleam from its surface, however dishonest, calling—no, demanding—his attention. He thought himself stupid for worrying about power tools in the face of the so-called apocalypse but found himself trusting in its draw, finding importance in its silent allure.

"There! Look at this fat fuck!" Tyler shouted excitedly, bringing everyone's eyes to him.

The cigar stuffed to the brim with overflowing green buds looked larger than a traditional Cuban, if it had been rolled by a sloppy child, its edges uneven and sharp angles bent into the center. He stuck an end between his lips and reached for his pocket, patting it flat. His face filled with confusion as his search came up empty. Raising his arms, he looked around the counter for some means of lighting his self-made treasure, but his eyes froze as he stared down into the bottom of the counter and went wide and bloodshot before he even took a single puff.

"Oh, fuck me!"

There was a growl, a mix of a diseased dog and scavenger bird, a carrion crow and vulture rolled into one hideous shriek, a large white mass of flesh following it. It rose from under the counter—a large man dressed in wide overalls that went over his checkered flannel. A beard, flowing white in life but in stiff bloody clumps in death, hung down to the center of his chest. His mouth was cracked wide in a snarl, his yellow teeth bared and dripping a type of thick mucus, blood flying from his throat in thick black clots. A thick, soupy mix of blood was pouring out from his bottom lip, down into the thick white strands of his beard, making his mouth seem cavernous and wide like a leech. Arms wide and covered with hair thick and bristled, he swooped down at Tyler, hoping to seize him up in one smooth motion, but Tyler was quicker and already had the Remington in his hands, forcing it into the large dead thing's face. The barrel went straight for the middle of his head and smashed right into his nose, drawing forth no blood from its still-crusty veins but causing the pale green skin to split and the cartilage to crack like cardboard. It sunk down and caught in the monster's teeth, before Tyler overzealously shoved it into the back of its throat, half of the steel disappearing into the dead man's gullet.

"Eat this, you zombie fuck!" Tyler said with glee, his finger slamming down on the trigger.

Instead of a boom that deafened the world, there was only a harmless click as the creature continued to struggle against the end of his gun. Panic seeped into Tyler's face as he realized his predicament, his hand reaching for the duffel bag before the creature's flailing arms knocked it out of reach.

Moving on instinct more than thought, Frank ran to the nail gun on the wall, light from the ceiling falling around it like an illumination of the holy, and seized it by its weighted handle. He almost turned and fired right then, before he stopped himself, running back to the box of nails that stood at the front of the store, grabbing a loose handful. Kicking over a nearby display for weather stripping, he found an outlet with an open plug behind it and practically threw the attached charger into it. A single green light lit, followed by a succession of three blinking red ones to indicate a charge.

Frank heard the grunts of the struggle behind him, whirling to face the zombie that was bearing down on Tyler just as Matt and Bruce finally realized the situation and started reaching for the guns at their sides. Matt knocked his own shotgun over, while Bruce fumbled at the strap above his own revolver. Frank poured several nails through the magnetized end and took aim at the monster's yellow, bloody eyes and squeezed the hefty trigger down as far as the base allowed him to, as many times as the flimsy trigger allowed him to, his fingers straining against the plastic so hard he thought it might crack.

There was flash, and before Frank finished blinking, the nail was embedded in the center of the creature's iris and at least a dozen more sticking out from the sides of his bald head, a deep sigh escaping its cracked lips with a final gurgle of blood that spilled out over Tyler's head. With a cumbersome slouch, it fell on top of Tyler like an infant taking a nap, his arms raised up in disgust and refusal to touch the bloody thing on top of him. When no one came to assist him, he finally pushed the dead weight to the floor, breathing heavily as he did so. When the body disappeared beneath the counter, he made sure to add a kick for good measure.

No one spoke, and Frank had trouble dropping his arm, the nail gun holding up his arm instead of the other way around. It felt numb, but hefty, as if someone had tethered him to the ground and he was the only thing holding it up. Matt was staring at him with a mix of admiration and concern, Bruce with a sense of mild amusement as he shoved his weapon back into its holster.

"Well, fuck," Tyler said, breaking the silence.

Without looking away from the man on the floor, he grabbed the blunt that had fallen from his mouth onto the glass countertop, which had somehow avoided the puddle of blood better than Tyler had, and placed it back in the nook between his lips. Pulling a lighter from the pocket on his hoodie, he brought it to the edge and inhaled deeply, letting the smoke sit in his lungs before letting it escape.

"Guess that greedy bastard did want his money back after all."

If Tyler had meant it as a joke, no one laughed, and the silence remained as he pulled two fresh shells from his duffel bag and slid them into the slide above the trigger. As they dropped into place, he gave the shotgun a quick cock and brought it down on top of the man's head beneath the counter and fired without a word of warning, a spray of blood completely coating him in the syrupy substance. The red geyser went everywhere, pouring out like a sputtering fountainhead splattering specks of red over every living face in the hardware store.

"What the hell'd you go and do something like that for?" Bruce said, his hand instinctively hovering above his own weapon as form of habit, one beaten into him so deeply that not even the entire world turning over on its head could stop him from doing it.

Matt simply brought his palm down the length of his face, trying to wipe as much of the sticky red drops from it as he could but only smearing it into a sinister-looking war paint.

Tyler took another hit from his blunt, its end turning a hazy red as he pulled in the smoke, and exhaled without looking at them, clearing the shotgun's chamber. The shells fell to the floor in a light clatter, and Tyler calmly loaded two fresh ones into their place. He sighed as he faced them, a weariness from the lack of sleep giving him the look of someone twice his age with the sagelike wisdom to boot.

"Since it seems I'm the only muthafucka around here who ain't had a deprived childhood and has actually seen a goddamn zombie movie, I guess I'm the nigga who's gonna have to do the explaining," he said, taking another long hit, exhaling slowly into silence before speaking again. "There are some simple rules to survive a bunch of undead muthafuckas rising up to munch on your innards and shit. I ain't gonna have time to explain him all, but let me get the preschool ones out the way first for ya'll since ya'll running around like kiddies that pissed their drawers.

"First of all, as I have just so expertly demonstrated for ya'll here, the first and most important rule is to double tap. Ya'll got that? Even if the bitch look dead, one more shot ain't gonna hurt you, but it's sure as hell gonna hurt it, you feel me, fam? Besides, these ugly fucks already look dead, so just staring at it ain't gonna tell you nuthin', but spreading its brains out on the sidewalk will tell you all you need to know, ya hear? Simple shit? Simple shit." He kicked at the squishy body beneath him, clearing a path out of the counter for himself as he grabbed the duffel bag, the blunt dangling from his puckered lips. "Now, the other more obvious rule is to aim for the head. Death ain't stopped these fuckers, so a couple bangers through the chest ain't gonna have much luck either. These guys make Fiddy look like some kind of punk ass from Long Island. The only thing that's gonna stop 'em is if you fuck up the brain. I'm talking bashin' it in, blowing' it off, stabbin' it, roastin' it, whatever, just get the mofo's brains separated from the rest of it."

"I thought they liked *eating* brains," Bruce said, pacing.

"Bruh, that was one time back in the 'eighties. It ain't your fault for thinking so. You can blame cartoons for that shit. These zombie fucks don't seem to really give a shit about what part of you they're eating, so I'd say keep yourself away from their mouths in general, homie. That's another thing we need to talk about…"

Tyler drifted off into a shaky silence, his eyes drooping and going to the floor, the drug already seeming to have its intended effect. However, there was heaviness behind those eyes, one that didn't reek of laziness but of broaching an uncomfortable subject.

"What is it?" Bruce asked.

"If you get bit, you turn, right?"

Matt said, answering for Tyler, who acted like he hadn't heard the question. At Matt's suggestion, he nodded, pulling the blunt from his mouth and blowing out smoke like a fire-breathing lizard.

"From what I know about zombies, there's a lot of different reasons for them getting up and walking around. But no matter what's causing it, virus or otherwise, if you get bit, you become one of them. From that moaning nigga in the jail cell, something tells me that shit applies here too."

"They brought him in early this morning for getting in a fight with another bum. Both of them were drunk, but he had killed the other guy by bashing his brains in with a trash can. Kept rambling on about the how the other guy bit him, so they cleaned the wound and bandaged it up before throwing him in the drunk tank," Bruce said, as if deep in thought. "Guess antibiotics don't do anything to stop it."

"Guess not," Matt said somberly.

"Is there any other important rules we need to know?" Bruce asked, his thumbs digging into the belt at his hips. There was a hint of sarcasm to the question, but it felt forced, as if he was struggling to make it more humorous than it was, like he needed it to be.

"Just keep moving," Tyler said, castling a worried look down at his leg tucked behind the counter. He took another hit, the ash crinkling from the end and spilling to the floor, blending with dirt and grime until Frank could no longer tell where it had fallen. "Keep moving and will all be sitting on a comfy bed with a ho sucking our dick before the night is over. Sounds good to you, right, homie?"

Bruce opened his mouth to say something but stopped, almost stammering, unable to respond. Matt looked at him strangely, studying him up and down, trying to read something in his movements.

Suddenly, he started sniggering to himself, threw his head back in a squawk of a laugh, and turned back to the door, checking the outside for any dead that had wandered too close. Frank hardly noticed; he had hardly heard any of the conversation past reaching for the nail gun. All he could think of was the weight of it in his hand, the heft of it as he moved it. It had been intoxicatingly simple to get what he wanted; he had taken it easily, acted on instinct. Now, all he could do was stare across the street, into the green living room, and lose himself inside it, in that life. So simple. So easy.

It took Tyler slapping his arm around his shoulder to shake him from his trance, the fantasy that had consumed him.

"I wanna thank you for what you did back there, Frog," he said, tapping his free hand on Frank's gaunt chest.

Letting the malice in his eyes speak for him, Frank merely let his gaze bore into him.

"Sorry. I wanna thank you, Frankie. That better?" Tyler said, smiling weakly. This time, Frank answered with a small, warm smile but remained quiet. "You got quick thinking there, Frankie boy, good reflexes. I also wanted to apologize about them things I said back in the jail cell about you. You saved me like a real OG would back there, homie. My life is your life, you feel me? I'ma make it up to you, dawg. 'Aight?"

Frank nodded, managing the outline of a smile as the haze of his dream began to settle and mix into the reality around him—the child he never had's math book soaked in a puddle of blood, his beautiful wife sitting on top of the hardware store counter, her form wasted away by time so that her skin looked like burned leather, a smile borne on her bare teeth, her pupils a milky white shade that made the grin that much more ingenuous. She waved seductively, the stalks of her fingers crumbling into gray chunks as she did so, her laugh rattling her bones and caving in her chest. The long ring finger that remained had a golden band still wrapped around the flap of skin outstretched toward Frank's chest and then turned back toward the banshee, curling itself temptingly like a ghoulish seductress. Even though she was hideous to behold, he felt her draw him in, her breath cool and musky but her touch warmer than anything he had ever felt. Tingles erupted from the stem of his brain and down his spine, his knees weak and shaking.

Tyler supported him as he fell to his knee, his head spinning and breath falling short. The spell passed quickly, but Frank was slower to rise, his head groggy and buzzing. He opened his eyes to Matt and Tyler's look of concerns, Bruce pushing his head outside and checking round the corner of the wall.

"You okay, Frank?" Matt asked, placing his hand on his shoulder.

"Yes, I'm fine," he replied, no matter how unsure he was himself, "just tired."

He looked back at the green living room across the way and found it empty and still, a deep sigh escaping him. As he stared hard at it, wishing it to change, he noticed the gray hand in the doorway was no longer there, having disappeared from sight.

"I think we should get going right now," he continued.

Matt looked like he wanted to press the issue, but Tyler simply slapped him on the back and started after Bruce, who had taken his first steps back onto the street, his gun raised and constantly dancing around the smoky horizon. Matt grumpily swallowed his concerns and followed, motioning for Frank to do the same.

Stepping out into the street, Frank realized just how much colder it had gotten since their departure from the jail that morning. Before, the wind had been the cold's harbinger, carrying it in every powerful gust into your bones, but now it was something deeper. It seemed to be emanating from the fog now. It bit at the skin and dug in until every part of you was red, raw, and numb from its arctic touch. Matt seemed to sense it too as he shivered, rubbing his arms in an attempt at heating them.

They moved up the street, stealthily shifting between abandoned vehicles and under awnings for cover whenever possible. There were no signs of life amidst the ruins. Hardly any signs of death, either. In fact, other than the hand in the green room, the four of them didn't come across a single body, only large pools of blood on the ground and painted across the walls in wide, scattered arcs. Doors were thrown open; skid marks adorned several driveways, both signs of wild flights of fear that had turned the picturesque dwellings of the

American Dream into the battered husks that remained, ghosts that hovered above their grave. They too had become death, hollow imitations of life, as much a cruel deception of it as a forlorn tribute to it. Frank still saw his own dreams in these two-story coffins, reflected like a dirty mirror, cracked and divided into different offshoots of reality, all stemming from one missed opportunity or another, into an infinite sea of possibilities that all lay behind him now. He was too far from the coast to see it anymore.

"Man, people sure cleared out of here fast," Matt said, his eyes darting from house to house, looking for movement in every ravaged abode.

"Mm-hmm," Bruce said with an air of insight, "you would've too, if you saw what the rest of 'em saw on their televisions. It's not often you see a newscaster get her face eaten off by her own story." He snorted, more a stifled laugh than sign of derision. "I was in the hospital still when the thing aired. People started panicking, throwing each other out of the way just to get to the front door. Didn't matter if they were sick or even children, they all just turned into wild animals, running on basic survival instincts. I barely made it out of there without getting trampled. Some people weren't so lucky."

"You pigs didn't release any kind of statement? Some kind of warning? You're telling me ya'll muthafuckas didn't do anything about this shit at all?"

Bruce shook his head. "Never got a chance to, the damn thing happened too fast. We might've been able to put a lid on it if we had learned of it before the media got its hands on it, because as soon as that happens, you can pretty much kiss any hopes of a logical and planned response good-bye."

They reached an accident in the road: two cars of ironically the same make and model, two Sedonas with their engines coiled around each other, their tiny metal parts melded into one by pressure and heat. Pausing, he tapped the barrel of his gun against what remained of the glass, but nothing inside stirred. As they rounded the twin beasts, both of the drivers' stood open, and no one had to speak to realize where they had gone or, more accurately, what was left them of them.

"The news pretty much whipped everyone up into a frenzy in less than an hour. It was the worst I've ever seen it, and I had been expecting it after last night's... well, after last night's altercations."

Matt seemed to perk up at this passing mention of their crimes, readjusting the heavy shotgun in his sweaty palms, an awkward cough soon after. Tyler hardly seemed to realize Bruce had answered his question and was walking far ahead of the others, dropping and rolling like a kid playing soldier. He dropped to one knee in front of a small one-story thatched roof, took aim inside the front threshold, and swiveled left and right before raising a fist as symbol to imaginary squad mates. Frank felt a mild distress at the disrespect on display but let himself drift into his cloudy fantasies, the fogs of uncertainty looking just like the thick mist that had covered the town.

"Well, at least somebody seems to be enjoying themselves," Bruce said, throwing a quick nod of his head toward Tyler's antics, just as he slid behind a car and checked for an invisible foe around his makeshift cover.

Matt gave a pained chuckle, but his eyes still held that glimmer of mistrust that had come with Bruce's admission of their crimes. Frank could read him like a book and knew what seeds had planted themselves in Matt's mind, but he did nothing to nip them in their bud, despite Matt's propensity for irrational thinking.

"Before you lost contact with your fellow pigs, did you hear anything about some kind of government intervention? My old man was on his way down here, and I wanna think he'd do something about his hometown being filled with flesh-munching assholes," Tyler said suddenly, still participating in his self-constructed game.

"As far as I know, the national news hasn't even gotten word of it yet. The station went off the air just a couple minutes after the feed ended, with a technical difficulties screen running on repeat. I tried getting ahold of the people stationed outside Saint Roma's, but all I heard was screaming and... something else. That was where most of the chaos came from. I was planning on driving by it but couldn't even cut through the traffic. I heard reports of over a hundred wounded coming over the radio before we lost contact. Apparently, most of the people in that basement never made it back out. They crammed into the doors and trapped themselves like rats in a fire, poor bastards," Bruce explained, visibly struggling to make sense where there was none.

"On my way back to the station, I had on NPR, and they were having their usual 'Here and Now' without even a mention of Loganville. Now, one would think the dead rising up and eating innocent folks would be a fairly big story no matter what kind of proposition Congress threatened to pass. So my guess is, nobody knows about what's happening here yet. We're completely cut off, isolated."

At this, a heavy quiet blanketed them, made all the more apparent by the suffocating nature of the mist that surrounded them. It made everything blurry and gave everything a metallic taste, a sticky wetness that clung to the skin but didn't dampen the clothes above it.

"So how many of those things do you reckon there are?" Matt asked, almost afraid of the answer, however speculative, he might receive.

Bruce stopped in his step, his hand scratching at the mild five o'clock shadow that grew lazily from his chin.

"Well, the town's got a population of what? A little under a thousand? Reports had half the town at least over at Saint Roma's, but that was probably an exaggeration… Then again, with all the cars I saw gathered out front… and the fact that they hadn't moved by the time I got there…" he trailed off without finishing, his lips moving as if he planned to but was physically unable to produce the right words.

"How long does it take to get to the nearest town by car? Less than an hour, right?" Matt said. "When did that report air? The one at Saint Roma's?"

Bruce lifted his arm and tugged at the bloody sleeve to get at the watch on his wrist. Wiping more of the red goop from its face, he studied it briefly.

"Around three hours ago."

"And if somebody had made it out and to another town…"

"Then the national news would've heard about it by now, yes. That's what I was thinking about on my way over to the station, when I first saw the gathering outside Saint Roma. My guess is, most of them are still trapped down in that basement, fighting and eating through each other to get out. That should buy us some time before we have to deal with the largest horde of 'em."

"Excellent terminology," Tyler shouted from up ahead. "Looks like you can train pigs."

Matt spoke before Bruce could address Tyler's brash rejoinder, "So what you're saying is, nobody's made it out yet? How the hell is that possible?"

Bruce looked him glumly, almost as if he was ashamed. "You remember the man in the cell, of course?"

"Yes, quite well, actually. It's easy to remember someone once you've seen their guts spilled all over the floor and their head blown into little pink chunks. What's your point?"

"He was bitten last night, and he wasn't the only report that we got. A lot of them had to be dismissed until this morning after the trouble at the bar." For once, Matt seemed too engrossed in the theory to notice the mention of their own escapades. "My guess is that, this has been happening slowly for some time now, so slowly that it went unnoticed until it reached its breaking point this morning. I mean, that girl they found at Saint Roma's—the one that ate the reporter—was Sarah Marsden, and her body went missing from her grave nearly a week ago now. We thought it was foul play for a while there, but if—"

"Wait a minute. What did you say the girl's name was?' Frank said, the dirty mirror of his lost dreams shattering like brittle ice on the surface of the lake. He felt himself slip through into the cold waters, splashing against his face, snapping him awake.

"Sarah Marsden, the girl who got dug up from the cemetery last Sunday. Why?"

Matt's head turned so quick he thought it would snap free from its shoulders, and their eyes met in solemnity.

"Goddamn it, Marshall," Frank said, hardly aware the words passed through his lips. "Any word on the guy they thought did it? Was he… was his body there with her?"

A look of confusion fresh on his face, Bruce opened his mouth as if he was going to inquire further, before everything seemed to snap into place. Instead, he shook his head as if it weighed a thousand pounds, leaving Frank's stomach to drop out from under him. Pain came, then numbness soon after, his emotions awash in a torpid tide that showed no signs of slowing. Part of him was thankful that the rumors of his friend's darker inclinations had proved as abhorrent and unfounded as he knew them to be, but at least in that scenario, there had been a chance of his friend being alive. Now, when the people who gave birth to the rumors were no longer around to make them, it seemed a weak consolation in comparison to having his friend grinning beside him. He expected tears to come, however shameful they may have felt, but there was only the numbness.

Moving so silently he didn't notice his approach, Matt placed his hand on Frank's shoulder and guided him forward. The steps forward were arduous at first before he settled into them, finding a pace that seemed normal. Tyler had gotten far ahead of the rest of them, nearly two houses down, his lopsided gait instantly recognizable, but it was hard to tell how far exactly as the houses seemed to blur into one another, each a copy of the last. The walls might be a different shade, one roof a thatched gable and the other a shingled pyramid; but they felt the same, especially when absorbed by the placid whiteness of the fog. The lawns stood perfectly clipped with hedges arranged, bikes left out front in childhood carelessness. Behind the thick walls, the families had been different in every possible way but alike in their hopes and fears—as much a product of their environment as their environment was product of them, all molded by this agreement we had called society. This place had always been ruins, long before they had been abandoned—ruins of an empire whose Golden Age had come and gone in the night. A way of living whose pulse had stopped many years ago, but its maggot-infested corpse shambled forward regardless, undeterred by its own slow, painful demise.

Back when he was young and foolish, he had truly believed that if he worked hard and did what was asked of him without a complaint or second thought, even things suggested by others—his so-called *superiors*, which stretched the loosest definitions of the word—he would be rewarded, based solely on his merit and his ethic. But time went on with no care for those poor souls drowning in its endless stream, and those above him climbed higher off of his successes, on the backs of his frivolous dreams. Of course, this meant he suffered below, forever stuck in his station, doing his so-bestowed duty, unable to afford even the simplest of luxuries, his own dreams pressing further and further into the horizon by promises of one day more, until now when they were nothing more than inklings of happiness based on things he had never taken the time to know.

Several small fires could be seen breaking through the fog, beacons leading them deep into the strange jungle they found themselves traipsing through. They saw messages scribbled into the walls of buildings—some in runny black spray paint that announced anarchy rising and declared death on the proletariat, but much more common were the ones written in crimson, similar to the shade that covered the hardware store floor, asking for help from the police, the government, anyone, but more than any, praying for help from God. Frank suspected that he had stopped answering prayers down here for quite some time now.

It was after they had gone several blocks like this, surrounded by fog and cryptic tidings, that they heard the explosion. The heat of it carried on the wind, brushing what felt like embers against Frank's cheeks, rippling through the grass, like an ocean of dirty green tossed about by the force of it. The windows rattled in their frames; the ground tensed as if bursting with anticipation, and some frames of smaller cars rocked back and forth over their tires. Frank had to grab hold of the mirror of the one nearest him, its trembling only making things worse as he tried to keep himself from tumbling over his own wooden legs. As soon as he did, however, its alarm started up in a series of metallic screeching, the sound echoing deeply into the white abyss around them. His hand slid off almost immediately, pulled back as if some venomous creature had sunk its fangs into it. Another alarm went off behind them, and two more than a couple blocks down, all singing a similar, unrelenting tune in a round like a quartet all too willing to take advantage of this rare silence.

"Well, that doesn't seem good," Matt said.

A horrible moan seemed to answer him, primordial and familiar in its terribleness. The sound of it alone evoked such pain, such a stirring of emotions deep within Frank's gut that he felt instantly like he needed to retch all over the concrete—mournful yet brimming with hatred, crying for a vengeance it neither understood nor desired but required nonetheless. Several more cries answered this one until the sound grew unbearable, pounding in his eardrums, like it was coming from a bouncing speaker right next to his skull. Blood pooled in the back of his head and made him dizzy, but he steadied himself with the car again, ignoring its squeals of protest.

"Yeah, that's definitely not good. We need to get moving now, or we're about to have a lot of those bastards swarming us," Matt said, shifting the shotgun's weight in his hands.

"It might already be too late for wishful thinking like that," Bruce said.

He had already pulled the revolver from its holster and was aiming it into the impenetrable fog, his eyes following something that Frank couldn't see. The horrible shrieking made it hard to focus; his vision was constantly wavering and fading into a hazy blur, his thoughts concerned only with making it stop somehow. Frank wanted to scream himself, to add to the chorus of inhuman monsters, to feel some kind of relief to the panic piling itself at the base of his spine, but knew it would do no good for anyone—least of all, himself.

Without warning, the moans ceased suddenly, disappearing into themselves like light from a room with the flip of a switch. Bruce's eyes remained steady on whatever he saw darting through the fog, but Frank's eyes were still struggling to make it, or anything, out amidst the milky veil. A growl pointed him in the right direction, and his eyes followed the end of Bruce's antique revolver straight into the snarling jaws of a man whose face had broken through the seal of mist. It hissed at them, a glistening mix of saliva and blood falling from his cracked, swollen lips. Moving on one broken and twisted leg, it threw itself forward shakily, its balance stronger than what it seemed. Its arm were outstretched, like a child reaching up at the moon he cannot touch, chipped nails and contorted fingers clawing at their faces.

Looking down his meager sights, Bruce readied his shot, letting his gaze flow with the swaying of the gun. His finger tightened, and there was a thunderous crack and a spark as the gun went off. Instantly, the creature's shoulder flew back, struck by some ethereal bolt, knocking it back and causing it to stumble over its own awkward shuffle. Despite this minor victory, Bruce's eyes never moved from their target but merely waited, waited for their prey to make the mistake of getting back up again.

Ignorant of this hunter bearing down on it, the monster in human flesh got back its feet, albeit difficultly, leaning back on its haunches as if stooped over in some kind of laughter. Frank knew this couldn't be the case, but he couldn't shake the idea and could hear the warped guffaws in his mind.

Bruce fired another round into the zombie, this one catching it in its stomach, knocking it back but not off of its freshly regained footing. The force was strong enough to tear its belly open and spill half of its guts into the cracks of the concrete, sinking into the dirt and grass beneath.

"What the fuck did I tell you?" Tyler hollered, cocking his own gun and pressing forward into the mist, trying to get within his weapon's limited firing range. "Shoot 'em in the head! In the head! Otherwise, you're just pissing the fucker off!"

"I'm trying, all right? After four years of being told to aim only for the chest, it's a bit difficult to switch to a target a quarter of the size, okay?"

His gun went off again, but this time, the bullet went wide and missed the creature entirely.

"Fuck this shit, I'll handle it if none of you other ni—"

Stumbling forward through the silky vapors of the fog, another zombie brought its rotting hands down on top of Tyler, catching him off guard and bringing his shotgun barrel down to the sidewalk. It went off harmlessly into the dirt, chunks flying up and slapping the entangled duo in the face. Grunting, Tyler managed to throw the dead woman off of him, her soccer mom haircut bobbing as her face slammed heavily against the pavement, teeth and blood spilling out in a torrent beside her. Using this momentum, he brought the barrel of his Remington against the back of the woman's skull and fired, blowing it into fleshy chunks spread out, like demented chalk art across the sidewalk.

"Ah, fuck! I dropped my fucking blunt!"

The creature that had weathered Bruce's shots fell on top of him then, its jaws snapping at his ear, spewing a black goop from its mouth that looked like a mix of slick oil and blood. Tyler's elbow snapped back into the zombie's ribs, breaking a hole in the withered skin that poured more of the sickening black liquid out onto the street. Half of it covered Tyler's bright sweatpants as he struggled within the creature's arms, pulling his neck away from its bites just seconds before the chattering jaws snapped shut around it. His head drooped to avoid one of its attacks, before flying back in a wild blow that caught the creature in the center of its face. Its nose caved in on itself, and the monster began to howl, not entirely in pain but running on some kind of instinct that recalled the sensation. Its screech was deafening, but Bruce's bullet silenced it quick enough as it flew through its extended gullet and out the back, making the gaping mouth a portal directly to the other side of the world. Without another grunt or groan, the zombie finally succumbed and slumped to the floor.

Frank watched the whole scene as if he was a spectator in some kind of prehistoric arena, engrossed in the seemingly doomed fate of his companion without moving a muscle to prevent it. He found it hard to look away, his hands gripped tight around the cold steel of the oversized magnum Tyler had handed him but without even the thought of lifting it, like he was certain it would make no difference—that his arms would be unable to bear the weight, that the shot would go wide and kill his friend instead of the wretched thing that would feast on him while he was still wriggling. He tried to force himself to action, remembering the hardware store; but his muscles where no longer his to control, marred by panic and Klunesberg's voice in his head: *Why waste a bullet on anyone except yourself? You wanna do them a favor? You wanna do all of us a favor, Frog? Turn that thing around, stuff it down your throat, and then pull the trigger.*

He trembled, feeling Klunesberg's presence crawling up his back, like he was standing behind him in judgment, eyes looking over every inch of work with a scrutiny that would make a prison warden proud. With sharp, acute tingles moving up his spine, it felt like an arachnid, a scorpion climbing its way up his back, jagged feet digging into his skin like anchors on a mountain side, its pincer bared and ready to strike at the smallest sign of fear or mistrust.

More and more of the awful creatures started emerging from the mist, figures appearing out of the ether, their forms floating listlessly toward them. Every one of them were monstrous—exposed and bloody jaws, dead crystal-white eyes, open chest cavities that showed their still organs, forever frozen in death. None of them had all their limbs intact. Some were broken; many more were ripped completely free from their slots, the broken remains of cartilage and muscle sinew in its place, a sickly yellow that reminded Frank of a dog's milk bones.

Tyler was checking himself for any kind of bite or incision, his hand slopping through the muck on his clothes, lifting sleeves and pant legs frantically as he ran his hand over his pale skin. Blood still stained his calf, an even deeper shade of crimson than before, as the weight he had been putting on it constantly must've restarted the bleeding. Bruce was sliding shells into the wheel of his revolver, one by one, far too slowly, and the pressure manifested on his face, dark furrows appearing in his brow. Matt had taken up the responsibility of firing at the oncoming horde, their numbers already growing larger than Frank could count. Right now, he made it to a little over a dozen; but more were coming into sight with every passing second, drawn to the cacophony of alarms and their fellow dead.

Bruce finally finished loading the entirety of his chambers and popped the wheel back into place and gave it a quick and final spin. He returned to his assault, firing round after round into the zombies, many falling to the ground; but only one of them had gone completely limp, while most thrashed on the floor. like fish thrown into the open air. Taking advantage of this, Matt ran forward to the zombies struggling like overturned turtles and unloaded his shells into their heads, their wild bodies going disturbingly still in a matter of moments afterward.

See, Frog, they don't need you. If anything, you'll only be a weight, dragging them down, slowing their steps, leading them into the quite literal jaws of death. Is that what you want? Come on now, Frog, I thought you were a team player.

Frank's breath ran short, sticking in his throat like syrup. It felt like someone was standing on his chest, forcing all the air out of him in staggered gasps. He tried to shake the voices away, but they only grew louder, accompanied by Klunesberg's sneering grin, his face that of a rotting, decayed beast, ears twisted into nubs and his glasses crushed into powder and shards that sealed his eyes shut. This was his true face—the one he wore underneath the mask, the one that delivered the smiling pleasantries to those who served his purposes and fooled any that might suspect him as anything less than human. But Frank had known the truth. He had seen this real face of his long before, even though only now, miles away in the bowels of a church, did it match its real-life counterpart. He had long suspected this to be the reason for Klunesberg's disgust, his constant abuse merely a gamble to destroy the poor fool that had learned the secret of his inhumanity. It was why he only showed this face to Frank, enjoyed tormenting with it, and used him as an outlet for the coldness that he felt within.

It's quite the cute theory, Frog. To think that your paltry existence makes any sort of impact on my life. Is a boot concerned with the ant caught beneath it? Does a tiger care if the antelope thinks it's vile, or evil? Do you think it even understands the concepts and, if it did, that it would even concern itself with them? No, because nature has a wonderful simplicity to it, Frog. One I thought you would be able to appreciate due to your namesake, but the meaning seems to have slipped past you, much like most everything else in your pathetic excuse for a life. The prey always blames its fate on the hunter, so terrified of accepting its fate in the order of things. Unable to be the link in the chain it was designated at birth. If the gazelle could understand the lion, it would be the lion. And if the lion empathized with the gazelle, it would be prey just the same. Just like you, Frog, so save yourself hours of pointless struggle. Turn that gun on yourself, and blow your fucking brains out.

Frank erupted in laughter, it consumed him like a fire, its intensity blocking out everything around him. Putting the gun to his head, he planned on giving Klunesberg exactly what he wanted, by blowing his brains out the back of his skull and Klunesberg along with it. He laughed again, manic and forced, knowing the joke wasn't as funny as his madness was convincing him it was. His finger danced on the trigger's edge, feeling an overwhelming emptiness when nothing of value passed before his eyes. In fact, nothing passed in front of his eyes, except for Klunesberg's rotting face bearing down on him, its jaws open in a distended laugh of their own.

The smell of its mouth, like rotten eggs being cooked on a stove top, made him realize that this monster was not one from his mind but one that had slinked out from the fog, catching him unaware and vulnerable in his temporary fit of insanity. Most of its face hung off in loose gray flaps, loose curtains pulled back to reveal the ghastly view underneath of bare red muscles coiled tight around pearl white bone. Pus leaked from its nostrils, and thick black blood frothed from its mouth as it fell on him. Its arms were outstretched, clasping for his jugular. As a knee-jerk reaction, he swung the heavy magnum and connected with the zombie's forehead, splintering the skull into a crater. A calm overtook the creature's movements, a mild, unpleasant twitch writhing through some of its extremities. Remembering Tyler's impromptu lesson, he clumsily twisted the butt of the gun back into his palm, stuck the barrel deep into his freshly made indent—a slow click as the steel touched sturdy bone—and pulled the trigger, turning the crater into a soupy mess, blood seeping through the crust like molten magma.

Tyler had freed himself from his attackers and was taking cover behind the wall of a two-story colonial, the siding pressing against his face as he inched his way to the edge to peer around it. As he did, he was met by three more of the monsters, pouncing on him in their sluggish, almost leisurely way. He dropped the shotgun to his waist and fired a round directly into the stomach of the dead woman leading the pack, annihilating her abdomen and sending her legs flying onto the house's porch while the remains of her torso flopped to the ground like roadkill, still wiggling and fighting to reach Tyler with broken nails and crushed fingers. The other two fell before Tyler even had a chance to unload the empty shell, a steady trail of smoke rising from the tight barrel of Bruce's revolver before disappearing into the all-consuming gloom. Tyler gave him a large, excited whoop as a form of gratitude before charging forward round the cover of the wall.

Frank, still shell-shocked from his struggle—if you could call it much of a struggle—with the bloody mess at his feet, was unsure of where to move next, of whom to help first, still unable to locate Matt among the chaos. He got his answer soon enough.

"Hey, I could use a little help over here, assholes!"

A zombie had Matt pinned to the ground, the only thing separating the two of them being the shotgun clutched in Matt's hands like a barbell held to the creature's throat. So far he was successfully keeping the monster's spitting bite away from his face, the shotgun digging deep into the loose folds of the creature's gray skin; and the zombie's wild thrashes was tearing the skin loose, drawing forth that same sick black bile. But two more zombies were approaching with three more just several yards behind them, making their ways through the remains of a rusted old swing set.

Without further hesitation, caught up in the adrenaline and with the memory of his brief victory at the hardware store propelling him forward on battered legs, he flew into the creature on top of Matt and tumbled to the ground with it. His fingers clung tightly to the gun in his hands, cradling it next to his chest, like a linebacker as the ground came up to meet him.

His landing was less graceful than planned, if he could even call his gung-ho heroism a plan. The force snapped his neck back into the concrete, turning his vision to fuzz and static. Consciousness faded for just a second, but the blur of the monster next to him, lifting itself from the ground once more, kept him in the world of the waking. His sight returned long enough to pick himself up from the ground, pushing off his hand hard enough to scrape the skin, and nearly crashing back to the ground from the momentum. Wasting no time, he shoved his gun into the zombie's snapping jowls, feeling the tug and pull of its yellow jagged teeth through the steel. After he pulled the trigger so hard his knuckle seemed to shatter against the finger guard, the jerking stopped suddenly, and the sleeve that once was the zombie's head fell into the dirt.

Matt was back on his feet as well, firing his shotgun into the group gathering behind him. A spray of bullets caught two in the face and a third in the chest, knocking it back and causing its legs to tangle in the chain-link of the swing. The steel coiled round its legs like serpent as it tried to free itself, only making the chain's grip tighter with each wanton tangle. The zombie seemed to ignore its entanglement and forced itself toward the two of them, the chain going taunt as he pulled the swing to its limit.

It surged forward suddenly with an intensity that made the both of them leap in their skins—Matt bringing his shotgun up defensively, while Frank nearly dropped his in a collision of his ungainly hands around the grip. Still, the chain held strong and pulled the iron bar that held it forward with the beast that led it, but not before its leg snapped free of the bone with a crack and lurch, dropping with the chain into the grass. The zombie tripped over itself and its loss of balance, its mouth swallowing a clump of grass as it extended its neck, desperate for their pulpy flesh between its teeth. It howled with what Frank thought was frustration, or some kind of pure animalistic rage, but it was cut short by the steel bar of the swing set snapping down hard on the base of its neck. The zombie fell limp, black blood oozing through the fresh wound in its neck, most of its collar bone jutting out from its center.

They turned to face each other with grins and guffaws, but their celebration was cut short by at least a dozen more of the creatures emerging from the shadows of the smog, all moaning with that same lifelessness that was disturbingly melodic in its simplistic, droning pitch.

Tyler whistled to get their attention, opening his mouth to say something; but he never finished as a scream rang out from down the street, louder and fuller than any one they had heard since before they had known the grimy walls of their cell. Vigorous and stubborn, the wail floated down the stretch of invisible landscape, slicing through the fog, like a thrown knife and just as sharp.

"Is that a person?" Frank asked excitedly.

Instead of an answer, Matt grabbed him by the collar and dragged him across the street to where Bruce and Tyler stood flat against the wall of another abandoned home. Matt followed their example as soon as they reached him, while Frank was still processing this new piece of information, this preservation of life after waves of unrelenting death.

"Is that a person? A living one, I mean?" Frank repeated before getting shushed by Matt and Tyler while Bruce checked the corner, beads of sweat forming at the top of his neck despite the bone-seeping chill.

"Quiet, Frog," Tyler said, "we don't want to draw any more attention toward us."

Frank started to correct him at the first sound of his nickname but restrained himself, finding a sliver of truth in his words, although he wasn't sure keeping quiet now would really do them any good.

Squatting low and shifting his weight behind Bruce, he leaned out from behind the large officer's back and tried to follow his gaze down the boulevard to the source of the scream but only saw the horde of bewildered zombies, moving like cattle through a field—no direction, no intent, just blind wandering in the hopes of finding food beneath its mouth. There were far too many for Frank to count now, even if he had the time, and their clustering together and moving apart like a giant multicelled amoeba only made it easier to miscount, as he found himself giving a tally to one of the zombies before remembering he had already counted one dressed exactly like it.

"Do you see anything?" Matt said, his eyes shut and his breathing heavy as he pressed himself against the wall. It looked like he planned to force and squeeze himself right through the boards and into the living room beyond.

"Nothing yet," Bruce reported, "well, except for a lot of walking dead people."

Matt pressed off the siding with his hand, leveraging himself over to the edge of their cover in the banal hope of catching something that Bruce's sharp vision had somehow missed.

"Wait, there's someone coming up the street, coming fast too, a lot faster than the rest of those freaks."

Frank's newfound courage was shaken—thoughts of some new threat, an interloping, sprinting zombie with twice as much blood and pus pouring from its orifices like a walking biohazard. The gun felt slick in his hand, so much so that he nearly squeezed the thing right out of his loutish fingertips and was thankful that freedom had found them before they had been transferred to their promised prison and its always-unguarded communal showers. He swallowed roughly at the very thought and nearly recoiled when Matt placed his hand suddenly on his shoulder.

"You still with us, Frank?" he asked sourly. "I don't need you going comatose on me again."

Opening his mouth to respond, he was cut off by Bruce's waving arms, shushing them agitatedly.

"Whatever that thing is, it's almost at the end of the block. Keep your voices down 'til we know who—or what—it is."

Matt and Frank gave pained nods, both struggling to hold their tongues after being rudely silenced but aware enough of the importance of their collective quiet. The scream came again, made hollow by the breeze, like it was being run through a filter, only the highest pitches breaking through the roar of wind. The anticipation grew too much for Frank to bear in ignorance of the situation, so he crouched low, his rusty knees cracking in protest as he skulked into view of the smog-ridden street.

Peering down its seeming infinite vastness, into the eternity of the fog, he made out a small shadow on the north side of the street, standing out against the hazy glow of the mist. Like Bruce had said, it was coming fast, growing larger every second and only heightening Frank's stress instead of providing any sort of relief.

The curtain of white parted for the figure as they burst into view, nearly spilling over themselves and at one point, nearly running on all fours as they crossed onto the sidewalk at the end of the same block of the house the four of them concealed themselves behind. The shade came closer, the orange glow of fire showing it to be a young woman, tears spilling down her porcelain face, torn khakis hanging in ribbons from her legs, clapping against them as she ran. She screamed once more, the muscles so tight in her throat you could see the veins bulging against it from half a block away.

"Good Christ, it's a girl," Bruce said, nearly running out from their hiding spot as soon as the thought of a threat left him.

Matt grabbed his shoulder and held him back with a stiff resistance that Bruce easily shook off.

"Hey, hold up there, cowboy. How do we know she isn't one of those things?" he asserted, looking beyond the porch and hedges to see this girl for himself.

Frank noticed an odd look take over his features as he looked at her, his eyes wide and shaking, his hands tugging at the legs of his pants.

"One of them? She was running away screaming!" Bruce protested.

"So what? I'll admit she looks normal from here, but who's to say she's not ten seconds away from turning into one of those things," Matt said. The girl cried out again while he was still speaking, loud enough to ring in Frank's ears like tinnitus. "Hell, she could've turned already. Maybe she's got a bite underneath those clothes of hers, a chunk of flesh missing or something. I mean, she already screams like one of them, doesn't she?"

"She ain't a zombie, homie," Tyler said, interrupting his casual lean against the house's side as he straightened up. "The bitch might be bitten, but she ain't a zombie."

"And how do you know that, since you've become such the zombie expert?"

"Zombies don't run."

"Now I know you're full of shit. In the few movies I *have* seen, plenty of zombies fucking run. In fact, all of them do."

"Nah, nigga, zombies walk. Infected run. Really big fucking difference there."

Bruce turned around to face them with a look of exasperation.

"While I'd love to stand here and debate the technicalities with you, idiots, I'm gonna go help that poor girl."

Without waiting for anyone to join him, he shot forward in a burst toward the dazed woman, who was wandering in the center of the street disoriented by the fog and screamed louder than ever, either in madness or the madness of hopelessness. He stopped before he took ten steps and backpedaled sharply—the woman's last scream drawing a deafening response from a dozen undead throats around her, all drawn to their wounded, squealing prey.

"You may wanna rethink that," Tyler said, as if he was aware of something that the others were not, or something they were unwilling to admit.

The woman's head spiraled in the hopes of finding her attackers, of even catching the briefest glimpse of them, but their laborious crawl of a walk didn't break through the veil of the fog until they were almost already on top of her. A particularly large zombie with a gut that shook and rumbled like tremors were passing through it, its mammoth arms descending on her and falling just short as she gave out a yelp of terror and backpedaled away from the hefty, inflated creature. It backed her up against the side of an old station wagon, snapping forward at her with an incredible speed that didn't match its immense weight. Ducking out of the way at the last second, she slipped out of the behemoth's path, its pale, flabby skin crashing against steel like a wave. The window fell to pieces beneath its weight, and shards shredded its bulging skin. Water poured from the wound, before being followed by the usual black, crimson bile, the creature's distended features returning to their natural, nonbloated form, or as similar as could be when death had taken the color from their veins and the water had destroyed the elasticity of their skin.

The thing moving toward the girl no longer looked human. It was a shapeless mass that slugged forward on appendages concealed beneath sagging, torn skin, coated in a layer of slime and black pus. Bones stuck out at odd angles from the mass of skin, its face stretched and pulled into something like a deflated blow-up doll, or one of those horrible burn victims where the breaks in the skin were melted together. A walking bag of flesh and bones, it approached the girl with a quivering trepidation, and more and more of its undead brethren appeared behind it, marked with burns and impalements, large gaping gashes that left their bodies mangled carriages for their insatiable hunger. Even the most normal and vigorous of them carried bite marks on their necks, or even whole chunks of their chests and limbs missing, with a loss of pigmentation of the skin, their complexion pale and dull.

"Oh, God! Please no, God, no! Somebody help! Anybody!"

The words cut through Frank worse than any one of the undead's blunted teeth, his chest seeming to implode, all his ribs cracking as they were pulled into the pit of his stomach.

"That's it! Fuck this! I'm going in there to help her!"

Bruce said, giving dark looks to Matt and Tyler before running into the street, or at least attempting to. Tyler caught his arm at the elbow and attempted to pull him back. He seemed caught off guard when Bruce fought him off and charged forward, like a bull in heat; but as he twisted away, Tyler caught both his shoulders and threw him heavily against the wall, resulting in a thunderous crash of body against siding.

Regret took hold almost immediately after, and his head darted immediately to the street side to see if any of the mindless horde had heard their small scuffle. Apparently satisfied, he brought his face close to Bruce's, so that their noses were practically touching, his amber eyes steady yet red and bloodshot, which Frank assumed wasn't entirely an effect of his short-lived smoking.

"So you're gonna go out there and save her, is that your plan, Dudley Do-Right? Gonna run right in and kill a couple of those fuckers, scoop her up in your arms, and then what, homie? Hmm? What are you gonna do when the rest of them gang up on ya? You just gonna turn and run and get cornered like her again? What are you gonna do then?"

Bruce tried to shake himself free of Tyler's grip, but Tyler pushed back and held him pinned to the wall.

"I'm gonna… I'm… I… I don't know," he admitted through gritted teeth, as painfully as if he had been driving a knife into his belly. "But I've gotta do something! I can't just let those things… *eat* her, for Christ's sake!"

"Let me tell you exactly what you're gonna do if you go out there. You're gonna run out there, kill maybe one or two of those ugly fucks, prolly the fat one and one of the slow ones behind him. If you're quick, you might be able to grab her and lead her out of that circle of cars, but how far you think you'll make it? The end of the block? Maybe, if you can get past a good couple dozen of them completely unnoticed, and then it's only a matter of time 'til they surround you again. From the way she's moving, that girl's got a busted ankle, foot, something that's only gonna slow you guys down."

Frank stepped cautiously back toward the sidewalk, looking for the girl and saw her backing up from the growing mass of blood-covered creatures; and he watched with a sunken heart as her foot collapsed when she tried to put weight on it, turning her escape into more of a slow hobble.

"He's right," Frank said, almost absentmindedly.

"I get it, fam. You wanna be the big hero. You wanna be everything that big, shiny badge is meant to be and then some, right? You wanna rescue that bitch over there, bring her home, and get a taste of that sweet snatch as a reward. I don't blame ya."

Matt chuckled oddly at this, a stifled laugh like some kind of shared joke, but only Frank seemed to notice it.

"But that ain't gonna work now, not in a situation like this. You know what's really gonna happen when you got out there? You're gonna save that dime piece from one gruesome death and lead her right into another one, one that also involves you getting your face gnawed off like that nigga on bath salts.

"Now let me tell you what you should do about that girl. You're gonna wait right here 'til those nasty fucks swarm her, and in the confusion, the rest of us are gonna sneak by while they get their feast on our poor homegirl there."

Bruce opened his mouth immediately to protest, but Tyler clapped his hand over his mouth to silence any resistance.

"You think I'm doing this to spite you, but I'm trying to save your life, you ignorant motherfucker. You can't make it in this place with your outdated sense of morals. You try and pull that 'protector of the people' horseshit here, you're gonna wind up another dead bastard whose brains I'm gonna have to blow out. And while it would be slightly gratifying to get rid of one more pig's ugly face, I'd rather save the bullet. Make sense? Am I finally getting through to you? You trying to be like Carl Winslow, when you need to be like Shaft, you feel me?"

As Tyler finished, Bruce yanked his arm free and cocked his arm back in a curled fist that he sent straight into his cheek. His face seemed to warp around it from the force, and for a split second, the two masses were indistinguishable before Tyler fell face-first to the rough patch of dead grass below.

"You have got to be the most racist sack of shit I have ever had the misfortune of encountering, not to mention a selfish, vile little prick at that."

From the ground, Tyler spat blood into the dust, a wet splotch that stood out on the dry grass.

"Fuck. Fine, less like Starsky, more like Hutch? Does that please your bland, black-and-white sensibilities motherfucker?"

Bruce sent a swift kick into the side of Tyler's head, sending it whipping violently in the opposite direction. His eyes rolled into his head as he crumpled to the dirt, but a moan soon after showed that he still clung to consciousness. Matt had his shotgun raised to Bruce's face, but Bruce looked at him as if he dared him to do it, a gaping void between them. His eyes were hard as ice and just as cold, permeating hatred that kept Frank from raising his own arms against him.

"If you're gonna shoot me, then just do it and be done with it. You scared sons of bitches wanna stay here and cower while that girl dies, then be my guest. I won't force you to come with me, especially since they'd be a bullet in my back before I stepped off the sidewalk. But me, I'd rather die than just sit back and watch it happen like some helpless nobody."

He pulled his .38 special from its holster, popped out the spin wheel to count his ammo and reload the necessary chambers before he started toward the street. Before he reached it, however, he turned back to look at the two of them—a forlorn, disappointed look at

Frank that stole his breath, and one of fury and righteousness as he gazed into Matt's—and said, "I should've left you in that cell."

With a mild reluctance, like he was still holding onto a sliver of hope that the two would change their minds, he turned back to the sound of the girl's cries and moved onto the sidewalk. Frank watched him go, the guilt eating away at his insides so intensely that he thought he was going to throw up his guts, like their friend in the cell. Bruce's words danced in neon in his head, especially those about the inaction of a helpless nobody, and Klunesberg's laugh soon overpowered them.

Living up to your reputation as always, Frog. Some things, and people, never change.

Then came the laugh, terrifying in its bottomless tenor, deep and low and brimming with a confidence that only made Frank's knees crack together more.

Anger suddenly filled Frank's stomach, clearing out the bile that had settled there. A fire had been lit beneath him, one he knew that he could not contain. It had been a spark in the hardware store and grew to a simmering ember, but now the simplicity of it all gave him a seemingly infinite supply of courage. His feet moved without his ordering them to, and he found himself being carried by his overzealous legs into the fray behind Bruce, whose head twisted back briefly to acknowledge him with a humbled grin.

A scream like the crack of thunder split the sky and caused the two of them to nearly leap free of their skin. They brought their focus back to the girl, who had fallen while their attention had been occupied with Tyler's plan and was backing up against the wall of a small deli. The fat zombie was crawling, its skin sticking to the ground and stretched like a crawling slug was, backing her into the small alcove beneath a red-and-white striped awning that held the store's entrance—a glass door with iron handle across it, a small "Will Return" sign hanging inside with the clock crossed out and "Never" hastily scribbled over it.

Bruce tried to work his legs up into a sprint, but before he could even move, the creature was upon her and sunk its misshapen jaw into her thigh. As it reared its head back, it tore the skin off with a sick tear that sent blood spraying like a fountain from the gap, strands of muscle still holding the pulpy piece in place, like a long strip of pulled pork. The girl screamed again, this time turning to a wail and a screech, pain leaking from every note.

The others were on her in moments, shoving the others out of the way, taking stray and wild bites that landed on each other instead of their intended target. However, many of them struck home, and soon chunks were being torn from the girl by flopping hands and wiggling heads. One tore her shirt and gripped her exposed breast by the nipple. But it pulled hard like it would on a pull top bottle, and the fat came loose and brought half of the skin from her chest with it. Another hand fell into her stomach and dug deep with its jagged nails, its hand disappearing completely within her and pulling up shiny red logs of intestines, glimmering in the overcast afternoon light.

Despite this torment, the girl's sharp cries came louder and more desperate than ever, but all of Frank's courage had fled at the sight of the undead feast. The pile of throbbing dead collapsed on itself onto the girl, burying her in tangle of writhing limbs—only her right arm, shoulder, and head visible. As fate would have it, her head twisted in pain, blood pooling from her mouth and falling out in splatters on the concrete, like raindrops, and her eyes met theirs, questioning and sorrowful. She reached for them with her free hand, her lips forming words she no longer had the strength to say.

Crawling over the pile was a legless, battered zombie, most of it nothing more than bare skeleton and skin that looked like it had rotted away more than a decade ago at the earliest. The girl's eyes went wide as she saw the thing's gleaming teeth nearing her face, unable to pull away from it while her body disintegrated beneath her. She turned to them a final time with panicked doe eyes, and as the crawling zombie slid down onto her face, she gave one more pitiful gasp as the jaw bones wrapped around her jugular in a surge of crimson blood that turned her howl into a wet, choked gurgle. She disappeared underneath the writhing column—wet, loose pieces of flesh being tossed out from between them.

Even after watching the entire gruesome display with unflinching eyes, Bruce jumped forward as if he meant to pull the mangled remains of the girl from their thrashing teeth; but Frank stopped him, having to wrap his entire arms around his chest to do so. This still proved a struggle to restrain the distraught officer, whose mouth hung open in silent protest, not daring to speak, his rationality still tugging at the reins of his emotion.

He sent an elbow into Frank's ribs, light but effective, and freed himself. He took several long strides toward the pile of undead before he stopped himself, his body fighting itself with each arduous pace. Frank used this lull in his dead-set heroism to grab him by the shoulder and guide him around the trail of parked cars, circling the squirming mass while tucked behind the painted metal. They moved quickly, with heavy, unburdened steps, but the ravenous creatures never looked up from their hard-fought meal.

As they ducked around an open car door, Frank peered inside and saw the keys dangling tantalizingly from the ignition, a green lanyard advertising Boise State and a collection of various chain-store discount hards hung beneath them, grazing the gray leather seat. He almost jumped into the driver's side and twisted the engine to life then and there without a hint of a second thought, but these thoughts came sooner than expected and stopped his hand, although not easily. Only the roar of the engine and the memory of the clogged streets ultimately dissuaded him.

Slinking around the front of the car, they stalked silently back into the damp grass and hard dirt of backyards. They darted behind a large set of edges, Bruce lagging behind, a conflicted mind still weighing down his stride. As they rounded into the yard, Frank was met by the dark tunnel of a gun barrel, meeting his gaze with cold indifference.

Matt's eyes raised quickly as he recognized him, and the shotgun fell to his side soon after. He grabbed Frank and pulled him into the cover of the hedges, crouched low behind the faulty wooden deck stretching out from the house's rear slide doors. Tyler was here as well, rubbing the side of his swollen jaw with back of his hand, struggling for balance on his bad leg.

He leaped up on seeing Bruce, like a chained attack dog, Matt flying instantly to him and stopping his blow before it even got close to Bruce's face. Shoving him back against the beams of the deck, he brought Tyler's arms to his side and held them firm so that, despite his shakes and struggles, he could not move.

"Cool it, all right? We got bigger and uglier things to worry about than him," Matt said calmly, his eyes searching for his friend's, whose own were darting about trying to get Bruce's attention.

Bruce's stare belonged to the ground, and he hardly seemed to notice Tyler's contention, save for a spared glance, before quickly drooping back to the dark, slick mud.

Tyler gave one final shake of dissension, the climax of his tantrum reached before slumping back against coarse cedar. A look of sour disappointment freckled his features, along with the addition of deep purple bruise that covered up most of the right side of his face. His usually handsome, if slimy and unkempt, features were tarnished by bloodstains and bruises, making him look like an old time bare knuckled boxer.

"I'm chill if he's chill. I ain't the one who's going around kicking niggas in the fucking face like some punk-ass bitch just 'cuz he got a stiffy for a soon-to-be stiff," Tyler said, a lisp twisting his words from his swollen lips.

This time, it was Bruce that leaped at Tyler, and it took the intervention of both Matt and Frank to keep him from wrapping his hands around his bare throat.

"See? What'd I tell you? Dude's gone fucking crazy. He's over here, trying to beat the fuck out of living people while there's dead ones walking around."

"I'm trying to save living people! You just wanna save yourself, even if it means other people die!"

"Yeah? Your point being?"

Frank had the wind knocked from him as Bruce charged again, his fingertips dancing right past Tyler's nose. Tyler hopped back into the boards of the deck as they pushed Bruce back, his arms crashing into them as he fought them. Eventually, he threw them off, stomping around like a caged, extremely virulent tiger.

A malaise set in, the foundation of their union shattering from under their feet. Frank saw darkness, poised to swallow them all, and nearly screamed.

"We need to keep moving. Those things back there… It won't be long until they're… finished," Frank said.

Without looking up, he felt Bruce's stare searing his skin.

"That's right. And whether you like to admit it or not, *Officer*, Tyler was right too. You went out and tried to save her. You couldn't. He tried to spare you the trouble of watching that lovely thing die, but you tried anyway. While I can't say it wasn't admirable, it was also damn foolish, and you nearly got my friend Frog here killed on your foolish sense of moral obligation," Matt said.

Frank felt a mixed bag of emotions in his chest, a warmth stemming from Matt's genuine concern, but also the utterance of that name brought Klunesberg's satisfied smirk into his head.

Instead of answering, Bruce merely paced around the yard, coming dangerously close to the fence, like he intended to leap right over and carry on alone; but he came to a slow, faltering halt and knelt against the gleaming white post, his head lightly resting against it. He sat like that for nearly a minute without moving or speaking, the wind tearing ripples through the baggy brown uniform.

When he did finally stand, he didn't speak; but laboriously, almost dutifully, he approached Tyler and held out his hand, his bare palm facing the sky. Tyler grinned like a hyena stumbling over a fresh carcass and eagerly slammed his hand into Bruce's, doing his best imitation of every equality poster from the late 'eighties.

With a look of disgust, Bruce tossed his hand aside and pointed to the duffel bag that sat at his feet, buried under the extra fabric of his spacious sweatpants. Tyler followed his finger and, after a moment's contemplation, realized its meaning and gave a snort that was both insulted and amused. Reaching into its confines, he pulled out another large magnum, similar to Frank's, except instead of having a clip that slid up into the grip, it bore a cylinder similar to Bruce's revolver and a front sight with small vents in the barrel.

Inspecting it, Bruce gave a grunt of approval and moved grumpily back over to Frank, settling at his side but refusing to look at anyone or anything except the gun. He tested the sights and the weight of it, juggling it in his fingers, tensing them against the trigger. He reached into his front chest pocket and pulled out a small box of ammunition, only to shove it back shamefully upon realizing they no longer matched his weapon.

"All right then. If everybody's finally happy, maybe we can make it to the hospital I've heard so much about and gather up some supplies and get into contact with somebody that can send in some reinforcements, although it looks like they might need a small army at this rate," Matt said sheepishly.

He strolled forward to the small door in the fence, grabbing its Victorian-style, coiled steel handle and pushing it open before peering out into the street.

After nothing ripped his head from his shoulders, he stepped cautiously out onto the sidewalk and signaled for the others to follow without looking back to check if they actually had. Reluctantly, Tyler crawled out from the brush and slunk past Frank and Bruce but stopped and turned as if ready to rekindle their tensions. He quickly slammed his hand into Bruce's chest, hard enough to make the cop take a step back and for his own hand to seize it, ready to pull it from its socket. However, as he relaxed his grip on Tyler's wrist, he saw that clutched in his fingers was two new boxes of ammunition. Bruce stared down at them in bewilderment, making Tyler laugh with a hint of condescension as he tapped his finger gingerly over the boxes, slung the shotgun over his shoulder, and followed his friend out of the yard.

Frank thought to wait for Bruce, but the thought of losing track of Matt and Tyler seemed worse now than it had in the face of saving that limping woman. So he rushed forward to the gap in the fence and turned back to give an excited signal to the gaping deputy. With a bitter shrug, he trailed after them, moving back into the streets as they continued northeast through the fog.

For several miles, they passed relatively without incident, only encountering four or five of the undead, and all were sluggish and dull enough to be lulled back into death's arms by means of a quick, unseen blow to the back of the head with the butt of a gun. Frank even dispatched one of them himself, wielding his magnum's grip like a club as he brought it down over and over again onto the creature's skull until red covered his vision and the remains more closely resembled Jell-O than anything that could once be called human. Bruce had to drag him away from the motionless corpse so that he would stop grinding the brains into mush and the bone to powder.

As they neared the town's center, the woods began to creep back up on them, the shadows of trees stark against the pale-gray horizon, always giving the illusion of something moving just out of sight. Often, Frank felt eyes on him, and whether they were living or not, he could not be certain. But it was a persistent feeling he could not shake no matter how much he tried to settle his worries.

Fires burned on every street, giving much-needed light in the darkness of the clouded sky. The sun had yet to break through the fluffy shroud above, and combined with spending the early morning inside a cell, it felt like the world had fallen into a long, continuous night from which it would never wake. Cars burned, with flames licking from the skeletons of their engine. An entire block of houses stood with doors open, portraits of the horrible violence that had gone unnoticed until it was far too late. Frank felt a quick wince of sadness but mostly found himself happy that there were no dead there to greet them. The thought make him feel uncomfortable, like he should care more than he did.

"I hear shouts again," Matt said suddenly, interrupting their blocks' worth of silence. He stopped in place and began to look around them, his gaze settling on the line of trees that stood on the south side of the street. "Farther away, but there's more of them. Distinct ones, I mean."

"Living or dead?" Tyler said. His latest blunt was pressed between his lips and muffling his speech into a barely intelligible slur.

"Hard to tell. There's no way I could be sure, not at this distance."

Bruce came up behind the lot of them silently, still somber and disinterested.

"Coming from the forest?" he asked. "I can hear them too."

With a resigned sigh, Tyler hefted the shotgun into the cradle of his arm and took aim into the tree line of the forest. Matt followed suit, raising his own weapon and staring down its sights into the mist-covered woods. Bruce remained still, as if he barely noticed any of them were there, but his eyes were alert and swallowing up the greenery before them.

Shadows shifted behind the misty veil, becoming one then breaking apart, the rustle of pine leaves crisply tottering into the underbrush. There was the slick slide of footsteps on wet grass and damp twigs, and Frank raised his own weapon in a poor imitation of those around him, feeling foolish as soon as he did so—especially considering he probably wouldn't be able to land a shot into a zombie's head even if it grabbed the barrel and held it against its temple.

The fog parted, a shadow stepping into the hollow light, giving it a clear, delicate shape. Whatever it was, it was skinny, decayed almost to the point that only bones remained.

"Veronica?"

Matt's gun practically fell right through his fingers as if they'd gone transparent, running forward to the young girl with matted brown hair, shiny to the point of gleaming but also frayed and spotted with cow licks.

"Matt? What are you… I thought you…"

The girl's eyes darted about spastically, trying to take the entirety of the lurid scene before her. Her hands trembled and jerked at the smallest crunch of leaves or drop of dew, and she kept spinning back to the woods as if looking for something.

"It doesn't matter, you've got to help me. You've gotta get me out of here. They're coming. I saw them behind me. One of them was eating a wolf while it was still alive. We saw it. It kept screaming and whimpering, and then it started…"

She was cut off by her own tears, and Matt pulled her into his arms, wrapping his arms tenderly around her and cupping his head against his chest. She buried herself in his brown leather jacket, the tears turning the cracked material a dark black. Her nails dug into him fiercely, so deep that Frank thought about running back to the hardware store to fetch a crowbar.

"You know this girl, I take it?" Bruce said, sneaking up behind them.

"She's my baby sister," Matt said with affection.

He pulled back enough to look down at her, nuzzled against him, a serene smile on his lips. Haughtily, she pushed away from him, crossing her arms and wiping the corners of her eyes to dry them but succeeding only in making the dark smears wider. Frank choked back a laugh when he pictured her as a disgruntled raccoon.

"I'm not a baby," she said firmly.

Matt seemed taken aback by this, hurt even, far more than he should be over such a small slight; but there were barbs strewn beneath it, meant to cut deep and hard as they had done.

"You most certainly are not, aren't you?' Tyler said.

His cheeks were split with the widest grin, one that seemed coated in slime. He lightly plucked the blunt from between his lips and cooly exhaled a trail of smoke from the side of his mouth as he took several lazy steps toward her.

"You remember me, Vicky? Come on! Big Uncie Ty? I used to swing by while Matty was babysitting that fine ass of yours, and…"

"And steal my dad's vodka and hotbox his private bathroom, yes, I remember," Veronica replied, with thinly veiled disgust.

Tyler slunk up beside her, ignorant to her brisk dismissal, and coiled his arm around her shoulder.

"Matt didn't tell me that you grew up to be so beautiful. In fact, it seems like Matty doesn't talk about you at all anymore. But what he should'a been doing, he's making sure you had my digi—"

A quick punch to the gut from Matt finished the sentence for him.

"Ew," Veronica said as he slumped to the ground in an emasculated heap.

"Sorry to interrupt the reunion, but you said '*we* saw something.' Are there other people with you?"

Veronica's mouth fell open in a silent gasp, but she slammed it shut quickly as if she hoped no one had noticed and went into a state of deep thought, continuing as if it had never happened. Bluntly, she shook her head, a mask of exasperation worn on her pretty face.

A tree branch shook, and there came a moan from behind it. Before the branch even fell, Bruce's gun was pointed at, it went off just as the raspy moan came to a slow, rattling halt.

"Whoa! Whoa! Whoa! What the hell was that?" came another girl's voice from beyond the pines, along with the shuffling of many more feet on the crowded forest floor.

"I thought you said you had no one with you?" Bruce said calmly despite the angry scowl he wore.

Veronica shrugged leisurely as if it had been nothing more than a momentary lapse in memory, but Bruce pressed into the tree line and pulled the bullet-ravaged branch aside. In an awkward pile on the ground, there was another young girl, an older one at that (one that Frank recognized from the diner out by the highway), and a young boy cowering in a fetal position behind them, warily sparing glances up at Bruce and his magnum.

Upon seeing them and the steady rise and fall of their chests, Bruce rushed forward and helped them up with quick utterances of an apology, abashedly avoiding eye contact.

"These friends of yours, Veronica?" Matt asked, briefly checking out the three of them as Bruce helped them to their feet.

"Matt?" the older woman said as she hobbled toward the group.

"Vel? What in God's name are you doing with Veronica? And who the fuck are these other two kids?" Matt said, pressing his palm against his forehead to hold it from bursting apart.

"Wait? So this is your brother? Then why the hell did they shoot at us, Veronica?" the young blond girl asked, her hands in tight fists at her side.

Her sweatshirt was torn and covered in blood, more so than Veronica's, and dark circles surrounded her eyes—sunken pits, instead of makeup, like she'd been up for days. Still, there was an elegance about her, one that she was trying her hardest to hide.

"I must've forgot that you guys were behind me," Veronica said snidely, barely looking at them.

"You bitch!" the blond girl shouted, nearly tackling Veronica before Matt jumped in between them.

With a heavy shove, he knocked the girl aside and lifted the cold steel shotgun to her face. Her eyes went wide from the shock of the whole motion, but a bitter resilience took over soon after, her face melting into a sneer that dared Matt's already-jumpy finger to action.

Bruce knocked the barrel down into the dirt and put himself in front of the blond girl.

"Are you goddamn crazy? Put that fucking gun down. She's a teenage girl, for Christ's sake—a *living* one, in case you couldn't tell."

Matt avoided his accusing gaze, but Bruce kept after him until their eyes met, and shame took root at side of Matt's mouth as he backed away tepidly.

"So this the same brother that was sent to jail this morning for murdering his boss, right?" the young boy said, looking cautiously from face to face. "How'd he get out of prison?"

Matt glared at him, and the boy's gaze quickly descended to his feet. "I'm sorry, do I know you?"

The boy shook his head quickly, as if the speed of his refusal implied its sincerity and his innocence.

"I released them," Bruce said, "in light of the town's current situation. Figured they'd be more help than harm, although I admit I am starting to think I was mistaken."

"Well, I'd say he's certainly living up to his reputation," the blond girl said hotly.

"Hey—" Matt snapped, pressing forward against Bruce's chest again.

"Enough!" Bruce boomed, his disappointed stare flowing over both of them. When silence finally settled in the small grove, he dropped his arms that held them apart. "Now, didn't you also say that something was chasing you?"

Veronica's half-shut, disinterested stare turned to one of fright in an instant, their squabble forgotten to the perverse terror on their heels. All began speaking at once, giving what they believed to be the most vital information in a long string of connected rambling. Somehow, after several repetitions and questions for clarification, they understood the gist of what had happened, including the panic at the school yard, the collapsed bridge, and the trek through the forest.

"The wolves… They were eating the wolves," Veronica finished. "Then they noticed us and started following after us. One of us led them away so the rest of us could get away, but more than half of them were still following us."

At the mention of the other member of the group, the blond girl's strength seemed to leave her, and she faltered in place, catching herself on Bruce's arm.

"How many is half?" Bruce asked, looking uncomfortably down at the girl attached to his arm.

"At least fifty of them."

"Fifty?" Tyler said through clenched teeth as he struggled to his feet. His hands were still at his stomach, his face wincing with each pained breath.

"We need to get moving. Now!" Bruce said, but Frank supposed no one really needed to be told to do so.

Without a word of protest, they all shuffled out of the forest clearing anxiously. After several nervous steps, the blond girl stopped suddenly, nearly leaping back from them.

"No, we can't leave yet! We have to wait for him!"

They all turned back to look at her with puzzled gazes. "Wait for who?"

"Her stupid boyfriend," Veronica said with an air of contempt, "the guy who ran off to distract them. For some reason, she thinks he's still alive."

"He is still alive, you ungrateful bitch!" The girl ran at Veronica again, but Bruce held her in place, having anticipated it at this point.

"Hey! Hey! Listen to me! What's your name? Huh?"

"It's Bible Bitch," Veronica answered quickly, and the girl's hands stretched past Bruce's reach and nearly got hold of the loose strands of her dirty brown hair.

"It's Gwen," the boy said frantically as he tried to calm everyone with exaggerated waving of his arms, "and I'm Billy. We're Veronica's classmates."

"This that girl you were always talking about? The prophet freak's daughter?" Matt asked, leaning in close to his sister's ear.

She looked him stubbornly and gave a nod that was just as labored.

"Listen… Gwen, I'm sorry about this boy of yours. Believe me when I say that no one here would love to go and look for him more than me. But we don't know where he went, and if he had brought half a group of undead down on him… well, his chances aren't the best. And if those things are as close behind you as you said…"

The girl stifled tears, bit her lip to hold them back, not giving any of them the satisfaction of admitting they were right. Her lip went out in a pout, but she kept silent, resolute in her stillness.

"You guys shouldn't have waited."

The voice caught most of them off guard and sent several reaching for their firearms, but the pale, lanky boy that pushed through the underbrush was breathing so hard no one had to wonder whether he still carried a pulse. Gwen ran to him immediately, embracing him suffocatingly before stepping back with a face that was two shades past crimson. He smiled warmly at her, but when he faced the rest of them, his face was as stern as a statue's.

"Good Lord, is that Range? Range Barnfell?" Frank said, but his lips hardly felt themselves making them.

They poured out of him like a breeze, simple and sure. His stomach tied in knots, tight twists that made him squirm. He wasn't sure if it was relief he felt, or white-hot guilt.

"Frank? What're you doing here?" the boy said in surprise, an odd smile playing on his features.

He stepped gently away from Gwen and toward the lively old man, giving him a quick but welcome embrace.

"How the hell do you know this kid, Frank?" Matt said quizzically, one eyebrow raised to the middle of his forehead.

"He's Marshall's cousin, that's how, don't you remember him? He used to stop by the bar from time to time. I supposed he never came inside, though." He tilted his neck back to answer Matt's query but kept his eyes on Range and his hands tight on his shoulder, unsure of what to say, still debating whether or not the boy was real or the final crack in his splintering mind. "It's good to see ya alive and well, boy. I hadn't talked to you since that night you came asking after Marshall. I'm glad to see you among the living."

Range nodded with that easy smile of his, but it sunk quickly and was replaced with a strained look fraught with worry.

"We need to move quickly, or else none of us will be able to make that claim much longer. If what was chasing me catches up to us, we're not gonna have a chance."

"What do you mean? The zombies?"

"Sort of."

"Sort of? Sort of! What the fuck else was chasing you, motherfuckers?" Tyler whined.

"Well, there were zombies, quite a lot of them, in fact. I'd say over a hundred by the time I lost most of them near the creek. I circled around and tried to lead as many back in the opposite direction, but the horde was too large, and a lot of the stragglers at the rear caught wind of me and turned a good chunk of them back toward me. But for the most part, they've been tangling themselves up in the branches and tripping over any stray twig or root that gets in their way. If it doesn't slow them down, it at least makes it easy to hear 'em coming. That's not really the most pressing issue right now, though—"

A howl drew his speech to a shuddering halt, one that was unlike any of the others that Frank had heard but intrinsically the same. There was still that same cold to it, one that sunk deep into chest and sat there, pressing itself down on top of you. But it was more basic, more natural in its animalistic nature, brimming with a power that awoke even the deepest, most well-buried fears deep within a man's bones, ones based purely in millions of years of genetic evolution, meant to guarantee its hosts survival. Frank shook, heavier than he thought possible, so much so that he thought he had been struck by a sudden fever; but when it passed and the chill remained, he realized it was merely the trembling grip of terror that seized him.

"That's our cue to get moving," Range said, urging everyone forward with his example.

His hand went to Gwen's in an instant, and he pulled her forward into the street with an elongated gait that conveyed his haste. Frank followed quickly after him, along with the boy Billy, but the others stood awkwardly near the forest's edge, stern looks of disbelief crowding their faces. Half of them looked ready to protest until the second howl rang out, along with the rustling of the underbrush.

In fact, it looked like the forest had sprung to life, the trees' branches propelled by the breeze and whatever's feet were crunching through the forest floor, what little of the forest was visible through the mist seemed to be shaking with laughter at some cruel joke none of them understood.

Breaking into sprints, they all joined Range across the street. He was looking for a break in the high wooden fence that protected the yard tucked behind it but was struggling with the latch. Frank noticed the guitar sticking clumsily out the top of the bag on his back and fought a smile, even with whatever horror lay snapping at their heels.

"Here. Let me get that so that we don't, you know, fucking die," Tyler said hastily.

He brought the butt of his shotgun down on the edge of the fence post, cracking the wood around the shiny black latch, but it held tight. Three tries later, and it lay at Range's feet as he pushed through the gap in the door into the yard. He raised his hand for the others to wait as he scoped around the small but spacious yard, spotted by fallen bikes and daffodils growing through them, a shed tucked away in the back corner next to a stone bench. A statue of a young woman wrapped in wreathes stood next to it, along with a birdbath tucked beneath a dead hedge.

After seeing nothing to threaten them, Range waved them in after him, which the others quickly obliged, pouring in like water through a hole in a dam. As soon as the last of their scraggy group stumbled through the gate, Range slammed it shut behind them. His eyes scanned the ground around him for something to hold it with, and fortunately, there was a shock cord on a small bench at the gate's side, an indication that they had not been the first people to experience difficulty with the latch.

Range set to work securing the door, sliding one hook through the fence post and pulling it back through the other side when they heard the footfalls. Steps wouldn't be the proper way to describe them; they were too light, too quick. They patted against the concrete, splashing through the puddles, both clear and red; and just as Range attached the end of the cord together, something crashed into the fence and made the whole thing tremble like it was a model made of Popsicle sticks.

Matt's sister fell back over herself in shock, and Matt and Bruce both had their guns up, ready to fire at anything that broke through. Range stepped back slowly, his arms spread, keeping everyone calm as the creature moved silently along the length of the fence, its shadow slinking underneath. Frank tried to make it out through the gaps but only saw shadow pressing against the fog.

They stood tense, nobody daring to say a word to incur the wrath of whatever lay in wait behind the spruce panels. Frank's heart was pounding against his uvula. Everyone was desperately searching for some kind of escape but saw only the white paneled fence, now their prison as well as their sanctuary. The blond girl at Range's side was looking oddly at the house, so much so that Frank followed her gaze, expecting to see monsters pounding against its windows but only saw the dark, occupantless chambers behind the glass, its walls completely unremarkable save for the blinding shade of blue.

Without warning, the creature began to slam against the fence again, this time in a string of attacks that succeeded in tipping the flimsy wooden structure inward toward them with every thunderous bash.

"Shit! It's gonna smash its way in!"

"Not if I shoot the ugly fucker first, it's not," Tyler said with an air of confidence, winking at a disgusted Veronica as he did so.

"What street are we on?" Gwen said quietly, still lost in her own thoughts.

Range looked at her, following her gaze to the house but leaving just as stumped as Frank.

"What does that have to do with anything?" Matt asked angrily.

He was twisting his body in every direction, looking for some kind of escape, but he was coming up short, and the frustration hung heavy on his features.

"I know where we are. This is the Tenelli's house, isn't it? That means we're off Cambridge and Naragansitt." She ran her finger through the air like she was tracing a route on an invisible map, mumbling to herself. "We need to get to the alley."

"Great idea!" Matt said sardonically. "Now how the fuck are we supposed to do that?"

Thrashing came from behind the fence, fingers and claws tearing at the wooden barrier that now stood limp, half of it caved in on itself already, the point of breaking coming at any second. The crashes were coming fast enough now that Frank knew no one person, or thing, could be responsible for it all, and the dance of shadows in the mist only confirmed his theory.

Gwen scanned the back wall of the yard and stopped when she got to the shed and ran toward it.

"We can climb over the shed. Now, let's go!" she said.

The words came as a command, but no one questioned them, all simply waiting for any excuse for an escape attempt—even the faintest, impossible chance looking better than waiting for whatever was behind the wobbling fence.

Bruce went over first, his gun up as soon as he landed. He whistled, just loud enough for the next person to hear. One by one, they all climbed to the top of the shed, balancing between its crooked steel folds, and leaped to the gravel alley below. Frank was fourth after Vel and whistled for the other young boy to follow. Eventually, they were all standing in the alley, all ready to run but without a direction, conscious of the shifting darkness near the street. Range was finding his footing on top of the roof when there was a long, arduous groan as the fence gave way and the beasts behind it flooded in. Whatever they were, they made Range's normally placid eyes grow large and bloodshot as he looked at them.

Not slowing once they broke through, they crashed into the shed and nearly knocked Range right off back into the yard, a fall that would surely mean his doom and make him something's squirming dinner; but he leveraged the shifting steel and leaped forward, nearly falling onto Matt and Bruce. Matt grabbed him in his arms and steadied him, placing his hand on his back before pulling it away sharply and looking to his sister.

"Are you okay?" Gwen said, approaching him frantically.

"Yes, thank you, but we need to get going right now," he said with pained breaths and added another, "Right now," to stress his point.

Gwen nodded and looked around to regain her sense of direction. "Come on, we just need to cut through the Drent's backyard."

As they headed into the open grass, they heard a moan and saw the mass of zombies milling around in its center. They all tried to stop themselves but only collided with one another, drawing the monsters' ire immediately.

"Come on! Run!" Gwen shouted, abandoning caution in the face of death.

They surged forward past the small horde, their slow reactions bringing swinging arms that grasped only air and dives that only left their broken, pale bodies in the dirt.

Gwen led them into the next yard and up the small flight of stone steps to the screen door as she threw it open. A small stone shrine of the Virgin Mary sat encased in white Christmas lights at the bottom of the stairs, tucked beneath the low-hanging spruce branches. She reached back into the pockets of her hoodie and began to dig through them, her hands moving underneath like a mouse beneath a rug.

"What are you doing, you psycho? Open the door!" Veronica said at the point of tears.

Her eyes were locked on the horde shuffling closer, more than a dozen of the grotesque creatures, each covered in dark blood and broken limbs.

"It's locked!"

"How do you know? You haven't even tried it!"

"Because this is my house!" she said bitterly, pulling loose a small ring of keys from the confines of her pocket and sliding it into the keyhole.

With a twist and push, the door was open, and everyone crowded inside, shoving one another to be the first one in. Range and Bruce waited at the bottom of the steps—Range to push everyone forward and keep them from knocking themselves back down, and Bruce to fire stray rounds into the heaving masses of flesh bearing down on them. Some went down, but many of the dead merely began crawling toward them, unabated by the loss of trivial things like limbs.

Finally, they were the only ones at the bottom of the stairs when Frank called for them. Bruce turned and saw the opening and practically threw Range up them, backing up as he did so. In a flash, they were both behind the sturdy wood of the door as Gwen slammed it shut behind them, pulling the chain into place and dropping the latch like a guillotine.

The history of Loganville is long and spotted with misery, much like any small town in America. They don't teach you much about it in school. Local history was never as important as instilling the monomyth that is America into the youth—making sure they knew of our God-given manifest destiny and the lofty ideals set forth in the Constitution, promising rights for all while denying them to an entire race of people deemed subhuman.

Sorry. I hate to sound like an edgy teenager who just read their first copy of Howard Zinn, but it still slips out now and then, especially when you're in a place like this, where time seems to stand still. God, at that age, I thought I was so damn clever. I think everyone does. They see the world a little smaller for the first time in their lives, and they finally feel big—powerful, like everything is finally within your seemingly infinite grasp. The world is your plaything, a tool ready for your disposal, and you can fit the pieces into whatever shape best fits you. Even things that have already happened can be shifted, changed into something that resembles only the smallest semblance of truth, but one that feels real enough and is steeped in good intentions, a crystal statue placed on a pedestal of invincibility that they alone possess. They can be molded by those around you, to the point where you're merely following step-by-step assembly instructions provided to you—something you can believe in and whisper to yourself in the dark on the nights when your views are challenged, shaken like glass. But when they're shattered, broken completely into shards so small and insignificant, they cannot be reassembled, even if you know the shape and color they once took. And the illusion of invulnerability goes with it. You no longer balance your views on something as flimsy as the thought that death won't come for all men and that good intentions don't wash out the evil actions committed in their name. They become malleable, easily changed, steeped in self-awareness and a broader understanding that buffers them from the rumbling evils of the world. But even then, it doesn't mean that they can't be broken again, and no matter how much you wish to see the world as you once did, the broken shards will slip through your fingers, leaving bloody gashes on their journey toward oblivion.

Of course, that doesn't stop some people from trying. People will stubbornly cling to the bow of a ship, looking up at the clear sky, as the deck cracks and crashes into the waves beneath. It also doesn't stop them from passing their own shattered, hastily reconstructed statues, ghoulish remnants of their former untainted selves, marred by harsh, conflicting reality that leaves them broken, hideous husks, down onto the generations to follow. They put them on new pedestals, golden ones marked by their prestige. They marvel at the cobwebs, claiming that they add to the piece's beauty, to its artistic integrity.

Coincidentally, it seems like those people are the ones who are also responsible for the writing of the history books, as foolish as that seems. They say the winners are the ones who write history, but I ask, what's to stop the losers from writing their own, save death? What's to stop the winners from changing the way the game is played? What happens when no one wins? Once it's been set, who has the authority to change it? How many truths have been lost to time? Is the history of man truly determined by men, or by God? Or is time simply a river, constantly pressing forward, spurred on by the current behind it, guided by none but its own inclination?

I find myself asking these questions to no one in particular. I can't come up with any answers, of course. I doubt anyone could, without also discovering the reason for human existence, the meaning of life and all that. I suppose all my free time has turned me into some kind of pseudo philosopher. When you spend your days with nothing to look at but blank walls, wide and encompassing, like white projector screens—watching your memories, however horrible, played out in front of you like a movie marathon in a seedy theater—you try and think of anything that will give meaning to it all.

Right. I've started rambling again, haven't I? You really should just stop me when I get like that. It's not often I get visitors out here. And most of them are nosier than you are, and those are the ones that aren't even journalists, just some nuts who read about the "Loganville Disappearance" fifty times on Wikipedia and desperately wanna hear what it's like to kill a zombie in real life, hoping it matches up to the voyeuristic fantasies in their head.

Anyways, you probably want something as close to the actual facts as possible. I mean, you are a journalist after all, wouldn't want any exciting embellishments on it, no, sir. Well, I might be a shitty philosopher, but at least I can dig up dusty, old historical documents from old library basements. It's amazing what you can ask for as long as it isn't your freedom. It helps when you've got a lot of free time and know what you're looking for, but… a feat I'm somewhat proud of nonetheless.

Loganville was founded in 1756 by Malachi Longwarden, an English settler from Lincolnshire that originally settled his own plantation in Virginia in the early years of the eighteenth century. After serving as a militiaman in the French and Indian War, later rising to the rank of brigadier general and leading several scouting missions into the wilderness that always ended in the complete and total annihilation of any Shawnee Indians that he encountered along the way—much to the approval of his superiors, who always rewarded these conquistador-like expeditions into the unknown—Longwarden would often come back with key pieces of enemy intel. Rumors mentioned his affinity for torture in regards to obtaining this information. Some of his most famous techniques involved a more archaic form of waterboarding that involved encasing the victim's head in a small wooden box, usually hastily made filled with loose nails and chipped piece of wood, that would slowly be filled with more and more water from a nearby pitcher with every useless answer. The subjects hands were restrained, left to struggle and flap heedlessly against their bonds as the victim struggled to keep his head above the rising pool. Sometimes they'd leave them with the box half full, the poor soul inside the box able to keep his mouth and nose above the water line if they kept their head as high as possible—a simple proposition that becomes more sinister as the muscles in your neck start to scream, the gentle tide against the sides of the box filling their ears with its alluring lullaby, urging them to let go of their worthless and ultimately meaningless struggle.

The sad thing is, this was probably the most humane of his various forms of… data extraction, usually reserved only for the White Christian French that had the misfortune of running afoul of his death march. The Indians faced a much more harsh punishment, no matter their willingness to provide Longwarden with information, however vital. He saw it as an opportunity to cleanse them of their sinfulness while helping his country in one fell swoop. In fact, he considered himself the arbiter of true Christendom. The man who was single-handedly bringing the light of God down on these baseless savages that had turned their back on him.

The Native Americans that survived the total slaughter of their village, after having to watch as everyone they've known and loved was brought forth and killed before their eyes, by men who laughed and claimed to love some benevolent creator as they did so—even if they understood English, I doubt any of them could understand why this was happening to them. I'm not sure any of them would've felt better if they did.

Well, after being dragged on the ground through the bloody piles of everyone they once knew, he would bring them to a pit and throw them in. The walls would be smoothed down, dug in deep enough that no man would be able to reach the lip of the pit.

He would leave them there for several days, hoping that he was "starving out their resistance to God's glory," or so he liked to claim in his various journal entries on the subject. If you were one of the lucky ones, you would succumb to hunger before the third day when they pulled you out for your "conversion to the faith."

They would tie the man, or woman, in a few rare cases—almost all of which included several rapes, the religious purposes of which have never really been clarified—to a long pole in the center of the camp. Longwarden himself would come out, dressed head to toe in baptismal robes, carrying his King James Bible in one hand and a large scythe in the other. He was known for looking like a skeleton that had stolen someone else's skin, his features gaunt and tight against his pale flesh. If there ever was a walking embodiment of the grim reaper, it was Malachi Longwarden.

He would ask them a series of questions—starting small, asking for names, if they had any family. Most would respond that he had killed their family just several days before. Longwarden would often write how amusing he found this, claiming that they were angry with him when they should've been thanking him for sending their loved ones into the wide, loving reception of God's caring hands. Of course, he also believed God to have promptly thrown them down into the fires of hell with the rest of the savages and sinners; but to him, this was a kindness, a reprieve from their life of sin.

These questions would continue—most seemingly without purpose, meant to keep the subject from simply telling them what they wanted to hear. He would listen intently to the answers, if they were in English, of course; but then again, if you didn't speak in God's gifted tongue, then you most likely wouldn't have survived that long, and he would form his opinion on the salvageability of their soul. As night came on the third day, Longwarden would finally ask the questions regarding the enemy intel.

I don't know how expansive your knowledge of the French and Indian War is, but many tribes would work with French settlers, mainly due to their respect of the land and the customs of its native people, sharing strategies with its members in regards to raids on the enemy's supply lines or isolated townships. Longwarden often got the date and time of these raids from his first prisoner, but that wouldn't stop him from testing the rest, just to be sure that he wasn't jumping on any false leads. After receiving the same date and time from three screaming mouths, he figured it would be safer just to ask them all, just in case there was some collusion formed in their pits, even though all were separated by more than twenty feet with a guard between them.

As soon as dusk fell, Longwarden would ask his questions, and if the answer was one of silence, or reluctance, or anything other than the answer he wanted—no, expected—then he would raise his scythe and take a pound of flesh from the sinner, usually a long piece of flayed skin from the chest. Every undesired answer would end in the same result, taking more and more of the person's flesh, even to the point when some soldiers in his unit would swear that men would still be clinging to life, drool and blood hanging from their lips, as their entire rib cage lay exposed to the open summer air.

Longwarden, always a man of his word, would often request a scale brought out to him to weigh the flesh, carving off more and more and slapping it wet and heavy on the scale until it came out exact. He was quite a fan of Shakespeare and romanticized his method of retribution against the conniving Shylock, "the perfect representation of the savage that has hidden his ugly face from God." However, this form of torture bears more in common with a form of Chinese torture known as *lingchi*, or death by a thousand cuts—a punishment so heinous it was usually reserved for those that committed treason or murdered their own parents.

After the questioning, Longwarden, being the generous man that he was, offered redemption to his captive prisoners, his congregation of the damned, and give them his spiel on the Lord's mercy while they bled out from their wounds. Those that lived through his long-winded speech would be offered communion, a single cracker and a cup of wine, topped off with blood from the bodies of their dead tribesmen.

Those that accepted his gift and chose to walk in the light of the Lord, after swallowing the concoction of fermented grapes and the blood of their family and friends, would be sent to God on a chariot of flames, just like Jesus himself ascended.

This, of course, meant they tossed a torch at the kindling around the base of their posts and let the flames hollow out their bones. Longwarden considered it a tribute worthy of thanks, and if they did not thank him for it, before he burned them, of course, they joined the rest of the nonrepentant sinners in the pits.

The pits they had occupied before, huddled low and alone, its walls barely wide enough to stretch your arms all the way out, would now house two of the Shawnees. Crushed against each other, their space was limited, and any movement meant the pair would crash into each other in some way, elbowing ribs or knocking skulls. Members of Longwarden's unit—his clergymen, as he dubbed them, even handing out white collars for their uniforms—would poke and prod the poor souls in the hole with the tips of their bayonets, the rusted ends tearing through their already-mangled skin.

Longwarden himself would then preside over them, pacing back and forth, giving a sermon as he was wont to do for most of his life, this one on the price of turning one's back on God and the crushing darkness it brings. For an insane, sadistic masochist, Longwarden had some fairly progressive ideas on hell and damnation. He believed hell to be a complete disconnect from God, in the form of drifting through an infinite void of blackness, each eternity inseparable from the last. Every waking moment spent apart from the source of all light in the universe, speech choked by the suffocating darkness, a constant fight, an endless struggle to retain your sanity in a place that had long abandoned it. All I can say about Mr. Longwarden's idea as a nonbeliever is that it's a lot easier to imagine hell on earth that way. But then again, I've seen the more literal interpretation as well and would consider the former a much better option.

After this grandiose and eloquent elocution, Longwarden would offer them one final chance at their salvation. Quite generous, wasn't he? All they had to do was prove their devotion to God by following in Longwarden's footsteps and destroying the sinners besmirching God's bountiful gift to man. Simply kill the other man in the pit, and you would be guaranteed medical care, a meal, and a hot bath.

On hearing this, many instantly turned on their cramped neighbor, clawing at their face, wrapping their hands around their throats; but many more resisted, looking up at their captors with fierce, shining eyes. Longwarden once said he saw those eyes in his dreams, looking up at him from beneath his boots as he crawled up a hill of severed limbs. Those that choose not to participate would be given encouragement in the form of new bayonet wounds, with plenty of Shawnees dying beside one another, mumbling chants and singing from their throats as their life escaped through the gashes.

The winners were left to gloat over their fallen comrades to the sound of applause and whooping cheers, the drunken soldiers falling over themselves in mirth and laughter. Longwarden would consent and give them what he promised. He would throw them scraps of bandages, mostly used and still coated in the previous wearer's blood, and sometimes a needle and thread if he had enough to spare, but nothing more. His inaction would draw questioned grunts from the bloodied victors. He explained their meal had already been delivered and was lying at their feet, advising that it would be better to start eating sooner rather than later, as maggots made their way into the meat quickly if it wasn't salted.

He gave them the night to enjoy their meal, coming back in the morning to find that there were a few holdouts that had left their food untouched, to which Longwarden would give fatherly tsks of his tongue, disappointed that they wasted a perfectly good and well-prepared meal and that they wouldn't be getting any sweets that night.

However, more often than not, the bodies would be missing fingers, whole hands, whole limbs, even entire chunks gone from separate portions, like a late-night untended buffet wagon. Longwarden smiled at these mangled forms of men, satisfied with whatever point he was trying to make, and declared that they would be the first to be washed—the first to be reborn beneath the waters of baptism.

The men would gather up large cast-iron pots from the mess tent, taking it down to the nearest well or water source and filling them to the brim, leaving a trail of spilled excess all the way from the banks of the river. They would hang these over freshly made fires, grease fires built on top of the bodies of those slain in the battle—which, in Longwarden's case, were mainly women and children.

Once the water began to boil, Longwarden would walk among them, blessing each drop of water with silent prayers and quick flashes of the cross over his temple. Once the bubbles covered the top, with steam pouring into the sky, making the air stick to your skin like wet blankets, he signaled for the men to give the remaining Shawnee their baptism and welcome them to the Kingdom of God.

I tell this story like it was an isolated incident, a single journal entry buried away in the officer reports from the battlefield, hidden along with many of the atrocities of war, best observed behind the veil of righteousness.

But this was a common day in the life of a soldier in Longwarden's unit. Many of these reports come from his own men, some haunted by the things they did, after settling back into the normalities of life after the war—when peaceful sleep began to be disturbed by the screams of a thousand Shawnees as they watched their skin broil off their bones, curling up like a shade. Plenty came from Longwarden himself, as he often wrote of his times in the war and how those experiences shaped him into the man of action that he was. He took pride in them—a terrible, vindictive pride that continued on well after the war's conclusion in 1763.

While Shawnees definitely did not have a voice in pre-Revolutionary politics, possibly even less so after the war, there were enough rumors spread by survivors of Longwarden's raids—terrible tales about burned and scalped men, usually reserved as horror stories meant to invoke fear of the native populace, except now they were about one of their own: a white Christian Englishman torturing and maiming, like a blight on the countryside, modern-day Vlad the Impaler.

This brought pressure down from Longwarden's friends in Birmingham. Many refused to act, especially after he reminded them of his contributions to the war effort, including personally removing Indians from land that they bought for a cheap turnaround afterward. Their cold, hard fortunes softened their decision, merely issuing Longwarden a cease and desist against the native tribes; and if he refused and continued on his crusade, they would send the entire state militia after him, with orders to either bring him back in chains that would remain for the rest of his life or as a head short a body.

Longwarden condemned them, insisting that they had turned away from God, tempted by the base impulses of the savages, lying with their women and lowering themselves to bartering with their appointed leaders. These decrees, along with his growing disappointment with the colonies' growing rebellions against God's queen and country, finally drove him to leave Virginia in the final months of 1769, his final crusade taking place just a year prior.

Selling off most of his estate, Longwarden began the long trip into the north in 1770 along with the most devoted of his clergymen, settling briefly in Pennsylvania before the pacifism of the Quakers nearly drove him mad. Around 1772, Longwarden reached what is now Maine but was still part of Northern Massachusetts back then. He set up a small trading shop near Portland, increasing his fortune through timber and fur trading while also actively sabotaging French territories by causing conflicts among the natives through coordinated raids. Many suspect him to have had some kind of secret agreement with England, working for the crown to restore most of the Northern territory to British rule, although no concrete proof of this arrangement has surfaced, other than uncredited reports from after the Revolutionary War.

When the war did finally break out, Longwarden found himself again fighting for England and quickly returned to his well-worn strategies of hunting and converting the French and Native Americans. One of the generals fresh off the boat from London, who ended up fighting alongside Longwarden, jokingly remarked that Longwarden had actually been given a white coat, with instructions to color the uniform himself.

There aren't as many reports from this period of time due to the massive scale of the conflict and the lack of interest in the suffering of native tribes. The ones we do have are all hearsay—stories told over drinks in occupied taverns, rumors passed from camp to camp that spoke of terrifying markers found along the Northern routes into the wilderness; markers made of Algonquin body parts, limbs strung together in queer shapes that were hard to make out even if you stared at them for some time, a feat which many were not able to accomplish without vomiting. One man claimed they looked like angels, but there's no more on the subject outside of his sparse testimony. Another story tells about a tribe that was decimated up near Quebec, their land found completely abandoned as if the tribe had simply upped and vanished. Fires simmered on piles of mostly ash and rocks. Wet clothes hung from the sides of adobes and doorways stood open as if people had been gathered around them, lost in some story of their own god's ambivalence. Later, a small band of raiders dressed in bones came out of the hills and descended on a small unit of colonial soldiers, devouring the dead midbattle before reinforcements ultimately overpowered them. Upon inspecting the bodies, they found decoration similar to that of the missing tribe—pants sewn with the same hide, bows strung with the same twine. The only difference was the jingling suit of bones, too big to be from wolves and too small for bears, their circular, grinning skulls terrifyingly human.

Longwarden helped expel the American invasion of Canada with his clergymen executing their particularly famous brand of guerrilla warfare, but this experience wore him down and began his disillusionment with the British monarchy. After repelling the Americans, he learned of the British forces' acceptance of the native tribes and even slaves, going so far as to offer uniforms to men willing to serve. Longwarden went to his superiors about this, arguing about polluting the waters of God's army with the oil of sinners, but he was brusquely dismissed. He considered it offensive after all his years of service, all his years of purging the countryside in God's name; and they thought of him nothing more than a dog that could be heeled, holding him by the chain and pointing him in the direction they wanted.

He wrote in his journal of his change of heart as

> The most profound vision that God has ever given me. As I sat in my armchair, a fire crackling near enough for the sparks to sizzle to ash against my skin, I saw through lids half closed, a face upon the cinders—a noble face, stern and unrelenting in its intensity. I knew that I was staring into the face of God and could not look directly into his brilliance. Suddenly, the coals turned gray and rolled over themselves, steam rushing up from beneath as they folded inward. The heat was enough to make me think the skin was broiling on my bones. The Lord's fiery

> visage disappeared in a rush of brimstone and was so replaced by one half its size but just as bright. A crown of thorns sat upon its head, and tears fell down its face, a knife with no handle clutched in its teeth.

"I understood then," he writes, "I understood then that God's favor had passed to England's children."

Longwarden and his unit disappeared during the Saratoga campaign, moving south into New Jersey where they joined up with Sir William Howe's troops at Morristown. Afterward, he was given command of over a thousand Hessian troops, which he brought up the Delaware, stationing them on the bank on Christmas Eve, 1776. The night was one of the hardest for Longwarden to endure. He wrote several long entries into his journal, decrying the sin and debauchery that went on in his camp, the Hessians boozing and gambling the entire journey. He was disgusted by their lack of resolve, by the fact that their only motivation in the war was the gold that would fill their galleys on the trip home.

> A man who fought for God and country gave his life for something greater than himself, a man who fought for money was simply a cur, biting and yipping at anyone that passed in the hopes of scraps.

Did you like my impression? Maybe I'm going a little overboard on the gruffness, but I imagine that's how you'd sound with that much self-righteousness cramped up your ass. Still, probably a little less cartoony wouldn't hurt.

Well, anyways, as sunset came on Christmas Eve, Longwarden dispatched one of his clergymen across the lake in a small dingy, cutting through the fog with a single lantern. While he did so, Longwarden exited his tent for the first time in their journey (when they weren't riding, of course) and walked among the men, distributing wine by the barrel in celebration of the Lord's birthday.

He gathered everyone around tables for a feast, something uncommon during the winter years of the war, so the Hessians took advantage of the occasion by getting stinking drunk and engaging in revelry that might make a sailor squirm uncomfortably in his chair. Longwarden silenced them all with a speech of his own, one speaking of God's Son and his ascension to the throne of his father, his duty and obligation to the world and mankind bestowed upon him. As he raised his glass in toast, Washington's army rowed across the Delaware unnoticed, landing on the banks silently, coming up on the enemies unaware.

The Battle of Trenton was more of a slaughter than a battle. The Americans killed around a third of the camp before they surrendered. He captured the rest and sent them to the barracks, all except for General Longwarden, of course, who was given a prestigious place in Washington's tent, where terms of the surrender were discussed, along with arrangements for Longwarden's conversion to the American army. Pleased with such a monumental victory and the boost to his troops' morale, along with fighting alongside Longwarden in various skirmishes during the French and Indian War, Washington assented to most of his demands, handing out pardons to him and his clergymen, giving them positions of equal or greater rank within the Continental Army, and the smallest but most import piece of Longwarden's surrender: a settlement of land that he had scouted out during his time in Maine—a plot of former Iroquois land that he had occupied, something he hoped to craft into the perfect example of the American town.

The deal was struck and signed in the same day, over drinks and stories filled with laughter. Longwarden went South with Washington's army, fighting in several key battles, including Yorktown and Lexington. Rumors of his savagery followed him for the rest of his days, but his place of prominence in Washington's army tempered his methods and kept him opposite British troops, good Christian men deserving of a soldier's death.

After the war's end in 1783, Longwarden gathered the surviving members of his clergymen and started his trek back north, stopping in several cities along the way and gathering followers to his new brand of Christian extremism that gained popularity after the gruesomeness and destruction of the war. He also found himself a wife in New Hampshire, a Ms. Rosemary Castavet, whom he married in 1784 just a month before their arrival at their gifted settlement. None of the horrible angelic markers that had once surrounded it remained. Many of the first-timers believed it only to have been idle gossip passed about by bored townsfolk, still clinging to the horrors of war as their only interest. However, the lone poles standing in the shapes of crosses, slick with dried blood, seemed to tell a different story.

Construction on the town began almost immediately. Nestled between the Roeg River and the surrounding forest, they would be cut off during the winter, and if they wished to survive without a critical depletion of their numbers, under Longwarden's guidance, they planted several fields of maize too close to the river—which in the late spring flooding, brought the destruction of over half of the crops. Winter came quickly, striking in early September; and by November, nearly half of Maine was buried under several feet of snow.

Reports from the larger cities believed that Longwarden's crazy commune was doomed and didn't expect them to last through winter, especially not one of the harshest winters in the fledging country's history. Even the Iroquois were struggling, as their numbers began to dwindle and disappear. Fur traders passing through the woods would find tribes missing, some too elderly or too young, frozen solid in their wraps, the rest of the village disappeared. Many believed they must have simply moved South, leaving those that they were unable to carry; but when the frost began to fade, the snow melting into the rivers, the Iroquois did not return.

Yet emerging from the woods on the first day of spring was a small collection of Longwarden's clergymen, looking to trade furs and skins with anyone that had leftover stores. Many were dumbstruck as to how they survived out in the wilderness, especially as far north as they had, but they gave no answer as to their miraculous survival. Whenever asked, they would simply give the sign of the cross and whisper the Lord's Prayer while looking at their feet.

People started talking about Longwarden's town and its grim, tight-faced residents. Their prudent lifestyle was ideal to some looking to connect themselves with God and his so-called gift, and the settlement's numbers began to grow again until they were nearly double what they were before winter. Its furs, usually from animals that lived deep within the wilds of Canada, skinned and framed with a perfection that many compared to the natives, gained popularity and spread throughout the north, giving the town an economic boom that lasted into the nineteenth century and made the name Loganville known throughout the country.

Now, you might be asking yourself, why would a man like Longwarden, a man set on bending beneath the will of God, whose devotion to him was second only to his devotion to himself, would give the town such a name? Why not Wardensville? Or why not just name it Longwarden and call it a day? How could such a petty, self-aggrandizing man miss out on his opportunity to forever make his name known to the annals of history as anything more than a bloodthirsty beast?

The town was his; it was his own great creation, the ultimate proof of his devotion to the Lord, the culmination of all his life's work. It was more than just the dirt and mud beneath his feet; it was his blood.

It seemed only fitting that his town would bear the same name as his son.

"I feel like I walked into Kirk Cameron's vacation home, well, you know… if he was poor."

"Who's to say he isn't, by this point?"

"That's a good point. 'Ey, Gwen, girl, is your pops Kirk Cameron?"

"Can you put that down please? You're gonna drop it."

Gwen strode up haughtily and grabbed the small Virgin Mary from Tyler's hands. While giving him a reprehensible stare, she placed the statuette back on top of the dais that stood in front of the fireplace, taking extra care to avoid the numerous candles that covered the length of it like a bad breakout of acne. The entire house was filled with them. Every table, every cabinet and countertop, shelf was absolutely covered in the silk white wax candles, some already burned halfway down their wick. Most of them were several inches wide, and the newer looking ones were all nearly half a foot tall.

They gave the entire house a rosy glow, a feeling of sacredness that felt like stepping into another planet after escaping from the hellish fog. It was as if a bubble had formed around them, separating them from the nightmare outside, the few windows with their drawn shutters being their only indication that the world outside still existed.

Light music was coming from a radio in the living room. An AM channel that specialized in playing hymns and other famous songs of praise was playing "It is Well," by Spafford, a song Gwen had to pretend not to recognize when it came on.

She was still struggling to adjust to the idea of strangers walking around in her house, her greatest shame exposed to scrutinizing gazes. Veronica's thin eyes drifted over every nook and cranny, surveyed every wall with tight, drawn lips, her face a mix of boredom and smug satisfaction. Her brother and his boorish friend had started picking over everything as soon as the back door had shut behind them, the scratching at the panels dying down only moments afterward. No one spoke for what seemed like days afterward, but eventually, they had dispersed throughout their new surroundings, leaving Gwen to suffer her embarrassment alone.

Frank, Range's friend, who had known his cousin—an old man of over fifty with more gray hair growing out of his ears than his scalp—introduced himself as the others filed into the living room, the two of them standing awkwardly about the kitchen. Dishes from that morning's meal sat in the sink, slow, monotonous drips pounding against them as the house settled into silence after the commotion of new guests pouring inside it.

Frank's eyes settled on her for several awkward minutes afterward, his mouth constantly twitching as if it meant to say something, but all he ever did was force a cough and rub his shoulders. Eventually, Gwen gave up on waiting for whatever speech he planned to give and decided to see what part of her horrific childhood the rest of the group was picking through.

Stepping into the living room was almost blinding from the candlelight that filled it. An oddly calming haze had settled into the house, no longer giving it the feel of a prison but the church that it was always intended to be. Gwen felt strangely at peace with the house, more so than she ever had in her life, as if a demon had been exorcised from it, a darkness drained from its foundation.

"Um, excuse me? Gwen, right?"

Gwen turned and saw Vel's sorely red face peering into hers, her nose bent slightly askew with a trail of blood falling from one of the nostrils.

"I'm sorry to be a bother, but do you think you could point me to the bathroom. I don't want to just wander around, walking into rooms I'm not supposed to," she said with a warm but withered smile.

"I can't say I blame you," Veronica said, appearing from the hallways by the stairs, her flat tops clacking against the hardwood as she leaned lazily against the bannister. "I wouldn't wanna get lost in this freak show either. Might walk in a room full of skin suits made to look like Jesus or Paul or whatever."

Gwen did her best to avoid looking at her, realizing the energy to put up any sort of argument would simply be wasted.

"It's the third door on the left, down the first floor hallway. If you hit the laundry room, you've gone too far. If you hit the basement door, you've definitely gone too far."

Vel nodded sheepishly before disappearing in a strange waddle down the corridor, passing by Veronica, who spared a look of disgust that followed her out of sight. Disappointed by Vel's lack of interest in her biting stare, she pushed off the carved chestnut knob at the top of the balustrade and moved toward her brother and his friend, who had settled into the armchair near the window, his leg tossed over its arm so his whole crotch was spread wide. As Gwen looked, his hand went to his groin and began to scratch feverishly, causing her to look away quickly in a mix of disgust and embarrassment.

"So this is the big, bad abode of the Peggy Sinais, Prophet of Loganville?" Billy said, swooping out of corner near the door.

Gwen nearly jumped from the surprise, his wide grin popping up from the furthest reaches of her peripheral vision.

"I was honestly expecting a lot worse, from the way you talked about her."

"Well, I'm sorry my house isn't living up to your, oh, so high expectations, Billy."

"Whoa, jeez, I was just saying. I mean, I was expecting something like a "drink the Kool-Aid' type place, but this more just like… a stuffy Christian bookstore." His eyes went wide as he seemed to fumble over his words, making Gwen feel guilty for snapping at his jests, however ill-timed.

"Right, right, I'm sorry, I'm just a little on edge right now, as I think all of us are."

"I don't know about ya'll, but I'm in a damn good mood right now, actually. I mean, I just got to blow a dead mo'fucka's face off with a shotgun, I just scored me a couple ounces of dat loud, and of course, the best part, I ain't rotting in prison, waiting to get my salad stuffed by some burly nigga who ain't seen pussy in a decade. Hell, who'm I kidding? Matty'd probably bend me over after a couple more hours, that cock smoker."

"Well, if only we could all be as optimistic as you," Veronica said bitterly.

Bruce shifted uncomfortably in the chair he had pulled out from the dining room. He had turned it around and was sitting with his head in the cradle of his arms laid across the top of its backside, his stare a thousand yard away. Frank came in from the kitchen with a glum look sewn to his face. He shuffled over to Bruce and propped his hand on his shoulder reassuringly. Bruce looked up at him and gave a brief, if forced, smile, before floating back into whatever dark fantasies occupied him.

"You know, this place actually looks a lot like my grandma's house up in Vermont. We'd drive down there for Easter and all the other super religious holidays. Her place was a lot like this, small knickknacks everywhere, usually with big eyes and rosy cheeks, like little *chibi* characters. Has the same smell too, mothballs and peppermint candy, although the candles definitely leave a strong scent, obviously, but that's underlying aroma, a smell as dull as its appearance," Billy continued, as if Tyler had never spoken.

In fact, Tyler had continued his debate with Veronica, citing that he knew a way to make her more optimistic if he wanted to show it to her; but Billy hardly seemed to notice, talking excitedly next to Gwen's ear, so close she could feel the warmth of his breath beating against her lobe.

"They would always make sure I didn't bring a book or a Game Boy or anything with me when I went up there. Thought it'd be rude of me to act like I wasn't interested in spending every waking second with my grandma. I remember one year, I saw these ducks gathering on the lake right before winter so there just a hint of frost on top. They looked so beautiful out there contrasted against the dirty gray lake that I wanted to run out and feed them, touch them, anything really, but my grandma grabbed my wrist before I even made it past the screen door and chided me. She kept going on about how I'd ruin my nice clothes and that I was so desperate to avoid spending time with her. God, it was so annoying. I can definitely understand how frustrating it must be in a place like this."

Gwen's mouth fell open as he finished, her mind trying to process what was going through Billy's at that time. She could feel how dumbfounded she must look. She saw it in Billy's reaction, the sharp backpedal that came whenever he saw that he had upset her.

"I'm just saying, I can relate, you know? To all this? Not trying to downplay what you went through or anything. Sorry, it was a bad time to bring it up. I've just never been in your house before, and you were always talking about it, so I just thought I'd mention that. Try and take your mind off of everything."

"You're right, Billy. You haven't been here before," Gwen said, a little harsher than she meant to. "Maybe I should show you around a little bit then. You see that closet in the corner over there? The first door in the hallway, see the cross hanging on the front with my name on it? Looks like my room, right? Well, you'd be wrong. My room's upstairs. That's the closet my mom would lock me in if I forgot to pray before bed. She said I was already walking without the light of God anyway, so I might as well sleep without it too. When I was six, I changed the words of the Lord's Prayer to a dirty version I had heard some older kids singing at Sunday school, and she locked me in there for a week, told the school I had gotten measles."

Billy started to speak, his hands raised in effort to get her to stop; but she went on, her uneasiness fueling the wildfire inside her stomach.

"You see the picture on the far wall? The one with Jesus holding the lamb in the desert?"

"That's totally Willem Defoe. Matty, ain't that the faggot from *Boondock Saints* up there? The dude from Platoon who threw his hands up all dramatic and shit?" Tyler said, his hands at work on another cigarillo wrapper held over his lap.

"Definitely looks like him, I think he was Jesus in a movie once too."

"Do you see the switch hanging from the wall next to it? The one hanging from the hook?" Gwen said, quieting the rest of her newly attentive audience as she let the words spill out of her like a freshly plucked scab. "She'd use that on me when I forgot the words to prayers. Or when I told her about a boy at school I thought was cute back before I even understood what that meant. She used to keep going until I started crying, sometimes until my voice was hoarse. For a while, I'd try not to cry at all, just to see what she'd do, but I always broke. I thought it made me weak until I realized that it was only because she'd never stop until she won.

"One day I nearly made it. I swear, it seemed like she was going at me for about an hour, and I barely made a sound. If you were a neighbor, you might even wonder if we were home with how deathly quiet it was. The backs of my leg were red and raw, most of the skin had already started to peel and bleed by then. Her arm was tiring. I could tell because the space between each hit grew longer, the seconds stacking on top of themselves, and while I was mostly numb to the pain, they started to become nothing but static under my skin 'til I couldn't feel anything.

"I don't know what came over me, but... I guess I thought I'd won. She was tiring. I could taste the victory, however small and however petty, and it was more real than ever before. So I smiled—a big, wide happy-go-lucky smile, like I didn't have a care in the world. She saw this and gave a grunt, a sharp, bitter sound, and brought the switch above her head, and—"

She pounded her fist into the palm of her hand, flinching despite herself, the thwack of her skin colliding too close to the real thing for her liking. Her lower thigh burned as if the wound had happened yesterday. She swore she could still feel the rush of blood down the back of her leg.

"Now that shit is fucked up," Tyler said bluntly, much like the green-wrap cigar between his lips.

Matt's eyes were in the fireplace sifting through the soot, but Veronica's gaze met hers, unblinking, her face a storm of emotions, never settling onto one that was identifiable. Billy's lips were still fumbling for words, his hands buried in his pits, which had sprouted dark stains around the loose flannel.

"Your mother really did that to you?" Frank said. His soft eyes seemed wider than usual, glistening the candlelight.

Gwen nodded. "I still have a scar on the back of my thigh. The cut needed stitches, but my mother refused to take me in. She said, 'If God wanted me healed, he would have me healed.' So I went and found the crocheting kit she gave me... I used the pink thread because I thought it was the cutest. Thought it'd match my skin the best. Pretty dumb thing to be thinking about when sewing yourself up, but I guess it kept my mind off the actual job.

"I was nine years old. I hadn't even had my period yet, and I was already trying to stop myself from bleeding when I had no idea how. I don't even remember what the argument was about that got me in trouble in the first place anymore. But I've got a scar for the rest of my life from it now, so hopefully, it was worth it."

No one said anything for a while, frozen in the bubble to another time Gwen had opened before them. It was hard not to see herself back then, sitting hunched over in the small stool in the corner, always dressed in the best Sunday school clothes—big, black dresses and socks with frills, always with frills. It reminded her of angels for some reason. Maybe just because it had seemed white and elegant, but she had always felt comfortable in it, like she was truly beautiful, until it only made her think of the meetings with the switch that came after.

"You know, girl, I'm sure that scar ain't all that bad. It probably ain't even noticeable, and you're just thinking it's making you a Frankenstein for no reason. Why don't you bring me somewhere private and show it to me, and I can tell you just how beautiful you is."

Gwen sent the tip of her gym shoes into Tyler's shin, causing him to reel back instantaneously, his body a slave to his own reflexes. The cigar wrap in his lap flew up in the air before crashing to the floor, spilling its tiny green contents into the white fibers of the carpet.

"Ah… what the—you made me spill my bud, bitch!"

Veronica brought her open palm across the back of his head, knocking the tiled cap off in a wild arc that ended with the bill slapping him in the face.

"Serves you right, asshole, you can be a real fucking pig, you know that?"

Matt gave a short intake of air that came with a placid smile, but he quickly went back to his engaging stare-down with the fireplace soot, his fingers dancing across the bulging muscles in his neck.

Gwen looked up at Veronica, struggling to not seem entirely grateful. Veronica met her gaze again and replaced her enthusiasm with a halfhearted scowl, a sneer missing its edge.

"Besides, she's already taken by that blond weirdo."

"What? The li'l wimp with the guitar? You're fucking with that scrawny piece of shit? Man, I thought that mo'fucka was autistic or something. That nigga is seriously fucking weird."

"Oh, you're one to talk."

"Psh, I ain't gonna be insulted by a dollar-store Carrie White. Unless you got some psychic powers that could rip off my junk and shove it down my own mouth, I ain't too concerned with what some basic bitch thinks of me."

"Where is Range anyway?" Frank said suddenly.

His head wobbled to attention and circled the room, looking hopeful as Vel traipsed noisily back in from the hallway, the sound of rushing, gurgling water following her.

"I didn't see him anywhere in the hallway," she said, struggling to fix the button of her jeans, pressing her stomach up into itself.

"Last I saw him, I think he was at the foot of the stairs. I'd say the second floor's probably your best bet," Bruce said.

He shifted back in his chair and crossed his arms in front of him, a passive anger in his features that Gwen almost missed. She wondered if it was directed at Range but saw his tight eyes drifting over to Matt and Tyler by the bay window and took it as all the explanation she needed.

"What's he doing up there?" Billy said, a restrained nervousness causing his voice to tremble near the end.

"He's probably going to meet the prophet. Introduce himself to his future freak of a mother-in-law. I'm sure she'll be happy with how easily he'll fit in with this side of the family," Veronica said.

Gwen opened her mouth to tell Veronica a fine list of sharp objects to place up her ass when Frank spoke up hesitantly.

"That reminds me, Gwen, where is this mother of yours?"

The mismatched group looked at each other, their eyes darting from person to person, trying to assemble an answer between them. The floorboards groaned and rattled as a weight shifted between them, creases forming in the stiff hardwood planks upstairs. Gwen felt a chill pass through her. She waited for another groan to confirm her worst suspicions, one longer and more drawn out, drifting through tones that the human throat couldn't reach while breath still pumped through their lungs.

"What the hell was that?" Vel said shakily, wiping her hands on the sides of her jeans.

"You don't think it's—"

A thunderous crash cut Bruce off before he could say the words Gwen dreaded, the thought of which seemed to make her body shut down and turn into nothing more than a lumpy mannequin. The whole house seemed to quake and shook loose a small Jesus statue that tumbled free from the shelf. It crashed onto the soft white wool, the soft fibers doing everything they could to slow the descent, but it shattered into pieces so small they became invisible save for the glint of reflected sunlight. Gwen swore she saw blood gushing from behind the plaster pieces, thick rivulets of crimson pouring out on the carpet; but when she blinked, it was gone, and all that remained was the minefield of glass and wool.

"Something's upstairs," Matt said, announcing the obvious.

"Maybe it's mother dearest, looking for her holy vibrator before she leaves," Tyler said.

He snickered to himself as he got to his feet, putting the mangled green blunt in the space between his lips, and grabbed the shotgun he had laid against the side of the chair.

"Sorry about that," came a shout from upstairs, bouncing down the stairwell like a super ball. "Everything's fine."

Range's voice sounded muffled and distant when obscured by a floor's worth of drywall, but Gwen recognized it nonetheless, mostly by the twisting knots it sent through her stomach.

"What the hell is that kid doing upstairs?" Bruce said.

He had leaped up from his seat at the sound of the crash, visibly shaken, and now he was struggling to sit back down without drawing any more attention to himself.

"He's trying to introduce himself to her family, like I said," Veronica said, smiling wolfishly through deep, strained breaths, "which reminds me of something I've been meaning to ask you, Gwen…"

That chill came again, more debilitating than before. It swept up through her legs and settled in the nape of her neck, her muscles shivering and stiffening. She placed her hand back there and found it covered with sweat and hot to the touch. Pushing the feeling aside, even though the chill persisted, she braced herself as Veronica sauntered toward her.

"Your mother, as we all are well aware of, fancied herself a prophet, right? *The* Prophet of Loganville? Always going on about how the end of the world was coming, the day when her god would punish all the unclean and the sinners of the world would be doomed to face its worst horrors for all eternity. I remember that point specifically from those times she'd pick you up from school. You remember that? When she'd stop and give a sermon from top of the stairs? She stood on top of the stone handrail so she could tower over us, her hair down to the bottom of her back and frizzled out so she looked like Moses in that old movie."

"Does this have a point, Veronica?" Gwen said, her impatience slipping into her words.

"What's wrong, Gwen? You can tell stories about your old lady, but I can't? I have a few, you know, like the time she called me a slut for wearing shorts above my knee. When was that again? Oh, right, third grade. Or the time during the band concert intermission where she declared that everyone in the audience was going to have the flesh peeled from their bones and their souls ran through fire by the devil's minions for listening to the devil's music. All because the director thought it'd be fun to have the kids play a version of 'Smoke on the Water.' She also said the band instructor would be struck down by a heart attack, which happened three days afterward. It seemed like she knew what she was talking about from time to time, so much so that she was brought in for police questioning for that one, wasn't she?"

"Ew, you was in band? I almost wanna retract my earlier dick offering," Tyler said.

"My point is, Gwen," Veronica said, ignoring Tyler's intrusion, "is this…" she said, waving her hand toward the windows and the veiled world that lay behind it, "all this… Is this what she was talking about? Is this the end of the world? Huh? Is now the time when all the good folk are raptured up while the sinners are left here to rot as the dead rise and add us to their ranks?"

The group went silent, shifting uncomfortably at the thought presented, Veronica more so than the rest, like she was disturbed by her own behavior. Gwen became suddenly aware of their eyes on her, swallowing her up with their prying glances, unable to hide from the accusations she had faced many times before in her life.

"Don't tell me you actually believe her," Gwen said, the smile on her face crumbling as she finished.

She tried to laugh, to tell herself how silly the notion was—that Peggy Sinais, Patron Saint of Loganville, had ascended into the sky on a chariot of fire, to be welcomed into God's wide but surprisingly rippling arms, while the world descended into fire and death beneath her.

She had spoken of it so long, with such tenacity and belief, it was hard not to take her seriously—especially when Gwen had been younger and, like any child, the word of her mother had been infallible. There had been a time when she had been expecting the world to end at any moment, not afraid as most children would be, but reveling in the idea of a reset button for the whole world, one that might put an end to the life she suffered through. Remembering those thoughts now made a chill seep throughout her body, deep into her bones, into the marrow so thick that it was practically a part of her.

"Well, where is she then? Huh, Gwen? Where is your mother? Why wasn't she there to greet us with a Bible and a switch at the back door after we came stomping in? If she's hiding, why hasn't she come out and said anything to us? Even after hearing us talking and using her bathroom, something those geeks out there are incapable of doing?

"And why didn't she mention any of this to you, huh? The Great Prophet's been calling for the end of the world for years now, and here it is upon us, without even a squeak from a woman who was famous for predicting tragedies and spewing scripture whenever she had the chance? Doesn't seem right, does it?"

"You do believe her, don't you?" Gwen said. She tried to laugh, but all that came was low rumbling, her insides contorting over themselves.

"After what I've seen out there—what we've all seen out there—it's hard not to make the connection. And your mother seems to have simply vanished, which certainly fits into the theory."

"You're crazy, almost as crazy as she is."

"Well, what's the alternative, Gwen? That she did know this was day was coming? That she was prepared and waited for you, her sinful wretch of a daughter to go to school so she could sneak off without you? Or maybe you're right, and she didn't know, and she saw that dumb-ass reporter get her hand bitten off on live television and decided then, to take the car—you know, the one missing from your driveway—pack it up with her figurines and sermons and her sister, everything actually important to her, stopping for one final prayer before fleeing and leaving her daughter to fend for herself among all the blood and carnage, without a care as to whether she lived or died?

"Either that, or this is the Rapture and she was magically transported up to heaven, like an even lamer version of *Star Trek*, which one sounds more plausible to you, Gwen?"

In her head, Gwen had already charged at Veronica, tackled her to the ground, and began pounding her fists against the bone until they had melded with the muscle into a jelly-like substance; but in reality, she had barely taken a breath since she had finished speaking. Every part of her body seemed to be fidgeting, as if trying to escape, to throw itself against something in frustration. Violence seemed much simpler than trying to process Veronica's poison-coated diatribe.

Her temple burned, and her vision blurred. The lights seemed to flicker, and the glinting haze of candlelight become one giant beacon through the darkness. She nearly stumbled but caught herself with a step forward at the last moment, moving toward the stairs, as nothing other than ascending them and smashing Veronica's brown skull against drywall seemed to make any sense.

Bruce stood from his chair, the legs sliding soundlessly through the white wool carpet, his eyes darting between the two of them. His face was hard and solemn, a sadness etched into the lines there that made Gwen forget her own doubts for just a moment. However, looking beyond into the kitchen and seeing the empty driveway and the oil stain left from Peggy Sinais's Honda, she thought of the woman speeding down Highway 60, a smile on her face and a psalm on her lips, delighting in her daughter's hopelessness.

Gwen shook the thought away and found dampness tugging at the edge of her eyes. Even though she hadn't thought it possible, her legs began to carry her away faster. She reached the stairs and started up them—walking past Billy, who tried to flag her down with a concerned wave, and Vel, who followed her up the first several steps after catching the tail end of the argument on her walk back from the bathroom, not backing off until Gwen turned her icy gaze on her. When their eyes met, Vel seemed to shiver then fell back down the stair she was currently climbing.

"What? I was just saying what we were all thinking. I don't know why you're all looking at me like that…" Veronica's voice gratefully trailed off as Gwen reached the landing and turned the corner sharply, her shoulder colliding with the wall.

She pressed on into the second floor hallway, stopping as soon as she was out of sight to let her body slump uselessly against the wall in a fit of sobs. She allowed herself three good and heavy ones, letting the tears warm her cheeks. Finding it hard to stop now that she let them come, it took her a moment to collect herself as she moved into her mother's room.

The door was half closed, a crack of light illuminating against the black, sunless hall. Gwen thought she saw a shadow sweep past the bottom of the door, but when she waited for it to come again, the phenomenon did not repeat itself. Tepidly, she placed her fingertips against the wood panel, pressing lightly against it with a soft click from her nails.

Peering inside, part of her expected to see her mother's clothes laid out over the bed, almost like someone had been preparing them for a trip and wanted to see what an outfit would look like, to be strewn as if a body had simply evaporated out from under them, their owner simply vanished from the face of the earth.

The thought made her chuckle harshly.

As she crept into the room, she found it empty—nothing out of place. The curtains dappled against the window, fluttering with the breeze filtering through the small crack of glass that carried wisps of fog into the room, like translucent fingers probing the room. Striding over to the closet, she slid the door along its flimsy hinges by the small brass circular indent of a handle and found nothing missing, save for the clothes she had seen her mother wearing before school that morning.

Wearing a look of derision, she closed the door slowly, confused as to why she even cared enough to wonder, enough to let Veronica's barbed words penetrate her thick skin. With a sigh, she moved out of the room and back into the hall, catching her bedroom door, recoiling as if someone had darted past it and caught it in the wave of its momentum.

Gwen approached it silently, unsure as to what questions awaited her behind it. Even the thought of Range's jovial grin, as calming as it usually was—when it wasn't causing her stomach to churn, at least—did nothing to relieve her concerns now. In fact, it only made them worse, as she knew the rawness of her cheeks wouldn't be able to convince a legally blind man that she hadn't been crying just moments before.

Wiping her thumbs against her cheeks and feeling the bitter sting, she sniffled as quietly as she could manage and pushed open the door to her room.

Sitting on the edge of her bed—looking out at the rolling hills of Loganville through the small window on the east wall—Range waited, not even turning her head as she entered. She shuffled in, barely lifting her socks from the carpet, enjoying the tingle of static in her legs. She sat herself lightly down on the opposite corner of the bed, opening her mouth to say something; but the only things that came to mind were stupid, frightened questions about her mother. Feeling incredibly disgusted with herself, she sat in silence, choosing to follow Range's stationary gaze out the window.

The fog clung to the ground as if it had claws, with hills breaking through its peaks, small, jagged little houses piercing its luminescent veil. In the sky, the sun hung low, barely visible through the pockets of clouds cast over the sky, its light diluted into shade.

The graveyard stood as if on the edge of the world, the tops of tombstones and mausoleums cracking the surface. Gwen stared into its depths, transfixed so that she found herself unable to peel her eyes away. She saw what looked like ants from this distance, moving about beneath the stones, dark shapes flitting out of view beneath the lofty green hills. She squinted, even leaned forward on the bed as it creaked in protest, and nearly gasped when she realized what the dark formless shadows were.

"There's still a few stragglers trying to pull themselves through six feet of dirt. I'm guessing the ones that are the most decomposed and missing the most limbs, but it'd be a pretty poor hypothesis from this distance."

Gwen nodded absentmindedly before realizing that with his back to her, he probably hadn't even noticed it. A deep, sonorous wail echoed over the rooftops, in and out of streets, adding to a chorus of howls that had become so constant it sounded like white noise, a gentle static that set you on edge. When she turned back to Range, his head was turned toward her, the dark, hollow sockets that were his eyes settling on her reclined fingers.

"This is your room, isn't it? I'm sorry for bursting in without asking. I... I wanted to look out at the graveyard, to see if it was still happening, if the dead were still rising. Doesn't really excuse it, though."

Gently, Gwen lifted her hand and placed it on his, almost taken aback by the roughness of his knuckles, the firmness of his wrinkles. They felt smooth but aged considerably past his years. His fingers twitched at the touch of hers and recoiled slightly, but she coiled hers around them regardless. A small smile crept its way onto his face, but his emerald green eyes still seemed restless, like staring into murky water in a hurricane.

"Is everything all right?" Gwen prodded, hoping to keep the subject as far away from her puffy cheeks as was possible. "You disappeared up here as soon as we got in. And you look... well, troubled's the polite way of putting it."

"And the impolite way?"

"You look like shit."

He laughed then, a quiet murmur that grew louder as it went on. It sounded so musical, like everything he did; he almost seemed to embody it.

"I guess the lack of sleep finally caught up with me. I hardly recognized myself when I looked in the mirror this morning. I did shower, though, so I at least attempted to look... well, not like shit."

It was Gwen's turn to laugh, almost forgetting everything that had lead up to that moment, all the blood and terror. All that came to mind was this—this moment and the comfort that came with it, immutable but vulnerable at the same time.

She ran her free hand up to his hair, letting the knots tie around them, entangle her. With a ruffle and a smirk, she ran her hands through the locks of hair and out the other side, taking delight in the rose color that crept onto his cheeks.

"What were you talking about down there? I heard you shouting about something with Veronica. You two weren't fighting again, were you?"

"Not physically, at least, although I certainly wanted to. I've never wanted to punch a girl right in the boob more."

"All right," he said, trying and failing to stifle his laughter, "that's an improvement, at least. What was she going on about this time? It obviously got to you."

"How can you tell that?"

Instead of answering, he untangled his hand from hers and brought it up to her cheek, brushing his thumb and forefinger against it. Caressing the length of it and wiping away the remnants of tears that still clung to the raw skin, he cupped her cheek in his palm. The warmth was almost intoxicating, the steadiness of his hand holding her up as she nuzzled her face against it.

The tears came again then—in long, hard, messy sobs that made Gwen cringe in embarrassment just as much as they rocked her body. Bringing her in close, he let her bury her head in his shoulder, his scent like mint dashed across pine leaves swam in her head and took all her thoughts away. She wasn't sure how long they sat there like that, letting the silence envelope them, but Gwen would've been happy if the world, basking in the hopelessness of its current predicament, decided to end right then and there, preserving that quiet for all eternity.

"My mother... she just left me here to die. I can't... I can't believe she knew this was coming, but I can believe that she didn't want me to come with her. She never wanted me. She made that perfectly clear my whole life, reminding me every day that I was a mistake, born of sin and all the devil's worst temptations. You know, it was one thing to deal with the insults from others, the whisperings behind my back, the judgment behind their eyes, people like Veronica bringing up my family at any chance they got to remind me just where I came from. But to hear it from her... the one person who's supposed to care about you no matter what, to not even have that to come home to. How was I supposed to come out normal? People act like I've done something wrong, when all I've ever done is try to be normal. I've failed miserably apparently, but when you've never even seen what normal really looks like, how…"

He cut her off by squeezing her lips closed with his thumb, her watery eyes looking sheepishly up into his, almost losing themselves in that emerald green forest.

"Let me ask you something. When we met at the graveyard, you told me all about your mother and how much she seemed to hate and despise you. You told me about the things she did to you. Do you hate her for that?"

Sniffling and stumbling for words, Gwen let her lips stammer uselessly as the neurons in her head fired for an answer to a question that seemed so simple. Did she really hate her mother? Even after all the things she did, she supposed her mother deserved some kind of familial recognition. She let her stay under her roof and fed her, gave her clothes and heat and the basic, bare essential amenities.

But so did prisons. And the lack of freedom, the derision, the beatings all seemed in line with that interpretation. And who was to say that if her mother had given her up, things wouldn't have been better in the home of someone that actually wanted her around? Her mother hated her from conception and was too cowardly, too headstrong in her backward belief, to think of anyone other than her own salvation.

"Yes. Yes, I do."

Range nodded solemnly, and Gwen almost expected him to turn away from her with a face of revulsion and disgust.

However, instead, he wore that charming grin of his as he said, "Then why do you care that she finally left you alone?"

Gwen didn't know how to answer him. Everything seemed lighter, less important than it had before. Even the room seemed to take on a sort of ethereal glow, similar to the kind that pervaded the rest of the house. Her thoughts were racing, trying to find some loophole in his argument, but each thread led to a frayed end and a deep pit in her stomach.

"Maybe trying to be normal was the problem. Because you're right, you aren't normal. You're very far from normal. You're extraordinary. You're wonderful. You're beautiful. You're all the words that sounded stupid and cheesy until I met you, and I realized they only sounded that way because I hadn't seen the face to match them yet. I hadn't met the girl they described so perfectly yet.

"You try to act like you're cool and indifferent, but the problem is, you care. You care too much. You care what everyone thinks so much you've already let them decide who you are for you."

"God, you're corny when you want to be," she laughed, turning her head to choke back the fresh tears.

Her attention floated over to the open window and out into the wide expanse of fog and abandoned buildings. One of the dead shambled into view on the streets beneath them, one of its legs dangling from a thin thread of muscle behind it, like a child pulling a wagon.

"How can you say things like that during all this? How can you be so damn positive? It's weird, you know."

He smiled softly, turning back toward the window.

"When I was young, my mother told me that I had a very unique talent of finding beauty in tragedy. My father did the same, apparently. I guess it's why that song in my head is always so mournful, so sorrowful. Sadness just has this loveliness to it, in a way—a kind of tenderness, honesty. It's something real, no matter what your lot in life is. It connects us all. A few lucky people find happiness, but sadness finds everybody at some point. See? I don't always have the cheeriest outlook.

"My mom used to say it was a gift, but I figured out pretty quickly she was wrong. Beauty's a wonderful, amazing thing, but it isn't happiness. It looks like it, so much so that people spend their whole lives confusing the two, but true happiness is much more elusive, I think, and I don't quite have the power to find that as easily. Instead, I have this unwanted fascination, this obsession with sadness, desperate to find this beauty that I've convinced myself exists within it—this nobleness to it. It seems like something I can't escape from sometimes… like this cruel joke someone's playing on me.

"I keep thinking... I think that if I can somehow finish that song, that melancholic tune I can't get out of my head... maybe that'll make me forget about it all. But being with you... I don't know. Maybe I've been going about it all wrong, focusing on the sadness to get rid of it when I could've just been out trying to find that same beauty in other places."

He squeezed her hand hard then, his eyes peering into hers. She noticed his other hand was wrapped around the fretboard of his guitar, his thumb skirting over the strings, producing that same sorrowful melody she'd heard so many times before.

"And maybe the rest is just supposed to follow. I don't know, maybe I'm overthinking it."

His expression became one of pain, the first sign of weakness she had ever seen him show—a lingering doubt that clung to him like condensation on a muggy day, something that inched its way into every thought. Her heart fluttered, almost ashamed for having observed this blemish in his armor, but she didn't turn away.

Instead, she slipped her hand under his chin and turned it sharply toward her. His eyes tried to turn away from her, to escape, but she held him there until he forcibly met her gaze. His sunken eyes seemed to droop even further, glistening in the dim midday light that broke through the clouds.

"You do overthink a lot of things."

Her hand dropped to his neck, resting against the thick tendons. With a respectful hesitation, his head fell against hers, their foreheads colliding gently, the bridges of their noses connecting. She could feel his breath against her lips. His musk—a mix of pine needles and hickory that reminded her of the playground near the elementary school, inhaled deep inside her—was almost intoxicating.

"Now who's the one being corny?"

The world disappeared into a shift of time and space, everything important in her life spiraling into nothingness and replaced by only that moment. The window seemed to stretch beyond the horizon—an extension of the infinite, the horrors behind it no more real than they had been a week ago. Her fears became doubts became worries, which fell away like shed skin, like blossoms falling from a tree in a tragic yet gorgeous spiral. All she knew was the all-encompassing embrace of his eyes, small chips of jade surrounding a vast ocean of black, and the heat of his breath, brushing against her lips as the space between them closed…

"Hey, would you two stop sixty-nining and get the hell down here already? Seriously. What the fuck? It's been like twenty minutes. We're trying to figure out what to do other than hang out in the Manson family bungalow all day, this some total bullshit. Homie gets to bust a nut, and I'm down here, looking at pictures of that mo'fucka from *Platoon* with sheep and shit. Goddamn travesty is what it is, you know what I'm saying? I'm up in here, dogging these ungrateful bitches…"

The voice trailed off, and the moment was dragged along, kicking and screaming behind it.

Range's hand had curled into a tight, trembling fist, gripping the edge of his pants with white knuckles. He sighed, and his palm went flat against his jeans, pulling away from her as he pushed himself out of the soft folds of the mattress. From his vantage point in front of the window, the light seemed to give him an ethereal outline, a trace of light that made him seem even more mythical than before she had even spoken to him.

"Come on, we should be getting back. Not that I don't…" he cut himself off there, even though Gwen placed her hand on his arm in a last-ditch effort to get him to continue. "We have to figure out our next course of action. The library's still a good couple miles away, and the sun will be going down soon."

He started toward the door, pulling loose from her hold, her fingers digging uselessly into the skin. Begrudgingly, he stopped inside the frame, resting his hand against it, as his head drooped, his tangled mess of hair spilling over and shading his features.

"When this is done… if we… when we fix it, or we make it out of here, I wanna take you somewhere—someplace cheerier than a graveyard, hopefully, unless you'd prefer that, someplace we can sit and talk and say corny things to each other, if you'd like that."

Gwen smiled, even though each beat of her heart was slow and burdensome, like someone had tied weights to the bottom of it. It felt as if someone had reached down and scooped out a hollow part in her chest. She felt as if something was wrong, like something had slipped by them, but she smiled nonetheless, telling herself that everything was going to work out in the end. His own mirrored smile only made the thoughts easier and feel less like she was lying to herself.

"Come on, the others are going to be waiting for us."

She stood calmly, taking one last look around the room she had spent her childhood in. The nakedness of the walls seemed to bother her much more now than it ever had, the tossed-about manner of the closet, the crumpled bedsheets. Still, there was a coziness to it, a familiarity drenched over every corner.

Slipping to Range's side, they moved down the stairs gracefully, practically floating as if suspended on strings. When they reentered the living room, the small group gathered in a lopsided oval in the center of the room—Matt, Tyler, and Veronica standing opposite Frank, Bruce, and Billy, with Vel awkwardly mingling next to Matt and his sister.

The floorboards creaked as they danced across them, causing everyone to turn with gleeful or resentful suspicion on their faces. Veronica opened her mouth immediately to comment on their approach, but Bruce swiftly cut her off.

"Ah, good, you're back just in time. We were just talking about things we're gonna need once we go back out there. Basic things like food and water, some things that can be used as weapons, flashlights, for once the sun goes down."

"Well, all the food is in the cabinets and the fridge, plus some perishables in the pantry out back, but we'd need to head back out the back door if we wanted to get at it."

"I volunteer Owen Wilson be the one to do it! Hansel looking motherfucker," Tyler said through a fit of giggles, taking the blunt from between his pouted lips just long enough to scatter gray and black ash on the pale wool carpet.

Range shot a sharp look at him but kept his mouth shut.

"We don't need that much food. Some kind of law enforcement or emergency response team will show up by tomorrow, and once nightfall comes, I doubt we'd even have enough time to stop and eat, not unless we wanted to feed those dead bastards as well."

"I know we have some flashlights in the basement. I can run down and get them. As for weapons, you probably won't find much, but there's knives in the kitchen and some scissors in the drawers by the sink. Some wine in the cabinet above the sink and some isopropyl alcohol in the one underneath it. Any other blunt objects lying around are yours for the taking."

Tyler let out a loud wheeze of laughter at that last statement and began waving his wrap around like a police baton. Seemingly satisfied by her answer, Bruce gave his usual stiff nod and hobbled over into the kitchen, giving light tugs on Frank and Billy's shirt collars to get them to follow.

Gwen turned and started back toward the hallways by the stairs, but that feeling of something amiss that she had gotten in the bedroom grew louder than ever. She looked back for Range, almost certain he'd have disappeared from existence in the brief second she had turned away and half expected an absence of light in his space.

"Go on, I'll be waiting for you when you get back," Range said, with a smile that was as real and genuine as the rest of him.

Her hand drifted back on its own accord, feeding on her desire to touch him, to graze his skin just to make sure he wasn't just a trick of the light.

Feeling foolish, she pulled her hand back as if bitten and resumed her brief respite to the basement. Circling the staircase, she dodged an eager-faced Veronica, who started to say something that disappeared into the hum of the pipes as she turned the corner.

She reached the plain white door that separated the hall from the staircase to the basement, on the opposite side of the lower landing, the stairwell upstairs suspended just above it. Her finger danced over the clear glass knob, folding over its sides until the whole thing vanished inside her hand. With a last-minute shake of hesitation, she pushed the door open and peered down into the inky blackness that swam below.

The shadows seemed to possess tendrils that had worked their way up the wooden bends of the stairs, hands trying to pull her down in their depths. Anxiously, she flicked the switch on the inside wall; but other than a brief click, the darkness remained, laughing at her.

Trepidation slowed her steps, especially when she crossed the threshold, placing her almost naked foot on the cold wooden step; and a sound wormed its way into ears, one that she hadn't been aware of before. Quiet and crackling, it sounded like the buzz of simple static until she descended and it formed syllable by syllable into a half-intelligible voice rambling away.

By the time she got to the bend in the stairs, the voice had taken shape into one she recognized, be it mildly, its owner's face obscured by the haze of time and faded memory. The darkness was so absolute it was hard to see the wall directly in front of her, and she nearly tripped down every stair as she came around the corner leading to the final descent.

However, a glow had made itself known, the bottom of the formless gap appearing as she took slow, measured steps into the basement. When she reached the bottom landing, she saw that the candles that had been placed upstairs had been child's play to the display down here.

Candles covered every inch of space around the room—on shelves, on windowsills and old furniture. They even covered the entirety of the floor, save for a path that led to the laundry machines at the back. The voice she had heard on the stairs was now booming so loudly that she had no idea how she hadn't heard it upstairs. A man's voice was speaking feverishly with cracks of distortion, making his already-harsh voice something out of an old emergency radio broadcast.

"The people of this world like to think they've got it all figured out. They cling to that idea like a life raft in this vast sea that we call existence, waters that are churned by the Lord himself, to a rhythm that we may never understand. And you know what, I hope we never do. I don't know about you, good people, but I enjoy my ignorance. People will like to throw it against you, like it's some kind of badge of shame, but it is a medal of honor, my brothers and sisters, one to be worn proudly, as a tribute to God and his desires."

Gwen stepped cautiously through the small patches of candles, the fire licking at her ankles and causing sweat to trickle down her legs. The basement had always been plain, terrifying only in that way that every child's basement is terrifying—a dark home to the strange and unknown.

Peggy Sinais kept her rotation of Christian store memorabilia down here, stuffed away in matching boxes, marked only with dates and Bible passages. Yet now, nearly every box had been overturned, half of their contents strewn across the floor. Busts lay in powder-white pieces; paintings lay torn, their ripped edges floating dangerously close to the flickering flames of a thousand candles.

"These nonbelievers, they find solace—false solace, I might point out—in their theories and their inventions, the same solace provided by any of the devil's favorite temptations. They place themselves on the same level as God, claim to be able to understand the mystery that he has given us as if it is something meant to be solved.

"Well, let me tell you, ladies and gentlemen. It. Is. Not."

The surviving memorabilia hung from the walls, the largest paintings and statues all bearing a common, easily noticeable theme: the crucifixion of Jesus, including a life-size wooden recreation. His face, nearly as tall as Gwen, stood leaning on the wall across from her, his eyes wide and pleading. Streams of blood came from the tears in his forehead, flowing down into the corner of eyes. His mouth hung open as if he was screaming out in anguish or pain, of which she couldn't be certain.

A painting on the other side of the basement bore the same pose, almost the exact same scene—the same look of terror present in his face as the life drained from him, his cause looking less and less noble as the blood poured out of him onto the dirt below. Gwen tried to imagine herself up there in his place, a thought so blasphemous her mother would've given her fifty hits from the switch just for thinking it; and all she could think of was the regret he must have felt, his faith in the supposed goodness of his Father's kingdom slipping along with his consciousness.

The painting beside it was a retelling of the story of John the Baptist and Herod, Herod's daughter holding John's head on a silver disk before her father, a maniacal grin on her face. On the other side was a sloppy watercolor from a crafts fair, a poorly etched carving of Solomon splitting a baby down the center to settle a dispute between two arguing mothers. The sorrow on the mothers' faces was stark against the rest of the carving, a greater detail put into the tears on their cheeks than anything else.

"Our original sin was trying to piece together a mystery that God did not want solved. A sin men carry, thanks to the traitorous women birthed from their ribs, their weaknesses made flesh, and we carry that weakness with us now for the rest of eternity.

"And now, having figured out the reason the sun sets and rises, and the similarities between God's design, they think themselves invincible. Immortal. They believe that they are the pioneers, leading us into the unknown on chariots of fire, when it is the fire that they are dragging us into with their endless thirst for knowledge.

"Call me ignorant for believing in something my father believed in, and his father before him. Call me foolish for revering the very thing that has carried us so far. Call me naive for believing in the all-powerful."

Gwen stepped into an open circle of candles, the tips of her toes barely squeezing between the biting flames. As she moved through the slapdash cathedral, she saw the table set underneath the famous depiction of the cross bearing INRI at the top—saints Paul and Francis pointing up at their savior like he was an interesting tourist stop, instead of their esteemed friend and mentor.

On top of the small desk was a tape recorder, an old piece of machinery long obsolete, covered in a layer of dust save for the front near the glass and square buttons—six white, one bloodred.

"I give myself over to a higher power. Something that requires the strength to believe in something you cannot prove—a strength that these terrified searchers, so desperate for a meaning to their sinful lives they cannot accept the easy one in front of them, one that's been written and passed down for generations before us. They look to the future, when they should be looking to the past."

A blurry photograph stood in a gilded frame on top of a lone stool beside the desk. Crumbles of a thick, white powder—less transparent than dust and twice as heavy—covered the stool beneath it, handprints pressed into the pile. Behind it was another large crucifix with another frightened portrayal of Jesus, bloodier and ganglier than the rest, balanced against the drawers of the desk.

She stepped through the sea of candles, feeling hot wax crisping the bottom of her socks. She could smell the burned fabric. A small ray of light poured in from the slit of a window, showing the drifting dust mites that flitted through the air.

Bending over, she stared intently at the photograph, but the layer of dust was too opaque, other than a brief trail of finger marks that circled its center. Gwen grabbed it by the golden vines of its frame and gave a short huff of air that she instantly regretted, as the dust flew back into her face, placing a vicelike grip around her chest.

She coughed and nearly fell over the stool into the pile of candles but caught herself on the edge at the last moment.

"That does not mean I do not concern myself with the future. In fact, it is quite the opposite. I worry for our children. I worry for my daughter, like you all worry for your sons. I worry so much it seems like something I cannot contain with God's reconciliation. I ask him for forgiveness for our transgression, but there is only so much appeasement a man can provide on his own. I am worried about the future, ladies and gentlemen, of this congregation, because I have seen it."

The man in the picture stared back at her, a wide smile on his wrinkled face that showed not even a single tooth. His eyes shone even without their color, the black-and-white shades showing the photo's age. Gwen's breathing slowed to the point where she could no longer feel it, a deep-seeded fear taking hold of her. She knew this man. She had spent her whole life living under his shadow.

"God has given me a gift, one I plan to use to lead his flock back into his good graces. I see them as a warning, a darkness that can be avoided by circumventing the sins that lead to it. To this goal, I have dedicated my life. I have dedicated my children's life to it, and their children's children, and so on, the cycle persevering."

Gwen set the photo of Reverend Sinais back down on the stool, her breath caught in her throat, as if he had reached out from the photo, across time, and wrapped his sweaty palms around her neck. She stumbled backward, tripping over a collection of candles as she did so, the concrete floor extinguishing the flames as they smashed against it.

There was thud as she reached the soft barrier behind her, the mushy feel of wet cardboard on her back. A crunch echoed from under her step, and as she looked down, she saw the bottle of pills her aunt had taken under her socks, cracked into a million orange pieces. The pills labeled Dermoxitil had been crushed into a fine powder, one that looked eerily similar to the kind that lined the stool.

Looking back toward it as the man on the tape reached his terrible crescendo—his voice booming as if it was the voice of God himself—she saw the shattered bowl beneath the wooden legs, its squashed contents spread across the floor, along with two overturned glasses with a damp spot beneath them. Fresh footprints spotted the mush, and when Gwen looked at her feet, she saw similar stains; and the horrible puzzle started to piece itself together, almost unwillingly, in her mind.

"But no matter how much we fight it, the end of the world is coming. That, I have seen, and even that, I cannot prevent. It is as inevitable as thunder after lightning. Many would have you fight anyway, to give yourself into the sin of false hope, a defiance of God's will. They ask you to stand at Judgment Day, ready to fight the unending tide, instead of taking your rightful place at God's side.

"And that is something I cannot allow. We must always give ourselves willingly to the Lord when he calls us, or risk eternal damnation. So I implore you, when that day comes, give yourself to God. Your family, your friends, do not let their quest for knowledge doom them.

"Walk in the light of the Lord, and deliver unto him his people, whatever the cost."

With a hiss and a shriek, someone pushed through the pile of boxes behind her, knocking Gwen to the ground in a rain of white pills and cardboard that crashed into the candles and sent them scattering outward across the cement floor, like split atoms. Her mother's decayed form fell on top of her, black bile pouring out from her mouth, like a dark fountain, her eyes misty pits that held nothing but resent and spite. Her teeth clacked and snapped next to her nose, sending flecks of pus over Gwen's reeling face.

Sliding back on her hands and knees away from the rotting corpse of her mother, a scream dug itself into the pit of her stomach and nestled there, but it would not come. Instead, she found herself squeaking like a cornered mouse, hating herself for that almost as much as she did for being so foolish as not realizing her mother's twisted intentions as soon as she walked into the empty house.

The rounded curls of her mother's hair bobbed as she tried to push her freshly paled body forward onto her prey, but Gwen was on her feet first, backpedaling toward the stairs. However, her escape was short-lived as she collided with her aunt, knocking the two of them into a nearby shelf.

They fell to the ground in a tangled mess of limbs and steel, candles sending hot wax and flames over their skin. The creature attempted a throaty howl as a burning wick embedded itself into her aunt's eye, turning the lumpy white ball into a bubbling pile of jelly.

The gooey remnants of her eye dribbled down her wide cheeks, pooling in a fold of loose skin above her neck. Her aunt's throat was swollen like a bullfrog's, a throbbing lump that distended it to nearly three times its size. Veins, slick and purple, bulged against the surface, thick fluid frozen and visibly swirling through the dead arteries in the afternoon light. Like claws from a cornered animal, her hands thrashed and swung at Gwen's face, drawing blood as the nails tore up part of her cheek.

This time, it was Gwen's turn to scream, pain searing through every ripped-up nerve. The lingering feelings of familial compassion receded back from her conscious mind, down to where Gwen could no longer find them—a brief flash of her aunt's grinning face alongside her husband, Greg, going through her head as she brought her fist down on the quivering lump in her throat.

It exploded in a torrent of blood and pus, the coiled-up mass of organs bursting out through the newly opened gap in the twitching carcass. What Gwen could only guess was her spleen, swollen and turned a sickly green, slid up into her snapping mouth; and she began lackadaisically chewing on it, like it was a treat placed on the nose of an obedient dog. Her jagged, broken teeth—coursing with foaming spittle from her burst throat—bit down into the tough meat, tearing it in large chunks that leaked a sickly red slime down her chin.

Nearly gagging, Gwen fell to the side for just a moment, but it was long enough for her mother to seize her shoulders and throw her across the room. She crashed into the desk with her spine, the pain turning her vision to a blinding white haze. The recording of Reverend Sinais ended with an abrupt whirring as the tape player tried to continue its only function even as it was crushed under Gwen and the weight of the collapsed desk.

Weak and dazed, Gwen tried to fight her way to her feet, but her strength seemed to have been completely exhausted. With heavy footsteps reverberating through the concrete beside her ear, she started to accept her end, however bitterly ironic it was—the thought of her mother devouring her still-twitching body seeming oddly fitting.

You care what everyone thinks so much you've already let them decide who you are for you.

Her hand shot forward, reaching for something, anything to grip between her fingers as some kind of weapon. This new well of strength seemed almost bottomless, her fingers jittery and clumsy. At first, her hand slapped helplessly against the cold ground but finally thwacked hard against something firm and unmoving. Her hand shot out and coiled around the heavy object, square and sturdy, and swung it wildly over her head, like a makeshift mace.

She felt the end connect with something, heard them fall back into a steel shelf as it clanged loudly against the floor, like a crash of thunderous cymbals. Her eyes fluttered open, struggling to make sense of the light entering them.

A shadow that nearly took up her whole vision made her lash out with the heavy piece of wood in her hand, smacking whatever creature that lay in front of her to the side. The shadow tumbled and fell onto the table beneath the window, directly into a spiral of candles.

In an instant, flames engulfed her entire body, catching on the thin fabric of the dress—one of her aunt's Sunday best, made of yellow satin—something that would set a normal person to thrashing and screaming. Instead, the monster that had once been her aunt gave several oddly indifferent, inhuman shakes as her head caved in on itself in a rush of embers and a cloud of ash rising from its charred remains. Sizzling like serpents, the flames burned themselves out unnaturally quick, as if an unseen gust had washed over them. Sparks sizzled from the blackened husk, the clammy skin refusing to burn any further

Using her hard earned respite, Gwen used the heavy cross in her hand as shaky cane to get back on her feet, her mother's flailing limbs already upon her. Gwen raised the cross, ready to swing, but stopped as her mother pounced on her, the milkiness in her eyes gone to reveal the deep hazel underneath.

In that moment, she was plain, old Peggy Sinais, the Prophet of Loganville—her mother, no longer a nameless, faceless member of the undead but a monster still the same. The dark mole that hung like a rival to the moon just below the bridge of her nose, a beauty mark most women would appreciate but had forever gone under the cover of blush, had burst in her last tumble; and pus and bone poked through, like a drunk white earthworm that couldn't make it to the bathroom in time. The golden cross earrings, ones her grandmother had worn every day for twenty-seven years, dangled from her lobes, even though one of the ears had fallen to her neck on a ripped patch of skin that clung stubbornly to a fraying strip. Her breath reeked of rotting meat and chemicals you'd find in a janitor's closet—no worse than usual, really, crumbles of white mush still swimming in her dripping bile. The sadness that framed her eyes—always small, bitter things with depth only if you considered a bottomless pit of black truly deep—remained; but the life behind them gone, the glint she had noticed on Christmas Day Mass and her first communion, the days when her mother had been only that, instead of her tormentor.

With all her weight, she pushed her mother off of her with the edge of the cross, her mother's corpse spinning on its shattered ankles and landing in a heap on top of the stool in the center of the room.

Taking no more time, Gwen descended on her mother, kicking the candles aside, raising the cross high above her head until it was bathed in the glow from the window, Jesus's mournful gaze looking down on her with indifference as she brought it down on her mother's skull.

Warm drops of blood splattered against her face, the taste of copper and chalk on her tongue. With a heave and a pull, she yanked the cross free from its sticky prison of caved-in flesh and brought it down again, harder than the last.

And again.

And again.

And again until all that lay before her was a headless corpse and a deep, shimmering puddle of red with pulpy chunks floating on its surface. And as she stared down into that red mirror that had once been her mother's head, she saw herself staring back at her.

ACT III

From Romero with Love or (The One Where Everyone Dies)

The tombs were also opened and many bodies of the saints who had fallen asleep were raised. And they came out of the tombs after His resurrection, entered the holy city, and appeared too many.
—Matthew 27:52–3

They were ordered to torture and not kill… When this happens, people are going to prefer death to torture, look for ways to kill themselves. But they won't find a way—death will have gone into hiding.
—Revelations 9:6

Something came out of the fog and tried to destroy us.
—Stevie Wayne, *The Fog*

No tears please. It's a waste of good suffering.
—Pinhead, *Hellraiser*

Choke on 'eeemmmmmmmm!
—Captain Henry Rhodes, *Day of the Dead*

The Barnfell's genealogical history is just as dark and spotted with misery as my own, maybe even more so. Tracking down all the different cousins and offshoots from the main line that were quickly married off to other townsteads across the state when they came of age or even before it, it's hard to trace all the roots and construct an accurate history.

For the most part, the Barnfells that originated in Loganville and resided there over the centuries from its inception are very straightforward and easily traceable as long as you're not easily discouraged—which I wasn't—especially when you had as much free time as I did in the hospital.

The first record of the family came from an 1823 census of the county that reported a father, mother, and child residing in a small farm near the edge of town. Ironically, it seemed that they produced only meager amounts of corn and wheat meant for subsistence and didn't actually have a barn, leading the inspector to note that maybe "it had fallen down before he got there."

It was quiet for the next fifty, or so, years until 1868, when Jacob Barnfell—a supporter of the Confederacy during the Civil War—lynched a couple that were caught partaking in the sinful practice of interracial "fornication." What newspaper clippings could be found about the incident say that the woman, Lydia, reportedly worked for Barnfell, in an arrangement that resembled slavery in every way save for what they called it. Some reports even asserted that the woman—a Haitian immigrant with skin like charcoal and a smile that was just as smoky—had been Barnfell's lover, living on his property in return for services that women have been providing men for most of their partisan history.

The man she was caught with was a worker from a small, despairingly poor family that didn't even reside in the county. He came from an Indian reservation several miles north, brought down by the allure of work and a bar that had more than several deposed, solemn Native Americans, joining their ancestors by drinking themselves into an early, vomit-crusted grave.

The night in question, Barnfell along with several other Confederate cronies were celebrating a recent harvest, one that was particularly better than the rest. The yields had been especially good for the Barnfell estate, which had been notoriously unprosperous over the course of their settling into the river valley.

This, of course, called for an even wilder and more exuberant celebration than the ones before it, their cautions thrown onto the same wind that had brought them their fortune. One of his named associates, Franco Norois, was famous in the region as a hunter, known for bringing in record numbers for the hunt each year that ultimately ended up being the main reason for legislation that culled the amounts of animals killed per season as Franco's hunting of the jack-eared rabbit in the winter of 1882 nearly drove the species to the brink of extinction. He was also famous for his near-death experience from a bear at the age of fifteen that left half of his face in tatters as he attempted to crawl back into town for aid. He was followed by hungry, yipping wolves for the entire four-mile hike, with one of the beasts even managing to get ahold of a side of the mangled flap of skin that had been his face and tore off an ear. He killed that one, along with others from his pack, but that was the one whose skin he wore at his belt for the rest of his days.

Because of this traumatic experience, Franco Norois was left with a face that was said to make women cross to the other side of the street to avoid him. Locals lovingly referred to him as "Handsome Frank," as he became something of a local legend, albeit more of a boogeyman than a saint.

Well, you see, Handsome Frank goes walking out of whatever bottom-feeding saloon he and Barnfell had found themselves sloshed in. That night, he circled around to relieve himself on the side of the building when he heard rustling off in the woods. Thinking it was a varmint whose skin would net him enough to pay for the night's refreshments and still come out ahead in the end, he decided to investigate.

So he went to his horse and grabbed his rifle from the saddlebag and moved to the edge of the brush, poking around with the end of the barrel, when he came across Lydia and her lover. Handsome Frank was inebriated enough and probably so foreign to the sight of intercourse that he took several shots at the two of them, critically injuring the man from upstate's femur. The two tried to escape into the woods, but the shots had already drawn the attention of Barnfell and other patrons, expecting Handsome Frank to be carrying in one of his fresh, bloody trophies.

Instead, they stumbled upon what many of them considered an abomination. Barnfell himself equated it to sodomy with beasts in his testimony, and he was one of the first at the scene. As Lydia tried to dress herself, he grabbed her and the unknown white man, berating them severely as he did so, inspiring his drunken posse to join in with jabs and barbs of their own.

Leading the group deep into the woods, the drunken men—thinking as most drunken men do—thought this was the perfect example of exactly how the world had gone rotten, the perfect summation of all their long-winded, spit shrapnel–filled rambles over amber glasses. And when you already get the thought in your head, you think of a quick and easy way to fix it too.

The man, whose name I can't recall—something French with an accent that makes it a mouthful—he was the one they focused on first. From his own admission in his journals, we know that Handsome Frank Norois took Lydia off on her own, away from the group into a small clearing. While not part of any sort of plan of theirs, this action was supposedly followed by cheers and encouragement from the other members of his pack, talking delight in toying with their meal.

The man was beaten within an inch of his life, mostly by Barnfell himself. Later, doctor reports compiled from the incident indicated that he actually broke several of the knuckles on his right hand from the beating, and both were swollen to twice their natural size.

The state of Barnfell's hands were very similar to the man's face, which made identification difficult, especially since he had traveled so far south of the reservation he had grown up on. A poor man from a well-renowned family of drunks, he had found himself despised by the natives that called him neighbor with distaste and belittled by those of his own race for failing to rise to his supposed station. He had met Lydia on a drunken gambling binge and had begun to make several trips down to Loganville in the months that followed. The night in question took place roughly ten months after he met her.

They strung the man up afterward, supporting his back to draw the process out as long as possible. He kicked and squirmed. His eyes bulged out of his skull, while his neck turned a shade of red that would make a dahlia jealous; but he lived, forced to hear Lydia's screams has Handsome Frank showed her just how handsome he was.

All Handsome Frank writes of the incident is that he "had his way with her and sent her back to her mate." Apparently, it wasn't a sin when you used it is a form of punishment. When she was found hanging from the tree the next day, Lydia was missing her left eye, both of her breasts, and a hand. Her intestines and ovaries had been pulled out, and her right leg had been removed. A coroner report—while done hastily due to pressure from many in the legal system that took a special interest in the case, some even before the news had broken of the story yet and should've had no way of knowing about it—indicated that Lydia had been still alive when these injuries had been inflicted. Due to the swelling around the lacerations and the blood loss, he speculated that these were done before she was hung, and asphyxiation and blood loss were the true causes of death. A report published on a later date contradicted this one, however, saying that the cause of death had been from a previously unreported cut to the throat, and indicated that it tied in with other killings in the area—of which the killer liked to display his victims as monstrous trophies, akin to a hunter taking pride in a big kill.

Surprisingly, despite many people having witnessed the event of vigilante justice take place, no one ended up persecuted, save for a couple days of jail time for Barnfell for assaulting a police officer during his arrest. Most testimonies were thrown out beforehand before many of the witnesses got a chance to testify in court. In fact, none of the witnesses did, as an actual court date regarding the murders was never scheduled; and the whole incident was quickly brushed under the rug while more important issues, such as the building of a town road, captured everyone's attention instead.

Jacob Barnfell stayed out of the newspapers for several years, so much so that I thought he had died in prison back when I was originally doing my research. But as it turns out, that wouldn't be the final time Barnfell's picture would appear next to a headline announcing a bloody murder.

In the years 1877, a story broke out about a small farmer on the edge of town killing two intruders as they tried to enter his house. Normally, this would just be another example of the glories of the second amendment in action, but the odd discovery of the murder scene raised a lot of questions with the investigators.

For example, there were no broken windows or locks on the house. It appeared that nothing was really amiss or out of place, like nothing had been touched or moved around for years. One of the robbers was found outside, near the edge of the woods, fallen forward in such a way that it was obvious that he had been trying to escape into the safety of their shade when a round of buckshot caught him in the back.

The other man was found in the living room, the round that did him in taking off most of his face in the process. There were several deep cuts in his chest, with severe hemorrhaging around the wounds, so much so that normal man would've died, indicating that this intruder was superhuman or Barnfell had destroyed his face with another shot after his death. When questioned about this, Barnfell spat and said he "wouldn't waste the bullet."

Again, the case was only paraded through the papers briefly, a small blurb written more out of obligation to the dead men's families than any sort of journalistic intention. Barnfell himself married later that year to a woman barely older than thirteen, and they begot a daughter, Cynthia, the following summer. He died several years later after catching gangrene from a rusted piece of farming equipment, succumbing unusually fast for a man of his size, with some even speculating that he simply gave in to the disease in an attempt to find himself closer to God, the devout Catholic that he was—a man after Malachi Longwarden's own heart.

His daughter went on to marry into a prominent family, passing over her father's land as a dowry. And the son-in-law Barnfell never met, a Mr. Montgomery Clifford, soon took over the farm and took on several migrant workers, much to his mother-in-law's chagrin, to work the fields and increase crop yields by over half the year's previous amount. Business boomed, while rumors began spreading about the farm's new owner and his workers, most notably their nocturnal activity and the large crowds that formed out in the newly built barn, Clifford's major contribution to the farm's namesake. His clientele seemed to extend past the usual market owners and shop keeps, with many of the town's men giving him giddy pats on the back and hearty handshakes as he went through town, thanking him for services rendered, ones his wife spent many nights thinking on. She writes of it briefly in a small diary of hers, but like her father before her, her flirtations with literacy are brief and, overall, uneventful.

Clifford and his wife were gifted with a son in the year 1893, and in the following months, tragedy struck the family again when Clifford was found murdered in his bed, more of his throat outside his body than inside. Cynthia was found hysterical, covered in blood and clutching her child as she gesticulated wildly into the woods, babbling wildly to herself about intruders in the house, dozens of them or more. The police initiated a search in the woods that lasted for several days but ultimately ended up empty-handed.

Cynthia reports that the murderer snuck into their room at the dead of night, hoping to work out a previous dispute over wages with Clifford. Apparently, he was moving sluggishly and reeked of booze, something the cops also noted about the crime scene, one of the few pieces of evidence that matched her story.

She claims that the man was fired from the farm in the early spring—which, while corroborated by other reports, those same reports claim that the man left on his own terms, looking for more prosperous employment up north in the hopes of relocating his family, arguing about his morals being tested by his working there. Clifford had raged and fumed until he was red in the face, but he let the man leave peacefully, although his eyes wished death on him as he walked the stretch of land to the highway, so much so that the witnesses thought the man might burst into flame.

This same man was reported missing several weeks later, having never returned to his small rented room above a local market. The landlord claimed that he was usually very regular in his schedule, and he was all paid up for the month, so had no reason to skip out of town. The police simply believed his offer of work upstate had revealed itself sooner than anticipated and the eager men had run off to claim his American Dream.

Apparently, the dream itself wasn't enough for him, and he came back to town to collect his final paycheck, vouching for blood instead of cents, and after arguing heatedly with Clifford, brought a dull straight razor across his throat, tearing roughly at the edges of flesh as they blossomed outward, like poinsettias in bloom.

Somehow, during this heated exchange of words and the ensuing struggle, Clifford had remained stationary in bed, not even standing to face the man. Also, the jagged tearing of the throat was noted as unusual as the man's job had involved husking cornstalks, tying hay, and the like, something that would give him some proficiency with a blade, especially a dull one.

The mystery was only complicated by the discovery of his body by a local stream several days later. A small boy came across him and fainted from the sight, having to be hospitalized after nearly splitting his own skull on the riverbed. The man was found torn to shreds, his head placed on the top of his shrunken, half-consumed pieces of flesh that used to constitute a human body. The official report claimed he was attacked by wildlife, but the clean bites and odd arrangement of the body gave rise to many whispers of hauntings of old Native American spirits, claiming the land was tainted by the bloodshed that birthed it.

Many other whisperers about town liked to believe in a much more realistic, rational evil—however surreal it seemed—and began to speculate that Cynthia, having gotten word of her husband's late-night dealings in the barn and taking note of the many supple women in his employ, all dressed in an usually short dresses and exposed necklines, finally built up the nerve to pay the bastard back. The fact that he had finally given her a child only added fuel to the wildfire, but the police dismissed the idea outright, claiming her "too frail and timid to harm even a foal," and stuck to the story of the scorned worker and his unfortunate escape from one jaws of death into another, more literal one.

After the incident, Cynthia took her maiden name, one that she shared with her son. It was her way of honoring the grandfather she never knew but her mother told her so much about, speaking of him as an angel that dared spare time for us mortals. She gave the boy his name and set him to managing the farm when he came of age, doing an adequate, if unspectacular, job of it herself until said time came.

Young Jacob Barnfell's life was relatively uneventful when compared with that of his father's and grandfather's but a much more admirable one in that regard. He married a young girl named Margaret Rivers in 1902, who gave birth to triplets in the fall of 1903—just eight months after the wedding, leading to some gossip around town about the wedding ceremony being partially inspired by a shotgun held to the groom's back. Others even claimed that the birth of that many children was an obvious sign of the woman's infidelity, her erotic escapades being wholly responsible for the split zygote.

The birth of the Barnfell triplets was quite big news at the time, as it was the first documented case of triplets being born in town; and in a place as sheltered and as isolated as Loganville, news can be hard to come by. It's a place where rumors can sprout up easily, buds that could be easily nipped if the mundaneness of everyday life didn't inspire others to nurture them with half-earnest, drunken whispers in boisterous tavern halls.

Talk died out around 1905 when the shoe factory was built near the edge of town, famous for using a leather made from beaver pelts indigenous to the region, with some designs from a famous designer that was born in Quebec, a couple hundred miles away from Loganville. He grew up near enough to the place to hear the stories about it. In fact, he was probably well versed enough in them that I should have no sympathy for building his monument to industry on its outskirts.

Most of the town began working there, creating an economic boom that nearly lasted into the roaring 'twenties. Every family in town seemed to have someone working there, the wave of industrialization finally crashing into the barren wasteland that was Loganville.

The Barnfell triplets, Matthew, Mary, and Paul, were some of the many children employed by the factory—back before the widespread industrialization of the nation gave rise to the rapid misuse of child labor—where they and the other children worked on machines twice their size, their nimble fingers darting in between assembly lines of crashing, crunching machinery. Many kids lost fingers and entire hands, and many contracted various diseases, like gangrene and an outbreak of polio that resulted from unsanitary working conditions. Despite all this, many residents saw the factory as some sort of salvation for a town whose resources had taken a beating over the year as a demand for steel grew nationwide while demand for crops dwindled, along with the yields being so small and miserable that many subsistence farmers succumbed to hunger in the decades before its arrival.

Many people put their hopes and dreams into that factory as some sort of retribution, and for a while, at least, they were correct to do so, with the income from the factory being used to build schools, a hospital, and many other pieces of infrastructure that are still in use today—if not heavily altered in the 'fifties during the modernization movement that turned the town into the suburban wasteland that it is today, despite the nearest city being over a hundred miles away.

That, of course, all changed on the hot, boggy summer day in 1917, when the factory's owner, Malcolm Winthrop—an entrepreneur that had invested in the factory prior to its construction—decided that even though it was nearing a 120 degrees near the machinery in some of the more cramped corners of the factory, he would push production hours through lunch and on into the twilight hours, when what little light still remained was hidden behind the rolling ridges of the town cemetery.

There are varying reports of what actually started the fire. Some experts say that it was due to a spark from faulty machinery wiring due to the cramped conditions—the result of there not being adequate spacing between machines, not allowing the heat to be diffused between them and to instead build to the point that it melted the safety insulation around one or more power lines. Other equally decorated experts claim that the fire must've been started by a disgruntled employee, one lost in the quick shuffle of bringing in new workers to replace the overworked or injured, or had simply reached his breaking point in the sweltering heat and long hours. Either way, once the fire was started and stretched up into the upper alcoves and catwalks that overlooked the factory floor, there was no way to stop it from spreading across the entirety of the facility.

In a matter of minutes, it had spread to the rafters, and the entire ceiling had become an inferno, a sick reversal of the beauty of the Sistine Chapel, a portal to hell opened above them. Of course, once it got to that point, many of the employees began to flee through the three exits located on the northwest, east, and south walls. The south wall soon became inaccessible due to a collapsing walkway, and the eastern door was one of the first things to be consumed by the fire, leaving one exit available for those still trapped inside.

As Mr. Winthrop made his way out of the building, he noticed several of his employees fleeing with extra product, crisped leather or burned shoes. And being the truly prudent businessman that he was, he decided that the best way to protect his insurance on his burning goods was to make sure that they were found burned. Taking inspiration from one of the worst massacres in American history, he put a lock over the remaining exit, trapping over twenty-five poor souls inside of the raging inferno, ten of them at least being children. Three of which were the poor Barnfell triplets.

The fire burned through the rest of the facility, charring it down to its steel bones, with any attempts to extinguish it proving futile. The fire kept burning, shining well into the night as glimmering beacon, one that seemed to promise hope or some other bright-eyed emotion but was actually a harbinger of the death contained inside it. The following morning found the building to be nothing but brick, mortar, and ashes, looking more like the charred remains of some prehistoric beast than something that had once been the prosperity of an entire town.

Now here's where it gets really strange. I'm talking like *X-Files*, "hear me out, Scully" strange. Reports from the day of the accident claim that every one of the workers that was trapped inside the factory perished with it. These original reports include the Barnfell triplets in the list of casualties. In fact, I think they're the first three names listed, although I guess I could be wrong. Once you've seen one autopsy reports, you've seen 'em all, I suppose.

Of course, this would mean that the Barnfell line ended with them; but of course, that raised the obvious question of where Range came from. For a while, I thought that I had completely made him up, that maybe all the things the doctors had dismissed as symptoms of stress and insanity were really just that—machinations of my deluded mind, no matter how real it felt at the time.

These thoughts plagued me for months, to the point that I gave up my research entirely, hitting a dead end—no pun intended—on something as simple as a family lineage. I mean, they have websites that can do that stuff for you, and here I was struggling to figure out the identities of his great-grandparents that were born at the edge of the century.

That was when I went back and worked backward, first finding records of Range's birth at hospital several miles from the Canadian border. That alone was enough to inspire me to keep digging. At least, I wasn't so crazy as to have made this whole thing up, just crazy enough to have had it happen to me. I don't know why I doubted myself in the first place. It wasn't like I was the only one who could see him or anything. But when you have so many people telling you the same thing, day in and day out, under lights so bright they turn everything else black, it's hard not to believe them. Even if it goes against everything you think you know as a fact, sometimes agreeing just seems… simpler.

From there, I was able to find both of his parents, Kent and Rosemary Barnfell, both born several summers apart and went to school several towns apart from each other—Kent Barnfell, in

Loganville, while Martha Shepardson, hailed from up north near Blaine. The odd thing about their marriage is that even though both of them went to separate schools for the entirety of their academic career, both ended up engaged and wed in the summer of their graduation, despite never sharing a class or even having a shared sporting event between their two schools.

Obviously, something like this wasn't unheard of—although for the time, it was especially more rare, since most small suburbs remained isolated from one another, kept apart by the distance and the manmade bubble that surrounded every suburb, the belief that the darkest terrors lurked just outside its borders but none could pass through into the modern-day sanctuary. This was made even truer by the advent of McCarthyism that began to spread through the nation, the threat of Communism seeping its way into the quiet streets in the guise of smiling neighbors. Distrust was at its paramount among citizens, even in the quietest, most harmless of neighborhoods.

This brings me to the link that ties the two Barnfell threads together: Kent's father, Paul Barnfell—who was a major voice of McCarthyism throughout rural Maine.

Yes, the very same Paul Barnfell that supposedly perished in the factory fire that claimed the lives of his brother and sister. Trust me, I was just as shocked as you were when I saw the name. At first, I thought it was simply a shared name or one given in his honor. In her grief, had Margaret given birth to another son and named him after his fallen brother to sort of carry on his memory or something sentimental like that? It might make sense if the triplet's father, Jacob, hadn't died in the year previous to the fire due to an onset of typhus.

So where did this new Paul come from?

During campaign rallies from later on his life, he claims that his brother and sister are the ones who died in the factory fire of 1907, claiming to be the original Paul that survived the fire, using it to garner favor from the voters always sympathetic to a local tragedy. From his own admission, he claims to have been able to escape the inferno by climbing on top of the bodies of the dead around him, including those of his brother and sister, to reach an exposed window. He smashed through it and crawled to safety, heading straight home to his mother before the authorities even got a chance to look at him—which is why the reports listed no survivors among the wreckage.

While this background was definitely outlandish and implausible, he certainly seemed to act like a Barnfell—famously using religious doctrine to help back the idea of American unity and togetherness against the faceless enemy, the ones always lurking just beneath the shadows. Of course, these shadows seemed to always wear skin that matched and always took the form of an outsider despite supposedly trying to fit in to dismantle us internally. Funny how that works out, huh?

Paul Barnfell personally denounced several state legislatures as Communists—including Jack Thompson, for his socialistic views on health care, and Marty McDougall, for daring to suggest an African American man take a position in local office. Both men ended up being chased out of their respected districts in disgrace, many also losing their license to practice law and whatever assets they held, usually stripped of their dignity as well, as they were chased out of town like a stray, infected dog. Some found new jobs in places so far from New England that no one knew their name, drinking themselves to a slow, disgraced death.

Charges were later raised against Barnfell in 1958 when he personally led a mob against an African American family he claimed to be informants for Stalin and the KGB, claims he based on hearsay from a supposed confession given to a local chaplain who often frequented Barnfell's political rallies, so much so that he can be seen standing behind Barnfell on his podium in several photos of the man. After the accusation, a mob gathered on the family's lawn, which some witnesses claim was actually led by Barnfell himself, although even I think that's highly unlikely. While I don't doubt he played some part in it, the man was smart enough to keep himself away from a situation that was meant to incite violence for the sake of his political career. I also don't doubt that it pained him greatly to do so and that he would've loved to have been at the front of the pack, holding a burning torch high above his head to set on the driest, most rotted section of that poor family's house himself.

The charges against Barnfell were later dropped, but his political career never fully recovered. He lost his race for governor in 1960, and while holding several small positions in local government over the years, he mostly isolated himself to the family farm 'til his death in 1974 by his own hand. He was found in a seedy motel room with a revolver in his limp hand after deciding to redecorate the room by painting the walls a slightly less tacky shade of red. Range told me his mother told him that his grandfather was humming that song in his final days, the same one that Range heard his father singing in his own final hours, the one he loved to toy around with on that guitar of his…

Of course, there are no records of anything like that—not officially, at least. However, the coroner reports did uncover something slightly odd about Paul Barnfell. Apparently, the man was incredibly healthy for his age. At seventy-two, the dead man looked healthier than most fifty-year-olds he knew. Also, for a man who supposedly survived a fire when he was younger, reportedly having escaped through an open window engulfed in flames, his body bore no burns or even any scars that would indicate cutting himself on broken glass.

Range didn't know about that, but he had already had his suspicions about Paul Barnfell—mostly from stories told to him by his mother who had always spoken oddly about her father-in-law, with a guarded tongue and air of caution even when they were alone. He had also learned of the fire at the Manoa factory and the death of the Barnfell triplets due to his time spent researching in the library's catalogues before the disaster; but the part he couldn't figure out was, why anyone would want to impersonate a child—let alone one that came from a family famous for being indignant farmers that had more gruesome murders centered around them than any normal family should.

He found his answer, though. I know it's silly, but I find some solace in that, however ridiculously trivial it seems—that at least he knew the truth about his family before he died.

The door creaked loudly as it opened, a squeal of protest as the dull glow of the basement stairwell was flooded with false sunlight, the pale rays that managed to break through the layer of cloud and fog. Her damp socks sunk into the carpet as she pulled herself from the dark depths, the sticky substance squishing between her toes like mud. There was a soft splat of her feet as she walked, and she could feel drops of the stuff rolling down her face, even if she dared not admit to herself what it really was.

The smell of iron was thick in her nostrils, the taste of copper fresh on her lips. Moving gracelessly, she stamped into the nearby bathroom and spun her hand round the glass knob above the sink labeled with a giant *H* and threw her face under the rushing stream from the faucet, without so much as a glance at the mirror that covered the whole of the wall before her. Letting the water trickle and fill her hands, she splashed it over her face, rubbing it deep into her pores. She felt the blood… so simple to think of it like that, something you get from a small cut or wound, even though she probably had several liters of the stuff covering her, all from her own…

She washed the thought away with the rest of the grime, ignoring the feeling of digging the blood in deeper into her skin, or merely pushing it around. It felt like it had sprouted claws and started to cling to her skin, like a tick burrowing its way into her flesh, festering deep down while it lay its eggs within her. Grabbing the towel and pressing it to her face, she gave out a small scream, muffled by the fabric but ringing in her ears so loud that it blocked out the world around her and left her only to the ghastly images that had been replaying themselves in her mind like a highlight reel.

Gwen let the towel fall into the rim of the sink, settling into the murky brown water near the drain as she looked up into the mirror. There were still streaks of red across her forehead and through strands of her hair. An entire side of her head was dark and matted, and when she brought her hand to it, it came back absolutely covered in the stuff. Her nose, small and mousy, had been coated to the point that she had a hard time seeing it until she rubbed her thumb against it, revealing her porcelain-white skin underneath. Her green eyes, usually so vivid and bright despite every other plain aspect of her, seemed to have grayed and dulled so much that she hardly recognized them.

Silently, diligently, she finished washing her face clean, save for a few heavy splotches that the ruined towel couldn't get without leaving a streak of red just as deep, and then moved back into the hallway quiet as a ghost. Without a word, she moved into the living room, into a conversation that had already devolved into petty arguing, her approach unnoticed by everyone in the room—except, of course, for Range, who looked to her as soon as she entered but kept silent. His dark eyes seemed to stare right through her, seeing everything.

"All I'm saying is that there's a difference, mo'fucka, it's not that complicated."

"Well, obviously, if you're lecturing me on it."

"And what I'm saying is that I still don't even see why it matters."

"Shiet, man, of course, it fucking matters. All a nigga's trying ta do is figure out what those ugly mo'fuckas out there are exactly."

"I thought you already knew what they are. You went on that whole spiel of yours back at he station about how 'nobody ever believes it's zombies' and whatnot."

"Well, yeah, but are they infected, or just regular, old bitch-ass zombies."

"How is that any fucking different?"

"Man, and you all be calling me the stupid one, like I'm the one that ain't know nothing. Ya'll mo'fuckas don't even know the difference between a goddamn walker and an infected. Let me see if I can break it down in real simple-to-understand, laid man terms for you, niggas. Who here has seen the movie *28 Days Later*?"

Matt, with his eyes practically rolling all the way up into his forehead, raised his hand unenthusiastically—along with Veronica and Tyler, whose hand was up before he even finished asking them the question. With a look of reproach, Range eventually raised his own hand as well, before his wide eyes came back to Gwen, who did her best to shrink away from them.

"C'mon? That's it? How the hell have half of you not seen that shit?"

"Is that the one where Julia Roberts has the baby with Hugh Grant? The pregnancy movie, right?" Vel asked.

"Why would I be asking if ya'll had seen a movie with corny-ass Hugh Grant?"

"I figured you were planning on confessin' how big a fan of his you were," Bruce said with a sly grin wrapped around his cheeks.

"No, I ain't talking about the movie where some English pansy ass knocks up some ginger. The movie with some other English guy walking through London, all abandoned and shit. And he's all screaming 'Hello? Hellooooooooo?'" Tyler mimicked this action by cupping his hands tight around his mouth and producing a tinny wail. "'Is anyone out there? Wah, wah, wah.' That movie."

"Oh, where he's wearing the blue hospital gown?" Billy asked meekly.

"See, this little bitch knows what I'm talking about!"

Billy smiled glumly from the pseudo compliment paid to him, burying his hands into his armpits after briefly raising his own with the others.

"Why do you care if we've all seen some shitty movie, shithead?" Veronica said, her impatience coming easily.

"Whoa, whoa, whoa, *28 Days Later* is far from a shitty movie, beautiful." Tyler brought his hands up to try and run his fingers through the hair around her ears tenderly, causing Veronica to swat at him with a plain look of disgust as if his hand had been a cockroach flying too close.

Undeterred, Tyler continued, "*28 Days Later* is what changed the fucking game. It's what turned zombies from the slow, shuffling motherfuckers always going on about brains into slimy, fast-charging, uber violent beasts. It gave 'em street cred, if you feel me on that. They went from some clumsy mofos you could knock over with a quick push into something that would chase you into a corner where thirty more of its friends would start tearing you limb from limb while you're still squirming."

"They did that shit in *Day of the Dead* too. We saw that shit in theaters when we were skipping class."

"True, but I'm talking, like, violent tearing, 'shaking of the jaw'–type shit. Rabid dogs in human skin, you feel me? They move fast. They sprint, and they ain't dead."

"What do you mean they're... not dead?"

"I mean, they ain't dead. Damn, open you ears. This shit ain't rocket science. They're infected, thus the name. Is that so complicated? Shit."

Tyler took another long drag from the blunt in his mouth, although if this was the same one from before her trip to the basement or a new one that he rolled after finishing his previous one, Gwen couldn't be sure. With the speed of which he was going through them, she'd be more surprised if it wasn't the latter.

"They're infected with what?"

"I don't fucking know, nigguh. It depends on the movie. *28 Days Later* has some rage virus, or some symbolic bullshit like that, while most others just have it as some random undiscovered virus that somehow has the power to reanimate dead tissue or some generic science lingo like that."

"So what? You think those things out there are infected or something like that? Not dead?"

"They seem pretty fucking dead to me," Gwen interjected, not even realizing she had done so until the group turned to face her, their piercing gazes cutting through her like razor wire.

Her hair stood up on the back of her neck as she anticipated the inevitable flurry of questions regarding the flecks of blood that covered her clothes, but the group merely nodded in agreement, ignorant to the deep crimson stains that covered her as if they had been there the whole time. In fact, when Gwen looked herself over again when everyone's attention returned to their no-nonsense, contemplative debate of the dead human condition, she could admit that she had trouble picking out her mother's blood from the rest that she had picked up in her trek across town. However, to Gwen, the difference was as obvious as the difference between types of movie monsters was to Tyler's drug-fueled brain.

"I ain't saying they're infected. If anything, I'm saying the opposite."

"So you're saying what? They're just plain, ol' regular zombies? Well, isn't that a relief, you guys! They're just regular, run-of-the-mill zombies, nothing to worry about here."

"Go fuck yourself, Matty. I ain't saying they ain't dangerous or any shit like that, but the strategies to survive are different, depending on what type of bloody mo'fucka you got trying to eat your ass like it's a five-piece chicken meal." Tyler took another drag and exhaled a cloud of smoke through a shit-eating grin as he eyed Veronica again, much to her chagrin. "And in your case, sexy, I ain't talking about myself."

"Ugh, you're repulsive. I don't know why my brother hangs out with you."

"He's a great wingman, makes you look like Gandhi by comparison."

Matt tugged uncomfortably at his jeans as he stepped between Tyler and his sister, his eyes glazing over and disappearing into his own thoughts. As he neared Veronica, she herself took several steps back from him with darting eyes, placing Vel between the siblings—a betrayal that went unnoticed by Matt's distracted gaze.

"So what you're saying—at least, what I think you're saying," Bruce said, trying to redirect the derailing conversation back onto its broken tracks, "is that you have some kind of contingency plan for a zombie outbreak, in the very, extremely, highly unlikely case that one ever took place? One that varied depending on types of zombies that I didn't know existed until five minutes ago."

The silence that filled the room was thicker than the fog beyond the window panes, so thick that a buzz saw would have trouble slicing through it neatly. Several eyes looked back and forth between their ragtag assembly of survivors, all trying to weigh their chances of survival based on the occupants of that small, jasmine-scented room of flickering candles and sweating when the odds came up heavily stacked against them.

"You say it like I'm the weird one. Honestly, it's much more weird that ya'll don't have a plan for the zombie apocalypse. Seriously, what the fuck do ya'll do with your free time except be a bunch of boring fucks, I'm tellin' ya."

"So can we get back to the original question of what the hell those things outside are? Are we all in agreement they're zombies then? However fucking stupid it sounds to actually say out loud?"

The circle of souls gave slow, stubborn nods to the question, while Tyler sat in his armchair, deep in thought, or his version of it, a stern look decorating his hard features.

"Somewhat. They seem to be sorta trans-zombies. You feel me? A little of both."

"Yeah, I don't feel you on that one at all."

With an exasperated grunt, Tyler shifted in his chair, leaning forward like a professor giving a lecture to a particularly troublesome student, a situation Gwen had no doubt Tyler had been on the opposite side of many times in his life.

"I'm saying they've got aspects of both—the bite thing. While not exclusive to the motherfuckers, that's an infected thing. The virus usually travels via saliva or whatever, some dumb shit like that. Then again, they also did that same shit in *Return of the Living Dead*, but it's the fast-moving, vicious motherfuckers that really adopted it.

"Now these slow-moving, nasty mo'fuckas with exposed brains and shit, they seem like your typical zeds. As dumb as they are ugly, really only a threat if they gang up on ya in large numbers, like bitches you find at the bar at 4:00 a.m. I know you feel me on that one, Matty. These are your typical flesh-eating, walking *Dawn of the Dead* zambonis."

"Hold up a minute. Now, I've seen *Dawn of the Dead*, and those bastards moved pretty quick to me."

"Well, yeah, in the remake, which came out after *28 Days Later*, when fast zombies was all the rage and shit. It's the reason why the 'seventies version is always gonna be superior, fam. Give me a classic half-decayed geek over some bloody-nose sick patient any day, motherfucker."

"Well, that's usually always the case, isn't it? The old stuff is usually always better," Billy said, nodding to himself.

"What is that supposed to mean?" Veronica inquired.

"Well, you know, just like in general, I guess? You know what I mean, everything in the past was just simpler, you know? Music was better and actually required some kind of talent to produce. Literature was actually important, with authors like Hemingway writing about the fruitlessness of war instead of whatever new adventure some shitty teen wizard is getting into. People actually seemed to give a damn about culture. Women went out dressed in clothes meant to make them look elegant. Now they go out dressed in clothes tight enough to make a prostitute blush."

"I think you might be a little confused," Veronica interrupted, Billy's rant cut short with a sharp look that turned his cheeks to crimson as if they'd been struck by an open palm. "Girls from the past probably wouldn't have fucked you either."

Billy sputtered helplessly, his tongue carelessly throwing out syllables in an attempt to counter Veronica's verbal jab; but heavy, animated laughter from the hyenas besides her already began to fill the room. Even Vel had to stifle a few laughs behind curled fingers held to her petite lips, a lazy attempt to cover her overexposed gums. Left speechless and exasperated, Billy whirled to face Gwen, his beady eyes tearing into hers for some kind of meaning. It was impossible for Gwen not to notice, but nothing seemed to be registering—all her nerves burned out to such a degree that it felt like the world was simply a play put on in front of her, caught in throes of an early, drunken dress rehearsal.

Still, Range's gaze held her, for he alone seemed to actually see her, to actually tell just whose blood was thrown over her, whose blood was slowly settling into her pores, burrowing its way into her flesh…

"Hey, now, leave the kid alone. He's just a little idealistic, that's all. Let me tell ya, Billy, was it?" Frank asked, groaning slightly as he shifted himself away from the wall, a pale bust of Jesus himself wobbling as he did so. "I get what you're saying, but you can trust me when I tell you that people are the same now as they've ever been. We're interesting creatures, unique from God's other creations in that we seem to preserve things that we determine to be greater than us, but we have to filter out a lot of shit to do so. That's why the past always seems better, or more refined, as you would have it. You remember Led Zepplin, but luckily, most people have forgotten

Captain and Teneille. They remember Donna Summers, but they forget the fifty women who sounded exactly like her—trying to capture that same spark, fill that same niche, that flooded the airwaves week after week. Although, and I hate to sell you up the river here, kid, but I think she might have your number on the whole women thing."

There were several more snickers from Veronica's camp, and several more spastic stutters from Billy's; but afterward, the room became uncomfortably quiet, as if everyone was squirming in their own skin.

"That mother of yours," Frank said, breaking the silence like a rusty tire iron scraping broken glass. "I remember her. I didn't at first, but I've been thinking about it, about my own time at Sunday school and the like. My father knew your grandfather. Reverend Sinais, correct? Thought quite highly of him, if I remember correctly. Of course, I was just a child, and you don't question much at the age I was at, but I remember him coming to our house one afternoon to bless our new house. I was terrified of him for some reason I couldn't put my finger on. He tried to talk to me, but I was a shy child. Like I said, not much has changed."

He wore a sad smile on his face, his eyes intently watching a scene play out before them, one that had taken place many decades before.

"I don't think I'll ever forget what he said to me. Gosh, I was so terrified it's as vivid in my mind now as it was back then. 'Listen up, Frank,' he told me, 'you have to be a good boy, the very best boy you could be. Always do as your parents ask, but more importantly, always do what God asks, because only by doing what God wants can we ever appease him. To give in to temptation, that is death. To turn yourself away from God, that is the very death of the soul. Similarly, only through God can true happiness ever be found, and anyone who didn't accept him or his teachings is doomed to a fate worse than death, of fire, brimstone and suffering for all eternity. If I didn't change my ways,' he said, 'stop getting in trouble in school and the like, the devil would pick his teeth with my bones every day while I wailed endlessly for God to save me. A cry he would turn his back on, just like you turned your back on him.' Keep in mind, his words. not mine."

"That's some pretty heavy shit for a kid. You didn't actually believe that shit, did you, Frankie?"

"I did, for a while, at least. I think everyone has a falling out with the church once they get older, old enough to realize the basic hypocrisies and the dated ideologies. It doesn't take a particularly smart man to notice how odd it is that a book mentions stoning women as an acceptable punishment for disobeying her husband in one chapter and instructing you to love thy neighbor in the next. But for a few years there, I did. I cleaned up my act, started living in fear of what God might think about everything I did, to the point where I was scared to do anything anymore. I'd stop sneaking deserts after dinner. Stop thinking of which girls at school I thought were pretty. Sometimes I wonder…" he trailed off, his voice soundlessly moving on without him as an air of melancholy took over.

A deep sadness filled his eyes, like saucers of sour milk, a deeply troubled gaze that warred on with some internal battle. Even with silence, Gwen stood enraptured, her knees shaking as soon as she heard mention of her grandfather's name.

"I still have my faith," he said after a violent shake of his head. "Sometimes I doubt it's there myself, but it is. I think it's as foolish now as I did when I left the church, but it's something you just can't seem to shake. The more I've thought about it, the more I think that the reason I can't is because maybe that's the part that seemed the most real to me—the most authentic. It didn't seem right to label others as evil, to declare them damned for all eternity, just because they didn't go to church the same day of the week we did or didn't stop eating meat for forty days. But the idea of holding on through the worst of times, hard set in the belief that things will get better—could get better—that's the part I liked. That's the reason I still believe. It's hard to, now, especially in the face of all this, but it's a comfort. I'll give it that, at least."

"No, you're right," Vel chimed in, meekly. "When I was… well, back when I was… going through a bit of a hard time… emotionally, I was sent to a support group that prayed before and after every meeting. A lot of the members would get together and go to mass together at this local rectory. They invited me to come with them at least ten times before I finally gave in and went, but I gotta say… there was something… comforting about it, right? I mean, the rituals and all the kneeling and stuff seemed odd at first, I'll admit, and I probably embarrassed myself there more than I'd like to admit, trying to recite prayers I'd never really learned. I don't know how they convinced me, but I went back with them the next week, and… I don't know. Nothing was really different, but I felt… accepted there, like I belonged to something larger than myself and all that. I knew some of the words and some of the motions. I knew some of the names attached to the smiling faces around me, and I felt… safe, I guess, more so than I had in a long time.

"I went for several more weeks after that, but… I'm not sure why, but I guess the zeal just disappeared. I got my job as a waitress a little while after that and had to work the night shifts on Saturday, and I told myself, 'It's okay, you'll go twice next week,' then three times, and four, until I couldn't remember the last time I went anymore. I didn't feel guilty exactly—almost disappointed. And that was almost worse, like when your parents get a phone call from school telling them you were reading magazines in study hall instead of doing your required work.

"I still go sometimes, though, mostly holidays, or the days when everything seems especially gray. Today would've been a nice day, although I guess it was a good thing I didn't, in retrospect. I'm not sure why I still go, really, but I guess that means I believe, at least a little bit."

"Maybe you both should switch to Buddhism then or something, one of the less crazy religions, one that doesn't involve killing or maiming those that don't agree with you. So Islam's definitely off the table," Matt said glumly.

"You guys should subscribe to Rastafarianism, like I do. It's definitely more relaxed than all this shit with switches and nailing dudes to crosses and all that ish."

"You realize Rastafarianism is based on more than just smoking a retarded amount of pot, right? Ideas that sort of clash with the whole 'shooting a bunch people' thing."

"Nigga, all I've shot is a bunch of nasty-ass, cheese-dick zombie mothafuckas that have been trying to eat my ass and the motherfucking sheriff. You know who else shot a sheriff? Bob Fucking Marley."

"While I do love me a good philosophical discussion about the ethics of shooting cops, now may not exactly be the best time for it," Bruce said sharply, sliding the chair out from under him as he stood.

The legs of the chair dug into the carpet and produced a sound like a rough tear as they dragged across the sinuous wool fibers. The gold badge on the lapel of his shirt seemed to almost produce its own light now, borne proudly across his chest as it caught the light of the room.

"We need to figure out what our plan of action is. I'm not entirely opposed to just holding up here 'til morning if need be, but I'm open to any better suggestions."

No one spoke immediately, everyone leaning close to the other with the mild anticipation that someone else would serve them their salvation on a silver platter in a nicely wrapped bow. As the seconds ticked passed and a plan didn't materialize out of thin air, a cold sweat began to appear on several already-slick brows. The heat from the candles seemed almost oppressive, a thousand flickering heat sources centering on the small group gathered in the living room.

Gwen's throat felt raw and haggard, but something compelled her to speak. She wasn't entirely sure if it was because she knew no one else would or because the silence was giving her too much time alone with her thoughts and the images that danced across them.

"Range mentioned something at the library that might be useful in stopping these things, if they even can be stopped."

"Stopping them? Bitch, I already know how to stop 'em. A shot of lead to the head and the dead stay dead."

"I mean, all of them at once, dick bag."

"What? You mean like a cure?" Bruce asked.

"I don't know. Ask Range."

All their eyes settled on him, his blond hair drooping over his eyes so that they were covered by a sheer yellow curtain.

"Not exactly, but something to a similar effect."

"I don't think I follow…"

"Listen. It doesn't matter," Gwen said, surprised at her own tenacity. Turning back to Tyler, she asked, "You talked about having a plan to deal with these things."

"Well, sorta. I mean, they're your typical slow-moving zombies, so the best course of action would be to hole up somewhere and try and survive until help arrives. That way, you can keep the fuckers off you without having to waste all your ammo to do so."

"Will the library work? As a place to fortify?"

"Bitch, you think I've ever been to a library?"

"Hey, can you do me a favor and not call her that?" Range said.

Tyler scoffed and shook his head while exhaling a voluminous column of thick smoke. "I didn't mean it as an insult. Bitches is just what I call bitches, 'aight? Damn."

"Trust me. You're not gonna win this one. It's better just to pretend he said something an actual decent person might, like, 'sure' or 'whatever,'" Veronica said snidely.

If Gwen hadn't been so light-headed, she might've thought of her words as a form of kindness; but she knew it must simply be her rattled, oxygen-deprived brain playing tricks on her.

"The library's three stories tall, has two double doors and a revolving one at the front entrance, two fire exits round back, and a fire escape that extends down from the second and third floor on the northeastern side. It's the building with the gray roof in the center of a large parking lot—one so large that even if everyone in town suddenly got the urge to actually pick up a book, they'd still probably only be at half capacity," Bruce said.

Tyler's face took on the look of a man deep in thought, a look that oddly suited him, like someone that managed to pull off a uniform that they weren't keen on wearing in public.

"Where is this place again?"

Looking about with a sudden burst of urgency, Bruce rushed over to a small table near the front bay window that was relatively candle-free compared to the rest of the burning wax–adorned living room. With a brisk flick of his arm, he cleared the small pieces of china from its surface, small angelic figurines falling deftly onto the carpet in soft bounces, some losing their fragile wings and loosely administered halos in the impact. As they lay in the fluffy whites fibers of the dirty shag carpet, they almost seemed at home, save for the cracks that ran up their backs, splitting them from all that made them holy.

"Sorry about that," Bruce said to Gwen abashedly, his dark skin paling in the incandescent glow of the room.

"I'm just angry I wasn't able to smash the things myself," Gwen said, giving him a forced smile.

Bruce returned one just as strained and uncomfortable, his eyes darting back and forth from the floor.

Pulling a folded square of paper from his back pocket, Bruce hurriedly began pulling it apart at the corners. The small square doubled, then tripled in size, and so on until it covered the top half of Bruce's body while the table obscured the bottom. When fully straightened, the paper stood two feet wide and at least a foot and a half tall, divided into many small squares the same size as the paper when it had been pulled from the dark pit of the deputy's pockets. Laying it flat across the glass tabletop and smoothing the stubborn folds with the butt of his palm, Bruce displayed the map for all to see.

With several slow, wary steps, the group gathered round it like children circling a campfire for warmth and light and the promise of safety from the darkness of the woods behind them.

"So if my bearings are as intact as I think they are, we should be… right around her, correct?" His finger was square in the center of Gwen's cul-de-sac, tapping impatiently. Gwen gave a quick nod as confirmation, which seemed to satisfy him. "The library… is up here, past Essex and near Victoria Boulevard on the corner."

Leaning over the map, Tyler's red, sagging eyes moved lazily over the overhead view of the town, following the trail that Bruce's finger had made across it. Placing his own where the library supposedly resided, he dropped so low to the table that his cheeks were practically resting on it.

"Yeah, I have no idea where this is."

"It's a couple blocks northeast of the hospital, right across from the flower shop owned by Mrs. McCreedy."

When this two landmarks failed to produce any sort of reaction from Tyler's slovenly features, Bruce sighed and rubbed the bridge of his nose with tightly sealed eyes.

"It's a block before the Wendy's."

Tyler's mouth opened in a wide "Oh" as he looked back to the map, tilting his head like a confused dog, as if he was seeing the map in a new light.

"Well, I think I know where the Wendy's is, but I don't remember seeing no library or shit."

"We used to smoke in the parking lot every day after high school. The big parking lot with the pine trees on one side and the oaks on the other. We used to get drunk and bring girls there on the weekend."

Somehow, despite the gears clearly working behind the still mask he wore, Tyler struggled to place the spot in his memory.

With a groan, Matt mirrored Bruce's sentiment and ran his hand down his face, dragging his fingers through the short stubby hairs of five o'clock shadow.

"The place where you fingered Marla Gainsborough in my backseat."

As if a bolt of lightning burst through the ceiling and struck his frontal lobe, an act that would've brought a sick smile of validation and praise to the late Peggy Sinais's face, Tyler excitedly slammed his hand down on the table, setting its flimsy legs to trembling.

"*Oh*! The gimp with the bad leg? Oh, shit, I totally forgot about that. And I didn't know that bitch was splitting the red sea and she got those bloodstains all over the upholstery? Good times, man. Good times."

"I still don't know how you didn't notice," Matt said with a sly smile that made vomit rise to the back of Gwen's throat.

Veronica gave him a stare that could melt a glacier, one that turned his cheeks hot with shame as soon as he noticed it.

"I thought paraplegics didn't do that shit. How the hell was a mothafucka supposed to know that?"

"She wasn't paraplegic. Her father broke her leg when she was, like, three."

"All right, all right, so you know where this place is now? Can we just leave it at that?" Bruce said, cutting the story off before he learned any more of the enrapturing details.

"Yeah, yeah, yeah, I know the place, fire escape, three stories, and all that shit."

"*Two* stories. Is it going to work?"

"Man, I don't fucking know. Any building big enough should work as long as you got spots to back up if you get overwhelmed, not like that shit's gonna happen with a nigga tough as me, but for the ladies, you know?"

He put a particularly proud emphasis on the word *ladies* while giving a smugly satisfied gleam at Range. If Range even noticed, he didn't show it. Instead, his eyes were embedded on Gwen, his face a torrid storm of emotions that was hard to pin down as either debilitating anger or devastating sadness.

"Well, we can use the second floor as a retreat point. Hopefully, we can set up some kind of fail-safe to block the areas off if they start to swarm us. I don't know how much time we'll have, or if we'll be able to make it there without leading an army behind us, like a Pied Piper leading rats, if the rats decided to eat him instead when he grew tired of playing.

"We can use the fire escape then to head back down even if we lose both floors. The tightness of it should funnel them enough to clear out a few more on your way down, and the rest will probably clog themselves up, like arteries, knock themselves off, and the ground will take care of the rest.

"I actually think it might work. I'm still not entirely sold on the whole 'travel across town' part of the plan, but I'll admit my own don't seem to be any better. Does the building meet the requirements of this plan of yours?" Bruce said, peeling his eyes from the map and forcing them on Tyler.

Tyler's head was drooped low, his eyes playing on the floor, a dull smile on his lips. As the stretch of silence grew deeper, his head snapped up and darted between the various heads all locked on his.

"Uh… yeah, sure, I guess."

"You guess, or you know?"

"Uh, I know? Whatever one gets you off my dick about it."

Bruce's hand slammed down so hard on the table a crack went through the thin plate of glass that protected the fragile wood frame beneath. It had belonged to Gwen's grandfather, and her mother had opted for any way to preserve it for as long as they would need it—which, to her, would only be several decades until the Good Lord decided to destroy the world that he had made for mankind, a classic move from history's greatest Indian giver.

Trembling and bloody, Bruce lifted his hands from the remains of the glass, several deep shards buried in his skin, lacerations falling open as loose pieces slid from the wounds. Veronica turned her head away sharply at the sight of it, her hand leaping to her mouth. Vel began sprinting into the kitchen faster than Gwen had ever seen her move, disappearing through the archway while Range turned and trailed behind her.

She quickly reappeared behind him, carrying a crumpled clump of paper towels in her talon-like grip, holding them out in front of her like they were some kind of toiletry bomb. Range moved into the hallway, casting another long, sorrowful gaze at Gwen as he went past. She had to stop herself from following him—a part of her knowing where he was going, and a deeper part of her that she didn't like to acknowledge wanting him to see it.

Bruce grabbed the towels from Vel and pressed them to his palm, going to work on the shards still protruding from his flesh. His fingers twitched and spasmed uncontrollably, shaking as if Bruce had decided to stand on top of a tumbler.

"Sorry about that too, Gwen," he said, barely able to look at her.

With a smile he couldn't see, Gwen ran her hand down his shoulder, feeling the knots and scars and resisting the temptation to pull back from them.

Range returned, holding a trail of gauze that he had salvaged from the bathroom cupboard.

"I found these," he announced, "but no disinfectant."

"My mother wouldn't allow any alcohol in this house, except for maybe wine, but that was only after a priest had blessed it and deemed it the blood of Christ."

"So she'd rather have blood than alcohol in her house? And I thought you were a freak. But apparently, it gets diluted the further down the family tree you go," Veronica said, sounding more like her usual self.

Her face still seemed squeamish, constantly on the verge of losing whatever small breakfast she had managed to force down her throat that morning.

"Logic wasn't exactly her strong suit," Gwen said, stifling the harsher obscenities that had came to her mind first.

With a loud tear, Tyler unzipped the duffel at his feet and stuck his hand inside, digging around for something amidst the drugs and automatic weaponry. A smile grew on his face when he found what he was looking for, and he pulled out a slim bottle of clear liquid triumphantly.

He tossed the bottle of vodka to Bruce, catching him off guard, but somehow the deputy managed to get his hand up to stop the bottle in midair and catch it in the nook of his arm as it slammed into his chest. Looking the bottle over and cringing when he saw the proof and the price tag that was well under fifteen dollars, he reluctantly twisted off the cap. Bringing the top to his nose, his face shrunk into itself as he let out a long, hard, regretful sigh.

Still, he brought the bottle to his lips and threw it back, taking deep gulps before he pulled the stuff down into his stomach, practically dropping it as his body seized up in disgust. He held Vel and Gwen at bay, wearing a veneer smile as he did so, before placing his hand flat on the glass table.

With another long, mournful sigh, he upturned the bottle on his hand, gritting his teeth hard as he did so. Even so, his hand began to writhe like a trapped spider, his fingers extending and slamming against the glass and twisting themselves in an unnatural positions.

Somehow, he didn't scream, even though his teeth ground together hard enough that Gwen was sure filings would begin falling from his mouth like early snowfall.

"Easy there, mo'fucka, you're tough as fuck, but save a little for me, that's my only bottle."

Sharply, Bruce turned the bottle back over and slammed it onto the table, shaking it again to the point that Gwen was more impressed that it was still standing than upset in any capacity.

Bruce gave out a low rumble of pain, the most that he allowed himself, and dropped to his knees so fast that it looked like he had lost consciousness. Instead, he stopped just above the ground and let his hand tremble on the table above him, flexing his fingers in and out as he did so.

"You need to start taking this seriously," he said while hobbling to his feet.

He nearly collapsed, but Vel was fast enough to catch him, putting herself under his arm for support. As soon as he righted himself, he gave her another formal pleasantry and sent her away, ignorant to the look of hurt that flashed across her face.

"I don't care if you don't care about your own, worthless life. I can understand why you wouldn't. But there are other people's futures at stake here, and even if you somehow can't give enough of a rat's ass to at least pretend like that matters to you, then maybe I made a mistake by letting you out of that cell, although I think I already knew that."

Smiling, Tyler got to his feet, pulling the blunt from his lips and tapping the ash from its tip arrogantly on the floor.

"Maybe you did, pig. Maybe you did."

Their gazes met—Bruce's hard and resigned, while Tyler's seemed almost jovial as if he understood something that everyone else did not. In that, he reminded her of Range, to the point where she was beginning to feel sick just thinking about it.

"But I'll play along," Tyler said with that jester's grin of his, grabbing the bottle from the table and taking a swig of it himself. Grimacing, his smile finally faded, but the buoyant attitude remained. "At least for now."

Bruce nodded, prying his hand from the puddle of vodka on the table and placing it into the folds of his arm.

"Now then," he said, dropping the index finger of his good hand on the map near Gwen's street, "we're here, and the library…" he dragged his finger northeast across half of the map at least to the upper right corner, circling a building larger than those around, "is here. It's about five or six miles away. Moving as fast as we could, we'd probably be able to make it there before nightfall, but it's been getting darker earlier than usual, and the fog isn't doing us any favors."

Moving his finger back across the imaginary road between the library and Gwen's house, he stopped at a larger structure in the middle of town and tapped his finger mechanically, "We can stop at the hospital along the way to gather supplies. If things go bad, we might even be able to hold up in there instead."

"In the building where they store a bunch of sick and dying people? Yeah, no thanks, I'm actually trying to avoid the zombies instead of running right into their dining room," Veronica interjected.

"The girl raises a good point. That place has gotta be swarming with the bastards. I mean, how many bodies do you think they had in the morgue, let alone how many helpless patients that were confined to their beds when this whole mess started," Frank said.

"Wait, why would the people in the morgue matter? They were already dead, weren't they? Are you telling me that *any* dead thing is coming back to life? Even people that've been dead for what? Decades? Centuries?"

Gwen's heart leaped into her throat, trapping her words there before she could answer. If she had given more thought to it and been able to go back in time, along with many, far more important things, she would stop herself from ever saying anything. But the group had noticed her twitch and stunned silence, and their eyes were firmly focused on her wavering lips.

Instead of cleverly excusing herself with any kind of easy excuse, she said, "Yes. I think so, at least. Range and I saw… the dead rising from their graves in the cemetery near the edge of town."

"You saw what?"

"Oh, Jesus fucking Christ."

"Careful, nigga, he might actually hear you in this place."

"How long ago was this?" Frank asked, more calmly than the rest, even though his fear was brimming just beneath the surface of his easy facade.

Gwen looked at Range, unsure as to whether she had made a huge mistake or a monumental one, and expected a disapproving look that would send what little remained of her into a dark abyss from which there was no escape; but none came, only a troubled one to match her own.

"Last night. But I'd been observing it for about a week now," Range said, answering for her, his troubled eyes still floating above the map as if he was taking himself on a private sky tour of the town.

"You've been what now? Did you say for a week? You saw dead people rising out of the fucking ground for a week, and you didn't say anything?" Veronica shouted, exasperated. "I take back the autistic thing. That's an insult to autistics. You're full-blown retarded, aren't you?"

"Hey, a lot of people find that word really offensive," Tyler said.

"That means a real lot, coming from you."

"What was I supposed to do? Run to the police and tell them I saw a zombie in the graveyard? Especially following the news that my cousin supposedly ran off with one of the bodies he was supposed to be burying there? How well do you think that would've gone over?"

"Well... well... you could've showed them or something!" Veronica sputtered angrily.

"I showed someone," Range said, his eyes finally enveloping Gwen's and turning her insides to a sticky, sweltering mush.

"So you're telling me that not only do we have to deal with a good chunk of the town's population as undead, blood-slobbering freaks—if not *all* of them—but also everyone who's ever made the mistake of dying in this shithole? I mean, what the fuck? How many of those fuckers does that make? Over two thousand at least, and that's me being optimistic here," Matt said.

"Well, I mean, actually the town's got a base population of a little over a thousand already, a number that's been pretty constant throughout the town's history, if not higher during its boom times.

And given the amount of tragedies recorded during those times, I'd say the number would easily be closer to five thousand or so," Billy said, his fingers doing figure 8s in the air in front of him, as if writing on some invisible chalkboard.

Gwen noticed he did it a lot when he was trying to explain something he was particularly nervous about. He had done it during every presentation they had ever given, even when he was hiding himself behind an oversized piece of white poster board.

"Thanks for that, Rain Man. I'll make sure to bring you to Vegas and buy you a monkey suit next time I go," Matt said heatedly, the bloom of the candles matching the intensity worn on his face.

"Leave him alone. He was just trying to help answer your stupid question," Gwen said.

Upon hearing this, Billy's back straightened, and he seemed to grow at least a foot taller, his gentle sway turning into what was close to a drunken swagger.

"Stupid? Sorry that I care about how many of the zombies that want to peel my skin from my bones, like an orange, are out there. Guess I'm just be overly cautious."

"How many there are isn't gonna mean shit when we're actually out there. Either they find us, or they don't. There's what? Nine of us? What difference is two thousand versus five thousand gonna make? If we get overwhelmed, we're done for. The only thing we can do is keep moving and make sure we don't get bunched up."

Matt's mouth started up even though he had no words prepared for it, and all that came out was a frantic stutter, his groundless position crumbling out from under him. With unbidden frustration, he gritted his teeth like sandpaper and slammed his fist into the wall, knocking frames from their hooks and turning the picture of Jesus breaking bread with his disciples on its side.

"Can we not break everything in my mother's house?" Gwen said, the words turning to ash in her mouth.

It sounded strange to say, like a charade she was playing, trying to pretend that everything was normal while her mother's blood decorated her shirt like spilled paint. It felt wrong. She had spent so much time dreaming of her escape, the release of this weight chained to her back; and now, here she was, acting like nothing had changed, almost believing it herself.

"Send me a fucking bill," Matt mumbled, moving to a chair in the corner and plopping down into its center as angrily as one can relax into a chair.

"All right, that's enough. We don't have time for this. It's already nearly four thirty, and we haven't even left yet," Bruce said, clapping his hands together, like a teacher trying to gather his unruly students. Turning to Tyler, he asked, "How many more firearms you got in that duffel bag of yours?"

With the red-hot glow of his cherry taking up all his attention, Tyler barely noticed the question, and it wasn't until Bruce snapped his fingers excitedly in front of his face and the long trail of ash fell into his lap.

"Uh… I got plenty. What's your point?"

"We should distribute them out before we leave."

"Distribute them out? The fuck? The two mo'fuckas who don't have one can just come and grab 'em. I ain't picky about my pieces."

"You're worse at math than I expected, and they were already as low as I thought they could possibly go. Five people need guns, moron," Veronica said, her chuckle so filled with condescension that it seemed almost natural.

Tyler's face seemed to go blank, his eyes glossing over as his weed-roasted mind tried to work out the difference in his head, the obvious answer eluding him. Like a lightbulb going on in a room filled with dead animals, Tyler's features changed from comprehension to disgust so fast that the two were almost impossible to distinguish.

"Nah. Nah. Nah. Nah. Nah. Nah. Nah. Nah, nah, nah, nah, nah! There ain't no damn way in hell that I'm giving a goddamn gat, my goddamn gat, to a bunch of goddamn hoes!"

"You've got to be fucking kidding me."

"Do you want us to die? Because if half of our group can't defend itself, we're basically walking right into death, and you know it."

"Actually, I don't wanna die, and that's exactly why I ain't about to give a gun to no damn girl. That's practically asking for a bullet in the back. If we're lucky, only half of their shots will come close to us, and I'd rather not waste the ammo on bitches that don't even know how to hold a gat, let alone actually spray a couple geeks. Besides, the way I've been treated so far, one of 'em will probably try and shot me with it as soon as I hand it to 'em."

"Well, I wasn't going to before, but now…" Veronica said.

"I've actually been to a gun range before," Vel said, raising her hand weakly. Stepping forward from the shadows that swirled around the hall, she rubbed her arms tenderly as if for support. "Only a couple times, but by the last time, I only missed the target twice."

"You went to a shooting range?" Matt asked, quizzically. "You don't really strike me as the 'guns n' ammo' type of girl."

Abashed, Vel added, "I'll admit I wasn't too into it. I was really just trying to impress this guy that worked there, even though I kinda hated it, honestly."

"See? Vel already knows how to shoot, and I'm a quick learner, although I can't really say the same for Veronica," Gwen said, the grin feeling uncomfortable on her face.

"Ha-ha. Give me one, and I'll show you how fast I am, Gwennie. Probably not as quick as that boyfriend of yours, though."

Luckily, Billy said something before Gwen could share her own comeback, leaving her to swallow it and mildly fume with blushing cheeks.

"I mean, I've never even fired a gun before, so she's already probably more help than I would be."

"Well, I already knew your scrawny ass would be no help, so that ain't much of a surprise, Pee Wee Herman–looking motherfucker. Maybe I should just hol' on to the guns I got left. Save 'em for when I run out of ammo."

Bruce strode over to where Tyler was standing, placing himself square in front of him, his broad shoulders towering over him like a monolith. Slowly, with a hint of malice but enough gentleness that put even Gwen on edge, Bruce brought his hands down on the arms of the chair, his finger slowly coiling around the carved wood, his back arching with him.

"Either you give the guns up willingly, or we'll take them from you."

The umbrage in Bruce's throaty growl was enough to cause Matt to stir from whatever fantasy had occupied him since his outburst. He hopped up from his seat in the corner, but Bruce barely looked up from Tyler's hardened visage.

"Even if your friend there decides to help, it's the two of you against the rest of us. Do you think the both of you could handle that? I mean, physically, you might have a chance, but could you really do it? Huh, tough guys?" Pausing with a grin that would make a fox nervous, his mind seemingly having snapped and finally given way to the madness, Bruce looked up at Matt. "I mean, your sister's one of the people who wants a gun. You gonna kill her too? Like you did your boss? Solve your problems the easy way? You gonna protect her the whole way even though she can't bear to look at you half the time?"

This final question seemed to deflate him, his grizzled face sagging into one of dejected sadness that took any intimidation he might've had and turned it into a bitter self-resentment that dragged his shoulders down with him.

"Just give him the guns, Tyler," Matt said slovenly, plopping himself haughtily into his chair and burying his head into the flats of his palms.

With one final look back, Tyler sighed dejectedly and kicked the duffel bag out from between his feet. The contents spilled onto the floor, the steel dancing with the light of the candles in a kind of aural ballet.

"All right, all right, just fucking take 'em, like I give a shit."

Ponderously and with great caution, more so a respect garnered only through appropriate fear, Gwen stepped forward toward the pile of weapons and looked down the barrels staring up at her. She swore that if she stared hard enough, she could see the glint of a bullet looking back at her, but she knew it couldn't be the case. Half of them probably weren't even loaded. Probably.

Taking another look at Tyler as he grumpily mumbled to himself, rolling more of the sticky green crumbles into an unwrapped cigar, she started to believe that maybe she wasn't seeing things after all.

"I want the biggest one," Veronica said, pushing her way past Frank and Billy, knocking the latter into a side table as she did so.

Stepping up to the pile across from Gwen, she knelt and started pulling the loose contents of the bag out onto the floor. As she did, a rifle that looked more at home in a video game than her Christian mother's living room floor tumbled out, the clack of its grip sounding too much like gunfire for Gwen's taste.

"No automatics. We're trying to move unnoticed, not to throw a ticker tape parade announcing our location," Bruce asserted.

"Ugh, fine," she said, like a child forced to eat an especially unappetizing pile of vegetables before dessert.

After minutes of browsing, sliding steel over steel, and a near scare where Veronica would've blown Vel's head off if the safety hadn't been on, she finally decided on a standard .38. Gwen was unsure what made it different from any other pistol, save for the clips that fed into the bottom of the grip instead of a six-shooter revolver, but Veronica seemed pleased with it.

Gwen herself picked up a silver magnum after seeing Range choose something similar. She felt somewhat silly for doing so, but she knew so little about guns that she was merely trusting his analysis of the situation. Plus it was adorable, in its own odd, demented sort of way. Veronica initially scoffed when she saw that the gun Gwen had chosen was larger than her own, but she quickly turned it into an assertion that Gwen needed one much larger to get herself off, making sure to produce an obnoxious "whooshing" noise as she strolled past Range, turning Gwen's cheeks to embers.

Vel quietly approached and left with a shotgun, the same kind that she had reportedly used at the range, notable for its range as well as its power. At least, that's what she claimed. Even with her supposed expertise, the gun looked out of place in her hands. She nearly dropped it twice as she walked back to her place in the circle.

As Billy approached, Tyler sat up in his chair, waving his hand wildly as he brought his lips across the pseudo cigar held in the other.

"Oh, no, you don't. Since you're so useless, apparently, I don't wanna waste a good gun on a fuckboy like you."

Bending over to the pile of deadly weaponry at his feet, he shuffled through the guns until he found a small .22 at the bottom and pulled it to the top.

"Here," he said, chuckling to himself, "thought I'd give you a little something to match your… personality."

"Can a bullet from this thing even kill one of those things?" Billy asked despondently, the color draining from his face.

"You better hope it can."

Tyler continued to laugh wickedly as Billy strode away, his body quivering, like a whirlwind had passed through the house's cramped corridors.

"You can pretend you James Bond or something. Tell all your boyfriends you like your ass shaken, not stirred, you know what I'm saying. Ah, shit, Matt did you hear that? Shit was classic, fam, I swear."

"All right, everybody, we've gotta move out soon before we lose what little daylight we have left. I'll give everyone five minutes to gather themselves before we go. Use the bathroom if you need to, because I don't know when we will stop next," Bruce said, sauntering over to the stairwell like John Wayne trying his best to play John Wayne.

"Jesus, you sound like my mother," Veronica said, her face scrunching to half its size.

It was an improvement in Gwen's book, but she decided to keep the thought to herself. It didn't stop her from grinning like an idiot, though.

Moving away from the hallways toward the kitchen, she saw Vel making her way to the back laundry room, eyeing the door to the basement. Gwen's legs went weak, and her head felt like lead as Vel's hand dropped to the knob.

"Stay out of the basement," Gwen said sharply, sharper than she meant to, but the intended effect remained as Vel recoiled from the door like a shock went through it.

Feeling the fluster return to her face, she started walking quickly toward the kitchen archway, hoping to dodge any questions about her rebuke. However, as she ducked under the smooth white paneling and her feet hit the cold, wet tile, Range was there, his eyes locked on hers.

"Did you find those flashlights?"

"What're you talking about?"

Stepping closer, his feet pounding on the tile and reverberating inside the dark caverns of her head, he replied, "You went down to the basement to look for flashlights. Did you find any?"

Gwen's stomach ached, bubbling and twisting inside her like a dying animal.

"I did, but they weren't working properly," she said dismissively.

She went to step around him, but he followed her and blocked her path with his body.

"You were down there awhile."

"Yeah, and? Why are you prying so much? Why do you even care? It's just a couple of stupid flashlights," Gwen said, losing control halfway through, tears tugging at the corners of her eyelids.

Trepidatiously, he moved closer, his hand raised almost defensively. He brought his fingers to her cheek and dragged his thumb across it, smearing the warm blood that coagulated there, making its coppery aroma fresh again.

"What the hell happened down there?"

His fingers danced up and caught the tears there, wiping it through the blood in an attempt to clean it. She pulled away from his touch, even though it was almost painful to do so, acidic on her already-raw skin. Every part of her begged to give in to the weakness, even more than before when it had seemed so easy; but she hadn't given in then, and she sure as hell wasn't going to now.

There was a thump—a heavy plop and slide, like a wet sack of bloody flesh being dragged across hardwood floor. It happened quickly but shook the wall behind them, setting the cabinets and the glassware within in them to wavering.

The thud came again, louder and more forceful than before, knocking loose several glasses perched above the sink, scattering shards of glass across the floor. The sound of dull scratches followed, nails clawing against the wall in fast, jagged repetitions. This thump and scratch continued and built to the point that it was all Gwen could focus on. Range himself had taken on a harder, more aggressive stance, his eyes wide as saucers that reflected the room around them. Gwen could see the fear in her face, the sweat forming on her brow even though it was cold enough to chill your very bones.

"What was that?" she said, nearly stuttering.

Another heavy thud. The others hustling and darting around the living room, previously oblivious to the crescendo occurring just outside, finally took note of the wall's tremors. Many of them stopped in their tracks, turning toward the east wall, confusion fueling their curiosity as much as unbridled terror.

"I think they found us," Range said quietly.

"Who found—"

The glass in the kitchen window disintegrated as a furry gray lump broke through, the glinting reflections of sun falling and adding to the field of shards that had once been the kitchen floor. Leaning over the sink, with the yellow frilled drapes framing it like a hideous picture from a delirious Dali on his deathbed, was the chittering head of a wolf.

Its fur was dirty and matted, clumps of mud and dead, crumbling leaves tangled in its twisting, greasy hair. Its jaw was twisted and distended, hanging open wide like that of a jackal or hyena, a monstrous grin that seemed mocking in nature. Its eyes were icy smears of white—not a pupil to be seen in that unending pureness, like fresh, unbroken snow that hid a decomposing body underneath.

Every feature gave the wolf an oddly human quality, like that of a disheveled madman. Its mannerisms and its struggle to squeeze its body through the cramped window frame made its grinning face look like one trapped in a permanent cackle, and the low rumble that echoed from its throat only added to the illusion.

Its body shook back and forth as its hind legs tried to push it toward its prey, the strained grunts and groans sounding more and more like laughter, until Gwen could fool herself no longer. The creature's paws bounced haplessly against the steel sink as its mouth bounced happily along with the terrible cadence, its laugh mocking them, destroying everything they once considered sacred and pissing on the ashes.

In one final, horrifying motion, the wolf's body arched and its back pressed up against the glass of the window, the remnants of glass tearing through its spine but drawing not even an ounce of blood. Bulging and straining against the tight space, a sickening mass moved through the lifeless thing, catching in its throat and choking its laughter.

Those who were wandering the living room and front hall had pushed their way into the kitchen and stood in stunned silence at the sight of the cackling animal and its bull froglike throat, its face moving from person to person, like it was taking in each of them, remembering who they were, marking them for death.

With a laugh that was quieter than the rest, almost like a small chuckle of amusement, the decaying beast gave a breathless heave; and out of its mouth poured a stream of writhing bodies and legs, dark masses pressing against each other, squirming as they forced their way out of the wolf's broken jaw. Looking down into the cast-iron sink, you could see a slowly building pile of spiders, snakes, and centipedes—all falling from the wolf's mouth, like a faucet with a broken handle.

Veronica screamed, which seemed to cause the creature a vast amount of delight, its muffled laughter returning even though its throat was home to millions of biting, twitching creatures.

Without hesitation, Range raised the gun in his hand and pressed it to the wolf's temple. The wolf's eyes narrowed and seemed to understand what it was that he was doing, causing it to laugh harder, its smile growing with the stream of insects and serpents that fell from its maw.

With a swift click of the trigger, and explosion of gas and fire, the wolf's head disappeared—leaving only its still carcass and the few remaining creepy crawlies that continued to descend from its remains, briefs flaps of fur and skin being the only suggestions that the cackling wolf once had a head.

"What... in the *fuck*... was that?" Tyler said, his hand seizing his heart, fingers clenched and balling up his T-shirt into a mass above of his chest.

Almost as if they were answering him, another wolf leaped in behind its friend's body, getting stuck in the window but snapping and snarling its elongated jaw just the same. It wore a smile similar to the one before it—a sick inversion of the noble, solemn creature that it once was.

Another broke through the sunlight in the living room, the breeze following with it. The drapes caught it and twisted it to the ground, where its legs spun uselessly in the air, an act that would've been comical if the wolf hadn't been missing half of its skin and leaving its innards in a trial behind it.

Not giving it a chance to recover, Bruce ran up to the beast as it tried to chew its way through the thin lace of the drapes, its muzzle scraping against the gun's barrel right before it sent a bullet into its skull, leaving a spray of blood and chunks of bone in its place.

"Everybody move! Now!"

Range corralled them all to the back door, urging them forward like a man on a runway. He practically shoved everyone past down the small alcove of stairs toward the screen door, stopping only to take a shot at the wolf trying to squeeze its way over its brother's body. Its ear disappeared, and instead of a howl, there was only that same twisted, all-too-human laughter.

Two more wolves leaped in through the living room window, their faces half bone and muscle, but even their skulls still wearing that same horrible grin, chuckling over a joke that only they seemed to know. They backed Bruce up into the kitchen, with the wolf above the sink taking a bite at his arm as it went by, but missed wide by several feet.

Nevertheless, Bruce still pulled back sharply, firing a round from the shotgun he carried into the living room and catching the creatures off guard.

One of them was split nearly entirely in two, its legs sent to one side of the living room and its head and left front limb went to the other, held together solely by a single stretch of intestine. The legs continued to thrash and kick as if nothing had changed, while the head merely slapped its paw against the ground, a cackle like that of a mischievous child.

The other wolf leaped aside, and the blast only cost it half of its back leg. It charged forward, its recent loss of limb doing nothing to slow it but only to change its direction. Instead of its low head barreling into Bruce, it crashed into the doors beneath the sink, its head splitting the wood in two.

The beast tried to shake itself loose, but the splinters and jagged edges held it tight, refusing to let go. The group backed out the now-open screen door, their portal back into the hellish world of which they had earned only a momentary reprieve—Tyler and Matt leading the charge, with others following fearfully behind them.

Bruce started to back up, falling over his own legs as he did so. He crashed into the door by the stairwell, causing Range to jump back up the steps between them and pull him to his feet. By now, the wolf had nearly freed itself from the cracked wood of the cabinet, its eye from the freed side of his head already focused on them with a morbid glee.

"Come on! Grab him, and we've gotta go!" Gwen found herself saying, reaching for Range and pulling him down by his shoulder.

As the three of them descended to the landing, the wolf pried itself free with one final, heavy yank of its head, tumbling over its backside into the counter behind it. Its legs excitedly slid over the linoleum tiles, trying to find a footing, just as Gwen backed out the screen door, feeling it slap against her side as she pulled Range and Bruce out with her.

The three fell back, out into the yard where Frank, Vel, and Billy waited to catch them just as the wolf leaped down the stairs. Its glistening, pus-coated teeth snapped right next to Bruce's face, but it crashed into the opposite wall hard enough to leave a dent in the drywall, powder falling down from the spreading cracks as the wolf rolled down the stairs into the basement.

As soon as Bruce and Range tumbled out of the house, the screen door slapping shut against it like muted applause, Gwen ran forward and threw the screen open again, reaching for the small brass knob that stuck out from the cracked white varnish like a sore thumb.

Wrapping her shaking hand around it, she slammed it shut, watching with wide eyes as the wolf, its loose tongue flapping around its distended jaws like a banner, burst up the stairs at her—the thick wood door turning its relentless charge into nothing but a soft thud, muffled laughter, and the quiver of long dead pine.

His breath hammered in his chest, reverberating through him until it was thunder in his head, crashing with every ragged gasp. Every inhale was to swallow fire, his lungs screaming out at him to stop, to slow down, to do anything to get the pain to stop. Still, ignoring this reprieve, he pressed on through the ache, urging his legs forward by willpower alone.

He had long lost track of who was still running alongside him. He had heard their pounding footsteps beside his own several blocks back, but soon, his heartbeat had been the only thing pounding in his ears.

A cold wind was bittersweet, cool to the touch but stinging in nature, leaving him numb as it passed through him. It whistled down the alley like a banshee, removing any thoughts Frank had of slowing his pace, even if he knew it to be something other than those creatures.

He could still see the laughing faces of the wolves, chasing behind him, their gaping smiles delighting in the chase of their prey. One had nearly gotten its teeth around his ankle. He had felt the rush of air as its jaws had snapped shut like a trap, long strands of saliva wrapping themselves around his skin instead.

Unable to push his body any further, Frank's feet stomped themselves out, slowing to a rigorous halt that almost threw him forward. He noticed a large green Dumpster near a service door tucked into an alcove and figured it a good enough place as any to hide himself away and catch what breath still remained to him.

Shuffling over to the small, shadowy nook, Frank collapsed inside it, his back hitting the wall as he slid down its bumpy length. The bricks dug into his spine, causing him agony all the way down;

but compared to what he had just been through, it seemed like a gentle massage from rough, callused hands.

When his rear end finally hit the pavement, the first thing he noticed was the dampness. Looking about and underneath him, he brought his hands to his face, haphazardly at first, before he noticed the smell.

Sticky crimson covered the wholeness of his palm, his nose rising in disgust as that copper aroma forced its way into his nostrils where it seemed to cling to the very hairs there. After literally catching himself red-handed—Frank, using his top-notch skills of deduction, looked at the cold ground beneath him and saw that he was in a puddle of the stuff. It stretched from the steel door with faded green paint to the end of the small alcove, with large bubbles forming at the edge of the door and rolling lazily across the surface toward him. Not wanting to find out what was making them, he managed to hoist himself back to his unsteady feet, taking a deep breath to steel himself as he did so.

Leaning his head round the corner, he scoped out the alley for any creature that lurked in its shadows, his ears sensitive to any stray noise outside his own disorganized breathing and the whistle of the wind. Upon first glance, nothing seemed awry or out of the ordinary—save maybe for the fog, which was thicker than any Frank had seen in his life, even when he had lived near the coast when he was younger, but that was another lifetime ago now.

A small thump and scrape from behind the door caused Frank to jump but catch himself at the last minute, backing slowly into the alley before he could inspect it any further. This haste seemed to be his undoing, as a formless shadow crashed into him out of the corner of his vision before he could even react, knocking him to the ground. His face slid through the puddle of cold blood, half the stuff going up his nose as he tried to breathe while the other half filled his mouth.

Sputtering, he tried to spit the substance out of his mouth, but the taste and the slick feel remained, making him gag with every breath and replacing it with the more familiar taste of vomit. He was sure he would've thrown up if he had any food to spare to it.

"Ah, Jesus Christ, Frank, are you all right?"

The voice was familiar, but he couldn't place it until he saw Matt's bewildered face looking into his own, wanting to laugh bitterly when he saw his own forlorn expression reflected in the young man's wide, relfective eyes.

His face was a matte painting of blood, fresh specks of the stuff splayed across his forehead, with drops of it falling from his cheeks. One eye twitched as a drop rolled down, hanging from his lashes, hindering what little visibility he already had.

"Yeah, I think I'm fine, a little worse for wear, but fine," Frank answered, patting himself over as if he needed to verify himself.

Matt gave a pained nod of his head, struggling to wipe the blood from his face as he did so, almost comically. Backing him toward the wall, Frank did his best to wipe the blood from the boy's face, but no matter what he did or how much of the stuff he smeared around, there always seemed to be more to take its place. It was only afterward he remembered that his hands were already covered in the same stuff he was trying to sop up, and he abashedly wiped them on his bands, his crimson cheeks hidden beneath his veil of blood.

With an annoyed grunt, Matt swatted his hand away, scowling darkly. "I said I'm fine, Frank. Now, where are the others?"

"I don't know, I lost them as soon as we hit the alley," Frank answered, doing his best to mask the hurt in his voice.

"Goddammit."

He slammed his fist into the wall hard enough to break the skin, but he hardly seemed to notice. His lips were twitching, and along with the faded blood that decorated his face, like tribal war paint, he looked like a genuine madman.

"One minute, she was right next to me, then I was by myself, with three of those nasty bastards on my heels."

Seeing Frank's concern that he hadn't lost his canine entourage, Matt gave a swift shake of his head, stooping to catch his breath as he did so.

The sharp clack of footsteps against asphalt made them both jump. Matt had his shotgun raised toward the intruder before Frank even had a chance to turn himself to face it. Suddenly aware of his own lack of weapon and feeling practically naked without it, like a dream where you realize only too late that you forgot to wear pants that morning, he patted the back of his jeans, hoping to feel the cold touch of steel. When instead he felt merely his own sweat-drenched, overheated skin, the memory of his fall replayed itself in his head as he watched all too attentively as his gun clattered to the ground, swirls of blood forming around it.

Looking to his feet, he saw the gun there, beckoning to him. The sound of charging footsteps was louder in his ears, more rapid with less space between them, and more human in that it sounded like shoes pounding the pavement instead of leathery, decayed paws. Of course, that could only be because their soles had worn all the way down to the bone, but the thought made his spine curl.

Dropping low, both out of the path of Matt's shotgun and within reach of his own firearm, Frank fell to one side and leaped awkwardly toward the dark, onyx-like steel, his fingers grazing it as he fell heavily to the ground. His joints ached and screamed at him for acting like such a damned fool, but he pressed on regardless, even without quite knowing his motivation why anymore, fumbling to get the slick weapon into his hand.

When he finally managed to get a grip that he was sure wouldn't slip as soon as he pulled the trigger, he raised his head, his arm following as if attached by string, and aimed down the sights—the barrel pointing into the center of Billy's zit-scarred forehead.

His hands went up defensively, shaking them back and forth as if he planned to push the bullets back with a gust of wind. His face was dirty and splattered with mud, save for the tracks of tears down his cheeks, his red eyes darting around the small alley from end to end and everything in between. He held his own small pistol limply between his fingers and bounced and twirled about his finger as his hands shook, so much so that Frank was sure it was going to fall and shoot the terrified kid in his foot.

"Whoa, whoa, put the gun down, Matt. It's one of ours."

Matt ignored his command and fixed his grip on the shotgun. "How do we know he hasn't been bitten? By those… things?"

"Well, for one, he isn't in pieces."

"Don't fuck with me, Frank."

"Oh, come off it, Matty. Look at him. He doesn't have a drop of blood on him. Maybe a good bit of dirt, but that ain't no reason to shoot a man. Now put the damn shotgun down."

Hesitating as if he needed more thought to sway him from action, for the first time that day, Frank was truly frightened as to what the boy was truly capable of. Still, he lowered his weapon all the same, even if it seemingly pained him to do so. He seemed to age physically at least a decade, his face a scrunched-up mask of self-control that was slowly being chipped away at by a furious rage from beneath it.

When the gun fell, Billy seemed to droop with it, his breath pouring out of him, like he had sprung a leak. His eyes remained on the gun that was dangling loosely from Matt's fingers, his nonchalance with it more terrifying than his fury.

The wind whistled through the alley, making them all visibly shiver. Frank took note of the quiet that seemed to surround them—oppressive in its totality, ready to give way at any moment. The calm seemed almost… too calm, its placidity an omen in itself.

"Did you see where the others went?" Matt asked, his voice stiff and unwieldy.

Almost embarrassed, with reddening cheeks and eyes that spent most of the conversation on the floor, Billy replied, "I was with them for a while until we hit Dearborn. I was trying to stay close to Gwen, but those… those fucking monsters, they split us up! I tried to cut across them, but they practically charged me. Next thing I know," he sighed, defeated, "I ended up here."

"And Veronica? Did you see what happened to her?"

Billy grimaced then flushed when he realized that he did so, Matt picking up on it almost immediately. Seeing weakness, he pounced on it like a viper in the grass.

"Tell me what you saw, faggot. Now is not the time to be testing my patience."

"Last I saw, she was with Gwen, and… the wolves chased them into a yard, and I saw someone fall. The wolves pounced on something. I couldn't stop to see what it was, but…"

The younger boy broke into harsh sobs again, ones that rattled his whole body so hard that Frank was certain he would break apart at the seams. Matt cursed bitterly, and his eyes went to the ground, closed so tight and hung so low that Frank at first believed him to be sharing in Billy's misery.

Instead, he turned and sent his fist into the wall again with a sickening thud. Even though he must've broken several knuckles with the first blow alone, he hammered three or four more hits into the unflinching wall, his voice rising in an awful crescendo that was similar to that of the very monsters that chased them, if it had been only one or two octaves deeper.

"You just left them there? You didn't stop to help them?"

"Huh?"

Matt sent another wayward fist into the wall, his clenched fingers trembling so violently that his veneer of invulnerability was failing. Frank's own hand was dancing around the pistol in his waistband. He kept telling himself he was foolish for even thinking he might need it, but for some reason, his hand hung there all the same.

"You left them there. No, you left her there, my poor, helpless sister. She was being attacked by those sick fucks, and you just fucking left her, like she was a piece of meat that might distract them long enough for you to escape," Matt said through a jaw as tight as his fist, the grinding of his teeth almost audible from across the alley where Frank stood, the situation spiraling out from under his control.

"I told you, I tried, but… the wolves… they just… lunged at me. I swear! I swear to you, I tried, man! I really did, I swear it!"

"You didn't try! You ran to save your own ass! Don't try and fucking sugarcoat it. Admit it. Quit being a little bitch, and own up to it, or I swear to God, I'll shove this shotgun up your ass and split you in two."

"That's enough! This isn't gonna solve anything, Matt. Any rational thinking person would know that," Frank said, putting himself between the gun's dark circular pit of blackness and the boy cowering with his arms wrapped around his skull.

Frank felt his legs almost give way, but he regained his composure quickly, the thought of that lovely green living room adding weight to his stance.

"Any rational person, Frank," he spat with a venomous emphasis. "Any rational person would've killed this useless sack of shit as soon as they heard they left their fucking sister to die. You know, since I *am* such a rational fucking person, I'm starting to question why I haven't already. The fact that I haven't, really should qualify me for some kind of sainthood. If this is the fucking Rapture, I should've been beamed up into a seat at God's right fucking hand by now. Jesus would be the disappointing child compared to me with how sharply I have turned my cheek. And while all that sounds quite promising, something's telling me I'd enjoy making street art out of his brains a lot better."

He pressed forward, gun raised and levied against his shoulder. Standing tall with a baneful black shadow cast onto the cherry red bricks behind him, Matt seemed to tower above the two of them, his very presence making the world seem more entombed in shadows than it had before.

With a wide sweep of his arm, he knocked Frank aside, juggling the gun on his shoulder blade. Billy gave a squeal of fear and shrunk into a ball, his head tucked into his chest and his arms shielding his head as if he intended to deflect bullets with them.

Off balance, Frank stumbled and landed awkwardly on his back foot. He felt a slow, rigorous snap and the familiar burn of pain up the back of his thigh. Hot webbing stretched up the length of his leg, seizing him and holding him in place. Part of him wanted to collapse, to give in and accept that he tried, that he did the very best he could do and that was all that mattered, maybe not to the boy. But not much would matter to him in a couple of seconds.

Frank watched the whole scene play out behind his eyes, frame by frame, like he was watching in slow motion. He stared into the pit of the boy's eyes as the bullets tore through the skin, ripping it into red, fleshy chunks that burst like zits in a thousand different directions. The shells rolled against the cold bone, splitting it, cracking it, before shattering it as if it was no more than glass. The brains separating, exploding like confetti in ripples and shreds that danced through the air like hellish fireflies.

He remembered something Tyler had told him in one of his drunken rambles at the bar one night several months ago. He wasn't sure what exactly Tyler had said that made him start paying attention to him. Everything that had come before it had been the typical stuff to expect from Tyler—what girl he supposedly ravaged that night, despite supposedly treating her worse than he did his dog; what illicit substances he had abused his body with that week; just how "street" and "gangsta" he thought he was—things assholes like him had always boasted about, only the vernacular had changed in recent years, as it always did.

However, this night, the existential side of whatever drug Tyler had imbued that night was making itself known. He began speaking of the meaning of life and the constant struggle between life and death in nature, the contrast between them and things that even someone has slow-witted as Tyler must ponder from time to time in terms of their own existence. He started to tell Matt about some drug he was trying to get his hands on, something relatively new—a chemical cooked up in a lab, except it wasn't entirely new.

Supposedly, this chemical was also produced naturally in the body when we dream, but only during waking hours on two very rare occasions: the first being your birth and the second being your death. The drug, called Dimethyl-Dimethyla-Dime, something, or other—he couldn't remember the specifics, just the abbreviation Tyler had used like a chant or a prayer: DMT.

"DMT," he raved.

A psychedelic compound so intense that mere minutes spent under its influences were said to have felt like ages, even an eternity. The "trip," as they called it, at least back in his own psychedelic experimentation days, would include visuals so strong that it felt like one was in another world—one composed of objects from the real world, twisted and melded and shifted into shapes more grandeur than human consciousness could comprehend. It stretched time into observable matrices, slipped you between dimensions, gave you access to all the deepest, most intimate parts of your mind—the ones that made you, you—the truths you held closest to your soul. Overall, anyone who took the drug came back changed, always for the better, he said—if you didn't count those that died from seizures after taking it, of course.

Apparently, a new, more potent form of the drug had begun appearing in some of Tyler's many social circles, especially since most of those connections were only made due to the wealth behind his father's name. Taking the form of a pill instead of a liquid that had to be based to be inhaled properly, it served as a less harrowing alternative, one that didn't conjure up images of junkies and scarred mugshots. Derived from a mix of DMT and another chemical released upon brain death, reception of the new drug was far more mixed, with any reports of unwanted side effects being squashed just as quickly as they appeared. This only interested Tyler more.

Frank wondered if Billy's mind would have enough time to release such a chemical before it was obliterated by several grams of cast-iron buckshot. If so, would time slow into the sea of infinity, his mind forever trapped in the moment of its own destruction? The tearing and ripping of lobes spread across eternity, his thoughts trapped behind never-ending agony?

Knowing that he would carry the weight of this inaction until his own date with the infinite, Frank threw himself forward, pushing off his ruptured ankle, his muscles reaming. His hand flailed out in front of him, his grace forgotten as the pain that reverberated through his legs. Gritting his teeth, he ignored the pain as he shoved the shotgun's muzzle into the dirt.

Matt followed Frank's awkward heroics with his eyes the whole way, his finger hovering over the trigger, a still obelisk that promised only horror. And yet, he did not pull the trigger—even when the gun, while shaken, still danced in front of its intended target's bared skull.

"Leave him the hell alone!" Frank managed to say through a clenched jaw. "If you're gonna shoot the boy for abandoning your sister to those things, you might as well turn the thing right back on yourself afterward because I didn't see you going after her neither. Instead, I found you back here, hiding, the same as me."

Taking a step back, almost dazed, Matt let the shotgun snap into the dirt, falling forward along with Frank, who began to growl in discomfort. Shock waves of pain racked his lower extremities, his ankle bulging profusely from the top of his sock, the skin a shade of red and purple.

Cavorting like a man that had just drank half his weight in whiskey, Matt fell backward into a slump against the wall, his head resting against the Dumpster beside him. His eyes sifted through dirt, wide and empty, his hand fidgeting at his pants as a sweat started at his forehead. He slammed his eyes closed, only to open them moments later, seemingly more afraid of whatever lay behind them.

Looking more like the young man that entertained him with conversations and a compassionate ear as they drank their sorrows away, Frank felt a modest sense of pity for him.

Billy was still curled into a ball, like an armadillo, at Frank's side. Pressing his hand to the ground to right himself, Frank found his hand damp and submerged in a puddle of the boy's making. Raising the hand to his nose, he recoiled and gagged, almost spilled the contents of his stomach into the pile, making an even more cancerous mix.

He shook his hand until it was moderately dry, or dry enough for him to put up with the smell, and pushed himself back to his feet, stumbling on his bad leg when he reached them. He grimaced but stood tall.

"Come on now, kid. Time to get up," he sighed.

Extending a hand out to the boy that went unnoticed as he cowered inside his chest, Frank gave him a quick slap from the back of his fingers, giving into his frustration. With a snap, Billy was looking up at him with eyes as big as moons, unsure if what he was seeing was part of this world or the next. Frank's false smile seemed enough to alleviate his worries as he quickly took his free hand and the help up.

"Th-thank you... for that."

"Don't mention it. I know it probably doesn't mean much from a guy like me, but you can't let guys like that push you around, or else... or else you'll end up as a guy like me," Frank said, his grin widening into an authentic one that fringed on demented sadness. "And you might wanna try and look for a new pair of pants next opportunity you come across."

Too stunned and caught up in his brush with death for embarrassment, Billy gave a quick nod of understanding, one that made it seem like he was apologizing for some imagined slight. Frank wanted to say more to the boy to clear up any more fears he might have, but something told him the words of a balding, disheveled man like him wouldn't be enough to calm anyone when the dead were eating the living and the animals chased men with looks of glee stapled on their drooling maws.

Turning his attention back to Matt—who was slowly, lecherously pulling himself up the wall like a drunken cockroach, clawing at the indents in the bricks for finger holds—Frank offered him a hand, one that Matt swatted away without hesitation, not even sparing it a glance.

"Get the hell away from me, Frank."

"Listen, Matt, I'm sorry for what I said. I don't blame you for your sister's death, just like I don't blame Billy. The only thing—"

"Stop talking, or I'll take this shotgun and turn your brains inside out."

The voice that rumbled up from the pit of Matt Métier's throat was slurred and cracking, as if he had traveled through a desert, swallowing sand in his dehydrated desperation. Frank barely recognized it, and he thought, if he had, maybe it wouldn't have frightened him so damn much.

With a heavy lurch, Matt stepped out past the Dumpster, grabbing the flimsy plastic lid for support when he nearly fell back onto his ass. Without a word of explanation, he headed around the alley's corner, into the gap between buildings, his dark figure disappearing around the wall before Frank had chance to stop him.

Signaling for Billy to follow, Frank started after him, slipping into an exaggerated hustle—one as fast as the pain in his ankle would allow—while his mind started to imagine what exactly someone in Matt's state of mind might do. When he rounded the corner himself, the light at the end of the street caught him off guard. Despite the heavy fog, the last ray of sunlight were still broadcasting their radiance onto the hallowed earth below, breaking through the low line of clouds broken up by the Maine tree line. The pines stabbed at the sky, drawing forth red rays of light that gave the world a tint of sepia tone. He could hear the moans coming from behind it, from beyond his field of vision—that same horrible cry that he heard in that cell, the ones that had followed them the entire day. The voices felt like hot wax dripped into his ear, searing them and filling them with their muted echoes even in the deepest silence.

In the center of this blinding-light piercing the wisps of fog, stood Matt, still moving forward as if stuck to a track that carried him forward endlessly, bound for a destination that Frank knew all too well.

"Matt? Where are you going? You gotta wait. Those things are still swarming the street!"

Switching to a frantic yet cautious sprint, Frank caught up to the ghost of a man floating above the ground and grabbed his shoulders, trying to keep him from his intended destination. Matt bucked him off, knocking into him with his elbow and casting him into the wall. He bounced and rolled off his shoulder and landing badly on his ankle, the sound of tearing and ruptured nerve endings filling his ears along with the moans of the dead.

The horrible groaning reignited his resolve, along with the idea of bearing Matt's slow, agonizing death on his conscience—hearing his pained, piercing screams in his nightmares every night, coming from Klunesberg's gaping mouth.

In his head, Klunesberg was watching, laughing, his face obscured by the laughing mask of a jackal he wore. The laugh grew louder and louder until it was all that he heard, no matter how much he ground his teeth and pressed his hands against his ears.

He wanted to scream but knew that in doing so, he would be bringing the doom Matt wanted on him sooner than even he intended, and the creature's unnatural appetite would not be satiated by their willing victim alone. And he would be dooming himself and, more importantly, Billy, to that same horrific fate.

He leaped forward, pressing off against his bad ankle hard enough that the pain blotted out his vision into a wave of mercurial static but low enough that his head was level with Matt's stomach. The two connected, Frank's shoulder and neck crashing into Matt's hips. He tucked his head in and slammed it into the young man's stomach, knocking the wind from him and causing his body to fold inward.

The two of them tumbled into the wall on the opposite side, landing in an amorphous pile of black trash bags, slick with the juices that formed on the most nauseating of waste. Their doughy composition softened the impact and muffled the sound of it to the point where even Frank had a hard time telling when they had stopped falling, his equilibrium disturbed by the mind-numbing pain in his leg.

Matt let out a gasp of pain, his hand reaching for his back to move some sharp object sheathed in thick plastic, darker than shadow, which was digging into his spine. Frank rolled away from him, propelled by gravity and a small, halfhearted shove from Matt, his doing summersaults along with him.

"You're a crazy bastard, you know that, Frog?" Matt said through heavy breaths.

Frank tried to tell him that wasn't his name, but all that came out was a weak sigh of assent. Billy had made his way over to them and crouched beside Frank, his hands dancing over him, unsure of what to do, how he could help.

You should've let him die, Frank. Who are you to stop him? Who are you to stop anyone? To tell anyone what to do? What advice can the dead give the living? Well, I think that's unfair. Even the dead have lived at some point. You, on the other hand… well, you've certainly played at it. You've always been content with helping others before yourself, a truly noble idea in theory, less so in practice, especially an all-consuming one. So why don't you help the fool get what he wants? What you've wanted so many times before in the past? I've seen your thoughts, Frog. I've heard them. 'Ribbet, ribbet, maybe this world will be better off without me.' 'Ribbet, ribbet, I have more regrets than I do happiness.' 'Ribbet, ribbet, I've wasted my life.' There are even more pathetic ones, but I'll spare us both the embarrassment. Well, now's the time you both can get what you want. Just stay down, and let the pain carry you where you've always belonged.

Groggily, Frank tried to open his eyes, catching blurred glimpses of Billy's worried nursing above him. He saw Matt rise from the garbage bags at his side, angrily knocking aside Billy's hands with a look of annoyance. He felt a hand press against his back from under him and soon, weightlessness, as he was dragged to his feet.

There was another bite of pain as he steadied himself. Matt was knocking the clinging remains of garbage and its slime from his and Frank's back, his eyes avoiding Frank's at every opportunity.

"Feeding yourself to those things isn't gonna bring your sister back. You know that, right?" Frank said, the words sliding out his lips like they were numb and coursing with Novocain.

Matt didn't reply for a while, his body remained so still and intent on his task at hand that Frank wondered if he was being ignored, something that wouldn't exactly surprise him and would make Klunesberg cackle.

"I know," Matt said softly.

Frank was startled but stopped his body from showing it. He let a smile creep across his face but hid it behind his usual veil of saddened indifference when Matt's face finally met his own.

"It almost seemed like… retribution, if you could call it that. Fuck, if I understand philosophical shit like that, but… I already owe her, for what I… for the things I've done. The thought that I'd never be able to make up for it, to never see that smile of hers again, back when she thought the world of me. I can't remember the last time I saw that smile. Sometimes that was the only thing that kept me going. And with that gone… it seems like all my hope went with it."

He opened his mouth, as if he wanted to say more, but shut it quickly, his eyes glistening as he turned toward the open street. Frank saw his lip quiver and put his own frail, wrinkled hand on his shoulder.

"You've got to be shitting me."

Taken aback, unsure of the cause of Matt's sudden outburst, Frank brought his hand back quickly as if touching a stove. However, he soon noticed that Matt's attention was held by something across the street.

Running forward, Matt tucked himself against the wall, giving a small wave of his hand for Frank and Billy to follow. Frank did so hastily, while Billy moved with an air of reluctance, his darting eyes showing his apprehension.

"What are—"

Matt sent a punch into his ribs that Frank mistook as a petty revenge for the earlier tackling, but then he saw a decaying pair of legs shuffled past, the fat of the thighs hanging like loose sheets from the side of a bed and baring the staunch yellow muscle. The creature passed by them without notice, a solitary cell of a massive herd moving through the empty streets. For a moment, Frank thought Matt's focus was on the decomposing army that blocked their passage, but something kept his eyes still and steady across the street.

As soon as it passed from their sight, Frank, in a hushed whisper, tried his question again, "What exactly are we supposed to be looking at?"

Not daring an answer, Matt brought his hand up to the side of Frank's face and traced a line with his finger to the tree line opposite them. Giving his eyes several moments to adjust to the twilight haze, Frank began to notice branches ruffling and cracking as if something even larger and more sinister moved behind them.

The foliage trembled and shook, branches bending inward while large shadows rustled behind them. Saliva caught in Frank's throat, forcing him to swallow heavily as he watched the formless darkness take familiar shapes beneath the underbrush. The thin black stalks became legs creeping through the hedges. The darting shifts of shade became heads tucking themselves under stiff pine needles. The dark masses forcing aside the greenery around them became pale hands with red lacquered nails, sliding through the bush like a serpent.

Range's face was the first one he was able to make out distinctly, the boy's gleaming blond hair catching and reflecting the sunlight with ease. The girl at his side was most assuredly Gwen, her own dirty blond hair standing out against the verdant backdrop that shielded them from the horde making its way through the streets.

When he saw Veronica's anxious and weary face, still beautiful despite the wear and tear it had received, with a natural pout that always seemed to denote frustration, he couldn't help but smile and enthusiastically shake Matt's shoulder.

Matt turned, baring that mischievous grin of his, tempered by his own relief into something all the more charming, a rare view of the young man with the world in front of him he had met all those years ago—the boy who he had once envied, despite the vast gap in their experience, but it was that same easy charm that won Frank to his side.

Then there was the week when he disappeared from the bar. Just stopped showing up to work, causing his boss—whose own head now bore a hole, thanks to Matt—to rage indolently every night to the customers he was now forced to serve. Frank would be lying if they didn't get a kick out of it at the time, all assuming the boy had simply gotten fed up with Caplin's bullshit and decided to quit without having to deal with a final helping of it to swallow.

He showed up the following week, however, acting as if nothing was different, arriving for his usual shift with an awkward grin that seemed a bad caricature of the one he usually sported. The abuse he took from Caplin that night could be heard all the way across the bar, but somehow he managed to keep the job. Still, whatever happened to him that week seemed to stay with him, marring every smile, every joke. There was a hint of resentful sadness behind every word, one that he tried to hide and did a good job of it for the most part; but whatever had changed him had done so by the roots, a scar that cut too deep to ever not be noticeable, no matter how tough the skin that replaced it.

"Is that everybody? I only see the three of them."

"Which three?"

"Range, Gwen, and your sister."

"Gwen's over there?" Billy said, a mixture of excitement, relief, and what Frank thought was embarrassment, or was at least close enough to it, where someone well versed in it could easily recognize.

"And here I thought you'd be happy to hear my sister was still alive," Matt said glumly, sparing the boy a shaded glance through eyes no bigger than slits, before turning back to the street. "Tyler's over there as well. I'm not sure about the deputy."

"Bruce."

"Yeah, whatever," Matt said with an easy dismissal, and just like that, the Matt he had come to know too well was back, fidgeting and anxiously tugging at his clothes. "We've got to figure out a way over to them, or at least a way to get their attention. Is there a rock around here or something? A loose brick?"

"You're gonna throw a brick at them?"

"I think there's a smarter way to get their attention than that, Matt, preferably one that won't take their head off if they don't notice it."

Range was crouching low near the edge of the tree line when his eyes met Frank's and lit up. Quickly, he turned back to the rest of the group and began directing them toward Frank and the others, the excitement mirrored in their faces. Tyler's snowcap appeared beneath the underbrush, with his curious face following just behind it. When he saw Matt, his face exploded into giddiness, bringing his fist to his mouth as he bounced excitedly.

As terrible as it made him feel, Bruce was the last face Frank noticed, his caramel skin obscured by the forest's shade. He wore a stern expression, the slight curve of his lips the only thing that could be considered happiness to see them.

Range turned and started whispering to the rest of the group. There seemed to be a long debate about something—something that Veronica, most of all, felt especially passionate about to the point that her impassioned words bordered on audible shouts. Gwen, of course, was also starting to get angry with the way the conversation was headed, waving her arms at Frank, Matt, and Billy while mouthing her words like they were acid.

Finally, a consensus seemed to be reached, however tenuous, one that seemed to leave bad taste in Range's mouth from the look of displeasure he wore. Silently, he motioned for them to cross the street, waving his hands toward them, like he was signaling for a plane to land.

"What is he doing?" Billy asked, nervousness sending his voice into the upper octaves.

"It looks like he wants us to cross over to them."

"They want what? Why don't they just come over here?"

"Something tells me that's exactly what they were discussing," Frank said, a cold shiver going down his spine as he did so. He blamed it on the biting gust that passed by.

"Well, that shouldn't be so bad," Matt said confidently.

Pushing off the wall and back onto his feet with a drunkard's grace, Matt stood and stared into the dull gray of the empty street, his fear appearing only in the moment of action. He hesitated long enough for Frank to grab his arm.

"We need to be careful here. We don't know what's moving in the fog."

"Who needs to be careful when you got a gun that could blow a man in half?" Matt grinned, giving his best imitation of confidence while he lifted his shotgun onto his shoulder.

"If you use that thing, you're gonna bring the entire town down on us. I'm assuming those things can see just as little as we can, but they seem to be able to hear pretty damn well. Only use that thing if you really damn have to."

"You always struck me as a bit of pacifist, Frank."

"You told me once a pacifist is just a fancy title for a pussy."

"That does sound like something I'd say. So if we're not allowed to use our guns, Frank, how would you suggest we get across without one of those things getting a taste of our insides? Just hope they walk around us?"

Billy whimpered, his legs shaking as if he was trying to wet himself again but forgot that his bladder was empty.

"If we can find something blunt, preferably sharp…"

Frank let his gaze wander over the alley's ground, the hard asphalt a sea of cracks and stubborn blades of grass refusing to be buried. In an alcove similar to the one that he had taken shelter in earlier, he saw a door illuminated by a flashing halogen. It was covered in muck and grease, dark-brown stains seeping into its green varnish. The glass window that it held in its center was broken, the pieces dashed and scattered over the ground.

Walking over to it, he heard the soft crackle as it snapped and shattered beneath his boots. He noticed a particularly long shard and grabbed it, feeling it slice into his hand, hard enough to draw a thin line of blood.

Satisfied with his makeshift weapon, he brought his head up to look for more long pieces when his eyes were drawn to the hallway behind the door. The light from the alcove shone in through the modest window, making a wreath of light down the shadowy corridor. Another halogen flashed and sparked at the opposite end, firing at odd intervals. The longer he peered into that hall, the more he realized the light was actually far more frightening than the dark.

The walls were stained with blood, gallons of the stuff dripping even from the ceiling. Rib cages and spines and other bones littered the floor, like the lair of some ancient beast, a cave fit for the worst of demons. The heads that belonged to these bodies remained intact, frozen in their final moments of abject horror. Long mouths frozen in screams, eyes clenched in fear of looking at the monster that was tearing them limb from limb. He could still see the tears on their faces. Their necks seemed to be stuffed with red straw, scarecrows made of blood and flesh.

At the far end, near another wide door with a small window, the only difference being the blue paint that decorated it and the enormously obtuse man that lay against it. His stomach was so wide that it had literally burst, the belly button at its center blossomed outward, like a cartoon character that had swallowed dynamite. Its mouth still moved, and its fat still quivered, the bloody contents of its stomach spilling out onto the floor with each quake.

Frank held his hand to his mouth for fear of involuntarily screaming, vomiting, or a sick combination of the two. He backed away from the door, stopping just long enough to notice another blade-like shard underneath the toe of his boot. Taking care not to crack it any further, he slid it out from under his sole and tucked it into his pocket with the other one.

Refusing to make the horrors of the hallway real by speaking of them, Frank instead silently handed Matt one of the shard of glass, avoiding his eyes.

Matt shook his head and instead pointed toward Billy. "Give it to the kid. He'll need it more than I will."

"I told you, you can't fire that thing—"

"Calm down, Frank. There's more than one way to kill a man with a gun."

"These aren't exactly men we're killing here, Matt."

"They sure die like them. They might need a little more coercion than most, but they die all the same."

"How do you know they're not men, though?" Billy said suddenly. "What if part of them is still in there? Aware of what they're doing but unable to stop it? I mean… don't you feel bad? Killing them? Knowing they were people once?"

Matt shared an annoyed glare with Frank, before turning it on the frightened boy. "Honestly?"

Billy nodded his head while reaching out to take the piece of glass from Frank's extended hand.

"Not really."

With that, he stepped out into the street, his feet cracking against the sidewalk as he moved through the sea of fog. The other side of the street seemed deceptively close—close enough that Matt started out into a light jog, reaching the street before Frank and Billy had even left the alley.

His carelessness proved dangerous quickly as he stepped out past the line of parked cars, only for one of the dead standing motionless behind an old Toyota to descend on him. With a loud moan, the creature's jaws opened wide, like a python trying to stretch itself wide enough for its prey, tendrils of spit and foam forming over the stained yellow and black teeth.

Rot had eaten away at its chest, its entire midsection nothing more than a glorified rib cage. Loose straps of skin held its hips to its spine, with a cavernous pit of air where the stomach should have been. Dangling from his throat were several chunks of flesh, bouncing against the bones. More pieces and organs sat in collected lump above its waist, pieces spilling over and slapping its legs.

With an angry grunt, Matt shoved the butt of the shotgun up into the monster's chest, shattering the ribs into debris that flew up into his face. He sent two more blows into the creature's heart until it fell and then pounced on it, his bulky form pinning it to the ground. Lifting the gun above his head, he brought it down on the zombie's skull, splattering it over the concrete like some kind of bad impressionist painting.

Frank had enough time to catch up to him and see several more of the creatures shuffling up the other side of the street, noticing their fallen comrade and altering their slow but deliberate direction toward them. Charging them, Frank shoved the blade of glass up underneath the thing's jaw, a hot spray of blood covering his face.

The creature collapsed limply, still spraying blood like a geyser over Frank's clothes. He felt it sliding down his skin, sticking to it with that overpowering aroma of copper. It dripped from his fingers, his hand gripping the blade so tight he wasn't sure how much was the creature's and how much was his own.

Its screeching companion clawed at him, its nails torn up into rows of keratin knives that whistled as they split the air around Frank's face. He ducked the creature's blow, feeling a burst of adrenaline at its grunt of frustration that compelled him into another wild slash of the glass in his hand.

In one swift, heavy motion, he brought the glass down into the curve of the zombie's forehead, its gray leathery skin splitting as easy as paper and the skull beneath it crumbling away at the slightest pressure. Thick purple clots of blood gurgled up from the wound, pulsing around the see-through blade. The monster soon collapsed in a ragged heap, just like its brethren.

Dropping to the ground, Frank struggled to get his bloody, damaged hand around the glass shard, his fingers numb and useless from the deep wound across his palm. The glass had truly been a double-edged weapon—one that had cut Frank's hand down to the bone, a heavy price for clutching it tight enough to bury it in someone's skull. The nerves in his fingers misfired and kept his fingers jittering. He tried to make a fist but found that it was complete agony to even attempt to do so.

Still, he pressed his fingers to the glass's edge, trying to find a sturdy-enough hold to pry the thing loose from its pulpy sheath. His sausages for fingers slapped uselessly against it, sliding helplessly across the smooth pane.

There was a crunch, and as Frank whirled, he saw one of the undead fall onto the pavement, the back of its skull connecting with ground first and splintering the bone, like a bomb had gone off inside it. Matt dropped on top of it like a wrestler going for an early pin and crushed the skull into paste with the butt of his gun, brains and blood already dripping from its end before he set to his grisly task.

Frank tried to find his bearings, looking around desperately for the tree line. His eyes settled on the deep hazel of the bark and the green contrast and saw that they had only made it halfway across the street. Two more lanes, plus an extra filled to the brim with parked cars—whose owners would never come to collect them or be able to pay the page-long parking lot ticket soon to be owed to them—was all that stood between them and the cover of the forest.

Range was standing now, visibly struggling to restrain himself as he watched the struggle, hopping from foot to foot to quell his anxiousness. Tyler shared a similar resolve, with Bruce actually needing to restrain him as he tried to shove through the hedges, with what looked like an Uzi straight out of the movies in his hand. Veronica's face, however, wore a passiveness that was almost unsettling.

When Frank finally turned back to Matt, he had tackled another one of the unfortunate zombies that had crossed his path, resorting to his very effective strategy of smashing his gun into its head until the said head was a fleshy soup drizzled over the concrete. His ferocity was that of an untamed animal relishing in its kill and the blood that now decorated it. All of him was thrown into each heavy blow, his eyes wide but focused, shaking only from absolute concentration.

Because of this focus, he was unaware of the small family that had hobbled out of the fog—a child and its parents walking in tandem, the familial obligation keeping them together even in death. The mother was missing the lower half of her jaw, her tongue flopping lazily around her throat, twitching occasionally, like a sleeping serpent. Her hair seemed to be more blood than actual strands. The whole thing was one wet, matted mess that curled into a ridiculous crimson swirl around the top of her head that would've been comical if half of her face hadn't been missing.

The father was even worse, as his wife's jaw was stuck protruding from inside his own, stabbed right through the center so that a row of teeth curled out from his mouth, like a ram's horn. His eyes were like rotten grapes, chewed up then spit back out into their sockets, dripping out like egg whites. His scalp was peeled back, bits of the pink muscle covering the skull chewed away, like plastic from the foam insides of an old gym dodgeball.

His limbs swung like pendulums, cracked at the joints and newer joints made from fractures that punctured through the skin in their severity. The buttoned-up flannel was torn open, revealing a chest that had received a similar treatment. The skin had been flayed—no, peeled—in rabid chunks from the muscle, some spots even showing the organs beneath. His spleen was even bulging, like an ulcer, from an abrasion in his side, squishing pus from it with each step.

The boy was almost normal in comparison but far more terrifying in its pseudo innocence. You would hardly be able to know that he was dead if it wasn't for the small hole in the center of his tender forehead, the chalky skin flowered outward and a small sliver of dried blood leaking from it that traveled the length of his face like a river, splitting itself into smaller rivulets that were reminiscent of the veins that once contained it.

They saw Matt's savage ballet almost immediately, seeming to take the same delight in his splashes of blood as he did. Their mouths dropped open in animal-like hisses of delight, pointing and aiming their excuses for limbs in his direction.

Frank's stomach dropped out into a gaping pit where he could no longer feel it. The way they were moving, they would be on top of Matt within a moment; and even with the wide, careless arcs he had been throwing, there would be no way he'd be able to handle all of them at once. Even if he took out one, the child would sneak up in his blind spot, or the two remaining would simply overwhelm him. Much more likely, he would see the group and fire a booming shell into them, drawing forth the entire horde moving through the fog, like predators swimming just beneath the icy blue surface of the deep.

Just let him die. The fool's caused you enough trouble already. I mean, it's his fault you spent last night in a jail cell, all because he dragged you into some harebrained scheme of his, using your goodwill to his advantage, using you to his advantage. Tsk. Tsk. C'mon, Frank, I'm the only one allowed to do that, aren't I? You're trying to make me jealous, aren't you? That's it, isn't it?

Matt remained ignorant of the encroaching monsters, still devoted to the task in front of him—which was now an icy, reflective puddle of crimson. Frank looked down at the shard extending from the creature's skull in front of him, forever lost to him and his useless fingers.

He reckoned he might be able to take one of the family members but would soon quickly find himself outmatched by the other two, especially when one of them was small enough to lose track of, even when you were staring right at it. The dead boy was closest to Matt's swaying arms—its mouth a pit of blackness that seeped up, black mucus spilling from its lips, like drool dripping tantalizingly from a hungry dog.

What do you owe him anyway, huh? A few beers now and then when you left your wallet at home? A couple pitiable women, scraps tossed your way from his own misguided sexual conquests, ones that you were doomed to strike out with anyway, just like you always have? Some foolish sense of camaraderie despite the fact they've never seemed to see you as anything more than just a pawn? These "friends" of yours, who use you for jobs that you could never say no to—not because you were afraid or needed the money, but because you could never say no to someone who had displayed on you even the smallest measure of kindness. They knew that as well as you did, yet they dragged you kicking and screaming into the maw of the beast all the same.

Frank righted himself, pulling himself awkwardly to his feet as he debated whether to attack the oncoming zombies, ensuring his own demise, or to shout and doom them all, or to leave Matt as an unwilling sacrifice for the "greater good" Frank had always heard about and never seen.

Think of all I've done for you, Frank. I have given you purpose, attempted to impart on you a certain knowledge of how the world works, tried to save you from your own… baser limitations. I gave you a name that people actually remember. I made you somebody instead of the nobody, the nothing, that you once were. I was the one that gave you a job despite that spotted arrest record of yours. Along with the rumors about you and your certain… oddness, I doubt anyone would've given you a chance like I had.

It was then that Frank noticed Billy, slowly creeping his way through the swirling strands of fog toward the group of undead, the shard of glass extended in a trembling hand held out in front of him, like a child holding its own dirty diaper out in disgust.

And how do you repay me? With unconditional hatred, with indignation, by declaring me the bane of your very existence. Stare at me with those dark, beady eyes of yours, turning your own regret into bitterness on your tongue. I've tried to show you the error of your ways, to teach you by example, but it seems the lesson had proved just as useful as all the others life has granted you.

Frank slammed his fist into his own forehead, willing Klunesberg's nasally voice to cease its endless tirade that sounded more and more convincing by the second, trying to lure him back to that life of shameful hesitation he had endured for far too long.

Any kind of hesitation was off the table now. If he did not act, Matt would be surely consumed by the approaching zombies. Billy's sluggish, halfhearted approach would cause more trouble than it would assistance; but it would serve as a good-enough distraction, allowing Frank to attack the creatures again, weeding out their numbers into something more manageable.

In fact, if Frank took out the first and Billy the second behind him, all that would be left would be the child—an easy-enough, if slightly unsettling, proposition. The idea was getting more attractive with each passing moment, to the point where it almost seemed like a good one; but that was most likely Frank's foolish optimism, something he had never really been quite well versed in.

Waving his hand to get Billy's attention, Frank finally succeeded by pressing his lips together and giving off a small whistle, one that was louder than he intended but still went unobserved by the small family of undead. Billy, however, whirled around to face Frank, swinging his transparent weapon around in long, wild arcs that slid through nothing but air. The boy even slammed his eyes shut while doing so.

Frank whistled again, the sound's repetition and the fact that breath was still creaking its way through his lungs seemed to snap Billy out of his spastic defense mechanism, his eyes going wide as he looked for the whistle's origin—when his gaze settled on Frank, a look that was a mix of relief and pleading, a desperate plea for an end to the madness that had seeped into their world to someone who had just as little power to change it as he.

Even though he felt just as helpless as the crying boy, Frank attempted to steel himself, to give off the appearance of fortitude with his actions even though his insides felt softer than melted butter. He motioned toward the small collection of death marching toward Matt, who was panting over his fresh kill.

Frank pointed to himself, trying to impart the idea silently, that he would go and attack the nearest of the slobbering beasts, causing a distraction of sorts—one that would most likely put them all in more danger than if they just sat back and let the problem resolve itself—although, luckily, he didn't think that second part translated as well.

Billy followed Frank's wild gesticulations and gave a confused but confident nod as Frank smashed his fist into the palm of his open hand and then pointed at the zombie with the blood-matted hair. However, when Frank indicated that Billy should follow with an attack of his own, he began shaking his head so violently that Frank had thought their luck had really gone sour and the boy had been struck by some kind of seizure.

Yet his head stopped, and he began mouthing the word *no*, like a panicked child throwing a tantrum. The gap between the nearest, fleshless zombie and Matt was almost nonexistent as was Frank's patience, his own plan being rendered useless by Billy's wanton cowardice.

With a gruff look and more forceful expressions, Frank reinforced his point; and without waiting for Billy's response and hoping to force him to action with his own crazed heroics, he burst into a ragged sprint, hobbling off balance on his swollen ankle to the point that his own run was probably more savage looking than the dead.

Slipping his hand to the back pocket of his jeans, he dug his fingers into the edge and ran them along until they clumsily fumbled over the cold steel of the magnum that rested there. He pulled it loose and managed to slip it around in his hand like a club that he swung up into the first zombie's chin. The blow connected hard, sending a cocktail of teeth and that sickening black bile into Frank's eyes. The jagged edges cut loose skin just above his eye, and the bile that entered it burned like hot tar burrowing into his flesh.

He wanted to howl like Michael Jackson after a kick to the groin but somehow held it in, biting down on his tongue until he tasted blood. As he swallowed it, he prayed that it was his own, but it was far too late to worry about something so trivial as the creature recovered and pounced onto Frank with its teeth bared out in front of it.

Bringing his hand up defensively turned out to be a blessing, as the zombie bit down hard on the gun's stock with the remains of its mouth, thrashing its head about, like a shark with a seal between its teeth. Frank juggled the gun, trying to keep it at the perfect angle to hold back the snapping jaws of his attacker. He pressed forward, pushing the gun deeper into the creature's gullet, until its neck bent backward, and it toppled over itself.

Frank followed it down, holding its chest down with his legs as he brought the butt of the gun down across the zombie's skull, shattering a chunk the size of a baseball and flipping it over onto the pavement. He saw the exposed pink matter beneath, the folds of it pressing out through its alabaster shell, like it was trying to escape. The creature moved and snapped at him as if it had been nothing more than a light smack across the nose, its gray eyes trained on him with what resembled hatred but was far closer to rabid hunger.

The other zombie was nearly upon him, its disjointed limbs coming into view in Frank's peripheral. With a wild swing, he swung the gun into the zombie's knee, turning it into powder that disappeared into the fog as the creature collapsed into a heap. The sound alerted Matt who, as he turned, first noticed the fallen zombie clawing at the ground, trying to slither at Frank like a snake while half of its intestine lay tangled around its shoddily amputated leg.

While Matt went to work, crushing the former father's skull in, Frank focused on his own kill beneath him. The woman—if you could still call this ghastly thing that—was still trying to bite at his thighs that were pinning her, screeching like a bat and waving its tongue about as if it was tasting the very air around it. Frank raised the gun high above his head, making sure that the barrel was firm in his fingers; and in that moment, as it looked up into the gleam of the stock with childlike innocence and confusion, he almost pitied it—but not enough to lessen the blow as he crushed its brain into the back of its skull, straight through into the hard pavement.

When the creature began twitching, Frank fell off it, only for it to drop limp soon after. He felt a little foolish at this last-minute retreat, his relief so palpable that he wanted to laugh. Somehow, his plan had gone off without a hitch, as perfectly as any plan could go—one that he surely would've dismissed years ago as misguided pride. And it had worked, just as good as Bruce's or anyone else's. He almost felt like cheering, until he remembered the boy with the bullet hole in his forehead.

He felt the teeth pierce his skin—the canines slicing through flesh, the incisors gnashing against bone as they pulled up the skin and muscle above it. This time, Frank screamed, unable to keep the pain from forcing his throat open. The monster pulled its head back, tearing the skin from bone, pulling the muscle into stringy sinuous fibers that stuck between its teeth. The blood welled up from the wound, like muddy water rising up from a clogged drain, sticky purple clots sliding over Frank's skin like slugs.

Frank saw the boy smiling with glee as it clenched his flesh between its teeth, delighting in its kill, a human vulture. He tried to push it off of him but found his arms to weak to do so. In fact, he couldn't feel his left arm at all—only the air passing through where a chunk of his shoulder had once been.

Turning back to Billy, he saw the glass tumble from his fingers and crash to the ground into a million stars, the bewildered boy backing away from it as if it were acid. The word *no* still dripped from his lips like a leaky faucet, until his hands went to his mouth, like a stopper.

He heard Klunesberg cackling, the tenor of his voice dropping into octaves lower than he had ever heard before—rumbles that he felt on his skin more than he heard in his own head. A deep cold began seeping into his feet, filling him like an icy wave, but he was too weak to shiver.

When Matt bashed the last bit of life out of the dismembered zombie, he looked over to Frank and cursed heavily, scrambling to his feet as he did so. The small imp went back in for another bite of its succulent feast, an act that Frank saw but did not feel. All he felt was the swaying of his body as the goblin chewed his very bones.

His vision started to blacken from the pain when Matt reached him, sending a boot into the small creature's face that sent it rocketing backward into the curb. Without the little monster supporting him—even if it was only as a meal—Frank lost his balance and fell onto his back, looking up at the mist-shrouded sky, marveling at the yellows and reds that that had broken through, giving the clouds a wound of their own.

Frank coughed and felt blood fill his throat to the point that he nearly choked on it, sending him into an even harder spasm of coughs that rattled his chest and started the pain up again in his shoulder. He screamed again, knowing it made no difference now. If anything, it would only lessen the agony by sending in more of those damned things to devour him before he became one of them…

His thoughts were cut off by a sickening squish as Matt slammed the heel of his boot into the curb, the dead boy's skull serving as a buffer. He tried to look for Matt, but his vision started to sway and twist, worse than any inebriation he had ever experienced, his head lighter than air.

The feeling spread throughout his whole body, and he realized that he was airborne, his first thought being that he was ascending to heaven in a ray of light, breaking through the crimson clouds, and that idea was absurd enough to get him to chuckle despite the pain.

"Don't go loopy on me now, Frank. You hear me? Stay with me, buddy. I'm getting you out of here," Matt said.

Weightless, he floated beneath the sky, which seemed to be standing still as the earth moved beneath it until all he saw were trees above him, the bloodred sky being overtaken by one far more verdant. The leaves split the light into dazzling stars, blinding in their radiance, turning his vision into a field of white.

He felt himself come to rest on the ground, his eyelids fluttering and turning the world into a corridor at a cheap haunted house, with strobe effects ran through cheap color filters. Shades of purple and yellow and red tainted his sight. Even when he closed his eyes, they were there, spinning around in time to Klunesberg's disheartening, animated laughter. Flashes of heat shook his body, sweat dripping out of every pore so intensely he could feel it, each drop like a pinprick in his skin.

"What the hell happened out there? What happened to hi— Oh, sweet mother of God."

"He's losing a lot of blood. I need something to put pressure on the wound... Now! Why the hell is everybody just standing around?"

"But he... he was bitten."

"Thanks for explaining that. I don't think I would've noticed unless you pointed it out there, Sherlock."

"You know what I mean."

"No, I don't think I do. What do you mean? Please. Enlighten me."

"What I mean is that I don't think stopping the bleeding is going to help him that much."

Frank coughed again, so hard that it felt like his lungs were coming loose and about to tumble down into the pit of his stomach. Every part of him felt old, more so than usual, as if he was already rotting from the inside out. The taste of bile was thick in the back of his throat, and yet when he gagged, nothing came up except for more pulpy clots of blood.

He struggled to open his eyes and keep them open, a task that was increasing in difficulty by the second. He was slowly becoming aware of a fever in the back of his head, a thick cloud brimming with thunder, fog rolling underneath that simmered and cracked with electricity. Behind its icy veil, rage and malice incarnate brewed, radiating its vileness like a cheap and especially foul cologne.

Embrace it, Frog. Let it fill you up until there's nothing of the old, pathetic thing known as Frank Rogers left. His voice was an arctic wind, so deep and sonorous it could be mistaken for an endless drone. *You've always wanted to belong. Well, now you can belong to something greater than you or I will ever be—a single piece in the large expanse of the collective ether, a place where even the high and low can serve one greater purpose. And that purpose is hunger.*

Gwen was standing over him, looking down at him with big, puppy-dog eyes that emanated concern but hidden behind unassailable walls of tension that made her face seem twice as old as he knew it was. And still, the way her muscles tensed when she moved her neck was so lithe and lean. Her cheeks were pudgy, not enough that you would call it fat, but he bet there was plenty of skin in them—greasy, fatty skin peeled right off the bone and slid down his waiting throat…

He shook his head, giving a defeated groan as he did so. His thoughts were no longer his own, a foreign presence in his most private of hiding spots. He could feel it there, hanging over his mind, a cloud ready to burst at any moment, but it was becoming harder to distinguish which were purely his own and which were those of the creature he would soon become.

Suddenly, Billy's idea that the dead might be fully aware of what was happening to them without any control over their own bodies seemed far more frightening and far more real. However, his coughing up blood contrasted with the image of the man in the jail cell lying facedown in a pile of his own guts was oddly comforting—at least, in terms of present circumstances.

"Frank? Frank? You still with me, buddy? Look at me. Look in my eyes if you can still understand me, pal."

Frank obliged, even though part of him wished the lot of them had just left him—saved themselves. He wanted to consider it noble, but it was mostly because he didn't want to have to suffer the embarrassment of them watching him die in agony.

"He's still responding. Maybe he's gonna be okay? Maybe he's immune, or something? Maybe we all are? I mean, we all haven't been infected yet, right? Maybe he's gonna be okay?" Matt said, trying on an awkward grin that made him seem totally mad.

"Yeah, Matt, and maybe I'm a long-lost princess who's the key to saving the world from an alien invasion too. You never know," Veronica sneered before her prideful face drifted back down to Frank's, and a look of something that might be considered guilt took over her features.

Don't worry about her, Frog. The hunger will consume her too. It will consume them all in time. You're just the lucky one who gets to go first. Heh, luck. Now, that's something new for you. You must be feeling ecstatic. Well, except for the mind-numbing pain of death and all. But the hard part will be over soon.

Range appeared above him, Matt giving him a shady look and opening his mouth as if he was going to say something, but he looked at Frank and decided that it was probably best kept to himself. Frank thanked him for that, at least. Instead, Matt turned his attention on Billy, standing up in a huff and pacing toward him as if he meant to walk right over him.

"What the hell happened out there, huh? Huh? You just left him to die, didn't you? You let him die! This on your hands, you hear me! This is on your fucking hands!"

There was the shuffle of feet pounding the dirt, and with Frank's ears pressed to the ground, it sounded like train running off its track. He tried to tell Matt to leave the kid be, but his strength was almost nonexistent. When he tried to speak, all that came out was a dull croak.

Hearing this startled Range, his own usually passive eyes filling with life and glistening. He grabbed Frank's hand and squeezed, the warmth beating back against the chill that had taken his body. Frank felt a smile fill his face, taking all the little energy he had and feeling like someone was shoving icicles into his cheekbones.

"I'm sorry this happened to you, Frank. I… I thought I could save you. I thought I could save everyone… but I didn't even try. And for that I'm sorry. I can never apologize enough."

Frank put his own hand over Range's, letting the fingers twist and interlock.

"Marsh… Marshall… Mar… proud," was all that he managed to spit out through his jellied lips, his throat closing up and filling with warm, sticky blood that bubbled up between his teeth.

Range shushed him and lifted him off his back, shifting the blood back down into his lower half where at least he could no longer feel it. Tear welled in the young man's eyes, tears that Frank knew he didn't deserve but touched him nonetheless.

"I… I can…" he started, taking time to wipe tears from the corner of his eyes, "I can put you out of your misery, if you want it."

He nodded his head toward the gun resting at his side, barely looking at it himself as if he could go on denying what it was while still offering to use it. Frank would've laughed if it wouldn't have hurt so damn much.

The offer of mercy was what finally made it all feel real. He was going to die; slow or quick, it didn't matter. This was the day he was going to die. It was almost funny. He had spent so much time wishing for an end to his misery, long before the dead started walking the earth; but now it seemed absolutely terrifying, the finality of it all. Like going down a slide, you could psyche yourself up all you wanted, but when you hit the drop and your stomach disappears out from under you, the fear hits you.

I'm glad you see the humor in the situation too. I was afraid the irony was wasted on you, Frog.

Frog.

Frog.

At least, with his death—even if he refused the mercy offered to him and became one of the nameless undead forced to wander the hell they escaped from—his name would die with him. He would no longer be Frog, the moniker that had clung to him no matter how much he tried to shake it off—Klunesberg's one and only gift to him. He would be nothing, another slave to the hunger. But even that was better than being Frog.

He knew that was as close to accepting his death that he was ever going to get, and he gave Range a quick, hardened nod, bracing himself as he did so with deep, shaky breaths. His blood quickened at the sight of death's deliverance, the silver barrel of the gun opening like a gaping pit of doom ready to swallow him up. If the alternative hadn't be so exponentially worse, the dark, menacing look of the gun might've been enough to dissuade him from his intended "mercy." The painful look Range wore was enough to convince him to be grateful and hold no ill will toward the boy for blowing his brains onto the forest canopy, but it was still hard to think very highly of him while he had a gun pointed in Frank's face.

He steadied his aim until the edge of the barrel was in the center of Frank's broad forehead, pressing it to the skin. It felt hotter than he expected. They must've encountered some undead of their own on the way into the forest, probably some of those damned wolves, laughing as the bullets tore their faces to shreds—obliterated, just like his own was about to be.

Swallowing heavily, Frank told himself that he was ready, closing his eyes and enjoying the feel of the wind on his face one final time. There was so much he had left undone. He had always been told it was best to live without regrets, especially when you were on your deathbed; but when you had has many as he did, it was hard to reconcile it in the meager time provided. At this point, life seemed more like one giant regret than a series of them, and while not exactly as a romantic death as he would've imagined for himself, it provided an odd sense of comfort.

He looked Range directly in the eyes and nodded, closing his own again to brace for the impact he would never feel. Each second passed like a century, the anticipation a disease eating away at him, his own violent thoughts becoming more lucid and gray, a slave to the storm that was making its way through his system.

He tried to think of the good things in his life, expected to find nothing but a blank slideshow screen when his life flashed before him, but was surprised when her face came to him—looking just like she did the day before she left when he had thought of proposing, even carrying the thing in his pocket the whole night. Instead, he had waited; and the next day, she was gone, her body turned into a sheet of paper overnight, one that spoke of broken dreams and unrequited feelings. She said she couldn't wait for him to decide how he felt, and he couldn't blame her, exulting in her escape not because he wanted her gone but because he knew she would find her happiness far easier without him as an anchor at her side. At least, he didn't regret that. He supposed he regretted not allowing himself a chance to make her happy, but never once did he regret his decision to give it to her.

God, that smile of hers was radiant, like a thousand suns compressed into one, a new day dawning every time she laughed. He could smell her hair on the wind, the mix of lilac and poppies; he could hear her laughter in the shifting of the leaves, light and jovial like the singing of wind chimes.

The horrible moan of the undead broke him from his state of bliss, its horrible connotation stirring images of fire and decay through his brain—a newscast of all of mankind's worst atrocities playing themselves over and over: children dying of mustard gas and napalm, a group of men stoning a woman for daring to threaten society's very foundations by wearing a pair of hot pants, brothers killing brothers over the rights to enslave their fellow men, taking land from one's neighbor and condemning them to death by mutilation and disease.

He grabbed the barrel of the gun and moved it aside before the boy had a chance to react. His speed startled Range, made him reach for a rock or branch behind him to use as a weapon against what he thought was simply another of those hideous creatures.

"Wait," Frank croaked, his throat seemingly catching fire to do so.

His voice gave them pause, with most of the group having moved in, ready to defend the still living from those whose death was already certain. It was hard to stifle resentment, even when he knew he would've done exactly the same as them.

Clearing his throat with more painful hacking, blood started to leak out over his lips, a sight he knew must've made him look even more wonderful than he did normally. He understood why Range had been so readily prepared to put him down, with how much he resembled death.

"T-ty-t…" he sputtered, annoyed at his basic inability to form even the simplest words. "Ty… tyle… Tyler," he finally managed, raising his trembling arm toward the pile of baggy clothes on two legs that was pacing just outside the circle of onlookers.

"What did he say?"

"I'm not sure."

"I think it was Tyler."

"Really? I heard *tire*."

"Well, considering that makes no fucking sense and we have someone named Tyler standing ten feet from him, I think I'm gonna have to side with the Tyler theory."

"What the hell would he want with Tyler?"

Tyler seemed to know just as little as they did, which Frank expected, but he wasn't planning on enjoying the look of bewilderment etched into Tyler's face as he approached so damn much. He looked to the others, almost like he was asking approval, before kneeling down at Frank's side, his eyes darting nervously as he did so.

"What, uh… what can I do for you, Frog?"

He wanted to tell him to never say that horrible fucking name again, but he knew he wouldn't be able to gather the strength to manage it. Instead, he focused on one word that he knew would get the point across in a way that even someone as dim and inebriated as Tyler could understand.

Frank pulled him close and tried to whisper in his ear, but the syllables were fighting him every step of the way, his breath leaving him in mere seconds. Tyler's eyes squinted as he tried to listen, leaning in far closer than any of the other, more rational members of the group would've, and Frank admittedly admired him for it.

"What? I can't hear you, Frankie. Do you want me to end it instead of this fag here? Is that it?" he asked, Range's face souring but only for a moment.

Frank shook his head vigorously, coughing as he did so, before grabbing Tyler's collar and yanking it until his ear was next to Frank's teeth. This caused even Tyler to jump, Frank included, as he thought his body would betray him and begin chewing away Tyler's lobes like grapes. But he stopped just as he intended, and using one last burst of breath and energy, he whispered one word in Tyler's ear before slumping back to the ground.

A sly grin spread like weeds over Tyler's face before he broke out into a fit of manic laughter. He stood and walked over to the duffel bag near the edge of the clearing, hoisting it over his shoulder as he carried it to Frank's side.

"What did he say?" Matt asked, but Tyler ignored him, turning his attention to the bag and unpacking its contents.

"I'm gonna be real with you, Frank. I didn't think you had something like this in you. For that, and a lot of other things, I apologize. I owe you a debt, and it's a damn shame I don't get to repay it in a way other than this," he said, placing something small in Frank's outstretched fingers.

He cupped his free hand over the both of them to make sure Frank held it securely, giving him a look of authentic respect that almost brought tears to his old eyes.

Frank nodded and mouthed the word *thanks* before sending him away. The others started to ask questions of him before looking down at the small egglike package in Frank's tight grip.

"Is that a fucking hand grenade? Because that looks like a fucking hand grenade."

Range understood what Frank planned to do immediately and dropped to his side, an intense look in his eyes. There was an outburst of arguments around him, but he focused on Range's placid features, smiling at the tenderness he found there, wishing he had more time to act like a father to the boy, who—if Marshall's stories were to be believed—desperately needed one. He placed his free hand on his cheek, wiping away the ghost of a tear as he held it there.

"You don't have to do this," he said, his voice wavering. "I don't want you to do this."

Frank smiled. He wanted to tell him that, in his sad excuse for a life, he had few things that he didn't regret; and this decision, as unpleasant and difficult as it was to make, was definitely one of them. He wanted to tell him a good many things about his own mistakes, about Marshall, about how great a man the boy was going to be. However, he liked to think the silence said it better than he ever could anyway.

"Come on. Let's keep going," Range said, his eyes still locked with Frank's.

Slowly, he stood, as if he was waiting for Frank to change his mind; but Frank only smiled, laying his head back on the grass and relishing in the cold autumn breeze.

He heard the shuffling of feet as the group left. He heard muffled protests from Matt and Bruce—both of which were finally, but gruffly, persuaded to respect Frank's wishes, as ludicrous as they might seem. Soon, as the silence fell again, Frank found himself alone.

He sat there for a while, enjoying the peace, when he heard a low, rumbling growl. He wasn't sure how much time had passed. The world around him had become nothing more than a fever dream. Sitting himself up on his elbows, he stared into the shade of the trees around him and saw those pale white eyes looking back at him.

Stepping out of the shadows, one of the grinning wolves stalked its way up to him, a small snigger coming from between its grisly teeth. More laughter echoed around him as the wolves began appearing from the shadows, joining the chorus. Frank thought he heard Klunesberg's hearty wheeze among them, but whether it was simply a part of his own fractured mind was impossible to determine.

The wolf leading the pack's grin disappeared, morphing into a hideous snarl at the drop of a hat—its jaw extending, stretching out, elongating even further than it had. Its green, rotting gums protruded from the tufts of furs covering its lips, looking like an alien out of those movies. Its teeth kept going well past their normal length, blood and mucus appearing where gums had been. It looked like its skeleton was trying to pull itself from the sack of skin that had once held it.

Frank figured this was as good a time as any, and fumbling with the small ball in his hand, he found the small silver ring and, with a tug that required all his strength, pulled it loose from the top. The wolves seemed to understand this, or at least, found the motions comical enough to break into another resounding chorus of cackling.

They set upon him, their jagged teeth tearing into his aching flesh and shaking it violently to more easily pull it from his bones. The pain exploded into pure agony before turning to a constant that faded into the background of his mind.

He thought of her, and his days at the bar, Marshall and Range's exciting stories and nervous energy, Matt excitedly telling of his sexual conquests as he poured them all another shot of cheap whiskey. He even thought of Tyler, telling his audacious stories in the animated way he did.

He remembered too late Tyler's avid description of DMT—the drug that turned your final few seconds into an endless eternity, at least, by our own limited perception, regret pouring in like a broken levee as the small object clutched in his hand exploded outward, engulfing his face in searing, burning flames that ate away the skin.

Veronica wanted to scream when she heard the sound of the explosion but clamped her hands over her mouth to keep from doing so. The others in front of her turned back to look, their ears perked and eyes wide, but Veronica found herself unable to. She knew that if she did, the guilt that was already eating away at her would only worsen—its decay becoming more pronounced, its odor more fetid and vile.

She felt more than a little naive and overly dramatic, blaming herself for the old man's death. But seeing him lying there, half of his shoulder hanging off his narrow, listless frame was almost too much for her to bear, reducing her to a strained, guilty silence. Embarrassed by her display of weakness, she had kept her distance from the rest of the group, afraid of what she might say or how her voice might crack. She couldn't afford to appear fragile now, after she had held it together for so long. She was still in better shape than that pathetic loser Billy, who shared Veronica's affliction of muteness but was also constantly wiping his sleeves over his mucus-covered face, like a toddler that bruised its knee.

He sickened her. She would not end up like that.

And yet, she could not get that poor man's face out of her head—the scared expression he wore when he knew his death was certain, imminent even. It was so real, so utterly real and unlike any of the trite meaningless trappings they wore in high school, playing offense at imagined slights. Everything that had seemed to make up the structure of her world was suddenly revealed to be nothing more than wet sand, playthings that could be swept away heedlessly by the tide. Amanda getting upset because Tim Markerson didn't say he loved her after she let him finish inside her was an invention of boredom and the feeling of entrapment—an endless repeating of the same routines day in and day out, until you can't remember a time in your life outside of that unrelenting cycle. But that old man's face… that was something else entirely. Something that bore actual consequences, carried actual weight.

Weight that was thrown right onto her shoulders.

"Do you think that was… ?" Gwen started.

Her voice trailed off, and her gaze fell to the sidewalk, almost as if she didn't want to know the answer—typical Gwen. She looked twice as heartbroken by the old geezer's sacrifice, and she wasn't even responsible. She didn't even know what it's like to have to bear someone's death on your conscience, but ignorance of other's problems had never stopped Gwen from assuming her own were always at the top of the totem pole.

"Yep," Bruce said softly, "I'm guessing it was. Poor bastard."

"I'd make a toast if we had something to drink with it," Matt said, not looking up.

His arms were crossed in front of him, hugging his chest as if he was shivering. His fingers tapped against the folds of his arm and scratched at itches that covered the length of his body. Despite their years apart, she remembered enough about her brother and his… habits to recognize what was happening. She made sure to keep her distance.

Tyler raised the blunt between his fingers into the air as he exhaled a large puff of smoke, giving a small, empathetic cough.

"For Frank."

"How… quaint," Bruce remarked, giving Tyler a reproachful stare before he moved into the intersection ahead of them, moving around an old Toyota station wagon to do so.

"It was my fault."

Veronica had to touch her own lips to make sure she hadn't spoken without realizing it. They were dry and cracked but firmly sealed. A sob from behind her made her whirl about, to see Billy falling to his knees, his face a moist mess of tears and snot.

"He wanted me to get his back, but… I just couldn't. It's my fault he's dead."

"You bet your weaselly fucking ass, it is," Matt said, hocking a giant lob of spit into the street.

Billy cried as if struck, but his self-pity soon festered into a hollow rage as no one supplied any comfort—even Gwen, his greatest ally, who merely stared at him with eyes that were as expressionless as the dead.

"All I had to do was take care of the… of the child, but I… I couldn't. It was a child, for fuck's sake! I mean, he looked just like my little cousin. For all I know, he might've been. How the hell was I supposed to just stick a goddamn piece of glass in its head?" he shouted, not daring to look at anyone while his rage was directed at them. He was too much of a coward for that.

"You think I wanted to stab that woman? Huh? Do you think I enjoyed doing that? Do you think I enjoyed splitting that little fuck's head in two across a curb? That this is how I get my kicks? Huh? How I get my rocks off? Well, fuck that. I didn't want to hurt those people—if you can still call the dead people—but if I didn't, I would've been just as dead as them, along with the people I care about." Matt spared a glance, however fleeting, at Veronica—which was enough to make her skin crawl. "I did it because we were left out there, with no one to help us."

From the way he turned his back on Billy, and toward the rest of them, he appeared to be addressing the lot of them now, his fingers scratching at his neck.

Veronica felt her cheeks get hot, the shame mixing with the guilt in her stomach for a violent cocktail of nausea. She wanted desperately to change the subject, to avoid the darting eyes as the others looked to her, condemning her. Matt still hadn't figured out it was her who had insisted that they leave him in the streets, her opinion providing the most sway over the rest, especially Bruce, whose rationality and enmity toward Matt provided few objections. Gwen and Range had made the biggest scene, neither for Matt, of course, but for the decrepit old man and a pussy big enough to rival Sarah Hyland's floppy beef curtains. When told that they themselves could gladly volunteer to help them, they shared a glance and sat reluctantly in passive-aggressive silence while Victoria had relished her victory, be it a minor one.

"I don't know about that. You seem like the type of guy who enjoys his violence," Bruce said through a mocking grin, "especially when you can make yourself a good-enough excuse for it."

"Oh, come off your high-horse bullshit, cocksucker. You've shot just as many people as I have, or have you forgotten?"

"Only the dead ones, though."

Matt resigned himself to a constrained silence, his own brooding tantrum he liked to throw when confronted with his shortcomings. It was the same reaction he had when their father called him out on the late nights and bad grades and all the women that kept coming through the living room just after dinner, leaving just before sunrise, many of them twice his age. Matt gave no explanation for his behavior. He simply wore that blank, labored scowl as he packed his things, leaving the house without a word as to where he was going. Their parents had run after him, their mother to the front lawn and their father all the way to the end of the block where Matt parked himself on a bench, waiting for a bus. When he was unable to convince him to return, receiving only more of that contrived silence, he threw his hands up in a huff and walked back, slamming the front door behind him, throwing the dead bolt as if it served as a final sentence, the slamming of his gravel. Veronica had heard the whole thing from her room, even through the closed door. She saw him pass by the window but didn't care enough to see where he was going. She was afraid that if she did, he might change his mind and come back, or the whole thing would reveal itself as another cruel joke the universe decided to play on her.

"Well, it doesn't matter now whose fault it is. The important thing is, we use Frank's distraction, make sure it wasn't a waste. We need to get to the hospital quickly before—"

A rancid, clicking groan cut him off, timed almost too perfectly, like a cue from a bad high school play. From the swirling mists that covered the sea of abandoned cars in front of them, they saw shadows start to form, their opaque forms becoming fuller, denser. First there were two. Then there was five. Then eight. Then eighteen.

Veronica saw the futility in counting once she got past twenty-five.

The rattling groan fell away, and several more took its place, but each individual groan sounded like a thousand painful wails merged into one pitiable sob. Some wavered with anger, others with cold indifference; but sorrow dripped from them all, rolling down Veronica's skin as it crawled.

"Oh, noooooooo," the old waitress moaned, her own slobbish voice mixing far too well with the cries of the undead.

Veronica wanted to tell her to shut her cock trap but was too afraid to draw any more attention to herself from the shadowy onlookers. She still entertained some naive hope that they might just pass them by, or even that she might just wake up in her bed, drenched in sweat, telling herself it was just a dream—a sick, twisted, and hyper-realistic one that would probably result in therapy; but it was just another thing to add to the list, she supposed.

The first one to appear was far wider than its shadow implied: a fat, slovenly creature with gray flaps of skin rolled on top of each other, like a decaying Michellin Man. A festering hole had been made in the center of its stomach, its edges raw and crated with yellow pus that dripped down its jiggling belly and onto its nubs that it called feet. From the depths of the literal pit in its stomach, crawled forth centipedes and their million-legged brethren, spiders and the like, circling the edges before retreating back into their damp, cavernous abode.

Behind the wobbling tub of zombified lard came a woman, naked save for a pair of bloodied panties. At first, Veronica thought they had been cherry red; but she soon realized from a dry spot on her hips that they had been a brand of unflattering granny panties stained by a downpour of blood and bile that had turned the fluffy cotton into a sticky, clinging sop around the creature's legs.

As the small husk rambled toward her, she saw that the choice of underwear had been appropriate, wrinkles covering the monster's skin like crumpled wax paper. Her already-drooping face was slunk more than usual, her jowls flapping loose from her jaw at the sides, torn from its moorings, swaying uncomfortably with the heavy breeze. Her breasts sagged nearly down to her stomach and were smeared with dried, crusted yellow vomit.

Despite this, her cool black hair still shone in what little sunlight they had, a gleam that pierced the fog and made Veronica squint against its brilliance. While the rest of her body had been ravaged horribly—her arms turning to leathery flaps like the wings of a bat, thighs that looked like jellied fats slapping against each other, the wrinkles reminding her of tectonic plates crashing against each other—her neck was something of a cross between a turkey's gizzard and Sarah Hyland's source of locker-room embarrassment.

"Where the hell are they all coming from?" Matt hissed, a bad attempt at keeping his voice low enough to avoid drawing the ire of the dead.

"They must've been drawn to the sound of the explosion. We probably could've snuck right by him, but the noise was enough to send 'em right toward us," Bruce said while throwing his back against the wall of a nearby alley.

He had his pistol in his large, ungainly hands, dropping small brass-coated bullets that caught the light into the cylinder.

"Way to go, Frog!" Tyler cursed loudly.

The wobbling, walking tub of fat turned its head, the rolls in its neck squishing together to twice their size as it turned its head toward Tyler. A fat snake of a tongue wriggled its way out of the creature's open mouth as it gave out a tremendous groan, flopping lazily against the side of its neck, bulging blue veins dispersed between the enlarged cilia of the dark-gray skin, looking like something you might pick up at the meat department of the supermarket.

Another zombie had made its way out of the fog and was moving toward Veronica with an outstretched claw, swinging at her as if they were mere inches apart, even though as many as half an entire block separated them. This one's skin was bloated, its head settling down into its neck in such a manner that it was hard to tell where one ended and the other began. A bright-green moss was clinging to parts of its face, going up half of its caved-in cheek, growing over the bit of exposed bone and the crater beneath it. She saw more of the stuff up and down the length of its arm, giving the creature an almost-alien appearance.

When it tried to illicit the usual moan, water bubbled up from its throat, pouring over its open mouth in a swirl of blood and that thick black bile. As it took another hobbled step, more of the murky water bubbled over with a sound that reminded Veronica of choking on your own spit.

Another loud boom ripped through the air next to Veronica's ears, startling her bad enough to cover them and cower defensively. She scolded herself for this after the fact, annoyed at her own fragile instincts. Looking toward the source of the clamor, she saw Bruce firing round after round into the walking blob, his teeth ground and his eyes narrowed.

The bullets either whizzed by the beast's head or embedded themselves into its globulous shoulders and chest, sending shock waves of rippling fat throughout its body but barely putting a dent in its laborious forward march. One round entered the gaping hole in its belly and mushroomed out the folds on its back, shaking loose more of the centipedes making a home in its entrails.

With an angry grunt, Bruce's final shot ripped through the center of the creature's open gullet, sending chunks of brain and spinal cord out the back of its neck. She even saw several limp vertebrae hanging through the exposed innards as the creature fell back on itself, the rolls of fat absorbing one another until its corpse looked like nothing more than a tall pile of gray flesh, crumpled like trash strewn across the sidewalk.

Veronica remembered her own firearm, shoved hastily into the back of her jeans, like she had seen so many times on television and at the movies that it seemed almost like second nature, something she had been doing her entire life. However, when she patted her hands against her backside, she found nothing there but the rough burn of denim on her palms and her own, still-intact spine.

Looking over her shoulder, she saw that her jeans were empty, and all she succeeded in doing when digging her hand into the fold of her jeans was making herself feel like some kind of slobbish dyke and giving herself the most inappropriately timed wedgie. She quickly realized her search was futile and that she must've dropped the gun while fleeing from Gwen's House of Holy Horrors. It had probably slid right out the top of her jeans when she had been running, or maybe when they had been crouched practically to the ground in the bushes, when her back was arched low and her butt pointed out. She had been conscious of Tyler's voyeuristic stare but had learned to ignore such a gross distraction as that as soon as the boys had first started taking interest in her, with their covetous stares that always ran her up and down, even some of the more lecherous adults that weren't as keen at hiding it as others. She had taught herself to take pleasure in it, not entirely a sexual one, but one of liberation. Thinking of it as control, or leverage, made it easier to bear. She thought of it as power, her taking control of those that sought to use her as an object of sexual gratification.

However, lately, she had begun to doubt if that was really the case or simply a well-developed narrative she had concocted to convince herself otherwise, to take some of the shame from the enjoyment away. She did her best to hide it when Matt was around; she wouldn't dare give him the satisfaction. Besides, it was his stare she feared most of all…

"Veronica!"

His voice shattered the silence like glass, its echo crashing into her ears, like sharpened shards drawing blood. She turned toward

Matt, met his stare with one of indifference, one she knew he could easily see right through, but she wore it all the same.

With an animated underhand throw, he tossed something shiny over a small pileup of cars, the small silver gun bouncing off of the nearest Honda's mirror and landing conveniently at the edge of Veronica's feet, scuffing the white plastic with its wooden stock.

It had been the old man's gun before Matt had taken it from his dying hands, the man who had died because of her—no, because of Matt. Matt was the one who hadn't been paying attention. It had been because of Matt that no one had dared to step out into the street to alleviate the threat, Veronica most of all.

When she picked up the bloodied weapon, a stain decorating the end of the barrel and the hammer with a crimson crust, her resolve weakened; and she thought of the dying man's face and the way he stared at them, at *her*, before burying the useless hindrance down in the usual spot in the back of her mind.

The heavy heat washing over her neck alerted her to the zombie standing over her. What she originally believed to be its ragged breath beating across her skin was merely its putrid stink, radiating off its body to the point where you could feel it digging its way into your pores.

She noticed the wrinkles sagging next to her face as soon as she saw the creature, recognized the harrowing toothless smile as dark sludge slid and dripped from its raw gums. The thing fell on her, dropping face-first toward her with its loose jowls flopping in the wind.

Defensively, like she was pushing off a drunken suitor, something she was more familiar with than she would've liked, she raised the gun and her free hand and pushed back against the wrinkly leather beast, her knuckles and the barrel of the gun nuzzling into her sagging bosom.

It took her a second to note that the gun was pointed directly into the creature's chest, but when she did, she pulled hard on the trigger, caught off guard by the recoil that sprung back and nearly threw the explosive steel from her grip. Despite this loss of control, she fired another round as the gun pulled upward; and this time, it flew from her finger and clattered to the asphalt. Neither bullet got anywhere close to the old woman's head, the first burrowing through its heart and the second tearing loose part of its shoulder.

"Aim for the head! The head! Shooting a dead person in the chest isn't going to do anything!" Matt called out angrily from behind her.

"Oh, because the head makes *so* much more sense, foolproof logic right there," she said, finding time for sarcasm as she gathered up the gun from the street.

Merely fazed by the carbonized steel that had burst through its skin, the geriatric zombie pressed toward Veronica, hissing through its glistening gums. She fired another round at the creature's head, trying to line it up under the gun's tiny sights, but the bullet went wide and struck only air.

"Just do it!" Matt said, offering one of his always-insightful pearls of wisdom.

"I'm fucking trying! I've never even fired a gun before! I can't exactly just choose to hit them in their stupid fucking heads."

"Fucking Zambinis!" Tyler shouted, cutting their heated exchange short with his usual gibberish. "You dun' fucked with the wrong son of a bitch, you feel me? You like the taste of that lead dick, don't cha? Choke on my fiery cock, bitch!"

Gunshots erupted from all around her, Matt and Tyler turning to deal with a horde that had started to approach from the rear, drawn by the sound of gunfire. Billy was pointing the small pea shooter of his at the approaching dead menacingly, even if his hand was trembling like a leaf in a hurricane and his face was that of a man who had just shit himself. But she never saw him actually fire the gun, and whether he was simply out of ammo or living up to his pathetic reputation was up for debate.

The freak Range, with his hardened face and chin, his features still set and stern, was firing into several zombies slinking in from an alley between him and Bruce. She hated to admit, he did look somewhat handsome—especially as he grit his teeth with each buck of the firearm, his forearms tensing and showing the lean muscle he hid beneath his bulky jacket. Gwen was, of course, at his side, seemingly unable to function without her man, taking aim at the same small group.

Surprisingly, while most of her shots went high, hitting car windows or unlit lamp posts, at least two connected with the skulls of members of the undead horde, one entering through the eyeball and turning it to a pale jelly and the other going up through the jaw and out the top of its buzzed head.

She saw the little twat's eyes dart over to where Veronica was standing, staring like an awestruck, gawking moron. They shone with life and smirked as if she was so damn pleased with herself. When her lips curled to match the beaming look in her eyes, Veronica almost turned the gun and put a bullet right between her weasel eyes. God knows there was enough room to do so.

Instead, she turned back to the old woman sliding her decrepit legs toward her, the right foot dragging on its side with part of the ankle protruding like a famous Pizan tower. Raising the gun to the creature's face, she shoved it in between its lips, letting the slimy gums slide harmlessly over her hand, feeling the sickening tongue prod and taste her. Disgusted, she pulled the trigger and watched blood explode from the back of her liver-spotted skull, raining down on her in a light drizzle.

A feeling of elation, the likes she'd never experienced before, rushed through her—an excitement that was almost impossible to decipher, impossible to place and understand. She had reveled in the power her looks had given her before, but this… This was something else entirely, something far more intoxicating and alluring.

She refocused on the gun in her hands, the metal clicking from the way her arms trembled. It wasn't fear, she knew, but pure exhalation. Still, she needed to steady herself, or her shots would continue to fly harmlessly by their targets.

Exhaling slowly, she stared down the gun's short barrel, over the small nub of a sight at its end, doing her best to line it up just below the nearest zombie's nose. She eventually decided on the one with moss growing over half of its glossy skin, water still bubbling up from its bulged throat.

Gently, she eased her finger over the trigger, gave it a sharp pull with her finger, bracing for the recoil. She handled it better, the barrel only pointing up at a forty-five degree angle at most, in an arc that lasted no longer than second; but the shot still went wide, crashing through a car mirror just beneath the drowned creature's elbow. She thought it looked like a woman from the curves beneath its clothes, but its skin was lumpy even in the exposed areas, dark splotches like bruises rising from its flesh. Its face, as she observed it through the sights once more, was too formless to place any sort of gender to it. Everything was sagging, and there wasn't a chin or jawline to speak of, only a stretch of skin that went from the bottom of the face to the shoulders.

This time, she pulled the gun up in the opposite direction of the car mirror, hoping she could compensate enough for her own inexperience. She waited to exhale until after she pulled the trigger, keeping the breath tight in her chest as she lined up her shot. Her muscles tensed as her finger squeezed around the trigger, her breath fleeing with the expelled bullet.

The zombie's nose cratered inward, flaps of flesh furling inward, like a hole punched through paper, black pus bursting through the newly opened orifice. Its mouth fell open, the lower teeth extending out past the upper as its skull caved in. The projectile exiting through the back of its neck was enough for the already-weak, bloated skin to come apart in wet chunks along the neckline.

Falling forward then back into its disconnected spine, the top of the monster's head wobbled like a hat in the wind, its already-pale eyes icing over into pure snow. A river of crimson caramel came pouring through the wound as it crumpled to the ground, the skull cap rolling off like a soup lid from the impact's momentum.

"Fuck, yes!" Victoria cried in triumph.

Spurred on by her sudden victory, she felt almost invincible, like death incarnate, ready to rectify the previous jobholder's foul-smelling, groaning mistakes. She laughed in her bloodthirsty glee, amused by the thought that Tyler—as much of the ignorant, debased brute that he was—at least knew how to embrace the pure thrill that came with it.

From a low, especially disconsolate groan, she noticed another one of the undead make its way out the fog and into her field of vision. Moving over the sidewalk near Bruce—who was still struggling to take down the group of three large, hulking zombies that surrounded him—the noticeably thinner creature, wearing long black robes and the white collar of a clergyman, walked with a gait, its leg twisted and hanging loosely by a yellow tendril of muscle to the exposed bone. Blood and bile made his robes glisten in the lowlight, but Veronica blocked out everything but the center of his forward, topped off by a larger-than-an-average-widow's peak. Veronica had always liked that in older men, but now she was almost thankful for it and the larger target area it provided.

Aiming high and to the left again, she fired three shots, slamming the trigger against the stock until she heard the empty clicks of the cylinder. She couldn't be sure which, but one of her volleys successfully scalped the top of the fallen priest's head and the bone beneath, the brains underneath sliding out like congealed honey. As he fell face-first into the cracks of concrete, she saw his gold cross, large and ornate in its design, go bouncing over the hard slabs, the movie's stories of its power over the dead as exaggerated as most everything else in cinema.

"Ha! Take that, you pasty sons of bitches! Did you see that one there, Gwennie? Right in the center of its goddamn head! And that dumb prick said girls didn't know how to use a gun! I'm like Rambo with a better ass!"

Gwen was giving her an odd, frightened stare, trying to shout something over the cacophony but muffled by the ringing of gunfire. Veronica merely laughed, sure that Gwen was trying to argue her kills had been better, more precise, or much more likely, how hers had been much more difficult and traumatic, always playing the victim.

Still high off adrenaline and spilled blood, she turned back to face the street and the slowly growing shadows pressing against the fog.

"Any more of you dumb bastards wanna try me? There's plenty more where that came from, you slobbering idiots! I've dealt with drunk college guys more threatening than you and twice as ugly! I wasn't aware, dying turned people into bigger pussies than th—"

A high-pitched squeal cut short her gloating, coming from right beside her ear, so close she could feel it and how abnormally cold it was. With a whirl, she was face-to-face with one of the dead, its hair a stunning brown, freshly permed and done in a way that had to be professional. Dressed in a bright-yellow jacket with a laminated ID hanging from one loose pin on her lapel, Veronica quickly recognized the reporter from the television, even with half of her face missing.

After the feed had been lost, the missing girl had apparently continued its feast of the young reporter's pretty face, chewing away her right cheek and the eye above it and removing her lower jaw completely; so all that remained was shiny red muscle around a hole for her throat, just beneath the roof of the mouth and teeth that still remained to her. From the dark hole meant to be her throat, a tongue flopped and slid around like a worm on a hook.

Veronica tried to raise the gun to the creature's face, crying out in a confident smirk as she slammed the muzzle into its forehead. It was only then that she remembered that she had run out of bullets.

Another horrifying screech erupted from the dead reporter's throat, its tongue shaking and quivering with fury as it charged her, swinging its arms wildly. One of its clawed hands with its lacquered nails caught in Veronica's mouth, filling it with the taste of nail polish and dirt and vomit. With a tug, it caught on the edge of Veronica's cheek but kept pulling and prying, the sharp nails slicing their way through the skin slowly but surely.

Her scream became one with the beast's as she felt her cheek being slowly ripped in half.

Not all of Loganville's history is some dark mire of death and tragedy. Most of it was. You can't really argue that. But there were bright spots, flowers that managed to grow up from the cracks in the concrete.

The fur trade was a booming enterprise in the early nineteenth century, and there were several notable French traders that operated in the forests outside of Loganville—the most famous of which being Auguste de Vraille, who fought for the preservation of wildlife. Unlike most of their contemporaries, they saw the importance of keeping a balance in the decimation of wildlife, having understood the importance of their environment by spending time with the many of the native tribes of the area. De Vraille would often speak for them at legislative meetings that they themselves were banned from attending and would keep poachers off the land in the off season. The tribes themselves didn't dare go into the forests in which de Vraille made his trade. There were too many stories about it that kept even their bravest from its borders.

De Vraille himself had never shared the tribes' superstition, especially regarding nature. He was of the mind that, while mankind was meant to protect nature, he was also master of it, as ordained by God after its creation. His passionate reverence is what kept him on the citizens of Loganville's good sides—most notably from the town's namesake, who had been elected mayor in 1824, just several years after his father had relinquished the position after six consecutive terms. The two were often seen loudly arguing scripture over poker—one thinking the fiery Logan Longwarden, with his bushy amber-blond beard, was about to snap the fur trapper in two with his bare hands right before he broke into a fit of riotous laughter, clapping the slovenly Frenchman on the back like he was his own brother.

De Vraille ultimately failed in his attempt at preservation, however, with many of the native species dwindling or going extinct throughout the area before his death in 1843. He disappeared during one of his expeditions into the woods, traveling deeper in than he normally would in the hopes of locating some of the migrated animals tucked away in the forest's bowels. Some speculated he took his own life, choosing to hang himself from a cedar tree after seeing the forest's devastation—an outdoorsman defeated by bureaucracy—but that was mostly due to legend the natives told, de Vraille becoming one of the very stories he always scoffed at.

During the Civil War, Loganville was noted for its food production and its contribution to Northern efforts, with General Grant himself personally thanking the newly elected mayor, Rhodes, or something like that. Of course, knowing Loganville, there was plenty of opposition to this support, the town having one of the highest secessionist populations in the North. Many of them organized into attacking shipments of the food, some even bold enough to ride them straight down into Virginia, although many found themselves arrested or gunned down before even reaching their destination.

Of course, the town's biggest claim to fame was Jonathan Longwarden—born in 1878, the grandson of Logan and son of Christopher, younger brother to Charles and Logan II. The town's sole redeeming feature amidst a history of death and mutilation, Jonathan Longwarden was what put this town on the map of American consciousness in the final years of the nineteenth century. While the foundations of the factory were still being laid, Longwarden was already composing such famous pieces, such as, "Fugue in A Minor, op. 167" and "Midnight in the Garden of Eden." He wrote both of these before his eighteenth birthday, and both had been played in Carnegie Hall before the end of the century.

His most well-known piece, "Die Unausweichliche Zyklus," wasn't written until the end of his life, coming after a long hiatus of nearly five years. A lot of music historians account for this lack of productivity with the turmoil in his personal life, mostly the death of his wife in 1906, which is said to be the inspiration for "The Labyrinthine Waltz," although Jonathan never confirmed this, he himself passing away just several months before its premiere in Trotsky Hall in Vienna. Jonathan was meant to attend the premiere, having received an invitation from the conductor to do so, signed by the owner of Trotsky Hall, Augustine Baumgartner, who wrote his own correspondence hoping to convince him, along with several other famous composers who were in attendance—including Louise Japha, Antun Dobronic, and Atanas Badev; but Longwarden died before ever receiving it.

Like most of Loganville history, Jonathan's life was marred by personal tragedy that heavily influenced his work—which, let me tell you, expansive as it is, shares the unique trait of being wholly depressing throughout. This guy could make "Flight of the Bumblebee" sound like Satie's "Gymnopedie" if he wanted to. He had a way of dragging that same tragedy, that same sadness he felt out of any piece he worked on. Despite this, his popularity grew with each piece he produced, the emotion in the melodies inspiring enough to break up the humdrum of marches and sousaphones, which had become all the rage at the time.

And with the life Jonathan had, even by Loganville standards, one really can't blame him for reflecting the tragedy in his own life in his music. His troubles started the very day he was born, his mother receiving an ovarian cyst during childbirth that went unnoticed for several days afterward, with even Maria Longwarden herself unaware of the complication, writing off her abdominal pain as simple postnatal aches and not seeing them for the problem that they were. Several days after his birth, while his mother was feeding him in the family's library, the cyst ruptured, inducing massive amounts of internal bleeding and trauma that rendered her unconscious. Of course, she had been holding young Jonathan at the time, feeding him with her own body when she lost consciousness, and fell right on top of the poor child, nearly suffocating him before a servant noticed the muffled screaming.

The doctor did his best to save Maria to no avail. She had simply lost too much blood before he arrived, so much so that they had found Jonathan surrounded by it while still clutched in his dying mother's arms. When they pried him free, he was dripping with the stuff as they carried him into another room, trying desperately to resuscitate him. The doctor tried to revive him for more than five minutes before finally and ashamedly declaring the child deceased. They had to drag the screaming Christopher Longwarden from the room, along with the child's curious brothers, who had lost their mother and their new brother in the same fell swoop, with little thought that death would soon be a familiar face to both of them.

The boy sat in that room alone for five minutes without anyone going inside it, save for one maid from Haiti—a medical practitioner of sorts, one that dabbled in fields that modern medicine wouldn't dare to tread. No one was quite sure what exactly she did, but sure enough, crying was heard throughout the house, reverberating through the dining hall, the living room, kitchen, and every square inch of hallway in the house that made everyone leap to their feet and sprint to the room in question. When they entered, they found the child at the maid's breast, nursing peacefully while she wore a look of serenity that was almost disturbing. They quickly separated the two of them, the servant receiving a stern punishment for entering the room without permission and for daring to nurse a white child with her tainted milk, but Christopher himself walked in and stopped the assault—although he waited long enough for her to learn her lesson. But for a Longwarden, that was the closest to saintly behavior you were going to find.

After a week of worried nights spent with doctors waiting just outside the child's door, things finally seemed almost back to normal at the Longwarden house, except for the death of the family matriarch. Years passed without much incident, Jonathan growing into a scrawny, troubled young boy who was often at odds with his brothers, who took more after their father with their large frames and cold hearts. They often blamed Jonathan for the death of their mother—as cruel, unsupervised boys are oft to do; and Jonathan, of course, blamed himself—as confused, troubled boys are wont to do. This led to many minor scuffles and conflicts, so many that Christopher had to keep their rooms at separate ends of the house, with Jonathan's room in the empty east wing near his mother's old room and the brothers in the west. Because of this physical separation and the already-widening personal divide between him and his family, Jonathan went into isolation in his abandoned wing, pouring his time into music and the theory around it. He played records at all hours of the day—Beethoven, Mozart, Bach, whoever he could get his hands on. He listened, and he learned, writing out each piece over and over until he could do so by ear.

One day, near his seventh birthday, he came home to find his records missing, not the entire collection; but his most treasured pieces had all disappeared, along with the rest of his room being turned upside down in order to find them. When he asked the maids if they had been in his room, they told him that they hadn't been there all day; and if that had been simply feigning ignorance, they did it well enough to convince young Jonathan of their innocence. When he went to find his brothers and found their room empty, he begrudgingly made a trip into the woods in the back of the house to find Charles and Logan smashing the plastic discs over a rock while humming Schubert's "Unfinished Symphony" and cackling like cherubs.

Jonathan confronted them, and a scuffle ensued, one that left Jonathan with a broken lip but his brother Logan with a compound fracture in his skull. Logan had sent a brutal haymaker into the side of his brother's head, knocking him to the ground; and Jonathan, in his innocent retaliation, kicked the large boy off and over him. Logan quickly lost control of his momentum and fell down the embankment into the creek, splitting his head on a rock at the bottom. His blood mixed with the stream water and sent Charles running back to find their father while Jonathan watched the life drain from his brother's body.

Afterward, the divide between his family and him couldn't have been any wider. His remaining brother never spoke to him again, avoiding Jonathan whenever possible—either out of hatred or fear—until his death in 1898 in the Battle of San Juan Hill as a member of Teddy Roosevelt's Rough Riders. Jonathan wrote a piece for the funeral, entitled "Deces de la Cruate," but he himself did not attend.

His relationship with his father was a tenuous one at best. Jonathan understood his father's mistrust and could even understand his revulsion and took no further insult at his father's attempts to keep their relationship one based purely in familial obligation. After the death of Charles, all the spirit seemed to leave him—a mere shell of a man, a ghost that moved about his own house, lamenting that which never was. Neighbors said the sight of him in the windows was far more chilling than any ghost story—a gaunt, frail man who looked like nothing more than skin stretched tight across shambling bones, his piercing eyes looking down at you with enough malice to make one's stomach sick.

Jonathan, now the sole Longwarden heir to occupy the estate, tucked himself away from the world, leaving his house only to mail off a new piece to his publisher. Throughout this time, he was able to produce such classics as "Eros' Lament," "Pugnare Fatum," "Flight of the Northern Fulmar," "Tempore est suus morbo propio," and "Gregorian March." These works would go on to define him, often cited as his best, save for the final piece he ever produced, which is unanimously praised as his magnum opus and is easily his most well-known arrangement—although I'm getting a bit ahead of myself there, as he wouldn't write that piece until after meeting his lovely wife, Anna Luxington Clark, in 1903.

Their courtship lasted nearly a year, with Jonathan even coming out of the dark shell of his manor to lavish gifts on the young woman, unafraid to show the public that someone of such profound sadness was capable of the same exuberance as everyone else when under love's guiles, something I can relate to a little too well. He asked Ms. Clark for her hand in marriage in 1904, which she joyfully accepted along with her overjoyed father—who provided a more-than-generous dowry in order to mix his blood with that of the town's founder and its most famous citizen, a benefit to him as much as it was to her. In fact, if he could've married the boy himself, he probably would've from the way he gushes over him in his journals.

The only thing out of the ordinary about their engagement came just several days before the marriage, when Jonathan unexpectedly called the whole thing off, refusing to explain himself and retreating into the closed-off wings off his manor, taking no callers and having his servants turn away everyone before they even had a chance to enter the foyer. His young bride was absolutely heartbroken and just as confused as everyone else about Jonathan's sudden change of heart, spending her days sobbing for most of her waking hours, her cries echoing over the stretch of Loganville.

Suddenly, a week after canceling the engagement, Jonathan showed up at Anna's front door dressed to the nines in a horse and buggy so encumbered in roses and orchids that it nearly tipped over from the weight. He apologized profusely for his actions, claiming to have simply been unsure of the future he could provide for his family, especially after the first years of his life had been so marred by tragedy. Anna, being the good-natured woman that she was, scolded him harshly but forgave him soon afterward, as even she could understand his reasoning; and if she had given more credence to it, she might have done the smart thing and ended the engagement herself right then and there.

Instead, like all of us foolish girls in love, she threw herself into it wholeheartedly. Their wedding was attended by nearly everyone in Loganville, an event whose pictures still hang in town hall and in several of the back study rooms of the library. It looked like some kind of carnival—hundreds upon hundreds of people, all laughing and cavorting with one another, all except Jonathan of course, who looked as somber as ever, if not more so. When you think of all the pain and death that was monumental in Loganville's founding, especially those directly caused by its founder whose very great-grandson was at the center of the jubilation, all the darkness and tragedy that had spotted every inch of the town's history—it's almost odd to see them so happy and carefree, like when you see a picture of a dictator relaxing in their civilian attire, the illusion of their terribleness shattered by one image of them in jean shorts.

The couple entered into marital bliss for several years, happily appearing at public events like the celebrities that they were, like pre-Depression Kennedys of Northern Maine. Many people expected them to conceive a child almost immediately. With how they carried themselves in public, many thought them to be going at it like rabbits while they were in private, but complications made conception difficult for Anna. It wasn't that she was infertile—quite the opposite, in fact. The zygote would replicate itself too quickly, splitting itself too thin, into too many separate cells until its very existence was no longer sustainable, resulting in a bloody and consistently dangerous miscarriage. They lost three children this way before nearly giving up hope.

In the summer of 1906, however, the pregnancy finally took; and in the fall, when Anna Longwarden's belly began to show, the town went into an absolute frenzy, celebrating as if the child was their own. And in a way, it was. It was the great-great-grandchild of their beloved town founder, the son of their most prominent and celebrated citizen in the town's history, the living embodiment of all their pride and hope for the future.

The months passed with the buzz growing to a fever pitch. People were making bets about the child's gender, having naming contests over drinks until the suggested names became nothing more than strung-together slurs; some even suggested a festival complete with Ferris wheel, and all, just to celebrate the joyous occasion. Of course, this meant that when the time drew near, people began regularly reporting to the Longwarden estate for news of the child, only to leave disappointed and with a growing concern that began fidgeting just beneath the joyous, celebratory surface.

When the ninth month came and went without the baby's arrival, those concerns started to boil over—not just with the citizens, but with the Longwardens themselves, who had the doctor on call every day stopping in to check the child's vitals. Halfway through the tenth month, Anna collapsed due to cramps in the west-wing hallway, her water breaking in a rush of fluid and blood.

For the next few days, Anna's cries once again echoed over the hills and valleys of Loganville—although now they were not haunted by grief but by terrible, agonizing pain that chilled anyone unlucky enough to hear. Labor lasted several days, Jonathan himself barely ever leaving the darkness of the room, allowing only the doctor and a few of his most trusted servants to enter. With the cries that came from behind the door, not many were really itching to get inside in the first place.

Those that were stationed outside reported hearing a terrible screaming, even worse than the cries that had been a steady constant before but far more drawn out and bitter, deeper and guttural like a beast's. Blood began to seep out from underneath the door, until the servants were standing in a puddle, unable to resist entering when the pool started to turn into a lake and then a waterfall as it reached the stairs.

When they entered, they found the doctor catatonic in the corner of the room, unable to speak or even focus on anyone that was speaking to him, his eyes a blank canvas. Anna lay on a futon in the center of the room, her legs spread wide with a bloodied white sheet covering them. Her mouth was frozen in a scream, eyes wide and bloodshot, and her unhinged jaw hanging loosely. Jonathan himself was standing by the bay window, holding his lifeless child in his hand with a look in his eyes that said that the world had finally betrayed him for the final time.

The whole town went into mourning, burying mother and child together in a grave at the top of the tallest hill in town so that they might be closer to heaven to make the unborn child's ascent easier. Dante believed all the unbaptized children wound up in purgatory, but the people of Loganville were not known for their literary minds.

Jonathan went into further isolation from the world, leaving only for the funeral procession and whatever other arrangements needed to be made. He had many visitors, none of which he saw or admitted into the house. Many claimed to hear him working away furiously at the piano, saying it was the most heart-wrenching thing that'd ever graced their ears.

A year and a half after Anna's death, Jonathan emerged from the shadows, walking the streets in the dead of night to deliver his final piece—his magnum opus—to his publisher that had relocated to a house in the center of town a couple of years prior. The stunned man knew quickly the importance of the piece placed in his hand, but still, his thoughts were on Jonathan, attempting to get him to speak and talk about his disappearance and his long hours spent in solitude. But he barely pried a word loose from his tightened lips. Defeated, he abided Longwarden's request and set to publishing the piece almost immediately while Jonathan returned to his shadows, apparently satisfied.

Jonathan's final piece, "Die Unausweichliche Zyklus," premiered at Loganville town hall in 1908, organized by the publisher in coordination with the town in the hopes of drawing the reclusive composer out of his manor for a night meant to celebrate all the joy he had brought to the town with his music, despite its melancholic nature. The ploy worked, with Longwarden himself attending the event—as captured in pictures of the night that still hang beside those of the wedding in the town hall and library's back corridors. Longwarden himself seems relatively happy, bearing a harlequin grin in the few photos of him alongside other illustrious members of the town—including the mayor Kenneth Grosting, industrialists

Michael Carpenter and Jason Cunningham, and owner and operator of the shoe factory that had burned down several months before, Marcus Savini, wearing an expression as slimy as his hairpiece.

Several thousand people squeezed into the small auditorium for the thirty-six-minute piece, with hundreds standing in the back just to be able to get a chance to hear the masterpiece during its first performance. After the final crescendo, the crowd erupted into a thunderous applause and standing ovation that lasted nearly half an hour itself, the entire crowd moved to the point of tears, showering and heaping their praise on Jonathan, congratulating him on producing something so beautiful from something so tragic. He took each compliment in stride, shaking the hand of every person who came to him and sending them off with that weak smile of his.

When the night finally came to an end, Jonathan was the last one in the auditorium, standing on the stage as the lights went out, engulfing the room in darkness. As accustomed to it as he was, this was his cue to leave; and calling for his servant to bring the carriage around, he returned along the rough dirt roads to the Longwarden manor at the edge of town. He thanked the driver profusely, tipping him nearly three times the usual amount, an equivalent of a month's pay, while he retreated to his room. Staring out of the bay window that overlooked the town his great-grandfather had raised from the bloodstained dirt, Jonathan swallowed a sifter worth of brandy and gave the town that had given—and taken—so much from him one final, longing stare.

And then, Loganville's most beloved and celebrated citizen, their favorite son that had given the town new life, hung himself from the rafters—his lifeless body staring out the bay window for all the town to see with the rising of the sun.

Bruce saw the creature tear the poor girl's face apart, its fingers poking through the cheek and out the other side as it dragged its fingers through her skin like a rake. The cry she made was one he knew he would hear in his nightmares for years to come, if he lived long enough to have them, the pitch distorted by the blood being funneled down her throat.

The dead in front of him were making their usual howls but were easily eclipsed by Veronica's wailing, even distracting the walking cadavers from the meal in front of them. While Bruce's skin was still roiling from the sound of the young girl's screams, he knew that to waste the opportunity that had fallen into his lap would be incredibly foolish and a death sentence in its own right.

Rushing into the nearest corpse, he crashed into its chest, its nauseating stench turning his stomach over as he knocked the flailing creature into the dirt. Its wild movements snagged the other zombies surrounding it, dragging them down with it until they were a pile of thrashing limbs struggling to untangle themselves. Bruce ran toward the girl, making the mistake of stepping too close to one of the creature's hands, which was loose enough to strike at his ankles like a waiting cobra.

Despite looking like nothing more than burlap sack of assorted bones and vaguely human features, its strength was greater than Bruce would've ever anticipated for something of its size. With a swift yank, Bruce's leg had been ripped out from under him, dragged despairingly closer to the zombie's chipped, blackened teeth that were snapping like a trap.

Bruce levied the momentum in his favor and twisted his boot so that his foot collided squarely with the creature's gaping maw, crushing its nose up into the back of its skull and sending its rotted teeth bouncing over the pavement. Its grip tightened, so sharply and suddenly that he thought it squeezed the tendon to the size of a straw, but it went limp soon after.

Pushing off the asphalt hard enough to tear the skin, Bruce felt the gun digging into his palm, almost weightless, just another part of his arm, so familiar and fitted to the folds of his hand that he hardly noticed it anymore.

He reached the girl in a matter of moments—the snarling reporter trying to free itself from Veronica's skin, its fingers tangled in the muscle, coated in the blood. Veronica's throat had gone dry, but she was clinging to consciousness, her fluttering eyes looking up into the demon's half a face, its tongue rolling around the dark abyss of its throat, like some kind of flatworm. The creature, once a pretty young thing like Veronica until something had torn off its jaw, was attempting to twist the poor girl's neck to an angle deep enough to crush its remaining teeth into her bared neck, scooping up the chunks of muscle and skin like a spoon through a cantaloupe.

Time slowed, adrenaline pumping through his veins like a drug, giving him enough time to decide against firing his gun while the living girl was still entangled with the dead one. Cracking its skull with the wood stock of his revolver seemed the much more sensible idea, one he indulged in as soon as the back of the monster's permed head was visible.

The blow knocked the creature from its feet, what little balance it had retained in death leaving it almost immediately; but instead of falling, it floated in midair, held by its snagged arm straining its victim's flesh to its limit. Veronica began to scream again, even more piercing than before, as its still-twitching fingers pulled down the remnants of her cheek, the remaining strips of skin and muscle tendrils tearing and unfurling like streamers. Finally, with a sickening plop, the remaining pieces of her cheek gave way and tumbled to the ground clutched in the zombie's hand, blood pouring from the wound and splattering on the road like raindrops.

Bruce grabbed the crying girl away from the fallen creature still trying to right itself, looking more like a turtle trying to roll on its back than a bloody reanimated corpse. Cradling the trembling girl in his arm, he lifted his boot over the remaining half of the zombie's face, its slobbering tongue slapping against its neck, with black bile rising from the shadows behind it. He slammed his foot down with a satisfying crunch, one he might've enjoyed a little too much, as its head caved in around the plastic sole of his boot, blood flowing in through the rivets. Some even splashed up onto his face, catching on his eyelashes, which he almost instinctually rubbed right into his corneas.

He had to pry his foot loose; the skin and bone that had been the creature's head coiled around his foot like a cast. Looking down at the thing, he hardly even recognized it as human. It was mostly just pulpy red chunks and scattered teeth, white goop that looked like it had once held a colored iris in its center. A puddle of blood had formed around the body, staining its bright-yellow lapel, dulling the colors that seemed to shimmer in the reflected light of the fog.

"Hey! Hey!" he said, turning his attention to the sobbing girl at his chest. "Can you move? Can you walk?"

She made to lift her head, before jerking to a sudden stop. Embarrassed, she nuzzled deeper into his pit—ignoring the aroma, if she could even smell anymore, and the dampness there—and nodded slowly, woozily. Bruce felt a terrible shame for the girl but knew that if they stayed in the center of the street, it would only be a matter of time before another walking corpse would come to finish the job that had already been started.

"Hey, I need you to walk when I walk, all right? Just feel it out. There ya go, one step at a time, all right? We're just gonna head to the alley, and I'm gonna try and stop the bleeding."

She moved as if she wanted to protest his final amendment but was in no state to protest and obediently mirrored his steps, her face still buried in his chest and her eyes watching his feet. They stumbled several times but quickly reached the alley that Bruce had taken shelter in—even managing to avoid the thriving pile of dead he had left in the sidewalk, the two dead with their brains intact still valiantly struggling to free themselves from their unmoving comrade.

When they reached the dirty green Dumpster, Bruce put it between them and the street and tried to sit the girl down. However, she clung to his shirt with her manicured nails tearing into the fibers of his uniform.

"Hey, hey, it's all right. I just need you to sit down so I can take a look at you, okay?"

She shook her head gently, pressing herself harder into the pressed fabric. Bruce knew that he had some time before any of the dead noticed them but not enough to deal with the girl's newfound self-esteem issues. He wasn't old enough that he couldn't remember his time in high school. If anything, he remembered it too well sometimes—the pain and the confusion that came with hiding your differences. And his only crime had been enjoying a different set of genitalia than most, while this poor girl had just had half of her face nearly ripped off.

"I'm just gonna look at it long enough to stop the bleeding and patch you up, okay? That doesn't sound so bad, right? You have my word that I won't tell anyone what I see. It'll be our little secret, all right? That sounds fine, doesn't it?"

The girl was trembling like a leaf, but she finally relented, letting herself drift away from Bruce's tightened chest but covering her face with her dirty hands as soon as the fresh air touched it. She fell back against the wall, slumping down into a sitting position, quiet sobs muffled against her palms.

Bruce looked at his sleeve, decided that he was never going to wear the damned uniform again after today anyway, even if he didn't manage to avoid getting any more liters of blood on it at this point, and tore it off at the shoulder. He quickly realized he didn't have anything to clean the wound with, save for a small puddle of what he at least hoped was water that lay beneath a slowly draining gutter. Tearing the sleeve into one long strand, he dipped it reluctantly into the dirty water, unsure if it would clean the wound or just smear more bacteria into it.

"All right, sweetie, I know you don't want to, but I'm gonna need you to move your hands, or else I can't get at the wound."

She shook her head, buried it in her knees with more gushing sobs, but kept her hands pressed firmly against it. He could see the blood dripping out from between her fingers, rising like that globulous alien creature from that old James Dean movie.

"Hey, come on now, it's just like we talked about. It's gonna be our little secret. If you don't let me do this now and get this bandage around you before the others show up, then everybody's gonna be able to see, and I don't think you want that."

Bruce almost felt guilty for using her own insecurities against her but deemed it necessary, at least enough to ease his conscience for now. Begrudgingly and labored to the point where it was hard to tell if she was moving at all, Veronica pulled her hands from her mangled face, strands of blood sticking and stretching as she separated them.

He did his best not to show his disgust, but his fastidious breakfast came up in his throat and almost gave him away. She would never be beautiful again; that was for sure.

From her right lip, the skin was split nearly up to her ear—a sloppy half of a harlequin grin, the cut jagged and misshapen, lumps of flesh pressed and pulled from its place that made it look like scrunched-up fruit pulp than skin. Through the open wound, you could see her teeth pressing through the ragged flesh, the upper half of her jaw nearly entirely exposed as the upper cheek seemed to have been ripped clean off with only small shreds dangling over the gap. Her tongue would occasionally slither through the chunks of torn skin, apparently unintentional, a reflex trying to probe the recent destruction and make sense of it all.

The ear had been disfigured as well, the bottom half of the lobe lacerated clean off and the upper half oval of cartilage was left with a serrated chunk in its center, crusted with dark crimson blood, a chipped edge of dirty yellow fingernail embedded in the wound. Bruce went to pry the jagged shard loose but thought it might start another spurt of bleeding, one that the girl might not survive, especially if the wooziness prevented her from walking any further. From the way her pupils were dilating, he could tell her bonds to this reality were already wearing close to thin.

Instead, he wrapped his hand in the wet cloth and slowly dabbed along the edge of the wound, being careful to press as lightly as his trembling fingers would allow. The sound of screaming in the distance and that dreaded moaning did nothing to steady his hand. More than once, the girl pulled back as if struck, the pain causing her eyes to squint and water and a low whimper to rise from her raw throat. One time, she pulled back so hard that she nearly cracked her head open on the red bricks behind her, the bits of blood and brain being almost indeterminable against the bright crimson concrete; but luckily, she received no worse than a slight bruise.

"All right, now, I'm going to wrap this around the… around the wound, okay? The only way to do so would involve covering up your mouth, like a gunslinger from those old Western movies, although those are probably before your time. Hell, they're before mine, but you can thank public-access television for that one."

The girl gave him a quick nod, a dazed one that reminded him of his own, sharp and to the point. Smiling lightly enough that you wouldn't notice unless you really looked, he reached behind the girl's head to fix the wrap when he noticed how dirty the cloth had become. Small clots of blood and splotches of mud decorated it from one end to the next. Looking at his already-uneven uniform, he figured, evening out the other side couldn't hurt, even if it did make him look like one of those douchebags that wore sleeveless tees here in Maine though the temperature barely made it above eighty even on the hottest summer days. Oh, well, the only ones around to judge him now were the dead.

Tearing loose the other sleeve up the thread line, he tore it from the center and wrapped it hastily around the back of the girl's head. He took special consideration to make sure it fell over every inch of the bloody gash on her face. It was only long enough to go around her head twice, but that seemed to be enough. He tied it off in a small knot in the back and checked his work with a critical eye. It was loose, ragged, and already soaked with blood, but she did look almost stylish and a little imposing. The comparison to an old gunslinger was an apt one.

"There ya go. Like I said, it'll just be our little secret, all right? I'm almost jealous. That bandana makes you look like one tough son of a bitch. I'm sure even the dead would think twice about fucking with you now, you know that?"

She looked up at him with bright, expressive eyes, ones that almost took him by surprise with their brilliance and broke his heart all the same. He saw tears forming at their corners, ones she held back. He respected her immensely for that and gave her a small smile to show it. From the way the sash moved, he thought she smiled back; but for all he knew, it might have very well been another sob.

"The wrap should hold you over for now, at least until we get to the hospital when I can clean you up a bit better. Hopefully, we can find some stitches or something less cumbersome that won't cover up the rest of that pretty face, all right? But if we wanna get there, we're gonna have to get up and out of this scummy alley, you got that?"

She gave a slow, labored nod, one of extreme pain, which was understandable when any sort of movement caused a gash that covered half of your face to reopen. Still, without even another word, she was clawing her way up the wall behind her—nails digging into the cracks of sediment like a house cat as she pulled herself to her feet. She became unsteady, leaning so far to one side that Bruce was sure she was going to tip past the point of recovery and went to catch her. Swatting his hand away like it was no more than a gnat buzzing too close to her ear, Bruce could only chuckle as she righted herself, brows furrowed as she did so. Bruce thought of telling her just how much she reminded him of himself—especially at that age, when his disconnect to the black-and-white world around him had started to feel like superiority—but he didn't want to come across as some overly gushy sentimentalist.

"Time to get going then. You wait here while I check the street and clear out whatever dead might still be hanging out near the entrance to the alley."

She moved like she was going to protest but stopped herself, either because she knew her words would hold no weight, or something as simple as the words probably caused the half of a Glasgow grin to erupt in a fire of pain.

Bruce turned to face the alley's entrance, his gaze drifting into the depths of the swirling mists and the shadows that moved silently through it. Counting the remaining shells in his cylinder and replacing the empties, he steeled himself for what awaited him where the street and alley met—groans already filling his ears along with all-encompassing pounding of his heartbeat, a drum that urged him forward like those used at war, building his bloodlust to the breaking point.

Before he could even reach the very crest of the alley wall, a figure twisted around it like the flit of a shadow, a wave of darkness breaking against him. A hand wrapped itself up in his collar, twisting until he felt the fabric digging into his neck, cutting off the circulation there. With force, he was thrown against the wall of the alley, so hard the wind blew through him like a blustery autumn day.

His first instinct was to bury his fist into his attacker's face but thought better of it when he considered that he would basically be playing a deadlier game of "here comes the plane" with whatever undead horror had him in its grip. Flinching, he stopped his blow short, watching his fist dangle in front of Matt Métier's creased brow.

With a howl of rage, Matt threw Bruce into the wall again, letting him sink to the ground much like Veronica had moments earlier. Bruce thought, based on his boundless fury and animalistic grunts, that the amateur thief had joined the ranks of the undead; but a swift kick from Matt's wet and crumbling gym shoes was enough to dismiss the idea outright.

"Where's my sister, you fuck?" Matt spat, further disproving Bruce's "he's a zombie" hypothesis but providing fairly damning evidence for his "he's a jackass" theory that he formulated some time ago.

Tasting blood when he opened his mouth to speak, Bruce instead spat the crimson liquid he had become so familiar with the past twenty-four hours onto the concrete, where it mixed with an already alarmingly large puddle of the stuff that Bruce had landed in.

"Would you just calm down? She's ju—"

Matt gave him another sharp kick that sent his head into the bricks behind him, turning his vision to black with flashes of turquoise and magenta and a million other blinding colors that nearly stole him away from the land of the conscious. Somehow, biting down on his tongue kept him awake although the pain was tremendous. He was becoming so used to the taste of blood he had almost forgotten what his mouth tasted like otherwise.

"I don't wanna hear another word from you, you conniving faggot! I saw what happened to her, and I saw you drag her back here! Now, you point, you got that? Point me in her direction, and if she's not harmed, I just might let you live."

Bruce was starting to regret his own charity, especially when he felt one of his front teeth come loose and slide dangerously close to the edge of his throat before he spat it out. The small incisor bounced off his open palm and landed in the puddle of blood beside it, a ripple spreading across the surface.

Lifting his arm was harder than he expected. Those cheap shots had left him woozier than he would've liked to admit. But with what little strength he did have, he angled his arm toward Veronica in her spot near the Dumpster, who had just begun to take note of their new visitor.

As he extended his finger as shakily as that of an old crone, Matt traced a line in the air and followed it to his sister, who was using the Dumpster's lid for support as she stood, or made an attempt to. The sleeve fashioned round what remained of the lower half of her face hid most of her expression, but not the fire that burned in her hazel eyes.

Grinning like a hyena, Matt turned back to face Bruce, his own eyes aflame with a malicious glee. "Thanks a bunch, asshole."

The punch came so fast that Bruce wasn't sure if he felt it first or his face smacking against the bright-red puddle, the liquid filling his ears and giving him the feeling of being totally submerged. He heard the crack of another and felt his chest cave in, but the pain was lost to him, his entire body tingling with numbness.

Somehow, he forced his eyes open, out of some sick fascination to watch as his body was broken. It hadn't been the first time he found himself beaten on the ground. It also wasn't the first time someone had proudly declared him a faggot beforehand either. If anything, it almost made it feel more familiar; he would gladly suffer the beatings of a hundred bigots than endure one more minute of the hell he had found himself in.

Unfortunately for him, Veronica appeared, awash in an ethereal glow, grabbing Matt's forearm as he reeled back for another blow. Matt looked at her with a strange conviction, raising his hand to her as if he didn't even recognize her. It lurched to a slow stop just before striking her, freezing just in front of her bloodied brown bandage. His whole body quivered as if he had been shot, his muscles going limp and his mouth falling open.

Bruce knew to never let a good advantage go to waste and hobbled hastily to his feet. Balancing off the alley wall, he made sure he was level with Matt, even though every part of him wanted to double over and give in to the pain. As soon as Matt noticed him rising, Bruce sent a haymaker right into his cheek.

Matt flew hard into the concrete, so much so that he bounced off like a cheap dime-store super ball. Bruce wanted to say something clever, like, "Visiting hours are over," but he thought he would have to punch himself in the face for that something that cheesy. Instead, he settled for a kick to the ribs, one that left Matt squealing in pain.

"What's going on back here?"

The blond boy had appeared at the alley's edge, a lone shadow given form against the pale backdrop. The fog's wisps curled around him, making him stand out even more through its translucence. Gwen appeared behind him, her eyes still checking the street, enraptured in some unseen monstrosity. When she reached the blond boy, whose name escaped the bewildered and battered deputy, Gwen nearly crashed right into him, unaware of his presence or any of the scene in question before them.

Her eyes went to the squirming man on the floor, his hands buried in the curve of his stomach, his face a strained mosaic of agony. She then saw Veronica standing above him, a tough but determined look in her eyes, the only part of her face that wasn't covered with the garish makeshift bandage—which was steadily dripping blood down the girl's chin and neck in two thin, winding rivulets as if some kind of vampire had sunk its bared fangs into the meaty flesh.

The rest of the group sprinted up to where Gwen was standing, nearly colliding as she had done, sliding into an almost-comical skid as they tried to stop their momentum and dart into the protection of the alley's walls.

As soon as Tyler showed his face, Bruce let out a slow sigh, one of bitter resignation, as the vagabond's eyes immediately went to the body at his feet, his face slowly broiling over with fury. Bruce raised the flimsy pistol in his hand, which he couldn't remember when he had even loaded it last, using the delay caused by Tyler's recent smoky indulgences to get the drop on the furious brute.

"Calm down," he said before explaining himself, hoping that it might be enough to dispel whatever tension there was with wishful thinking. Not surprisingly, it didn't work.

"Nah, fuck that, what the hell did you do to my boy Matty, you Oreo motherfucker?"

"Listen, for one, I'm gonna pretend you never just called me that, and two, your friend here attacked me for the heinous crime of saving his damned sister's life. For some reason, he decided to show his gratitude in that cheeky way of his, you know, by attempting to beat the ever-living shit out of me. Your 'boy' Matt's a real charming fellow, now, isn't he?"

Tyler's push forward came to an abrupt stop when he noticed the bruises Bruce wore and Veronica stepping over her brother's side like he was nothing more than a gum wrapper that had spilled out the top of the nearby Dumpster. Dropping his shotgun into a lax position at his side, he walked past Bruce, eyeing him suspiciously but keeping his distance, his own face awash with doubt at his chosen side.

He grabbed ahold of Matt's arm at the elbow and hauled the groaning, grumbling man to his feet. The other, older woman—Bruce thought her name was Vel—walked hurriedly over to the duo and looked over Matt's wounds, fussing over them like a worried mother trying to get grass stains out of their child's soccer uniform. She kept casting hurt, bitter looks over at Bruce with each new bruise she tended, despite the fact that many of them had nothing to due to with Bruce and more to do with the dead trying to devour them. From the way she was looking up at Matt, he wouldn't be surprised if even that argument didn't divert her mistrust into more reasonable avenues of investment.

"Is this true, Matty?" Tyler said meekly.

Matt raised his head and glowered at him with eyes that seemed darker than the most opaque of shadows and just as all-consuming in their hunger, swallowing Bruce into the void of darkness that lay behind him.

"I thought... I thought he was going to..." he paused, trying his best to formulate the proper words for his intended meaning, "put her out of her misery."

He shifted his devilish gaze to Veronica, whose eyes traveled guiltily to the alley floor. The makeshift bandage moved, and a muffled voice was heard, but only for an instant, so brief and silent you could mistake it for a stray breeze whipping against a wall.

Her eyes clenched afterward, hot tears appearing at the edges, fresh blood dripping down her neck. Bruce moved near her and wiped it away with his thumb. The frown he wore on his face felt like it weighed several tons, dragging him down into the dirt and muck.

"Unlike you, I don't solve all my problems by killing the other person. Besides, your sister's fine. She didn't even get bit. One of those things got a bit too close and gave her a small cut on the cheek, that's all. It's a good thing I got to her before you did, otherwise, she'd have a bullet in her head alongside it."

Matt gave him a stare that promised death—a slow, particularly drawn-out one—but kept still, even if his muscles did tense. Tyler kept his nervous eyes on his friend, his own grip tightening, wrinkles forming in the sleeve wrapped around his fingers.

Gwen stepped forward, eyeing Veronica teasingly, something Veronica noted with an irritable glare.

"Well, whatever you did, I think it's a vast improvement. I mean, I can barely hear her when she talks."

Gwen backed away laughing as Veronica clawed at her, held back only by Bruce's quick intervention. Her nails buried into his arm as he held her, not hard enough to draw blood but enough to make bright-red indentations in the skin. Bruce made sure to give Gwen a particularly disapproving look, even if he did find the light jab funny enough, making him feel a little too much like his mother.

"That's enough of that. We need to focus on getting to the hospital. There are some supplies there we could use, and who knows, we might find some other survivors. I mean, what better place to survive than a place stocked to the brim with medicine?"

"Oh, I don't know, a place that isn't filled with sick and dying niggas?" Tyler said.

"We talked about that word, remember? Racism aside, he brings up a good point. The place is probably going to be crawling with undead, so be on your guard. We don't wanna waste the supplies as soon as we get our hands on them."

"How much farther to the library from the hospital?" Gwen asked, looking at Range, who was keeping watch over the street.

Upon hearing mention of the library, he turned, saw Gwen, and grinned before giving a small salutatory nod to Bruce.

"Just under two miles. From the looks of it, we've got about an hour or two of sunlight left, so we can't waste it. Luckily, the fog seems to make it bright enough that even twilight should be well lit enough for us to get around, although if the power goes down and we have to wander in the dark… well, let's just say, I hope we've got enough bullets left—enough for whoever's left, I mean."

A silence passed between them, the usual after Bruce said something they didn't want to hear but knew to be true all the same. Bruce knew he had a knack for delivering news that many others would find unpleasant, and while it had its benefits, Bruce often saw it as more of a burden than a skill. Now was one of those times.

"We got dinner guests!"

They heard the moans first, the crumbling bodies of the undead forcing themselves into the tight alley corridor. There must've been at least two dozen of them, all moving ignorant of the others around them, wedging themselves into a living wall of flesh that clogged the thin artery-like veins of the back alley.

Tyler untangled himself from Matt, staying just long enough to make sure he didn't crash to the ground without him; but Vel caught him with her shoulder, supporting him as if he weighed half of her size when the opposite was more likely true. Readying the shotgun with a swift pump of the fore-end, a small silver capsule flew from the port and bounced off of the top of Bruce's shoe. He could feel the heat through the leather, enough to make his foot slide back through the shifting crimson waters.

Range wheeled back, loading his own shotgun, as he dodged a fast swipe of one of the creature's yellow nails, which flew over his head and into the bricks of the alley wall, a horrible screeching sound emanating from their touch. One of the shambling undead lunged at them, only to trip over itself and smack into the pavement, its jaw splintering against the concrete, sending teeth scattering outward, like stray comets hurtling across the dark vastness of space.

"Get back!" Range shouted, motioning briskly with his hand.

No one waited for a second appraisal and started immediately moving back further into the alley's depths until they were at the edge of the buildings, in the nook of a small parking lot with two or three small spaces that you would've been lucky to fit anything more than a small compact in.

Matt nearly fell, still dazed from Bruce's blow, something he felt quite proud of, even if the sight of Vel tending to him and straining to hold the weakened man up didn't exactly make him feel like Ghandi or anything.

His thoughts were silenced by the small explosions of the shotguns firing, almost in tandem as the creatures finally pushed their way into the alley, stepping over their already-fallen compatriots in an effort to seize the easy meal in front of them. The round tore through them, ripped heads from shoulders, limbs from torso, and shredded anything in between into jellied bits of quivering flesh that smacked uncomfortably onto the pavement.

Tyler and Range fired round after round into growing crowd of undead, a thunderstorm of gunfire and moans with the splattering of blood taking the place of rainfall. Bruce recognized one of the zombies, a middle-aged Asian man he recognized from a traffic stop earlier that week, whom he pulled over for going twenty over in a car pool lane when the only thing in his passenger seat was a bag of McDonald's and a heavy dose of self-loathing. He tried to give him some spiel about being late for some important business meeting. He remembered the way his cheeks reddened when he had asked if he was bringing his McDonald's into the meeting. Now his cheeks were pale and starchy, covered in a dampness that reminded Bruce of mildew. They blossomed into a more violent shade of red as the buckshot passed through them, turning his vaguely Korean features into a pulp mush. It cut through the slabs of fat around his neck like they were paper, swinging his head back like a human Pez dispenser.

Afraid of seeing someone else he might recognize and care about more than the grumpy office worker whose day he ruined, Bruce started toward the back of parking lot in the rear of building—which, by the looks of a sign above one of the barred back windows, was a kind of fishing shop—and started looking for an escape route that would put some distance between them and the slow-moving dead.

There was a flimsy gate with a horseshoe lock that was covered with a light-green plastic, preventing him from seeing what lay beyond it. Poking a hole through the mesh with his finger, he peered through into a segregated part of the alley complete with a collection of Dumpsters and trash cans near the back exit of a small Indian deli. The cacophonous booming of gunfire continued behind him as he looked up the length of the alley his makeshift peephole allowed him, surprised when he spied not even a single walking corpse and later amused that not seeing a walking dead person had become unusual for him.

"Yeah! Suck that lead dick, mo'fuckas! You like that lead cum all over your face, don't ya, you dead fucks? Ah, shit, I ain't had this much fun since House of the Dead 3! You ever play that one with plastic blue shotties? Hey! Blondie? You even listening to me?"

From the sound of Tyler's bullshit, the zombies had backed them all the way to the end of the alley; and when he turned, he saw Range stepping back into the parking lot, desperately trying to slam more of the small red shells into the loading port. With a pump of the fore-end, he went right back to firing at the unseen horde that was forcing them back, a look on his face that didn't seem to ensure success.

"We need to get moving! There's too many!"

"Speak for yourself, bitch! I'm holding off these ugly cunts just fine! Did you see that shot? I blew this nigga's head off so hard it blew back and killed the nigga behind him! Goddamn, Thugger's 'bout to right a goddamn banger anthem about me!"

Motioning for Gwen, who was standing closest to the fence, Bruce kicked the gate open, the hinges screeching like a banshee. One of the undead that had been standing just out of sight from his tiny vantage point was knocked back, bouncing off the fence in a way reminiscent of a toddler that runs into a screen door. The zombie couldn't have been older than twelve when it was alive, its legs scrawny, wobbly stalks that crumpled inward as he fell.

Wasting no time on his conscience, he sprinted up the groaning, dazed monster and emptied two bullets into its forehead. Drops of blood speckled across his face, tasting rotten on his lips, but he kept down his lunch even when looking into its glassy eyes as they stopped their sickly twitching.

A hiss alerted him to another zombie approaching from behind the gate. It lunged and missed, Bruce taking an easy step back over the child's ruined head, foot sliding through the gravel and catching on a sturdy rock buried in the dust. He brought the revolver up to the spot directly between the zombie's dull eyes, a hint of green behind their otherworldly paleness. It stopped his itching finger, but only for a moment, as he blew the creature's brains out right after.

As it fell, he noticed the similarities between the two and realized that the newcomer had been the first zombie's mother—at least, back when their lungs held air and their veins pumped blood instead of holding it like a fleshy medical bag. She had come at Bruce right after he had emptied two rounds into the poor kid's head. If he hadn't known any better, he might've thought she was trying to protect him—except they weren't *he's* and *she's*, not anymore, only things, dead things trying to devour the living. And it was the living he served, not the dead. All the dead asked for was justice, and two bullets seemed to be the best distributor.

"Come on! Through here!" Bruce shouted, waving his arm over the top of the fence to catch the others' attention.

Unfortunately, he also drew the ire of another pair of undead coming out of the building opposite him. They were large and bloated, layers of fat swinging as they shuffled out of the building's bleak shadows.

His first shot ricocheted off the back wall, and his second went through one of the creature's breasts, although whether it was male or female, he couldn't be sure, and the shot seemed to be absorbed and devoured by the folds of skin. Another shot was swallowed by one of the monsters and exited through its cheek in rivers of black bile, bursting forth like a broken levee.

"I got him!"

Gwen ran up from behind him, sliding into a sturdy stance while she lifted the shotgun to her eye line. With a slow breath, she took her shot and turned the nearest zombie's head into wet confetti with a satisfied smirk.

Not wanting to be outdone, Veronica pushed the grinning girl out of the way and lifted the hand cannon that seemed absolutely gigantic in her slender hands. The creature roared, tendrils of spit flying forth from his open maw, and fell forward, its weight leaning into his momentum and carrying him toward her like a slow wrecking ball.

With the cloth tied around her mouth, the girl looked like a bandit, more fit for robbing trains than slaying the undead, but it suited her sultry frame. She fired, and the bullet smashed into the monster's shoulder, knocking it back and sending him reeling but doing nothing to slow him down as he quickly righted himself. Her second went right into its belly, causing nothing but a slight ripple and for her target to roar even louder, spittle hitting Bruce in the face even though he was still several yards away.

The dead behemoth continued his labored assault, its speed only increasing with its enormous belly carrying it forward, leaning over so far with its head down like a kamikaze. Panic had crept into Veronica's eyes, the trembling of her arms showing through the rattling of gun. Bruce and Gwen went to lift their own weapons, scrambling for the trigger hold when Veronica gave a sharp grunt.

Her eyes narrowed, and the barrel of the gun dropped as the bullet exploded out of it. It crashed through the creature's knee, bursting it like marrow-filled balloon that cleaved the leg in two. With a squeal, the creature fell stomach-first into the gravel, rocks and dust swirling up around him, a cloud moving low over the ground. As it slid to a slow, lurching stop at their feet, Veronica dropped the gun to her side and emptied two more rounds into the zombie's tiny head, stopping its turtle-like flailing in an instant. Her finger kept slamming against the back of the gun, even though all that came was the soft click of an empty clip.

"I think you got it," Gwen said.

Boils covered the creature's body, glistening and gelatinous in the way they shook even though the body had long since come to rest. The force of its fall had created a long divot in the ground, a crater that it had come to rest in, a shallow grave for a man that might've had trouble squeezing into your standard six-footer. The smell from the body was worse than anything he had ever had the misfortune of smelling in his life. Something close to a dead, soaking wet dog that had been run through a garbage disposal and composted in lard for a particularly hot and sunny week.

Bruce turned away, the awful aroma reminding him of their need for urgency. Moving up the small length of alley, he saw that it led out into another small cross section of shops and businesses, with a couple of large Victorians on the other side, visible only by their garrets and spindly weather vanes. One had windows that watched him like eyes, made yellow by the effulgent paint behind them, the uneven siding adding malice to its glare.

Other than the disapproving stare of a couple of empty windows, the way seemed clear. He wasn't sure what street it led out to, but anything was better than the way they came from. There was a small garden nook, complete with a flimsy wide awning with bright-green vines wrapped around its diamond pattern. Several families of flora grew underneath it: gardenias, orchids, lilacs, hydrangeas, and every kind of lily he could possibly think of, and even more whose names escaped him.

It contained a small path that ran underneath the plastic white arch, one made of stepping-stones comprised of pebbles cobbled into discs that led around the side of the building, which seemed to be a type of historical society based on the old-fashioned sign that hung from its side. He couldn't make out most of it. There was too much blood splattered over its chiseled lettering.

It was quiet, disturbingly so, after having seen a man's head rupture just several minutes before. The only determinable sound was the swinging of the old wooden sign on its cast-iron hinges, the thin chains rusted to an orange haze.

The footsteps behind him made him jump, his hands fumbling over the revolver while he tried to remember just how many bullets he had left. When he finally whirled about, he was not met with the face of the dead, decayed and rotting beneath grayed flaps of skin, but something far worse: the scowling visage of Matt Métier, his eyes focused on him so intently he could feel them burning a hole in his skin.

"Did you find something?" he said, calmly but through gritted teeth.

Vel was still at his side, clutching his hand fiercely, like it was some kind of life preserver in the middle of a tsunami; and from the way Matt's hand was making indents in her flesh, the edges turning bright red, he was surprised his grip hadn't broken in her hand in two.

"Just a small path, looks like it leads into the street, but I can't be sure without checking it out further. Might be safer than just the alley."

"Well, is it, or isn't it? It's not like we've got a lot of time to decide here."

"It looks quiet, but like I said, it could infested out front…"

Matt pushed past him, roughly bucking his shoulder into Bruce's chest, knocking the breath right out of him. His feet strode from stone to stone as he reached the edge of the Victorian structure, when he turned around with a devilish grin.

"Seems fine to me."

"We don't know—"

"No, I think, I do know. Yeah, I think I understand perfectly, actually. You want to be the hero. I think you made that pretty clear from your last performance. You know, I might not be the smartest guy or the most knowledgeable when it comes to stuff that happens in this town, especially for a bartender, but I do hear things. I know who you are. I knew from the moment I saw the way you reacted when Tyler talked about shooting that sheriff you love so goddamn much. I've heard the stories, about your promotions, how they all seemed to happen so quickly. Sure, you were good, did the job well, but it takes something special to grease the political gears enough to get them moving that quickly.

"As weird as it sounds, I think I actually believe that you didn't do it on purpose. From all your self-righteous lectures and your annoyingly optimistic attitude, I think you actually do give a shit about the job, and your sheriff, I guess. And the two just sort of happened as a happy coincidence one late night over some white wine and the sharing of some good, ol' ultra masculine service stories.

"Most people in your position would've just shut their mouths, enjoyed the perks, and ignored all the rumors that anyone with a right mind wouldn't say too loudly in public. But you, you actually wanted to earn it. You wanted to be the hero your rank made you out to be. I guess I can't blame you, really. I know what it's like to live a lie, how it can eat away at you…

"But if you wanna relentlessly cling to old-world ideals of chivalry and the self-made man, that's fine, but I won't have you dragging me through the dirt to do so, especially when it involves you putting my sister's life in danger. So while you take your time, being indecisive, trying to think of the best way to reveal your fabled shortcut that will save us all, rekill every one of those dead fucks, and cure cancer all in one go—I think I'll be the hero this time and lead everybody through here and save us all some time and, hopefully, our lives."

Before Bruce had a chance to argue, Matt put his free hand between his lips and whistled, a shrill piercing noise that carried over the wind, down and through the alley. The hair on Bruce's arm stood on end, the world descending into an eerie, unmitigated silence broken only by the bursts of static gunfire and frenzied shouts coming from the parking lot behind them.

Gwen and Veronica, adjusting her flimsy head wrap as they clumsily sprinted up to the archway that Bruce found himself under, gave Matt a quizzical look when they saw his dissembling smirk and the way he moved confidently through the old manse's leaf-strewn backyard. A large, lush scarlet oak—which bore the classic "two-frayed ropes holding up a dirty plank of wood" swing from one of its highest branches—towered above them, swallowing what little sunlight broke through the fog and its canopy; moving to the small stairwell that led up onto the expansive porch that stretched around the length of the house, spotted with large bay windows that normally would've showed off the entire interior of the thick, impenetrable white curtains that seemed to shroud its interior with the same fog that had seized the rest of the world.

"What the hell is this place?"

"You're asking the wrong guy. History was never really my strongest subject."

"Who gives a fuck?" Matt said as he mounted the stairs that groaned loudly in protest.

Vel was still close behind him, cheeks inflamed from the leech-like grip he had around her fingertips. Every step, she would cast a nervous, open-mouthed stare at Bruce and the girls as if ready to protest, before Matt yanked her up higher onto the porch.

"The place is deserted and leads straight through to the street. What does it matter what it used to be? Just suck it up, and grow a pair."

Turning to Gwen and Veronica, Bruce mumbled, "Charming as ever, isn't he?"

The girls gave a small chuckle, Veronica's being muffled and wet—which drew the ire of Matt, who pretended not to notice despite his spiteful glare.

There was a crash of metal and grunts that caused even the overzealous Matt to look toward its source like a frightened puppy. Range had thrown himself against the gate, holding back the horde that was cramming itself against the other side, causing the flimsy steel barrier to shake as if caught in a storm. The loose gravel was doing nothing to help his footing, his ratty tennis shoes slowly losing more and more ground as his body slid out from under him.

Falling onto his rear end, he shoved off and back against the gate, the cheap steel ringing out like a sloppy sword fight you could see at local Renaissance Fair. The other boy, Billy, was cautiously attempting to place his hands flat against the gate in an attempt to aid his struggling compatriot but kept pulling back with every slight shudder and sway. Gray and green putrified fingers jammed their way through the holes in the steel mesh, wriggling like worms and petrified snakes. Some were just inches from Range's face, with several last-minute flinches saving him from having one of the slimy intruders burrowing into his skin, like poor Veronica.

"Hey! Clear a couple of those ugly niggas out for me, will ya."

Tyler was fiddling with a small object in the palm of his hand, his other free hand holding up his slowly drooping sweatpants, the shotgun tucked neatly under his armpit like it was nothing more than an umbrella. He stepped casually in front of the struggling Range, whose feet kept pushing helplessly through his freshly made ruts while the fingers came closer and closer to his exposed face.

"All right, I guess I'll do it myself," Tyler mumbled, looking pitiably at the brown-haired boy. "Now, get your bitch asses out the way. I ain't about to ask you twice."

Reluctantly yet gratefully, Range slid away from the gate with a burst of speed, scooping up his shotgun from the grass beside the gravel road as well. Tyler unloaded two shots into the gate, with the horrid cries of the undead and the stillness of the gate being the only signs that they even made contact. Range fired another round of his own, a flash of blood flying over the top of the fence.

Tyler set to work immediately after, while the sound of the gunshot was still ringing in the air. Sliding the thick shackle through a diamond nearest the edge of the gate, he clicked it into place and backed up with a leap just as the fence began violently convulsing once more.

The three of them quickly began to look for the rest of the group before Range finally spotted Gwen's waving arms just beneath the flower-covered archway. Dragging the frenzied Tyler by the back of his hood and dragging him toward the pathway, Range led the remaining members of the group to the large Victorian backyard.

"That lock will buy us some time but not enough for sightseeing. The gate itself probably won't hold them more than a couple minutes, but that should be enough time to at least lose them."

"How many of those damn things is there, fam? I must've blown at least twenty of them into fucking dumplings, but there's still more than I can count banging on that piece-of-shit gate."

"Well, that really doesn't mean much, coming from you."

"It doesn't matter anyway!" Matt declared, stunning the group into an awkward and dreaded silence. "Let's just get ourselves onto the street and figure out where we are. Follow the path on the right alongside the house, and meet us around front! Let's go! We don't have time to argue!"

Despite their lack of time, Bruce felt plenty like arguing but resigned himself to following the rest of the group as they started toward the side of the house. He had a bad feeling about this place— one that he couldn't get rid of, one that sat in the bottom of his stomach, crying out with every step and jostle. He knew there was something wrong, but he also knew that starting another fight with Métier would only cost them what little time they had bought with a cheap chain-link fence.

Surprisingly, it was Tyler that spoke up for him.

"Hey, Matty… yo, I don't think this is such a good idea, fam. I think we should just head up the alley and stay as far away from this place as possible."

"I never thought I'd say it, but I think I agree with Tyler on this one. Something about this place is giving me the creeps."

Matt's laughter boomed beneath the porch canopy, filling the entirety of the property, like it was coming from some kind of static-filled sound system.

"Oh, no! The creeps? Say it ain't so, Gwen, say it ain't so! What's next? The fucking heebie-jeebies? You guys wanna get a talking dog and investigate which old man is trying to scare us off the property? It's just a fucking house and an old, ugly one at that. And we're not even going inside it, so how about you guys just grow up and follow me before I lose my temper."

"Is that supposed to be a threat?" Bruce asked, trying his darnedest to keep his voice from wavering.

The placid, dull eyes that Matt wore were devoid of any and all emotion, like those of the dead except with the slight amount of color that showed that life stirred behind them. They just no longer cared about the lives in front of them, looking right through and past them.

"Why don't you find out?"

Without waiting for another word of protest, Matt started around the porch, grumbling to himself as he pulled Vel along behind him like he would an unruly child. She cast a forlorn look back at the rest of the group as she shuffled forward, feet clumsily colliding with the back of Matt's pounding feet.

"Oh, shit!"

As soon as they rounded the veranda, disappearing around a vine-covered wall, Matt cried out in shock and came flying back into view, crashing into the railing with a snap as loud as thunder as the balustrade caved in beneath him. One of the undead had seized him, grabbed him by his shirt, and toppled the two of them over the edge of the porch and onto the grass below, where they struggled like drunken dogs. Vel was screaming from the porch, clinging to the oaken support beam near the freshly made hole in the railing, her hand outstretched and reaching for the pinned Matt.

"Fuck that! Stay the fuck away from my nigga Matty, you slimy, undead shitheads!" Tyler said, charging toward the conflict with reckless abandon, his eyes only focusing on the shotgun in his hand as he shoved several of the small red cartridges inside it.

"Wait!"

Range grabbed Tyler by the hood once again, trying to hold the rambunctious lunatic back; but with a quick shake and bucking of his shoulders, he cast the woolen shroud off and continued his boundless run toward Matt and the zombie trying to chew his face off.

Instead, Range grabbed him by his free arm, giving him a rough pull back. Tyler, growing more impatient, merely turned and sent a quick backward elbow into the boy's face, colliding with his nose and sending up a spurt of blood before Range could cover up the damage. Gwen ran to his side almost immediately, but he ignored her, going once again to stop Tyler's relentless charge.

Bruce couldn't understand the boy's hesitation, until he noticed the growing buzz of voices, muffled tones in a disastrous harmony that traveled through the entire length of his body. He shivered as he realized it was another chorus of terrible groans, not from the group of undead behind them, but from in front, in the lawn beyond the house. As soon as this realization came upon him and drained all the blood from his head, the first of the mob made its way to the side path, slowly making its way into view in all its twisted, demonic glory.

One became two, two became ten, ten became many; and soon the entire horizon was spotted with undead, moaning with a horrible sadness coupled with indifference—pale, glossy eyes frozen in place like those of porcelain dolls. They were crawling over the ground and over each other, fighting to get forward at the free buffet that had been laid out for them. Bruce saw one fall beneath the all-consuming mass of green, leathery flesh, disappearing into a mess of crunching feet and shadows as it was ground into the dirt from whence it had come. Many had already made their way onto the veranda, crowding it to the point of knocking themselves over the edge, much like Matt had done moments before.

Vel's screams became shriller as the crowd enveloped her. Bruce saw her leap down onto the ground beside Matt, but in a matter of seconds, the two of them were swallowed up by the horde, which had quickly taken interest in the rest of the group instead of the measly appetizers.

Tyler was shouting and still struggling to free himself as he watched Matt disappear into the sea of bodies and twisting, snake-like limbs, streaks cutting through the blood on his face. Finally, he relaxed enough for Range to loosen his grip and immediately righted himself, shrugging as if having suffered some kind of cruel indignity as he lifted his shotgun and fired into the crowd, hitting some of those at the front of the pack, bullets tearing their faces into even more distorted, nightmarish visions right before they popped like spoiled grapes.

Bruce turned and started back down the path toward the alley, suddenly very aware of the sweat pouring down his forehead. He wiped it away with a quick arm across, feeling the moisture stick and cling to his skin like a parasite.

The fence with the small gate had almost been completely knocked onto its side, the chain-link curled inward like the crest of a wave just before it crashes onto shore—except instead of water washing over sand, it would be undead flesh spilling out onto the gravel and whatever living creature that was misfortunate enough to be caught beneath it.

He reckoned, they only had a minute or two before they were completely surrounded. However, the path leading straight down the alley was still eerily clear, where even the fog seemed lighter than usual—a clearing in the forest of mist that had overgrown the town.

"Get your asses back to the alley!" Bruce called back to the others, but most of them had already begun filing in behind him, pushed back by the encroaching horde.

"Ohhh," the brown-haired boy groaned, "they're everywhere."

"Just stay calm. If we lose our cool, it's already over, especially since they have this much ground on us. We just need to move forward down the alley and see what street we're on."

"And if we have no idea where we are? What do we do then? Just keep running in circles?" Gwen asked, her attention caught between the conversation and firing several shotgun rounds into the faces of the undead, some of them exploding like chestnuts held too long over a fire.

"I've patrolled this city nearly every night for a year. I'll know where we are as soon as I get a street name. It looks like we're in the historical district, but I don't recognize any of these stores from the back."

"Well, enough talking about this stupid shit, let's get our asses movin'!" Tyler said, running up with Range behind him, firing shots of crowd control into the shifting mass of bodies that grew ready to swallow them.

His face was stiff and still looked like something out of a *Mad Max* movie, twisted patterns of blood giving it a drawn, haunted look that almost twisted Bruce's gut into what could've been mistaken as sympathy.

Tyler was first to start down the alley, kicking up dust almost as thick as the mist as he went until all you could see of him was a small sliver of a shadow where he once stood. Veronica was ready to follow but hesitated when she heard the gunshot ring out.

"Come on! Let's go!" Tyler called, reappearing briefly as a silver figure wavering in the sun's minimal light.

Veronica nodded, still looking unsure of what horrors awaited her in that glowing veil, but with a small adjustment of the bandage around her mouth, she ran until she too became nothing more than a wisp that looked human only if you were willing to stretch your imagination. Billy motioned for Gwen to go next, but she declined, her eyes set on Range who was attempting to tip over the vine-covered plastic archway. With a flash of anger that soon melted into fear when a skull-shattering moan broke the tenuous silence, Billy dashed off down the alley.

The dirt he kicked up shot into Bruce's face and caused his throat to burn and his eyes to water, but he kept them open and stifled his coughs to muffled throat clearings that wouldn't draw any more attention to them than they already had.

There was a sharp crack, like bristled thunder; and when Bruce turned, he saw that the cheap chain-link fence had folded onto itself, with several undead scrambling over only to be snapped back by the malleable steel. One fell back hard enough to topple the entire center of the wriggling crowd over onto itself, like a pile of squishy bowling pins, and Bruce had the sickening desire to laugh—not just laugh, but to cackle like a madman, like the doomed protagonist in a cheap Lovecraftian horror story.

"It's time to go now," Bruce said, grabbing Gwen by the arm and pushing her toward the street.

She protested, looking back just as Range succeeded in toppling the flimsy architecture on top of the horde, which had seemingly grown to the hundreds. They covered the lawn, more numerous than blades of grass and dandelions, tripping over themselves as their massive numbers became their greatest weakness as well as their greatest strength.

"He'll be fine! I've got him! Now get going! We're gonna be overwhelmed if we stay here, and I don't fancy being pulled apart like a turkey on Thanksgiving, now go!"

Reluctantly and swallowing her pride along with her tongue, she was gone, another victim of the mist, slipping inside its constantly moving entrails. Bruce ran to fetch Range, who was stumbling back from two large members of the undead horde swinging their bulging, veiny arms like sledgehammers poised to take his head clean off with their curled fingers.

Bruce fired two rounds into the center of each of their foreheads, closing his eyes before the spray of blood even reached them. Without wasting any time, and as if he hadn't even noticed his brush with death, Range started firing at the nearest zombies, dismembering them like a surgeon with Parkinson's performing a heart transplant with a machete. One of the undead, wearing a dress that indicated its lumpy, globulous form had once been that of a woman, had its stomach blown straight through, the stomach and liver spilling out and dangling from gray sausage intestines. They bounced near her feet and tangled up the twin stalks, bringing the groaning beast to the ground in a skid of dirt. Several more had tripped over the tipped archway, and along with the fallen woman, there was a small blockade, a levee of human flesh that kept the zombies on the lawn back long enough for them to walk quickly back into the alley.

Bruce's slow jaunt became a quick sprint when he remembered the caved-in fence and felt their limbs dancing across his back. Range had already taken the lead, and when Bruce gave out a small yelp as a hand wrapped around his ankle, he turned back and fired another blast into the unseen creature's face. He felt hot blood sticking to his leg and the inside of his crotch, the thought of which made him squirm. Even though he was almost completely out of breath, he kept his pace with Range, not wanting to be shown up by a high school kid. Soon, he was even with the boy, even though he suspected it was because he slowed his pace considerably, and the zombies became nothing more than the distant patter of displaced stones behind them.

"We're on Macintosh, by the way."

"I'm sorry, what?"

"Macintosh. Macintosh Boulevard. You said earlier you didn't know what street we're on. We're on Macintosh, just two blocks south of Main Street and three east of Truffle Avenue, which is where the hospital's emergency room entrance is located."

"And just how the hell do you know that?"

"That house, I've been there before, quite a few times as a kid. My grandmother used to bring me before she passed. And when she did, we took her to the hospital via the entrance on Truffle. Well, my mom did, at least. I went back to that house to be by myself."

"A kid running off to go to a historical society, now I've heard everything."

"In case you hadn't noticed, I'm a little… odd."

"I didn't really have time to, but out of all the crazy shit that's happened to me today, kid, you are definitely one of the more normal parts of it."

"Well, since you've most likely seen dead people feasting on and ripping the living apart piece by piece, that doesn't exactly fill me with confidence."

"Just take the damn compliment, kid."

From behind an alley wall lurched forth an undead abomination, strips of flesh falling out of his still-chewing mouth. Apparently not satiated by the meal rolling around in his petulant cheeks, he lunged at Range, only to be met with the butt of his shotgun. The pieces of skin and meat flew from its mouth along with several teeth as it spiraled down into the dirt. After several more seconds of running, its squirming form, still trying to lift itself from the ground, disappeared into the belly of the fog.

Bruce watched it fade into the mist, and when he turned back around, he almost had his nose snapped off by one of the creature's rotten yellow teeth. Its breath—or the illusion of it, as he knew no air moved through its frozen lungs—was worse than any odor he had been misfortunate enough to come across in his years of service, and that included a murder in a truck stop up Highway 90 that involved body parts being hastily shoved into a toilet. The mellow lowlight gave its face enough illumination to bring out every greasy, bloodied pore, every scratch and abrasion, so that it looked more like a demon than human. A pair of glasses had been broken and crushed into the monster's face, the half-splintered bridge protruding from its eyeball at an obtuse angle that sent it clacking against its snapping jaws.

Instinctually, so quick that it surprised even himself, when he felt the splash of blood across his eyes, he brought his revolver to its forehead and fired a round deep into the back of its skull. His second and third shot gave only shrill, empty clicks. Fortunately, the monster fell and stayed down long enough for Bruce to spring over its emptying head, being careful not to slip in the congealing blood.

When they reached the street, they came to a slow skid of a stop, Bruce's leather loafers cracking against the black top almost as loud as the boy's ratty gym shoes that seemed to echo like they had stumbled into a cavern instead of an open street.

"Where did the others get to?" Range asked, panting.

"Don't tell me you're out of breath after that light jog," Bruce said with a small smile.

A hand coiled around his shoulder, and Bruce wasted no time in spinning around and sending his fist into the undead's face, only wishing he had remembered to use the butt of the gun instead of his tender, exposed knuckles. The creature fell back, screeching like a child, moving its hands to its nose as blood trickled down and onto the cracked pavement.

"Ow! What the fuck, man? You fucking hit me in my fucking nose! Ah! Shit! The fuck is wrong with you, homie? You turn around punching everybody who taps your bitch-ass shoulder? Fuck," Tyler said in a high-pitched nasal of a voice as he tightly gripped his fingers over the bridge to stop the bleeding.

"When there are zombies trying to chew on my face like dollar-store jerky, I do. You should've said something."

"Well, shit, excuse me! Didn't realize I had to announce myself to avoid getting punched in the goddamn face. Ah! Ah! I think you fucking broke it! I'm gonna look like that guy from those Shanghai movies."

"Jackie Chan?"

"Oh, don't say that. You're making me almost feel sorry for the guy," Bruce said, fighting the laughter.

"Man, fuck ya'll, treating me like shit even though I just saw my best friend get devoured by those zamboni bastards."

"Yeah, and you and your 'best friend' shot my boss this morning, so don't expect an outpouring of sympathy on this end, pal."

"Man, you still pissed off about that shit? Shieeeet, it's not like I knew ya'll at the time. I thought we was niggas now?"

"Hey! I'm not anybody's 'nigguh,' you got that? And if I'm counting correctly, that's your third strike, so I'd owe you a punch in that gaping face of yours anyway. So let's just say we're even, how about that?"

Tyler nodded begrudgingly as he hobbled to his feet, struggling with his left foot—which had blood running out the bottom of his sweatpants, spilling out onto the gravel—still rubbing the top of his bridge. The others appeared from behind him, emerging from the fog like ghosts, pale spirits becoming whole once again.

"And where were you guys?"

"Looking for a street sign. Apparently, we're near the corner of Burlington and Macintosh," Gwen said, letting the comically large shotgun rest at her side.

The amount of blood on the girl would've looked shocking on any other day, but after what he'd seen today, she seemed almost primped and pampered.

"Well, now, it looks like you were right," Bruce said, slapping his hand over Range's back. He gave him an awkward but grateful smile, its coldness stemming for from a lack of acclimation instead of a bored dismissal. "That means the hospital's only three blocks to the east."

"And how are we supposed to figure out which way is fucking east? I wasn't aware we were gonna need fucking compasses."

"I think I have an app that has a compass on it," Bill suggested.

"Good luck with that working. Even if you could get a signal, I doubt you'd be able to reach a satellite uplink."

"Where was the street corner at?" Range asked, twisting his head for any hint of green street sign.

Gwen's brow furrowed in thought while she too let her eyes glaze over the dulling horizon, before finally pointing down the street in front of her. The group turned and followed the trajectory of her extended finger into the depths of the fog, hoping for a clear sign through the icy veil, only to be disappointed when none presented itself and all they saw was the swirling tendrils of mist, a bed of snakes made of pale smoke devouring one another in a constant struggle.

"Well, we'll have to take your word for it. C'mon, if we don't hurry, we might lose the light."

The thought of being stranded outside with those howling creatures in the night—especially the wolves, whose sneering laughter still carried on the wind from time to time—was enough motivation to get the rest of the small, dwindling group moving again without protest or disagreement, even from Tyler, who was saltily rubbing his jaw and muttering to himself as they made their way up the street.

Bruce did his best to try and make out the houses around them, feeling naked without having some kind of idea what part of town he was in. While never a fan of his town, the kind that proudly sported high school bumper stickers on their car and carried pennants to whatever sports team was currently trying to make its way to state that year, he did take pride in knowing the place like the back of his hand.

But nothing seemed familiar here. Even the house that carried a vague hint of sentiment seemed dark and dreary, like the owner had packed up and moved brick by brick, board by board, from a sleepy little Eastern European burg called Transylvania. Windows were shattered, some completely covered in blood that Bruce mistook for curtains; though he supposed they were, in a way, curtains for whatever bloody show awaited inside. Some doors swung on hinges; others were thrown completely off of theirs, onto the overgrown grass yards littered with toys not put away and remnants of bodies too far deteriorated and devoured to join the ranks of undead hunting them.

A smell like sulfur filled the air, rolling around in Bruce's nostril like wisps of the flame. Mingling with the overall rotting odor that had persisted since they started their misguided attempt to reach the hospital, it produced an odor that almost required a shirt over the nose to keep from gagging.

"The fog seems worse over here, thicker, almost."

"This stuff smells like shit, like straight ass."

"I keep expecting some gross-ass tentacles to reach out and grab me or something," Billy mumbled with a forced machismo.

They crossed another block, this one even worse than the last when it came to the signs of decay and death that hung like ornaments over the lawn. On one yard, there sat a tricycle, a small red number that seemed right at home on a Norman Rockwell postcard, except for the small arm that was still clinging to the handle bar.

A van sat in the center of the road, causing the group to break around it. As Bruce peered inside, he saw the family still inside, frozen in the middle of their escape: the father in the front seat with his head cracked open, bits of brain spilling out onto the dashboard and the mother leaning back in her seat, hands clutched in a death grip around the arms of the chair, her throat torn open and left hanging halfway down her throat like a turkey gizzard. As Bruce leaned in for a better look, a child no older than twelve slammed its face against the glass, a crack forming around its forehead as a thin line of black blood trickled from the center of the wound. It gnashed its teeth against the glass as Bruce jumped back, but it did not break; and soon, like a disinterested dog, the child went back to its meal—its former brothers and sisters in the back.

Bruce shivered violently.

"Jesus Christ, how did things get so bad so quickly? I was supposed to protect these people, to serve them, and now here I am, putting bullets between their eyes like it's some kind of goddamn courtesy. How did I not notice what this place was becoming? How did nobody notice it? Were we all just blind?"

"It's because this place looks the same alive as it does dead," Range said over his shoulder from the front of the group.

"What do you mean by that? There's some shadier areas and some run-down parts of town, maybe, but it never looks like this. This… looks like we landed on some kind of alien world, one that's similar, but there's something just… off about it."

"Maybe that's because you're really seeing the place for the first time."

"Listen, kid, I've lived here my whole life. I've spent nearly every day of the past five years driving up and down these streets. I know them like the back of my hand… Well, when there isn't fog thick enough to cover up an entire block, that is. And I've never seen anything like this."

"No, he's right," Gwen interjected, looking contemplative. "There's always been something about this town, something lingering just beneath the surface that just felt… wrong, like you said, Officer, like something was… off. I used to chalk it up to my feelings of isolation, but after seeing this, I have to agree with Range. The town doesn't feel different, because it isn't. It just isn't hiding its true nature anymore."

"With the way you guys are talking about it, you make it seem like the town is alive or something."

"It is, in a way. All towns are. They're molded and shaped by the people within it and by the secrets they keep, and the smaller the town, the more secrets there are. You just have to dig a bit deeper to find them. Sort through the stories we tell ourselves over and over again to the point we can regurgitate them without having to actually think about them anymore to find the actual truth they contain, only to find it's a dark and rotten thing, and you see why they buried it in the first place. They doll it up, make it look nice, try and hide what it really is, like putting makeup on a corpse, but they can't cover up the smell. It rots and rots underneath the town built on top of its very bones, filling it with its stench—a subtle one, one you only notice when you really look for it, but one that is as much a part of the town itself as the people living within it. That's what I think he means. Whatever is the cause for Loganville's rot, it's been here the whole time. Like our bloody, hungry friends back there, it just no longer felt like staying buried."

"Wait. Wait. Are you trying to say this place is cursed or something? That there's some malignant force responsible for this? Do you kids have any idea how ridiculous you sound?"

"Any more ridiculous than the dead coming back to life and eating everyone?"

"You know what I mean."

"I don't think we do. Obviously, a virus seems more realistic, but how do you explain the people who've been dead for years? Does a virus that infects the dead really more ridi—"

"More ridiculous than the idea that the whole town is cursed? Built on an ancient Indian burial ground? No. I'd say the idea of a virus infecting the dead is much more viable than some magic mumbo jumbo. I think you guys might've just read *Catcher in the Rye* one too many times and are letting your suburban malaise and teen angst get the better of your fear. I mean, I can't believe I'm having a serious discussion about whether or not Loganville is cursed or not."

Desperate for any vindication, he surprised himself by looking to Tyler for support against the lunacy these two troubled kids were suggesting. "You don't seriously believe in any of this stuff, do you? I mean, you're our 'zombie expert,' right? Tell them this is ridiculous."

"I've seen and heard a lot of ridiculous shit today, fam. This shithole being cursed is not one of them. In fact, that's one of the least ridiculous things I heard. I mean, the oldest zombie movies don't have anything to do with curses. It deals with voodoo, black magic, all that bullshit, but all that virus stuff is only the recent shit, all brought on by the classic Romero shit, but those are all just movies anyway, and most of 'em all contradict the others ones. All I'm saying is, if I found out this piss-ass little town was cursed, I wouldn't exactly be fucking surprised. Even a gangsta-ass muthafucker like me can tell there's always been something wrong with this place."

Bruce knew when he was defeated, even if he had logic and rational thinking on his side. Deflated, he looked up to Veronica, his hope getting the better of him when he made eye contact, finally believing he had found some support in this ridiculous exchange, until she abashedly and ashamedly cast her eyes to the ground and avoided his stare for the rest of the slow trek through the mist.

They remained in a tentative, fearful silence for the rest of the trip, which, fortunately, consisted only of another block before they reached the hospital.

Its sleek yet massive form seemed to materialize out of the fog, like some kind of desert mirage, its dark towers of glass and rebar appearing as dark gray stains on the horizon before becoming whole—what little light there was catching off the glass that made up the side of the building giving the place a luminescent gleam that made Bruce's eyes strain after so many hours spent in the murky autumn fog. It towered high above the modest houses surrounding it, the few towers contained within its grounds dotted with dozens of small windows on each floor. It looked like a creature with a thousand or more eyes, all following them as they grew closer, enforcing their malicious will upon them and drawing them in further, like a spider watching its prey entangle itself it its webbing.

Bruce knew behind each of those frosted glass panes was a patient, who, at the start of the morning, believed themselves safe on the road to recovery—a slow and arduous one filled with pain and tribulation—only to be thrown back into the jaws of death, either from the loss of power or the sharpened, gnashing teeth of their former physicians and caregivers. Then to make it even worse, they were now stuck in between: puppet to some virus (Bruce refused to believe the cause could be anything else; it was the only piece of sanity he had left in this madness) as their conscious mind rotted from the inside out. He imagined all of them, in their paper-thin gowns, heads pressed flat against the glass, dull, lifeless eyes watching them but not seeing them as they neared the sliding doors.

For a moment, Bruce thought of John as well, standing above his bed as a ghoul with half of his face torn off by shell and shrapnel. His brilliant amber eyes, turned into black, accusing beads digging into Bruce's chest as he dragged his bloody and beaten body across the room, mouth watering with that slimy black goo as it poured over his fine white whiskers that grew whenever he went a day without shaving.

I knew you'd come, Bruce. She tried to tell me you wouldn't. But I knew you would. I knew you owed me that, at the very least. You owe me everything. I told her you would come.

"We're here," Range announced to no one in particular. From the way he said it, Bruce suspected he would've said it even if no one else had been there.

"How's it look in there?" Bruce asked, pushing past the skittish Billy and Tyler, who had taken the brief respite to prepare himself another cigar out of his seized confiscated materials.

Almost by habit, Bruce thought of pulling up the small radio at his belt, clicking the button and reciting the code for illicit drug use in public. Even after the instinct had passed, he still considered it, especially when he thought of the look it would bring to the distracted Tyler's face.

Range made a lid for his eyes with his hand to better see inside the frozen glass doors, pressing his face almost completely flat against the double doors.

"Seems quiet enough," he said.

"It seems, or it is?"

"Well, we won't know for sure until we go inside, will we?"

"This seems like an incredibly bad idea," Billy said from behind them.

His saucer-like eyes were looking straight up to the roof of the building, and Bruce wondered if he too saw the eyes and troubled souls that lay in wait behind them.

"Holy shit, you can talk?" Tyler said, while exhaling a cloud of smoke that disappeared instantly into the mix.

As Billy looked at him bewildered, he went into a spasm that couldn't be called a laugh or a cough but something awkwardly in the middle.

"My bad, nigga, I just don't think I heard you say a damn thing this whole time. I thought you was one of those, you know, Helen Keller people or was, like, Gwen's retarded cousin or some shit."

"I'm not retarded!" Billy said, his voice wavering between anger and embarrassment.

"Shit, son, I said I was sorry. I forgot you was just a little bitch, that's all."

Billy shook his head violently and threw his hands in the air with an exasperated sigh. He looked toward Gwen, who was absentmindedly loading her shotgun with bloody shells from her back jean pockets.

"Listen, all I'm trying to say is, why the hell are we going into this place? They have a morgue in there! A morgue! A place where they keep fucking dead people! And in case you guys didn't notice, the dead are currently fucking eating everyone!"

"Hey! Language, fam."

"Would you shut the fuck up! God, do you people want to die? Do you? Because it sure seems like it. 'Hey, guys, where should we go to bunker down and keep ourselves safe during this zombie apocalypse?' 'Well, gee, I don't know. How about we walk right into the building where all the dead *and* dying people are, put ourselves in a confined space and hope for the best?' 'Well, shit, fuck, ass sure sounds good to me, *fam*. Can't wait, *fam*. Because all I'm good at is shooting things and being an asshole to everybody, *fam*.'"

"Damn, dawg, do I really sound like that?" Tyler asked, looking to Range.

"Hey! I didn't hear you coming up with any better ideas, kid. If you've got an idea, let's hear it, but don't just tear this plan down when it's all we got because that isn't helping anybody, all right?"

"I got a plan. How about we get the fuck out of here? Why are we still in this godforsaken place?"

"We already talked about that, Billy. We can't just leave, not when the bridge is out and half of the town is surrounded by forests that are filled with wolves that laugh while they're chasing you," Gwen said, doing her best to placate him. "Besides, Range thinks he knows a way that we can—"

"Oh, yes, perfect Range, the guy who has all the answers, the guy who's here to solve all your problems, whom you trust completely despite having met the guy two fucking days ago. Meanwhile, you ignore the guy who's been there for you every damn day, listening to you bitch about your crazy-ass mom day in and day out, hoping that someday you'd stop whining enough to notice me, who's trying to warn you about walking into a goddamn death trap, because why? Because I'm not some weird, mysterious freak who has no friends? Because I don't have pretty green eyes and shiny blond hair, huh?

Because I'm not a piece of shit trying to put you in danger and actually cares about keeping you safe?"

"Jesus Christ, Billy, are you really doing this now? First of all, I don't need anyone to keep me safe. I can handle myself, all right? And I'm so sorry I bored you with stories about my crazy mother when I obviously should've been paying more attention to you and your dick, is that it? Is that what you want to hear, Billy? Does that—"

Before she could finish, Billy cut her off with more of his frantic rant, pacing back and forth as his voice grew louder and louder with his increasing, wilted fury.

"You know what, Gwen? I hate to say it, but I'm starting to think your mother was right—about this, about everything, this being the end of the world, mankind's final days, the culmination of all our sins. She had the right idea speeding off like she did, leaving this shithole behind. She's probably laughing all the way down the highway—"

"My mother is dead," Gwen said blankly.

Range, who had only been half listening before, his cheeks burned a fierce crimson and his eyes darting uncomfortably between the arguing friends and the ground, now focused his eyes solely on Gwen's drawn, sorrowful face.

Billy stammered, his planned-out speech that he had clearly practiced over and over in his mind suddenly failing him; but his rage had turned into bitter frustration, and he was not about to let the poor girl off so easily.

"Just proves my point. Your mother knew what she was doing. She was right about this. She was right about a lot of things. She was right about *you*."

Gwen looked up at him, the hurt etched into her face like stone. Range started moving toward her, but Billy took no notice, his eyes flashing with delight at his well-placed blow, reveling in her despair.

"You're just a whore, Gwen, that's right—a harlot, as your mother would say, just like all the girls you despise. You're no better than them. In fact, your ego makes you worse. You're just a trumped-up slut who can't—"

A sharp crack rang through the air as the palm whipped from one side of his face to the next, knocking the words right off his lips along with a small trickle of blood. Veronica brought her hand back across in the other direction, just to make sure her silent point was made.

"Thank God, someone hit that little bitch. I thought I was going to have to…" Tyler said with a puff of his strawberry blunt, if the unusual smell was any guess.

Stunned, Billy brought a slow, reluctant hand to his face, gently touching the bright-red handprint on his cheek and using a finger to dab at the blood that was smeared across his cheek. Without a word, Veronica moved over to the front of the building, past a grinning Range, and shoved her way through the revolving door to the side of the nonfunctioning automatics. Tyler called after her and followed her inside, righting his shotgun and pulling up his drawers as he did so.

Range gave an inquisitive nod to Gwen, who returned it with a warm but bemused smile. Seemingly contented, he turned, sparing one sly smile with the still-trembling Billy. Gwen went to follow him when Billy's hand slid like a worm around her wrist. Bruce prepared himself to charge the scrawny bastard if he made a move; but instead, he gave a sob that was almost pitiable.

"Gwen! I-I-I'm so sorry! I-I di-didn't mean it, I swear! Y-you have to believe me! I'm just stressed, is all, and I was tired of nobody listening to me, and I-I took it out on you. Please. Please believe me."

Without even looking at him, Gwen yanked her arm free of his grip and strode into the revolving doors, quickly moving out of sight into the hospital's vacuous entrance hall.

The boy slithered down into a heap on the ground, his body racked with sobs and curses as he slapped his fists aimlessly against the ground. All disgust for the boy left Bruce's stomach and was replaced by a slow drip of pity that compelled him forward, putting his hand softly on his shoulder.

With a snap of his neck so quick and wild he thought he might've broken it, Billy looked up at him with red-ringed eyes and a pouting lower lip, looking like a raccoon you find digging through your trash.

"I didn't mean it. I swear, I didn't mean it. I swear it," he said, half to Bruce and half to himself. "I'm just stressed, that's all. I'm not used to all this stress, and I just want to help her. I'm at my wit's end, you know?"

"Yeah, yeah," Bruce said, his empathy disappearing in an instant. He grabbed the boy by the scruff of his polo shirt and hefted him to his unsteady feet before giving him a light and forceful shove forward. "We all are, pal. Now, get inside."

With a sniffle and a light nod, the boy hobbled forward into the nook of the revolving door and pressed himself against the glass until he was inside, Bruce following in his wake. When they finally stepped through onto the damp black carpet that served as an entrance mat, Bruce suddenly realized just how drastically things had changed.

The room he was in looked almost nothing like the one he found himself in that morning.

The small plastic chairs were all overturned and thrown about, their spindly steel legs high in the air, like beetles trapped on their backs, except they remained still and silent. One was even embedded in the drywall, apparently thrown and impaled there during some kind of scuffle.

On the wall beside it, there was a large coating of blood that covered half the wall and most of the ceiling tiles, almost like something, or someone, had exploded in a volley of human insides. There were intestines dangling from the ceiling, like streamers at Charles Manson's birthday party, and bright, shimmering puddles of blood and of that strange black saliva that spotted most of the floor, submerging chairs and thrown-about magazines, their pages sealed by the hot, sticky liquid. Footprints covered the floor, well trodden into the very tiles, some in dirt, others in blood—all moving toward the door and out past the small entrance mat's borders.

Even though the room had seemed dark from outside, several lights were, in fact, working. Some gave the room a dark purple aura from the blood thrown across them, but any light was better than none. Confused as to why the automatic doors hadn't opened with their approach, he turned round and quickly saw that it was not a lack of power that kept them shut but a severed arm protruding from one of the sliding door's edges, the fingers jammed into the tight crevice, bruised skin bunched up against it. A small trail of smoke rose up from the door's edge, the gears most likely having burned themselves out from the strain. Given the fact that whatever body it was once attached to was nowhere to be found, Bruce could only figure that its former owner had made the difficult decision of life with one arm or no life at all and escaped with the rest of the maddening crowd through the revolving doors. He must've been a straggler; otherwise, someone would've broken the glass to get out instead of dealing with the cylinder's slow, cramped rotations.

A television suspended from the wall, an old flat-screen that was cracked in the bottom right corner, obscuring some of the picture, even if that picture was only a wash of static and irritating buzzing. Bruce made his way toward it, thinking he finally found a way to show just how ridiculous the younger members of the group were being. They outnumbered him now. The only one near his age was Tyler. And while Bruce almost would've preferred the idea of being alone against them than having the support of Tyler, he had to admit, despite his buffoonish appearance and mannerisms, he knew how to handle himself, and others, when the time really called for it. Still, he needed to calm them down with a bit of logic before their twisted fantasies started luring them down dangerous, suicidal paths just to get to a library that was still half a township away.

And the half-broken television set was just his ticket to do so.

He ran his hand along the plastic casing, looking for a small series of switches and found them at the very bottom near the stand. Fiddling with a few, he finally found the one for changing channels, indicated by the fact that static became a startlingly beautiful mountain landscape with the number 3 plastered in a small black box in the upper-right corner.

"Hey, you guys might wanna come over and check this out! I'm gonna see if there's anything about an outbreak on the news," Bruce called, loudly enough to get their attention but quiet enough to avoid anyone else's. "If there even is any news stations left," he added solemnly.

The group gathered behind him, looking over the walls and the spacious front desk, which also stood deserted. Range slowly made his way behind it and gave it a quick once-over, his shotgun leading his eyes, even going so far to check underneath the desk. Finding nothing, he slowly moved back into the group, watching as Bruce made his way through the channels.

He passed all the infomercial channels and went right past Telemundo but stopped as soon as he got to a major network. For some reason, there was no news on—only a daytime soap opera he didn't recognize, in which two women were trying to decide whether to kill their family matriarch to steal a piece of the inheritance away from their illegitimate children. Maybe the disease just hadn't reached that part of the country yet, or had been hit so hard that execs were still scrambling to get someone covering the story. Either way, he flipped right on to the next one with an anxious sigh.

"Why is this place so empty? I'm glad it's not overflowing with the bastards, but I still expected some kind of welcome party. The quiet's starting to make me uncomfortable," Gwen said.

"I guess all those dead mo'fuckas heard I was coming and ran off," Tyler replied.

Bruce could hear Gwen's eyes roll without even turning around.

The smell of formaldehyde and blood was starting to get to him, along with a potpourri of other nauseating odors blending together: vomit, excrement, sweat, fear. Every channel he passed was on its regular daytime programming schedule, showing talk shows hosted by celebrities long past their prime, relegated to interviewing the very people that replaced them in the limelight, and reruns of sitcoms that were already reruns themselves, just with a different cast and different set of names stamped at the end. The only one that seemed affected, the local station that had aired Lacey Chabert's early-morning exposé on getting one's face chewed off by the undead, was still declaring technical difficulties—which made sense as the station was on the outskirts of town, buried deep in the woods, which were now filled with cackling, snarling wolves.

Bruce had made a trip out there once on a report of some stolen property, and there had only been a small group of four people in the control room with one man giving them all orders and a janitor who didn't show up until after the sun had gone down. It was at least a fifteen-minute drive through the backroads to get back into Loganville and an hour in any other direction, so Bruce doubted anyone was successful in their escape. Hopefully, they had holed up there and were waiting for rescue, a plan that was looking smarter and smarter by the second.

Finally, just when he was beginning to feel like pulling the television off of its wobbling stand and smashing it into a pile of chips and wires, its insides spilling out into a puddle of human insides, intermingling in sparks and smoke—he came across a view of a large colored desk with two strained, grinning faces smiling back at him from behind it.

"Here we go! Here we go!" he said, quieting those that were already silent, getting the attention of those who had already given it. "They're gonna say something about the disease, or outbreak, or whatever it is. They're gonna tell us what's going on."

He could feel the looks of concern and hear the unsaid rebukes of the group, wiping his hand over the length of his face and then drying it on his slacks. They were wrapping up some story on firefighters putting out a fire up on Interstate 43, one of the raging infernos cutting through the forest that had been put out after only claiming several dozen acres and the lives of several emergency responders and hermits too stubborn to move out of the way of the blaze before it arrived.

Bruce waited eagerly for them to change the subject, but they just kept on talking as if there were no other problems in the world, their smiling faces making it seem as if peace had been declared just minutes before Bruce tuned in and this recent fire was the worst tragedy to befall humanity in its known memory. He noticed the shuffling of feet behind him, knowing that the others were getting impatient, even more so than he was. But the reporters just kept talking on and on about the wildfire, their voices slurring into a steady drone...

At the sound of footsteps he nearly leaped, twisting around to see Range slipping down the north hallway toward a sign marked stairs, rounding the corner and disappearing from sight. Bruce didn't stop him. He already knew there was no convincing that boy. He could see the conviction in his eyes when he spoke of the library and whatever placebo he hoped to find there. It was easier than accepting the truth, he supposed, one that was about to be revealed on national television, which was about as irrefutable as you could get.

Except the reporters had already finished discussing the fire in the brief moment it had taken him to watch Range's escape and were now going on about some crazy new health craze that proved that foods mankind had been eating for centuries were actually killing us. The woman was speaking to these supposed peddlers of immortality as if she had never heard anything graver in her life, despite just having discussed the grisly, painful deaths of several men up in the foothills.

With what could only be described as growl, Bruce angrily turned to the next channel to find a cop drama discussing the rape and pregnancy of some underage girl, all while spouting witty one-liners and throwing passing flirtations at their coworkers. The next was more daytime soaps and after that, a cheap daytime game show where a woman was being shown the kitchen dinette set she might win if only she could use her knowledge of capitalism and the free market to ballpark the price of a bocci ball set.

Fortunately, for the sake of the television set and his own stable reality, the next channel contained a news program, and from the serious face of the old white man sitting behind his cylindrical desk, it looked like he was the answer to Bruce's prayers, which is something he never would've expected in a million years.

But then he started speaking, and as the words rolled out of his wrinkled, liver-spotted mouth, they turned to ice in his ears that made his whole body quiver. He was talking about the recall of some kind of failed pharmaceutical, how there were several reports of insomnia and even a type of cancerous growth that went unnoticed during extensive FDA testing. In fact, the company, Carpenter-Hooper, even falsified several reports from the FDA regarding its readiness for human consumption, leading to many members of the board being brought in for questioning by the DEA. They prepared to move on to a panel with several experts in the fields of pharmaceuticals and pharmaceutical laws about what might happen to the company's executives and shareholders, as if they were planning on spending several more hours on the topic.

"No, no, no, no," Bruce said, his mumbling trailing off to nothing as the program continued without even a mention of the dead, or an emergency, or even so much as reports of a bad cough.

They were alone, without anyone even aware that their whole town had swallowed itself up. This was no global epidemic. It wasn't the end of the world. This was just death—pointless, meaningless, ceaseless death.

With a cry, he shoved his fist into the screen's circuits, watching the screen flash a final gurgle of static before the life left it. Satisfaction rolled over him when the screen went black and stayed that way.

"Fuck, man, I was watching that shit. My boy Steez was selling that shit for crank prices just last week. Supposed to give you a wicked fucking buzz, from what I hear. This other guy I know, Ricky Cunts, said he saw ants crawling out his own damn dick and took a fucking hammer to it, like some kind of tweaker. I don't know how they saved it, crazy puta."

"Swhat doesh… that mean?" Veronica asked, the bandana muffling the slur in her words. She blinked hard several times during the simple question, the pain from speech more than apparent.

"It means asshole."

"I'm tashking… about the shtuff on TV, ashole."

"It means that nobody knows about this, which also means nobody's coming to save us."

"What? How could nobody know about… about *this*? Half of the town's dead, and the other half is feasting on them, at least until they get up and start looking to eat as well. But you're saying nobody knows?" Billy asked, disbelief clear in his tone.

Bruce wanted someone to smack him again, but no one stepped up this time. They all shared his doubts, his fears.

"Has anybody been able to get a signal? Tried calling someone from out of town? I know they might not believe us at first, but all they'd have to do is try calling the cops, fire department, city hall, *anything*, and see that something's wrong. Hell, we could get a video of zombie by sticking our damn phone out the window and upload it to YouTube and get people talking."

"I hate to admit it, but those are actually good points. I feel a little dumb for not thinking about it sooner. My phone's in my locker. Does anyone else have one?"

"My mother never even thought about giving me a phone, thought it was the devil's way to distract people from God."

"They confiscated mine at the prison. That probably explains why that shit wasn't blowing up last night while I was hitting up all my bitches."

"Yes, I'm sure *that's* the reason."

"I dropped… mine back… at the school, but it wouldn'sht matter much anshyway," Veronica said, taking a long pause before continuing. "Haven't had anything… but pockets of service all morning. Nobody at school… ugh… could get on the Internet, Wi-Fi, or anything… and… and plenty of people… were pisshed because they thought their friends… weren't answering their texts when they just weren't getting them."

By the time she finished, she was nearly on the verge of collapse, her knees shaking and a fresh trail of blood leading down her neck had sprouted up, but she stayed standing.

"Somebody had to have gotten some kind of message out. I got plenty of calls this morning on the landlines, at least. There were whole crowds of people gathering at the hospital and the church."

"She's right. I can't get anything. I tried half my numbers, and it said all the calls failed. The Internet just brings me to a refresh page every time, no matter how many times I click it," Billy explained while tapping at the screen like a curious primate.

"That doesn't make any sense. The radio was still working. The television's still working. I even got a call on my walkie-talkie, telling me to get my ass back to the station. What's special about the cell phones?"

They sat in silence for a moment, trying to grasp at what little straws that had been presented to them and trying draw some logical conclusion with it. But it was like trying to suck up a frozen milkshake; with all that struggle, all you got was frustration and a headache.

"Maybe… and I'm using *maybe* very strongly here, but… maybe whatever is causing this… has a way of blocking them. That would explain why everything else works except the things that might get us out of here or get us help," Gwen surmised.

"Oh, don't start with that curse nonsense again!" Bruce chided.

"Do you have any better explanation? You just saw this isn't from some stupid outbreak!"

"That proved nothing! All it means is that nobody knows about this yet, this disease, virus, whatever it is. I refuse to believe this is some kind of magic mumbo jumbo because this is the real world and shit like that doesn't happen in the real world."

"But zombies do? Are you listening to yourself? How does an outbreak explain the phones not working or any of the other weird stuff that's been going on out there?"

"How does a curse explain it? A ghost was messing with the text messages? Spirits invaded the World Wide Web?" Bruce said bitterly, his temper getting the better of his self-control.

"This thing can bring things back to life after they've been dead for hundreds of years, but the idea of it manipulating a couple of telecommunication waves is too far-fetched for you?"

"It all is! None of it makes any damn sense! At least, I'm still trying to find a way to make sense of it, instead of sinking the rest of us further into madness based on some diluted fantasy of a kid who's probably read too many bad Stephen King books. I honestly expected a bit more from you, though, Gwen. You know better than anyone how dangerous it is when people believe in crazy stories, and yet here you are, defending one in the same crazy way!"

He knew he misspoke before he even finished, but the words spilled out anyway. Gwen stared at him as if he had danced over her grave, the edges of her eyes reddening from the struggle to hold back tears. Surprisingly, she didn't cry, not even a drop; she merely turned and followed after Range around the corner, her short, sharp steps reverberating through the empty hospital.

"Damn, bro, that was harsh. I think she's going to find some ointment for that burn."

"I didn't mean for it to be," Bruce said softly, part of him wanting to chase after the poor girl who had suffered far too many betrayals that day, but this wasn't the time for sympathy.

This was time for cold, hard truths; and if she couldn't face them, maybe time alone was what was best for her, although he seriously doubted her time would be spent alone.

"But she needed to hear it. We can't give in to delusions, no matter how harmless they may seem. Now, does anyone have any other ideas? Practical ones?"

Veronica looked at him sorrowfully, but without any kind of judgment, thankfully, as he wasn't sure if he would be able to handle her distrust as well.

"Do you think... think anybody could've gotten out? Out of town, I mean? Either they were just passing through... saw how bad things were, and turned around? Or saw that the bridge was out and told someone?"

"I think that's our best hope. Obviously, if someone had just been passing through, they never made it back out, but they'll hear about us sooner or later, that's for sure. That just means our main job is surviving until that happens. Now, I still think the plan is sound, especially since we're moving toward the highway, but I think there are a few things we could work on in regards—"

"I think you guys need to come back here and see this."

The voice echoed out from the nearest hallway and was clearly a warped, spacious version of Range's; but it made them all jump, regardless, Billy even raising his small pistol toward the doorway defensively. Range's head appeared soon after near the stairwell along with his hand waving them over, but his eyes were on something at the far end of the hall.

Bruce had a bad feeling in the pit of his stomach, his insides churning and the hair on his arm rising as if by magnetism. He was worried that they were walking themselves into another debate, or worse, some kind of trap. He knew firsthand how defensive others got about their deeply held beliefs, even the most ridiculous ones, and faced the persecution from those because of it. Still, his instincts told him that neither Range nor Gwen were that far gone... yet.

Moving into the hallway toward the stairwell, Bruce was first taken aback by the terrible smell and how much worse it was than in the entrance hall. It smelled like cooked meat and burned hair, adding to that already-charming bouquet of blood and feces, and Bruce nearly threw up after his first two steps over the threshold.

Billy, following just behind, did not share his iron stomach and quickly retched in the corner, only making things worse and nearly tipping Bruce's gut over the edge, but he held firm. Veronica followed them in, and from the way she acted, you'd think it smelled like a bubbling brook on a spring day.

They rounded the corner and saw the cause of the aroma wafting through the halls: a pile of roasted corpse stacked nearly halfway to the ceiling at the far end. Bruce gagged again, putting his hand to his mouth to catch whatever bile escaped.

As he backed up, he noticed a dampness soaking into his leather soles and heard the slosh of water against his feet. The entirety of the hallway floor was covered in nearly two inches of water that nearly reached the top of his shoes, as the center of the hall seemed to dip, making a small, barely noticeable crater for the water to settle in.

Billy made his way round the corner too swiftly, his feet sliding out from under him and sending him spiraling into the corner where the wall met the poorly tiled floor. The smell seemed to hit him when he landed, and coupled with the loss of equilibrium, the boy vomited again into the already-murky water.

The offensive odor—a mix of rotten eggs, moldy cheese, week-old meat, and gallons and gallons of antiseptic—made even Bruce woozy as he noticed a sway in his step and his left eye blurring. Throwing his shirt over his nose gave him temporary relief, although his own body odor was nothing to start a perfume line with. Moving forward past the stairwell, Bruce spared a glance upstairs, only to be met with a wall of furniture that went nearly to the ceiling.

"What in God's name... What happened here?"

"I don't know. That was there when I found it," Range said calmly, his eyes drifting between Bruce and the end of the hall.

Moving close enough to smell the varnish, Bruce ran his hands over the desk that formed the base of the structure and up the backs and legs of the chairs stacked one over the other, giving it a gentle shake to test its durability. Surprisingly, it was fairly resilient. It barely moved in an inch from all of Bruce's spastic tampering.

"I wouldn't stand so close if I were you."

Bruce was about to ask him what he meant when a hand made almost entirely of bone, adorned with loose strips of yellowed and frayed skin dangling between its fingers, forced its way between the legs of chair and stopped just short of Bruce's nose, so close he could smell the must and decay.

Falling backward and into the hallway lagoon with a heavy splash, he backed himself against the wall, as far from the flexing, spindly fingers as possible. The hand thrashed wildly, trying to squirm its way through the small gap to get to the meal on the other side. The desks and chairs that made up the makeshift fortification trembled and shook but held strong, and after several long seconds of silence, it slipped right back through the gap, like an eel retreating back into its cave.

Bruce tasted his heart in the back of his throat, and with his breath pounding in his ear, he got to his feet and braved the stairwell again, getting close but keeping enough distance to stay out of reach of any more probing limbs.

"How many of them are back there?"

Looking through the small gap that had once held the skeletal attacker, he saw several shadows passing in front of each other, the light dance of shifting fabrics as several of the undead bumped and collided with each other in their crowded prison.

"Couple dozen, at least. I'd be willing to bet that the entire second and third floor are still trapped behind that barrier, though. With how empty this place has been, I figured they'd have to be cooped up somewhere."

"Who do you think did this?"

"That's what I wanted to show you. Come on."

Silent as a ghost, Range moved through the water toward the pile of burned bodies, covering his own nose as he grew closer. With one last trepidatious glance at the barrier that looked flimsier and flimsier by the minute, Bruce begrudgingly followed behind the stalwart youth, who was so focused on his destination that he didn't even spare a look to see if Bruce was following him. The rest of the group fell in place behind him, the splashes of water echoing through the hospital corridor like it was a small cavern.

When they reached the human bonfire, Bruce gagged again and managed to ask, "This isn't what you were trying to show me, was it?"

Again, Range didn't even look back. He merely shook his head and continued forward as if no one had a said anything, alone in his own, strange world.

"It's just a little further now, just around the next bend, actually."

He turned at the next hallway, the sign above it indicating that toxicology, radiation, and the morgue were all in this direction, the last word catching Bruce's attention the most.

"This is where the morgue is. Are you sure it's safe to be walking around back here so nonchalantly?"

"I'm sure."

Sharing a worried look with Veronica, who quickly adjusted her bandana down out of her eyes and kept her shotgun ready in the nook of her shoulder, prepared for whatever terror Range had in store for them. Clearing the corner, they were faced with a hallway about half the distance of all the others they had passed through, cut off by a pair of silver double doors made of the glossiest steel Bruce had ever seen. On the small windows that lay just above the door's center was a collection of handprints, some bloody, others simple white streaks, but all covering every blank piece of glass. Between the curved handles and the door, there was a long piece of broken steam pipe, supported and cradled by the thin strips of metal.

And at the door's side, crumpled on the floor was the body of a man in a police uniform, his head blown off by a shotgun that rested haphazardly in his lap.

"Jesus Christ," Bruce said, running his hand over his face in the hopes that it might wipe away the image from his mind.

Unfortunately, it remained even in the darkness of his eyelids, the ghastly sight of the man's ruptured head reminding him of an exploded party popper stomped flat into the grass.

"Do you recognize him at all?" Range asked.

"Well, it's a little hard to, now, I'll admit, but let me see…"

Kneeling far closer to the corpse than he would've liked, so close that he could still catch a whiff of morning breath coming from the remains of the man's exposed throat (a cocktail of coffee and bagels tainted by the overpowering smell of copper that clung to the air). Blood had spilled down most of his tattered uniform, rips and tears in the fabric over fresh wounds that still glistened with pus and dried sweat. Over the right lapel was a small bronze plaque of a nameplate, the weight of it causing it to droop to one side, obscuring the name. Slowly, with a dread that weighed him down like tar, he pressed his finger gently against the side of the tag and turned it toward him, a chill running down his spine as he mouthed those two simple syllables: *Asworth*.

"Ah, fuck," Bruce said despondently, "it's Asworth."

"You know 'em?"

"I did," he answered, his focus remaining on Asworth's twisted remains as he stood, his knees cracking and sighing in protest. "He was with the sheriff when he got shot, got relegated to hospital duty as a way to give him some time to calm down. They should have sent the guy home, but we were already stretched too thin with the fires upstate. Poor bastard blamed himself for it too."

There was an awkward scuffling of feet that Bruce could only assume came from Tyler's oversized gym shoes, and he'd be lying if he didn't enjoy his discomfort, but his mind was still centered only on Asworth and his final moments.

"What do you think made him do… well, this to himself?" Range said, as if he were reading his mind.

The kid seemed to do that a lot. As awkward as he could be, he seemed to have an uncanny read on people, invading their thoughts with that deceptively dull gaze and understanding them intimately.

"I can't say. Like I said, he blamed himself for what happened to the sheriff, called himself a coward. Didn't think he was as serious as this, though. Unless…"

Bruce knelt beside the body again and inspected it closer than he had originally. The man's head was obviously lacking in the clue department, as it hardly even resembled a human head anymore. It looked closer to the underside of an octopus, strips of flesh and bone spilling out like tendrils. One even had an ear dangling from the end, like some kind of sick ornament, but Bruce's eyes danced over that grisly sight as quick as lightning.

His arms bore several small scrapes and cuts; some were matted in blood but didn't look any worse than what you might see from a bad car accident. As he moved down to Asworth's soaked-through khakis, something caught his eye, but only briefly, so much so that he thought it to be a trick of the light, until a nagging from the back of his mind made him look again.

There was a spot on his uniform—one that, from a distance, looked like a simple crease in the plain auburn pattern but, if you moved to the right angle, was a large gash that nearly split the shirt in half. Bruce let his fingers slip inside the tear and felt a sickening squish on the skin beneath, his fingers sinking into a boglike wound. He tried to explore further but found the shotgun to be in his way and set to moving it by prying it from the dead man's stiff, plaster fingers. There was a dry crack as the thing came loose, the hands lolling lazily down his thigh and landing with a soft splash into the puddle of blood and drain water.

"I think that answers your question," Gwen said from behind them.

Behind the shotgun, the gash was clearly visible, not only in Asworth's shirt, but through his stomach—a cut so deep that you could see the different organs pressed against each other, trying to squeeze themselves out of their fleshy prison all at once. The edges were black and in the shape of bite marks, leaking a thick green paste that made the skin clammy and slick.

"Looks like he got bit by one of those things," Bruce said, pulling his hand from the hole in Asworth's guts. "Knew what was gonna happen to him and decided that he didn't wanna end up like one of 'em, crazy son of a bitch."

"Do you think he's the one who barred the stairwell?"

"He's gotta be. It looks like he sealed these doors off as well, although I'm not sure why."

"The morgue is down there," Gwen said, pointing to the sign that hung on the east wall. Sure enough, there was the word *morgue* written in a boring white font with a small arrow aimed in the direction of the double doors beside Asworth's body. "He was trying to make sure none of the dead got out."

"Guess that means he burned the bodies too," Range said, turning behind them to the still-smoking pile of charred remains.

"So you're telling me this motherfucker sealed off the walkers upstairs, the ones crawling out of the damn morgue, *and* burned the rest that he could find? And then he got bit and decided he'd rather blow his head off with a 12 gauge than become one of those ugly fucks? This nigga was the hardest motherfucker I've ever seen," Tyler said, as politely as Tyler knew how.

"And he thought he was a coward," Bruce said, a sad grin appearing on his face without him realizing. "Well, let's not let his efforts go to waste. Let's start searching the place before those things break through the barriers."

"Wait… you really think… they're gonna break through…" Veronica said, straining to finish and failing to do so. The pain was more obvious on her face from her attempts at a nonslurred speech, her eyes turning into thin creases above what could only be a harrowing grimace hidden behind Bruce's torn sleeve.

"They're stronger than they look, but they're not that strong. One or two by themselves won't be able to make a dent, but if they all pile on it at once, it'll go down in a matter of minutes. So we'll have to make the most of the time we've got… Jeez, that sounded better in my head, you know what I mean. We need to spread out and gather what supplies we can before this place becomes overrun. Only grab what we can use. Everything we take, we'll have to carry ourselves, other than what we can fit in Tyler's duffel bag. I'm taking antiseptic, bandages, anything that can be used as a weapon."

"What about pain pills?" Tyler asked, raising his hand lackadaisically like an unruly student.

"While I can already imagine what you plan to do with them, I have to admit they might come in handy, so that's fine. Just don't go overboard. We need room in the bag, and we don't need you getting so drugged out we can't tell you from the zombies."

"'Aight, man, I know how to handle my shit. You ain't gotta babysit me."

"Fine then. We'll meet back in the lobby in a half hour. That should give us enough time to search what parts of this place aren't infested. Now, be careful. Just because the barriers are up doesn't mean that every inch of this place is safe, and it'd be a dumb mistake to think so. We'll split up into pairs. If you hear anything, or get outnumbered, call out as loud as you can, and somebody will come running. And if you hear anybody screaming, you go and assist them, okay? The only way we're gonna get through this is by working together, whether we like it or not."

He made sure to look at Range and Gwen with that last line, a thinly veiled attempt to ease the tension between them, but neither of them reciprocated this peace offering in any noticeable way, so Bruce let the issue lie. With some final last-minute instructions about what types of antibiotics they might need and what brand of gauze worked best, they split themselves into pairs and drifted off to their separate corners of the first floor. Range and Gwen agreed to search toxicology and the cancer ward beyond it, while Tyler and Billy, although much more reluctantly than the first pair, relented to searching the pharmacy on Tyler's request, a concerning look of glee on his sunken features as he limped down the southern corridor. Finally, Bruce brought Veronica to the emergency room on the pretext of looting the supplies there—although from the group's sideways glances, he believed they suspected their true intentions, despite their secrecy.

Still, Bruce played it off like he didn't notice them, keeping his head high on his shoulders, walking forward with such purpose that it demanded respect. Veronica matched his pace, her cheekbones high above the torn fabric the only indication of her once-lovely smile. After traveling through three long hallways, around four desks, and through eight double doors, they finally reached the emergency room.

Leading the slim girl over to the patient exam table in the back of the room, he easily lifted her off her feet and set her gently on top of it, her back leaning against the pale plaster wall behind her. She fidgeted as the bare leg from under her shorts touched the cold metal table and slouched as soon as she found a place of comfort. The walk had taken a far greater toll on her than Bruce had originally thought. Her breaths were rapid and frighteningly short, her chest moving in static, jittery rises as she desperately tried to catch her breath.

"All right, I'm gonna take the bandage off now, if that's okay?" Bruce said, as calmly as possible.

In reality, he was terrified of what he might find behind the once dirty-brown sleeve that had turned a deadly shade of dark maroon.

Veronica gave him a hard nod, one that was more for her than it was for him, and Bruce started untangling the knot near her ear. It came away easy enough, the material dampened and loosened by the massive amount of blood that had soaked through it. It fell off all at once, pulling apart like a curtain on a stage of the damned.

Just as Veronica's condition was graver than he thought, the wound was far worse than he could have ever imagined. The blood around the edge of the tear in her mouth had congealed into sticky black tar that glistened in the low fluorescent lights. He saw exposed jawbone jutting from a spot where her cheek had been ripped clean off and all the exposed teeth beneath it. Flies flew from some of the redder, fleshier parts of the wound, buzzing around Bruce's face, like bees defending their hive. Small yellow maggots moved through the remains of muscle and skin, their small creamlike bodies burrowing deeper and deeper into the flesh. Some parts of loose skin had already turned a sickly shade of green and others an even more ghastly yellow that reminded him of animal skeletons after they'd been stripped clean by scavengers.

From the hurt look in Veronica's saucer eyes, and the way she turned, covering the lower half of her face with her hands while she broke into a slobbering fit of sobs that sounded more like an out-of-breath pug, Bruce could tell that he did not hide his disgust very well at all and instantly felt a fever of guilt lighten his head.

"Hey, hey, now, it's not that bad. Really, I just… I just wasn't as prepared for it as I thought I was," Bruce said, wishing he could grab the words from the air and shove them back down his throat along with his foot right after he said them.

With surprising tenacity, the girl choked back a sob and gave a stiff but not discourteous nod, allowing him to proceed. There were a few sniffles and tears still streaked through her bloody cheeks and over her wound, but for the most part, she held her face perfectly still while Bruce examined the gash in the poor girl's face closer, probing with his finger and trying to remove as much of the maggots without the girl seeing their writhing forms. How they had gotten there so quickly, Bruce couldn't be sure, but he knew it wasn't a good sign. The skin was tough and leathery in some spots already, with entire sections of skin having been torn loose by the creature's claws or fallen away in their hurried march toward the hospital.

Once the wound had been cleaned of all the visible parasites, Bruce started searching the room for a needle and thread, along with some kind of staple gun to give the suture a better hold. After checking several drawers and cabinets near the far wall, he finally found them in a small plastic container next to some disposable gloves and antiseptic that had been knocked over in some unseen scuffle.

As Bruce gathered the materials for the quick operation, he paused, his thoughts turning against him as he pictured the wound again—the green hue to the skin, the infestation of maggots and flies. Was he actually helping this girl or merely prolonging the inevitable? He knew that a bite supposedly turned you into one of those things. It had been at least a decade since he'd watched any kind of horror movie—be it zombies, machete-wielding maniacs, or a man playing straight to impress his son's in-laws—but he knew that much at least. But did a scratch, especially one as deep and grisly as the one Veronica bore, carry the same consequences? And even if it didn't, how long would it be until she succumbed to the infection and heavy blood loss?

The thought passed in a moment, but it was long enough to make him angrily slam the cabinet door for even considering it—whether it was fruitless or not, he was not about to give up on this girl, like he did that girl screaming the streets. He was going to get her, and the rest of the kids wandering the hospitals corridors, out of here—even Tyler, as much as he loathed the idea.

Veronica hopped lightly on the table from the sound of the crashing cabinet but didn't ask him about it. From the constrained look on her face, he knew that she was having the same thoughts and that if she fell into the same mind-set, the girl would be well and truly lost.

"All right, sit up for me, beautiful, and let me get a good look at this scratch of yours," Bruce said, wearing a forced grin.

She rolled his eyes at this, making him feel like some kind of awkward uncle, but the small glimmer in the whites and the lack of tears turned his fake smile into one of genuine warmth as he started on his less-than-desirable task.

Pouring the antiseptic into a cloth, he told Veronica to brace herself, his own skin rippling from the imagined pain. The girl's back straightened, and she took in one deep breath and released it like a slow, serene summer breeze. After another one of her hardened nods, he pressed the damp cloth into the center of the wound.

The squirming and squealing started immediately, her breath turning into a high whine as she gritted her teeth against the pain. He did his best to move it up and down the length of the wound, but her twisting head only made it more difficult, along with the gnashing teeth that clamped down on the tips of his fingers on more than one occasion. Grabbing her chin gently but firmly, he held her head still while he finished his unsavory work, scrubbing the disinfectant deep into the furthest reaches of the wound. Several maggots had risen to the top of the flesh, but he scooped them harmlessly into the cloth, crushing the life out of them with a satisfying squish.

As soon as he pulled away, Veronica's hands rushed to the wound to caress it, but he stopped them forcefully. She struggled against him, but he did not allow her to dirty the wound again, reminding her that if she did, he would only have to apply more antiseptic—

which got her hands to her side quicker than a child told they'd get ice cream for being well behaved. Bruce threaded the needle without much effort, something he had previously struggled with, so he counted that as a small victory amidst an ever-increasing stack of losses.

The girl braced herself again as he started silently at the top of the wound, pinching the wound shut with his gloved hands and counted another win when no maggots surfaced. Veronica gave a grimace and another high-pitched squeal of pain as he pierced the rotting flesh, his victory vanishing as a thin stream of black pus broke from the suture point and ran down the curves of the gash and onto his hands. Bruce did his best to ignore it but could not keep it hidden from Veronica as each jab of the needle raised more and more of the black muck from her skin. Her light sobs returned, causing her face to tremble and her body to shake; but Bruce did his best to work around it, shushing her quietly as he did so.

After fifteen minutes of dedicated sewing that reminded him of a slightly more chaotic version of home ed, Bruce finished up and grabbed a pair of scissors from the table beside him, ignoring the already-thick, marmalade-like pool of blood they sat in, to clip the end of the string, tying the rest of it off in the smallest knot he knew. The staple gun was a much more harrowing endeavor, each staple bringing forth a scream of pain that was sure to echo down the maze of hospital hallways and empty rooms; but he kept the number to the bare minimum, using them only in places where the stitching was already loose. Fortunately, no one mistook her cries for ones of needed assistance—although that almost worried Bruce more, as they either felt like not responding, couldn't hear, or were already in far worse dangers themselves. He kept his mind focused on the task at hand and set about getting a bandage over the wound, pulling one from another drawer above the cabinet that held the suture supplies.

Taking a moment to examine his work, he had to admit he didn't do that bad of a job and almost regretted his choice of profession, however briefly. The stitching was rough and jagged, zigzagging this way and that along the wound, but it returned the cheek to its natural shape and contours, which restored some of her natural looks.

He didn't think she would ever be called beautiful again—at least not in the traditional, superficial sense—but it was a close-enough reflection, one found in a dirty mirror or murky puddle. A pale imitation at best, but it seemed like the best the poor girl could ever hope for.

"There we go. Good as new. Can you try speaking for me? See if it's any easier?"

She swallowed, readying herself and opened her mouth before closing it again quickly from the pain. After several slower, more cautious attempts, she finally tried to mouth a few words before attempting to actually speak them. After this, Bruce asked her to try several tongue twisters to see if the lisp and slurred speech was going to be permanent or just another symptom of half of her cheek being in literal shreds.

"Sally sells seashells by the shea… Sally sells sheshells… Sally sells seashells by the seashore! Sally sells seashells by the seashore!" she proclaimed triumphantly.

Bruce couldn't help but laugh as he pressed the square bandage over the wound, his own mood lifted by her enthusiasm.

"Like I said, good as new, I'm guessing, in a couple days, after some proper treatment by an actual doctor, you're speech will be good as new, and with some cosmetic surgery, you might not be able to tell that there was anything wrong with you to begin with. And remember, this is just our little secret, so I won't tell anyone if you won't. With the bandage, I'm sure most people won't even be—"

She leaned in and kissed him then, with all the timing of an awkward teenager who believes themselves in love, her tongue pressing against his lips, waiting for an invitation. He could taste the bile gathering against his pursed lips as he pulled back, jerking his head away as if she had struck him. The look on her face as he reeled back was quite similar, like he had spat in her face and thrown her into the dirt. The hurt in her eyes was palpable, full of misunderstanding and doubt, like the world had come crashing down around her.

"Whoa, let's hold up there. I'm sorry to disappoint you. You're a very pretty girl, any man would be lucky to have you, but I can't do this," he said as she descended into more heart-swallowing sobs. "It's not you, I swear, it's me," he added, instantly regretting it.

The girl stood up and pushed her way past him, but he grabbed her, holding her still as she fought to escape.

"Just listen to me. I'm sorry to have hurt your feelings. I really am. It's not you, and it's not your wound, that, I swear, no matter how cliché it sounds," he said, trying to skirt around the real issue. "I… I just don't go for that type of thing, if you catch my drift."

"No, I'm sorry. I was just being stupid. But you don't have to make up some bullshit excuse," she said, shaking free of his grasp and chanting this mantra to herself as she slipped into the hallway and out of sight.

His first instinct was to sprint after her, to protect her from whatever terrors lurked within the darkened hospital rooms; but at this point, seeing him following her would be worse for her than seeing one of those groaning, decaying monsters.

The room seemed darker when it was just him contained within its boring white walls. For the first time, he noticed a chill coming from the vents, a light rumbling that sounded like breezes and whispers in his ear. The coolness of it on the back of his neck sent chills down to the core of his spine.

With a deep sigh, he started gathering what was left of the antiseptic, needles and thread, along with a couple rolls of gauze that he stuffed into his back pockets. When he touched the blood-coated scissors on the small steel tray, he shivered, fully aware of the room's subarctic chill for the first time. He soon recognized the feeling as one of acute paranoia, one that seeps into your very consciousness and makes you aware of everything wrong with your surroundings. In Bruce's case, the first thing he noticed was the eyes boring into the back of the skull and the shadow standing behind him.

He turned to face it slowly, cautiously, but without urgency, for reasons he could not exactly explain. Sure enough, standing in the small doorway was a tall shadow that seemed to stretch up into the very ceiling. It did not move, and it did not speak; it merely stood and watched as Bruce looked it over. There was an air of familiarity about it despite its oblong shape and inhuman form, but Bruce couldn't put his finger on it—at least, not until he heard its voice.

Still on duty, are ya, Vencini?

It was the sheriff's voice—the same tenor, the same small whistle over his *s*'s that often made the grumpy old man blush, the same sharp tone whenever he used his last name. The only thing it was missing was the warmth that infected every coarse word and stiff command, the spark that made you want to follow the bastard over a bottomless pit into hell and back, the very thing that had allowed Bruce to drop his guard in the first place.

But it was the sheriff's voice; of that, he was absolutely certain. There was something else about it, though: its mannerisms, the way it watched him with invisible yet sinister eyes.

Are you gonna save the day, Brucie? Huh? You gonna save me, Bruce?

Acid dripped from its dark lips, its liquid edges melting into the shadowed world behind it, like an oil stain on a charcoal canvas. Bruce watched it move soundlessly out of the doorway, receding like the tide back into the hallways that birthed it, slinking out of view. The air rushed out of him, as if this dark vision had stolen it from him, attached itself to his very being and was dragging him along by a string. Compelled to the point of near obedience, he trailed off after the thing, watching it disappear around another corner, while the lighting flickered above it.

It occurred to Bruce that he was simply losing his mind, but he always heard that the truly insane don't think they're crazy but that everyone else is, and thinking that you were crazy was a good sign of your own sanity. He clutched at this thought like a totem, despite knowing deep down that it was a complete and total lie.

He moved down the hallway after his spectral guide, every muscle in his body urging him to stop, run back to the others, and get them out of this hellish fun house he had dragged them to, but he would not give in to the fear he felt. He had shown weakness in the lobby, futilely beating his hands against a TV screen, like a child in a tantrum, because the show had not ended the way he expected— no, *demanded* it to. The way they had looked at him then… No, he would not give in to this encroaching fear again. If he did, there was no chance, for any of them. If this was madness, let him face it. Let him tell it to go to hell and take this damned blight on the town, *his* town, with it.

He pressed forward, repeating this mantra to himself, truly embracing this new life as a madman, of which he was oddly accustomed to. As he rounded the next corner, he caught a glimpse of the shadow again; and hustling after it, he nearly fell backward as he turned the corner only to come face-to-face with it once again.

It was smiling. All of it was one, fluid mass of darkness, yet he could feel its smile pressing down on him all the same.

Come on, don't stop now. The hero wouldn't quit. The hero never quits this easily. You don't want them thinking you're just some fag, do ya?

Bruce blinked, and the shadow was at the center of the hallway, watching him as it traveled down another corridor, leading him further into the hospital's corroded heart. He wanted to follow, but his legs felt like hardened, useless gelatin. Now he recognized what else about this shadow had been so familiar.

It reminded him of Matt.

He no longer carried vigor in his step as he followed the shadow's descent into the darkest reaches of the hospital. What he had so easily shaken off as fear before, he now knew was something far worse: unmitigated, unshakeable terror. Matt's final words kept replaying themselves in his head, like a broken answering machine outputting more static than understandable sentences. He felt no sorrow or remorse for what had happened to the bastard; this was not guilt that was plaguing him. Instead, it was the truth, tucked away in his hate-filled rant, like venom in bared fangs, which was slowly eating away at his insides.

Sarah Nottingull's spiteful glares at every police ball, barbecue, get-together of any kind kept playing themselves over and over in his mind, along with her tear-streaked rant over her dying husband's body. Bruce now wondered which nightmare would be worse: the one he found himself in then, or the one he found himself in now.

Suddenly, he knew where this darkness was leading him and let his legs drag him along begrudgingly, accepting whatever horror awaited him.

Come on, Brucie. You've got to save everyone. You've got to save me. Why didn't you save me? You've never been one to follow orders when they don't suit you. So why didn't you ignore mine and come and save me when I needed you?

While the ruins of modern medicine had never been exactly pleasant, now they appeared to be the very gates of hell—dark, cavernous, and intertwining as they burrowed deeper and deeper into the earth. And he was spiraling down with it.

The angles of the wall seemed to bear down on him, oppressive in the way they seemed to feed off every breath, every thought, like he was traveling through the bloated, sterilized corpse of some ancient beast.

"Mem'ries, light the corners of my mind..." it sang in a minor, offbeat drone, like B. B. King poured over sandpaper. "Misty water colored memories, of the way we were..."

As he neared the double doors marked "Intensive Care," his heart was nearly beating from his chest, prying at his ribs in an attempt to at least save itself from this certain oblivion. The door, despite being incredibly heavy, was swinging gently before settling into place beside its brother. From behind, he could hear scuffling, sharp squeaks of turning feet and another small buzz of white noise he didn't recognize.

His breath caught as he stepped forward, pressing his palm flat against the door's flat steel plate that served as a makeshift handle for a door that was never locked. Gently, silently moving it forward, Bruce slipped through, catching it as it swung shut behind him and letting it glide softly back into place.

As soon as he took in his surroundings, however, he instantly regretted the decision and almost leaped right back through. In front of him lay some smorgasbord of the damned; the very sight of which tried to knock down the remaining walls of sanity and make life spent as a babbling, drooling fool preferable to the horrors of this new reality.

Sarah Nottingull's body lay several yards in front of him. Her face was gnawed down so that all that remained was the skull—save for the eyes, one of which lay on the ground beside its bare socket while the other was loosely clinging to its home—surrounded by what little flesh remained to her, along with her scalp and frizzy brown strands of greasy hair. One of her arms had been tossed in the corner, half devoured; and one of her legs was completely missing beneath the knee.

The worst sight was at her stomach, where the two saddened, frightened children he had seen earlier that morning were feasting on her insides, pulling them out like taffy and stringing them through their teeth. They gnashed on the entrails, squeezing the juices out with a childlike glee, their gray sagging faces mimicking those of innocence.

As Bruce took a startled step back, they turned in an instant and set their eyes upon him, searching him like pale chips of frosted headlights. Their cheeks were bulging like squirrels, forced that way by the chunks of meat they were shoving through them, making bloody, pus-filled holes so you could see the act of swallowing. Their bellies were distended, and blood covered them from head to toe, making them seem more like small demons than children.

There was a deep and crushing silence as they watched him, both sides waiting for one another to make even the slightest motion.

Can it be that it was all so simple then? Or has time rewritten every line? If we had the chance to do it all again, tell me, would we? Could we?

With a hideous howl, the small imps meandered toward him, their stubby legs waddling over the tiles with a pitter-patter that was almost comical. Bruce started wheeling backward, unable to strike something that still looked so innocent, even with black bile seemingly pouring out of every pore. The little girl still resembled her living counterpart, still had that gleam of innocence, even though blood trailed from her eyes where there had once been sour tears.

The boy tripped over its own stunted legs and started dragging itself along the ground, pushing with its back legs as it squirmed its way toward him like a worm. The girl snapped at his hand, Bruce yanking it away at the last second; and like an instinct, he swatted her with the back of his hand, sending the creature flying into the wall, landing hard against it with its back. There was a sickening snap as the thing that was once a girl folded in the wrong direction and flopped onto the ground in a bent heap, still twitching like a crushed cockroach.

The boy had gotten back to his feet just briefly enough to fall forward again, but his awkward momentum carried him into Bruce's legs, nearly knocking the two over in a knot of bodies. The child pulled at his clothes and crawled its way toward his face, its small claws tearing at his flesh while its mouth, still only half filled with baby teeth and dripping with blood and his mother's flesh, came ever closer. His sympathy toward whatever these monsters used to be evaporated, and he grabbed the little beast by the stomach and threw it hard into the glass that made up half of the hallway wall.

It crashed hard against it, the whole blood-streaked pane shaking and warping without even a crack appearing. Hopping to his feet but sliding in the mix of water and blood, Bruce stumbled forward toward his miniature attacker still struggling to pull its brittle body back up and let his foot rest on top of its head, pressing it down into the tile.

His eyes drifted up to the glass and the room behind it; even though he told himself not to look, his eyes were drawn instantly toward the broken door and the empty bed. His heart stopped, and his stomach turned over when he saw what was left of him—nothing but bones, still spotted with yellow muscle and chunks of flesh, some even of his face, torn and thrown about the room.

Mem'ries! Mem'ries! May be beautiful and yeeeeeeettttt! What's too painful to remember! We simply choose to forget!

Bruce screamed, his lungs emptying like a piston, as he raised his foot and brought it crashing down with a nauseating crunch. As soon as his foot hit tile, or maybe bone, he brought it up, just high enough to bring it crashing back down again. He repeated this several more times, feeling the small head disintegrate beneath his heel.

As his breath failed him, he stopped, having to grab the wall for support from falling into the puddle of brain and bone he had made at his feet. Looking down nearly cost him his lunch, or lack thereof, but he had to see what he'd done; he had to look at it, take it in so he couldn't forget it.

A slow, sick wheeze came from behind him; and when he turned, he saw the broken girl—its back twisting over its useless, spasming legs as it tried to pull itself toward him, its nails burying themselves in the cheap plastic tile. Its body uncoiled and folded back over itself like a slug, or something even more alien.

As the girl looked up at him, his back twisted toward the floor, he felt a pang of sympathy again. All he had to do was think of Hank's dissembled body, and it left him, bringing his work boot high above the girl's bouncing head. Bringing the heel down so that it landed in the girl's mouth, her small mouth chewed on the leather, trying to wrest it free; and Bruce thought one last time of the timid girl crying into her mother's shoulder, wondering if her father was going to live.

And now, here she was beneath his boot, with pieces of her mother and father dissolving in her stomach—or just sitting there, rotting, depending on however these abominations of nature functioned.

With one last final kick, he separated the top of her head from the bottom at the jaw, wincing himself as he did so. The top of the creature's skull skidded across the floor, sliding to a slow halt on the other side of the room.

Silence and darkness enveloped him. All that he could hear was that voice, so like and unlike the sheriff's, humming a tune he did not recognize, growing in a steady crescendo. And like a crash of cymbals, there came a booming thud from the hallway behind him—one that sounded eerily close to furniture tumbling down a flight of stairs.

He inhaled deeply and found ash, soot, and cobwebs pouring into his lungs. A coughing fit seized him, and he tried his best to stifle it with his hand. The small shed was coated in darkness, but he could still hear them, their melancholy droning becoming as second nature to him as the sound of his own breath, their twisted feet being dragged through crisp fall leaves, taking him back to the time of Halloweens spent running joyfully through streets filled with monsters and turning it into a sinister reality. He would've laughed if he hadn't been so busy coughing.

His skin itched and pulsed with heat in time with his rapid heartbeat, magma pouring through his veins. Despite the cold winds that shook the small shed to the point where it seemed ready to collapse at any moment, sweat was rushing from every pore, soaking him and washing him clean. He felt twice as sticky, but he could see the blood sliding off him, and he found some comfort in that.

So far, that was the only comfort he could invent.

Working against it was the fact that they had been chased through a forest by wolves and a horde of mangled, decaying bodies that swallowed the horizon without an end in sight and cornered them in a ramshackle shed outside of an old, run-down factory. The old steel workbench digging into his side wasn't helping much either, and neither was his loss of control, his mind already drifting into visions that were becoming harder to distinguish from the world around him. He heard their soft sighs, felt their steamy breath on his neck, their lips working their way down his chest, inviting him to lose himself as he always had, in the basic pleasures of the skin. So simple and so pure, how he had ever seen it as something wrong was completely beyond his current comprehension.

Matt Métier slunk low in the darkest recesses of the old shoe factory maintenance shed. Or had they made ammunition here? The stories mixed often. That was part of his job, mixing drinks and mixing stories to see what truth you got out of both of them. The truth found at the bottom of the glass always seemed more… honest.

Vel sat trembling beside him, clutching his arm and jumping at every stray scrape or bump that she had no immediate answer for. He couldn't really blame her for it, yet he despised her for it all the same. Everything about her was making him angry—her constant useless screaming and pointless crying, falling to her knees to sob and wax poetic when they needed to be putting as much distance between them and those creatures as possible. He had already twice considered throwing her to them to increase his odds of escape, but neither time had seemed desperate enough to require it, and he'd rather save that idea for when death was almost certain.

For now, he had to admit, despite her homely appearance—make that *extremely* homely—appearance, the touch of her cheek on his arm was quelling the fire building inside him, one he had not satiated for nearly two days now. Its embers were creeping into his skull, roasting their way through, fueling certain desires that were of no use to him now—not when his life depended on it, whatever it was worth at this point.

"How much longer do you think we'll have to... we'll have to stay here?" Vel asked, sniffling.

Goddamn, he wanted to choke the tears right out of her.

"How the fuck should I know? As long as it takes for those fucking things to leave us alone."

"You don't have to be so mean."

"I don't have to be nice either. Now shut the hell up, or they'll hear us."

They dropped into silence, Vel pulling away into a corner on the other side of the room but not daring to venture out into the other room, the one that held the door that led outside to the factory grounds. Again, he couldn't blame her but hated her nonetheless.

Part of him regretted it, lamenting the loss of her soft caress on his broiling skin, but whether that was actually him or the urge was becoming harder to tell. The lie was becoming harder to tell.

Old nun, blood seeping from between her legs, no teeth, yet a skeleton grin, grabbing your dick and yanking 'til she tears it up by the roots.

"How many of them are out there do ya think? A hundred? A thousand?"

"What does it matter? There's more than two, which means that they outnumber us, which means we're fucked," *blood pouring from between your legs,* "either way. Why are you even worrying about it?"

"I just thought we could try and make another run for it. We've gotta be near the edge of the woods, and I mean, we got away before, didn't we?"

"We got lucky. My shotgun went off, killed the fucker on top of me, and the dumb shits started feasting on his dead guts instead of mine. If they swarm us again, and they will, they're gonna pick us apart like a kid playing with his food. And it's gonna hurt, let me tell you that."

That seemed to shut her up, and they fell into a familiar silence, listening to the crunching leaves and each other's intermittent breaths. Matt began to doze, his mind drifting in and out of consciousness for what he knew must've been at least an hour, when a sound—or the absence of—caused him to stir.

It was dead silent outside.

He couldn't remember the last time he had heard a single shuffled step, and a quick look at Vel's wide-eyed face was enough to confirm his suspicions. Slowly, he hobbled to his feet and moved toward the door that separated this room from the next, peering through the glass to make sure nothing lay in wait for him on the other side. He found nothing, but something made him wait all the same.

A crash came from somewhere beyond the door, and Matt practically pressed his face flat against the glass to find its source. The room stood still, not even a dust mite dancing through the air. He waited for nearly a minute, waiting for their unseen assailant to make itself known, but none came.

Five more minutes passed, and still the room was silent; the whole world was silent, and Matt decided to try and brave the entryway. He'd rather at least make an effort at escape than simply lie down and accept his fate, even though he had started to wonder *why* he was even trying anymore. For now, at least, he pushed those nagging thoughts aside and pressed into the next room.

"Stop! What the hell do you think you're doing?"

"I'm checking if the coast is clear. You were wondering when they were gonna leave, well, now might be the time. So either stay here and join me once I say the coast is clear, or just stay here and die. Either one suits me just fine."

He didn't wait for her answer and stepped over the threshold, nearly tripping over a spilled chair near an overturned desk that must've served as some type of workman's station. His first thought was to check the door, and he nearly retreated once he saw it standing thrown open, one of its rusty hinges torn from the frame and lying in a pile of leaves in the nearby corner. The door itself was hanging at a forty-five-degree angle away from the struggling bottom hinge.

The doorway, however, remained empty, and Matt began to check the rest of the room, turning over furniture and debris for any sign of undead hidden beneath them or in the shadows. He tossed aside papers, some that went back all the way to the nineteenth century. There was even a folder that listed casualties, which Matt could only assume was from the fire that had taken this eyesore of a building more than a century ago. Flipping through the pages, he saw employee records—some for children under the age of six with falsified birth reports, some with mental disabilities, even an entire family of triplets. He threw it back into the rubble, throwing up soot, and started to head back toward the door to check outside when he saw it.

Standing in the doorway was a wolf, smiling at him with its clear, pale eyes, its tongue lopping lazily out of its grinning mouth and over its dripping teeth. Matt stared it down, sure that he was going to be dead in a matter of seconds, if he wasn't dead already, and felt an odd relief. But the wolf stood like a silent watchman, observing him without movement, smiling like it knew some secret that made this whole situation roaringly hilarious.

Testing his luck, or inspired by his own fearlessness in the face of death, he took a step back toward the room, the wolf's dead eyes following him, or at least it seemed like they were. It was hard to tell with eyes without pupils. Its ear twitched, but still it stood, no breath escaping its ruined lungs. He took several more paces forward and found himself at the edge of the door frame when it put one of its padded paws forward.

Matt instinctively reached for his shotgun, even though he knew he lost it in the chase, but the wolf did not charge. Still, it only watched. And smiled.

Then its head began to roll to the side, twisting up at an odd angle, as a slow chuckle started to undulate from its throat. Unlike the laughter from before, these cries were nearly indistinguishable from sobs, so sharp and bitter that they seemed to pierce your very soul.

It walked toward him, its spine rising and bending unnaturally beneath its torn, blood-matted fur, shaking off dirt and twigs as it bent itself into some unholy abomination, laughing as it crawled across the ground like a spider in a wolf's body. Its legs cracked and spun and twisted themselves into long spindles that pushed its trembling body across the floor in a way that was so unnatural Matt was sure he had stumbled into a nightmare and would surely wake up at any moment. Soon, its whole body was shaking from its wild cackling, and Matt found himself sprinting back into the room, slamming the door shut behind him.

He knew the flimsy door would not be able to hold off that creature. If it wanted to get through, it would get through. He waited for the inevitable crash of body against glass, watching the glass for any sign of the abomination, but none came.

The world had fallen back into silence.

Then, as if the ground had opened and spewed forth all the souls of the damned, there was a howling so loud that it seemed to cause the shed—no, the whole world—to tremble in fear of its intensity. His brains rattled like marbles inside his already-boiling skull, turning his thoughts into vapor that his fumbling mental fingers could no longer grasp.

Without even seeing her move, he felt Vel slide in beside him, wrapping her arms around his midsection as the world continued to explode around them. At first, he thought of tossing her to the ground, having his way with her there, whether she wanted him to or not; but instead, he pressed his fingers deep into her flesh and clutched her closely, reveling in meshing of their slick (*dead nun, blood seeping from between her legs, her eyes are missing so you can tell she'd dead*), sweaty skin.

The walls began to pound from fists slamming into the other side. Nails could be heard running themselves down to the bloody nubs against the rotted wood, along with the mournful howls of the undead as they raged against the thin walls that kept them from their latest meal. He could see individual planks rising and warping—twisted, gnarled fists slipping through the gaps that appeared, only to be squeezed back out by the board's failing strength. One of the hands even lost several fingers as the board snapped back into place on its wriggling digits.

Matt tried to take note of their surroundings, looking over the shelves for the fiftieth time since they arrived, hoping this time he would find something to defend themselves with. And just like the other forty-nine times, all he found was the buzz saw with the singed-off power cord and the chainsaw, conveniently out of gas without a single can in sight.

Through the glass, he saw shadows thrown across the wall, stretched-out specters that served as harbingers for the demons that created them. They slowly surrounded the door, their black and bloody faces, with bile dripping from their eyes and pouring from their mouth like a polluted waterfall. Gnashing their teeth against the glass, the dead fought each other to get a view of their prey—all failing to understand the concepts of a barrier made of transparent material, but even that would not save them for more than a couple of minutes.

All the fire in his stomach had left him. His body still felt like it was being slowly submerged in a slow cooker, but his desire to survive had become a terrible acceptance of their fate—a resignation that almost felt like retribution. But for what, he still wasn't willing to admit.

The pounding on the wall became a hypnotic rhythm, a pulsing beat that matched the one pumping through his veins, urging him to action, but not one that would save them. No, what he had in mind would save only him, taking him away from this awful world for those several seconds of rapturous bliss. He could live in those few seconds forever.

His lips knew the motions too well. Even with his head turning itself over like a cooked egg, the lines came to him easily, the same one he used practically every night—every weekend, at least. He couldn't remember a time when it wasn't this way, when he wasn't controlled by this… thing inside of him.

His mouth fell open to speak, but what came out was not what he had prepared. In fact, he wasn't entirely sure he was really speaking to Vel or just rambling to himself.

"I met this guy one night, at the bar, relatively late into my shift. I'm talking, like, one or two in the morning. He came in, looking like shit, reeked of booze so badly that I could smell it on him even when sitting behind the bar, which had been soaked in the stuff all night. Wasn't what you would consider traditionally handsome in the first place, but I mean, this guy was fucked up. He had this comb-over that looked like he'd fallen asleep and a dog licked his head for an hour. Real big nose, tiny eyes, big gut, old as shit. The drink gave him some bright-red cheeks, and if he had a beard, the dude might've passed for Saint Nick but instead came off like John Wayne Gacy.

"He stumbles up to the bar, plops himself down, and orders a vodka on the rocks—a double, of course. A triple, if I'd allow it, he said while sliding a five across to me. I'd been making shit tips that night, so, of course, I served the guy, poured him a triple like he wanted and figured maybe I'd sober him up by talking to him a bit. At least, that's what I told myself. I figure I just really wanted to know what could inspire a guy as old as him to get as piss drunk as he was.

"Surprisingly, he wasn't as loose lipped as you'd expect a man of his lowered inhibitions to be, but after another triple, he started to warm up to me. Told me he came from Germany, took me by surprise when he said that. At first, I thought he was bullshitting me. Guy didn't have even the slightest hint of accent. He had moved to the States over thirty years ago and did his best to acclimate by taking ESL courses down at the local community college down in Vermont. Said he liked it there, real quaint, quiet place where you could hide away from everything."

A palm slapping against the window made them both jump and stunned Matt into a momentary silence, but he continued nonetheless, more or less ignoring the horrible creatures about to break in and consume them. Vel was too entranced to care herself, it seemed. Even though these words were not some rehearsed spiel about her life goals he had absolutely no actual interest in, she still wanted him, craved him.

"I asked him what Germany was like, and he gets all quiet again. I figure I just missed out on my chance to hear this guy's story, so I go back to tending what other few customers we have before close when the guy waves me back over. He pulls out his wallet and shows me this picture of him and his family in an old house back in a small town named Brandenburg. Said he lived there during World War II. Told me a story about his neighbors, who just happened to be Jewish during one of the many times when it's terrible to be Jewish. His father, being the strong, virtuous man that he was, took them in and hid them up in the attic, even when the inspections started. He had been only eight or nine at the time.

"One day, a Stasi officer came to the house when his father was not home. He knew he was supposed to not tell anyone about the family staying upstairs. It was fun game that his father had invented, one that he loved playing. So he denied all existence of this hidden family for several minutes, but then the officer invited more men in, all of them carrying rifles and machine guns as they searched the house, turning over tables, chairs, not just hiding spots, no. They were trying to make a point.

"And it struck home. The game no longer seemed very fun. The officer began to warn him about what terrible fate would befall his father and mother if it was found out that they had been hiding a family from the SS, about how he would be taken away and put in a foster home and never see them again, while they spent the rest of their short lives in prison as traitors before meeting a firing squad.

"So of course, he told the officer where the family was hiding. He led them right up to the attic and moved aside the stacked boards over the rafters and watched as they pulled each member out by their feet, kicking, screaming, clawing, doing anything to free themselves. They all spat at him as they were dragged away, whispering curses in Yiddish and German alike, wishing the boy a fate worse than death for his betrayal. The officers told the boy they were simply relocating them, and for all he knew, they were, as they loaded them up in a truck and carted them off before his father even got home.

"The look he got from his father was far worse than any from the family. For several days, he locked himself in his room and wouldn't come out, and the man could hear him sobbing from behind the door. His father was killed in a bombing later that year during one of his visits to that room, and he and his mother immigrated here soon afterward.

"The guy was even older than he looked, if you could believe his story. I hardly did myself. Figured he was just a drunk making up sob stories for a lightened tab. I asked him why he was drinking himself to death now, of all times, and why he hadn't done so earlier back when it might've made a damn. He already lived most of a full life now. Expected the guy to rage and bitch me out, but he only smiled.

"He pulled out another photo. This one was a little more gruesome than the first. It was a picture from a concentration camp he found in a magazine he had been reading the other day, *Time* or *National Geographic*, one of those old-people rags that spend more time on coffee tables than in people's hands. A bunch of emaciated people, so skinny you could see every rib, the skin tight as a drum beneath them, horrible, horrible shit.

"He takes his finger and points to a guy in the middle and tells me, 'This. This is why. This is the man I gave to the SS.' He recognized him after all these years, despite his ravaged face, because he had seen that face over and over in his nightmares his entire life. For years, he had held out hope that they had never been sent to those terrible places, that they had somehow escaped. But there was the proof, staring him right in the face with dark, hungry eyes.

"The article attached said that the men in the photo were the only survivors, and many of them, including the man, died from injuries less than a week after their rescue. There was another photo, one that he could not bear to look at again, of a pile of bodies thrown lazily into a mass grave. And among them—not on top of them, but buried amidst dozens of other gray, lifeless small children—was the dead man's son, whom the man had played with many times when he was young. He had lived so long on a lie that he told himself that now that it had been shattered… he didn't know what to do anymore. He—"

The glass gave way, and a bony, half worm-eaten hand crashed through a corner at the top of the door, the zombie behind it trying to force its way through but still tangled up in the mob around it.

"He left me a damn good tip, a hundred dollars, I think. I called him a cab and wished him well in his future endeavors, still convinced that he was just a lonely man looking for a good story to tell.

But then I turned on the television the next morning, and right away, the report's about a suicide at a local motel. They slapped a picture of the victim on the screen, and sure enough, it's our German friend from the bar. Apparently, he rented out a room, finished off another bottle of schnapps, swallowed the barrel of a .45, and pulled the trigger. Left a note that only instructed to give away the remainder of his money to a local synagogue and an organization that specialized in aiding refugees."

The hand that had broken through was tearing itself to shreds on the glass, tearing what skin it had left off, like cellophane; but it was making the hole bigger, and its hand was dancing dangerously close to the hinges. Vel moved in closer and looked up at him, her big doe eyes suddenly looking like nirvana.

"Matt? What are we going to do? Why are you telling me this?"

Matt started to laugh, even though he didn't understand the punch line.

"Because I used to think I was like him, that all the bad things I'd done... they weren't my fault, I didn't know any better, I didn't know what I was doing, or that things would end up as bad as they did, that I'd hurt as many people as I did—even Veronica. How I ever thought that she would forgive me... that I even asked her to. God, I was ignorant. I blamed all my shortcomings on this desire I had inside of me. I dressed it up as something greater than it was, even gave it a ridiculous name—the urge. Ha! Like it was the guitarist in some shitty rock band. But I know the truth now.

"I'm nothing like that stupid bastard. I knew what I was doing. I liked it. I enjoyed it. I was always willing to make excuses for my vices, to let them control me. It was me. I'm the one who decided to give in and do what I did. I was the one who lost control. There is no monster inside of me. There's only me."

The words felt like sandpaper on his throat. Once he finished speaking them, it felt like he weighed several tons less; the world seemed slower, off balance, unnatural.

Vel's eyes warped with concern, constantly darting back and forth between Matt and the jiggling doorknob as the creatures threw themselves against the thin wooden defender. Not a word of what he said had sunk into her. Despite their depth, his words had washed over her like a bitter wave, none of it sinking beneath the surface. The dumb bitch was still consumed by the fear of death, ignorant to the pleasures that still lay in front of them if they were only willing to reach out and grab it.

His mind set, he switched tactics, remembering what little he could about Vel from their brief but barbed conversations from the diner, dripping with desire on both ends—although hers had always seemed more desperate, more consuming. He saw the way her eyes followed the flashing faces of the television, eyes like dinner plates, so she could take everything in, hide herself in it. She took solace in soap operas and dime-store romances. She would not be swayed by the truth but merely a dressed-up version of it—which was a shame.

She had seemed interesting for a second when she was caught in his rapturous spell, hanging on every word. But she hadn't understood him, not really. This girl never would. The people she considered real all wore their emotions on easily readable sleeves, with ethics of black and white that never mixed into gray; they had perfect looks to match their perfect spirit. Basically, as far and away from a real person as you could actually get, her mind devoted to a fantasy. He supposed that did give them some common ground.

"I'm… I'm sorry that I got you into this," he said, laying the coquettishness on like syrup that would make a normal person gag.

Vel, with a sweet tooth of a preteen girl, swallowed it greedily.

"You don't have to apologize, Matt. I know you were doing your best when you brought us here. Honestly, I wouldn't even have made it this far without you, so I should be thanking you, not forgiving you."

"Well, that's kind of you to say."

The glass shattered completely as one of the zombie's threw itself headfirst into its jagged remains, his scalp being sliced to ribbons of flesh that hung from his skull like glistening red streamers. The creature collapsed in on itself, its stomach folding up into the remains of the glass and tearing the skin open and spilling his guts onto the floor of the shed. Steam rose from the entangled insides as they plopped like fresh waste onto the ground, the zombie's writhing never faltering as if it hardly noticed the loss of its internal organs.

Vel turned away in disgust, burying her small nose into Matt's skin, her hot tears cooling him. Their skin rubbing together created a friction that turned Matt's smoldering ashes into a blistering wildfire that was growing out of his control, like a wild horse that had outgrown its reigns and rebuked any orders from its rider. He had to work quickly. Fortunately, Vel took care of the rest herself.

"I'm so scared, Matt. I don't want to die like this. Do you think it's going to hurt when it happens? I've heard people say it's just like gong to sleep, but that doesn't explain all the screaming, does it?"

"I won't lie to you, Vel. It'll probably hurt like hell, worse than anything you've experienced before, for sure. But that's the thing," he said, putting on his best puppy-dog face, "it doesn't have to."

"What are you saying? You have a plan to escape? To get out of here? Or are you talking about… ending it?"

God, this girl was denser than a pile of bricks. No wonder she had spent so many years alone when she was oblivious to even her dream guy's attempts at seduction. He scratched at the burning skin on his forearm so hard that he drew blood, surprised when it didn't come out as a steaming red vapor, like he expected it to.

"No, unfortunately, I have no contingency for that. What I was referring to is a lot simpler than that. What I meant is, we don't have to die like… like… this, huddling together in the corner, trembling with fear and terror at the prospect of our imminent doom. We're already about to spend an eternity in oblivion, so why go there early when we can enjoy ourselves one last time?"

Finally, the wheels started to turn in her hand. Her expression changed to one of slow understanding but mild trepidation. The idea excited her, obviously, but even someone as starved as herself was having a hard time getting into the mood while a crowd of bloody, dismembered bodies watched from outside.

"We can't… we can't do that here, Matt. Have you lost your mind? I mean, I'm flattered, more than flattered. It's like some dream come true, if it twisted and fused with a nightmare when it was born. I just don't think this is the time—"

"What other time is there?" Matt said, struggling to keep his frustration out of his dulcet tones. "Now's the only time. I've been a fool waiting this long, but I thought we had more time. Can you blame me? I don't want to leave this world with any regrets, especially none as big as this, and I know you don't either."

Vel's eyes were pulled to his, drawn in like magnetism, or the sinking gravity of a black hole that pulled her down into the depths of darkness with him. Knowing that he had all but won, he prepared his final assault, his main artillery strike that would leave the poor girl defenseless to his guile. He supposed he could just force himself on her, like he had done so many times before in his drunken rage, but where was the fun in that? If this was to be his final time, he would enjoy it pure as it was meant to be.

"If we're going to die, we shouldn't be afraid to live, should we?"

He practically gagged as he said it, but the naive girl bit the dangling worm hook, line and sinker. With a passion that suggested this had been her idea all along, she smashed her face into his, their lips locking in a wet, sloppy display of lust.

Matt's skin began to sing, tingles spreading down his spine like a natural drug, one that he had been fixing for worse than even the most desperate of junkie. Delighting in his successful conquest, he grabbed the collar of the girl's shirt and tore the garment in two, exposing her boring Kohl's brand bra that amply covered her modest bust. He threw his face between them, the contact of skin sending his senses into overdrive.

This was what he lived for, what he ached for. He was whole again.

His fingers unhooked the troublesome bra and threw it aside, burying his face again in her sumptuous breasts, his tongue toying with her tiny pink nipple as she moaned in ecstasy. Forcefully, he lifted her up and carried her to the desk, which he cleared in one swift sweep of his arm over the surface, knocking the clutter to the ground. She bit into his ear hard, taking even him by surprise and causing his member to harden in response, her fingers taking an immediate interest as she started to guide him into her.

Taking the cue with relish, his own hands flew down to her dampened panties and slid them just low enough so that they were out of the way, while he slid out of his own pants entirely with a series of quick, awkward kicks of his leg.

"I want you inside me now. I need it. I've never wanted anything more," she moaned, her sighs of pleasure uncomfortably blending with the crying of the dead behind them.

He slid inside of her, feeling her wetness, her tightness engulfing him. All his thoughts turned into white-hot bliss that took over his body. His hips crashed against hers so hard he thought they might shatter, and from her painful gasps, he knew it was less than perfect for her, but this was just as he needed it to be. He looked down as she writhed and squirmed on the table, her breasts spilling out from her torn shirt and shaking with each of his thrusts—which he began to notice were in time to the pounding on the wall, almost seeming to be egging him on. But he was too far gone now to notice anything like that.

"Sl-slow down, you're... you're hurting..."

He went faster and harder, his teeth gritting as he bucked his hips into her like a piston. Tears started to moisten her cheeks, and with her dirty black hair and plump face, he couldn't help but think of that horrible mistake from all those years ago. He nearly vomited as memories of that night poured into him, the night that had sent him across the country in an act of makeshift repentance. He could still hear her desperate pleas ringing in his ears, but he couldn't stop; he was so close now to those perfect seconds of bliss.

His eyes fluttered over to the filing cabinet beside them, and Matt nearly broke out into a fit of hysterical laughter. Tucked behind it, leaning against the wall were several cans of gas for the chainsaw on the shelf. Salvation had been an arm's length away, but instead, he settled for a cheap refuge in the pleasures of the flesh.

The door finally gave way behind them, the sound of the dead tumbling over themselves as they rushed into the room and surrounded them. Matt was dangerously close to finishing and didn't even bother to turn and face those rotting bastards. Instead, he shut out everything but these final, wondrous seconds of delight—his desires spilling out over the edge just as their nails dug into him and began to pull.

As his all-encompassing desire took control from the dark recesses of his mind, urging him forward despite his imminent destruction, he began to feel the pain as he was torn apart, looking down on Vel's screaming face as she tried to slink away from him. He saw his arm ripped clean from his socket in a geyser of blood and bone fragments, but his hips kept at their task, trying desperately to make those last moments of bliss even a second longer.

He looked at the zombies nearest him, their skin charred black as ash down to the bone. Their skulls had been nearly totally hollowed out by an explosion of flames, save for their brains spilling out through the unevenly fused sockets. But they chewed on his limbs all the same, ignorant to the fact that all their organs had been incinerated long ago. He could only guess where these monstrous creatures had risen from but tried to lose himself in the fleeting flashes of pleasure that still remained to him.

Their hands buried themselves into his belly, their fingers tightening around his stomach from the inside, unspooling his small intestine and stringing it like spaghetti into their groveling mouths. His entire midsection was nearly split in half as the zombies pulled him apart, Vel screaming underneath him the whole time. He felt their nails digging into his scalp and start to yank backward by his hair and neck, his vision blurring and turning to infinite grains of static as he felt the muscles in his shoulders pull apart.

Ecstasy flooded his veins as he finally finished, feeling the muscles in his groin tighten and contract for the last time, his thoughts disappearing into the clear, white void.

With one final escape of air through his neck, his head was pulled clean from his shoulders, his eyes watching as he drifted away from his body, his hips still set to uncontrolled flailing despite Vel being completely catatonic, screaming and swatting at her distracted attackers.

There was no pain, only an absence of feeling.

He tried to take in air but found none, only felt the slow wheeze as his final breath slid out his ruined throat. Merciful darkness closed in around him, his bliss turning to terror as Veronica's sobs, as clear and sharp as he remembered, echoed infinitely in his ear.

Billy tripped and threw himself into a car's rearview mirror, bashing his head hard against it and knocking it to the ground with him. Pain unlike anything he'd yet encountered in his short, pitiful life exploded through his forehead. Bells rang in his ears, intense and booming, and his vision faded into a pale white light that made his eyesight useless. He nearly dropped the small pistol in his hand but clenched his fingers tightly together by some unknown instinct and caught the gun midbounce. Somehow he pushed himself off the ground even without any sense of equilibrium, and as his washed-out vision returned, he saw blood spilling from his forehead onto the ground, leaving a trail as he loped forward like an injured gazelle.

He could hear the death rattles getting closer behind him, some so loud that he had to look behind him to make sure a dead man wasn't salivating over his exposed skull. His fingers reached up and gently danced around the wound, feeling a mix of limp, ragged skin and slimy, jellied muscle that had been pulled up and exposed. He felt faint, just imagining the gruesome sight in a mirror, his mind skirting the edge of panic, his chest tightening and his legs sapped of their strength.

Even though he told them to move forward, his legs dragged to a slow stop in the middle of the sidewalk. His vision narrowed into the shape of a cramped tunnel, the world shrinking to the size of the dying lawn he had stumbled into, the brown grass being torn up beneath him with every heavy step. His heartbeat pounded in his ears, louder than a tribal drum and nowhere close to as steady. He tried to breathe in deeply, but his lungs contracted and would hold no more, expelling what little air he had gathered in a sickly wheeze.

"What are you doing? We don't have time for resting! Get your ass moving!"

Billy tried to ignore this mysterious and, frankly, unwanted savior, hoping they would simply leave him to rest just a little while longer. He would find some way out of this, just like he did every other problem that seemed greater than the scope of his imagination.

Besides, there was so much for him left to accomplish in his life; it was not his destiny to perish here. Something would save him. The answer might come to him at the last possible moment, but it would come.

This nagging savior was persistent—if anything—however, and he felt a hand coil around his arm and drag him forward, over the remains of what had once been a family dog spread out across the grass. His first reaction was to swing at this attacker, until he realized it was Bruce's steel grip that was pulling him forward, his legs barely keeping up beneath him, and he stopped in fear of retaliation.

Gunshots rang out from their right across the street, and Billy caught brief glances of Gwen blowing the head off of a zombie near her, with nearly a dozen more pushing through to take its place. Range was even further behind her, cracking a dead woman's head open by shoving her nose up into the brain with a blow from the butt of his shotgun. A hot wave of jealousy soured and congealed in the bottom of his heart, putrefying the already-awful scene and turning it into something diabolic.

Angry at his own uselessness, he yanked his hand free of Bruce's grasp and kept pace beside him, trying to figure out how to release the clip from his own meager firearm and check what ammunition remained to him. Eventually, miraculously, the clip slid into his palm; and peering down into its length, he counted eight rounds, three less than he had been expecting. He conceded that it was better than having no rounds whatsoever and shoved the clip back into the slot under the grip.

The weight still took him by surprise, even after carrying the thing for hours. He wasn't sure he would ever get used to it. There was a time when he would've daydreamed about wielding a firearm, having enough power to save those around him, to fight back, to decide whether or not someone who opposed him lived or died. Now, he just dreamed for the day when he would never see another one.

With another quick look across the street, he saw a tuft of long blond hair darting past a crowd of gray-skinned ghouls and made his way toward it, his mind running through every bad action movie and cheesy video game it had ever soaked up. He tried to convince himself he felt powerful, but his wobbling legs told him otherwise, shattering an already-dubious illusion.

"Where the hell are you going? The library's this way! Jesus Christ, is anybody listening to a word I'm saying?"

"It's not exactly at the top of my list, fam!" Tyler went shuffling by behind him, another one of his cigars (at least Billy thought they were cigars, although he kept calling them something different) dangling from his lips as he dispatched several of the undead encroaching behind him.

With a deep sigh, he pulled a lighter from his pocket (a pirate skull emblazoned on the side with the words "Live Free or Die" in a banner that ran through its hollowed sockets), flipping the top with his thumb and relighting the tip of his cigar. This all took place in a matter of seconds, but the dead were on top of him again soon after.

Billy kept close for a while, the black top blistering his feet through his ratty gym shoes with tears in the soles. When they reached the opposite side of the street, he saw Veronica being backed into a corner between a chain-link fence and the attached house by three large, slobbish zombies that were so large there was no way for her to slip by one without slamming into another.

He turned toward her, gun raised and ready to aim for the center of the cheap buzz cut on the largest one in the center, when he remembered the sting of her fingers across his cheek and sprinted past her as she howled in maddening terror. His conscience slowed his step, like he was chugging through frozen molasses; but he pressed on regardless, slipping into the alley after Gwen. The sound of gunshots made him turn, and he saw Veronica leap, frogging over the small fence—large, ungainly shotgun in hand—as one of the boulder-sized zombies fell to his knees, his tiny head removed from his body like a popped zit, blood erupting from his open neck. As she ran by, her eyes pierced Billy's chest with a ferocity that frightened him more than the legion of undead behind them, and she raised a hard middle finger in his direction.

With scalding cheeks, Billy disappeared into the alley, catching sight of Range and Gwen at the east end near a small cul-de-sac of identical flats pockmarked by hedges that turned the series of yards into a maze of greenery. As he slid to a halt in the white gravel, a low groan alerted him to the mob of zombies behind him, taking up the entirety of the wide expanse of the alley. Their numbers were so dense that, with the fog obscuring the twilight horizon, it was impossible to see where their numbers ended. Not wanting to stick around and count them like pus-filled jellybeans in a jar, he turned on a heel and fell forward, just as a skeletal claw flitted past his collar.

He reached the next street easily, his breath becoming noticeably shorter; but Gwen was still in his sight, and that was enough motivation to draw him forward. There was still a chance to make good on his intentions, to show her that it was just stress that had spurred him on earlier—well, that and dissatisfaction at her choice of protection. Honestly, how long had he been there for her in the past? And there she was, always running to some handsome stranger who would've been considered a total creep if it weren't for his baby-blue eyes and shining locks. He was just trying to protect her—from herself, if necessary. It was for her own good. Besides, maybe that way, she would finally pay him the attention he deserved for all his years of loyalty.

More gunshots from his far-off left, beyond the view of the thinning fog. There was an enthusiastic whooping that followed, and Billy knew it must be Tyler and turned back toward where he had last seen Gwen, making her way back north by cutting through the nearest backyard. No fence protected this small square of grass and faulty wooden deck complete with tacky umbrella, and the dead had invaded accordingly.

Billy slipped past the first so quickly and silently that it never even noticed the living flesh behind it, content to merely clack its jaws at the fresh air. The next nearest swung at him so quickly that it nearly took his head off, but he ducked at the last second, losing balance on his chicken legs and having to jump forward like a tumbling toddler.

Rolling onto his back, he raised the small pistol and took quick aim at the snarling monster, not even bothering to look down the sights at this close of range—only to have the bullet ricochet off its exposed shin bone, shattering it in a flurry of shining filament and deep-red marrow. The thing collapsed on top of Billy's scrambling legs, his sliding feet pushing him out from under its dripping maw.

Grabbing the deck for support, he pulled himself on top of it and fell back against the glass for a chance to catch his breath. With his luck, however, there was a heavy crash as a zombie threw itself into the slide door from the opposite side, its nose exploding into blood, pus and mucus that seeped into the freshly made spiral crack. Not waiting to see if the glass would hold from another suicide blow, he charged and leaped over the opposite edge of the wooden structure and bolted around the side of the house, expecting to find Gwen's radiant face but finding only a small corridor between houses of identical white siding littered with still-twitching undead, face-down in the slick mud. Watching his step, his legs made wide arches as he tiptoed past these crying corpses, until he was able to slip out in the front yard and into the street, which was surprisingly absent of undead activity.

To the east, he saw Veronica catching up with Bruce, her hand pressed against her bandaged cheek, which had started to bleed again during her pursuit. Shouting tore his attention away to a small bungalow on the opposite side of the street where Tyler was swinging his shotgun like a club, knocking a slender zombie into the bushes, a spray of blood decorating the house's spotty, chipped paint job. Another two of the undead took the fallen creature's place almost immediately with a longer queue behind them—a chain of gray, dead flesh that linked around the side of the house, a thrashing trail of breadcrumbs that tracked Tyler's escape route. He swung wildly at his two snarling attackers, catching one in the jaw and sending small white shards spiraling into the fog where they quickly vanished, while his other swings flew harmlessly in front of their faces, barely keeping their slobbering teeth at bay.

Tyler sent his next blow directly into one of the monster's guts, which were already hanging half exposed from its belly—the butt of the shotgun landing against what appeared to be a spleen, pancreas, or some other purple, lumpy organ you see in tattered science textbooks. The zombie fell back, not from pain, but from momentum, falling into the line of undead behind him and dragging them down with him as he flailed about.

The other creature saw its advantage and seized Tyler by his hood, which had been thrown over the front of his shoulder in the chase, and dragged him toward him, its jaws nearly clamping down on his neck if he didn't fall out of his loose sleeve at the last minute. Like a newborn dog, the zombie stuffed the garment into its mouth and began to chew and shake its head viciously, the stitching falling to shreds between its gnarled teeth. As soon as it realized it wasn't the juicy flesh it craved (badly enough to shake off death like it was a common cold), it spat the mangled sweatshirt into the dirt, several thin white threads still trailing from its jaws, like banners whipped by the wind.

Tyler tripped over his own feet as he stumbled backward, crawling on hands and feet, much like a crab-walk exercise their drunk of a gym teacher had made them do several times during presidential fitness week—save for the fact that he was dragging his rear through the grass more in the style of dog trying to scratch an itch where its teeth won't reach.

Just when it seemed like Tyler was about to meet a similar fate as his jerk of a friend, Range appeared beside the zombie and fired a single round into its ear canal, its brains liquifying and bursting from the other side, like cherry glaze. He turned and fired several more rounds into the crowd of stumbling zombies behind them until they heard the dry clicks of an empty chamber—light, clacking metallic laughter that instilled more fear than the actual groans of the dead.

While he was so focused on the scene across from him, Billy never even noticed the presence behind him, its silent footsteps muffled further by the dewy grass. It was only when he heard one of those terrible groans again, an inch from his earlobe, unbelievably loud without the rush of hot air that came from breath escaping, that he knew he had been mistaken. Those horrible moans were terror incarnate.

Billy turned and shoved his small pistol into the zombie's gut and slammed his finger against the trigger, the vibration and immediate gush of blood making his hand flinch and several of his shots fly harmlessly into the walls of the two-story. The creature was unfazed and continued its assault, bearing down on Billy so that he could smell its putrid stench in the back of his nose, feel it seeping into his brain.

With his trembling hands, Billy tried to hold the monster back as more and more of the blood and bile poured from its fresh wound; but it was slowly overpowering him, its recesses of strength seemingly endless. Billy was tiring; the zombie was not. It craned its neck and bit down hard on Billy's hand, causing Billy to scream before he even felt the pain.

However, when the pain never came, he was forced to open his sealed eyes and look dumbfounded as the monster tried to chew on the pistol's muzzle, its teeth sliding harmless off the sides, leaving only small nublike indents in the cheap steel.

Turning away, he pulled the trigger again and felt the gun leap back and smack him in the face, hot blood splattering next to his own that began to trickle down from his nostrils and over his already-caked lips. Billy sprinted away without opening his eyes, afraid to look at the empty shell of a human head that he created and felt his legs tangle up in something unyielding and found himself eating concrete. A tooth in the back of his mouth came loose and went down his throat before he could stop it, its jagged edges slicing up his throat to bloody ribbons as it went down.

As soon as his vision refocused and the ringing in his ears subsided, he opened his eyes and rolled onto his back, ready to face this new threat, only to see an awful wooden gnome, spotted with blood, staring him in the eye with a reproachful laugh, and to find his knees caught in the spoke of a bicycle, left out in the yard by its owner that would never get around to putting it in the garage like their father asked. Feeling a new, stronger disdain for the aluminum contraption, he kicked until his legs came free and ran to meet up with Bruce and Veronica before any more of the wailing creatures ambushed him.

Bruce was tending to her cheek, dabbing at it with a strip of gauze and pulling it back bloody before folding it under itself and dabbing the clean side of the wound again. If they saw him approach, they ignored him, and it wasn't until Tyler and Range came running up to meet them that they turned away from their task.

"How much farther is this shit? I feel like Action Bronson after doing two miles on a treadmill. Out of breath as shit," Tyler said while taking another puff of his cigar, which was beginning to smell like a skunk.

"Just a couple more blocks down this street," Bruce said, motioning with his head down the street they found themselves in the center of.

A layer of cars surrounded them, some parked against the side of the street and some left abandoned in the center with their doors open wide, hazards flashing neon in the fog, making a small steel haven that shielded them from sight but not for long as gray shadows began to appear on the shrouded horizon.

"Should only take us another minute or two if we sprint."

"Oh, thank God, Buddha, MJ, whoever. Let's fucking get there so I can put my damn aching leg up. The fucking vicodin's starting to wear off."

"Where's Gwen?" Billy asked, looking at Range with narrow eyes.

His face went pale, and his head whipped back in the direction he came from as he realized something must be wrong. A scream answered both of their growing concerns, even if it was an answer neither wanted.

Running around the nearest car, they soon caught sight of Gwen struggling with four of the undead, and Billy's stomach sunk so deep that he expected to step on it as he ran forward. One of the creatures had her arm and was pulling her backward, the shotgun having fallen earlier in their scuffle, so far out of reach that escape seemed her only option. The other three zombies were almost on her, their teeth bared and pale eyes feverish.

Gwen fought against the one holding her, pulling away from his bites but unable to untangle herself completely, every broken hold leading to another, stronger one. Gwen screamed again as it wrapped its hands around her wrists and dragged her forward so hard that she fell to her knees in a squeal of pain.

She tried once more to get up but was knocked down by a blow from its arm that sent her crashing into the pavement, the creature setting on her as its fellow undead grabbed hold of her as well. They lifted her up as she kicked and struggled against them, raging and screaming curses at them as they held her down—a look of stubborn, painful resignation set on her soft features, one that broke Billy's heart into pieces.

Range leaped over the back of the abandoned vehicle and started charging toward her, brandishing his weapon like Tyler had earlier, except he was much too far to make it to her in time. They would tear her to shreds before he ever got near her; why couldn't he see that?

"Range!" she screamed, the sinking feeling in Billy's heart deepening tenfold.

Even now, in her final moments, she was calling out for him—the fool whose sacrifice would serve no one except the dead, who were lucky enough to get a 2-for-1 special. He was her last thought, the last thing she longed for.

Despite this heartbreak and every fiber of his being telling him to turn away, to leave the two to die together like they wanted, another part of him told him to watch—to revel in the sight of this cruel temptress being torn limb from limb and consumed, to take solace in her screams of agony as they curdled into broken gasps—but he knew he couldn't bear it. Despite all her vile manipulations, making him think he had a chance and always keeping him at arm's length until she needed him, he could not watch her die in such a terrible way.

And it was then when he knew what he must do.

Raising the pistol to his nose, he tugged back the slide and saw the shimmering bronze bullet nestled in the chamber and let it click back into place. Lifting the pistol while cradling it in his hands, like he saw at shooting ranges and in the movies when the hero wanted to steady his shot, he brought it eye level so that he could stare right down the sight to the small nub of metal at the end.

Lining it up, he moved the nub past the gray, bloody flesh and settled it on the pale white skin of Gwen's forehead. He tensed his finger, stretching it, waiting for the butterflies in his stomach to settle as he steeled himself for what he was about to do.

A quick death was a mercy in light of being ripped apart, like a shank of meat. This was a courtesy that she barely deserved yet one he felt obligated to give nonetheless. Yes, he was the hero, even if it meant making the tough choices no one else wanted to make. That was what separated him from Range, what Gwen was too blind to see. He knew what the world was really like, how it really worked. Range was as much as a fool as Gwen, both believing their carnal lust was actual love. But Billy knew better. He had seen enough successful relationships to know what actual love was, read enough real, classical romances to fill an encyclopedia. He had spent his whole life observing the world, studying it and everything about it that he could. He understood it better than the other kids his age, too caught up in thinking that each of them was the first kid to stay out all night and get drunk to actually understand the world they so cravenly inhabited.

And now he'd seen so many terrible things, watched so many people die, even those he could save... He had hesitated in the past, doubted himself and his plan. But no longer. Gwen needed him to be strong. She needed him to be who he was always meant to be.

He was a hero. And he was going to save her.

Gwen felt the bullet rip through her shoulder blade, a hot, blinding pain that numbed everything else around it. It became her world, a world of searing tendon and blistering bone that made her feel like her whole body had been set alight with gasoline. At first, she thought it was the ravaging bite of her attackers; but it was too quick, too focused. Her eyes strained to blink away the blurriness, to hold on to the thinning strands of consciousness, as sweet as its embrace might seem in light of her situation. She was not about to give in until she saw yellowed, decaying teeth piercing her pallid skin.

The first thing she saw was Range, running with his shotgun; and her first thought was her worst, but when she saw him smash it repeatedly over a decrepit zombie's forehead as it pinned him to the window of a cheap liquor store, she knew his ammo must've run out quite some time ago. Looking past the violent struggle, she saw a small shadow at the edge of the fog, the cool wisps of smoke shielding their face.

A gust of wind swept through the street, and Gwen felt it batter against her open wound and heard the dead salivating over it; but for some reason, they hadn't decided to finish her. Craning up as much as her constrained neck would allow, she saw that the bullet had also entered one of the zombie's chest, the mystified creature probing it and licking the blood from its fingers enthusiastically. The others were either watching their injured comrade closely, pining with jealousy at its free appetizer, or looking around aimlessly—their ears, or ear holes, for those that had had they outer ear ripped free from their skull, following the echoing gunshot.

Turning back toward the gunman at the end of the street, the wind had cleared away some of the thicker fog, revealing the small, glinting pistol that Gwen recognized all too well. Billy's squirming face materialized from the mist next, his eyes hard yet glistening. Part of her wanted to call out to him and ask him what the hell he thought he was doing, but she risked drawing the ire of the zombies that still had her pinned and outnumbered four to one.

Besides, it's not like he had been trying to hit her or something. Knowing Billy, the idiot probably just tried to pull off a shot that his inexperienced eyes thought was easier than it actually was. His hand had jerked back at the last moment.

When the next bullet whizzed right next to her eye, so close that she felt it graze her skin and draw a thin line of blood, her hypothesis suddenly seemed like the ramblings of an optimistic fool.

"Billy!" she screamed, her voice hoarse and grating on her throat. The consequences of her shouting no longer seemed to matter; the zombies had already started trying to pull her apart. "Just what the hell do you think you're doing?"

The zombies made slow chirps of attention as they remembered the meal beneath them. The creature that held her right arm—an old woman with wild white hair and a mouth coated in black slime—pulled her hand up to her mouth; but Gwen pushed past and punched the hag in the side of her jaw, dislodging the brittle bone and sending it spiraling across the road. The zombie harmlessly pressed its teeth against her skin but still kept Gwen tangled in her grip, while the others tried to shove their way past her to get a chance at the feast.

"I'm sorry, Gwen! I really am!" Billy said, with a grimace that said he regretted saying anything at all. "I couldn't let you suffer. It's for your own good. You have to trust me!"

"What the hell are you talking about, you crazy bastard?"

Another shot rang out, causing Gwen to duck as much as she could allow herself; but it proved needless when the bullet destroyed a car window far to their left, the glass particles sprinkling down on the odd banquet like fallen snow. This distraction was enough to make the zombie on her right drop her arm on her injured shoulder, a jolt of pain flying through as it slapped against concrete, and turn to face the howling car alarm, believing another meal had shown itself, one that would feed him and him alone.

"I'm going to save you, Gwen! Those things aren't going to devour you on my watch."

"So shoot them! Not me! Have you gone completely insane?" Gwen shouted angrily on the verge of tears that dared not show the sick boy she had once called friend. As she finished, another bullet flew harmlessly over all their heads. One of the zombies behind her stood and followed its trail with its head but didn't dare leave its free meal for the slim chance of another. They may be dead, but they were still pragmatic, it seemed.

Billy laughed, an awkward sound between a chuckle and croak, his eyes dark and shaded by fog.

"You've seen how good of a shot I am, Gwen. Don't you think I'd considered anything else? With the bullets I have left, there's no way I can kill all of them… But I can spare you. It's the only way, can't you see that?"

"All I see is a crazy asshole shooting at me while I'm held by down by fucking corpses!"

The words seemed to have some effect on him. The gun fell to his side; his head dropped into his hands; and choked, bitter sobs rose from his throat like a gurgle. Gwen fought to free herself now that most of her captors were distracted, with only the jawless woman still attempting to chew through her wrist. However, as soon as she moved, the zombies took notice and lurched on top of her, their hands falling down on her shoulders and knocking her to the ground.

"Shoot them, Billy! For the love of God, shoot them!" Gwen looked up at him, pleading, hoping that whatever remained of her friend in that husk of a body would do the right thing.

"I'm sorry," Billy said, raising his head from his hands. "I'm sorry you couldn't understand." He raised the gun again, his left eye squinting down the sights. "I love you, Gwen."

"Well, I think you're a piece of scum-sucking sh—"

The bullet hit her side, warm blood rising from the wound almost instantaneously and spilling onto the sidewalk underneath her. The zombies fell back only for a moment before they realized what had happened and noticed the stream of blood coming from their expiring meal, sending them into a frenzy of groans and wet gurgles as they descended on her.

Gwen tried to fight, but the pain was too great. Every muscle she moved seemed to be connected to one of her wounds, pain turning her brains to unusable mush, only good for feeling the terrible things that were about to befall her. All she could do is scream and wait for the end.

There was a loud smack that sounded like it was miles away. She felt rain on her face, soft patters that rolled down her lips and tasted like the sweetest copper, reminding her of penny jars and old rolled candies from her mother's nightstand. Some force made her body quake and tremble, her mother's switch snapping down her back over and over until it was scraping bone. Behind her, her mother was shouting something that sounded like scripture, but every other word was her name. Her mother came closer and closer, her words becoming a nonstop stream of Gwen's name pouring from her pursed lips into Gwen's honeyed ears.

"Gwen! Gwen! Wake up! We've gotta move! Can you walk? Can you move at all?"

"M-Mother?"

"I'd give you two more guesses, but I'm almost afraid of what your other answers might be."

"Ra-Range?" she coughed and felt something hot and slick in her throat, making her breaths feel like swallowing tar.

"The one and only. Can you walk? Or do I need to carry you?"

"You made it here in time?"

"Well, one of 'em might've drooled on you a little bit, but I'm afraid that couldn't be helped. But other than that and the bullet wounds, you seem fine, and honestly, they seem like an improvement, very badass."

"Don't make me laugh, asshole."

"So we've established laughing's out the picture, but how does a nice walk sound? More of our friends are coming up the street, more than I'll be able to deal with."

"I think it sounds fucking fantastic."

Slipping his hand into hers, he lifted her slowly to her feet. Her legs quickly gave out from the pain, but he wrapped his arm around her waist, catching her and keeping her from tumbling back onto the black top. Unknowingly, his fingers dug into her side, pressing up against the wound, causing the world to go white around her. Her vision returned in short bursts, the world coming in and out of focus like a cheap lens clouded by steam. She saw a steady splatter of thick, red water, spilling from her side in wet bursts onto the ground, which was moving away from her like threads. Weightless yet heavy, she could feel herself being dragged forward, her feet slapping against the pavement in a drunken imitation of walking.

The sound of the bullet cleared her head, a shot of adrenaline in her veins, her wounds tensing and singing in agony at the very thought of gunfire. Lifting her head was more than a chore. Every muscle she moved seemed to disturb one wound or the other; but she managed it, her sight allowing her to barely make out Billy standing several yards away from them, his gun still pointed squarely at Gwen.

"What... what do you think yo... you're doing, Billy?" Gwen said, blood in the back of her throat.

His eyes narrowed, flicking over Gwen as quickly as a lizard's, before centering on Range. "She's bleeding out. She'll die and turn into one of them. I have to finish it."

"She's fine. You didn't hit anything vital. If we stop the bleeding…"

"We don't have time, you moron! We're surrounded! She'll die before we make it anywhere safe! You know I'm right, don't you? I can see it in your eyes. I have to do it, even if you won't."

"Billy," she said, gently, tempering her fury, "I'm fine. I'm used… to… to dealing with stuff like this… Admittedly, nothing near as bad…"

The gun sang, and the bullet brushed past her arm, grazing the skin and adding another small rivulet to the blood pouring from her side.

"Put the goddamn gun down, you crazy asshole!" Range said, angrier than Gwen had ever seen him. She had never seen him lose his composure before; but his eyes were shaking, unsure, a feeling he was not used to, one he didn't know how to handle, and it made Gwen absolutely terrified.

"I'm not crazy, I'm just rational. And I'm not going to stand by and let you make her suffer by dragging her around, only for her to become one of those horrible, ugly… monsters! She deserves better, and I'm going to give her something better."

"If you wanna kill me with that thing, Billy, you'll have to actually look at me."

Billy's arm dropped for half a second, enough for Range to try and move forward; but like a taunt rubber band, it snapped right back and feverishly moved between the two of them.

"That's why you're missing, isn't it? You can't even look at me. I can't say… why… why I'm surprised. You never could. You always were… a coward." She coughed and felt the blood splash against her teeth, but she swallowed it forcibly. "You wanna know why I never… gave you a… a chance? Because you seem… so terrified by me. For someone… who… who claimed to love me… you couldn't even look me in the eyes for more than a second. Even now… your grand romantic gesture… and you can't even look at me. You're pathetic. You've… always been pathetic."

Billy stepped back, his hand shaking, his eyes darting left and right across the ground. Mumbling to himself, shaking his head, and slamming his fist against his head, and pulling out tufts of hair— Billy had gone from a frightened boy into the visage of an absolute madman.

"You're wrong! What do you know anyway, huh? Always complaining about your damn mommy like any other brat! I'll show you just how pathetic I am, all right? That sound good? Yeah? I bet you'll love that! You always loved being right!"

"You're not gonna do it," Range said coolly.

"I am gonna do it! I am!" Billy said, waving the gun like a child waving a stick during a game of cops and robbers.

"Not anymore, you're not."

A quizzical look passed over Billy's face before Tyler's fist connected with his jaw. He stumbled forward, carried by the weight of the blow as Tyler seized his hand and wrested the pistol from his squirming, flinching fingers. Terror and tears swept over him at once, his mouth stretching into an awful wail and starting to spout wavering apologies, all spilling together into an incomprehensible mess that inspired more pity than malice.

Tyler pulled out the clip and did a quick count of the rounds before loading it again. After pulling back on the slide and popping out the empty shell, he finally turned his gaze on Billy, the gun still held high in his hand, his blunt still burning in the other.

"I didn't give you this piece to be shooting fine young women with it—not living ones, at least."

"I'm… I'm sorry… I just wanted… I… I was gonna… save… She was dying… You'd understand… you would… If I… I explain myself, it'd make sense… I was saving her… You under—"

The shots caught him in the stomach, swirls of red appearing through his shirt around them. His mouth fell open in a noiseless gasp of pain and shock as his head drifted down to see the wound, to see that it was real, his hands slowly pressing over it and being covered in the rising pool of blood from his insides. Stammering silently, his mouth tried to form questions, but his voice was gone.

Tyler lifted the blunt to his mouth, the cheery roasting in the haze of the fog, and he kicked Billy in the chest, a geyser of blood erupting from the wound as he fell backward onto the cement. As he exhaled a curling cloud of smoke into the mist above him, he motioned for the two of them to move forward with urgency.

Gwen could hear the moans behind her, but craning her neck to see was more effort than she could presently manage. From the sound of their feet and their horrid cries, they were far closer than she would've liked. Range shifted her weight in his arms, pain exploding from her side, but she gritted her teeth and did her best to bear it. She couldn't be dead weight. Not now.

As they shuffled past the writhing Billy, his hand shot up toward Gwen, his fingers rolling helplessly. "Pl-please, Gwen… I'm… I'm so… soooorrrrry," he said, blood bubbling up from his mouth between his teeth.

"I am too," she said as they continued past him. "And don't worry, Billy," she added, turning her head back only enough to catch him in the corner of her eye, "unlike you, I'll look at you as you die."

A sob rose from his throat, his chest shaking and bringing up more blood as they walked by. When they approached Tyler at the edge of the circle of cars, he threw his arm around Gwen and helped them pull her deep into their junkyard sanctuary. Gwen put a hand on Range's shoulder and told them to stop, forcing her body to twist around just as the horde reached the crying boy.

He didn't notice the legs shuffling around him, trapping him in like a cage, not until their hands descended on him. He swatted them away like you would a bug, his weak arms slapping uselessly against their starched, pox-ridden skin. His legs skidded helplessly against the ground, trying to push himself away, but they were slipping and sliding through his own blood.

Two creatures held him down, and a third plunged its hands deep into Billy's open wound, its fingers cupped like someone reaching into a cookie jar. Billy's eyes widened as he saw them pulling his skin apart, still screaming and begging for someone to help him, but his resistance was noticeably slowing. Another gray husk moved around to his front and reached in from under him, forcing its hand inside him by his nails at the midsection, a spray of blood spurting out around it.

Billy began to scream, his hand still flailing at the zombies above him as the ones behind held him in an awkward full nelson. One of the creatures seized his hand and bit into it, consuming nearly half of it in one bite, pulling away fingers with strings of muscles and pulled tendon, as his thumb wiggled like a frightened survivor.

The color drained from Billy's face, and just when it seemed like he was ready to slip into the throes of death, a hand attached to the crowd behind him fell over his face, the curious fingers catching in his nostrils. Like a fisherman feeling a snag, they pulled back greedily, the cartilage giving way easily and peeling with the skin. As the hand pulled back, Billy's nose and the top of his face came with it, peeled back like a can of tuna—all while piercing, frantic screams echoed from his mouth until an overflowing gurgle of blood cut them off.

Gwen could watch no more and turned away, burying her head in Range's shoulder. She let the tears come, but only briefly, before sniffling them away and giving them a satisfied nod. They pulled back deeper into the line of cars, the horde drifting back into the fog but ever present on the horizon.

The pain threw Gwen into a state of semiconsciousness, her body floating above the ground as the wind crashed against her face; its cool touch against her sweat-soaked skin became something she longed for constantly, her fever breaking and turning her head into a thunderstorm filled with cracking thunder and piercing lightning that permeated her nervous system.

She became somewhat aware of being set down, the world and her settling into a shaky truce where both promised to stop spinning aimlessly. The slick-painted steel of a car pulled and tugged at her skin, and she knew someone must've leaned her up against one. She felt the breeze brush against her bare midriff and knew someone must be lifting her shirt, but she was too weak to fight them off. This didn't stop her from trying, her hands swinging at whoever was unlucky enough to find themselves in front of them, while they had to softly bat them away to get at her gunshot wound.

Her breath froze and broke in her throat when she felt the fingers stretch deep inside her, circling and stretching the wound as they dug deeper for the small bronze cylinder pressing up against her organs. A stiffness unlike anything she'd ever known permeated her body, where even the slightest movement meant agony and the disturbing feeling of someone probing where they shouldn't be.

"Into the bag and fetch some of the hypodermic needles... Clamps too, if someone got them. Yes, yes, the string as well... What do you mean? Speak slower, calmer, so I can actually understand you. What do you mean there's no morphine? How did nobody grab morphine?"

Gwen's eyelids fluttered open long enough to see Bruce pacing angrily in front of her outstretched legs. Range was at her side still, his arm keeping her slouching body from falling completely to the ground, her equilibrium still forfeit. Veronica's nose was buried in the duffel bag, lifting and shifting its contents about, hoping that the miracle drug might suddenly appear from some stray pocket or nook, but Gwen had seemingly used up all her luck for that day.

She breathed in and was sent into a spasm of coughs that racked her body and felt as awful as a second barrage of gunfire. Her very bones ached and seemed to be stiffening, for each movement became jilted and unwieldy, her motor control slipping into nonexistence.

"Tyler, didn't you find any morphine in the emergency room?"

"I mean, I found some, but I didn't think to grab any. I'm not a fan of that shit, gives you too intense a high, especially for something like this with all the running and shit. Even I got some limits, dawg."

"You what? Are you kidding? You didn't think it would be useful as a painkiller in the event of something like this?"

"Nah, homie, the only painkiller I need, I gots right here," he said with a smile and a drag of the shrinking blunt clasped between his fingers. The cherry glowed like a beacon on a lighthouse, a guide through the thick fog, blinking on and off with Tyler's labored puffs.

There was a scream from the undead—a low, trembling wail that pierced their ears and snapped Gwen back to attention, despite the pain it caused her to do so. The smell of death was carried on the wind, their putrid odor a sign of their approaching arrival—one that nobody wanted to be the first to admit, their worried eyes darting between scanning the haze-obscured horizon and the ground.

"Either way, we don't have enough time to get her stitched up before they swarm us again. It looks like they've noticed us, including the group from the east end of the street."

"So they're gonna meet in the middle? On top of us, you mean?" Veronica said, finally looking up from the duffel bag. Her eyes seemed to double in size at the sight of whatever lay beyond Gwen's back and the car she was slumped against.

She strained to raise up above the hood of the old Toyota to try and catch a glimpse of the size of this second horde, but the pain swallowed her vision before she even got halfway, Range stopping her as soon as he realized what she was trying to do. He tried to tell her that it was nothing for her to be worrying about, but she knew better. The fear in his face was all she needed to see to know that they had reached the end of their journey. They had been blocked in from both sides, all because they had wasted time, trying to save her.

"You guys should... should just leave me," Gwen managed to say, nearly choking on the words. "You've already wasted enough time... trying to help me."

Bruce moved in front of her, a painfully false smile on his face, so hammy that it was almost patronizing. "Don't you go saying stuff like that. This isn't your fault, and we're not giving up on you as easy as that, all right? We're gonna find a way out of here, you got that?"

Gwen knew that the words weren't for her but was a desperate attempt by Bruce to convince himself of what he knew simply wasn't true. It showed on his face as plain as day. It was clear in the fear on all their faces, sweat dripping over their tortured visages. In fact, the only one who actually seemed calm was Tyler. His face was so peaceful and serene that Gwen assumed he must've have taken one hit too many from that bag of his, or he had completely lost his mind.

"Welp, I guess that's my cue," Tyler said, getting to his feet.

Pressing off his knees, the blunt sliding from one side of his lips to the other, he stood, pulling up his baggy sweatpants and patting them off, only to realize most of what he thought was dirt as actually deeply stained blood and stopped trying.

"Your cue? What are you going on about this time?" Bruce asked haughtily.

"You know what I mean, boss. Now, slide me that duffel bag, Veronica. Daddy needs to grab a few things before he leaves."

None of the others spoke. Nobody was quite sure if what he was saying was true or some cruel, elaborate joke, or which one of those possibilities was the better of the two. Speechless, Veronica slid the bag across the ground, the supplies clinking loudly against each other as she did so.

"Thanks, babe."

With that, he started rifling through the bag and pulling up what was left of his arsenal, looking over each dealer of death with the greatest of care and attention to detail as he checked the rounds available, the condition of the parts, and what would even be useful against an enemy as large and spread out as the unending horde that had surrounded them.

"Okay, now that it appears that you're serious, you want to tell me just what the hell you think you're doing?"

Not even bothering to raise his head from his task, Tyler answered in a distracted voice, "Well, I thought it'd be pretty damn obvious. I'm gonna shoot those ugly undead motherfuckers, get 'em nice and pissed off, and then I'm gonna lead 'em away from you guys, while shooting the fuck out of 'em some more, of course."

"I don't think you realize the gravity of what you're suggesting."

"Nigguh, what the fuck does gravity have to do with this? I'm gonna run and shoot some zombies. It's every kid's childhood dream come true, and I'm gonna live it up," Tyler said, bemused.

He pulled two heavy-duty machine guns from the confines of the duffel bag, their extended clips getting caught on the zipper and nearly ejecting themselves. Gwen recognized them from several movies she would watch gleefully at some long-forgotten adolescent friend's house as Uzis, but she had no way of knowing if that was a technical name or just bad slang.

"You're crazy if you think it's gonna be as simple as that. You don't even have two perfect legs. I'm honestly surprised you made it this far on that thing, and what you're suggesting... You saw how easy it is for those things to surround you. What are you gonna do if that happens again, huh?"

"I'll shoot as many as I can and make a way over the corpses—well, the dead corpses, anyway, seems as good a plan as any."

"Then why don't you just help us shoot our way through the ones that are right in front of us? You don't have to do this. There's another way that keeps everyone alive."

"Who said I was planning on dying? I already told you, boss, I'm just leading the ugly fuckers away from you guys. The forest isn't much farther, and I can lose 'em in there as long as I'm lucky enough to miss the wolves, but those pups can chew hot lead all the same, you feel me? Once you guys sneak around and I reach the woods, I'll double back if I can and meet up with you guys at the liberry or whatever, and if I can't... well, then I'll just do my best to push through to the next town. It ain't that much farther once you hit the woods anyway."

Tyler stood, almost picking up the duffel bag, before sliding it back over to Range.

"You guys'll need that, for the girl. Feel free to use whatever's left in there ammunition-wise, but I'll warn ya now, there ain't much left to choose from, a couple pistols, a magnum or two. I think I saw a switchblade and a bowie knife in one of the pockets. One of you fuckers is gonna have to lend me a shotgun since you bastards took 'em all."

Range tossed him the one at his side without a second thought or a single word of protest. Gwen wanted to scold him for not handing him her own, which would be useless to her even if they managed to sew her up; but she quickly realized it actually *was* her own, and Range had scooped it up when he was ferrying her away from the undead mob.

Tyler seized it eagerly, grabbing it out of the air like a starving man would a piece of rotting meat. He inspected it quickly, turning it over once or twice, running his finger gently over a scratch or dent as a haphazard damage assessment. When he was apparently satisfied by whatever conditions he had on this mental checklist, he loaded several cartridges in the loading port and gave the fore-end a sharp pump, the shells sliding into place. While he had been doing this, his head was also stretching over the circle of cars, his buzzed head peaking just above the rattled hood.

"I'll lead 'em north, through that alley over there by the Old Country Buffet. That should funnel them, make 'em easier for me to mow a couple of 'em down and slow them down enough for you guys to sneak behind them on the other side of the street, but you'll still have to be quick. These fuckers are dumb, but that's because they're running on whatever instincts are left to 'em. If they spot you, some will break off and follow you, and if that happens, even my sexy ass ain't gonna be able to help ya, got it?"

They all gave short, startled nods—some reluctant, others understanding, but all heavy with sorrow. Bruce walked over to Tyler and grabbed him fiercely by the shoulder, his eyes widening in what almost looked like compassion, but it was only for a fleeting second before his eyes sunk back to their usual cocky glare.

"Let me just make this perfectly clear. You don't have to do this. I'll admit options are thin, as is our time, but we can figure out another way. I… I just don't want you running off because you think we want you to."

"Shieeeet, boss, I know it ain't like that. I don't know why ya'll mofos is freaking out so much. As soon as ya'll get to that library, you're gonna fix errything, ain't ya? So I just gotta make it on my own for an hour or so, tops. Shouldn't be hard."

"We don't even know if the library's gonna actually have anything to help us, or if it'll last even five minutes as a shelter. You could be doing all this for nothing."

"He's right. Don't waste your life on my hunch."

They all turned to look at Range, Gwen twisting her neck despite the protest of her shoulder, and she instantly noticed the displeasure on his face. These words did not come easily for him, a crack in his confidence, in his calm composure, doubt seeping into the cracks of his psyche—which Gwen had once thought he kept out simply as a show of strength but was because he had a hard time getting rid of them once they made their in, a scourge that lingered in the shadows.

Tyler's smile didn't flicker in the slightest but glowed with an understanding that seemed incredibly foreign on him. Of all the words she would've used to describe the guy before, she never would've thought *pleasant* and *reassuring* would be among them.

"I ain't worried about none of that stuff. Oddly enough, I think I believe you guys. This shit definitely ain't no virus, and I've got faith that you know what you're doing. Besides, in the movies, the guy who runs off on his own always turns up again sooner or later, so let's not act like you guys can get rid of this nigguh that easily."

Veronica moved listlessly over to Tyler and graciously planted a kiss on his cheek. She pulled back and looked at him with those disarming, puppy dog eyes of hers. "Be careful, all right?"

"You know I always am… And you also know I'm gonna tell everyone we totally fucked now when we make it out of here, right? Ow!"

Even after the quick punch to his stomach, Veronica wore a sterling smile, silver tears falling gently from her eyes, over the bloody bandage adorning her cheek.

Bruce approached him next, and Tyler stuck out his fist, waiting eagerly for Bruce's reciprocation; but Bruce smacked the hand aside and hugged him firmly, which turned his giggling face to one of confusion and discomfort.

Pulling away, Bruce asked, "For the last time, you're sure about this?"

"Shit, yeah, dawg, you ain't got act all fatherly on me and shit. I'm a gangsta, I know how to handle my steez, you got it? Hanging with you guys has been hurting my cred anyway. Seriously, what would the guys think if I told 'em I'd be hanging out with a damn pig? I'd never live that shit down."

Bruce gave a weak smile and ushered him over to the edge of the cars, with Tyler stowing the shotgun under his arm as he pulled his drawers up with the same hands that held his Uzis, the free forefingers hooking around the elastic waistband. As he neared the break in the cars, he turned back to Gwen and Range, taking one final hit of his roach-sized blunt, turning the end into a pillar of ash that crashed and broke against the pavement alongside the remains of the cigar, and gave them one last stare-down.

"You guys better fix this, all right? If you do, I'll personally buy you bitches a fucking room."

And with that, he leaped over the hood of the old Toyota, sliding over its rusted and dented frame like a cheap action stuntman, landing awkwardly and breaking into a broken sprint on the other side. He began hooting and hollering while firing off several rounds into the air, instantly drawing the attention of the chain of zombies just several yards in front of him.

"Whoo-whooooo! Hey, look over here, motherfuckers! You pansy-ass dead fucks! You wanna come get a taste of Ty-Ty's big black dick? Gonna give you some of this lead cum! Let's go!" he exclaimed like a wild man, intermittently firing off submachine gun rounds into the sky.

"Damn, you niggas ugly when you get up close. Actually, I think I remember you, yeah, you! The fat one on the right! And honestly, this whole being dead shit you got going on is probably a bit of an improvement, homes. You still look fuck ugly, don't get me wrong. Oh, you wanna get a taste of this fine white chocolate? Well, your slow, brittle asses gotta catch me first. And I know if some punk-ass cops ain't got shit on me, you ugly cunts sure as hell don't. Come on! Catch up, fatty! Catch up!"

They lost sight of him as he slinked through the alleyway and into a copse of trees on the other side. He was breaking into a slow jog when the trail of dead, following along like rats to a piper, got too close. The crowd of shuffling dead dispersed gradually; but soon, small pockets of bare street and fog appeared in the shadowy black mass. Their numbers were thinning out, filing slowly into Tyler's funnel, crashing up against the walls like a tumultuous ocean current being redirected through a narrow canyon.

"Look," Range said in a low voice, "there's a gap on the sidewalk over there. If we can get past there, it should be a straight shot to the library."

Gwen leaned over, fortunately on the side that didn't have a bullet hole in it, peeking her head above the trunk of the car. It was as Range had said. The sidewalk on the opposite side of the street, the one spotted with lavish houses—two-story Victorians instead of one-story businesses with more grease than shine—was nearly completely empty; and the ones that remained on the brown, dirty lawns had their attention solely on the escaping prey. The entire congregation of zombies had flocked to the alleyway that Tyler had escaped through, even drawing some of the crowd from behind them, the two seas of rotting flesh combining and rushing after the promise of living meat. From the looks of it, their desperation could be chocked up to the fact that he was one of the only living things left in the town, the first food many of them had ever laid eyes on in their second, abominable life.

"All right, well, let's not waste the opportunity that dumb son of a bitch gave us. Range, help me carry her. You take one shoulder, and I'll take the other."

Bruce bent down low (so low that Gwen caught a whiff of the sweat from underneath his pits and almost gagged); grabbed the duffel bag at his feet, slinging it over his shoulder; and wrapped his other arm under Gwen's, waiting for Range to do the same on the other side. One the count of three, they lifted her, and the pain returned twice as strong as it had ever been. She could feel the blood spilling out of her and hear the thick splash as it slapped against the asphalt. She wanted to scream but bit down on her lip instead, tasting fresh blood as it trickled down her throat; but by now she was used to the taste and almost welcomed it, as it meant she was still conscious.

"Switch with me. You're putting too much pressure on the wound, carrying her like that!"

"No, I got it."

"This isn't the time to be macho."

"I said I've got it."

Gwen felt herself rise and balance out, some of the pain alleviating as her weight was lifted off of the wounds.

"Put pressure here," Bruce said, grabbing Range's hand and pressing it into the wound on her side. "I'm gonna hold the one on her shoulder closed with my hand. We need to hold these wounds shut, or she might lose too much blood. Veronica, you're going to need to cover us. Can you do that?"

Veronica seemed to be in her own little world, sweat soaking her face and making it glisten in the lowlight. Her eyes were staring a thousand yards ahead of her, darting at unseen terrors, her breathing ragged and coming in short sharp bursts. She looked so different from the girl she had known her whole life, looking more like a refugee from war than a posh suburban girl without a care in the world.

"Veronica! Did you hear me? I need you to cover us, all right?"

Her attention caught; her eyes snapped up at Bruce, frightened, shaken, but she swallowed laboriously and gave him a nod of approval, lifting her shotgun like a tin soldier.

"You got ammo in that thing?"

Veronica gave another curt nod, which Bruce returned in his own robotic manner.

"All right then, let's move quickly."

They were moving again. Gwen watched as the ground shifted beneath her like a track, doing her best to take actual steps but being dragged along all the same, the tips of her toes scraping over the pavement. When they reached the curb, her feet cracked against it; and she was forced to bite her lip again, drool spilling down over her chin.

The three of them reached the lawn, most of the grass dead or dying, just like the owners who once tended it, with spots of hard, cracked dirt that looked like measles on a dead patient. In front of them, behind a row of hedges, there were one or two straggling zombies milling about. Either they hadn't yet noticed Tyler's distraction or did not care enough to join their brethren in the nearby street, but they made the journey much more harrowing than any of them would've liked.

Everyone held their breaths as they moved past, crossing over the stone pathway leading up to the residence's porch and onto the next segment of lawn. Now, Gwen tried only to lift her legs high enough so that they kept off the ground, not daring to give them away in the slightest. Veronica crept out past the hedges, nervously watching the zombie standing in between them, and tiptoed over the cement in her bare, bloody feet, her flat tops discarded long ago.

They were clear of the crowd of undead now, Bruce and Range guiding Gwen back toward the street where they planned on pushing straight on to the library. Peering into the fog, she could see the plain, featureless building already, a terrible sense of foreboding sinking down on her chest. Whether this was a sign or merely internal bleeding, she couldn't be sure, but she didn't like it either way.

Then, just as they reached the end of the lawn, Range's foot slipped on the wet grass, his foot sinking into the crevice where the dirt met cement and wedging there, dropping Gwen awkwardly on top of him, burying her elbow into her side.

Unable to hold back anymore, Gwen let a terrible wail escape her throat, the pain unbearable and all-consuming. It was all she thought of and all she believed she would ever think of. It seemed endless and infinite, and no matter how much she wished for it to stop, it merely subsided in tremors that grew less severe but continued unabated.

A series of groans answered her own scream, and before she even had a chance to register the pain and her surroundings, she was being lifted up again. She didn't feel any difference in the pain, simply because she doubted it could get any worse. If anything, the wind whistling against it that came from the rush forward was more a relief than a hindrance.

A shotgun blast came from behind them, as loud as thunder, and the three turned Gwen around slowly to see Veronica struggling with a zombie that had seized the shotgun and pointed it harmlessly toward the heavens. The weakened Veronica was being quickly overpowered, and it wasn't long before the monster wrenched the gun from her hands and tossed it aside, the steel clattering on the ground as it slid under a nearby Volkswagen. The members furthest back in the crowd began to turn around toward the commotion and, upon sight of the easier meal, promptly altered their course toward the trapped girl.

Veronica began to scream as the zombie set upon her, its hand thrashing against her torn face, clawing at her, trying to pull her apart by her already-loosened seams. Without thinking, Gwen pushed away from her two supports, her fingers staying just a little longer on Range's hardened shoulder, and rushed toward the zombie, every nerve and fiber of her body scolding and screaming at her, telling her that she was crazy, that she was going to die... and that she didn't care—not when this whole awful situation was her fault.

She barreled hard into the creature's back as it bore down on Veronica and knocked the lot of them into the ground in a tangle of blood and limbs. Her shoulder connected with the creature's leg and seemed to explode in a blinding white fury, and as she landed and rolled over her side, her vision left her again; and she sunk into a state of semiconsciousness, the pain her only thinning link to the outside world.

She blinked, trying to clear away the darkness, and only caught fleeting glimpses of Veronica rolling over in discomfort, the bandage on her cheek thrown aside and the wound ripped open anew, pouring more blood into the cracks of dirt. And the zombie—its bald head encircled with long white hair, missing half of its yellow, rotted, nubs of teeth, with blue leathery skin and a hole where its nose should've been—came crawling over the two dazed girls, moving right toward Gwen's face just as her last tether of consciousness came loose; and she slipped into dark, troublesome dreams marked with death.

I remember dreaming of my mother—not as one of those ghouls, but as she was. I think that's what made it more frightening.

She was following me—not chasing, just... walking behind me at this deliberate pace. She was wearing this plain white dress that she used to wear to church, except there was a sopping wet stain of blood at the base. There was so much you could see the dress sticking to her legs as she walked, even hear the wet smack as it slapped against her skin. I tried walking away; but no matter how fast I ran, whenever I turned around, she was there.

But I couldn't see her face—at least not clearly enough to make out what she was thinking, just enough to know it was her: the same high brows and those shelf-like cheekbones that she gave to me. It was her, all right. And if I didn't know any better… it almost looked like she was crying.

I'd never seen my mother cry, never even heard a sob from her. So I didn't really have anything to compare it to. And she was so far away; her face was a constant blur of movement, obscured further by that haze that makes dreams, dreams.

So I ran and I ran, even though I knew I wasn't stretching the gap between us, because every time I looked back, there she was—walking in that slow, unwieldy gait, creeping ever closer. I ran through abandoned city streets, overgrown forests that looked like something out of an Aesop fable—one that would have to have the ending changed in modern printings—and long, empty stretches of beaches, where the arctic water roared over my feet in waves that flowed in an odd, intrinsic rhythm.

Finally, I grew tired and decided to wait for it, for my mother. Running was getting me nowhere. I might as well see what the hell she wanted. So I planted my feet in the sand, sinking through the soggy clumps, and waited as she crept closer and closer. As she grew near, I saw that there were indeed tears falling down her face—but not ones of remorse or sadness. No, she was laughing giddily as if someone had stirred her brains up with a spoon.

My resolve quickly faded away after that, and I tried to turn and run again, but my feet were firmly encased in sand. It sucked me down deeper, the grains shifting and slurping around my ankles, like the beach itself was trying to swallow me. My mother was so close now I could see every wrinkle on her haggard face, her skin drawn tight and her eyes wide and bloodshot as tears continued to stream from their edges, marked by the occasional drop of blood that mixed and slid down her sullen cheeks slower than the rest.

I bent low to try and pull my legs free, but it only pulled me down faster, like it knew I was trying to escape and enjoyed taunting me. After realizing I was only antagonizing whatever it was that held me, I gave up and stood still, ready to face whatever fate my mother had in store for me.

But she was gone.

All that stood in front of me was the endless beach, a trail of soft footprints leading back through the sand. A seagull squawked overhead, and as I turned to look at it, I felt nails dig into my scalp and rip my head back. Something sharp pierced the bottom of my spine and began to drag itself up the length of my back, slowly, so slowly that I could feel it move every inch of the way. I tried to reach back and stop it, but blood began to pour from the center of my palms; and when I grabbed the knife or razor or whatever it was, my weak, shaky hands slid off uselessly.

After what felt like an eternity and a half, the blade hit the base of my neck; and whatever had my hair in its clutches relaxed its grip, letting my hair slump forward just enough to see the puddle of blood forming around my feet, a miniature lake in the sand.

They say you don't feel yourself die in dreams. But I felt that; that's for sure. Range told me it was just the pain of the stitches making its way through, but I haven't been able to convince myself of that yet.

For some reason, I didn't wake up but seemed to sink deeper into a black pool. It wasn't water but simply darkness that swallowed you down to the top of your head, the last bits of light disappearing when you sink beneath its stoic surface.

I felt hands pulling me down—unseen hands, but ones that pressed hard into your skin, hard enough to leave a mark but also seemed to pass right through you. They were colder than ice; even the most frigid winter breeze seemed tropical compared to the chill held in those fingers. Voices began to whisper in my ear—dark, angry voices speaking so fast that nothing was intelligible. Some words were sharper than others, like pins jammed in your ear, and others were softer than a rocking cradle and twice as bewitching. I couldn't understand them, but they're meaning was clear. I was to submit and let myself be pulled down into that darkness until I couldn't remember what light even resembled.

The idea of being plunged into darkness until the end of time, or as close as my puny mind could so determine, made a fire in my stomach and got me to start kicking my legs, fighting it, but it was like moving through molasses. I wasn't even sure if I was even moving upward or just treading endlessly in the muck, but I kept at it. Terrible things bathed in the seediest neon started to flash before my eyes—a crying infant that had the body of a cockroach; a wolf standing on hind legs, ripping apart a man's rib cage, like you would a pack of airplane peanuts; even my mother growling and screaming at me, chanting verses over and over, while darkness dripped slowly from her lips like tar. I forgot most of them as soon as I woke, but one stood out, one she kept repeating over and over. She read it to me plenty of times when she was alive as well.

Something like… "Therefore, the Lord shall have no joy in their young men, neither shall have mercy on their fatherless and widows; for every one of them is a hypocrite and an evildoer, and every mouth speaketh folly. For all this his anger is not turned away, but his hand is stretched out still…"

And then I woke up.

She nearly choked on saliva that rushed down her throat as she sat up, flying into a fit of coughing that seemed ready to reopen her wounds and rend her body asunder. Her hand rushed to her side and traced the grisly bumps of hobbled-together flesh; and when she pulled her hand free from her shirt, blood spotted her fingers, thick and soupy as she rubbed it between the tips.

The walls seemed to be moving in the dark. She heard scratching and rustling, and the whole building seemed to be trembling. There was a nagging energy to the place, one that made Gwen's muscles cramp up as soon as she felt it. She tried to sit up but collapsed after only the slightest exertion of energy. Sliding her hands behind her, she found a shelf and placed her palms flat against it, pushing herself straight until her neck was even with the shelf above it. The thin pieces of balsa wood dug into her back and especially irritated her shoulder, which had begun to bleed through her shirt—although since the entire thing had been painted red by their sprint across town, the only way to tell was from the dampness and the way it clung to her chest.

"You're awake then."

Gwen turned toward the voice, startled, as its owner was still concealed in shade. Their shadow moved forward into the light, scooting closer and closer on a pillow across the hard gray carpet, the fabrics scratching against one another as they drew closer. Eventually, the light spilled out onto the shadow's face, and even then, it took Gwen a moment to recognize Veronica's newly scarred face—the way the dark played across her features, highlighting the worst of the injuries, and the black pus leaking from their burning red edges, glinting from large steel staples that held half the loosely assembled flesh together into the shape of a human face.

Gwen kept her face stoic but was having a hard time looking directly at the girl, both from the sight of her gruesome appearance and from their shared history, making the words hard to place and assemble from the jumble of thoughts that came to mind.

"Looks like I am," she said, playing it nonchalant despite the fever pounding in her ears and the pain in every joint of her body. Looking around, she saw that they were alone in the darkness, shelves towering above them and making the room's size hard to judge. "Looks like we ma—ugh... made it to the library. Where are the others?"

"Bruce just finished checking your stitches a little while ago. Last I saw of him, he was heading downstairs to check some fortifications we made after getting you in here. Your boyfriend went straight for the back room when we got here and hasn't come out since. Don't worry, he made sure you were alive and well before doing so, but Bruce and I haven't seen him for at least an hour or so now. I think Bruce was starting to get anxious."

As Gwen tried to straighten herself further, a book tumbled from the shelf behind her and onto the ground pages down on top of her thigh. Picking it up, she saw it was a medical text with instructions on how to do a proper suture, which truly inspired her with confidence in her stitchings, which were practically howling furiously at her with every breath.

"So what the hell happened after... after I blacked out?"

She slid her legs out and noticed for the first time the tarplike blanket underneath her, drenched with blood—*her* blood—right through into the carpet below, the stain settling deep into the fibers. She suddenly felt very lightheaded but tried to put the thought of just how many liters of blood she lost out of her mind.

"Well, after your fit of heroics," Veronica began, "Range ran forward like a lunatic, took the shotgun from me, and blasted the heads of the zombies that were attacking us clean off. Of course, this drew the attention of practically every one of those freaks still in the street; even some of the ones that Tyler led away started slinking back out of the alley. Even the dead are smart enough to figure out that chasing after a closer meal is better than chasing after one you can no longer see.

"Anyways, your ass was completely passed out. I tried shaking you and slapping you, which I absolutely hated doing, believe me, but you were out cold. I thought you were dead and planned on leaving you there, but Range obviously wasn't about to do that. He grabbed you and threw you over his shoulder like a sack of potatoes and nearly dragged me across the ground to get out of there, while Bruce shot a couple of them to keep 'em off our backs.

"We made it to the front door, and it opened easy enough. Apparently, whoever ran the library made it in this morning to open the door but didn't make it long enough to even try and lock the doors to protect himself, probably died helping some older patron, thinking she was a little under the weather right up until she started chewing on his neck. We got the door shut and locked, but Bruce insisted they might make their way through the glass eventually and tried to tip a couple of book cases over to help with the fortifications, seems like he hasn't had much luck yet, though. We have a couple of benches in front of the door for now, but you saw how much they helped back at the hospital."

"So was this place empty or something?" Gwen said, taking a nervous look around the dark corridors they resided in, the seemingly infinite stretches of books leading back into the shadows.

"There were a couple stragglers walking around. Bruce took them out easy enough. Range recognized one of them as the librarian who first told him about… whatever the hell he was going on about, some journal in the back room. It was some decrepit old black guy with half his face torn off, so I don't know how he recognized him, but he was pretty adamant about it. Cried a little bit, it was kinda weird."

Gwen felt a smile break across her face but quickly wore an expression of disinterest as she continued when she remembered who she was talking to. "And where are we?"

"Second floor, by the medical textbooks. Bruce sewed you up easy enough, although there were a couple times when they had a hard time stopping an artery. To be completely honest with you, there were a couple times Bruce thought you were gonna die. Told me it in confidence while Range was busy pacing back and forth between the bookshelves, but he finally got it clamped and sealed by soldering it with a lighter from Tyler's duffel bag."

"Has he—?"

Veronica shook her head slowly, a defeated look on her face—except it wasn't just defeat. There was a weakness about her, a tenderness that she did not normally possess. While Gwen and Veronica had never exactly gotten along, Gwen would always begrudgingly admit that Veronica was stronger than most girls and carried herself with a purpose that was at least admirable, even if she didn't agree with her source of pride.

But now her face was drawn, tight, the scar seemed to cover half of her usually stunning features and somehow made them even more grotesque, the contrast only highlighting the gruesomeness of her injury. Her breaths were short and stagnant, her eyes watery and darting at shadows. She seemed like an entirely different person, one that had aged several decades in a day and was now weary of everything that she had once seemed to love so exuberantly. It was like all the passion had been drained out of her, spilling out like blood from a gaping wound.

Gwen turned away when Veronica started to notice her probing examination and, feeling the awkwardness in the already-musty air, decided to try and stand, using the shelf behind her as leverage. The sharp steel dug into her palm, and the sweat residing there nearly caused her to slide off, but she managed to hobble clumsily to her feet.

"Are you sure you should be doing that?" Veronica asked after her second stumble.

"Dead sure."

Steadying herself, Gwen moved along the length of the shelf toward the end of the small common area, slipping behind a set of large armchairs, their arms wrapped in leather with felt down the back and used them as crutch to lean her injured side on. She nearly tripped over a low table tucked in the corner near the railing, which was buried in shadows, but recovered quickly and let her body slump against the edge overlooking the ground floor.

It only took her a moment to notice Bruce as she heard him long before she saw him, his heavy grunts and the shaking of the large steel shelves coming at regular intervals as he tried to slide the book laden behemoths over to the front entrance. At first, Gwen thought the doors were made of a heavy oak, oddly stained and shaking from the weight of the monsters behind it; but her heart sank when she saw the supposed "wood" split and the last lingering rays of bloodred sunlight break through. She quickly realized that the doors were actually made of an alarmingly thin glass with the legions of squirming undead pressed up against it, gnashing and biting and trying to force their way in. Cracks and holes had already been made with wildly swinging arms of yellowed, dirty bone and stripped flesh, their fingers dancing over the inside surface of the glass and spreading streaks of that slick black sludge and blood making the door resemble a stunning portrait of stained glass. Her breath failed her until she saw that there was still a small entryway protected by another feeble glass barrier, the horde still throwing themselves against the door leading outside.

Just as Veronica had told her, Bruce had already piled some benches and a collection of flimsy steel frame plastic chairs from the tables in the entrance hall in front of the door. He had turned over some of these giant tables and shoved them up against the benches for support, but the tables were old, at least from the early 'seventies, and would've been considered cheap even then. The wood was chipped and marked from top to bottom in messy signatures, curse words, and arrow-pierced hearts, along with an assortment of calcified chewing gum, the legs made of rusted metal covered in a worn black rubber. If the creatures could get through glass, they'd get through them even easier with a simple show of force.

There was an eardrum-destroying screech of steel on linoleum as Bruce heaved himself into a bookshelf, all his might barely causing the side he was pushing from to budge a couple of feet. The other side of the shelf remained planted, the massive structure rocking back and forth as books tumbled from its highest shelves and crashed and split their spines on the tiles below. After a minute of little to no progress, Bruce dropped to his knees, breathing hard and weakly slamming his fist against one of the case's dented shelves.

This brief show of frustration did not last long, and Bruce was back on his feet, wiping blood and sweat from his brow as he reexamined the wobbling tower of books. He scanned around the first floor, checking the rows of tables in the center leading up to the desk at the back of the entrance hall, with a hallway that led to the historical texts in the back examinations rooms. Several bodies lay slumped over in a pool of blood at their tables, and several more dotted the floor, their bodies twisted in odd angles or shredded down to mangled piles of muscle tissue and splintered bones. Bookcases stood tall on either side of the entrance hall, but the one Bruce was working on moving was easily the closest, saved for its counterpart on the opposite side of the building beneath Gwen's feet.

As he was looking around the ruins of the library, Bruce noticed Gwen observing from above and gave her a quick wave. Gwen returned it and immediately regretted it, her shoulder giving her a stern lecture through jolts of trembling pain. Gwen watched him as his slow gait turned into a gentle jog up the staircases behind the information booth, working his way up until he disappeared between the aisles at Gwen's side, reappearing between the two girls a moment later.

"Ah, my patient is awake, but she is out of bed, ignoring the doctor's orders as I expected. I guess that means you're feeling all right?"

"Well, I feel like I've been shot twice, but I'm definitely a lot better than I was before. Thank you."

"Don't mention it."

"Doing some light reading down there?"

Bruce wore a grin, but his eyes weren't smiling. Instead, they seemed overwhelmingly tired.

"Ah, nothing that really strikes my fancy down there. A bunch of different Bible translations and religious commentary, most of them the kind that says you're gonna spend eternity engulfed in hellfire unless you're in church every other day and that we have a duty to look after God's poor, lesser creatures, like Indians—not exactly page turners."

"That section seems right up my mother's alley."

"Come to think of it, I think I saw her name on the sign-out list on some of the covers."

"Figures," Gwen said, nonchalantly, but also turning her head to look back down at the crooked bookcase near the doorway.

"Well, since you've got enough energy to walk around, you think you've got enough to help me move a half-ton bookcase?"

Gwen put her hand to her side, and a spasm nearly brought her back down to the ground. Bruce rushed toward her but stopped when she caught the railing and waved him off.

"Forget it. Wishful thinking on my part. I just wish that boyfriend of yours would hurry up with whatever he's doing back there. Or at least would've stayed a little longer to help me fortify this place. The doors are locked, but that glass isn't going to hold long. I'm honestly surprised they haven't gotten in yet. If I can't get this thing in front of the door in the next fifteen minutes, I'm gonna send you back there to get him. I don't care if he asked not to be disturbed, we're not gonna last the night in here if we don't get a better barrier put up. He can have all the privacy he wants once that's done."

"Why doesn't Veronica come down and help you?"

The two shared a glance that spoke where they did not. It was both fearful and mournful, and once their eyes parted, Veronica's drifted down into her lap and settled there, her wan figure looking even more ragged.

"She... she did her best already. She's going to give it another try after she's rested a bit more," Bruce said, fumbling over the words.

"You should do the same. I'm gonna get back to work for the time being. Remember. Fifteen more minutes, then I'm sending you to go get him, all right?"

Gwen nodded, and Bruce left satisfied, charging back down the stairs, seemingly reinvigorated. Using the chairs for support, she settled back down onto her blanket and grabbed one of the cushions and placed it behind her back to stop the shelves from digging into her spine. As she sat in silence, her eyes began to flutter, sleep holding out a warm, inviting hand that promised to relieve all her troubles.

"You didn't get all defensive that time."

"Huh?" Gwen said through heavy lips. She blinked away the drowsiness and saw Veronica staring at her intently from the shadows.

"You didn't get defensive… when Bruce called him your boyfriend. Usually, you freak out or something."

"Oh."

"It's pretty obvious you like him. Why do you do that?"

"Do what?"

"Get all defensive whenever someone points out that you like him. See, you're doing it now too."

"I am not."

"Are you even listening to yourself?"

Gwen stuck her lip out and wanted to spit back a crushing argument but found none. Slowly, as her knee-jerk anger began to subside, she took a deep breath and looked back to Veronica.

"I don't know. I guess I always felt ashamed of it. Like it was… weak, you know? Like if I admit I like a boy, and I mean, actually like him, I'm just another dumb girl who can't do anything without a man. I don't know. It's stupid."

"You're right, it is."

"You didn't have to agree so quickly, you know."

"Well, it is. You like this guy, but you're more worried about what other people will think about you than how you actually feel. I'd say I was surprised, but it's pretty typical of you."

"Jesus, are you really going to do this now, after everything that's happened?"

Veronica scoffed. "You're only saying that because you know I'm right."

"No, I'm saying that because most of our friends and family died today, I've been shot, and I really don't feel like spending what might be the last remaining hours of my life arguing with you over some stupid, petty bullshit!"

"Oh, and now you care about everybody all of a sudden? Those people who hated you just as much as you did them? Those people who you acted better than you every day? Or are you just using that as an excuse because you can't deflect with a better one?"

"You heard Bruce. There are better things we can be doing with our time than this bullshit!"

"Fuck that!"

Veronica exploded, rising from the ground like a furious dust storm. The rush from standing was too much for her in her weakened state, and she had to grab hold of a bookcase to keep herself standing, but her jagged face remained one of bitter rage.

"I saw you lying there, bleeding out! I thought you were gonna die! We all did! And while everyone else was getting upset at themselves or tables or bookcases by the way the slammed their useless fists against them, I was the only one smart enough to be angry at you! It was typical Gwen, acts so tough and then gets brought down after getting grazed by some pussy with a BB gun.

"I was angry that I wasn't able to tell you all this to your face. That you had somehow… won in a way, so I'm gonna take this second chance I've been given and tell you what I've been dying to say to your smug little face for years."

Veronica stopped and clutched her stomach as she doubled over in pain, but she pushed Gwen away when she tried to get near, mumbling, "No, don't you help me, not until I've said what I'm going to say." She coughed violently into her closed fist, a dark liquid spilling between her wrapped fingers, but she wiped it quickly on the back of her jeans and looked back at Gwen.

"You really just can't let it go, can you? You can't even stop being a bitch in your final hours. You always have to be the best person in the room, the person in control, and you've been losing your mind ever since you lost your little 'kingdom,' which you ruled over your little horny subjects," Gwen said snidely. What little sympathy she once had for the sickly girl quickly fled with the rest of her inhibitions. She felt lightheaded, but she didn't dare let herself appear weak after Veronica had already done so herself.

"Oh my god, you are the biggest hypocrite. You go on and on about how you don't care what people think, but you do. You care what they think and mold yourself around it just the same as me. You like a boy but tell yourself you don't because it might ruin your image as this bad girl that you've so expertly crafted. It's quite the persona, Gwen, real original too. Edgy Christian girl who hates her parents and smokes cigarettes. Where'd you come up with that? Which reminds me… I haven't seen you have a single damn cigarette since this mess began. Stressful situation like this, you'd think you'd need one. But it's almost like you only smoke them for show or something, like they're just part of this… this… image you've made of yourself for people. This image you've crafted to hide behind that you think makes you better than everyone else. You think that just because you make yourself into the opposite of what everyone expects that you're not letting yourself being controlled by them, but you still are. You're as much a slave to expectations as me, as everyone else.

"Do you know why everyone hates you, Gwen? Hmm? Do you? Do you really know why everyone hates you? I think that you *think* you know, but something tells me you really don't. No, you think it's just because your mom is the town crazy lady. You wear that chip proudly on your shoulder for everyone to see. You wear it like a goddamn fashion accessory everywhere you go. It's a goddamn crutch for you to treat everyone else like shit with a clean conscience.

"I gotta say, for as much of a whiny bitch that Bobby kid was, and as out of line as it was for him to call you a whore just because you wouldn't fuck him, he was right about you, even with his head all the way up your ass. For as much as you talked about hating her, you are exactly like your damn mother. You judge everyone else as beneath you before having spoken to them, just because you assume they all know about *you* and who *you* are, what *you*'ve been through. You shoot disgusting looks at everybody at the hall, and anytime anyone's dumb enough to show you any kindness, you act like they're trying to trick you or something and tell them to fuck off. Even your best buddy Stacey would tell us all about the horrible things you would say to her if she dared to compare her troubles to yours, and all the worse things you said about everyone else behind their backs.

"You act like you're the only person who has a shitty home life, the only person who's ever been struck or belittled by a family member. Like your problems are the only ones that actually matter. Do you even know what I've been through, Gwen? Everybody knows and sympathizes with what you've gone through. But nobody knows what I've had to endure, what guys have forced me into, saying I owed them, or that it was my duty to fuck them after a night out, what girls say behind my back just because their shitty boyfriend made lewd comments about me. Do you know what it's like to be called a slut and a whore just because you've dared to spread your legs, even the same people that condemn you are the ones who want you to spread them in the first place. They're just jealous it wasn't for them."

Veronica's breath was running short, and her lower lip began to tremble. "You don't have any idea what *he* did to me… And he was the one who was supposed to protect me. You know what that's like right? Huh, Gwen? When the one who's supposed to protect you destroys you instead? Ruins you just like they did themselves?"

The tears came then and washed her words into a stream of inaudible sobs and mumbles as she buried her head in her hands. Gwen barely heard any of her muted cries; her heartbeat was too loud in her ears. Her vision had narrowed to that of a darkly lit tunnel, and the world around her suddenly seemed more distant and yet more suffocating, all at the same time. She tried to pull in air, but her chest remained tight and constricted, her heart ready to burst from her rib cage.

She wanted to tell Veronica that she was wrong and a terrible, spiteful bitch who had no idea what she was talking about, but… she couldn't. She just couldn't pretend anymore. Her words had struck deeper than the bullets and torn out her insides, leaving them steaming in a black pile behind her. She pictured herself as her mother, standing in that old gym auditorium, standing above her classmates, looking down on them as she condemned them to a life of sin and debauchery, one she was so far above; and she made herself sick, emptying the contents of her stomach on the blanket at her feet.

Curling inside herself, she clutched her stomach, wishing it would settle when she knew it would not, and nearly collapsed in the puddle of vomit at her side. She tried to stammer out explanations or apologies, she wasn't sure which, but all that came out were pained gasps.

"You know something," Veronica said, "we were friends once. Do you remember?"

Gwen could only manage to shake her head.

"I figured you wouldn't. I'd been thinking about it a lot recently. Even before all... *this* started. It was in probably, I don't know, second grade? I remember you sitting alone at lunch one day and thought it was strange that no one was around you. And I mean, like no one, you had legit a whole table to yourself. I came over and said hi, and you were shy at first, but after I started talking to you about some dumb cartoon show, one you hadn't even heard of, you started talking more than any girl I'd ever met. We parted ways after lunch, and I didn't think much of it until the next day when I saw you alone again. You waved me over... and you gave me an extra pudding cup you brought from home. It sounds stupid when you talk about it now, but it was the sweetest, most adorable thing anyone's ever done for me. You said you sneaked it away from your mom's cabinet and everything.

"We talked every day after that for like a week, about everything little girls talk about—animals, music, even what boys we thought were cute and which were gross—until one day you came in with a bruise on your cheek and a black eye. Everybody had been whispering about it since gym glass that morning, especially the marks on your back as well. I figured the best thing to do was to try and cheer you up, so I stopped by your table again and before I could even say anything, you yelled at me to go away so loud that the entire cafeteria went silent. You couldn't even look at me, but you told me off all the same, told me to leave you alone and that I 'didn't have a clue what you were going through.' So I did, and it hurt. I'd be lying if I said it didn't. God, the way everyone was looking at me. And you hated me, not because of who I was, or even what I was doing, but just because you hated everything. And then when I saw you start to take pride in that… I guess I hated you too.

"I know I'm not the nicest person. I know I can be superficial, but I'm just so… afraid of being nothing, of not mattering, or being just another face in a crowd. I can be a bitch, too, because of that, that fear. But I was nice to you once, Gwen, and you threw it back in my face, just like you do to everyone else."

Veronica was sobbing heavily now, her red, puffy cheeks doing nothing to improve her tarnished features; and her frailness was more apparent than ever, but she was sincere, and Gwen's heart was shattering, crumbling into the bottom of her stomach and cycling the drain.

"I'm… I'm sorry. It's not easy for me to say, and I don't know if it does any good, but I'm sorry, all right? You're right. I'm not the nicest person. I can be unpleasant to be around, and I hate others for things they aren't even responsible for. It's… just hard, to separate yourself from… everything, if that makes any sense? I… I've been trying so hard, doing everything I can to make sure I didn't end up like my mother, and I've been acting like her my whole life."

Now, she too was crying, but she didn't feel ashamed. Instead, it was like a weight shrugged from her shoulders, her body feeling lighter than air, so light that she thought she might float away at any moment. Veronica looked up from her hands, her scar zigzagging across her face and redirecting the flow of tears down her cheeks; and she stretched her open palms out toward Gwen, welcoming her into the curves of her chest.

They embraced and cried into each other's shoulders, each issuing meaningless apologies, enjoying instead the warm cradle of each other's arms.

"I'm… suh… sorry, Gwen, I shouldn't have brought up all that now. I'm just so scared. I kind of… go into bitch mode when I'm scared," Veronica said tearfully.

"You must be scared a lot."

"Careful now," Veronica said with a light chuckle, "but you're right, I really am. For all the admiration and attention I got, it was the same that any attractive girl got. I saw the way they treated my equally attractive friends from other schools, and when I went to a party out of town, I became part of a flock of pretty hens that people squabbled over. I got so scared by that feeling that I stopped going to any party thrown by anyone outside of the district. I knew that most of the reason people liked me was just because of my looks, and I hated them for it. You see, that's the difference between you and me, Gwen. I play the part to their faces and hate them while their backs are turned. I knew it couldn't last forever either."

She gave a weak smile that quickly devolved into another hollow sob. "But now I don't even have my looks. I'm some fugly beast better suited for a sideshow than a fashion magazine. I have nothing, I am nothing, just like I always feared."

She pushed Gwen away and cowered in the corner, the shadows devouring her and her arched, heaving back. Gwen slowly tiptoed over to her, unsure if she should even say anything, of what she even could say. Part of her wanted to give in, retreat to her own dark corner in this labyrinth of printed word, and sob until they end came, praying and tasting scripture on her lips.

But she could not.

"Hey! No, no, no, no, you got it all wrong. You're scar makes you look badass! Are you serious? Any hot chick can lose her looks from wrinkles and warts, but you got a badass scar from killing a member of the living dead. You blew their heads off with a goddamn shotgun. Let's see a scrawny fashion model do that!"

"Fuck you," Veronica said with a tear soaked laugh, "now you're just making fun of me."

"No, I'm serious. Like you said, I like to act tough, but I don't think I'd be able to get right back up after having my face torn up. That takes guts as well as strength, you know?"

Cautiously, Veronica's head turned to face Gwen, her hands still dabbing at the tears in a futile effort to stop their flow. "Well… thanks, bitch," she said with a friendly inflection. Gwen winced but did her best to ignore it. "But you don't give yourself enough credit. I mean, you did get shot twice."

"Yeah, not anywhere vital, though, at least I hope so."

A loud crash cut their conversation short and jerked both their attentions toward the balcony and the floor below. The sighs and groans of the dead could be heard again, as pleasant as hearing a song that you had just gotten out of your head. Bruce was shouting something that couldn't be heard above the horrible wailing, but Gwen knew it could be about nothing good.

She sprinted forward and collided with the railing, pain shooting through her bullet wound, like someone had dug a knife down to the bone and decided to jiggle it around. She gasped sharply but clutched the cold brass rail guard tightly, sure that her fingers were making dents in the cheap metal.

The front entryway had become flooded with undead, their putrid forms clogging it like cholesterol in the veins as they fought and scratched and bit each other to get to the glass. The ones in front shoved their gross, slobbering faces against the doors, their tongues leaving a snail-like trail of black and yellow slime that slowly rolled down and collected on the floor. It slid through the cracks in the rattling doors and began to drip from the legs of the chairs that made up the barrier. The doors were shaking so heavily in their frames, the handles clacking loudly against the edge of the overturned table.

"Hey! Hey, Gwen!" Bruce called out from below. "Get Range now! Do you hear me? They're gonna get in! The glass isn't gonna last more than a couple minutes!"

While he gave these rushed instructions, he was darting out from behind the racks of books, circling the tables and flipping over the one nearest him. With one heavy grunt, he flipped the thing on its side and tried to shove it up against the rest of the barrier, but the spiderlike legs collided with that of the other tables wedged against the door and kept it from going any farther. When Bruce tried to give it another large, scrupulous push, the tower of cheap furniture nearly crumbled out from the bottom, and he desperately caught the falling pieces and haphazardly started shoving them back into place. After getting everything balanced again, he held out his hands until things steadied, before sprinting back to the bookshelf to give it another screeching shove across the floor. Somehow he had enough power to nearly tip the thing forward, but it swung back at the last moment and settled down into its rut in the floor.

"What the hell are you waiting for? Go! Now!"

Feeling slightly guilty for her dumbfounded observations, Gwen nodded even though he was already focused on his Herculean task and whirled about to start down the stairs. As she pulled away from the railing, she realized Veronica was not beside her and paused to look around for her, not willing to leave her behind after their spontaneous reconciliation.

She found her quickly enough as she had never left her dark corner. Her face was buried in the corner where the two walls met, her nose pressed flat against it; her long brown hair dripped over her shoulders, thin and glistening like a spiderweb in the morning sunlight. There was a dull thud arising from the shadows, and it took Gwen a moment to realize that it was coming from Veronica herself.

She was smacking her head against the wall.

The darkness had obscured the swift movement of her head at first, but now that her eyes, had adjusted she was sure of it. Each thud grew harder, and duller, the walls trembling, the studs rumbling—until the noise became a wet smack and crimson began to appear on the wall, trickling down to Veronica's bare feet. Another liquid, foul smelling and yellow, was also spilling out of her pant leg at her feet.

"Veronica... are you okay?"

Gwen felt dumb as soon as she asked it, but she barely remembered saying the words. Either she hadn't heard or she was simply attempting to spite her, but Veronica started to slam her head harder against the corner, until sick crunches started to be heard beneath the thuds.

"Veronica, I need you to talk to me right now."

She doubled over so quick that Gwen nearly fell back off the balcony onto the hard tiles beneath, but all she did was start retching, adding vomit to the rug full of petulant liquids pooling at her feet. They were hard, violent heaves, ones that sounded heart-crushingly pitiful, especially when cut up by moans and painful sobs.

"It's all right, it's all right. I got a little sick myself, just get it all out of you. But we have to get—"

Gwen was cut off by another surge of vomit that was filled with chunky red lumps that didn't look like food. She felt sick herself and nearly lost whatever meager contents her stomach still had over the railing, but her fear kept her planted, frozen.

Whispers started to fall from Veronica's lips, rising from the shadows like steam. The words were sharp and bitter, like pinpricks on your skin, insects crawling in your ears, stinging and biting and thrashing.

"You dumb bitch… always trying to belittle me… disregard me… *me*!… Bitch… cunt… whore… I'll laugh as the demons chew on your flesh… pull it apart and floss their teeth with the sinews… cunt… whore… slut… self-righteous bitch thinks she's better than me… I'll show her… Ohhhhhh… Ohhhhhhh, God, it hurts… it hurts… make it stop, make it stop, make it stop!"

She smashed her head against the wall again with a wet plop and drag as she slid it down the length of the corner, the blood allowing it to glide easily over the surface. Vomit spewed forth from her mouth again, her cheeks puffing out like a chipmunk as she tried to keep some of it down, but some even began to leak out through the bloody seams of her stitchings. It poured out from between her pouted lips, long blood tubes and chunks and gushes of quivering bile.

"Ahhhhhh, stupid fucking cunts… ass-licking faggots… peel off their skin with a nail file… cut off their dicks with a rusty butter knife… saw left… saw right… his dick goes plop, plop… Oooooohhhh… It's under my skin… I need to cut it out… Yes, cut my skin off… slice, slice, slice, good, good, good… chew the bones 'til all the meat is gone… don't waste good meat… We'll starve if you waste it… cunts… watching me… mocking me… I'll slice her open from ass to ear, pussy to mouth… spread her legs with a sledgehammer… fucking bitch… watching me… watching us…"

"Veronica…"

Gwen's hands were clammy and practically slid off the rail as she stepped forward, closer to the twitching girl in the corner. Her feet squished over the damp carpet, her shoes sinking down to slap against the hardwood boards that creaked beneath. She reached for Veronica's shoulder, knowing what she would find but wanting to face it all the same. As she moved closer, she grabbed the heavy textbook from beside her ramshackle cot made of old blankets, grabbing it by the center and shifting it until it rested comfortable in the curves of her fingers.

"Veronica, I need you to say something I can understand. Tell me what's wrong. How much you hate me, anything, just don't make me do this."

Gwen was standing over her now, static flying between their two heaving bodies, making her hair stand on end and, combined with the overbearing stench, making her stomach queasy.

Veronica's neck snapped back, her eyes pale and lifeless, clear shades of white where her dazzling blue pupils once stood, and a terrible, mournful cry came from the dark cave that was her mouth, saliva flying forth along with the smell of rot, a howling call and response to the groans still rising from the floor below. She crouched low, like a lioness, and pounced on Gwen, pushing her back until they collided with the chairs.

Gwen's back bounced off the padded arm and sent the two of their tangled bodies tumbling onto the floor. They rolled over each other in an instant—first, Gwen was on top, then Veronica. Then Gwen again, before Veronica finally slammed her shoulder into the carpet, drawing a splash of foul water up into the air.

Leaning in low with a curved spine, so low that the tips of their noses brushed against one another, Veronica reeled back and roared into Gwen's face, her lips shaking as if they had been caught in a wind tunnel. The force was so strong that the knot at the corner of her mouth that held her stitches in place began to loosen, pulled by invisible, trembling fingers until, one by one, the thread began to pull itself loose, the cheek splitting apart all over again.

All at once, the rest of the stitches gave way, and her face seemed to fall apart, and from this new gaping hole spilled forth piles and piles of wriggling maggots that cascaded over Gwen's face. She felt their bodies writhing between her lips, in her ears, on her eyelids. She felt them down her shirt and her back, and her whole body wanted to revolt out of her own skin.

With a kick to the gut, she threw what remained of Veronica off of her and tried to stand but lost her footing as her shoes slid over the giant puddle of piss and maggots. Bile reached the back of her throat, but she held it down, taking a deep breath and exhaling slowly as she tried to right herself.

Before she could even stand up straight, Veronica was on her again, taking bites out of the air beside her face as she yanked it back. They nearly fell over again, but Gwen's foot caught against the edge of the balcony, reminding her of where they were standing.

With a giant heave of effort, she dragged Veronica over to the edge of the railing and pushed her over the top. It all happened so quick that the already-dulled Veronica had no time to react, other than to reach up and grab at Gwen's hands; but they flailed by, merely slapping harmlessly at her fingers. She managed to briefly grab a hold of the concrete beneath the railing but only long enough to contort and twist her body around like top as she fell heavily onto the tiled floor.

There was a wet, heavy smack as her body went limp and a flower bed of blood blossomed out from underneath her, echoing out through the cavernous halls of the library, its ceilings stretching higher than a cathedral. It was abrupt and sudden enough to make Bruce jump and look away from his task of forcing the bookcase against the barrier to the horrifying sight just several feet away from him. Angry confusion seeped into his cheeks, his mouth open as he looked up at Gwen, frozen and unsure as the bookcase began to tip back toward him.

Before he even had a chance to speak, a snarling, thrashing head broke through the glass doors, knocking the brass handles across the room as his teeth clacked and snapped together, and it was like the very floodgates of hell had been thrown open.

The doors burst apart, the impact knocking the small barrier of furniture completely over, chairs flying in the air and back down on the heads of the undead as they fought to get through the cramped doorway; and the tables flew forward, crashing into each other and tripping any of the zombies that had squeezed the gap. Sliding over the floor, the rolling pile of furniture crashed into the base of the bookshelf and carried it forward along with the built-up momentum, and it began to tip heavily in the opposite direction, directly toward Bruce.

However, Bruce's attention was on the broken Victoria—whose cracked, insectile limbs were trying to raise the remains of her carcass to its crooked feet—and he noticed far too late the waterfall leather-bound pages that were raining down him. The top of the bookcase crashed into the top of the one behind it, and like dominoes, the entire length of shelves began to fall to the floor, one on top of the other.

Bruce disappeared beneath the books as the steel shelves came together, crushing him beneath their weight, his scream muffled by the screech of metal and the roar of the zombies. Gwen cried out in disbelief as she watched, still refusing to believe he was gone, even after the dust that rose up from the nearly century-old bookshelves settled once again and Bruce was nowhere to be seen. Several zombies had been crushed as well, their arms and legs rising out of the mountains of books, some still wiggling this way and that, trying to free themselves, and some as deathly still as the air around them.

This barely put a dent in the waves of dead pouring through the newly opened entryway, a cascade of mangled bodies scrabbling over the remains of their crushed brethren. None even thought to stop and assist them; they were focused only on the prospect of a living meal. Gwen wasn't sure how they still knew that there were living people inside, why they hadn't simply given up long ago; but somehow they smelled them, or sensed them, and they were going to catch up to them eventually, no matter how hard or far they ran.

She looked around wildly for some method of escape but saw that the stairwell she had used to come up already had a line of zombies making their way toward it and the information desk at its center. And standing there, behind the pens and lamps and overdue books, was Range, his face blank and dripping with perspiration as he looked out horrified at the terrible scene of destruction before him.

"Range! Range!" Gwen screamed at the top of her lungs, but it was no use.

He was in some sort of trancelike state, completely ignorant to the world around him and the hell that it had descended into. She tried waving her arms wildly, whistling, shouting, anything to get his attention, but he was completely shut off from everything. All she accomplished was drawing the eye of the dead below, which began eagerly moving in their slow, tortured gait toward the stairwell and the catatonic Range.

She couldn't understand why he wasn't moving. It wasn't like him to become paralyzed with fear. If anything, it only made him push harder, but something had shaken him. Whatever he had learned in the back room had not been what he wanted to hear, and Gwen could only guess terrible, awful, terrifying guesses at what that was.

"Range! Stop just standing there and run! Range! Raaange!"

Finally, like awaking from a dream, his eyes snapped up to hers, meeting amidst the chaos; and he gave her a wan smile and a hard, short nod of his head, like they were the only two people left in the world. Just as the zombies began pressing up against the information desk, he spun around and sprinted toward the stairs leading up to Gwen, leaping up them two at a time.

She lost track of him in the rows of books before he appeared in front of her, stooped over and out of breath, his body still shaking so intensely that the sight of it made her blood run cold.

"Where are the others?"

Gwen had words prepared, but all that came out was an alarming sob as she practically leaped into his arms, catching him off guard. "Th… they… they're… Veronica, she… turned into one of them… and I… I… and Bruce… and… Oh, God, Range it was terrible."

"Hey, hey," he cooed, his calming mantra returning, giving him an air of benevolence that filled Gwen with such confidence that it was intoxicating, "I'm sorry. I'm sorry you had to see that, and I'm sorry I wasn't here to help. I'm sorry for everything, all of it."

Gwen sniffed, pulling away from him. "What do you mean? What are you saying? This isn't your fault."

His eyes grew dark, shadowed by the heavy overhead lights, his features becoming nondescript and blank. Gwen took a step back as if shoved, confusion swirling in her head, muddying her thoughts and twisting her vision.

"Is it? Huh? This isn't your fault, right? It couldn't be."

"Gwen," he said, reaching for her hand, but she jerked it away from him.

"Is it?"

There was a crash from the stairwell, making both of them turn away just in time to see the first of the horde of dead reach the second floor landing, its head tilted back, exposing the large goiter in its extended neck as it sniffed the air around it, blood dripping from its lower jaw. The stairs were now packed with dead fighting to reach the top, throwing one another about, even knocking some of the less fortunate or smaller zombies over the edge, sending their body rag-dolling onto the hard tile where their heads split like eggs. For a moment, Gwen even thought she spied Veronica, her half split-open cheek flopping around as she clawed her way past her fellow dead, only to disappear into the crowd, one gruesome face lost in a sea of the damned.

"Do you trust me?"

Gwen had to pry herself away from the sight of their approaching demise, her wide, wild eyes meeting his and drifting into their aquamarine depths as she studied his face. He looked shaken worse than before, but he no longer trembled like a sickly leaf. He stared directly into her soul, baring his just the same, reaching out with more than just his sweaty palm.

"I'd be pretty dumb if I did."

"That's what makes it trust and not logic."

The zombie at the landing had begun moving through the aisle of books, bouncing off the shelves with its lazy, haphazard lope. Gwen watched it moving closer, watched its crooked, jagged teeth fitting their sharp ridges together, its exposed bones and torn flesh, and tried to imagine the fate that awaited them. When she turned back to Range, his hand was still outstretched, a disarming smile on his face that still made Gwen's stomach queasy and ready to burst in a flurry of jittery butterflies.

Soundlessly, she slipped her fingers through his and clasped tightly.

His smile grew into a satisfied smirk, and without waiting, he pulled her toward the back wall, tipping over a chair in front of one of the aisles leading back toward the stairwell. He also grabbed the duffel bag near the blood-spotted tarp and threw it over his shoulder, the contents smacking loudly against his back—a gentle ringing, splendid tone rising from underneath the zipper.

"Come on, we're getting out of here."

He dragged her over to the window and released her hand, setting to work on getting the century-old window open. He slammed his palms up into the top of the frame, but the glass barely budged. After checking the small silver latch at the top, he tried again and made some headway, if only a centimeter or two; but with a groan very similar to the ghouls that lay in wait behind them, the window started to open.

With a loud grunt of his own, the veins in his thin neck bulging as he pulled up on the pane, the window flew open with a scream of protest. Hurriedly, he threw the duffel bag over the ledge and threw his leg over, stretching his hand out for her to grab again.

"You've got to be kidding me," Gwen said, stricken with disbelief.

"Watch out!"

He grabbed her and pulled her toward the windowsill at the last moment, the zombie with the bulging goiter crashing into the wall beside them in a haze of blood and limbs.

Now satisfied with the plan, she slipped through the window feet first, her gym shoes catching on the sandpaper like shingles and keeping her feet from sliding out from under her at the odd angle she now found herself standing.

Range was right behind her, swinging his other leg through the gap and going to shut the window behind them when the zombie appeared, the clublike swings of his hands nearly toppling Range as he lost his balance. He fell backward onto his rear and rolled over himself, his legs kicking up shingles, leaves, and dirt as he rolled toward the edge on his side.

With her arms outstretched to keep her balance, Gwen moved quickly over to him, watching her feet on each tile, not daring to let her foot linger for more than a second. Only the tops of her toes ever seemed to touch the loose and shaky shingles. Moving past the duffel bag, she threw it over her shoulder, nearly knocked over by the unexpected weight of it.

Range had righted himself but still hadn't been able to slow his descent. He clawed at the loose shingles, pulling them up in his bloody fingers, his face growing more and more worried as the edge came up to meet him. Just as his feet went over, Gwen was able to catch his arms under his shoulders, stopping him at the last moment, but gravity was still trying to claim its wayward victim.

Gwen tried to pull him up but found her strength lacking. After readjusting her stance, she tried again only for her side to nearly tear itself open, pain shooting through her body. Glancing down, she saw a fresh stain of blood forming around the wound, drops seeping through her cotton tee and cascading down the tiles into the gutter.

"Move!"

The warning came too late as the zombie dashed itself into Gwen's back, knocking her forward with a gasp over the edge. The world shifted around her, the sky becoming the ground and her falling up into it. She was jerked to a stop before the ground rushed up to meet her, her odd perspective lingering long enough to watch the battered zombie slam into the ground, the goiter in his neck bursting like a water balloon of blood and pus.

Looking up, she saw that Range had caught her in one hand, his other still clutching the gutter, which was bending and straining to keep them elevated. Range's face was one of immense pain as the weight nearly tore his arm off, but with teeth grinding so loud that it sounded like static in Gwen's ear, he held tight.

"I can't hold on much longer," he said, strained. Opening his eyes and looking at the ground below, he motioned with his head toward a pile of leaves next to an oak tree whose branches stood just out of reach. "I'm going to swing you over there, all right?"

"What? Are you crazy? We'll die!"
"Just aim for the leaves."
"You say that like it's going to help at all."
"It'll help a little. Okay? You ready?"
"No!"
"Good."

With that, he started to swing her back and forth, slow small arcs at first, which grew wider and wider with each sway. Gusts of wind actually worked in their favor, pushing their awkward display of gymnastics from the back, as the gutter began to loosen and come free of the wall but in the direction of the old dead oak tree.

"Okay… on three! One! Two! Thr—"

A zombie roared from above, its decrepit skull appearing over the edge and swinging at Range, causing him to lose his grip at the worst possible moment, when the momentum was starting to carry them back away from the oak tree. They started to tumble the two stories to the ground below, twisting around each other as Gwen screamed out of pure instinct, her stomach dropping out from under her.

Range wrapped himself around her and turned their bodies around so that she was on top of him, their eyes meeting briefly as they bounced off of the chain-link fencing, the steel giving way beneath their legs and sending them crashing hard into the wet leaves and dirty mud.

The evacuation team went through the town sometime after word got out about it. The government obviously wanted something formal, something to quell the growing rumors of an entire town disappearing overnight. Like usual, it took them longer than it should've to get a group out there. I think it was a week or so after everything settled, if I remember correctly. At least, that's when they decided to tell me about it.

Yes, they did at least have the courtesy to tell me about it and not just leave me to rot in that awful place they sent me. They even made a special trip down to the sanitarium just to see little old me—

although I'm sure they probably would've just kept me swept under the rug if they didn't need my help.

Yes, they asked for my help with something, although I'm sure they regretted it afterward as I wasn't able to do much more than they were. You see, during their excavation of the town, one of the first places they checked was the library, mostly due to its proximity to the highway and from it being the destination of our little exodus. It seemed that despite their reluctance to believe my story, someone over there had enough curiosity to investigate exactly what it was that Range found and see if it produced a viable explanation for the plaguelike annihilation of an entire suburb. My guess was, they thought it was some type of medical notes he used in making whatever virus they thought caused the outbreak; but obviously, they didn't find anything as simple as that.

The place was mostly as we had left it. One of the soldiers that accompanied the FBI agent in charge of the case commented that there were more people inside that library than any library he'd ever been in. Something told me he hadn't been in many from the way he sniggered about seeing a large pile of dead bodies. The agent himself was more polite—or at least, reserved his snide skepticism until when my back was turned, for which I can't really blame the man. He spent his whole life finding rational explanations for unexplainable things, and then this case gets dumped in his lap. He could search for the rest of his life, and I doubt he'd find an explanation that would suit him, one that he could fully believe in. It must've been torture for him, working on it, growing more and more desperate to try and feed his uncaring superiors answers when there were none to be found.

It certainly seemed he was at the end of his rope when he came to me and put the journal they found down in front of me, like I was supposed to know what it was. They kept trying to get me to explain its contents, asking me questions about it, even though I'd never seen it before in my life. He seemed convinced that I had left it there just to throw them off whatever actual trail there was, that I was some kind of terrorist that had arranged this attack and was using this story to try and cover up my tracks. Because we all know if you want someone to believe your story, you tell them about the dead coming to life and eating everyone—airtight alibi right there.

Like I said, the guy was very obviously at the end of his rope. That was his last grasp on his tether to reality, and he wasn't about to let go of it without a fight. They grilled me for several hours, sending people in and out of the room, some who tried to sweet talk the nonexistent information out of me and others who tried to frighten me with descriptions of what might happen to me in a public prison, like I hadn't just seen people being torn apart and eaten like cattle.

After a day, the agent's resolve seemed to break, either from lack of sleep or genuine belief, I'm not sure, but he seemed to trust me enough finally to let me actually read the thing I was accused of writing. And seeing that I'd spent the last month in a room with white walls with nothing but pills and faded conversations with overworked orderlies to pass the time, any kind of reading was like a godsend to me.

But I still hesitated.

Silly, I know, but there was something about the book that made me feel… off for looking at it, like I was sticking my nose where it didn't belong, where Range wouldn't want me to. I know if the dead could want anything, he would want me to read the contents of that journal; but it still felt like an invasion of privacy, even though I had no idea what was inside it.

The first thing I remember about it is the smell. God, it was one of the foulest-smelling things I've ever experienced. I wasn't surprised when I found out it had been excavated from a grave site and was soaked through with bone rot and maggots for decades before being touched by human hands. When I opened the front cover, there was a page of ownership with a name hastily scribbled in the upper right corner, but a dark stain covered the top. Didn't take me long to decipher whose it was, though. The sheet music that spilled out when I turned the page was answer enough, even if it didn't have Jonathan Longwarden's name plastered all over it.

Yes, Jonathan Longwarden's journal. Well, there's a very good reason you didn't hear about it on the news, because according to the government, officially, it doesn't exist. If you ask to see what they recovered from the Loganville site, even with some of the highest clearances, all you'll get is a couple of tissue samples, phone recordings from a few unsavory characters they claim to be suspects despite a single investigation into their backgrounds, and my address—and that has a bright red stamp reminding you of my psychological diagnosis. I've seen that too.

Of course, I expected such skepticism about my claims, so I decided to make photocopies and hide them in my mattress. No, I'm not joking. If I was, I like to think I'd have a better punch line than that. Hold on a moment...

There. And there. Sorry about the tear on page 3. I had to rush to hide them from one of the orderlies a couple of years ago, and in my haste, the corner got stuck on the stitching. I made them by sneaking the journal out under my clothes during one of my trips out to receive my medication and darting into a back office when nobody was looking. Obviously, since they're just copies, there really isn't a foolproof way to verify their authenticity save for the signature. If you take it to a historian or manuscript analyzer, I'm sure they'd be able to confirm that his handwriting is the same.

The first dozen or so pages tell us nothing we already know about the guy. It was started shortly after his brother, Zachariah, died, and we get some nice insights to his feelings about his family members. Let me tell you, he was quite bit more uncouth about them than he was in his public comments on the matter. The guy knew how to play the public as well as he did an instrument.

The interesting part starts around the page dated August 14, 1903, in which our dear Jonathan begins to mention a young woman in his family's service: a Haitian maid named Madeleine. Even though you don't hear of her for the first few pages, when he does finally speak of her, he talks about her like he was continuing a conversation from a previous volume, hinting at this bond that binds them together. As the months pass, he writes of her more and more, his words growing bolder and more veracious. He even wrote her poetry, sonnets and ballads and the like. Some of them are quite risqué as well.

He writes of burying himself in her skin and living in her breath, their hearts conjoining and beating as one—the usual sap. To be honest, it was probably for the best that Mr. Longwarden kept his poetry in his journals.

Around February 3, 1904, he writes of an altercation with his father—something about wishing that Jonathan had died in Zachariah's place, the usual conversations with his father apparently. He drunkenly mentions the fact that Madeleine was in the room with them during this squabble and heard the whole thing, causing him some embarrassment. Fortunately enough for us, this got him rambling about their history and this "bond" that they supposedly share.

Well, it seems that the woman that helped bring Jonathan into this world. The wet nurse that pulled him from his mother's lifeless body and nourished him from her breast while he was young was Madeleine's mother. Madeleine herself was born just two days prior to Mrs. Longwarden's tragic demise, and this sharing of the teat was responsible for the deep connection between them.

Now, in his later years, with his thoughts and his body maturing, this connection had begun to blossom into something much more passionate. It wasn't long before they consummated these growing feelings, as Jonathan writes joyfully over their coupling in May of 1904. The next few pages are filled with scribbles of sonatas and more terrible sonnets, with very little actual updates into his life. If you look at the list of his published works, you'll see quite a few of his uncharacteristically joyous pieces that seem to correlate with his affair. It really seemed like he loved her. She brought out the best in him. She seemed to rid him of the demons that had plagued him since his birth, provided him a sense of security that was deeply ingrained in his psyche.

However, around September 25, 1904, he writes his first complete entry since his wooing of the maid Madeleine. From the first few somber words, you can tell that whatever brief joy he had has left him. He speaks of darkness and shadows and the evil of men. It takes him several pages to get to what is actually bothering him.

It seems he was present for the public lynching of Lydia and her white-skinned lover, watching firsthand as she was strung up until the very second when her legs finally stopped twitching. The detail he goes into... What he saw affected him deeply, severely. He muses on what would happen if the town were to find out about his relationship with Madeleine and whether his status or family name is enough to prevent the same fate from befalling the woman he loves. For now, at least, he seems to believe it will be enough; but he also mentions Anna for the first time, as a possible bride arranged by his father. He goes into detail about her callousness and vile nature, briefly describing an incident at her estate where she crippled a servant with a croquet mallet after interrupting the field of play to deliver a message to her father. It's quite a nice comparison to the stories I've heard about the famous Mrs. Longwarden, who's usually described as a nineteenth-century Virgin Mary.

These thoughts weighed heavy on his mind for several weeks. He only writes small-paragraph updates through the end of the year, mentioning the growing pressure by his father to accept Anna's family's proposal and the extensive dowry that came with it. Longwarden's equity was tied up in land and fur trading, neither of which had been profitable for decades. The soil had gone dry, destroying any harvest before they even had a chance to grow roots, and the local wildlife had slimmed so thin that even seeing a rabbit became a rare occasion. Anna's dowry would cover a lot of the family's growing debt and pay for Malachi's slow poisoning of his liver through expensive brandy and bootleg moonshine imported from Virginia.

After much coercing verbal reprimands from his father, including threatening to disown him, it seemed Jonathan Longwarden finally reached a decision. I... I think I should just read this one for you. There's a better chance you'll believe me that way.

> March 8, 1905. I write this in a mind that may be judged unfit to speak of such horrifying events, but I find it impossible to sleep without telling someone of what has just occurred. Unfortunately, there is no one who would believe me, or even listen without condemning me as a sinner, a relegation I might just deserve, so it seems that this journal had become the final bastion for my thoughts.

I'm not quite sure where to start. After thinking over Anna's, or—to do away with charades—Father's proposal, and while the thought of a lifetime spent with anyone other than my darling Madeleine seems like someone has wedged a burning poker through my heart, the thought of her dead at another's hand is too much to bear.

And oh, how fate has cursed me to have her death be at her own hands! The thought that I have driven her to this has shaken me to my very foundation. The guilt tugs at my eyes and keeps them from shutting, for fear I'll see her blade-pierced belly again. Or the way she stared at me, eyes accusing, even when the last of her sweet, sweet life passed from them.

But I am getting ahead of myself. I am letting my emotions get the better of me, but I cannot think of anything but her and my roiling insides.

After thinking of my Madeleine's and mine future together, I began to realize the burdensome undertaking it truly was, filled with running and struggling to survive until we can make it across the sea to Europe, and even there, our safety is nothing close to guaranteed. Every eye upon us would be a threat, one that even love cannot endure. It seems that there is nowhere we can escape but forward in time, where our love might actually be accepted, but that is impossible. This is the world we have found ourselves in, and inside its rule, our love cannot be.

I decided to accept father's proposal and to take Anna as my bride, both for the sake of my father and Anna, but also for Madeleine. And selfishly, I must admit, my own well-being factored into this weight on my heart as well. The thought of a lifetime of suspicions and hard labor instead of a life spent dedicated to my music, my one passion besides my love, filled me with a dread that I was unable to shake from my thoughts whenever I considered a life with my darling Madeleine.

Oh, to even write her name now feels like a betrayal! Like a curse on my lips that steals my very soul away!

But I must continue, despite my reluctance...

After coming to my hard-fought decision, I met with Father and agreed to his terms and wrote to an overjoyed Anna myself several days before. She is set to arrive tomorrow for the official engagement arrangements, although my mind will be miles way, tangled in thoughts of Madeleine's final embrace.

Knowing that I could not hide this secret from my clever Madeleine for long, I arranged to meet her in private in my study after the rest of the house has retired, when the moon was highest in the sky. It was a full moon—*is*, actually, as even now, his exuberant face mocks me from the heavens—and the light was plentiful enough to see without lighting candles, a benefit of any secret late-night rendezvous, of which I admit I've had very few. My belly was growling with nervous feelings, but I told myself that this was for love, all of it, and Madeleine deserved to know my reasonings. I owed her that much and more, but understanding was all I could offer.

She came in like a whisper, her feet floating over the carpet so silently. I was shocked when she slipped her bare arms under mine and began to caress me. I'm ashamed to admit that she came as God had fit to make her, and that seeing her there like that, her glory exposed for all to rapture in, I nearly caved in to my baser desires and threw the whole plan out entirely.

But no, curse me and my resolve, I shunned her and told her to wrap herself in something before I dared speak to her any further. She rebuked me at first, thinking I was merely feeling prudish; but after I starkly denied her once more, she realized I was being honest. Hurt and confused, she ran from the room as quickly and quietly as she had arrived and returned just a moment later wrapped in a shawl my mother had made before my birth.

Still transcendent even in such homely garb, it was hard to turn this goddess away, to tell her how much I longed for her while also pushing her aside. At first, in my naïveté, I wholeheartedly believed that I was the one struggling, while she remained hard and impassive. In fact, I almost felt angry with how little she moved and reacted to my declarations, which only made my message colder.

I finished in a growl, the beast that I am, turning away such a beauty, and as the silence came and she saw that I was not laughing or cracking smiles but standing as sure and unwavering as I had been during the baring of my heart, she soon realized that I was serious, and she broke into sobs so pitiable that my heart was rent in two as soon as they reached my callous ears.

Her frail, fluttering fingertips clutched at her stomach so tightly I thought that she, too, was coming apart at the seams, her hands rolling over each other like torpid waves flowing over the shore. I was blind! Both by love and by my own hubris, my damnable ego inflating to the point where I had a hard time seeing over it, like dark mountains of madness twisting my point of view into their own sickening horizon.

It was then that I noticed the knife that she had slipped free from the shawl, letting the blade twist and turn between her forefingers as gently as you would a utensil, carelessly like she wasn't even aware it was there herself. The way the moonlight reflected from the blade made it seem larger than it was, like it was the largest thing in the room, big enough to have its own gravitational pull that drew everything in the room toward it, the immensity of the object on the room plain enough to make it its center.

"You say you love me…" were the words from her mouth that made my blood run colder than an arctic wind.

The enamored fool that I was, I tried to calm her with gentle platitudes and cooing pleasantries instead of wresting the knife from her hands then and there. I believed in my hollow words too deeply, and for that foolishness, I paid a price too steep for any man to bear with breaking.

To my surprise, it seemed like my strategy was making headway. Her eyes are focused clearly on me, the pupils contracting in the night-light but never leaving my own.

"I believe you," she said, sweeter than a thousand incense-wielding cherubs. "You love me as deeply as I love you," she said, making my heart soar. "And I will be the only woman you ever love, just like you are the only man who will ever possess my heart…"

With those swift words, she charged at me, her once-luscious eyes stained by madness, and in my startled fright—oh, even now it hurts to write, as if it is making the deed even more permanent—I grabbed her hand and tried to disarm her. But instead, the damnable monster that I am, I accidentally plunged the knife into her breast, a crimson ribbon flying from the wound and draping itself around me, the streaming liquid turning my skin slick and clammy.

The ignorant fool that I was, I backed away toward the window, seizing the drapes for security, still believing it was my miserable life that had been tossed into a tumultuous state of jeopardy, even while my darling's pulsing life force drained from her slender body liter by liter. By the time my stress-rattled mind realized what was happening, Madeleine was already crouching on her knees, cupping the wound and collecting the blood in her palms like a bird bath found in hell's gardens.

Low, mumbled words slipped from her lips that I first believed to be prayers or whispered adorations. They became louder, growing into a thundering chant, uttered by a voice that no longer resembled my love but was far deeper and made my very bones shake within their fleshy confines. The words tunneled into my ears like worms, cockroaches, and other crawling things, burrowing into the viscous pink membrane and planting themselves there. Even now, I hear them, echoing deeper and deeper into my psyche.

I write them down now for my own reference, even though I am sure that I will hear them until the day death comes for me, but in the case that I myself cannot figure out their meaning, they will be jotted down for some scholar to unlock their meaning where I cannot:

Nanm sa a, mwen fe' reklam-
asyon ko'm pwo'p mwen an,
Pa menm tan ka vole li nan men m',
Pa gen anyen va vini ant sa ki pou mwen,
Pa menm renmen an na yon lo't.
Se pou van yo tounen
Peyi a dispare'tr, fe'nwa a enfiltrasyon nan fant yo
Ak lanmo' te't li ap sispann
Pa nenpo't ki moun ki oze yo nan
vole sa a ke' nam men m'ke'

Tan, yon rivye' andige pa dezi mwe,
Pou tout tan chanje gen tan soufran sa a,
Pou nenpo't moun ki oze yo nan
vole sa a nam men m'ke'

I don't know how they all come to me so easily. I've done my best to sound them out as best I can, but it's almost as if I know them already. They flow like a melody in my head, in a loop, each word clear as a bell, and yet blending into one sonorous exaltation.

My dear Madeleine repeated this phrase over and over, even when I wrapped her in my arms and tried to stop the bleeding. She wouldn't even look at me, her pupils already rolling up into her eyelids, staring off into the sky. I shook her, cursed her, cried for her to answer me, but she died in my arms, with those damnable words still on her lips.

And I with her.

The entry cuts off there. There seems to be several more words scribbled hastily underneath several splotches of dried blood at the bottom, but most are unintelligible; and those that I have deciphered are essentially worthless.

However, in the margins, along with several small corrections to his original transcription—which is a rough form of Haitian Creole—Longwarden also provided a translation of his lover's final words, which might shed some light on why our friend from the FBI looked so shaken.

It reads:

This soul, I claim as my own,
Not even time may steal it from me
Nothing shall come between me and what is mine
Not even the love of another.
May the winds turn back

The land erode, darkness seeping through the cracks
And death himself be deterred
By anyone who dares to steal this heart from me.
Time, a river dammed by my desires,
Forever unchanged be this hour,
For anyone who dares to steal this heart from me.

 Range pulled her along the vacant field, stepping over dandelions and crabgrass and patches of hard earth as they neared the twisted chain-link fence that marked the edge of the cemetery. The pain in Gwen's side was so intense all she could focus on was the rush of the ground and how tightly their fingers intertwined in their clasped hands as he dragged her forward. The duffel bag bounced heavily off his thigh, the fabric slapping against the newly opened wound that resided there, acquired in their fall from the library's roof. Somehow, Range was running as if he barely even felt it.

 They skidded to a halt as they reached the curvature of the gate, staring in horror at the barren landscape before them. Half of the tombstones had been thrown over or tipped on their sides, pieces of others thrown about like debris from a storm. Mausoleums had doors thrown from their hinges, stonewalls that had been collapsed from the inside, where some still-writhing bodies twitched underneath piles of heavy stone.

 The most unnerving sight was the ground, the dirt shifting and parting like an earthquake as the dead still trapped beneath the hardened earth struggled to reach the surface and begin their second, tortured existence. Craters spotted the hills, some so deep that you couldn't see their bottom; and more were opening every minute, clawing hands pulling the dirt away. It looked like the entire cemetery had come to life, slow arrhythmic breaths causing the ground to rise and fall in hypnotizing patterns.

 Gwen looked behind them, only to be reminded of the horde that followed, so wide that their shadows stretched as far as Gwen could see. It looked as if the entire town was stalking them now, desperate for their blood—their warm, pulsing flesh.

"Come on! The town ends on the other side! We're gonna have to risk it in the woods!"

With another sharp tug, they jumped over the breach and landed on the uneven ground. The shock wave from their awkward landing traveled up Gwen's body, jostling her already-punctured organs and causing her to fall to the ground in a yelp of pain. She gritted her teeth and stopped herself by grabbing her knee, but the pain rang in her ears and sent the world spinning out of her control.

She felt Range's thin but sturdy fingers tighten around hers and lift her to her feet, the useless stones stumbling and managing to keep her upright as they hobbled forward into hell. The moans of the dead roared around them, a chorus of damnation that sounded pleasant and empty, bombastic yet subtly sad, long howls that somehow pierced the ears like needles. Gwen did her best to tune them out, zeroing in on her own heavy breathing, which echoed in her chest cavity.

They reached a tree on a small patch of grass that had long turned a sickly shade of brown, but the roots kept the ground intact and ensured that no dead would sneak up from underneath them. Range carried her over to the chipped, gray bark, letting her lean up against it, the rough wood digging into and irritating her skin. But it held her up and kept her from collapsing, so she clutched it tightly.

Range had begun to dig through the duffel bag again, quickly finding a small pistol, and started rummaging for loose bullets at the bottom of the bag. Gwen tried to catch her breath, but the sight of the horde spilling over the fence knocked it right back out of her. Like a wave of flesh, they poured over the iron meshing, shattering apart and crashing back together as they slowly but hurriedly chased their wounded prey. Their dull faces were sparkling with bloodlust and hunger, their pale eyes turning red in the light reflected from the sunset. The sky itself looked like its veins had ruptured, the breaks in the clouds a terrible crimson that all too closely matched its syrupy counterpart flowing in abundance beneath it. Some of the dead wandering around the graveyard started to take notice of the commotion and the horde's direction, several joining their ranks and even more turning and facing the couple as they looked down from the hill.

Range finished loading the clip and slid it quickly into the bottom of the grip, giving the barrel a rushed slide before turning back to Gwen.

"Here."

Range shoved another revolver in her hand, showing her that only five bullets sat in the six chamber wheel, before closing it in her palm and giving it a soft spin.

"You only have five rounds, so use them sparingly, okay? You ready?"

Gwen answered with a strained nod, shoving her weaponless hand back into his. They started down the hill, the angle nearly causing Gwen to roll forward and down it like a toddler. With how sore and useless her body felt, she almost relented but kept her marionette legs moving.

A zombie with a bad comb-over and glasses appeared out of the fog, wisps of white swirling around it like a curtain as he waddled forward, its polka-dot tie sticking to the wet mound of blood on his black suit coat. Range raised the pistol's muzzle to the zombie's temple and evacuated its gray matter from its skull.

Another one of the undead, a blond woman in a trench coat, took its place only to have her formerly pretty face split in two by heated lead. They stepped over her blood-spurting body, feeling the hot liquid spray them like a sprinkler on a sticky summer day. They turned around the next headstone, which had been sculpted in the shape of a cherub, Range crashing into it as he turned a little too sharply, and reached the base of the large hill in the center of the graveyard.

A hiss arose from behind them, and Gwen spun to see a torso scrabbling over the cherub's head toward them, its spinal cord slapping against the statue like a stubby tail. It was mostly a skeleton with mere tatters of skin and tufts of hair shooting from the top of its skull, but it leaped at them, pushing off the cherub with its muscleless fingers. Instinctively, Gwen brought the up the revolver and fired a round that caught the creature in the chest in midair, sending it reeling backward and into the headstone. The force caused the statue to topple over itself, and while the zombie tried to jump away in time, it wasn't quick enough to save itself from being crushed beneath it, the dirt swallowing its twitching body once again.

Leaping forward, they charged the hill, Gwen struggling to keep up with Range's wide steps, her own energy fading quickly. She stumbled once again, Range stopping to catch her and steady her before they started once more. As soon as her head cleared, and the world came back into a reasonable focus, they continued their desperate burst to the top of the ridge.

A hand burst from the ground, shifting the entire length of grass and knocking both of them off balance. Range kept them upright, but another hand burst up behind them, its clawlike fingers closing around the air, hoping to seize hold of anything.

Range tried to rush around it, stepping on and crushing several of its finger joints in the process, Gwen deciding to sidestep it altogether. They could see the top of the hill just in front of them, and Gwen allowed herself a heavy sigh of relief—allowed herself to think they might make it.

This allowance proved premature, as another hand rose through the trembling dirt and coiled and snapped around Range's foot like a bear trap, the bony digits going straight through his ankle. Blood rose and poured out and down the chalk-white bones as Range began to scream, his leg buckling and sending the both of them hard into the dirt.

Gwen lost track of him as the ground rushed up to meet her, the hard smack of earth turning her vision dark and her roll back down the curve of the hill turning it into a nauseous blur. As she danced on the edge of consciousness, she tried to look for Range, tilting her head what she thought was left and right but might very well have been right and left or even up and down.

Slowly, his body came into focus, just several yards away from hers, the hand still clutching the top of his ankle. A head had wormed its way up from the ground a shoulder-length away from the hand holding his leg and was doing its best to shake the dirt from its eyes to look upon its prize. Range himself was dazed and unaware of the miniature fiend at his side, his head lolling from side to side as his eyelids fluttered soundlessly.

Gwen tried to scream, but all that came out was a low groan, the breath completely stolen from her lungs.

In a flash, the head bit down into Range's side, tearing into the flank and pulling loose skin and chunks of meat. His eyes shot open, and he howled in pain, his hands rushing to find the source of his agony and stumbling on the chattering skull chewing his side. He pushed and pulled at it, but its teeth had sunk in too deep and were slicing through more and more layers as he rocked it back and forth.

Spying the gun still clutched in her hand, Gwen stumbled to her knees and crawled up the incline toward the terrible scene and slammed the barrel into the remnants of the skull's ear canal. With the pull of the trigger ricocheted through her arm, she was knocked back while the skull disintegrated into powder and gray chunks of skin. The fingers wrapped around Range's ankle went limp, allowing him to pull his leg up to his chest.

Snapping off the finger that was still embedded in his skin, Range tried to get to his feet, only to have his mouth fall open in a silent gasp as part of his insides started to tumble out of the hole in his sternum. Gwen shouted in desperation at the sight, but no noise came out.

He clamped his hand over the wound and struggled again to stand, only to fall again as the pain crippled his limbs. Gwen tried to catch her breath as she crawled toward him, wrapping her arms around his shoulders and whispering in his ear about how they were going to make it out of there, about how he was going to be okay, even though she knew he wasn't. She held the tears at bay for a while but felt some escape nonetheless, ignoring them as she dragged them backward up to the top of the hill. Every slow drag brought gasps of pain from both of them as their battered and bruised bodies fought to reach the top. Gwen was carrying most of their weight, Range's arm draped over her shoulder to stop him from rolling back down when his body went limp from the effort.

Eventually, they rolled over the crest on to a flat plain, resting on their backs as they sucked in as much air as possible. Gwen was up first, looking down over the stretch of graveyard to see that the entire bottom of the hill was surrounded by the undead, all of them scrabbling to get to the top but falling over each other as the hill's steepness and gravity fought against them, buying the couple a brief respite.

Pressing down on her stitches seemed to relieve the pain, enough so that Gwen was able to stand; but when she pulled it away, she found herself doubling over again. Still, she grabbed Range by his armpits and slid him inch by inch over to the nearest tombstone that stood in the center of the hilltop. It was plain and square, wide as a bed frame and sturdy enough for Range to lean back against it—the name Jonathan Longwarden splayed in large letters above his shimmering, matted blond hair.

Already, the stone had been turned black from Range leaning against it, each one of his slow, deliberate breaths drawing more of the bile from his wound. He coughed heavily, nearly slumping over before he caught himself on the side of the headstone.

Gwen fretted over him, pressing her palm flat against the wound, feeling her fingers slip inside and collide with something slick and slimy that she knew she shouldn't be able to feel. Her heart skipped a beat, but she kept her face placid and calming, whispering in his ear that she was going to fix him up. She grabbed the duffel bag by its strap and dragged it across the dirt, barely taking note of the zombies gathering at the base of the hill, their repugnant bodies swaying as they tried to tackle the incline without a sense of equilibrium. Gwen unzipped the side pockets, finding gauze and a needle and putting them to the side, planning to continue the search for a spool when Range placed his blood-soaked hand on top of hers.

"You've got to get out of here."

The words twisted in her stomach like a rust-crusted, jagged knife. She had tensed herself for them, but the anticipation had only made them worse.

"No. No. I'm not leaving you. So don't even think about trying to convince me."

"You have to. There's no point in staying. They got me pretty good." He chuckled, stretching his neck out over his distended chest to see the hole in his side, grimacing as he looked upon its gruesomeness. "I don't think I'll be able to make it much farther without my guts spilling out. You have to leave me."

"Bullshit. They sewed me up, and I'm doing just fine. I can do the same for you."

"I think mine's a little worse than yours was."

"Well, I'm a lot better sewer than Bruce was, so I'm sure it'll even out."

She finished threading the needle with the last of their string and started toward Range's gash, needle bared, when his hand slapped it away, the needle becoming lost in the sparse blades of grass.

"Gwen! Stop it. There isn't time. You need to leave."

"I already told you, I'm not leaving."

"You'll die if you stay here. We both will."

"So then I'll die. We'll die together."

"You don't even realize what you're saying."

Gwen slammed her hands into the dirt and raked it with her nails. "Yes, I do! I'm tired of running. I'm sick of feeling out of place, like I don't belong. With you, I was the closest to happy I've ever been. I know it's silly, and it's ridiculous because I barely even know you… but if I were to call anything love, it would be how I feel toward you. I'm not just going to leave you."

He laughed, like ice that dripped in Gwen's ears and spread through her veins. She knew it was silly. She knew she was stupid for even thinking such a thing, for telling someone such a thing, for believing in such a…

"After everything we talked about, you still care about how something seems to other people. Who cares if it 'seems silly' if that's how you feel? Who's even left to judge you? Who's left to even hear you other than me? No one living, at least. And I certainly don't think it's silly. How could I, when I feel the same way?"

It felt like her heart was ready to burst from her rib cage and take flight high above the carnage raging below, blissfully unaware of all the destruction, the pain, and the death, and living in this one moment—this pure moment when everything made sense, when everything was as it should be.

And it only lasted a moment.

"You have to go. Please, I'm begging you at this point, Gwen. You have to—"

A pained expression made him curl his lips back as his hand flopped lazily around at his side. He found the pistol and took aim at something behind Gwen's field of vision, firing three rounds before his hand fell heavy as lead into his lap.

"*Go*! You won't make it if you stay here!"

"And I'll survive in the woods with the wolves? I'm not going to be able to make it without you. I won't even survive the night. If I'm going to die, it's going to be here, with you."

"Don't you get it?" he spat, blood and mucus hanging from his chalked lips. "It ends with me. All of it. That's how you fix it. It ends with me. It ends with me."

Gwen wasn't sure if what she was hearing was real or just the inane chattering of voices in her head. The world seemed to slide out of view, blur like a matte painting, the words elongated into incomprehensible moans.

"What are you talking about? You… you've lost a lot of blood. You don't know what you're saying."

"I know… exactly what I'm saying. You believed in the curse the same as I did. Well, this is the solution. I need to die. But you don't, Gwen. And when I do, you can live. You can live for ten, twenty, a hundred more years and be happy, but I… I can't do that with you. I don't have the time to explain it all. You just have to trust me. Trust me when I say it wasn't intentional. I didn't even know I was… Just trust me, and go while you can."

"I don't understand what you're saying. You're not making any sense. You did this, but you didn't know? You've lost too much blood. I'll stay and fix you up, all right? At least get you coherent, and we can try and escape from there, okay?"

"*No!*" he roared with what little might remained to him. "I need to… You can't…"

He fell silent, his gleaming green eyes falling to the ground in defeat. In fact, he drooped so suddenly and so severely that Gwen thought that life had left him, but his chest still rose in uneven intervals.

"You were right," he said.

"I knew you'd see it my way eventually," Gwen said, grinning. She began to dig in the bag again when he continued.

"Earlier, you were right earlier. When you said it was silly, that you loved me. You were right. It is silly. It's ridiculous. I barely know you. And as tough as you like to act, you're actually pretty weak from what I've seen, always caring about what others think of you, always complaining about the bad hand you've been dealt, even though others have it worse."

"What are you doing?"

"Seriously, to think I could love someone like you, and so quickly too? Talk about clingy. Guess I got lucky."

"Stop it," she said through stifled tears. "You're just trying to make me leave."

He laughed again, sharp and dismissive, thick as the tar that was pouring from his wound. "No. Before, I was trying to make you leave. Thought maybe making you care might be the best way. I thought if you really did love me, that might be enough to get you to leave, because if you really cared, you wouldn't just shrivel up and die in front of me. But it seems it's just made you weaker."

She clapped a hand over her mouth to stop herself from crying out, the sobs coming in sharp bursts that shook her entire body. Deep down, she understood, but it didn't soften the blows. Instead, it made them feel like they were fists coated in sandpaper.

Falling forward, she pressed her lips gently against his forehead, tasting the salt of her tears and the warm copper of fresh blood. She pressed her own forehead against his, letting the heat pass between them, feeling their breaths fall into rhythm one final time. She wrapped her fingers around the back of his neck and cradled it into her shoulder as she cried, really cried, letting herself go until she was a blithering mess. She let herself cry, let herself mourn, because it was not weakness to show sadness but to let it consume you. And that manifested itself in ways other than tears.

She felt her trembling lips sliding down to his cheek and edging toward his own, her hair spilling over her face. But she found herself gently kissing his fingers as he pushed her away.

"No. I want to, but the bite…"

As he warned her, he coughed again, and the black pile flowed over his lips, splattering onto his jeans. Gwen fell back, frustrated, and ran her hands through her hair, tugging at the knots until whole clumps came free.

"I'm sorry, Gwen. I'm sorry. You have to go. Please."

Nodding while she wiped her face dry with her sleeve, she stumbled to her feet, taking a glance down at the horde—which was forcing its way up the hill in bulk, the back rows preventing those in the front of falling backward. They had nearly reached the pitfalls at the center, where the grass was still stained red with blood.

Remembering the pistol in her hand, she placed it in the center of Range's chest, her finger stuttering over the trigger. Range smiled, seemingly pleased, but pushed the gun aside.

"No, you might need it. I don't know how quickly these things are going to die."

"But they'll—"

"I know. Trust me. The most painful part's already over."

Gwen felt a smile growing over her face like a weed, something her deep sorrow couldn't prune. She rubbed her thumb over his cheek one last time, finding fresh streaks of tears, before she stood and started making her way past Longwarden's headstone.

"It's funny," Range mumbled, "how we all just keep making the same mistakes as those that came before us, over and over again, like one big, endless circle."

His eyes went wide as if something had suddenly clicked into place, and his hand shot out like pouncing animal, catching Gwen's wrist and stopping her easily.

"I need you to do me a favor, though, if you don't mind."

"Of course not."

"I need you to go to the duffel bag and find my guitar. I threw it in there earlier."

Gwen dashed back over to the bag, checking to make sure the dead were still some distance away from the hill's crest, and slid the bag back over to Range's side.

"Well, I've got it," she said, slipping it out past the zipper, which bounced lightly over the wooden frame. "But it looks like some of the strings broke in the fall."

"Which ones?"

"I'm not sure. The thinner ones, I guess?"

"That's fine. I only need the bottom two anyway."

She set the guitar in his lap and helped him lift his arm over its wide body, making sure it wasn't digging into his side too severely. As soon as he was able, his fingers started dancing over the unbroken strings, starting to form the melody he had been playing earlier—the one he played the day they first met—except this version sounded fuller, more confident, as if he was playing a piece instead of composing one.

"That's the sound. That bittersweet irony. It's beautiful yet tragic. That universal thing that binds us together. My father heard it too, my grandfather, and his father before him. I'd call it ouroboros if it didn't already have a name."

With that, he began to play louder, the tune drifting through the fog, floating over its clouded spires, mingling with the air and giving it a heavier feel like a winter wind. It rose higher and higher until it blocked out even the groans of the dead, until Gwen realized that they'd gone deathly quiet. They still moved up the hill, but it was listlessly, lacking the drive they once had. They seemed almost… sad.

"Go on, Gwen, get out of here. You won't get a better chance."

Gwen nodded and turned away before she lost her nerve. She started down the backside of the hill, stepping over twitching limbs and bodies as she went. A zombie slowly wheeled about to fall on her, but it was moving so slow Gwen had ample time to place the barrel against its temple and pull the trigger. Sliding open the wheel, she saw she only had one round left. She looked back and thought about using it, but the crescendo of music kept her moving forward.

The town line stood on the other end of the fence that marked the cemetery's edge, and the fog swelled and swirled at the border, not daring to stretch beyond it. Gwen saw the final few rays of bleak red sunlight and moved eagerly toward them.

She was cautious enough to notice the torso making its way on worn-down hands and elbows to get to her, but she quickly dispatched it with her final bullet and kept on walking past the remnants of the horde, dropping the now-useless hunk of metal into the grass next to the smoldering skull.

The music stopped abruptly, and a sharp, wailing scream rose above the clouds, and Gwen stopped in her tracks. The shrill, piercing yell toppled her foundation, her wobbling legs unable to support her as she fell to her knees. She could no longer tell where one wound ended and the others began; they all felt like one giant sore, a bruise on her very soul.

The scream cut off, and the world descended into silence, but one that was unlike the others they had experienced that day. It was not pure. It was light and airy, broken by the sound of rushing wind and chirping birds. A trickling stream from just below the ridge past the fence line seemed so loud that Gwen thought she was kneeling in it.

She forced her eyes open, looking around her as the last few zombies stood still as statues, their washed-out eyes staring at nothing but the distance. One by one, they slowly started to crumble into bits of powder and bone and flesh, falling in a cloud like a collapsing building. An old, haggard woman that was standing near a stone urn shook as if the ground beneath her was splitting, but instead of falling through, her head caved inward, as if concaving from a black hole, swallowing itself until the body fell in heap at the base of the headstone. A zombie that looked at least four hundred pounds or more was wobbling like gelatin before his gut burst, sending entrails out like sparks as the two pieces of his body fell on top of each other before settling in the ground.

Gwen got to one foot, stunned at the sight happening around her—the dead disintegrating, crumbling, and bursting one by one as their moans were silenced and sucked from their reanimated lungs. She scanned behind her to see that the horde itself was falling victim to the same effect, even more rapidly. The front lines fell and tumbled backward onto the line behind it, until the entire crowd was nothing but still, useless bodies, crashing on top of each other as they rolled down the incline. Their heads popped like cherry bombs, exploding outward in a dazzling display of gore and color, red and black slime covering the dying grass.

As she rose to her feet, the fog began to dissipate, like curtains opening to the gravel highway that stretched deep into the woods. She threw herself over the chain-link divide one leg at a time, going out of her way to keep herself from looking back even one time more and landing on the uneven surface, losing her footing as the rocks slid out from under her. The highway led like a trail into the woods, curving far out of sight as it followed the bend of the stream. The smell of burrs and fresh grown leaves was so potent it stung her nostrils as she breathed deeply, taking in everything at once. She saw carrion crows flying eagerly in large murders overhead, but the trees were spotted with finches, chirping giddily before heading into their burrows for the night. Gwen's side still ached, and a fresh red stain spotted her T-shirt; but she ignored it, pushing it into the back of her mind. She kept her eyes set on the path before her, watching the shadows in the woods as she pressed forward, heading for the nearest piece of civilization she could find.

The Barnfell line truly ended that day in the fire of 1906. As if the conflicting death records and lack of birth certificate weren't enough evidence, Jonathan Longwarden's journal confirmed what a lot of people already suspected about Roger Barnfell.

I don't have copies of these pages, as my time in the copy room was cut short by a curious orderly, so you'll have to take my word from here on out. A dangerous proposition, I know, but necessary if you want the rest of your story. Besides, you don't really care if it's true or not, do you? As long as it sells papers or books or web page views or whatever you plan on doing with this. I don't particularly care. It's just nice having someone to talk to that isn't also pumping me up with drugs or constantly nodding apathetically.

You see, shortly after Madeleine's death, Jonathan continued to investigate her final words, which haunted him for almost every hour of every day. He heard them constantly, whispers on the back of his ear, softer than a kiss but stronger than a breeze. After finding himself a good translator, he even managed to transcribe himself a basic meaning out of them but came no closer to understanding what they actually meant. Fortunately, the translator knew of a man that lived up north, in the Quebec territory just over Le Fleuvre Saint-Laurent, who came directly from Haiti after a series of unsuccessful coups following President Boyer's ousting in 1843. They traveled to meet this man, believing that he would be able to provide a more direct translation; but he surprised them both by telling them that he actually recognized the words as part of an old Haitian song that had connections to Haitian mysticism, more commonly referred to as Vodou. Said that it was used in rituals—a sort of incantation, if you will—used to obtain something that the enchanter most desired. No one knew what went on at these rituals, as no one outside of the practitioners had ever lived to tell of what happened there. All the locals knew was that they could last for days at a time, the followers chanting their song over and over until their desires were fulfilled.

The man himself had been just a town over from where one of these rituals had taken place, causing him to delay his journey for up to two days until it was finished. He didn't believe in any of the stories about these rituals at the time. He considered himself a man of God and had thrown out worship of false idols long ago. So despite the warnings of the villagers, he tried to leave the town early by a backroad only to be stopped by a small congregation that he recognized from his time spent in the local church during his stay.

He tried to reason with them, imploring them that they were keeping him from his God-given duty, that by stopping him, they were giving in to the power of these false idols and spurning God; but they ignored all his pleas and would not let him pass. When he finally tried to push past them, they beat him so severely he spent three days unconscious in the care of the town physician. By the time he was healed, the ritual had finished, and he was free to leave town by any road he chose, and he eagerly took them up on the offer and fled as soon as he finished paying the man who treated him—an awkward proposition, considering he was one of the men who attacked him in the first place and one he wanted to put firmly behind him.

What he saw when he passed by the town in which the ritual had taken place, he would not say. Longwarden and his translator tried for hours to get him to tell them something about what the ritual was like, but the man would not budge. So they settled for asking if there was any more to the song that they had missed—another verse or something that could explain the ritual's length; but the Haitian had nothing more to give them, because there was nothing left to give. There was only the one verse, repeated over and over until the speaker's desires were met.

After this fruitless journey, Longwarden parted ways with his translator and headed back to Loganville, arriving just in time for his wedding to Annabelle. Of course, she was quite ecstatic to see him, while he was less so, but the proceedings went smoothly for the most part. Brightened by her good fortune, Anna was more jovial than her usual entitled self and spoke to even the lowest scullery maid with a sense of dignity. Whether this was an actual, albeit temporary, change of heart, or an act to impress her future husband—Jonathan was never sure, but it kept things pleasant, and that was all that mattered.

Part of him had thought of calling the whole thing off after Madeleine's death, since it was for her protection that he had decided to marry the girl in the first place. But now, to do otherwise almost seemed like it would render Madeleine's untimely demise even more pointless. So he soldiered on, doing his duty, to his family and to himself; and the wedding came and went, and Annabelle Silverbough became Anna Longwarden, beloved mother of Loganville.

The night of the marriage, Jonathan did his husbandly duty, and Anna's birthing hips lived up to their promised expectations, and the couple found that they were going to be parents just several months after becoming man and wife. This worried Jonathan at first, as in the past weeks, Anna had reverted quickly back to her old self, cursing their friends and callers behind their backs with hurtful rumors and whispers and insulting members of the staff even after they went out of their way to please her. The thought of her as a mother made Jonathan worry for their child's future, along with the thought of him as a father—something he foolishly hadn't considered when he accepted this misguided marriage.

The months passed, and Jonathan's obsession over the song was becoming worse. It was growing louder, and he heard it even when he slept, from the time his eyes shut until they opened again. His final reprieve had been taken from him. So he spent his twilight hours in his study, hiding from the world and from sleep, by burying his nose in ink and sheet music. He got the idea of composing a piece similar to the one he heard in his head, if not a direct translation. Yes, a direct translation would be best. A piece so grand to get so deeply ingrained in his mind would be a song that captured the attention of the world even decades after his own death.

He wrote many pieces—inferior ones, but still great by anyone else's standards—but couldn't quite capture what he was looking for. While he was working in his study one day, a maid came sprinting in, telling him that Mrs. Longwarden had gone into labor and it would only be a matter of hours before the child was born.

He admitted his initial reaction was one of fear, but he put on a smile and went joyously with his servants into the room where they had her laid out, a small bedroom in the west wing. Anna was complaining on the conditions, saying that the room was too small; and despite Jonathan's attempts to dissuade her, she arranged to be moved into the study. Jonathan was angered by the loss of his refuge, knowing that the room was of no matter to Anna, but the stealing of her husband's "distraction" was what truly motivated her.

Begrudgingly, he relented, staying by Anna's side but also working and enjoying the bitter looks she threw his way. As the night came, a thunderstorm rolled in, seeming to coincide with Anna's frenzied shouting as the baby started to crown. The wet nurse was set to coaching her and guiding the child out easily, while Jonathan paced nervously around the gruesome yet beautiful scene before him. For once, the song was at the back of his mind. He could barely hear it at all.

It was over in a matter of minutes. The screaming infant was placed gracefully in his mother's arms, who received him with uncharacteristic courtesy, in a way that almost lived up to her beloved reputation. Jonathan looked down at the family he had mistakenly talked his way into, and... something strange happened.

He felt genuine love for them—not just for the child, whose face was like a tiny mirror held up to his own, with shining blond hair and a smile "that could melt the ices of Antarctica," but even for his wife, who had given this wondrous gift to him. Despite her flaws, she cared for Jonathan greater than any member of his actual family had; and from the doelike eyes she made at their son, he knew she cared just as much for him as he did.

They handed the child back to the nurse to cut the umbilical cord when Anna began shifting uncomfortably. Soon, she started shouting, and then she began screaming. The child started crying at the sound of his mother's wails, and Jonathan ordered him removed from the room. The nurse was trying to figure out the cause of Annabelle's trauma but couldn't figure out exactly what was wrong. That is, until blood started spilling out of her cervix like a geyser.

Jonathan held his wife's hand as she thrashed, more and more violently until she looked like a woman in the midst of a fit. The nurse tried to stop the bleeding even though she couldn't tell exactly where it was coming from or what could be causing it. Anna kept on wailing, crying that she was being torn apart at the seams, pleading for them to make it stop, even if it meant killing her, but no one in the room could understand why.

That is, until her stomach caved in on itself.

A boil of blood appeared above her navel, a hole slowly growing in her stomach as something worked its way out from the inside. A small, deformed head slowly rose above the edge of her skin, its small teeth sharper than razors and its head twisted and bulbous. It was chewing on chunks of meat and flesh, ripping through it like a wild dog. It looked human and alien, a deformed creature that no one could believe. One man who looked at it supposedly went mad and fled from the room, leaping from a balcony in a room nearby and breaking his legs on the shrubbery below before crawling three miles into town, babbling like a fool the whole way.

Anna managed to look down and see this horrible demon protruding from her stomach, and the shock was enough to steal the last of her life, her head slumping hard against the back of the couch as the creature continued to chew through her gut.

Barely thinking, Jonathan looked about the room before seizing a paperweight from his desk; and without hesitation, he brought it down like a hammer on top of the shriveled monster's skull, splitting it easily in two. A gush of pink matter spilled out into his wife's stomach, the twitching abomination flopping onto her breast like a dying eel. No one moved, both from confusion and terror, until Jonathan himself approached his wife's corpse and peered at the horror that had slain her.

After picking it up limply and plopping it onto a nearby table, they recognized it as something resembling a human fetus. There were tufts of patchy blond hair on its deformed head, and somehow, its teeth had grown in already in the shape of jagged spikes, but it resembled a human.

The wet nurse, crossing herself several times before continuing, claimed that she had seen something like this before—not exactly like this, of course, but something similar to the monster that lay on the dead wood in front of them.

In the town where she was born, she had specialized in multiple births, or births involving more than one child—a much more complicated affair as it required just as much effort per child; and since birthing one child already threatened death for the mother, adding more children only made the odds worse.

Sometimes, even with a competent nurse, nature can derail things long before human hands ever have a chance to intervene. In the case of twins, sometimes one embryo grew too greedy and fed off the other or simply became stronger than its brother, leaving the smaller, weaker embryo to become deformed and die in the womb. In all the cases that she'd seen in her years, all the dead children looked like that creature, or worse.

It all clicked into place then. Jonathan finally understood Madeleine' intentions, her desires, and the cost they carried. Quietly, he swore his maid to secrecy, paying her several lifetimes' worth of salaries in one go, on the condition she fled the country and never returned. He then had his child removed from the house and paid for one of his maids to keep it with her own newborn, only for a week or so, again offering her more money than she would normally see in a lifetime.

The next day, word quickly spread of Anna's demise along with the child, and Jonathan turned away every visitor and mourner until the study had been cleaned. The funeral was a closed-casket affair so no snooping eyes would try and see the cause of Anna's death. While some gossip spread about this unusual choice for a woman esteemed for her beauty, most attributed it to the newly widowed Longwarden's unassailable grief, and any other less-than-flattering rumors were quickly squashed out of respect.

Knowing how the curse worked, he knew his time was short but did his best to work out a way to protect his son, even if it meant giving him up entirely. When he read of the fire at the factory and thought of the countless dead bodies just waiting beneath the ground, he knew he could wait no longer and arranged a meeting with one of the victim's families: a widow that was unfortunate enough to lose all three of her children in the fire, a woman by the name of Clara Barnfell.

He offered her the child, of course, with the condition that she never told anyone of the child's true origin, along with a list of other instructions to prevent the curse from ever causing issues for the town. Even the child would be ignorant of where it really came from—that is, until it was time for him to instruct the next generation. The woman, consumed by grief and desperate for anything resembling the family she lost, gratefully accepted, even refusing the offer of a money. That is, until Jonathan insisted for the child's sake.

After ensuring his child's future, he went back to his study and finished his work on the piece, the grief opening his mind to listen clearly to every key, every note, every intonation of the dark melody in his head, and allowing him to write his magnum opus. As soon as he finished, he scheduled a premiere at the town hall, offering a sizeable donation comprised of the last bits of the Longwarden fortune; and the rest, as you know, is history.

The rules set by Jonathan were simple enough but more difficult in practice. Marriages were to be arranged for the children with suitors from several towns over, ones that preferably clashed with their personality and ensured for a loveless marriage, something that would keep the line going, without risking the town in the process.

Obviously, things didn't always go as planned, and marriages had to be canceled when the children started getting too close. And there were several incidents, such as an incident in the 'eighties that resolved itself rather quickly, where Zeke Barnfell tried to leave town with a girl only to murder her after an argument. Fortunately, her rebuttal after the fact set everything right again. And of course, there was Range's father, who had a last-minute epiphany similar to the one shared by Jonathan Longwarden himself, and the sight of his son was enough to inspire feelings of genuine love toward his virulent wife. He quickly corrected his mistake, leaving Range to think he didn't care, when the truth couldn't be any more different. I wish I had been able to tell him that.

Range's cousin, Marshall, is a different story entirely—one that nearly caused things to go astray long before Range was born. You see, one of Roger Barnfell's children, the black sheep of the family, decided to leave home after an altercation with his father, packing his things and changing his name to Meers and moving into the woods near the outskirts of town. Somehow, by pure coincidence or luck, or whatever you want to call it, the Meers line continued with a string of loveless marriages entirely by happenstance—at least from what I can tell.

I went to the FBI with my findings—well, "they came to me" is the more accurate way of putting it. Of course, this wasn't an acceptable answer and only worsened my connections with them—although I think our friend, the agent who got me Longwarden's diary in the first place, almost started to believe me before his superiors shut the investigation down. They reclassified everything and locked it away under piles of regulations and red tape, gave some bullshit answer to satisfy the reporters about drug recalls or disease, something more normal like that. I think in one conference, a director even mentioned something about space slugs or something. You can look it up, I'm sure.

Either way, they provided enough nonanswers that the whole thing started to look like a ghost story. The years passed, and most people talked about Loganville like they would about Roanoke or a missing flight. It's a weird mystery, but that's all it is—something you're never gonna solve or understand, something that just happened.

And here we are. Well, here I am, at least, locked up in this room for years, counting away the days one by one. Could be worse, all things considered. Not much else for me to tell you that I hadn't already… What? Well, I guess, even though everybody already knows most of that, I don't mind covering it again for the sake of coherency.

A couple of police officers from Castle Rock picked me up a couple of miles out of town two days after I made it out of the cemetery. They brought me into the station, unsure of what to do with a girl covered in blood who claimed to have come from a town where every citizen was now a bloody pile of flesh. Eventually, the FBI came to pick me up and debrief me, before they put me on the carnival ride known as the media circuit. I had microphones shoved in my face every minute of every day for a week, constantly asking me what happened, what I'd been through. I'm sure you could find plenty of interviews online. I know I've been shown a few from time to time. My favorites are the ones where I just stare at the interviewer. People speculated I was shell-shocked, but I just liked messing with them after the umpteenth time.

After the government got wind of my stories and some of the things I was telling people, they quickly put a kibosh on the interviews and had me transferred here until they could determine the accuracy of my accounts and investigate further into the cause of the incident. Of course, the pictures coming from the site weren't helping, especially given the nature of the Internet and its ability to pull a conspiracy out of cornflakes commercial. People claimed the comet had something to do with it, or solar flares, or even the drug recall; but none were more vocal than the evangelists that rode the media sensation as proof of the coming apocalypse, most insinuating that it had already begun. My mother would be quite happy to see those taking up her cause so eagerly, but the movement's died out in later years since the earth was still, you know, here.

Tyler, as you probably know, was rescued a day before I was. They found him in the woods in a shelter made of loose branches and body parts. With Tyler's high-profile background and the destruction of the Loganville police, Tyler was hailed as a hero who was misidentified as a killer by the police, who bravely fought back against the horrors of the town, trying to save as many as he can. The fact that they found me specifically, one of the people he saved, only made him look better—along with the fact that his father, the senator, had perished in a bridge explosion on his drive into Loganville to claim his son only added to his profile and made him a bigger name.

Tyler, being the guy he is, ate it up and basked in the spotlight but in a way I don't think any of us quite expected. He started speaking like his father, turning interviews into heated political discussions at the urging of his advisors, and it wasn't more than four years before he had retaken his father's mantle and became a US senator himself. He obviously agreed to peddle whatever story the government needed him to at the time and kept his words about his experience brief—outside of the accounts of his epic feats of bravery, of course.

During campaign time, he always pays me a visit, more for the PR than anything, but when we talk in private, he's the Tyler I used to know again, and we lose ourselves in that before the world takes us away again. Yes, he's still crass and unbearable at times, but it feels familiar. And it reminds me of Range a bit, in a very strange way. He'll probably be upset about me telling you what happened, but I doubt he's too concerned with the allegations of mental patients.

They found Vel, as you know, the last out of all of us. It was nearly a month later when they found her, completely by happenstance, when two hunters came across her in the woods. She was crouched over like an animal, mumbling to herself, and—how do I put this sensitively?—she was trying to sew herself shut. And I'm not talking about a cut or wound or her mouth either.

Obviously, whatever she saw affected her, and they haven't been able to get a word out of her for more than a decade now. If she was anything like me, she got plenty of offers for interviews and movie deals about her struggle; but she refused them all, didn't even give them a spared glance. Last I heard, she was being kept heavily sedated at an institution up in Canada, but only one or two people have access to her. And she spends most of her time in front of an old television they allowed her to keep in her room, mostly because when she was around the other roommates, she would try and attack them, howling like a lunatic and forcing herself on them.

I don't know how she survived to this day, but whatever she saw must've been terrible; and for that, I don't envy her, despite my own lackluster situation. Part of me has thought of agreeing to the government's story, like Tyler has—just for a taste of freedom once again, but I can never really bring myself to do it. To lie about it all… just seems wrong, like I'm disrespecting those that were left behind. It seems almost… sacred, in a way. It's almost a part of me now.

But… honestly… I don't know if it's worth fighting for anymore. The past has a way of always seeming far worse or far greater than it actually was. I'm sure that my mother wasn't the Margaret White–like demon that I made her out to be. And I'm sure the ostracization I experienced wasn't severe as I believed. The few friends I had were proof enough of that. I know that whatever we survived was far less intense than the way I remember, only the sensationalized bits collecting at the top like buoys above torpid waters.

And I'm also sure Range wasn't as handsome as I remember, or as suave, or profound; but in my mind, he is, and he always will be. The past isn't always a perfect retelling. The highs always seem higher and the lows so much lower, with the truth buried in the gray, stuck somewhere in the middle.

The past is beautifully hazy, fuzzy like halogen lights far off in the distance. The details blur into a beautiful mosaic far more stunning than its real-life counterpart. And sometimes we look at it with such admiration that we forget what the real thing was actually like. Everything is either great or terrible, with no middle ground, despite the mundaneness we experience day in and day out. We make the past what we want it to be. We use it to shape who we want to be. We use it as a reminder to keep moving forward, although sometimes we forget that and wallow in its impossibilities.

I often think of Range, the version of him I keep in my mind, and I remember the things he said. From time to time, even I wonder, is that what he really said or has time made a fool of me yet again? I mean, I've been in here for so long now, so long that years have begun to run together... so, so long. But then I think...

If I hear it clearly in my head...

And I think it's real, truly believe it's real...

What's the difference?

ABOUT THE AUTHOR

Max Houdek is twenty-four years old and was born and raised (by a mother who is almost the complete polar opposite of the one depicted in this novel) in the suburbs of Chicago, Illinois. After spending several years at the University of Iowa and traveling across the country, he currently resides back in his hometown, which provided him with plenty of inspiration to write this book. He spends his time living on a diet of fast-food and cheesy horror movies and sometimes plays bad music at open-mic nights across the city. He finds time to write about zombies, samurais, and other nerdy things in between working full time and drinking with his friends on his days off.

CPSIA information can be obtained
at www.ICGtesting.com
Printed in the USA
FFOW04n1800081116
29095FF